She suddenly found herself quite unable to breathe...

His back was to the wall and her slippers were toe-to-toe with his boots. He ran his hand up her arm and around her back before gently stroking her nape, and all the while he stared at her as though he were very, very...hungry. "Daphne," he said. It was a plea for permission, or perhaps forgiveness.

With every second that passed, her heart raced faster and a heady warmth seeped into her limbs and coiled in her heart center. If a mere look could do this to her, what magic could his kiss do? Her gaze drifted to his lips and she leaned a bit closer.

And that was all it took.

He hauled her against him and dipped his head, covering her mouth with his own. There was nothing gentle or civilized about his kiss. It was needy, raw, and...wonderful.

"Anne Barton is a delightful new voice in historical romance! ONCE SHE WAS TEMPTED is a charming read with characters who are easy to love—a wounded earl and a determined heroine whose heart won't be denied."

—Tessa Dare, *New York Times* bestselling author

Once She Was Tempted

ANNE BARTON

FOREVER

NEW YORK   BOSTON

Copyright © 2013 by Anne Barton

Excerpt from *Scandalous Summer Nights* copyright © 2013 by Anne Barton

Forever
Hachette Book Group
237 Park Avenue
New York, NY 10017

www.HachetteBookGroup.com

Printed in the United States of America

First Edition: October 2013
10 9 8 7 6 5 4 3 2 1

OPM

Forever is an imprint of Grand Central Publishing.
The Forever name and logo are trademarks of Hachette Book Group, Inc.

The Hachette Speakers Bureau provides a wide range of authors for speaking events. To find out more, go to www.hachettespeakersbureau.com or call (866) 376-6591.

The publisher is not responsible for websites (or their content) that are not owned by the publisher.

For Sylvia,
the kindest, wisest,
bravest person I know.
Also, your eggplant parm
is happiness on a plate.
Love you, Mom.

Once
She Was
Tempted

Chapter One

Bristle: (1) A coarse animal hair used in making paintbrushes.
(2) To become agitated or irritated, as in
The young lady's innocent inquiries caused
the brooding earl to bristle.

London, 1816

*U*pon meeting Miss Daphne Honeycote for the first time, Benjamin Elliot, Earl of Foxburn, had two distinct thoughts.

The first was that she *appeared* to be a suitable match for his upstanding young protégé, Hugh. Her golden hair was smoothed into a demure twist at her nape, and the collar of her gown was prim enough to pass muster in a convent. Her entire person radiated light, goodness, and purity.

The earl's second thought regarding Miss Honeycote was that he should probably take down the nude portrait of her that was hanging in his study.

To be fair—and to his everlasting regret—Miss Honeycote wasn't entirely nude in the painting. She reclined on a chaise of sapphire blue, her gown unlaced all the way to the small of her back, exposing slim shoulders and the long indent of her spine. The look she cast over her shoulder was serene and wise.

And utterly captivating.

His butler had once nervously suggested that a less titillating painting—of the English countryside or a foxhunt, perhaps—might be more befitting an earl's study. Ben had explained to the butler—with uncharacteristic patience—that since he had no intention of hosting the next meeting of the ladies' Scripture study, he'd hang any picture he damn well pleased.

But now, as he watched poor Hugh fumbling over himself to impress Miss Honeycote at the Duchess of Huntford's dinner party, he realized he'd have to take down the painting. It would never do for Hugh to see the scandalous portrait and discover that the woman he was courting was not the paragon of virtue he imagined her to be.

Ben wasn't one to cast stones, but at least he didn't pretend to be anything other than what he was—a bitter, cynical bastard. *Everyone* knew what he was, and yet invitations were never in short supply. It was truly amazing what character defects people would tolerate if one had a title, a fortune, and a few interesting scars.

He preferred to eat alone but couldn't refuse an invitation from Huntford. Especially when he suspected the duchess had arranged the dinner party in order to further Miss Honeycote's acquaintance with Hugh. This dinner was the social equivalent of advancing a column of infantry and probably involved more strategy. It was the kind of maneuver that Robert—Hugh's older brother and Ben's best friend—would have skillfully countered. Ben tucked an index finger between his neck and cravat, which suddenly felt tight.

Robert was gone, killed in the line of duty, leaving his younger brother with no one to look out for him but Ben—a poor substitute if ever there was one. The least he could do was protect Hugh from the mercenary and morally suspect Miss Honeycotes of the world.

Ben kept a wary eye on the stunning blonde throughout the evening. If he didn't know better, he'd swear she'd stepped out of the portrait in his study and raided the armoire of a prudish vicar's wife before coming to dinner. The contradiction between the oil-painted and in-the-flesh versions of Miss Honeycote kept his mind pleasantly—if wickedly—occupied during the meal, which was otherwise predictably tedious. Huntford sat at one end of the table, looking more medieval king than sophisticated duke; his pretty wife sat at the other. The duke's two sisters—Olivia and Rose—and Miss Honeycote were interspersed among the remaining men—Hugh, himself, and his solicitor and boxing partner, James Averill.

It was the sort of social affair Ben had avoided since returning from Waterloo. Cheerful gatherings, replete with inane conversation about the condition of the roads and the prospects for rain made him feel like the worst kind of hypocrite. He sat in one of London's most elegant dining rooms enjoying savory roast beef while members of his regiment lay buried in the cold ground.

It seemed almost traitorous.

Ben's leg twitched, signaling its agreement.

Damn. That twitch was like a warning shot before

cannon fire. Sweat broke out on his forehead, and he clutched his fork so hard the fine silver handle bent.

Beneath the polished mahogany dining room table, he gripped the arm of his chair while the twisted muscles in his right thigh spasmed and contracted like a vise. He gritted his teeth, keeping his breathing even. The dinner conversation became muffled, as though he listened through a door. Objects in front of him blurred, and he could no longer tell where the tablecloth ended and his plate began. Silently, he counted. *One, two, three* ... The episode could last ten seconds or ten thousand, but he gleaned a shred of comfort from knowing it would end. Eventually.

He reached eighty-six before the pain subsided and the room slowly came back into focus. After a glance up and down the table, he relaxed slightly. No one seemed concerned or alarmed, so he must have gotten through the spell without grunting. As inconspicuously as possible, he swiped his dinner napkin across his damp forehead. Miss Honeycote cast him a curious look, but he ignored it, took a large gulp of wine, and tried to pick up some thread of the conversation around him.

Hugh was grinning at Miss Honeycote like an idiot. He seemed to fall further under her spell with each bloody course. At this rate, they'd be betrothed by dessert. "I understand you volunteer at the orphanage on Thursdays," Hugh said.

"Yes, I enjoy being around the children." She lowered her eyes, as though uncomfortable discussing her charity work. Little wonder. She probably wouldn't know an orphan if one bit her on her lovely ankle.

"The children adore Daphne," the young duchess said

proudly. "With a smile, my sister can brighten the darkest of rooms."

"I do not doubt it," exclaimed Hugh.

Miss Honeycote blushed prettily, while Ben just barely refrained from snorting. He had to admit, she did a fair job of brightening his study.

She probably wouldn't deign to bat her lashes at Hugh if a viscount's title hadn't been tragically plopped onto his lap. Hugh was so smitten he'd already sunk to composing bad poetry in her honor, which meant Ben would have to confront her about the painting—in private, and soon. With any luck, he'd spare Hugh the humiliation of learning that the woman he fancied himself in love with was, for all intents and purposes, a doxy.

"Lord Biltmore tells us you're something of a hero." Lady Olivia Sherbourne, the more animated of the duke's sisters, leaned forward, gazing expectantly at Ben.

He shot Hugh a scathing glance before responding to Lady Olivia. "Hardly. I had the misfortune of finding myself in the path of a bullet. Let me assure you—there was nothing vaguely heroic or romantic about it."

"Nonsense." Hugh sat up straighter. "The colonel himself came to visit Lord Foxburn, and he said—"

"Enough." It was a bark, harsher than Ben had intended. The duchess fumbled her fork and it clattered onto her plate. Accusatory silence followed. The women stared at him with owlish eyes and, at the head of the table, Huntford glowered.

Ben set his napkin next to his plate and leaned back in his chair. If they were waiting for an apology, they were going to wait a long time. In fact, his flavored ice, which had been cleverly molded into the shape of a pineapple, was already starting to melt. Instead, he said, "I'm certain there are more appropriate topics of conversation for a dinner party."

The duke arched a dark brow.

Ben responded with a grin but didn't let it reach his eyes. "Better to stick with less distressing subjects when conversing with the gentler sex." He sounded like an insincere ass, and no wonder.

"Must we limit our conversation to weather and roads, then?" Lady Olivia looked like a chit who'd discovered her diamond earrings were paste jewelry.

"Of course not." Ben scooped the spike of the ice pineapple into his spoon. "There are plenty of interesting, *appropriate* topics for young ladies."

"Such as?"

He froze, his spoon halfway to his mouth. "I don't know…the color of Lady Bonneville's newest turban?"

Every head at the table swiveled toward him, and no one looked particularly pleased.

Miss Honeycote cleared her throat, drawing the attention away from him like a matador unfurling a scarlet cape. She smiled, instantly raising the temperature in the room several degrees. "Lord Foxburn, I cannot speak for my entire sex, but let me assure you that my sister, Olivia, Rose, and I are not nearly as fragile as you might think. If you knew us better, you wouldn't worry about offending our sensibilities. You'd be worried that we'd offend yours."

The ladies giggled, murmuring their agreement, and even Huntford chuckled reluctantly. Miss Honeycote pursed her pink lips and tilted her head as she met Ben's gaze. Her knowing smile and heavy-lidded eyes were an exact match to those of the woman in the portrait.

And, coincidentally, to the woman who invaded his dreams.

Daphne took a sip of wine and, over the rim of her glass, marveled at the luxury surrounding her. A fire crackled in the marble fireplace of the duke's dining room, gilt-framed pictures graced the sea-green walls, and a chandelier glittered over the mahogany table.

Her sister, Anabelle, blushed prettily under her husband's appreciative gaze. If the new fullness in her cheeks and sparkle in her eyes were any indications, being a duchess suited her quite nicely.

Her sister, the Duchess of Huntford. The thought still made Daphne giddy.

A year ago she and Belle were living in a tiny rented apartment wondering how on earth they were going to be able to feed themselves, much less purchase the medicine Mama needed. Daphne had spent night after night in Mama's room, watching over her, as if that would keep Death from skulking in and snatching her away. Some mornings, when the air was thick with the pungent smells of strong tea and bitter medicine, she was afraid to approach Mama's bed. Afraid that she'd take her hand and find it cold and stiff.

Daphne shivered in spite of herself. She wasn't the sort to dwell on dark times, but remembering was useful on occasion—if only to make one appreciate one's blessings.

And she had many.

Mama was now the picture of health. She and Daphne lived in a town house twenty times the size of their old apartment and a hundred times more beautiful. They had a butler and a cook and ladies' maids, for heaven's sake. If a gypsy had foretold it, Daphne would have fallen off her chair from laughing. And yet here she sat, in a ducal dining room of all places.

Enjoying her first season.

Even she, the eternal optimist, never dared to dream of such a thing. Because of her sister's marriage—a love match to rival any fairy tale—Daphne would gain admittance to lavish balls and perhaps receive her vouchers to Almack's. She might even be presented at Court. The very thought of which made her pulse race.

Yes, it was *that* thought that made her pulse race. Not Lord Foxburn, or his bottomless blue eyes, or his irreverent grin. He seemed a jaded, bitter sort, but Lord Biltmore held the earl in such high esteem that he must have *some* redeeming qualities. Something beyond the broad shoulders and the dimple in his left cheek. She endeavored not to stare, but he was sitting directly across from her, and a girl could hardly gaze at the ceiling all evening.

If she was nervous tonight, it was only because her recent good fortune seemed almost too perfect, too fragile. Like a tower of precariously balanced crystal glasses that would come crashing down from the slightest vibration. She pushed the image away, inhaled deeply, and savored her last bite of pineapple ice, which was surely a spoonful of heaven.

Shortly after the dessert course, Daphne and the other ladies filed into the drawing room for tea. The moment the doors closed behind them, Belle drew her aside and, as only a sister could, began interrogating her without preamble. "What did you think of him?"

"He is a bit boorish, but I think that, under the circumstances, we must make allowances."

Belle squinted through the spectacles perched on her nose, perplexed. "Lord Biltmore?"

Oh, drat. Of course her sister was asking about Lord Biltmore—the kind, young viscount who'd sent flowers once and called twice. "I thought you were asking about Lord Foxburn." Daphne's cheeks heated. "Lord *Biltmore* is a true gentleman. Amiable, gracious, and—"

"Did you notice his shoulders? They're quite broad."

Daphne frowned, wishing her sister would use pronouns with a bit more moderation. "Whose shoulders?"

"Lord Biltmore's!" Belle made the pinched face again, then let out a long breath. "No matter. If he doesn't strike your fancy, there are plenty more eligible men I can introduce to you. I just thought he'd be—"

Daphne reached out and clasped the hand Belle waved about. "Lord Biltmore is the finest of gentlemen. Thank you for hosting this dinner. You arranged it all for me, didn't you?"

A mysterious smile curled at the corner of Belle's mouth and a gleam lit her eyes. "It's only the beginning."

Oh no. Belle didn't undertake any task halfway. Daphne had once asked her to replace the ribbon sash on a plain morning gown. Within a few hours, Belle had transformed the gown into a shimmering confection of silk and delicate lace. If matchmaking became her sister's mission, Daphne would not have a moment's peace. "You are newly married and a duchess to boot. Surely you have more pressing matters to attend to than filling my social calendar."

"Not a one. This is your chance, Daph. No one deserves happiness more than you."

"I *am* happy." But she wasn't happy like Belle was with Owen. That was a rare thing.

"You know what I mean."

Daphne bit her lip. "Yes." If her sister was determined, why not let her do her best? There was no one in the world Daphne trusted more. She gave Belle a fierce hug and extricated herself before she turned completely maudlin.

Needing a moment, Daphne poured herself some tea, wandered to the rear of the drawing room, and sank into a plush armchair near an open window. A warm breeze tickled the wisps on her neck, and the simple pleasure of it made her eyes drift shut.

This season *was* her chance, presented to her on a silver salver. She, a poor girl from St. Giles, would mingle with nobility. With just a smidgen more luck, she might marry a respectable gentleman. Someone kind and good. Greedy as she was, she even dared to hope she'd fall in love. With a man who viewed life the same way she did— as a chance to bring happiness to others.

Lord Biltmore seemed the perfect candidate. His manners were impeccable, and he treated her like a rare treasure, or a fragile egg that might break if jostled. His boyish smile held not a trace of cynicism, and the way his russet-colored hair spiked up at the crown—much like a tuft of grass—was utterly endearing. Although he'd lost his parents *and* two older brothers in recent years, he managed to see goodness in the world around him and reflect it back tenfold.

The viscount could have his pick of the season's debutantes, yet he appeared to be taken with *her*—a newcomer with few connections and no fortune to speak of. The advantage of being an unknown was that she had no reputation—so far, it was unblemished.

She could hardly believe how nicely the pieces of her life were falling into place.

A shadow slanted across the teacup in her lap, and she looked up. A torso clad in a finely tailored dark blue waistcoat appeared, precisely at eye level.

"Miss Honeycote, might I have a word?"

Daphne blinked, tilted her head back, and directed her gaze to the face above the snowy white neckcloth. What Lord Foxburn lacked in manners he certainly made up for in good looks. His tanned skin set off his startlingly blue eyes. The fine lines at their corners seemed to have resulted not from smiling, but rather from glaring, if his current expression was any indication. Although his mouth curved down at the corners, his lips were full. She was quite sure that his genuine smile—should she ever see it—would be dangerously charming.

His light brown hair curled, softening the angles of his cheekbones and nose, but it was his eyes that left her slightly breathless and off balance. Turbulent as a churning sea, they harbored a storm of accusation, curiosity, determination, and perhaps a glimmer of hope. And that was only on the surface. She could not imagine what else lurked below, and the mere thought of exploring their depths made her skin tingle like—

Lord Foxburn cleared his throat.

She started, and her tea sloshed, forming a moat in the saucer. Hoping to remedy the small lapse in etiquette— what was it the earl had just asked her?—she smiled apologetically. "How clumsy of me." Heat crawled up her neck, probably producing more than could be considered a fetching blush. She waited for him to offer a gracious word, or at least smile back.

He did neither. Instead, he sighed as though he were already bored with their conversation. If, at this juncture, it could even properly be considered one.

Ah, well, the earl had returned from the battlefield not so long ago. One could understand how his manners might be out of practice. "Would you care to sit?"

"If you have no objection," he said wryly.

"I'd be delighted."

As he lowered himself to the settee, his lips drew into a thin line. He moved with the natural confidence of an athlete, but she'd detected a limp earlier. "Does your leg pain you?"

He narrowed his eyes. Yes, the lines reaching toward his temples were almost certainly due to this sort of squinting. An unflattering look for most men, but it rather suited him.

"A great many things pain me, Miss Honeycote." His arched brow told her he wasn't referring to physical ailments alone.

Well. Although sorely tempted, she would not retaliate in kind. "I am sorry to hear it."

He studied her, no trace of remorse on his face. "I require a word with you, in private."

Daphne glanced around the drawing room. The closest person was several yards away, and her curiosity was piqued. "I'm listening."

The earl pinched the bridge of his nose. He was perhaps the most impatient person Daphne had ever met. "The matter I wish to discuss is of a delicate nature. I think it would be best to arrange a meeting for tomorrow."

"I confess I've never had such an odd or intriguing request." She'd received her fair share of improper advances from men, but Lord Foxburn didn't seem the type of man to force his attentions on a woman. With his striking good looks, Daphne was quite sure he wouldn't have to.

Perhaps he wanted to share some information about Lord Biltmore. The young viscount had mentioned that Lord Foxburn had been his brother's closest friend and that, after his death, the earl had helped him adjust to his new role. But what did that have to do with her?

"I realize this must seem forward. However, I think you'll appreciate the need for discretion once the topic of our discussion becomes clear. May I call on you tomorrow?"

Daphne pretended to regard him thoughtfully for several moments, in order to give the impression that a fierce debate raged inside her. In truth, she was much too curious to say no.

"I'm staying here, with my sister, while our mother is in Bath."

Concern flicked across his face. So, he wasn't as unfeeling as he'd like people to think. "Taking the waters?"

"No, Mama's surprisingly healthy. But she's not accustomed to the parade of parties and social engagements. I think she just wished to escape it all."

"Your mother's a wise woman." The earl rose and inclined his head in a manner that could be perceived as either polite or mocking. "Until tomorrow, Miss Honeycote."

Before she could ask one of the twenty questions swirling through her mind, Lord Foxburn walked away. For someone with an injured leg, he made an amazingly hasty departure. How vexing. And unpardonably rude to leave without giving some hint of what he wanted to discuss, some clue as to why he insisted on secrecy.

If he was toying with her, she did not care for the game. His brooding, cynical air might intimidate some, but a girl from St. Giles didn't survive long if she was the cowering type.

She'd never been one to shy away from a challenge.

Chapter Two

Daphne ventured to the duke's library the next morning, determined to pass the time with a book. However, after reading the same paragraph in *The Canterbury Tales* for the third time, she set the volume aside. Tucking her feet beneath her, she leaned back into the overstuffed armchair and breathed in deeply. Leather, parchment, ink, and lemon oil tickled her nose, and the shelves of books stretching out before her made her heart beat faster. To have such treasure at her fingertips was...a complete and utter waste. She couldn't concentrate if her next ball invitation depended upon it. More than a little vexed, she tucked the book into its space on the shelf.

What did Lord Foxburn have to say that was so secretive?

This morning at breakfast, Daphne had debated mentioning to her sister the conversation she'd had with the earl, but then Belle would tell her husband, and Daphne was sure the duke wouldn't approve of whatever game the earl was playing. And now Belle was upstairs sleeping—her third nap this week—which could very likely mean she was with child, and *that* would be too wonderful for words. Daphne sighed happily.

Perhaps she could persuade Rose—Belle's sister-in-law—to play chess. Daphne had little hope of winning against Rose—a wise, serene opponent if ever there was one. A dose of Rose's soothing calm demeanor was just what Daphne required.

She found Rose in the morning room dutifully plucking the strings of her harp like a redheaded cherub, while Olivia slouched on the settee, her legs sprawled like a hoyden's.

"Thank goodness you're here," said Olivia. "Rose has played every song she knows and we are both bored beyond measure. Play something for us on the pianoforte, would you?"

"Yes, please," said Rose, looking exceedingly relieved. She was already setting her harp aside.

"Of course," said Daphne, reaching for the sheet music. Any distraction from the earl's impending visit would do.

"I should like to hear a ballad—one that is sad and moving." After stating this preference, Olivia actually laid the back of her hand on her forehead.

"Has something happened?" Daphne eyed her distraught friend. "Just what transpired between you and Mr. Averill last night?"

"Nothing." Olivia sprang off the settee and paced. "*Nothing*! Don't you see? That is precisely the problem. I've waited over half my life for *something* to happen—and it never does." She plopped back onto the settee and hurled a pillow across the room, narrowly missing a vase of pink tulips.

Daphne exchanged a quick glance with Rose before situating herself on the bench at the pianoforte. Needless to say, a sorrowful ballad was entirely out of the question. Deciding on one of her mother's favorite Scotch reels, she said, "Perhaps this will cheer you." She launched into the merry tune, and despite Olivia's best efforts to remain miserable, she was soon tapping her foot in time to the music.

With each song, Olivia's mood improved. Meanwhile, Daphne grew more anxious.

Lord Foxburn didn't seem like the sort of man who would go back on his word, but he could easily have been detained by more important duties. Which was why she saw absolutely no point in flustering the entire household over the mere possibility that an earl might call on her today.

But then, that was probably overstating things. It wasn't as though the earl were courting her, for heaven's sake. She hoped her sisters-in-law wouldn't misconstrue the visit. Olivia, in particular, had a flair for the dramatic. Rose was much calmer by nature but was quite the romantic. Daphne adored both girls and had no wish to disappoint them.

Just as she was about to suggest a chess match, Dennison appeared at the doorway.

"Lord Foxburn awaits your company. In the drawing room." His tone was even, but his bushy white eyebrows had crawled halfway up his forehead, betraying his surprise.

Olivia gasped. To no one in particular, she said, "Oh my. A handsome war hero, in our drawing room. Why on earth would he be here? The earl does not seem the sort who generally pays social calls."

Rose shrugged her slim shoulders. "No man is an island."

"Perhaps not." Olivia cocked her head and twirled a brunette curl around an index finger. "But I should think the earl is a peninsula connected by the thinnest strip of land one could imagine. Even you must admit he is peculiar. Have you ever known an *earl* to purchase a commission in the British Army? I could understand if he were a second son who inherited unexpectedly, but—"

"I'm sure he had his reasons," Rose said. "As to the purpose of Lord Foxburn's call, he must want to further his acquaintance with someone." She arched a brow at Daphne, and her stomach flipped. So much for remaining cool and unaffected.

"Me? I do not think we have much in common. But then, the earl is something of an enigma, isn't he? He says little, and yet, those blue eyes of his are so intelligent, so intense, that I feel like he's capable of reading my thoughts."

"Precisely," Olivia declared. "I hope he read mine last night at dinner. *I* was thinking it a shame that his title and dashing good looks were squandered on someone with his ill manners."

"Olivia!" Rose cast a mildly scolding look at her sister. "He has been through much. Come, we should not keep the earl waiting too long."

As they made their way down the hall, Daphne concentrated on keeping her breathing even and her hands steady. Thank goodness Rose and Olivia were with her; although the earl obviously wanted a word with her alone, she was not feeling particularly brave.

Rose led the way into the drawing room and greeted their guest.

The earl unfolded himself from the wingback chair, rose to his full height, which was a head taller than any of the women, and bowed. "Good afternoon, ladies." His gaze went to Daphne and she resisted the urge to stare at the carpet. "I hope the duchess is well?"

"My sister is fine. Thank you for your kind concern." Daphne didn't quite believe his question arose out of concern. He was no doubt relieved to find her sister absent, since it meant there was one less person he needed to shoo away.

He raised a dark brow and to Olivia said, "Might I be permitted a brief word with Miss Honeycote? I realize it's a forward request, but I wish to convey a message—a private one—from my young friend, Lord Biltmore." The smile he flashed revealed his dimple and seemed to say, *We all know that the silly little rules intended to preserve ladies' reputations need to be bent once in a while.*

Daphne had to admire the impressive show of charm. It would never do to underestimate him.

Olivia crossed her arms in the imitation of a fierce chaperone. The effect was completely spoiled by her face, however, which was alight with excitement. "Your request is highly irregular, Lord Foxburn. One naturally wonders why Lord Biltmore did not come himself."

"Naturally," the earl said dryly. He stroked his chin, which was darkened by the slightest stubble. Daphne curled her fingers into her palms and waited to see what story he would concoct.

"My protégé is shy and not at all sure how his message will be received. I am only trying to play the part of ambassador. Like Cupid."

Of all the—Daphne suppressed a groan.

Olivia, on the other hand, cracked like an egg. "I see no reason why you should not be allowed a short visit. Rose, do you agree?"

Rose flicked her eyes to Daphne, clearly trying to ascertain her wishes in the matter. She gave a slight nod.

"If my dear friend is amenable, I have no objection. For propriety's sake, the door shall remain open, of course, and we shall be just across the hall."

"I would not have it any other way." The earl's expression was polite, at odds with the subtle bite of his words.

Apparently, she was the only one who noticed. Olivia gave a satisfied nod, took Rose by the arm, and departed, leaving Daphne and Lord Foxburn alone.

She waited for him to say something. Instead, he walked toward her, approaching her from the side. When he was an arm's length away, he paced in a half circle in front of her. One of his legs appeared stiff, and yet his movements were quick and sure. He studied her, his gaze roaming over her face and body in a manner that might be considered brazen if he didn't seem so detached—as though he were a botanist and she a mildly interesting species of flora.

When at last the silence and the staring became too suffocating, she cleared her throat. "There is no message from Lord Biltmore, is there?"

"No." He looked at her like she was some sort of simpleton. "I lied."

"I see. Is this ... lying ... something you do often?"

"When it suits my needs." His matter-of-fact tone was chilling.

"I suppose truth can be terribly inconvenient."

The corner of his mouth curled slightly and he stepped closer. She lifted her chin in order to look into his eyes.

"Spoken like a woman with something to hide."

"*I* have nothing to hide, Lord Foxburn. Perhaps *you* should reveal the reason you're here."

After a glance at the open door, he clasped her elbow and gently but firmly propelled her to the far corner of the drawing room. He leaned close to her ear, his breath warm on her neck. "I know about the portrait, Miss Honeycote."

The hairs on Daphne's arms stood on end, and her knees wobbled.

Dear God. No.

The earl stared at her, measuring her reaction. Her heart thudded in her chest. What was it that she'd planned to do if ever she were discovered? She screwed her face into a perplexed expression. "Portrait?"

"Shall I describe it in detail?"

"I'm afraid I don't know what you're talking about." Needing distance—and a moment to think—she turned and began to walk away. He followed.

"There's a painting of you, wearing a white gown. I use *wearing* in the loosest sense of the word. It would be more accurate to say the gown—which is little more than a night rail—is falling off your pretty little shoulders."

Good heavens.

Daphne sucked in a breath and whirled to face the earl. "You are mistaken, my lord. I have never had my portrait painted. If there's a resemblance, I assure you it's only a coincidence."

He gave a wry grin. "I don't think so."

"What are you implying?

"That I'm not the only one who lies to suit my needs."

Heat crept up her neck. "You are wrong. My sister and I do not come from a family of means. Before she married the duke, we couldn't afford sugar cubes for our tea. The idea that we could have hired an artist to paint my portrait is ludicrous."

"I'm not suggesting that you hired the artist. I'm suggesting that the artist hired *you*."

Daphne swallowed hard. The future she'd let herself envision—marriage to a kind, respectable man—was vanishing like morning mist on the lake. The paintings weren't supposed to be displayed in public—Thomas had promised. How foolish she was. And now she, and the people she loved, would pay a great price. Mama and Anabelle, who knew nothing of the portraits, would be shamed. Olivia's and Rose's reputations would be tainted by their association with her. She'd ruined *everything*.

"I think you should leave, my lord."

"Easy," he said. "Your secret is safe with me."

"I have no secrets."

"Miss Honeycote," he said smoothly, "we *all* have secrets. They're practically a form a currency."

Chapter Three

*Blending: (1) A technique used in painting that ensures
the gradual transition from one color to another.
(2) The act of appearing as though one belongs in a glittering,
privileged world—even when one clearly does not.*

Miss Honeycote glared at Ben impressively, but as she swept an errant strand of blond hair off her forehead, her hand trembled. "That sounds like a threat, Lord Foxburn."

"Not at all. I merely hoped we could reach an agreement." He cast a glance toward the open door, listening for the hovering Sherbourne sisters. He didn't have much time.

"I have already told you that I know nothing of this portrait. I grow weary of this conversation and of your insults. If you will not leave, then I shall."

"Wait." He had to admire her feistiness and the fire flashing in her blue eyes. A woman with her charms could easily snare a rich, titled husband. And why shouldn't she? Ben didn't give a damn who she seduced—as long as it wasn't Hugh. "Lord Biltmore is smitten with you. You must discourage him."

She shook her head as if she doubted her pretty little ears functioned properly. "What does Lord Biltmore have to do with this?"

"His brother, Robert, was my best friend. I made him a promise."

Only, it was more than a promise. It was a vow of the highest order.

One of Napoleon's men had charged and knocked Robert out of his saddle. He hadn't been struck down by a sword or injured by the fall—that was the hell of the thing. He'd been trampled by horses, some of them riderless, spooked by cannon fire. By the time Ben found him, grabbed him beneath his arms, and dragged him away from the reverberating clash of swords, a thin red line trickled from the corner of his mouth. He choked out his last request: *Take care of Hugh.*

Four words, punctuated by the gurgle and sputtering of blood. And then his soul—or whatever it was that had made him Robert—left, and his eyes turned cold and vacant.

"I'm very sorry about your friend."

Ben looked up, saw the sympathy in her expressive eyes, and flinched.

"This promise," Miss Honeycote said, "what was it?"

"To look after his brother. Which means I must ensure that Hugh marries a proper and respectable young lady."

It was her turn to flinch. The color rose in her cheeks, and she crossed the room to stand before the window overlooking St. James's Square. She rested her forehead and palms on the glass and remained frozen for a full minute. When at last she turned to face him, she clasped her hands loosely below her waist.

"Lord Biltmore is my friend. I refuse to be rude to him just because you happen to think I resemble a woman in a scandalous painting."

"Go about it as nicely as you like. As long as his heart is broken in the end, I shall be satisfied."

"And you think that's what your friend would have wanted?"

Ben bit his lower lip to keep a nasty retort from jumping out of his mouth. His leg, which hadn't hurt much this morning, began to throb. In a measured tone, he said, "Robert was very unlike me, Miss Honeycote. He was something of a romantic and wanted his brother to enjoy a long and happy marriage to a woman who would be faithful. But he knew that Hugh was—and still is—somewhat naïve. Robert once confided in me his fear that if something were to happen to him, Hugh would be blinded by an opportunistic, fortune-seeking beauty."

"I am not—" She stopped midsentence, and her gaze flew to his thigh, which he'd absently begun to rub.

"What happened?"

He removed his hand and shook his head firmly. The injury was *not* something he discussed. He had no desire to be an object of morbid curiosity or, worse, sympathy. "Do we understand each other, Miss Honeycote?"

"I understand you are of the opinion that I would not be a suitable wife for Lord Biltmore."

"And you will discourage his attentions?"

"I will need some time to think on the matter."

"You'll have no difficulty finding another rich, titled gentleman to take his place." He'd only meant to point out the bright side, but her narrowed eyes and clenched fists suggested she wasn't appreciative of his effort.

"It may surprise you, my lord, to know that I don't view gentlemen as replaceable commodities."

"Are you that taken with him, then?" The thought hadn't occurred to him, and damn it all if his leg wasn't hurting more. Like someone had stabbed him with a hot poker.

She frowned slightly, and a tiny dimple marred her forehead, just above her left eye. "I don't know—that is, we're friends and I'd thought perhaps…"

"It's settled, then. You'll let him down as gently as you can, and I won't breathe a word about the portrait." He could hear someone in the hall humming. Off-key. He should escape before the sisters returned to check on their charge. "I'm glad we were able to strike a deal, Miss Honeycote."

He would have liked some acknowledgment of their agreement, but she simply gazed at him with a slightly puzzled look. "What makes you so sure that the woman in the portrait is me?"

It didn't occur to him to lie. Not about this. "You reflect light."

"Pardon me?"

"In the painting, as in real life, you are…luminous." It was true. He'd never known a person who shined like her. It wasn't just her pale blond tresses or her radiant skin or gleaming eyes. She shone from the inside, and it made him uncomfortably and acutely aware of the cold, damp, dark foxhole that was his life.

Her pink mouth opened slightly as though she were… what? Surprised, insulted…touched? Whichever was the case, he'd take it as his cue to leave. He nodded politely as he walked past her, concentrating on making his leg move as naturally as possible instead of thudding across the floor.

"Lord Foxburn."

Damn. He'd almost made it to the door. He stopped, faced her, and arched a brow.

"I'm curious." She approached him slowly and his heart beat a little faster. Interesting. "Where did you see the painting?" Quickly, she added, "The portrait that you think is of me."

"Do not worry. It's part of a private collection."

"Whose?"

"Mine."

She let out a sound that was part gasp and part whimper.

"Good day, Miss Honeycote."

Daphne braced an arm on the back of a chair for support.

The earl had her portrait.

She breathed in deeply and tried to tamp down the panic banging at her chest. How on earth had he come to possess that painting?

And more importantly, where was the other one?

She'd known Thomas, the artist, since they were children, and he'd assured her that the paintings were for a wealthy squire who was something of a recluse. Of course, at the time she'd posed for the paintings, she was a poor nobody. She supposed she still was, but now her sister was a duchess and everything else had changed. Daphne never dreamed she would be rubbing shoulders with nobility. Even so, she'd naïvely hoped that the paintings would stay tucked away in the squire's country home. Conveniently locked away in an attic.

But somehow one of the portraits had ended up in the hands of Lord Foxburn. Which meant the other one could be circulating as well.

Olivia and Rose scurried into the drawing room and pulled her to the settee. Daphne linked her shaking hands in her lap and assumed what she hoped was a serene expression. The last thing she wished to do was worry her dear friends.

"Tell us," Olivia said, bouncing on her bottom. "What message did Lord Foxburn relay from Lord Biltmore? This is so romantic, is it not?"

Romantic, no. Ironic...perhaps. But Daphne smiled. And stalled for time.

"It was nothing, really." She searched her mind for some tidbit of her conversation with Lord Biltmore from the night before, something plausible she could use.

"Do not be coy, Daphne!" Olivia gave her a playful push on the arm that almost catapulted her into Rose's lap. "You spoke to the earl for at least a quarter of an hour. That's not nothing."

"No, I suppose it's not." Daphne fiddled with the sash of her lemon-colored gown. She could feel Rose's all-too-perceptive gaze reading her like the morning paper—or, perhaps, the gossip rags.

Daphne hated to lie, but the truth simply wouldn't do. "Lord Foxburn simply wished to let me know that... ah..."

Rose laid a slender hand on top of hers. "You needn't tell us if it's a private matter."

Olivia threw her hands up in the air. "Are you mad? Of course she must. *Especially* if it's a private matter."

And then Daphne recalled what seemed a rather innocuous, random snippet. And she used it.

"Lord Biltmore is making a short trip to visit his cousin. He'll be in Southampton for a couple of days but hopes to see us at the Seaton musicale later this week." There, that sounded reasonable. Or at least conceivable.

Olivia clasped both hands over her open mouth, and Daphne wished she could take it back. "Do you know what this means?" Olivia asked.

Daphne exchanged an apprehensive look with Rose. "That Lord Biltmore wished to explain his brief absence from the London scene?"

"No." Exasperation oozed out of Olivia's pores. "That is, *obviously*. But it's much more than that, don't you see?"

"I'm afraid I don't," Daphne said.

"He wanted *you* to know. You'll notice he did not ask the earl to convey the message to Rose or me. Which means he holds *you* in higher esteem."

"Oh, I hardly think—"

Olivia held up a forefinger. "Don't be modest. Rose and I are not offended in the least, are we, Rose?"

The hint of a smile danced at the corner of Rose's mouth and she shook her head.

"On the contrary, we are delighted for you," Olivia continued. "It seems a match is in the offing."

Heavens. Quite the opposite was true. How had the conversation taken such a drastic and unintended turn?

"You misunderstand. Lord Biltmore is a kind and considerate gentleman. I'm sure he meant nothing."

Rose tilted her head thoughtfully. "I must agree with

Olivia. It seems like more than a polite gesture, and the message *was* clearly directed at you."

Encouraged, Olivia sprang from the settee and began to pace with such vigor that she almost toppled a piecrust table.

Daphne had to distract Olivia before she could pursue the subject further. "Could we please forget about the earl's visit? Tell me the latest news of Mr. Averill."

Olivia was never happier than when she related the dashing solicitor's archeological adventures. With a dreamy, distant look in her eyes, she opened her mouth and... blinked. "You are quite clever. Very well, we shan't discuss Lord Biltmore any more today. Tomorrow, however, is another matter."

"Thank you," Daphne said sincerely. "Would you mind terribly if I went to my room to rest?"

"Not at all," Rose replied. "Would you like me to send up some tea?"

"No, I believe I'll lie down for a bit. Thank you, though." She hugged Rose. Both girls had become like sisters to her. To Olivia, she said, "And I do hope you'll tell me about Mr. Averill later."

Olivia flashed a saucy smile. "Have I told you about the time I pretended to trip over a tree root in order to—"

"Later, Olivia," Rose scolded. "Daphne is tired."

"Very well. Just don't bring up the tree root debacle in front of my brother."

Daphne chuckled and hugged Olivia. "I promise. I'll see you both at dinner."

Well, this was a fine predicament. She was supposed to discourage Lord Biltmore's attentions but had somehow led her friends to believe he was courting her.

And that was the least of her problems.

She walked swiftly up the stairs and down the hall to the guest bedchamber she'd been given. The room was spacious and decorated in lovely hues of blue and gold. Gilded furnishings glinted in the afternoon light, but for once, Daphne appreciated none of it. After closing the door and turning the key in the lock, she sat on the edge of the bed and clutched fistfuls of velvet counterpane. Her whole body trembled and her teeth chattered in spite of the day's warmth.

As quickly and unexpectedly as it had begun, her season was over.

She would have to pack her trunks once again and go live with her mother's cousins in a village whose sheep population outnumbered humans by a ratio of five to one. How could she possibly stay in London? Each time she was introduced to a new gentleman, she'd wonder if he'd seen one of her portraits and would therefore assume the worst of her, as Lord Foxburn had.

Everything had been going so well before she met the earl, but one conversation with him had left her future in tatters. He didn't even know her and yet he'd judged her and found her lacking the necessary morals. It would be easy to make him the object of her anger, especially since he was so arrogant and callous. He was a miserable, soulless person.

But this dilemma wasn't of his making.

She'd made this terrible mess, and it was up to her to rectify it.

She rushed to the desk beneath the window. As she withdrew a piece of paper from the drawer, her hands shook.

The earl had seen the portrait in which she was on the sapphire chaise. She wore a thin white morning gown— not hers—that gaped at the back. For countless hours, she'd posed, one shoulder leaning against the arm of the chaise, as she smiled over the other at Thomas. Her bare feet dangled over the edge of the seat, the lacy edge of the gown tickling her ankles.

She'd known the pose was scandalous, of course, but she'd never thought her reputation among the *ton* would matter.

She'd trusted Thomas—an old and dear friend— completely. He'd known her family needed money and suggested the arrangement, but he'd never pushed Daphne to sit for him or made advances. On the contrary, he seemed too consumed by his art to be distracted by lesser human emotions such as desire. He was an unknown, but she hoped—for his sake—that his passion and talent would someday earn him recognition among society's elite.

What was it he'd said about his patron? Daphne did not know his name, only that he was a wealthy landowner who shunned town life. He'd challenged Thomas to find and paint "the perfect English beauty" and promised a handsome reward if the portrait pleased him. Thomas had split the money with her.

She wasn't exactly ashamed of the painting. Under the same circumstances, she'd pose again. But so much had changed since then. Mama was well, Anabelle was a duchess, and Daphne was having a season.

If either of the portraits was prominently displayed, though, and she was identified as the subject, she would be completely and utterly ruined. No gentleman would court her. No lady would befriend her. She would be exiled to the realm of unsuitable persons. A lump the size of an egg settled in her throat.

She supposed her circumstances could be worse. Anabelle would always make sure she had a roof over her head. Lately, however, Daphne had begun to wish for something more—marriage to a kind and proper gentleman, a houseful of laughing children, and years of domestic bliss. Those dreams were shriveling like tender blossoms in the summer sun.

Worse, her reputation was inextricably entangled with her sister's, as well as Rose's and Olivia's. Belle's sisters-in-law, in particular, had endured such a difficult time since their mother fled to the Continent and their father committed suicide. With Olivia's propensity to speak her mind and Rose's extreme shyness, they'd never been embraced by society. This season was to be their chance to restore their own reputations after having been dismissed as too odd and eccentric to join the *ton's* inner circles. In fact, just last week they'd received an invitation to Lady Yardley's annual ball. However, if the portraits of Daphne were placed on exhibition . . . she shuddered at the thought.

Daphne had to get the portraits back.

She dipped her quill in the ink and scratched out a message.

Dear Thomas,

I require your help. The portrait of me on the sapphire chaise is now in the possession of an earl, Lord Foxburn—a highly distressing state of affairs, as I'm sure you can imagine. The earl has promised to keep the painting out of sight for now, but we must find a way to get it back.

In the meantime, I need to know who your patron is, and where the other portrait might be so that I can prevent it from being displayed in a home or establishment where someone might recognize me.

Please meet me tomorrow at four o'clock in the afternoon at Gunter's, under the pineapple sign in Berkley Square, so that we may devise a plan.

Desperately yours,

D. H.

While she waited for the ink to dry, Daphne paced. How she longed to confide in Anabelle. Her sister, two years older and infinitely wiser, would know what to do and, even better, would find a way to make Daphne feel less miserable. But Anabelle was newly married and quite possibly expecting her first child. She'd been the one who had sacrificed everything when Mama was ill. Her extortion scheme had paid their rent and kept a little food on their table.

Daphne had never told Anabelle about the money from the portraits. She'd used it to pay the apothecary and the doctor when the bills had piled up. But her sister would have objected to any source of income that could jeopardize Daphne's well-being, and now it seemed she was, indeed, in trouble.

No, running to Anabelle would be selfish. Daphne could not rely on her to fix all of her problems. She would handle this dilemma on her own.

Daphne folded the letter and addressed it, miserably aware of what it represented.

Her last prayer.

Chapter Four

The next day was precisely the sort that gave London weather a bad name. Clouds hung low and gray, spitting fat raindrops at will. Every half hour or so, the sun flirted with the idea of making an appearance, a debutante coyly peering over her fan. But then the wind kicked up and the clouds returned, casting shadows over streets and storefronts. In the duel between gloom and promise, gloom inevitably won out.

As Ben's coach rumbled through the streets toward home, he absently rubbed the gnarled muscles of his right thigh. After sitting through a two-hour appointment with his solicitor, his leg was as stiff as the whalebone busk in a spinster's corset.

His solicitor and friend, Averill, had tried to give him the card of a young physician who had newfangled ideas about how to treat patients with permanent injuries. Ben refused to take it. He'd been poked and prodded by a dozen different doctors already, and they all suggested the same remedy: cutting off his leg.

Those quacks could take a flying leap into the Thames. He'd almost died in order to save his leg, and he wasn't about to part with it, even if it routinely felt like someone was twisting a knife into it.

Maybe, in a decade or so, he'd grow accustomed to the pain. In the meantime, he should probably barricade himself in a cave like a wounded animal. If he lived in a cave, he'd presumably be exempt from balls and soirees and house parties. Conversely, others would not have to suffer his perpetually bad mood. All things considered, it sounded like a winning proposition.

The only drawback was that there would be no suitable wall on which to hang Miss Honeycote's portrait.

He hadn't taken the painting down yet. He'd planned to that morning, but he'd gotten absorbed in the review of a contract, and every quarter of an hour or so he liked to reward himself by glancing at the wall opposite his desk in his study. Now that he knew the subject was Miss Honeycote, he found the artwork more fascinating than ever.

He wondered about the circumstances under which she'd posed and whether the artist was her lover. It hardly mattered, and yet, the thought chafed like a pair of burlap drawers. Ben had used a magnifying glass to examine the scrawling signature in the bottom right corner of the painting but couldn't decipher the name—only the initial *T*.

At least Miss Honeycote would no longer have her cap set at Hugh. With any luck, his young protégé would meet a proper miss and be married before Michaelmas so that Ben could retreat to his country house, which, while not quite as private as a cave, was bound to be more comfortable.

He stared out the coach window at a few gray-clad servants scurrying in the pelting rain like mice dodging the paws of a menacing cat. Then, out of the corner of his eye, he spotted a glint of gold that made his heart trip in his chest. He pounded on the roof of the cab, and as the driver slowed the horses and pulled over, Ben craned his neck around to be sure he hadn't imagined her.

Miss Honeycote.

She stood outside Gunter's, beneath an umbrella that was proving less effective by the minute. The damp skirt of her light green gown clung to her, revealing the curve of her hips and the long line of her legs. Her pink bonnet covered half her head but the thick blond coil at her nape was practically a beacon. And she was quite alone.

Ben hopped out of the coach before it had even stopped rolling, ignoring the pain that shot through his right leg when he hit the ground. The rain plunked on his head and dripped down his neck as he strode toward her. When she saw him approach, her eyes grew wide, as though she'd been caught stealing a cake.

"Why are you standing out here?"

She glanced up and down the street quickly before responding. "Good afternoon, Lord Foxburn. I was supposed to meet someone at four o'clock."

Good grief, it was almost half past.

"It appears my friend has been detained." She deflated a little and sighed.

"Come. I'll give you a ride home." He jabbed a thumb behind him toward his coach. His warm, dry coach.

"No thank you." A huge drop rolled off the edge of her umbrella and plopped onto his nose.

"How long do you intend to wait?"

She looked down at her dress and frowned. "Another quarter of an hour, perhaps."

"You could float away before then."

"I'll take my chances." As an afterthought she added, "But I appreciate your kind offer."

He got the distinct feeling he was being dismissed, but damn it, he was not going to let her stand out here and catch her death's cold. "You could wait for your friend inside my coach."

She hesitated for a moment, probably weighing impropriety against the puddle forming around her pretty new boots.

"No one is about," he said. No one who was *anyone*, at least. "If we drew the shades, no one would be the wiser."

When she nodded—almost imperceptibly—he clasped her elbow and guided her toward his coach before she could change her mind.

He plucked the umbrella out of her hand and held it above her head as she stepped lightly into his coach. After a word with the coachman, Ben climbed in and eased onto the bench across from her. He lowered all the shades but left a narrow gap on the window to Miss Honeycote's right, allowing her to watch the front of the shop. Sure enough, her gaze flicked there every few seconds.

For a while, they sat in companionable silence—an impressive feat given their conversation yesterday afternoon.

Then, Miss Honeycote delicately cleared her throat. "I've been wondering about something."

He leaned back in his seat and crossed his arms as though he was only mildly interested. "Have you?"

"The portrait—the one that you believe is of me—where did you get it?"

"If the painting is not of you, why do you care?"

To her credit, she didn't cower in the least. "Whether the portrait is of me or someone else, it's clear that the subject at least resembles me, or I resemble her. I'll admit that it's distressing." The furrows in her brow confirmed she was, in fact, troubled.

"You're concerned that others might have seen the painting and also come to the incorrect conclusion that the model is you?" He didn't bother hiding his skepticism.

She raised her chin, challenging him. "Yes. A lady's reputation is a fragile thing. I've only just arrived on the scene, Lord Foxburn. I should not like to be ostracized from polite society before I've managed to attend one major ball."

He grunted. "Balls are highly overrated."

"I'd like to make my own determination," she retorted. "Besides, my reputation is not the only one at stake. My friends, Olivia and Rose, could also suffer from their association with me." Her pretty blue eyes, which were framed with thick blond lashes, clouded with worry.

"I have an idea," he said.

She leaned forward. "What?"

"You could simply explain to everyone that the painting is not you."

"What do you mean, 'everyone'? You said you would keep it hidden."

"And I shall—if you want me to."

"Yes. I think that's best. After all, people may not believe me."

Quite true. He did not.

"And I suppose that is why I'd like to know," she continued, "how you came to be in possession of the painting."

"It belonged to a friend. I found it in his study, along with several other paintings. He hadn't had a chance to hang them yet." Ben's chest ached, making him feel tired and old.

Miss Honeycote sat up straighter and her lips parted slightly. "Were there any others...that looked like me?"

"No." He would have remembered.

She frowned. "So your friend gave it to you...as a gift?"

"Not exactly, but I knew he would have wanted me to have it."

Understanding and sympathy shone in her eyes. "You're talking about Lord Biltmore's older brother—the one who died at Waterloo."

"Yes." As always, the mere mention of Robert sent Ben back to that god-awful day, complete with the taste of gunpowder and the sting of smoke in his eyes. The grunts of soldiers wielding their swords and the inhuman moans of patriots struck down in battle still echoed in his ears.

"I'm sorry." She reached across the cab and laid her slender hand on his forearm, instantly dragging him back to the present. The warmth of her touch penetrated the damp wool of his jacket sleeve and radiated through his body, heating his blood. He let his gaze linger on her hand, memorizing the way her tapered fingers curled around his arm and squeezed with light, soothing pressure.

Ben nodded. "Hugh couldn't bring himself to sort through Robert's personal items. He asked me to do it and encouraged me to take whatever mementos I wanted. I wanted the painting."

She sighed softly and withdrew her hand, leaving him surprisingly bereft. "You miss him."

"Every. Damned. Day."

She didn't flinch at his bad manners but merely nodded as though she understood. And yet, she seemed entirely too young and innocent to have been touched by death. As if privy to his thoughts, she said, "I miss my father that way." But then a smile lit her face, belying her words.

"And yet, you seem almost impossibly cheerful."

"My sister has often accused me of the same thing." She glanced at the shop and swallowed before continuing. "Thinking about Papa makes me happy. I remember his deep, kind voice and the texture of his beard. I miss him, but I know he's in a better place."

He should have guessed. "You believe in God."

"Of course. Don't you?"

"I don't know."

Rain continued to patter on the roof of the coach. He raised the shade to his left and scanned the nearly deserted street. "I don't think your friend is coming."

Miss Honeycote bit her lower lip, and he had the very improper urge to reach across and trace the fullness of that lip with the pad of his thumb. "No," she said. "It would appear not."

"May I give you a ride home?"

She cast her eyes downward, apparently defeated. "Yes, thank you."

Ben excused himself and stepped outside to give the coachman her address. When he climbed back into the coach, his damned leg cramped and almost buckled.

Miss Honeycote boldly reached out and guided him to the seat. Right beside her. The green silk of her skirt touched his buckskin breeches. "What do you do for the pain?" she asked.

"Pardon?" He'd heard her, of course. He just hadn't expected her to be so direct.

She inclined her head and slid her gaze to his thigh, causing his blood to thrum in his veins. "How do you treat your leg?"

"I drink," he said dryly. "Copiously."

His answer had been intended to dissuade her curiosity, but she smiled sweetly. "Do you find it to be an effective form of treatment?"

"No, actually, but it happens to be the best bloody option."

Glancing around the coach, she said quite seriously, "Do you have any spirits here?"

"Thirsty, are you?"

She blushed prettily. "I don't like seeing you in pain."

Ben did his best to hide his injury—his weakness. Most people seemed oblivious to his discomfort, or maybe they thought it impolite to inquire about it. Miss Honeycote, on the other hand, had no qualms about prying into his business. And she was too perceptive by half.

"Don't worry on my account," he said. "I suspect this is payment for past sins. If so, I'm getting off easy." Her doubtful yet calculating expression made the hairs on his neck stand on end. A change of subject was definitely in order. "Before leaving for Southampton, Hugh mentioned he wanted to return in time for the Seaton musicale Friday evening. I assume you'll be there?"

"Yes, I'm looking forward to it."

"Hugh is more infatuated with you than I had realized," he announced bluntly.

Daphne swallowed. "And you find this distressing."

Highly. "That may be overstating it. I find it problematic."

"Lord Biltmore is a kind man. He doesn't deserve to be treated poorly."

"Agreed. The fact remains," he continued, "that you would not be a suitable wife for him."

"You've made that exceedingly clear, my lord."

He gave a wry smile, then asked, "How do you feel about him?" He kept his tone casual, almost offhand, but there was a tightness in his chest. He wouldn't fool himself into thinking her answer didn't matter to him.

It mattered very much. And for more reasons than he cared to examine.

"Lord Biltmore is a true gentleman. He has many admirable qualities." Though she didn't make an outright comparison, her meaning was clear: *He is everything you are not.*

"Do you love him?"

"That is a highly personal question, my lord." Her cheeks flushed pink.

He stared at her for several moments, long enough to see that whatever she might feel for Hugh—admiration, esteem, respect—she didn't feel passion.

"That's good," he said.

"What's good?"

"You don't love him."

"Of all the—Do not presume to tell me what I feel."

"I'm not," he said matter-of-factly. "I'm telling you what you *don't*."

"A ridiculous distinction." She folded her arms across her chest.

"Hugh will be there. At the musicale," he said. "I trust you'll abide by the terms of our bargain."

A wounded look flashed across her face as the coach

drew to a stop in front of Huntford's house. "I haven't forgotten, Lord Foxburn."

Guilt—an emotion he'd long thought himself incapable of—gnawed at his gut, and he glanced away, reminding himself that she was not as innocent as she seemed. After all, she'd posed for a portrait half naked *and* insisted on lying about it.

Ben helped her from the coach and walked her to the duke's doorstep.

The silk flowers on her bonnet had wilted from the rain. Her smile seemed similarly affected, damn it all.

"Look, if I act like a boor sometimes, it's because I'm trying to protect Hugh. That, and I'm an ass."

She smiled serenely—just like in her portrait. "I know." Placing a hand on the door handle, she said, "Will you be at the musicale?"

Him? Good God. It was sure to be an amateur, if not torturous, performance. But if she was going to be there... "Perhaps. Good day, Miss Honeycote."

She arched a blond brow and said, "Good day," before stepping inside.

As his coach rumbled down the street toward his town house, Ben ran a hand over the velvet seat still warm beside him. A faint floral scent lingered in the coach, and regardless of what he'd told Miss Honeycote, the truth was that the hounds of hell couldn't keep him away from the musicale—or, more specifically, from her.

Damn it. Apparently, Hugh wasn't the only fool in danger of succumbing to Miss Honeycote's charms.

Chapter Five

Glaze: (1) A thin, transparent layer of paint used to add depth or modify color. (2) To become glassy, as in The quartet's lifeless—and somewhat torturous—rendition of Beethoven's concerto caused the earl's eyes to glaze over.

Two days later, when Daphne returned from her walk, Mama was waiting for her in Owen and Belle's drawing room. She'd returned from Bath looking better than Daphne could ever remember seeing her. She'd swept her shoulder-length brown curls—streaked with silver—into a pretty bun high on her head. Hand-painted combs added sophistication. But it was Mama's full cheeks and easy smile that made Daphne want to weep with joy.

"I'm so glad you're back, Mama." She hugged her fiercely, loving her recently increased girth. *This* was the Mama from her childhood—the one who'd sung to her at night and kissed her skinned knees. After her mother's long and horrible illness, Daphne had begun to wonder if she'd ever be the same. Seeing her looking so healthy and vibrant suddenly made Daphne long to cry into her shoulder and tell her about everything. The scandalous portraits. The fear that she'd bring shame upon her family. The deal she'd made with Lord Foxburn.

But she was no longer a girl who could run to her mother to make everything better.

"Oh, let me look at you." Mama placed her hands on either side of Daphne's face and studied her intently. Daphne could almost see her counting freckles, making sure that no new ones had popped up during the two weeks she'd been away. "I've ordered tea. Now, sit and tell me everything that you left out of your letters."

Daphne happily obliged—to the extent that she could without incriminating herself, that is. She recounted every social affair she'd attended in the last fortnight, playing up the bits Mama enjoyed best, such as the evening Lord Huxton stumbled into a Greek sculpture in Lady Fallow's dining room. Owen seized it just before it hit the floor, preventing not only a royal mess but also a rift between the families that might have lasted for generations.

Mama sighed happily. "I missed you and Anabelle, of course, but I was surprised to find that I missed town, too."

"You did?" Daphne blinked. In the event that her greatest fear came true and the *ton* identified her as the woman in the painting, she had comforted herself with the thought that Mama might actually *prefer* living in a remote cottage. But perhaps not.

"Indeed. Henrietta is lively company—as you'll soon discover—but we found little to amuse us. There was the occasional fete in the Upper Assembly Rooms, but nothing like the dazzling entertainments here."

Who *was* this woman who claimed to be her mother? Perhaps the waters in the Pump Room were more potent than anyone realized. Mama's traveling companion, Lady Bonneville, was no doubt partially responsible. The elderly viscountess was known for her spunk, and Anabelle was confident she'd be a good influence on Mama.

Daphne wasn't so sure.

"I do hope we have some engagements lined up." Mama placed a fruit tart on her plate.

"We do." Daphne scurried to the escritoire beneath the window, picked up a small pile of invitations, and shuffled through them. "Mrs. Reece is hosting a dinner party next Monday. Shall I let her know that you're back in town?"

"Ah, she and her husband make a lovely couple—they're so in love." Mama shot Daphne a brief but wistful glance that all but shouted, *You could be, too, if only you'd apply yourself to the task.* "Yes, darling, please do let them know I'll attend. Is there nothing else scheduled before then? An event at which we might see Lord Biltmore?"

Oh dear. "Lord Biltmore?"

"Anabelle wrote that he's quite taken with you."

"She did?" Daphne intended to have a word with Anabelle, who had apparently skated dangerously close to a violation of sisterly trust in her letters to Mama. "I don't—"

"Don't be coy, darling. It's wonderful!" The rapture that overcame Mama was almost frightening in its intensity. Her shoulders rose up until they were almost level with her ears and she pressed her lips together tightly as though she might explode with joy. "Oh, Daphne. He's *such* a gentleman! Kind and good-natured and"—Mama paused to fan herself—"a viscount! He's everything I've ever wanted for you." She sniffled, almost overcome. "My daughter, the viscountess."

Good heavens. "Lord Biltmore is all that you say, only...I don't think we would suit."

"Why on earth not?"

"I know you want me to make a good match but—"

"It's what every mother wishes for her daughter."

"But finding the right person might take some time." At the rate she was going, a decade or so ought to do it.

Mama deflated a little. "You have *some* time...but you've devoted too much of your youth to caring for me. Don't deny yourself the joys of a family for too long."

This was Mama's sweet but thinly veiled way of saying that Daphne would be on the shelf if she didn't apply herself to the task of finding a husband. And she was right.

After all they'd been through, it was only natural that she would want to see her younger daughter well settled and taken care of. Daphne used to think she wanted that, too, but now she yearned for something more than security and comfort. She dared to hope for love and... passion.

"I understand what a rare opportunity this season is for me, Mama. I'll try my best not to disappoint you."

"You couldn't. Just promise me that you'll give Lord Biltmore a chance to charm you." Mama's eyes twinkled so brightly Daphne was powerless to deny the request.

"I will."

"Excellent." Mama slipped on her new spectacles and gestured to the stack of invitations Daphne still held. "What else have we to look forward to?"

"There's the Seaton musicale tonight. However, I'm sure that you'll want to rest after your travels. We could plan an outing to Bond Street tomorrow."

"I'm not too tired for a musicale," Mama exclaimed, as

though slightly offended. "That's tame even by my standards. Are the Seaton daughters talented?"

Daphne shrugged. "I've never heard them play."

"Ah, well, it hardly matters. The important thing is I shall spend the evening with *you*." Mama stood and smoothed her skirts. "I'm going to take Anabelle some toast—it's the best thing for her queasy stomach, you know—and lie down for a quick nap. I can't have puffy eyes while escorting you about. We must make a good impression everywhere we go. The unfortunate aspect of being suddenly elevated to the pinnacle of society is that some are looking for the slightest excuse to topple us right back from whence we came. I'll not have anything spoil the happiness that we've been blessed with."

Daphne crossed the room to hug her mother. "I've *always* been blessed, thanks to you, Papa, and Anabelle."

"It's good to hear you mention your papa." Mama's voice grew thin. "You must miss him as much as I do."

She nodded. "Sometimes, living in all this luxury feels like a betrayal. What would he think?" Papa had given up his comfortable life when he chose to marry Mama— a common woman—and his family had disowned him until the very end.

Mama let out a long, wispy breath and tucked a stray tendril behind Daphne's ear. "He would say that everything *around* us is not nearly as important as what's *inside* us. Whenever you or Anabelle got into mischief or told a fib, he would invariably say—"

"Nothing is more valuable than one's integrity," Daphne finished for her.

"I'm glad you remember," Mama said, her eyes moist. "I'll see you at dinner." After planting a kiss on Daphne's forehead, she glided from the room in a light cloud of rose-scented perfume.

Daphne sank to the settee. She was a fine one to speak of integrity. In posing for the portraits, she'd flagrantly disregarded the rules of proper behavior. That was shameful enough. But now she'd also been reduced to keeping secrets and lying to the people she loved.

She wished there were some other way, but she'd chosen her path two years ago—the moment she'd shed her coat in that chilly abandoned factory and posed upon the sapphire settee.

All she could do now was locate the second portrait— and the trail began with Thomas. The evening after Daphne had waited for him at Gunter's, the artist's mother had returned Daphne's letter, with the seal still intact, thank Heaven. She'd also scrawled a note saying Thomas had embarked on a grand tour some time ago and would not likely return for several weeks. There was no one else she could turn to for answers, except perhaps the person who was in possession of the first painting...

No. She couldn't trust Lord Foxburn. He was too cold, too unfeeling. Worse, his icy blue eyes seemed to judge her constantly, like he was measuring her behavior against a checklist of etiquette for proper ladies and finding it rather lacking. No small wonder, considering he owned evidence of her most embarrassing mistake.

But trusting Lord Foxburn wasn't the only problem. Daphne wasn't certain she could trust *herself* around him. He seemed intent on provoking her and casting aspersions on her character, and yet, she couldn't help admiring his loyalty to his friend. Nor could she ignore the pain he stoically endured in his leg and his heart and the fact that he was devilishly attractive—*if* one cared about such things.

When Daphne entered the Seatons' crowded drawing room with Mama, Olivia, and Rose that evening, her nerves were wound tighter than a spring. She was all too well aware that at any given moment, someone could recognize her from the paintings and publicly brand her as a woman of loose morals.

So, after exchanging a few polite greetings, Daphne thought it prudent to take a seat in the back and attempt to blend in with Lady Worsham's pink and green wallpaper.

"I see Henrietta seated in the front row." Mama smiled; she was, perhaps, the only person genuinely pleased to see Lady Bonneville in attendance. "She requires room for her footstool, you know."

"Yes, we know," said Olivia, rolling her eyes.

The elderly viscountess took her red tufted footstool with her everywhere she went—or, rather, her long-suffering companion did. If the habit was a bit eccentric, no one dared label it as such. It was in the best interests of all to keep Lady Bonneville happy.

"She's quite by herself. I shall go keep her company. Would you girls care to join me?"

Daphne did not wish to be anywhere near the front row *or* the viscountess's scrutiny. "If you don't mind, Mama, I'd rather remain here where the music won't be as loud." Olivia and Rose enthusiastically nodded their agreement.

"That's fine, darlings. Be sure to mingle." She gave Daphne one last pointed look through her spectacles before joining Lady Bonneville.

In the seat beside Daphne, Olivia snapped open her fan and fluttered it dramatically. "That was a narrow escape."

"I admire the viscountess," Rose said, "even if she does frighten me a little."

Olivia snorted. "She would frighten Wellington himself."

"She has taken Mama under her wing," Daphne said. "I'm grateful for that."

"I suppose I am as well," Olivia said, a bit reluctantly. "Mostly, however, I'm grateful to be here with you and Rose." She put an arm around Daphne and gave her a brief, tight squeeze. "I knew the yellow silk would be perfect with your golden hair. Don't look now, but the gentleman by the fireplace can't take his eyes off you."

Daphne swallowed. She'd never met the man, but what if he recognized her from the portraits? Her palms grew moist inside her elbow-length gloves. "He's probably admiring you and Rose. You both look lovely tonight."

Olivia sighed. "This gown shall be wasted if James does not show." Her eyes strayed to the door. "Alas, he is not among the latest arrivals...however, I see that Lord Foxburn and Lord Biltmore are."

Lord Foxburn. Daphne had been thinking about him ever since he'd left her on her doorstep. More specifically, she'd been thinking about his hair—which was slightly too long—and the manner in which a few dark brown strands curled just behind his ear. She couldn't imagine why she was fixated on such a random and meaningless detail, but there it was.

She swiveled on her chair and watched as he approached, Lord Biltmore at his side. The earl walked smoothly; the only sign of his injury was a slight hesitation before he stepped on his right foot. His jacket of blue superfine complemented his tanned skin and made his eyes look as clear as a September sky. His expression was more suited to a funeral service than a musicale, but she'd come to expect no less from him.

"Good evening, Lady Olivia, Lady Rose, and Miss Honeycote," exclaimed Lord Biltmore. He tugged nervously on the front of his rich purple jacket and shuffled his feet. "You're all looking particularly beautiful this evening." He smiled shyly at Daphne. "I wonder, Miss Honeycote, if you would like to take a turn about the room with me?"

Egads. Lord Foxburn had decreed that she must not encourage the viscount, but she did not wish to be rude. Surely the earl could not object to a walk in a room full of people. Pasting on a smile, she said, "That would be lov—"

Behind Lord Biltmore, Lord Foxburn narrowed his icy blue eyes and gave a subtle but crisp shake of his head.

"—er, lovely . . . *if* I didn't have such a dreadful headache at the moment." Lord, how she hated to lie. Almost as much as she resented having the course of her evening dictated by an ill-tempered tyrant.

Lord Biltmore's brow furrowed in concern. "I'm most sorry to hear you're not feeling well," he said. "Shall I inform your mother that you'd like to go home?"

"No, thank you. I'll just sit here awhile and see if that helps."

An awkward silence followed, and Lord Biltmore shifted his weight from one foot to another.

"A suggestion, if I might be so bold," Lord Foxburn said dryly. "Miss Seaton seems to be in need of encouragement."

Lord Biltmore snapped to attention. "Which Miss Seaton?"

The earl made a pained face. "Damned if I know her name. The one over there"—he inclined his head toward the makeshift stage—"with the greenish pallor. She's been adjusting the strings on her violin since we came in, but I suspect no amount of tuning will improve the upcoming performance. At least if you calm her nerves, she will be less likely to swoon midsong."

Lord Biltmore gazed at the stage and nodded sympathetically. "That's Miss Louise Seaton," he said. "And she does have a rather terrified look in her eyes. Please excuse me while I endeavor to put her at ease."

"Of course. That's very kind of you," Daphne said.

Just as Lord Biltmore left, Olivia sucked in her breath.

"What is it?" Rose asked.

"It's not a *what* but a *who*," Olivia whispered. "Miss Starling. And she's walking toward us."

The stunning blonde glided across the room, looking like she'd stepped out of the June issue of the *Lady's Magazine*. Her sumptuous rose silk gown set off her creamy complexion perfectly, and rows of pearls glowed around her neck.

Daphne forced a smile and breathed through her nose. She'd succeeded in avoiding Miss Starling since arriving in London. While Daphne was not the sort to hold a grudge, she'd never forgive Miss Starling for trying to ruin Anabelle.

"Good evening, Miss Honeycote. I have seen neither you nor your infamous sister in an age. Where is the new duchess?" Miss Starling inquired, her eyes wide with feigned innocence. "I pray she hasn't taken ill. One would hope marriage agrees with her."

Daphne shot the woman a sharp look. "I can assure you that it does."

"Lord Foxburn," Miss Starling said, a little breathlessly. "A pleasure." She extended a pristine white kid glove and preened as the earl bowed over it. "I confess I am shocked to find you hanging about with Miss Honeycote and her friends."

The earl's eyes flashed dangerously. "And why would you find that shocking, Miss Starling?"

She gave a throaty laugh. "The Honeycotes are hardly good *ton*. Do you know what part of town they were living in a few months ago? Proper young misses do not live in that kind of squalor. However, I'll concede that their ill manners are not entirely their fault. Poverty necessarily breeds immorality."

Lord Foxburn narrowed his eyes and said in a low but lethal voice, "The only person displaying ill manners is you, Miss Starling. I suggest you leave. After all, you run the risk of sullying your reputation if you converse with us."

"Thank you for your concern. I shall heed your advice, but first I shall impart my own to Lady Olivia and Lady Rose." She leaned toward the girls. "Do not allow yourself to be duped by the Honeycote sisters' woeful tales and charming ways. They think that their newly elevated status protects them from scandal and disgrace. You may be sure they have secrets—dark, ugly secrets—and it's only a matter of time before they're exposed for all to see."

The pink and green walls began to close in around Daphne. Miss Starling couldn't know about Anabelle's extortion schemes. Could she? And she couldn't possibly know about the portraits . . . unless she'd seen one.

"Good evening, Miss Starling." Lord Foxburn stepped in front of Daphne as though he'd physically shield her from further insults.

Daphne's lower lip trembled. The night was proving to be as disastrous as she'd feared. She glanced toward Mama, happy to see her chatting animatedly with Lady Bonneville. While a few other guests cast curious looks Daphne's way, most of the room seemed oblivious to the confrontation.

Rose reached over and squeezed her hand. "Take deep breaths," she advised. "Do not dwell on Miss Starling or her insults. She cannot hurt you."

Olivia snorted in a most unladylike fashion. "Do not give credence to a word of the hatred she spewed. She is nothing but a bitter, jealous shrew. When you arrived on the scene, she was taken down a peg. She *used* to be the most beautiful miss on the marriage mart, but not anymore. You are more beautiful by far."

"Inside and out," Rose agreed.

Ridiculousness. She was no beauty, and at the moment she felt like a shell, hollow and empty. A huge fraud.

Miss Starling's tirade may have been ugly, but it also happened to be the truth. And the worst part was that if Daphne's wanton behavior was exposed, all the people she loved—especially Rose and Olivia, whom she thought of as her sisters—would suffer the most. Daphne longed to go home but feared a hasty exit would only call more attention to herself.

"The musicians are poised to begin," Lord Foxburn said. Turning to Olivia and Rose, he said, "You should stay and enjoy the performance. I'll escort Miss Honeycote onto the terrace for a few moments."

Rose sat up a little straighter. "Only if that is what Daphne wishes."

"Yes." Fresh air and a few minutes away from inquisitive eyes sounded heavenly.

The earl grasped her hand and pulled her to her feet. "The terrace is this way."

She and Lord Foxburn moved against the tide of guests drifting toward the rows of chairs. He stepped in front of her and used his broad shoulders to cut through the crowd like the prow of a ship slicing through ocean waves. When he reached the doors, he did not release her hand but pulled her away from the house to the far side of the rectangular flagstone terrace. The twining of their fingers felt terribly intimate, sending wonderful shivers up and down her arm. It was only because he was so...so...

Masculine. It was the slightest shadow of stubble on his face, the predatory look in his eyes, and the decisive way he handled every interaction. He said exactly what he thought and did exactly as he pleased and didn't apologize for it.

Of course, this behavior was also rather infuriating. But at the moment, while their palms were pressed together, all she could think was that Lord Foxburn was very attractive indeed.

The night air was warm but still refreshing compared to the stuffiness of the music room. Several lanterns strung around the perimeter of the terrace glowed like mischievous fairies, and the fragrances of roses and rich soil tickled her nose.

He pulled her to a small marble bench, which felt smooth and cool beneath her bottom, even through the layers of satin and crepe.

Daphne faced the earl, very aware that no more than an arm's length separated them. Her eyes were level with his neckcloth; she had to tilt her chin up to meet his gaze. His mouth was drawn in a thin line and his eyelids appeared heavy. His expression wasn't quite angry or bored or interested, and yet it was all three.

"Thank you," she said, breaking the silence. "I felt as though I'd scream if I had to endure another minute in that room."

"I don't think that would have helped matters."

"No, but I'm afraid Miss Starling knows precisely how to bait me."

"She isn't worth even a second of your worry."

No? Daphne couldn't dismiss her so easily. And if either of the scandalous portraits were made public, Miss Starling's disdain would seem trivial in comparison to the *ton's* condemnation.

She gazed at her skirt rustling in the breeze and tried not to dwell on the tingling warmth between their palms. In that instant, she knew what she had to do. If she didn't do it right away, she might never have another opportunity, another private moment in which to speak with him. But the greater danger was that she'd simply lose her nerve.

Steeling her resolve, she looked into his eyes. "I have a confession."

Chapter Six

$\mathscr{B}$en liked confessions. Especially from beautiful women. "Go on."

"The woman in the painting...is me." Miss Honeycote didn't hang her head or even blush, but instead looked straight at him as though she'd make no apologies for her behavior. Good for her.

"I can't pretend to be shocked. But if it would help, I could feign mild surprise."

Smiling, she said, "That won't be necessary. When you first confronted me, I was caught off guard. I suppose I shouldn't have denied it, but I didn't know what else to do. I was afraid that I might taint the reputation of my family. I still am."

"Understandable. However, I do not intend to publicly display the painting. I gave you my word," he said, mildly offended that she'd doubt him.

"I know. It's just that..."

"What?"

"I need your help finding the other one."

Good God. "There's *another* one?"

She heaved a sigh. "Yes. Just one, but it's equally scandalous. And I don't know where it is."

Part of his brain reeled from the shock of learning there was a second portrait, but the male part was busy imagining what the second scandalous painting might look like.

"Would you help me find it?" The slight tremor in her voice told him what it had cost her to ask him. The truth was that she looked so vulnerable—yet beautiful—in the light of the lanterns that he would have done any damn thing she asked.

"You think I can help you track it down."

She nodded. "I'm terrified that it will turn up somewhere—just as the one you have did. I have very little information to go on, and even if I were able to locate it, I would need someone to help me purchase it—not the money, you understand, just someone to take care of the transaction."

"I am vastly relieved to know that no special skills are required of me. Purchasing a painting doesn't sound terribly taxing. I think I could be up to the task."

She arched a blond brow. "Finding the painting could prove difficult. It's very important that we keep my identity as the portraits' subject a secret. I know this is all a lark to you, but I haven't slept well since the day you visited my sister's drawing room."

He wanted to say that he hadn't either. That he was tortured by dreams of her. But that was sure to scare her off. "I know what it's like—to be haunted by things you wish you'd done differently."

"I don't regret what I did, Lord Foxburn. I had my reasons. What I regret—deeply—is the trouble and pain that my actions could cause my family. And yes, I have my own selfish reasons for wishing that I could keep the portraits secret."

What reasons could she have had for posing? She had alluded to her family's impoverished state, but weren't there other ways to earn some coin? Mending, laundry, selling oranges? Not that he was one to judge, but her manners suggested that she was raised as a proper lady, and the painting that hung in his study was not even vaguely in the realm of propriety.

There were so many questions he wanted to ask her, but they couldn't remain on the terrace much longer. "I will try to help you."

"Thank you." The corners of her eyes were suspiciously moist.

"There's one thing I would ask in return."

Her expression turned wary. "What would that be?"

"I want to know the truth—about why you posed for the portraits and..."

"And what, Lord Foxburn?"

Damn it all, there was no subtle way to ask. "The nature of your relationship to the artist."

She drew up short. "Why would you want to know that?"

Why, indeed? "I am a student of human nature. I like to know why people behave the way they do. *You*, Miss Honeycote, are something of a puzzle." He also wanted to know whether Robert had some connection to her and how he'd come into possession of her portrait. What if his friend had loved her? It seemed as though that should change things, but Ben wasn't quite sure how. He needed information, and he needed time to sort through it all.

"I suppose that is fair," she said at last. "I will confide in you if you will do your best to help me recover the second portrait."

He faced her and ceremoniously shook her hand. "We have a deal. I will arrange a time and place for us to talk and send word to you."

"With each day that passes, the risk of discovery increases."

"I understand the urgency of the matter and am at your service."

She gave a smile that warmed him to his core. This could well be the most enjoyable assignment he'd ever had. And where his heart was concerned, it could also be the most dangerous.

Daphne and Lord Foxburn slipped quietly into the drawing room through the French doors at the rear during Beethoven's concerto, and thankfully, no one seemed to notice them.

Daphne returned to her seat in the back row, which was otherwise unoccupied—until Lord Foxburn sat in the chair directly beside hers. She endeavored to act indifferently, as though she couldn't care less where he chose to sit, but the truth was that delicious shivers swept over her whenever he was near.

She told herself that this strange and powerful response to him was only because he knew her secret and could ruin her, if he chose to.

But deep down she knew it was more than that.

It was desire.

He was so close that she could see the dimple in his cheek and a hint of stubble on his chin. She wondered what it would feel like and checked the wholly improper urge to strip off her glove and run a fingertip along the length of his jaw.

Good heavens. This would never do.

She flipped open her fan and leaned slightly toward the earl. Under her breath she said, "Please don't feel that you must remain here with me. I don't mind sitting alone."

"Neither do I," he said, flashing a wickedly handsome grin. "But I like this spot. It affords a nice view."

She felt herself flush.

"Of the musicians, I mean."

"Of course." She was starting to grow accustomed to his teasing, but not to her traitorous body's reaction. Her heart beat so loudly she feared he would hear it. She fanned herself lightly and resolved to turn her attention to the performance.

But instead, she found herself staring at the hand he drummed on his thigh in time to the music. What would it feel like to have his hands on her skin, caressing her shoulders or the swells of her breast? She swallowed and fanned herself faster. Though she was not normally prone to such impure thoughts, it was shockingly easy for her to imagine him stroking her legs, particularly the soft skin at the tops of her thighs and the curve of her bottom. Worse, she wanted to run her hands over *him*—to explore every inch of him, from his broad shoulders to his narrow hips to the hard length of his...

Dear *God*, what was wrong with her that she should think such wanton thoughts while her own dear *mother* sat a few yards away?

Daphne coughed, and Lord Foxburn leaned closer, which did not help matters in the least.

"Are you all right?" he asked.

"Just a bit parched," she lied. "I think the concerto must be over soon. I'll fetch a drink at the intermission."

He looked at her curiously for a moment, as though he were capable of reading all her wayward thoughts. Then he unleashed a slow smile that washed over her like a wave, leaving her skin tingling in its wake.

Daphne resumed fanning herself—with a bit more vigor—and kept Mama firmly in her sights so that she would not be tempted to let her thoughts stray to the earl again.

The quartet was composed of the Seaton sisters and two other young ladies, all of whom played prettily. As soon as the intermission began, Daphne stood and—eager to put some distance between her and Lord Foxburn—went to speak to Mama. "May I fetch you and Lady Bonneville some refreshments?" she asked.

The viscountess, whose feet were propped on her ottoman, waved a bejeweled hand. "No need. I have already sent my maid in search of sustenance. Something substantial shall be required if I am to endure another hour of mediocre talent."

Daphne looked behind her to make sure the musicians hadn't overheard. "Begging your pardon, Lady Bonneville, but I think the quartet is quite good."

The viscountess raised her lorgnette and, through it, glared at Daphne for several seconds. Turning to Mama, she asked, "Were you aware your daughter lacks a musical ear?"

Mama smiled. "My Daphne is an idealist." Funny, it almost sounded as though she were apologizing.

Lady Bonneville clucked her tongue. "Thank God she has sufficient beauty to balance out the deficiency." To Daphne she said, "Loveliness such as yours is rare, but it's both a blessing and a curse."

Daphne shook her head to clear it. "What's wrong with being an idealist?"

The viscountess harrumphed as though Daphne were quite hopeless. "Mingle, gel," she said, pointing the way with her lorgnette.

Olivia and Rose had headed for the refreshment table, so Daphne joined Miss Louise Seaton, who was once again industriously tuning her violin. "I'm enjoying the concert," said Daphne. "You must have taken up the violin at a young age to have developed such talent."

"Thank you. Mother thrust the bow at me when I was barely four. I wish I could say the violin is a passion of mine. The truth is, I'm dreadfully tired of practicing."

"Really?" said Daphne. "Then why do you do it?"

"Mother believes it is the only way Jane or I will gain a gentleman's attention. This whole evening is a blatant attempt to showcase our talents and catch the eye—or ear, as it were—of prospective husbands."

"Oh." Daphne glanced around the room. "Has any gentleman here captured your fancy?"

A blush stained Miss Seaton's round cheeks, and she twirled a brunette curl that dangled in front of her green eyes. "Lord Biltmore is very handsome, is he not? Mama was over the moon when he accepted our invitation."

"The viscount is as kind as he is handsome," Daphne added.

"Here he comes," Miss Seaton said in an urgent whisper, "and Lord Foxburn is with him."

"Good evening, ladies." The timbre of the earl's voice made Daphne's body thrum like the violin's strings. "Miss Seaton, you are to be commended for your flawless execution of the songs as rendered on sheet music."

"Why, thank you, Lord Foxburn." Miss Seaton beamed, clearly unaware that he was having fun at her expense. Daphne made a mental note to swat him with her fan later.

"It is a wonderful performance," Lord Biltmore said, "and I look forward to the second half."

Miss Seaton smiled shyly. "Thank you for your encouragement earlier. I realize my playing is far from perfect."

"Nonsense," Lord Biltmore said.

"The fourth string is a tad sharp." Lord Foxburn inclined his head toward Miss Seaton's instrument.

Her smile faded, and Daphne clenched her fan as she shot him a scolding look.

"Though it's hardly noticeable," he amended. "Miss Honeycote, I wonder if I might have a word?"

"Of course."

Placing his hand at the small of her back, he guided her to the side of the stage. She tried to ignore the breathless feeling that overcame her the moment the earl touched her, and as soon as Miss Seaton and Lord Biltmore were out of earshot, she whirled to face Lord Foxburn.

"You were very rude just then."

"Would you rather I be dishonest?"

"Yes! Well, no..."

"I must go," he said abruptly. "I just wanted to let you know that I'll contact you so that we may formulate a plan. Soon."

• • •

"I can't believe we're having supper at Vauxhall Gardens!" Olivia sat at her dressing table, scrutinizing her new pearl earbobs in the looking glass. "Are you eager to see Lord Biltmore?"

Daphne, who was standing behind Olivia, met her gaze in the mirror and shrugged. "I'm looking forward to a pleasant evening with our entire party."

Their party consisted of Lord Biltmore, Olivia, Rose, James Averill, Daphne, and Lord Foxburn. He'd arranged it all, of course, and Daphne was certain that he'd gone to the trouble just so that he could speak to her about the next steps in their quest to locate the second portrait. She hadn't realized that the undertaking would require this level of subterfuge and didn't like the idea of the earl going to such lengths and such expense. She would prefer not to be beholden to him—or any man. But that was the problem with secrets.

Lord Foxburn had invited Anabelle and Owen as well, but her sister had confessed she was quite possibly expecting—if her violent nausea of the past few days was any indication. Owen, ever the doting husband, had been simultaneously horrified and elated and insisted on calling for the doctor at once. Doctor Loxton confirmed the happy diagnosis and prescribed plenty of rest for the duchess.

Olivia turned her attention back to her reflection and pulled out the pink ribbon that Rose had painstakingly woven into her curls just a half hour before. "I think I should use the gold instead." She held up a length of shimmery silk. "Will you help me?"

"Of course." Daphne plucked the ribbon from her

fingers and plotted out a course through Olivia's chestnut tresses.

"It's a bit more sophisticated, don't you think? I want James to see me as a woman—not as the adoring girl who tirelessly dug up worms for him to use as bait."

"I should think he'd owe you a debt of gratitude after that."

"I don't want his gratitude, Daph. I want his admiration, his devotion...his love."

"I know." Inviting Mr. Averill had been a brilliant move on the earl's part. Olivia would be unable to focus on anyone but the handsome solicitor, and Rose would be busy keeping watch over her sister. That left just Lord Biltmore to occupy, and Daphne felt sure that Lord Foxburn would have a plan.

All she had to concern herself with was how much to reveal to him.

His carriage arrived at eight sharp. Dressed in a claret evening jacket, black breeches, and gleaming Hessians, he looked breathlessly dashing. He'd offered to escort Daphne, Olivia, and Rose. Mr. Averill and Lord Biltmore would meet them at the private supper box that the earl had reserved for the evening.

They took the Westminster Bridge route, and if Daphne was the tiniest bit disappointed that they didn't use the water entrance, well, that was absurd. The point of this excursion was to initiate their search; any fun that she gleaned from the evening's amusements was purely incidental.

And yet, the atmosphere at Vauxhall Gardens was too festive and exciting for Daphne to remain unaffected. The other gentlemen joined them and the party dined on ham, chicken, and hearty salads.

After supper, they ventured onto the promenade and enjoyed the many sights. Mr. Averill was drawn to the artificial ruins, and Olivia was drawn to Mr. Averill. Rather than chase after the pair, the remaining four chose to sit on a couple of benches where they could observe the amusements and hear the orchestra playing. Daphne was so caught up in the merry music that she was startled by the sound of the earl's voice.

"My leg is in need of a stretch," he said, standing. "Might I prevail upon one of you lovely ladies to stroll through the gardens with me?"

This was her chance, and yet she didn't wish to appear too eager.

"I should stay close by and wait for Olivia," Rose said.

Daphne let out the breath she'd been holding. "I'd be delighted to see more of the beautiful scenery, if you're sure you don't mind, Rose."

"Not at all. I could listen to this orchestra all night."

"I'm sure Averill and Lady Olivia will return soon," said Lord Biltmore. "We shall join you on the trails then. We'll want to secure a prime spot for watching the fireworks later."

"Quite right. Shall we, Miss Honeycote?"

Lord Foxburn might have been a little less abrupt, but Lord Biltmore was no doubt used to the earl's abrasive manner. Daphne took the arm he offered and gave Rose a reassuring smile as they wandered down a pebbled path, away from the music and the crowds.

When they were relatively alone, Daphne said, "Thank you for arranging this. You must have gone to a great deal of trouble."

"Indeed. Walking with a pretty young woman in

Vauxhall Gardens is a great sacrifice, I assure you. You look especially lovely this evening, by the way."

She checked his expression to be sure he was not mocking her. He was not the type of gentleman who handed out compliments freely. Or ever. "Thank you." She cleared her throat. "What would you like to know? I shall attempt to answer your questions as completely and honestly as I can."

"Who is the artist?"

"A family friend, Thomas Slate. Both of our mothers are widows and pooled what few resources they had in order to see that Thomas, Anabelle, and I had food in our bellies and a roof over our heads. The three of us were often thrown together, and when Thomas grew tired of sketching the chipped vases and ramshackle furniture in our apartments, he began drawing my sister and me. He was quite good."

"His technique leaves something to be desired. The proportions are off. For example, in the portrait I have, your nose should be slightly higher on your face."

Daphne blinked. She supposed she should have been offended, but he stated his opinion so matter-of-factly that she couldn't summon indignation. "I thought you liked the portrait."

"I do. In spite of the fact that it lacks technical merit."

"And yet you were able to identify me as the subject almost immediately. Were you bluffing, then, when you claimed you knew it was me?"

"Oh, I knew it was you. Your friend may not have the best eye for scale, but he captured your essence beautifully, as only a good friend—or a lover—could."

Daphne stopped in her tracks and whirled to face him. "What are you implying, my lord?"

"That this Thomas person was either an intimate friend or your lover. He would have to have been in order to paint you with that kind of clarity and truth."

He was trying to provoke her, and for that reason alone, she refused to be baited. Let him think what he liked.

They began walking again, winding their way down a narrow path lined with thick hedges. Lamps hung from festoons in tree branches, swaying in the night breeze like tremulous stars. He steered her to a bench in a little alcove formed by a semicircle of dense shrubbery, and they sat, admiring the softly gurgling fountain in the small clearing in front of them.

Daphne reminded herself of the business at hand. "So you will concede that Thomas is talented, then."

Lord Foxburn inclined his head noncommittally. "I admire his work."

Heat crept up her neck, dash it all. "He is the person I was waiting for at Gunter's."

The muscles in his forearm flexed beneath her hand. "Ah, yes. The gentleman who left you standing in the rain."

"It wasn't his fault. I discovered the next day that he's on the Continent having a grand tour."

The earl seemed to consider this. "Who did he paint the portraits for? Does he have a patron?"

"A country squire commissioned most of his work, including the portraits of me. I don't know much about him. Thomas said he wasn't fond of town life and spent most of his time rusticating in the country."

Lord Foxburn grunted.

"What?" she demanded.

"It sounds like the sort of thing a scheming artist would

say to convince a young woman to pose for a scandalous painting."

Daphne bristled. "Thomas isn't like that—he didn't coerce me in the slightest. You must think me quite dim-witted if you imagine that I would allow myself to be manipulated or taken advantage of so easily."

The earl's eyes flashed with interest and...something else. Perhaps respect. "Why don't you tell me the real story, Miss Honeycote. Why *did* you do it?"

Chapter Seven

Tint: (1) Any color or hue that is mixed with white.
(2) A pale, delicate color, as in Her skin, smooth
  as cream, had the tint of a ripe peach.

This was the moment Ben had been waiting for, the reason he had arranged the entire evening. He needed to understand why Miss Honeycote had risked her reputation—the only thing she'd really had. But mostly he needed to understand her. To be close to her light for a while.

The lanterns above lent a soft glow to the Eden-like setting. Her cheeks had turned a lovely shade of pink.

"It's quite simple." She flicked her tongue over her lips as though it were anything but. "My mother was sick—dying, actually. For months on end she suffered from raging fevers and violent coughing attacks. I'll never forget how pale and thin her face looked as she lay in bed. Her skin was like white parchment stretched over bone." Her voice cracked on the last word.

She paused for a moment, and when she resumed her

story, her voice was clear and strong. "Anabelle and I believed Mama had consumption. The doctor prescribed various vapors and medicines to restore her lungs and keep her comfortable. He was expensive, and so was the medicine. My sister was working twelve-hour days as a seamstress to try to raise the money we needed. I did the occasional mending, but my priority was caring for Mama. The money I made from the portraits...well, it was my contribution."

As Ben imagined Daphne's desperation and worry for her mother, his chest tightened. But the angle at which she held her chin told him she didn't want pity. "What does your sister think about your current dilemma?"

She grasped his wrist and locked her gaze with his. "She knows nothing about the paintings, and she mustn't find out."

He shook his head. This grew more interesting by the moment. "Where did she think the money came from?"

"It wasn't as much as you might expect. We owed everybody money—the doctor, the apothecary, our land-lady, and the butcher. I used the funds to pay down our debt, but we never caught up—not until the duke stepped in to help. Before that, most of the burden fell on Anabelle."

"I'm surprised you were able to keep your activities a secret from her."

"I keep very few secrets from my sister, but I couldn't tell her. She would never have permitted me to do it."

Using his cane, Ben drew small circles on the ground between his feet and hers. "Why do you want to keep the truth from her now?"

Miss Honeycote fingered the purple ribbon sash of her

dress. "Anabelle has always taken care of me, and I don't want to be a burden to her anymore. She would worry herself sick, and she's already feeling poorly because of her condition. I need to fix this problem on my own." She chuckled self-consciously. "With a little help from you."

He stroked his chin, debating how best to make his next inquiry, then decided to go with his usual method— bluntness. "May I call you Daphne?"

Her eyes went wide and her lips formed a perfect circle.

Before she could respond, he said, "When we're in private, I mean. Since we are to work closely together, it would behoove us to drop some of the formalities. Considering the nature of our mission, I see no point in standing on ceremony."

"What, then, shall I call you?"

He shrugged. "Call me what you like—nothing could shock me. If you lack imagination, you could always use my given name, Benjamin—or, simply, Ben."

She looked at him oddly, as though it were quite a surprise to learn that he had a first name. "Benjamin suits you. Very well, we will use our Christian names when speaking in private. What shall our first step be?"

"Wait. You never told me how your mother recovered from consumption."

"Er, she was misdiagnosed. Once the duke sent his doctor to examine her, he realized the mistake and prescribed a new course of treatment. It took her a while, but she is much improved."

He sensed there was more to the story—she glossed over it too much for there not to be—but he was willing to let it go for now. "Does anyone else know that you posed for the paintings?"

"No. Thomas nicked some sheets and lanterns, bought a worn settee at a pawnshop, and set up a temporary studio in the abandoned factory near our apartments. No one ever bothered us there, save for a few rats."

"Sounds charming."

She smiled wanly as if recalling the memory. "It wasn't bad. Although it was terribly cold during the winter months. Sometimes I'd shiver and Thomas would remind me to relax my shoulders and drape my arm just so."

He didn't care for the way "Thomas" just tripped off her tongue. The more Ben learned about the artist, the less he liked him, and he hadn't liked the bastard to begin with. Making a young lady sit in her nightgown in a freezing, rat-infested factory was inexcusable—no matter the circumstances. Lucky for Thomas that the English Channel currently separated them.

Ben stood and paced slowly in front of a tranquil fountain, stretching his leg and thinking. "Might Thomas's mother know who his patron is?"

"Perhaps. I can ask, although if I inquire out of the blue, it might raise some suspicion. She and my mother are still quite close, so I'd need to handle the matter very delicately. If Mama learned what I did, she'd be so disappointed. Worse, she'd feel like she'd failed to raise me properly. She mustn't find out about the portraits."

"Let me begin by looking through Robert's papers. I don't think he had the painting for long, so maybe I can find a record or receipt of some sort." And now, the question he'd been dreading. The one he really needed to know. "Did you know him? That is, were the two of you acquainted?"

"If our paths ever crossed, I'm not aware of it. I'm sure we weren't in the same circles."

He let out a breath and began to pace again, but his damned leg buckled and he just barely caught himself from falling to the ground. Daphne sprang to her feet and wrapped an arm about his waist like he was some sort of invalid. "I'm fine," he snapped.

She stepped back quickly and held up her palms. "Yes, I can see that."

God, he was an ass. "I have learned to deal with my injury in my own ways."

"Ah, that's right. I believe you alluded to one of your methods—alcohol—in the coach the other day. What other methods do you employ?"

"Cursing sometimes provides relief."

"Well, then, you should be halfway to cured."

"Unless you have a better suggestion," he said dryly, "I shall do what works for me. Or at least gets me through the day."

"Getting through the day is no way to live." She walked up to the fountain and traced the edge of the round stone base with her gloved fingertip. Then, before he knew it, she was tugging off her glove. He opened his mouth to ask her what the devil she was doing, but his tongue wouldn't cooperate.

She leaned over the pool of water and thrust her bare hand into the gurgling stream spouting from the center. The column chopped in half before regenerating itself. Droplets ran down her arm, toward her elbow. He stared, mesmerized.

"Water has many healing properties," she announced.

Good God. "If you think I'm going to drink that, you are sorely mistaken."

She laughed, a sound that made him feel about two

stone lighter. "I wasn't suggesting that you drink it. But I do think that you might explore other treatments."

"Like taking the waters in Bath? No, thank you."

"You shouldn't dismiss the possibilities so summarily. However, I had something else in mind. When Mama was ill, I went to the lending library and got every medical journal I could find. I wasn't able to help her, but I learned a great deal about the human body."

"Did you now?" He raised an eyebrow suggestively. "Please, tell me more."

"Shall I tell you about the effects of the croup or diphtheria? Yellow fever, perhaps?"

"I was hoping for something more titillating. And I fear I'm missing your point."

She turned her attention once again to the water and trailed her fingers back and forth across the bubbling surface. "A medicinal bath might ease the pain."

He held back a laugh. "Splashing a little water on my leg isn't going to fix it."

"Maybe not. But in combination with some other remedies . . . I'll need to do some research."

The last thing he wanted was for her to think of him as she read about horrid diseases. "You needn't trouble yourself."

"It's the least I can do, since you'll be helping me find the other portrait."

"Suit yourself." If she needed something to busy herself with and keep her mind off the fact that her reputation could be smashed to bits at any given moment, he saw no harm in it.

She narrowed her eyes and crossed her arms, one of which was still delectably bare. "You don't believe I'll be able to help you."

He snorted. "No."

"Have you so little faith in me?"

"I admire your enthusiasm for the task of healing me. However, I'm in worse shape than you know. Surgeons and doctors alike have advised me." And they'd all come to the same conclusion—he'd be better off without his leg. Hang them all.

"Surgeons and doctors may have extensive education and professional training, but in spite of their eagerness to cure their patients, they often overlook the healing power of the mind."

"You think the pain is in my head," he accused. He managed to control his voice, but fury, hot and seething, coursed through his veins. "It's not."

She closed the short distance between them and placed her hand on his arm. "Of course it isn't. I wasn't suggesting that. Just give me a chance, please, and promise me that you'll keep an open mind."

She looked up at him, her beautiful face imploring. In the light of the lanterns, the skin above her fashionably low neckline glistened, and he imagined what it would be like to hold her and cover her mouth with his, to lose himself in her warm, seductive glow. He longed to trace the lace edge of her pretty gown with his fingertip. Or, better yet, his tongue. The anger that he'd felt only seconds before turned to ash and a different kind of fire ignited in his chest. In that moment, he knew he'd do anything she asked of him, no matter how silly or hopeless. "Why should I?"

"Because you have nothing to lose."

"That is true." He took her bare hand from his arm, raised it between them, and pressed his lips to the back of it.

"What was that for?"

"I was simply sealing the deal. I shall search for the owner of the second portrait. You shall search for a miracle cure."

She smiled as though he'd given her a precious gift. Or a puppy. "Perfect," she said.

Before he knew what he was saying, he blurted, "I'll even sweeten the pot."

Her forehead wrinkled in puzzlement.

"If you find a way to ease my pain, I shall give you the portrait of you that hangs in my study."

"It's still hanging in your study?" Her voice held a note of alarm.

"Relax. No one has seen it. No one will."

"I *would* feel better if it were destroyed."

Destroy it? He hadn't considered the idea that she might want to get rid of the portrait altogether. It would be sacrilege. He understood her logic, of course. For as long as the painting existed, her reputation was in a state of danger. He just knew that he'd never be able to bring himself to torch or shred it. The very idea made his stomach clench.

"Let's take one step at a time," he said. "I'll visit Hugh tomorrow and concoct an excuse to look through Robert's papers."

Her face fell. "I feel awful for putting you in a position where you need to lie."

He laughed. "You're hardly responsible for corrupting me. I thought we'd already established that I'm quite without scruples—a lost cause, if you will."

"I'm not so sure about that . . . Benjamin."

The sound of his name on her lips unleashed a fresh wave of desire. He wondered how she'd react if he leaned in and kissed her tenderly—just a brief kiss so that he could test his theory that she'd taste like honey, pure and golden.

But before he could act, she withdrew her hand from his and slipped it into her elbow-length glove. "The rest of our party is probably wondering where we are. Shall we rejoin them?"

"Yes," he said, stifling a sigh. "I suppose we should." He offered her his arm once again, and as they made their way back toward the rotunda where the orchestra played, they saw Hugh, Averill, and the Sherbourne sisters walking toward them.

Lady Olivia waved with her typical exuberance. "The fireworks shall begin shortly. Let's secure a good spot from which to watch the show." She was on Averill's arm and yet, somehow, was two steps ahead of him.

"The advantage of shooting fireworks into the sky," Ben said dryly, "is that one has only to tilt one's head back in order to view them."

"I think Olivia is right. We should walk to the crest of that hill," Daphne said, pointing to a slight ridge. "It should give us an excellent vantage point."

"Quite right," exclaimed Hugh. "But will the terrain be too rough for you, Foxburn?"

Damn Hugh and his concern. Even if he meant well, it was beyond irritating. "Promise me that on the day a little grassy slope such as that one proves insurmountable, you will put a pistol to my head and end my misery."

The Sherbourne sisters gasped but Daphne merely clucked her tongue. "My, but we are dramatic this evening. How were the artificial ruins, Mr. Averill?"

As she made polite conversation with the others, Ben mentally calculated the distance from their current location to the crest of the hill. The hell of it was, he wasn't at all sure he could make it to the top without falling flat on his face. He would find out soon.

After he'd walked about a hundred yards, a sweat broke out on his face. His leg had gone mostly numb, which meant pain was close behind. Daphne flicked her gaze to him and sympathy registered on her face before she quickly looked away. "Oh, look at the minstrels!"

The merry band of five had drawn a small crowd, and each of the performers appeared to be playing some sort of pipe in addition to a second instrument. The brightly colored plumes on their hats seemed to jig in time to the music.

He might have enjoyed the number they were playing if he weren't about to keel over in pain.

Daphne drifted to a short stone wall where he could sit. "I'd love to watch them for a while. Would you mind waiting for a few minutes?"

"Good heavens, no," Hugh said gallantly. "We have all the time in the world."

Averill waved Daphne and her friends on, and the women wasted no time in joining the circle of observers, laughing and exclaiming over every banal trick the minstrels performed.

Ben had barely lowered himself onto the wall when pain seared through his thigh muscles. He bit the inside of his cheek to keep from howling like some sort of wild animal and within seconds tasted blood. As usual, the world around him blurred and faded. He dug his fingers into the stone ledge, trying to control the quivering of his entire body. *One, two, three…* Somewhere around eighty-two, the pain began to recede. Ever so slowly, his vision cleared and the shaking stopped.

Averill was sitting on his right, looking rather dumb-founded. "I had no idea."

Ben groped his jacket pocket for a handkerchief. "Damned inconvenient," he said wryly. "But at least I have both my legs." He mopped his face, relieved to see that Daphne and the Sherbourne sisters were still occupied with the minstrel show. Suddenly he was parched and craned his neck in search of a passing waiter.

"What can I get you, Foxburn?" offered Hugh, who probably looked even paler than he himself did.

"Something to drink. I don't care what." His protégé hurried off, his thin frame full of dogged determination.

"How often?" Averill asked.

"I don't know," Ben said, running a hand through his hair. "A few times a week, sometimes less, usually more. Exercise can bring it on, but sometimes, it just comes out of nowhere."

"You should get some rest. Why don't we call it a night and take the ladies home?"

"No," Ben said quickly. "I'll be fine. They want to see the fireworks, and they shall."

A few moments later, Hugh returned, holding a huge carafe in one hand and a stack of glasses in the other. "It's arrack punch," he explained. "It smells quite strong."

"Perfect." Ben took a glass and impatiently held it out while Hugh poured. When at last he drank, the liquid burned his throat and made his nostrils flare. While it did little to quench his thirst, he could already feel the numbing warmth spreading to his limbs. He raised his glass for a refill and Hugh obliged.

Shortly after, the ladies returned, and Averill convinced them all that they, too, must sample the punch.

"It's very potent," Rose warned after a sip. "Not too much, Olivia."

Daphne approached, and every step that she took seemed to magnify the punch's intoxicating effects on Ben. "I was thinking," she said to no one in particular, "that it's a rather cloudy night for fireworks. I wonder if we should forgo them and return on a more ideal evening." Her gaze swept over Ben, her expression suggesting that she was quite surprised to find him still upright.

"Oh, but we're here already, and it won't be long before they start." Olivia gave a practiced pout that he'd wager was for Averill's benefit. The solicitor took no notice.

"What do you think, Lord Foxburn?" inquired Daphne.

"Lady Olivia wants to see the fireworks," he said. "Don't you?"

"Yes, but it doesn't have to be this evening," she said meaningfully. Concern was etched in her otherwise smooth brow.

He pretended to miss her meaning. "A few clouds will not spoil the show. But we'd better continue on if we want to get a good spot." If Hannibal could march across the Pyrenees, by God, he could make it up a sorry hill.

He heaved himself to his feet, both surprised and gratified that he could stand without leaning too heavily on his cane. Daphne watched him closely, as though she feared he might topple over at any minute. After he managed a few steps, however, she seemed to relax and even sampled the punch. After which, she made a face.

"A little stronger than ratafia," he said with a chuckle.

She smiled and lifted the glass to her lips for another taste. His blood thrummed in response.

They continued strolling, with Daphne making an

effort to slow their pace whenever possible. At last, they reached their destination, and even if the view wasn't quite worth the excruciating pain it had taken to get there, it was rather…nice. As the night enveloped them, distant lanterns swayed in the breeze like fireflies. Clouds skittered across the moon, lending a hint of drama to the evening. They all stood quietly, catching their breath, taking in the scenery, and enjoying the relative tranquility.

Just as he was marveling at the unexpected moment of serenity, a drunken woman tripped and stumbled toward their small party. A moment before she would have crashed into Olivia, Averill caught her and set her on her feet. "Are you all right, miss?"

"Oh, I think so." The sleeves of her gown had slipped down her arms and her ample bosoms were one jiggle away from breaking free of her bodice. Averill attempted to adjust her shawl as he steadied her. "So gallant," she said huskily, "and handsome, too."

Averill smiled wanly. "Can I help you locate your party?"

She placed a palm on his chest. "I'd rather join yours."

"B-but, I'm sure your chaperone is worried about you." The solicitor craned his neck on the off chance anyone nearby was searching for a cheeky, inebriated chit. Finding none, he sighed and removed her hand from his chest. Well done of him, since Lady Olivia looked like she was about to leap between them and inflict some sort of bodily harm on the young woman.

She attempted to smooth her hair but it still resembled a magpie's nest. With the air of a princess, she said, "If you do not appreciate my company, I'll find someone who does." She staggered away slowly, looking over her shoulder in case anyone should entreat her to stay. No one did, of course, and everyone exhaled in relief. Everyone except Olivia.

"How rude!"

"I believe she's had too much of the punch," Rose ventured.

"That's no excuse. She should have a care for her reputation. One display like that can ruin a girl for life."

Out of the corner of his eye, Ben glanced at Daphne. Her throat worked as she swallowed nervously. "I don't know. Gentlemen routinely become foxed and their reputations don't suffer in the slightest. Shouldn't ladies be afforded the same leniency?"

Olivia stared at her as though she'd sprouted another head. "That *woman*," she spat, waving a finger in the direction she'd stumbled, "ought to be banned from polite society."

Daphne's face fell, and Ben knew exactly what she was thinking. "It just seems like everyone deserves a second chance."

"Do you think Rose or I would be given a second chance?" Olivia demanded. "Do you think *you'd* be given a second chance?"

Her eyes downcast, Daphne shook her head. "I suppose not."

Just then, the first fireworks blazed a path into the sky.

Rose covered her ears, but Olivia shouted above the crackling and booming. "This is spectacular!"

The women formed a front row while the men stood behind, all staring up into the brilliantly lit sky. Everyone became immediately absorbed in the show, except Daphne and Ben.

Daphne looked preoccupied—probably with her imminent fall from grace.

Ben—much to his surprise—found himself worried about Daphne.

He approached her on her free side and leaned forward to whisper in her ear. "Olivia didn't mean those things. She was just protecting her claim to Averill."

"Maybe so, but she was right. If the portrait is discovered, I *won't* be given a second chance." Her voice, which was only a whisper, wavered.

It could have been the punch, but before he knew what he was doing, he reached between them and took her hand. He laced his fingers through hers and squeezed reassuringly. A current shot up his arm and radiated throughout his entire body. "You don't need to be afraid. I'll find the other painting."

"What if you can't?"

"I always, *always* deliver on promises, Daphne." It was true. He had no idea in hell how he was going to deliver on this one, but he would. How hard could it be to find one amateur painting of a beautiful woman?

"Thank you for trying," she said. "Thank you for this night."

Her sad smile stirred something deep inside of him, a place he'd thought was long dead. He could see that she didn't believe him, and who could blame her? In her eyes, he was probably nothing more than a bad-mannered half-cripple who drank too much. But he'd prove he was worthy of her confidence. He would get her out of this mess.

"How are *you* feeling?" she asked.

"Better. Thank you for creating a diversion back there."

"It was nothing." She laughed softly. "We are a sorry pair, are we not?"

He chuckled even though he disagreed on one point—there was nothing sorry about Daphne. But he did like the notion of them being a pair.

Their clasped hands hidden in the folds of her skirt and the shadows, they stood and watched the fireworks. The red and white streaks in the sky briefly lit her upturned face. Her profile was enchanting—long lashes, a sloped nose, full lips, and a delicate chin. Even in the relative darkness, her light was irrepressible, as though she were a beacon that had been kept lit—just for him.

After a few moments, she leaned back toward him. Her head was so close that a few stray wisps of her hair tickled his chin. "Maybe you're right and all is not lost."

He rubbed his thumb lightly over the back of her hand. He felt uncharacteristically hopeful, too.

"If we can find the painting, there is a chance I could still find a decent, respectable man to marry me."

Ben's gut clenched and his hopes were squashed. *Decent* and *respectable* were adjectives that left him entirely out of the running.

Chapter Eight

The next morning, Daphne knocked gently on the door to Anabelle's bedchamber. "It's me."

"Enter."

Odd. Her sister's cheerful voice had not come from the direction of her bed. Daphne swung open the door and found her standing before a full-length mirror wearing a nightgown. "What are you doing out of bed?"

"Shhh! Do you want Owen to come running?"

"If that is the only way to get you to stay in bed."

"I've been very good, Daph. Honestly. I just wanted to peek at my stomach." She smoothed the nightgown, pulling it tight across her belly. "Do you see anything yet?"

Daphne hesitated, unsure of the proper response, but then decided on honesty. "There's a slight swell where there wasn't before, but I suspect that I'm the only one who'd notice."

Belle beamed. "I thought so, too! She's growing."

"She?"

"Did I say she? I meant the baby."

Daphne chuckled. "I gathered. Now, do you think we could relocate to your bed, or at least the sofa in your dressing room? If Owen checks in on you, I don't want to be blamed for your flagrant disregard of doctor's orders."

"Oh, it sounds horrid when you say it like that, Daph. I'd never do anything to jeopardize her well-being."

Her. Interesting. She let it pass.

They moved to the sofa and Daphne made sure that her sister put her feet up. "Would you like something to drink? A bite to eat, perhaps?"

Belle blanched and placed a palm over her stomach. "Maybe later. Right now I want to hear all about Vauxhall Gardens."

"It was a delightful evening. So much to do and see—the fountains and follies and fireworks—"

Anabelle swatted her arm. "I don't want to hear about the *scenery*. Tell me the good bits. Did Lord Biltmore make any advances?"

"Belle!"

"I'm not suggesting that he, or you, did anything improper. But it would be nice to know where you stand with him. Did you walk with him, perhaps, or exchange glances during the fireworks?"

"No. The group stayed together for the better part of the evening."

"Aha! 'For the better part of the evening' means that you *did* spend some time alone with him."

Heat crept up Daphne's cheeks. The only person she'd spent time alone with was Lord Foxburn. Benjamin. She blushed some more. If she didn't confess some of the details, Belle would just make Olivia tell. "Not with him.

Lord Foxburn's leg was hurting and he asked if I'd take a walk with him while he stretched it out."

Anabelle's eyes narrowed behind her spectacles. "Is that what he told you?"

"Mmm." Daphne busied herself untangling the fringe on a throw pillow.

"Just out of curiosity, how do you feel about the earl?"

She could have said she felt sorry for him. It would have been the easy way out, and yet, she couldn't bring herself to say the words. Benjamin wasn't the type of person to be pitied, even in a white lie. "I admire his courage and his loyalty to Lord Biltmore. His older brother was Lord Foxburn's best friend, and he died at Waterloo."

"Ah, yes," Belle said sadly. "Owen mentioned it. Is the earl putting up barriers between you and Lord Biltmore?"

Dash it all. For once, she wished Anabelle wasn't so shrewd. "He's very protective of his young friend. I believe Lord Foxburn wants to make sure his protégé doesn't fall victim to a fortune hunter."

"Of all the—" Belle tried to spring to her feet, but Daphne gently held down her shoulders. "You don't need Lord Biltmore's money. And even if you did, he'd be lucky to marry someone as thoughtful and kind as you."

"It's all right. I'm not sure that I managed to capture Lord Biltmore's affections anyway."

Belle rolled her eyes dramatically. "Please. You could capture the affections of any man you chose." She paused for a moment and then tilted her head. "But perhaps he hasn't captured yours?"

Daphne shrugged. "I don't think we have a...romantic connection." Heaven help her, her face must be as red as a beet.

"Oh." Anabelle seemed to consider this. "That's another matter entirely."

"Did you, er, that is, did you always feel that spark with Owen? Even before you knew that he was as smitten with you as you were with him?"

It was Belle's turn to blush. "Yes. It was there from the start."

Daphne sighed. Few couples were blessed with marriages as passionate as her sister's and Owen's. Daphne dreamed of a love match, but she supposed it was far more important to marry a man with a kind nature and a gentle temperament.

"It will happen for you, too, when you meet the right gentleman."

"What if you feel something like a spark...but it's with the wrong gentleman?"

Anabelle gasped. "That way lies heartbreak."

They sat in silence for a few moments before her sister ventured, "Are you speaking of Lord Foxburn, by any chance?"

Daphne couldn't quite bring herself to respond, so she gave a noncommittal shrug that Belle was sure to see through.

She reached for Daphne's hands and squeezed them affectionately. "Lord Foxburn is undeniably handsome, and the fact that he's a war hero lends him an even more dashing air. But regardless of the attraction you might feel toward him, he is *not* the man for you."

"How do you know?"

"Owen says he has a very dark side and that his mission in life is to make everyone as miserable as he is. You deserve better."

Belle *would* say that. But then, she didn't know about the portraits. Daphne wasn't the innocent her sister believed her to be. "Actually, I don't think it's a matter of deserving someone, but the point is moot. You're right— Lord Foxburn and I would never suit. I get the impression that he doesn't approve of me."

"Of course he doesn't." Belle flung her arms in exasperation. "He doesn't approve of anyone. I can't imagine living with a boor like that."

For some mysterious reason, Daphne felt the need to defend him. "He merely says what the rest of us are thinking."

"Perhaps, but exercising self-control is a requirement in civilized society."

"Which is why Lord Foxburn prefers solitude."

"But *you* do not," Anabelle reminded her. "You thrive on helping others."

Her sister was right. Daphne leaned her head on Belle's shoulder. "I don't know what I'd do without you."

"You'd do just fine. But you wouldn't have half as many gorgeous dresses. Do you want to see how the ball gown is coming along?"

Belle had insisted on creating an elegant new dress for Daphne. Her sister said the gorgeous gold silk trimmed in faceted beads would shine like a diamond in the sun.

Daphne sat up and shot Belle a scolding look. "In case you've forgotten, I will remind you that you're a duchess now. And you're with child. You shouldn't be working so hard on a ball gown for me."

Her sister pushed her spectacles farther up her nose. "I am quite aware of that. Do you want to see it, or not?"

"Yes, please!"

Belle glided to her armoire and withdrew the dress, which—even in its unfinished state—nearly took Daphne's breath away.

"Oh, it's..."

"Stunning?"

"Yes."

"Come see." Belle pulled Daphne by the hand and positioned her in front of the looking glass. Standing behind her, Belle placed the work in progress under Daphne's chin and sighed happily. "I *knew* the colors would be perfect."

"Thank you," Daphne breathed. "For everything."

"You see?" Anabelle said. "Everything is going to work out. You shall soon have the most beautiful gown in the British Empire—and in France for that matter. Mama is well and growing stronger every day. You are under the protection of your brother-in-law, who happens to be a strikingly handsome duke. Best of all, you're the kindest, gentlest, purest soul I know. What could possibly go wrong?"

Well...for one thing, her half-naked image could surface at any time, bringing shame upon herself and everyone she loved. Daphne swallowed past the knot in her throat.

All things considered, there was quite a lot that could go wrong.

Before Ben's injury, he never would have considered taking a coach to Robert's house, which was a mere three blocks away. But after the previous day's exertions, his leg was about as flexible as a log, and walking more than a few yards was out of the question.

Last evening had been successful, in at least one respect. He and Daphne had a plan of action. They'd forged an alliance of sorts, and he was beginning to understand her. A couple of questions still plagued him. How had her mother recovered? How had her sister, a lowly seamstress, ended up married to a duke?

Eventually, he would solve the entire puzzle, but for now he was content with knowing why she'd posed for the portraits. She hadn't been coerced, and she hadn't been the artist's lover.

And while he was greatly relieved on both accounts, he didn't care to examine why.

His coach drew up to Robert's town house, although he supposed it was actually Hugh's house now. Strange to think of it that way.

Getting out of the coach was something of a struggle, but Richard, the footman, knew better than to offer assistance. Any helping hand he extended was likely to feel the smack of Ben's cane. He clambered out, wondering how the hell he'd been reduced to a caricature of a dowager viscountess.

He walked to the front door and was immediately admitted by Hugh's butler, who'd known Ben since he was a lad. "Good afternoon, my lord. I assume you're here to see Lord Biltmore?"

Actually, he'd prefer it if Hugh happened to be on an errand. He wasn't much in the mood for a social visit. Come to think of it, he never was. "No need to disturb him if he's occupied, Randalls. I actually only need to look for a few documents in Robert's study."

The butler took his hat and hung it on a hook near the door. "The study is just where the master happens to be.

I'll let him know you're here." He dipped another bow before heading down the hall.

Ben tried to wrap his mind around the fact that Hugh was in Robert's study. In the months since Robert's death, Hugh had avoided it. Ben had taken care of all pressing estate issues and closed the door behind him when he left, assuming that all would remain as it was.

But nothing was the same as before.

A minute later, Hugh ambled down the hall. He walked like his older brother had, except that he lacked Robert's confidence and bravado. But maybe that, too, would change with time. "Foxburn! An unexpected treat, this— seeing you so soon after the wonderful evening at Vauxhall. Randalls said you're searching for some papers? I've been slowly familiarizing myself with the various accounting books and a few contracts. Is there something I can help you find?"

"No." He hadn't expected Hugh to be interested. In the past he'd been all too happy to give Ben free rein of the study, rummaging to his heart's content. "It's... something of a personal nature. Nothing you need to worry yourself about, but I wonder if I could see his receipts from earlier this year."

"Of course, of course," Hugh replied, all solicitousness. "Come this way. Can I get you a drink, some refreshments?"

"I'll pour myself a brandy from the sideboard in Robert's... er... your study."

Hugh looked at him strangely but ushered him into the room and waved him to the chair behind the desk. "I've filed most of the receipts in the top right drawer. Letters and other correspondence are in the small wooden box on the shelf behind you. I didn't feel right reading Robert's personal letters, but I couldn't bring myself to destroy them either."

Ben turned and stared at the little chest. "The box was a fine idea."

Hugh beamed as if the offhand compliment was the highest praise. "If you're sure you don't need any assistance—"

"No."

His face fell a little. "Very good, then. I'll leave you to your task. Take as much time as you need. I shall be in the drawing room if you need me." He swept a stack of papers off the desk as he left and quietly closed the door behind him.

Ben shook off his melancholy. He was here for a reason, and Daphne was counting on him.

But still, first things first.

He lumbered to the sideboard and poured himself a healthy splash of brandy, relieved to see the familiar decanter and glasses. He'd shared many a drink with Robert in this room, from this tray.

The receipts were stacked in the drawer, just as Hugh had said, in neatly bound bundles. Robert certainly hadn't done that. And neither had Ben. Perhaps Hugh was more competent than either Robert or he had given him credit for.

He untied the first bundle and rifled through the receipts. The papers itemized groceries from Fortnum & Mason, books from Hatchards, and boots from Hoby's, and dozens of other purchases. All were dated the previous month, and a quick check of the next bundle revealed they were separated by month.

Ben counted backward and reached for the twelfth bundle from the top. Christ, had it really been almost a year since Robert died? And if so, why was he still so miserable?

The stack contained nothing of interest, just more incidental expenditures—hats, fabric, snuff, and the like. He pressed his fingertips to his forehead. Robert obviously didn't buy the painting of Daphne on Oxford Street, so how had he come to possess it?

Ben stood and wandered back to the sideboard where he poured another drink. As he swirled the amber liquid in his glass, he scanned the shelves before him. Miniature portraits of Robert's mother and father, both of whom had died when their carriage overturned five years ago, stared back at him, seemingly pleading that he take care of their only living son. A portrait of Robert's older brother who'd died two years ago after falling off his horse. The accident was the reason that a few short months after purchasing his commission, Robert had unexpectedly become a viscount.

Ben, on the other hand, was already an earl when he'd purchased his commission—a fact that had sparked endless speculation about his sanity among his friends and acquaintances. His decision had earned him censure among most of the *ton*. The only person who looked favorably upon his choice was the distant cousin who stood to inherit if Ben died fighting for his country. But Ben and Robert had always done everything together; Ben saw no good reason why his title should prevent him from standing by his friend.

Small statuettes of Egyptian gods stood guard over another shelf. And as Ben marveled over the complete lack of dust, he wondered, how well had he really known Robert?

During their time on the battlefield, Ben thought they'd covered every conceivable subject: philosophy, politics, religion, and death. They'd discussed strategies for avoiding marriage as long as possible. And they'd almost killed each other in an argument over who had the better left hook. Turned out Robert did, and Ben had a black, swollen eye for the better part of a week. All that history together, and yet, Robert had never mentioned the portrait now in Ben's study or the beautiful woman in it.

On the shelf to the right of the statuettes was a neat row of leather-bound books, ledgers if he wasn't mistaken. He set his glass on the desk behind him, took one of the ledgers, and opened it to a random page. November, 1814. A year and a half ago.

The timing seemed about right.

Unfortunately, there were few notations about the nature of the purchases. Each entry had a name—or, more often, initials—and the amount paid or owed.

After he'd scanned a mere three pages, the numbers seemed to move before his eyes like ants swarming a picnic. He rubbed his eyelids. There had to be a better way to track the source of the painting. The artist himself couldn't be too difficult to find, even if he was touring the Continent. At least Ben had a name to work with.

He slammed the ledger shut and went to return it, but a paper that had been tucked between the pages floated to the floor. His stiff leg made reaching for it awkward, and he was grateful no one was there to witness his epic struggle to pick up a damned piece of parchment.

The scrawling handwriting read simply, "English Beauty Portrait."

And was signed "Charlton."

Charlton.

He knew that name. And he knew where to find him.

After heaving himself to his feet, Ben shoved the slip of paper into his pocket and left the study.

The glass of brandy remained on the desk, forgotten.

Chapter Nine

*Undertone: (1) The hue of paint when it is spread
quite thinly, especially when brushed onto a white canvas.
(2) The underlying suggestion in one's words or actions, as in*
The hastily scrawled note held an urgent undertone.

Ben wrote Daphne a note that morning, advising her that he would be at Hyde Park between four and five o'clock that afternoon. If she could arrange to be there, perhaps they could take a stroll together.

And so, he sat on a park bench in the shade of a fig tree, ignoring the pain in his leg and desperately searching the meandering pathways for a glimpse of sunlight.

He only had to wait a quarter of an hour. Flanked by the Sherbourne sisters, she strolled toward him, the picture of propriety in a white dress and a cloak of yellow and blue silk, topped with a fetching bonnet. The almost imperceptible sway of her hips and the graceful way she moved her hands as she conversed with her friends made his pulse speed up. It seemed impossible that someone like her should be oblivious to her own beauty, and yet, he'd swear she was.

For a split second, he considered tossing his cane behind a bush. Most of the men milling about the park carried them; the difference was they didn't *need* them. Ben preferred not to use it in front of Daphne, but since walking for any distance without it was nigh impossible, he swallowed his pride and used the blasted cane to hoist himself off the stone bench.

"Good afternoon, ladies."

"Lord Foxburn, what a pleasure," declared Lady Olivia. The brunette was pretty and good-humored but lacked an element essential for survival in the *ton*—disingenuousness. She couldn't hide an emotion if her Almack's vouchers depended on it. At the moment she exuded breathless excitement. Her sister, the quiet redhead, was the insightful sort. He doubted much escaped her notice, a fact that made her slightly frightening.

"The pleasure is mine." Surprisingly, he meant it.

"Thank you for suggesting a walk in the park," Daphne said. Even her voice seemed tinged with sunshine. "It's the perfect day to escape the confines of the drawing room."

"Agreed," Lady Olivia chimed in. "I spent so many hours embroidering napkins this morning that my fingertips are tender and my eyes are crossed. If I so much as see another skein of thread, I believe I shall cast myself into the Serpentine."

"Shall we stroll in that direction?" he suggested with a wave of his cane toward the river. "I don't recommend a swim, but perhaps we might gawk at the swans?"

"That sounds perfect!" exclaimed Lady Olivia, and immediately linked arms with her sister. She set off toward the river at a good clip, leaving him and Daphne to trail several yards behind.

Since he held his cane in his right hand, he offered Daphne his left arm. The slight pressure of her hand on his sleeve almost made him want to grin, which was not at all his custom.

Dappled light played upon her cheeks as she gazed up at him. "How is your leg feeling today?"

He stiffened. "I didn't ask you here to discuss my blasted leg."

"I was just making small talk," she said gently. "That's what polite people do."

"By now you should know that etiquette lessons are wasted on me."

"I am a hopeless optimist," Daphne confessed with a shrug. "People can change, you know."

"Some people don't want to," he said. But he was thinking that if anyone in the world *could* change him, she might be the one.

"We shall see. Have you learned something about the painting?"

"I have the name of the person from whom Robert obtained it."

Her breath caught in her throat. "Who?"

"Lord Charlton."

"I don't know the name. Are you acquainted with him?"

"He's a baron with an estate in Gloucestershire, not far from Robert's—er, Hugh's—country house. We hunted with him once or twice."

"Is he...in town?"

"I spoke with a few people at White's last evening. Charlton's at his estate—apparently, he rarely leaves it."

"That fits with what Thomas said about his patron." Her face turned pale, and Ben wondered if she realized that she had a death grip on his arm.

"Are you all right?" he asked.

"I suppose so. It's just that until now, all I knew was that my portrait was out in the world somewhere. To learn that it could be in the possession of a specific person at a particular location is disconcerting."

"Yes, but it's also progress."

A governess chasing her young charge darted across the path in front of them; Ben drew up short and pulled Daphne back. Her side bumped innocently into his, stirring all sorts of not-so-innocent feelings in him.

She quickly put a respectable distance between them and asked, "Do you suppose Lord Charlton still has the other portrait?"

"It's possible. If not, I hope he'll be able to tell me who does."

"Did you find a receipt?"

"Not exactly, just a slip of paper with the name on it and a general description of the painting."

"What shall we do next?" she asked.

He turned and gave her what he hoped was a stern look. "*We* will not do anything. *I* will attempt to discover the whereabouts of the second portrait."

"How?"

"By paying the baron a visit."

She blinked as though she had not heard him correctly. "You cannot just knock on his front door and inquire whether he possesses a scandalous painting."

He smirked at that. "It may surprise you to know I can employ subtlety when circumstances require it."

"Can you at least tell me what you plan to do?"

"I suggested to Hugh that we visit his country house and address any matters that need to be resolved. He hasn't been there since Robert—He hasn't been there in several months. Once I'm there, I can invite Lord Charlton to dinner and probe for information."

"Thank you. It could work."

"*Could* work? Your confidence in me is awe-inspiring."

She stared down at the pebbled path for several moments, apparently deep in thought. At last, she said, "I've done some research on remedies for limb pain."

"I see. And do these remedies involve satanic rituals? Virginal sacrifice?"

Color rushed into her cheeks. "No, I thought perhaps you should try something *new*."

"There is nothing new, trust me. Hugh and I leave for Biltmore Manor at the end of the week. I don't intend to stay for more than four or five days. I'll have news for you when I return."

Daphne stopped walking and faced him. "I wish there was something *I* could do."

He shook his head. "Leave it to me. You can trust me, Daphne."

"I know. Thank you." The smile she gave him heated his blood.

"Your friends are almost to the river. We'd better hurry if we want to join them in harassing the swans."

"I should not like to miss that," she said, her blue eyes twinkling.

Talking with her like this seemed so natural, so right. Under different circumstances—if Robert hadn't died, if Ben's leg hadn't been injured—he and Daphne might have spent a lifetime of days just like this. As it was, he probably had only a few weeks at best.

He would find the painting, and she'd have no further use for him.

Then the darkness would return.

Chapter Ten

The next afternoon, Ben sat in his study reviewing the papers that Averill had sent over for him to sign. Although they were standard, straightforward documents, Ben might as well have been deciphering hieroglyphics. He was distracted, and one unearthly beauty—with all-too-earthly charms—was to blame.

So instead of behaving like a responsible earl, he amused himself by spinning his seal stamp. The seal, an *F* with a fleur-de-lis behind it, made a surprisingly decent top. However, when Flemings, his butler, appeared in the doorway and cleared his throat, Ben accidentally knocked the iron stamp off the edge of his desk, and it plummeted into the wastebasket where it landed with a *thunk*. "Damn."

Flemings eyed the wastebasket without lowering his chin. "Would you like me to retrieve it, my lord?"

"Actually, I thought I'd leave it there."

"Very well, my lord."

Sarcasm was often lost on Flemings. Or maybe the old bastard was a lot cleverer than he let on.

The butler tugged at the bottom of his jacket, which strained to cover the belly beneath. "Lord Biltmore is here to see you. Shall I send him in?"

Ben considered this. He couldn't remember the last time he'd had a visitor. True, it was only Hugh, but heaven forbid that the social calls become a routine occurrence. Hades had his underworld, a dragon had his lair, and Ben had his town house. Guests were to be endured, he supposed, but definitely not encouraged. "I suppose you can show him back here."

"Very well." Flemings turned to go, but not before his eyes flicked to the portrait behind Ben.

Good God. "Wait."

The butler froze but did not turn around. Ben wondered why he tolerated such impertinence. Probably because Flemings tolerated his.

"Show him to the drawing room and offer him a drink. I'll join him there shortly."

"Yes, my lord."

"And, Flemings?"

He froze again. Still did not turn around. "Do not let anyone near my study. No one—no guest nor member of the staff—is to enter, except you. And that should only be under dire circumstances. Do you understand?"

Flemings reluctantly faced him. "I believe I grasp your meaning, my lord. I am to keep everyone away from the sanctum...er, the study. I myself may enter, should conditions warrant it."

"Good." Ben reached for the cane he'd hung from a shelf.

"Am I correct in assuming that choking would qualify?"

"What?"

"If you were choking on a quail bone—would that be a dire circumstance?"

"Why in God's name would I eat a quail in my study?"

"Because you were hungry, I suppose." The butler's lips twitched as though he slayed himself with his cheeky humor.

In response, Ben smiled with the indulgent sweetness he usually reserved for children who've botched the punch line of a worn-out joke. "Our visitor, Flemings?"

"I shall escort him to the drawing room at once." The butler walked down the hall at a stately pace.

Ben could not resist calling after him. "For the record, Flemings, you'd better hope I don't choke on a damned quail bone, because the next earl will not take kindly to your insolence."

The butler's reply echoed down the hallway. "Very good, my lord."

Ben took a quick look at Daphne's portrait before closing the door behind him and heading for the drawing room. If Hugh had seen the painting, it would have been disastrous. Daphne would never have forgiven him. He had to be more careful.

He found Hugh gazing out a window that overlooked the street. Upon hearing the *thump* of Ben's cane on the hardwood floor, he turned and smiled broadly. "Foxburn, you're looking well."

"Don't tell me cripple is the rage this season?"

"What?"

Ben sighed. "Never mind. What brings you here?"

"I thought we might discuss our impending trip to Biltmore Manor. Shall we sit?"

"What's there to talk about? We'll travel there in a coach. We'll check that everything is satisfactory. We'll return here."

Hugh walked in front of the sofa. "Are you sure you wouldn't like to sit down?"

"Would it make you feel better?"

"It would, actually."

Ben sat and immediately wished he'd helped himself to a drink before doing so.

As if he'd read his mind, Hugh went to the sideboard, poured a brandy, and brought it to him.

Hugh was a good lad. The least Ben could do was listen to him. "What, exactly, did you want to discuss?"

"I saw the Sherbourne sisters and Miss Honeycote at a dinner party last night."

Ben raised a brow. Now Hugh had his full attention.

"I mentioned that we were going to spend a few days in the country, and Lady Olivia had a capital idea."

"Lady Olivia—the loud one?"

Hugh winced. "I suppose she is, yes."

"Go on."

"She suggested that I host a house party."

"What for?"

Hugh smiled, obviously pleased to have an answer at the ready. "Why, for the purpose of entertaining guests and enjoying a respite from town life."

"The purpose of our visit is to take care of estate business—not to play charades. If you want to host a house party, I can't stop you, but I don't intend to stay for it."

Hugh's face fell. "I thought you'd be pleased."

"Why on earth would you think that?"

"Because you seem to like spending time with Miss Honeycote and the Sherbourne sisters. I like them, too."

"They are not as annoying as the majority of the misses on the marriage mart," Ben admitted. "But to say I like spending time with them is an exaggeration." Except when it came to Daphne. Was he that transparent?

"Lady Olivia thought that since we all had such a nice time at Vauxhall Gardens, a house party would provide an opportunity for us to get to know one another a bit better."

"And just who else would you invite to this momentous event?"

Hugh shrugged. "Lady Olivia seemed keen on having Mr. Averill attend. Huntford and his duchess won't make the trip, of course, but Mrs. Honeycote could accompany the young women. I thought I'd extend an invitation to the Seaton girls and—"

Ben arched a brow. "I don't suppose they could leave their violins at home?"

Hugh frowned—a look that was half scolding, half disappointment. Ben was accustomed to such looks; it wasn't unusual for him to receive a dozen before breakfast.

Only, he *wasn't* used to receiving them from Hugh.

"Their playing isn't so bad. You might like the Seaton sisters if you got to know them," Hugh said.

Yes, and the Thames might freeze over in July, but since it was rare for Hugh to take a stand, Ben kept his doubts to himself. "You like them, then?"

"I don't know Miss Jane very well, but Miss Louise has a sharp sense of humor—not unlike yours, if you want to know the truth." The sudden ruddiness of Hugh's cheeks suggested that perhaps he admired more than Lady Louise's sense of humor.

Ben breathed a tad easier. "In that case, she sounds utterly charming."

"I can round out our numbers with a few of my pals from Eton." Hugh smiled as though pleased with himself.

"It sounds like you've got it all figured out." Ben twirled his cane, balancing it in front of him. He glanced at Hugh, wishing his true motivation for wanting a house party was written on his face.

He seemed interested in the Seaton girl, but what if he still had designs on Daphne? Now that Ben knew her as a person—and not just a scandalous mystery woman in a portrait—he could no longer argue that she would be an unsuitable wife. If he had any reservations about her character, it was that she was almost too generous and kind. Too good to be true.

And yet, the idea of Hugh courting her made Ben want to slam his cane into his good knee and break the bloody stick clean in two.

"Did Lady Rose and Miss Honeycote agree that a house party would be a grand and welcome adventure?"

Hugh scratched his head. "Not in those words, exactly. Lady Rose is much more retiring than her sister—"

Ben snorted. "*Everyone* is more retiring than her sister."

"True," Hugh conceded. "Lady Rose seemed amenable, however."

"And Miss Honeycote?" Ben focused on the spinning handle of his cane and feigned boredom.

"She seemed enthused at the prospect."

"Did she?" Interesting. And dangerous. Didn't she realize that if the second portrait was near Biltmore Manor, it was the worst possible place for her to be?

"She said something about needing a reprieve from balls and the like." Hugh shook his head. "I thought young ladies lived for such entertainments."

"I'd advise that you don't attempt to figure out the workings of a woman's mind. Not only is it futile, but it will give you the devil of a headache." So, Daphne wanted to escape town and the constant fear of being recognized. He understood the desire to run, but it was too risky.

"If you are dead set on hosting a house party, I cannot stop you, but I don't think you know what you're getting into. The staff will not be prepared for a large gathering. Who would act as your hostess, planning menus and overseeing activities?"

"My housekeeper, Mrs. Norris, is accustomed to the role. She took on hostess duties after my mother died. I doubt anyone would be more excited at that prospect than she."

Ben held out his empty glass and Hugh took the not-so-subtle hint. As he retrieved the glass and walked to the sideboard, he said, "I do hope you'll stay, Foxburn, and not just because we're short on gentlemen. I think it would be good for you to get out of your study—and socialize."

Good grief, the last thing he needed was for Hugh to make him some kind of project. Didn't he realize it was the other way around? The sooner Ben could fulfill his promise to Robert the better. And, now that he thought on it, maybe a house party that included several potential matches for Hugh—excluding Daphne—was actually a step in the right direction.

"I will consider it."

Hugh beamed and handed Ben his glass, replenished with brandy. "I'm so glad to hear it."

"Not because I need you to save me from my lonely, bitter life. I happen to like my life this way."

"Yes, of course. I understand."

Ben tossed back a healthy swig, welcoming the warm sting that traveled down his throat and settled in his chest. "Are we done here?"

Hugh laughed and slapped him on the back good-naturedly. "I suppose we are. You won't regret this, Foxburn. We're going to have a grand time."

As his protégé bounded out of the room, Ben dragged a hand down his face. Damn, but he felt old. His leg throbbed and just the thought of traveling an entire day in a coach gave him the beginnings of a headache.

He had to talk to Daphne and make her aware of the risks if she attended. Charlton lived only a couple miles from Hugh's country house. There was every possibility that she'd run into him at dinner or while riding or walking the grounds. And if Charlton *did* have the second portrait in his possession, he would recognize Daphne just as surely as Ben had.

He swallowed the rest of his drink in one gulp and hobbled out of the room, back to his study. There was no question—another meeting with Daphne was required.

The problem was, Ben looked forward to it far more than he should.

Chapter Eleven

Hatching: (1) A shading technique in which the artist draws a series of thin, parallel lines. (2) The act of devising a plan in the hope of preventing one's monumental fall from grace.

The next day Daphne was blessedly busy preparing for her visit to the orphanage. First, she finished mending a pile of linens and blouses for the girls. Afterward, she ventured to the market to purchase some fresh fruit and a few other treats she'd promised them.

Anything to keep her mind off the latest note she'd received from Benjamin.

He'd hinted that he had a matter of some urgency to discuss with her and wanted to meet in the park again today. Since she already had plans to visit the foundling home, she'd written back, suggesting that they meet tomorrow instead.

In between her chores and errands, she managed to walk through the foyer at least thirteen times in the hopes that she'd find a letter on the silver salver on the side table. The butler had begun to look at her strangely, as though he resented her constantly encroaching on his territory.

But alas, there was no reply from Benjamin.

Mama planned to come along to the orphanage. She hadn't been since before her trip to Bath and was eager to see the girls, whom she said reminded her of Anabelle and Daphne when they were young . . . and poor.

Which was not so long ago.

The grandfather clock gonged four times and Daphne plucked her bonnet from a hook beside the door. "Mama, please hurry. I want to spend some time with the girls outdoors before they go to dinner."

"Coming, my dear." Mama swept into the foyer wearing a fetching feathered hat. "Sorry to keep you waiting. I was engrossed in my book. The chapter ended with the heroine chained to a dungeon wall."

"I read that one to you. Don't you remember, she—"

"Stop!" Mama slapped her gloved hands over her ears with a vehemence that made Daphne giggle.

She'd read book after book to Mama during the dark days of her illness. Daphne thought that Mama had liked the stories. She'd certainly *seemed* to be listening, but due to her opium-induced haze, she remembered none of them.

"Where are the items for the girls?" Mama asked.

"The footmen put them in the coach already. Shall we go?"

Mama linked an arm through hers and they climbed into the duke's luxurious cab and settled themselves against the plush velvet squabs. As they traveled across town, the buildings outside their windows became shabbier, and the streets became dirtier. With every week that she spent in the comfort of Mayfair, this part of town became more and more foreign.

As though privy to her thoughts, Mama said, "It seems so strange to ride down this street in a fancy coach, doesn't it? A year ago we would have watched the coach through the dirty windows of our flat and wondered about the privileged people who rode inside. Now we *are* those people. But this place is a part of you, too, and it always will be."

"I'm not ashamed of where I come from."

"Anabelle's worried about you. She thinks you've been much more reserved lately—as if something's troubling you." Mama patted her hand and gave it a little squeeze. "If there's anything you want to discuss, anything I can help with, you must let me know. For months you took care of me, playing the part of the caregiver while I left you and Anabelle to struggle."

"You did no such thing, Mama. You were ill."

"Yes, but two young ladies should not have to fend for themselves in a city such as this. Especially gently bred women like you and your sister."

"You must admit we did pretty well."

Mama's eyes grew suspiciously moist. "You did, and I couldn't be more proud."

Proud? Daphne felt approximately as big as a thimble. Mama would be so disappointed if she knew what she'd done, no matter how worthy the cause. Worse yet, Mama would blame herself for placing her daughter in a predicament where she deemed immoral behavior necessary.

"Anyway," Mama said with a sniffle, "it is my turn to take care of you. You must think of yourself and your future. With your beauty and grace, you will have your pick of gentlemen. Make no apologies for who you are. Let your inner light shine."

The problem was she *had*. She'd let it shine a little too much. "I'll try, Mama."

The coach rolled up in front of the foundling home, an old building that looked as neglected as the poor wee ones inside. The stone rubble front was crumbling in many spots, and paint was peeling on the few shutters that hadn't already come unhinged and fallen off. Imposing iron bars surrounded the ground-floor windows, whether to keep intruders out or the children in, Daphne couldn't say. Either way, a depressing thought.

She and Mama carried two baskets each to the front door and were greeted almost immediately by a ruddy-faced maid who cheerfully relieved Mama of her load. "Yer looking awfully well, Mrs. Honeycote. Wonderful to see ye again, it is. The children are in the courtyard getting their daily exercise. They'll be so pleased to see ye."

"We'll see ourselves to the yard, Maisey," Daphne said. "Would you please take these baskets to the kitchen? The other two are linens and a few new articles of clothing."

"God bless ye, miss. These girls grow like weeds, and the dresses they outgrow are so worn out they're barely worth passing down. Even this poor lot turn up their noses at 'em. They'd rather wear somethin' too small for 'em than someone else's rags."

"I should think every girl deserves at least one pretty dress," Mama said thoughtfully. "Maisey, would you ask the director if I might have a moment of her time? I have an idea. Daphne, I'll see you outside presently."

She and the maid walked upstairs while Daphne

headed down the long corridor leading to the courtyard. She passed several chilly, dark classrooms and other closed doors, which she supposed were the staff's living quarters. When she stepped outside, however, sunlight warmed her face and her heart squeezed at the sight of the girls playing hopscotch, jumping rope, reading, and gossiping.

"Miss Honeycote!" a little girl squealed, sparking a small mob of adorable urchins that surged around Daphne.

"Did you bring us some sweets?"

"Do you have the green ribbon you promised me?"

"Look at the awful scrape on my knee!"

Daphne smiled and embraced as many girls as she could reach her arms around. "Let's see. No to the sweets, but I did bring some lovely oranges. Yes to the green ribbon, and some other colors to share."

"But the green is just for me, right?" Mary implored.

Daphne cupped the young girl's cheeks in her palms. "Yes, the green is just for you—to match your pretty eyes. Now, Caro, let's have a seat on the bench and you may show me your skinned knee."

The girls gradually resumed their activities, while Daphne and Caroline sat beneath the shade of the courtyard's only tree—a small one at that. Caroline immediately placed her worn boot on the bench and bent her knee toward her body. The large scrape had scabbed over, and if Daphne was not mistaken, a little mud appeared to be caked on as well. "Look," Caro whined. "Did you ever see anything so ugly in all your life?"

Daphne placed a finger on her cheek as though pondering the question. "Yes. Yes, I have. I once saw a drawing of a two-headed snake, and it was uglier than that. But not by much, if you want to know the truth."

Caro nodded soberly.

"Now tell me, how on earth did this happen?"

"I was climbing the fence back there"—she jerked a thumb toward the wrought-iron fence that separated the yard from the alley behind the orphanage—"and I fell."

Daphne blinked. This was much more serious than a scraped knee. "Why would you do such a thing, Caro? Was someone bullying you? Were you trying to get away?"

"Nah." She grimaced as though insulted at the suggestion that she'd shy away from a fight. "Nan dared me, and I wanted to see if I could do it."

"Well. I guess we know the answer to that question."

She bobbed her head of short, matted strawberry-blond hair. "I can," she said proudly.

"From the looks of it, however, things did not end well," Daphne pointed out.

"I made it over the fence just fine—landed on both feet. But then I had some trouble getting back in. I couldn't go around to the front door. Mrs. Higgins would have taken a switch to my backside."

"I can certainly understand why that would be a deterrent."

"She doesn't hit hard, but it's humiliating."

"Of course," Daphne sympathized. "So, you injured your knee when you were climbing back into the courtyard?"

Caro nodded. "The lace of my boot caught on the gate's hinge and tripped me. You should have seen it, Miss Honeycote. Blood was oozing out right here, and it dripped right down my shin and stained my stocking." She yanked it up and proudly displayed the small brown stain.

"You are very brave, indeed." Daphne wrapped her arms around the girl's thin but surprisingly strong shoulders. "You remind me a little of my sister. She's very courageous, too. I will tell you the same thing I would tell her. You mustn't ever try something as foolish as that again. You could have been badly hurt, or kidnapped by a stranger..."

"Like him?" Caro pointed to the back door of the orphanage.

Daphne looked up, pressing a hand to her forehead in order to shield her eyes from the afternoon sun that had just started dipping behind the building.

"Benjamin?" She said his name aloud, momentarily forgetting that Caro sat beside her.

"Who's Benjamin?"

"Er, Lord Foxburn. He's an acquaintance of mine."

With his cane in one hand, he strode toward them, the picture of sinewy strength and masculinity.

"He looks important," Caro announced. "And handsome, for someone that old."

Before Daphne could formulate a response, he reached them.

"Hello," he said, as if it were the most natural thing in the world for them to meet in an orphanage. In a courtyard full of girls, he looked like Gulliver, profoundly out of place and outnumbered.

"What are you doing here?" Daphne asked. Caro jabbed her in the ribs with a pointy elbow. "Ow."

Benjamin chuckled. "Maybe you should introduce me to your friend."

"Forgive me," Daphne said between clenched teeth. "Lord Foxburn, this is Miss Caroline."

"Hadley," Caroline amended. "Miss Caroline Hadley." Daphne chided herself for not using her surname. Not all the orphans had one, but Caro did, and she was rather proud of it.

"A pleasure to meet you, Miss Caroline Hadley." Benjamin shook Caro's grubby little hand as though she were a countess and not a poor little sprite with no family.

"What's wrong with your leg?" she asked bluntly.

"I was shot." He inclined his head toward her knee. "What's wrong with your leg?"

She shrugged. "I took a dare. I don't need a cane, though."

"Pity."

"Yes." The little imp crossed her arms and stared at Benjamin, sizing him up. After several seconds, she turned to Daphne. "I like him."

"Caro, it's not polite to talk about a person as if he's not there."

"Isn't that what you're doing now?"

Daphne sighed. Caro was precocious. And correct. "You only have a few minutes until they ring the bell for dinner. Why don't you run around for a bit?"

"I shall try." She limped a little as she walked away but soon began chasing after a rubber ball, keeping up with girls a head taller than she.

Benjamin sat on the bench. "I believe she's cured."

Her mind still grappled with the idea that he was here. At the orphanage. The cut of his dark blue jacket emphasized his broad shoulders and tapered torso. His right leg—the injured one—was just inches from hers, and she couldn't help staring at his thigh. Covered in smooth, snug buckskin, it looked perfectly normal. In fact, far better than average.

Dragging her gaze away, she asked, "Why did you come?"

"I told you—we need to talk. I understand your mother is with the director?"

Daphne glanced over her shoulder at the building. "She'll probably join me soon."

"It's about Hugh's house party. I hope you're not planning to attend."

She drew back like she'd received a slap across the face. Hadn't they reached an understanding? Weren't they working together? Maybe he was concerned that she still had designs on Lord Biltmore. "I don't understand," she said. "Are you worried that Lord Biltmore will get the wrong impression?"

"No." He drew his dark brows together. "Though that's a distinct possibility. It's too risky for you to come. What if Charlton *does* have the second portrait?"

"I hope he does. Then we would at least know where it is, and you could try to purchase it for me. There's very little I can do to extract myself from this mess, and I dislike being so dependent on you—"

His head snapped up. "You haven't even given me a chance to prove myself."

Oh dear. "I didn't mean to suggest you are unreliable. I just wish I could fix things on my own. I liked the idea of attending Lord Biltmore's house party because then, at least, I could be near the action—feel like I was contributing in some small way."

"You *can't* help with this. In fact, you shouldn't be

within a twenty-mile radius of the painting. If Charlton saw you, he'd almost certainly recognize you."

"We don't even know for sure if he has the painting. I realize there are risks, but there are risks involved in staying here as well. If Lord Charlton is half as timid as Thomas made him out to be, he's not likely to spend much time socializing with Lord Biltmore and his house guests."

Benjamin's intense stare made her toes curl in her slippers. "You may have a point," he conceded. "If Hugh invites Charlton to dinner, you could always plead a headache."

"Precisely. And if I'm there, I won't feel like a prisoner in the gallows waiting to hear what's to become of me."

"That's courageous of you." He said it as though he hadn't realized she had it in her. Well, that made two of them.

"Thank you. But I must confess, I don't feel very brave. What if Lord Charlton has the painting but won't sell it?"

"If he's offered enough money, he'll sell it."

Daphne gazed at the children playing across the yard beneath orange-tinged clouds. "My funds are not unlimited."

"I'm sure we can reach some kind of arrangement."

She stiffened. "What are you suggesting?"

"That you could pay me back over time. Or not."

Oh. "That's very generous of you."

He shrugged as lending money to women he barely knew were quite routine. "If you say so."

They sat in silence for a few moments, and then he jerked his cane in the general direction of the girls. "There are so many of them—must be at least two dozen."

"Twenty-eight. The older girls help take care of the little ones."

"What happened to Caroline's parents?"

"They died in a fire when she was five. She went to live with her grandmother, but she became ill and passed away last year."

"She had no other family? No one else to take her in?"

Daphne shrugged. "I suppose not."

He grunted. "Do you know them all?"

"Yes, some better than others. Some of the girls, like Caro, remember their parents. Others have lived here almost all of their short lives."

A bell rang, and the girls immediately scrambled for a front spot in the dinner line.

"Good lord," he said. "I'm glad I'm not in their way."

She smiled. "They're growing girls—they need their nourishment."

"Obviously."

She had a thought then—silly perhaps, but worth a try. "Would you like to see more of the orphanage? That is, if you're not too busy. I could give you a quick tour while the girls are dining."

Before he could respond, Caroline popped out of line, ran toward them, and gave Daphne a quick hug before racing back to her spot. "See you next week, Miss Honeycote," she called. "And you, too, sir . . . er . . . my lord."

A look of mild alarm crossed his face. "I don't think I'll—"

"Good-bye," Daphne called back. The girls filed into the building, waving. To Benjamin, she said, "Never mind. I'm sure you have more pressing matters to attend to." His reaction to Caro's assumption spoke volumes, and she chided herself for even asking him about the tour. He was already going out of his way to help her; she had no right to make additional demands on his time.

When he turned toward her, his forehead was wrinkled, like he was deep in thought. "On second thought... I'd like a tour."

Chapter Twelve

Daphne wasn't sure she'd heard Benjamin correctly.

She blinked twice. "You want to see the orphanage?"

"Why not? I've never been in one. To tell you the truth, I haven't been around many children at all. As a rule, I don't find them very interesting."

"I doubt they find you very interesting either," she lied. Caro had taken to him immediately, so much so that Daphne felt an uncharitable twinge of jealousy.

"Caroline is the exception," he admitted. "She's scrappy and smart. A survivor."

Interesting. Maybe he and Caro were kindred spirits. "Come," she said, rising from the bench. "We'll take a quick peek at the dormitory while the girls are eating."

They walked side by side, up the back stairs to the second floor. "How is your leg today?" Daphne asked.

"Still attached to my body. Can't ask for much more than that."

"I'm in the process of writing up some instructions."

"For what?"

"Just a few simple procedures I'd like you to try. To see if they provide some relief."

He arched a dark brow. "I'll have to let my physician know that he has some competition."

His mocking tone stung, but she shrugged it off. "I'm not suggesting that I'm smarter than your doctor."

"You *are* smarter," he said matter-of-factly. "He's had more training, but you're more intelligent."

"Thank you, I think."

"You're much prettier, too." He flashed a rakish grin that made her heart beat faster. She was not accustomed to seeing his flirtatious side—had not even known he possessed one.

They reached the landing of the top floor, which had once been an attic. The entire floor was one huge, open room, with rows of beds under the low slanted eaves. Threadbare curtains hung from the windows at each end of the long room and the walls were a dingy color that might have once been blue, although they now appeared closer to gray. The blankets on the sagging mattresses were neatly folded and a few of the pillows had dolls napping on them. Trunks at the ends of some of the beds held the girls' precious personal belongings, but most of the orphans had little to call their own.

It seemed a little barren without the girls there. A little cold. And yet, Daphne saw the potential of the place. She hoped Benjamin saw it, too.

"It's clean," he said approvingly. "A boys' dormitory would never be this clean."

"The girls are quite industrious. The older ones take turns doing the laundry and the cleaning."

He walked down the center of the room, his head only a few inches away from the ceiling. "Sharing a room with twenty-seven sisters could be difficult."

"But also great fun," she pointed out.

He nodded, his intense blue gaze taking in every detail of the room.

They descended one flight of stairs in order to look at the classrooms, and quite literally bumped into Mama as she and the director were leaving the office.

"Lord Foxburn!" Mama exclaimed. "Maisey told us you were here. So generous of you to come and visit the girls."

"A pleasure to see you again, Mrs. Honeycote. I would not have you operate under the false impression that I am a philanthropist, however. Far from it. I leave that kind of thing to good people like your daughter."

"Oh, you are too modest, my lord. But my Daphne does have a very giving nature," she said proudly.

The director extended her hand. "Welcome, Lord Foxburn. What can I do for you today?"

He shook her hand smoothly and unleashed his most charming smile. "I happened to be riding by and saw Huntford's coach out front. I thought I'd stop in and see if he was here."

Daphne nearly rolled her eyes. What a thin excuse. But the director believed it, and so did Mama. "Since the earl is here, I offered to give him a quick tour. May I show him the classrooms?

"Please, allow me." The director, Mrs. Middleton, stepped briskly down the hall and swung open a door that creaked as though its hinges were a couple centuries old. For all Daphne knew, they were. The room was large and three tall windows let in the waning evening light. There were no desks but long tables surrounded by wooden stools, some of which looked like they might topple over at any moment. A map of Europe covered much of the back wall, and the row of low bookshelves housed a few meager supplies. Some paper, a few worn books, small writing slates, and chalk. "This is the main school room. We employ two teachers. Miss Humphrey works with the older girls and Miss Randles instructs our young ones." The director shivered as though she did not envy Miss Randles her task. "She has the patience of a saint, she does."

Daphne tried to see the room through Benjamin's eyes.

It wasn't much to look at, but to her, it represented hope for the orphans. The opportunity to learn to read and write was more than many of her friends growing up had. If the girls could read, all sorts of worlds might open up to them.

Benjamin walked to the wall of windows and looked down at the courtyard below. Then he strode through the room, running a hand over the solid slab of oak that formed the top of a table. He nodded approvingly. "It's a fine room," he said.

It wasn't exactly a ringing endorsement, but the way he spoke the words made Daphne want to hug him. He said *fine* like the room was fit for twenty-eight princesses, and even though all three women knew it wasn't, they sighed in agreement.

"There are several improvements we plan to make," the director said quickly. "But in the meantime, thanks to the generosity of benefactors like the Honeycotes, we've been able to take care of these girls and teach them how to survive beyond these walls."

"Thank you for the tour," Benjamin said. "It's been very…enlightening."

"It was my pleasure, Lord Foxburn."

"Thank you for your time as well, Miss Honeycote."

Mama stared at Benjamin with a mixture of curiosity and suspicion. It was the kind of look mothers gave when they were putting together the pieces of a puzzle one would rather they didn't. "My lord," she said, "I understand that you shall be at Lord Biltmore's house party next week."

"I'm accompanying Hugh there to assist with any business matters and may stay for a few days of the house party. If my schedule permits."

"Of course. You must have many demands on your time. However, I do hope that you shall stay for some, if not all, of the festivities. Daphne, Olivia, Rose, and I shall be there and would enjoy your company immensely."

"And I yours." He made a polite bow. "Good evening, ladies."

Without thinking, Daphne blurted, "I'll see you out." She was oddly reluctant to let him go without saying good-bye.

"Don't be long, darling," Mama said. "We're having dinner with the Mosbys this evening."

Benjamin was silent until they reached the stairs at the rear of the building. At the top landing, he stopped abruptly, reached out, and clasped her hand in his. The sudden tension in their arms pulled her toward him and she bumped lightly into the solid wall of his chest. She started to say "I'm sorry," but *she* hadn't been the one to cause the collision.

Besides, she suddenly found herself quite unable to breathe.

His back was to the wall and her slippers were toe to toe with his boots. He ran his hand up her arm and around her back before gently stroking her nape, and all the while he stared at her as though he were very, very... hungry. "Daphne," he said. It was a plea for permission, or perhaps forgiveness.

With every second that passed, her heart raced faster and a heady warmth seeped into her limbs and coiled in her center. If a mere look could do this to her, what magic could his kiss do? Her gaze drifted to his lips and she leaned a bit closer.

And that was all it took.

He hauled her against him and dipped his head, covering her mouth with his own. There was nothing gentle or civilized about his kiss. It was needy, raw, and... wonderful.

He thrust his tongue between her lips and explored her mouth. At the same time he cupped her cheek with his hand, sweetly coaxing her closer, seducing her with the brush of his thumb across her skin.

Never had she felt so powerful and at the same time, so utterly out of control. Desire curled in her belly and she suddenly understood why ladies of gentle breeding would risk their reputations for a few minutes of bliss.

Kissing Benjamin was akin to breaking a wild horse. Not that she'd ever done such a thing, but she could now imagine it. A little frightening, but mostly exhilarating and thrilling. Every inch of him, from his scratchy chin to his broad shoulders to his hard thighs was pure, unadulterated male. He smelled like leather and grass; he tasted faintly of cloves and brandy. His body was so different from hers and yet, every time they bumped together, they seemed to fit perfectly. So much so that she had to check the urge to fall into him.

Instead, she poured all her energy into kissing him back. The rhythm of his probing tongue was easy to imitate, and soon she became an equal partner in the dance, leading as often as he did. Nothing existed but the two of them; nothing mattered but prolonging this moment.

Until his hand slid down her spine and firmly cupped her bottom. In some remote part of her brain, a warning bell sounded, and she drew back.

His eyes were dazed and heavy lidded, his lips swollen. "Jesus," he rasped.

"What," she asked, trying to catch her breath, "was that?"

"That"—he laced his fingers through hers—"was a kiss."

"Obviously. But...why?"

"I don't know. A momentary lapse in judgment, I suppose. On your part, that is."

"Wait a minute. You kissed me, which makes it *your* lapse in judgment."

He flashed a cocky smile. "You were begging me to kiss you. I should add that I didn't mind at all."

She wrested her hand away from his and placed her hands on her hips. "I fear you are delusional. There was no begging."

"Not aloud."

"I see. You were reading my mind."

He leaned close to her ear and softly said, "Tell me you didn't want me to kiss you, and I'll take you at your word."

His breath was warm on her neck and the strange pulsing in her loins resumed. "I...I didn't expect it to be so..." *Consuming, powerful, knee-buckling.*

"But now you know," he said, nipping lightly at her neck. His hands spanned her waist and eased up her rib cage. "What do you think?"

As long as his lips were brushing over her skin, she was incapable of thought. "This is nice, but—"

He lifted his head and stared at her incredulously. "Nice?" Clearly, it was not the answer he'd been looking for. "Nice is a rich cup of coffee or a day without rain. That kiss was not *nice*."

She snorted slightly. "What would you call it?"

He stepped closer and kissed her lightly on the temple. "I'd call it 'a glimpse of heaven.' "

Oh. She had to admit it was a more apt description than *nice*. Although *heaven* sounded much purer than she presently felt.

"You should go. Mama will come looking for me soon."

"You say you want me to leave, but then you won't stop kissing me."

"Very funny." She tucked a few tendrils behind her ear and smoothed the front of her skirt. "How do I look?"

"Like you've been ravished."

"Benjamin!"

"Ben."

"What?"

"You could call me Ben. It's a little less formal than Benjamin. I'd say we've crossed over into the realm of informality, wouldn't you?"

"The girls will be charging up these stairs to their dormitory any minute. Do you want to be standing here when they do?"

He started walking immediately. "I may not see you for a while."

"Oh?" She tried to keep the disappointment from her voice but feared she wasn't entirely successful.

"We have a plan now. There's really no need for us to discuss anything until I have the chance to speak with Charlton."

"No, of course not."

At the bottom of the stairs he paused and faced her. "I don't suppose I could convince you to change your mind about Hugh's house party? It's risky for you to go."

"I know. But I'd go mad if I were to stay in town, sitting around and awaiting news of my fate. I'm going."

Ben nodded thoughtfully. "You're very stubborn."

Daphne might have taken offense if he hadn't spoken the words with grudging admiration. "Yes. I look forward to seeing you at Biltmore Manor." She gave a slight wave, feeling suddenly awkward and empty.

He walked down the corridor toward the front door but stopped after a few strides. "This"—he waved his cane in the air demonstratively—"what you're doing here, that is, it's . . . good."

Joy bounced in her heart. "Thank you."

"I'll see you next week." He gave a casual salute with his cane and left.

Chapter Thirteen

*Iridescence: (1) A quality that causes paint to reflect
light and, thus, appear to change color. (2) The bewitching,
beguiling property that enables a woman's tresses to glow like
amber in candlelight and pure gold in sunshine.*

Traveling any considerable distance was hell on Ben's leg, and the journey to Biltmore Manor was no exception. It was lowering enough to have to ride in a coach instead of atop a horse. Adding insult to injury, he needed to stop every two hours, exit the coach, and hobble about in order to stretch his leg. Beyond humiliating. Thank goodness he'd traveled alone.

He would arrive at the house in less than an hour. He and Hugh would have a few days to meet with the steward, inspect the grounds, and review the accounts. After that, a dozen or so guests would descend upon the house.

The only one he was concerned with, however, was Daphne.

He reached into the breast pocket of his jacket and withdrew the letter she'd sent him three days ago. It was less letter than prescription. Even so, it was infused with her irrepressible optimism and goodness.

At the top of the paper she'd written, "Treatment for Leg Pain." Beneath it were a series of simple steps.

> *Number one. Soak the leg in a bath of water as hot as can be borne (without scalding the skin) for at least ten minutes.*
>
> *Number two. While the flesh and muscles are still warm, vigorously massage the affected area of the leg.*
>
> *Number three. Apply a poultice (made from comfrey leaves soaked in boiling water) to the leg and cover with bandages overnight.*
>
> *Repeat daily.*

Each time he read the steps—and he'd read them several times—they made him chuckle. Especially the last line. As though he had nothing more pressing to do than soak in a bath and mash up comfrey day after day.

Not that he objected to her nursing advice. It was nice that someone cared enough to try to help him in spite of the fact that his was a hopeless case.

Of course, she'd probably only given him her prescribed treatment out of a sense of duty—payment in return for the favor he was doing her with regard to the portraits. She couldn't know that he'd latch on to any excuse to spend a few moments basking in her light.

The kiss had been a mistake. It was like opening a door and taking a peek at paradise, but knowing he could never, ever be admitted. Daphne herself had said she was looking for a kind, good-hearted gentleman. Someone decent and noble. Someone she could raise a family with.

That wasn't him.

But the way she'd felt in his arms, the way she'd responded to his kiss, was hard to forget. He'd kissed her without holding back, hoping to show her once and for all that she should keep her distance from him. Not just physically, but in other ways, too. She shouldn't introduce him to little ruffians with freckles or show him classrooms with barren bookshelves. She shouldn't involve him in her problems or tell him what kind of man she planned to marry. And she certainly shouldn't waste her time trying to heal him. No amount of soaking was going to fix him.

So he'd channeled the full force of his passion into that kiss. He'd greedily tasted her mouth, sucked on her bottom lip, pulled her hips toward his. Although he felt a momentary hesitation on her part—a split second in which she'd been too stunned to move—she hadn't run away screaming.

And she really ought to have.

Though he was fairly certain that it was the first time she'd been properly—or should he say improperly?—kissed, she hadn't cowered from him or pretended to be affronted. Instead, she'd met him thrust for thrust and stroke for stroke.

He shifted against the velvet squabs of the coach seat. The mere memory of that encounter on an orphanage staircase set his blood on fire.

The irony did not escape him. The kiss that was intended to get her out of his system would haunt him for the rest of his days.

As the coach crested a hill, Biltmore Manor came into view. The sight of the stately structure, with its gleaming white stone front and its Palladian lines, transported

Ben back a dozen years in time. As a boy, he'd often come home with Robert in between school terms. It was closer to Eton than his parents' house. At least that was the excuse he'd used. The truth was that Ben preferred Robert's family to his own. Robert's parents were cordial and pleasant, but they mostly left Robert and him to their own devices. They could ride, hunt, fish, explore to their hearts' content without having to endure endless lectures about not achieving one's potential that were punctuated by lashes from a leather strap.

Yes, Robert's family was preferable, and he didn't seem to mind sharing. So Biltmore was the place where Ben had spent summers and kissed the butcher's daughter and broken his arm after falling off a stallion he had no business riding.

It was somewhat like coming home. Except, this time, Robert wasn't with him.

The muscles of his thigh twitched like some awful premonition. He tucked Daphne's note carefully back into his pocket, reached for his flask, and braced himself.

Two days later, Ben seized the opportunity to ask about Charlton.

And got his first hint that some sort of trouble had befallen the squire.

Ben and Hugh were taking a ride around the estate—a short ride, since that was all Ben's leg would tolerate—with the steward, Nigel Coulton, a short, portly man with a shock of white hair.

"Are those Charlton's fields to the west?" Ben asked.

"Aye," said the steward. "He used to ride into the village regularly, but I havna seen him in a few months."

Hugh scratched his head. "The squire is getting on in his years. Perhaps he doesn't enjoy riding like he used to, or maybe he's ill."

"What about his son?" Ben asked.

The steward spat in an impressive arc. "I see the son, Rowland Hallows, often enough. He frequents the tap-room at the Hog and Crown. Canna hold his drink."

"What does he say about his father?"

"Nothin' I'd believe."

Ben stroked his chin. "I think I'll pay a visit this afternoon."

"I'll accompany you," Hugh volunteered. "It sounds like Hallows is something of a scoundrel. If he's in his cups, he could be a handful."

Ben rolled his eyes toward heaven and wished *he* were in his cups. God help him if Hugh felt the need to protect him from scoundrels and the like. "The more the merrier. I just want to see how old Charlton is doing. He used to hunt with Robert and me."

It was the first time he'd spoken Robert's name since arriving, and it had slipped out unexpectedly. It hung in the air between the three men, who each recalled his own fond but now-painful memories.

A few moments passed before Hugh said, "Charlton sent a nice card after Robert...died. I should thank him."

Nigel pulled his hat down low over the snowy white bush atop his head. "If you see him, tell 'im I hope to see him in the village one of these days. Ain't his fault that his son is an ungrateful brute. There be bad seeds that fall from every tree." The steward sniffed the air. "A storm's comin' in from the south. We'd better head back to the stables."

As if to confirm Nigel's prediction, a gust of warm wind rustled the horses' manes, and thunder rumbled in the distance. A prickling between Ben's shoulder blades gave him a sudden and inexplicable chill.

Instincts born on the battlefield warned him that something was amiss at Biltmore Manor. It could be something insignificant, but he wished it wasn't too late to cancel the house party. He didn't want Daphne anywhere near this place.

Unfortunately, at that very moment, she was probably on her way.

"Miss Honeycote and the Sherbourne sisters should arrive tomorrow." Hugh added a lump of sugar to his tea and took a seat in Biltmore Manor's drawing room across from Ben, who was also drinking tea. Not his usual fare, but it couldn't hurt to keep a clear head before visiting Charlton later that afternoon.

Of course, Ben's ears had perked up at Hugh's mention of Daphne, but he did his best to maintain a bored expression. "The rest of the guests, too, I imagine."

Hugh leaned forward, elbows on his knees. "Yes, but I thought you might be most interested in Miss Honeycote's arrival."

Ben glared over the rim of his teacup, which he feared was not nearly as effective as glaring over the rim of a brandy snifter. "Why would you think that?"

"I saw you with her at the Seaton musicale and at Vauxhall Gardens. You seemed...happy."

Ben almost spit out his tea. "Happy?"

"Perhaps that's a stretch. But you must admit you were less miserable than usual."

"What's your point, Hugh?"

Hugh set his cup on the table and tented his fingers, just the way Robert used to. "Though I am very fond of Miss Honeycote," he said, "she doesn't look at me the way she looks at you."

"Maybe if you were more of an ass."

"Ben. I'm being serious. I think she cares for you, and while part of me resents the hell out of you for that, another part of me thinks . . . you need someone like her in your life."

"Jesus, Hugh. Don't play matchmaker for me."

"I wouldn't dream of it," he said. "I just thought you should know that Miss Honeycote is only a friend to me. I once thought we might be more, but lately I've realized that it takes two people to fall in love."

Ben thought about making a flippant remark, because that's what he *always* did. But that would have been like rejecting the gift that Hugh was laying in his lap, so instead he set down his cup and said, "Your brother would be proud of the man you've become."

Hugh smiled wanly.

And then, because the mood had suddenly grown far too somber, Ben said, "Do we have time for me to beat you in a game of billiards before we head over to Charlton's?"

Hugh stood and handed Ben his cane. "I suspect it will take several attempts before you're able to defeat me—if ever."

"You grow cockier by the day," Ben said approvingly. "Robert really would be proud."

A few hours later, Hugh and Ben stood on Charlton's doorstep. The large, box-shaped house was constructed of brick, and ambitious ivy scaled each of its four chimneys. From a distance, Ben had admired the bay windows and the simple solidness of its design; upon closer inspection, however, he noted that one shutter had fallen off its hinges and tall weeds had poked up between the stones of the drive.

Hugh rang the bell and a woman—the housekeeper, if the large ring of keys at her waist was any indication— opened the door. Her round spectacles accentuated the round apples of her cheeks. "How may I help you?" she asked, her voice tinged with suspicion.

Hugh stepped forward. "I am Lord Biltmore, and this is my friend, the Earl of Foxburn. I recently returned from—"

"Lord Biltmore?" A cautious smile split the housekeeper's face. "Why, we'd heard you'd come back. Please, come in. I'm Mrs. Parfitt."

"Thank you." Hugh handed over his hat. Ben followed suit. The housekeeper was friendly enough and might be a good source of information.

"We were so sorry to hear about the passing of your brother," Mrs. Parfitt said. "Never was there a finer man."

Ben saw the sadness in the housekeeper's eyes and decided he liked her. He sometimes forgot that he wasn't the only one who mourned losing Robert.

"Thank you," Hugh said again. "He considered Lord Charlton a friend."

"Oh, indeed." She looked from Hugh to Ben and back again. "The staff was delighted to hear you'd returned to Biltmore Manor. But what brings you gentlemen here?"

"We'd like to see Lord Charlton," Ben said. "We apologize for not sending notice, but we hoped he might be available for a short visit."

"I don't know." She wrung her hands. "He hasn't had any visitors in a long time, although he is having a good day."

"I hope he hasn't been ill," Hugh said kindly.

"He's not been well, Lord Biltmore. Not sick, exactly, but he hasn't been himself. I can tell you that."

"If it's a bad time, we can come back," Hugh offered.

But Ben didn't want to waste an opportunity. If the baron was having a good day, this might be his best chance to ask about the portraits. "On the other hand, a little company might be just the thing to cheer him," Ben said. "And we wouldn't stay long."

"Mr. Hallows, his son, doesn't normally approve of visitors."

"Rowland and I used to play together," Hugh said.

"Is he out?" Ben asked.

Mrs. Parfitt pushed her spectacles farther up her bulb-shaped nose. "Yes. He rode into the village."

Ben smiled conspiratorially. "We'll be quick. A short visit will lift Lord Charlton's spirits, and his son need never know we were here."

"He could return at any time."

Ben shrugged. "If he does, you may tell him that you tried to stop me from going up to see him but I wouldn't take no for an answer."

The housekeeper clucked her tongue. "That's not far from the truth, now, is it?"

"No."

"Very well. I'll take you up to his bedchamber, but just for a short time. And if he is sleeping, you must promise not to wake him. He needs his rest."

"We wouldn't dream of disturbing him," Ben assured her.

As the housekeeper led the way up the stairs, a sudden panic gripped him. What if Daphne's portrait was hanging in the hallway upstairs or, worse, in Charlton's bedchamber? Ben would have to create some sort of scene and get Hugh out of the house before he had a chance to identify Daphne. He hoped it wouldn't come to that.

Mrs. Parfitt toddled down the hall where she pushed open the door to a spacious bedroom. Only one of the room's three windows admitted light. The curtains on the other two were drawn tight. The walls were utterly and blessedly devoid of artwork. The baron sat up in his large four-poster bed, a book open on his lap.

"My lord, you have two fine gentlemen here to see you." Mrs. Parfitt's voice bounced up and down as though she were speaking to a rather simple child.

"What's this?" Charlton slammed the book shut and sat up straighter. His gaze went to Hugh and the older man's glassy eyes grew wide. "Bless my soul. Robert?"

Hugh walked closer to the bed. "No, Lord Charlton, it's Hugh—Robert's younger brother."

Damn. Charlton was in bad shape.

He squinted, as if he didn't quite believe Hugh, then gave a loud sigh. "Of course you are. You looked so much like your brother for a moment, that's all."

Beyond the cleft chin, Ben had never noticed a resemblance. But maybe he was too close to the brothers to see it. It would be bloody inconvenient if Charlton were insane.

"Lord Foxburn and I have come to visit."

Ben stepped forward. "Charlton." The baron shook his hand, but a mild look of confusion clouded his eyes.

"We went hunting last year," Ben said. "You, Robert, and I. Robert shot a pheasant and your hound—"

"Molly!" the baron exclaimed. "Molly snatched that bird right out of the air. Yes," he said more softly. "I remember."

"We're sorry to hear you haven't been well," Hugh said.

"Ah, it's nothing. I'm a little weak. A little forgetful. But Rowland takes care of everything. I'm fortunate that Eleanor gave me a son before she left this world. If it weren't for Rowland, I don't know what would become of me or the estate or the staff. We've missed you around here," he said sincerely. "It's a tragedy about Robert. First the eldest brother, and then him. Devastating. But you'll do a fine job, Hugh. Make a fine viscount."

Ben hadn't thought the baron capable of stringing together several coherent sentences, but clearly he was having a lucid moment. How to steer the conversation in the direction of the portraits? "Did you see much of Robert, in the months before he went off to war?"

The older man bit his dry, cracked lip, and Ben could almost see him searching for the memories, like someone rifling through the contents of a full trunk. "I don't think so. Though, there was the one night we played cards."

"Will you tell us about it?"

"We were at The Thorny Rose, one of the village taverns—Robert, Hawkins, Ludwig, and I. Had a few pints in us, we did, and Robert suggested we play a few rounds of cards. Just a friendly game of vingt-et-un. We weren't playing deep. At first. Then Hawkins—he's a squire who lives a couple miles south of here—he said he wanted me to wager my English Beauty paintings."

The hairs on the back of Ben's neck stood on end. "What English Beauty paintings?"

"That's what I call them," Charlton explained. "I had a

pair of portraits. Painted by a London artist, of a golden young woman."

"Who is she?" Hugh asked, mesmerized.

Charlton smiled wistfully. "I don't think the woman really exists, if you want to know the truth. Probably a figment of the artist's imagination. Only a goddess could radiate light like that. Old Hawkins, he wanted those portraits in the worst way. I said no, of course. I wasn't going to wager them. But then I started drinking more, and losing more, and before I knew it, I'd bet *English Beauty on a Chaise Lounge.*"

Was the old man completely lacking imagination? "That's what you call it?"

"Seems obvious, I know, but it's an apt description."

"Did Hawkins win the painting?" Hugh had sat in a chair close to the bed and was perched on the edge of it, clinging to every word.

"No." The old man rubbed his chin thoughtfully. "Robert did. A bet is a bet, and although Robert probably wouldn't have held me to it, I sent the portrait over the next day. One of the hardest things I ever did besides burying my dear wife, God rest her soul."

"I don't recall seeing it at Biltmore Manor. I'll have to search the storage rooms," Hugh said.

"It's not in a storage room." The baron smiled knowingly. "Robert was half in love with the woman in the portrait. Foolish—like a mortal falling in love with Aphrodite. Anyway, he told me he'd taken it to town. Said I was welcome to visit her anytime." The balding man laughed at the memory.

Ben wanted to laugh, too. This was almost too easy. "Where is the other portrait of the English Beauty?"

"I don't know what you're talking about." The man's face turned red as a beet.

"You said you had a pair of portraits. What became of the other one? Do you still have it?"

"Aye," he confessed. "I keep it hidden." He craned his wrinkled neck from side to side, as though a French spy might swoop in at any moment. "Things have been disappearing around here. I cannot take any chances with the English Beauty."

"What sorts of things have disappeared?" Hugh asked, his eyes round as saucers.

"Small heirlooms. Cuff links. My pocket watch."

"That sounds serious, Charlton," Hugh said. "Have you informed the magistrate?"

"No, and I won't either. Rowland says I've just misplaced a few things and that they're bound to turn up. The magistrate would say my brain is addled, and I suppose he'd be right. But I couldn't bear it if anything were to happen to the portrait, so I'm keeping it safe."

"It wouldn't be easy to sneak a portrait of any substantial size out of the house," Ben mused, "but it doesn't hurt to keep it tucked away. Very wise, if you ask me. It *is* still here, isn't it?"

Much to Ben's relief, Charlton nodded enthusiastically. Thank God. Assuming the baron wasn't entirely out of his mind, Daphne's reputation was safe for now.

"Hawkins would probably love to get his hands on it," Ben said conversationally. He needed to know who else might be able to identify Daphne. "Who else has seen the paintings?"

"No one I can recall. Well, the staff obviously. The painting's not fit for public rooms. Not that I'd characterize it as indecent, you understand, but the woman is not fully dressed and I couldn't offend the sensibilities of the parson's wife if she stopped in for tea, now, could I?"

"I should say not," Hugh exclaimed.

Ben found the entire exchange fascinating. In the five minutes since they'd begun discussing the portrait, the baron seemed to have an increase in energy and mental acuity. It was as if Daphne had managed to reach out of the portrait and heal him.

Ben was absurdly jealous. And curious. But he couldn't just come out and ask how she was posed in the second portrait. Or, maybe he could.

"What's the title of the portrait you still have?"

"Ah," Charlton said fondly, "it's *English Beauty beside the Looking Glass.*"

"And is it your favorite of the two?" Ben had to know.

The old man focused on a spot in the distance as though he were conjuring up the portrait from the recesses of his mind. "Indeed. There's something deeper about this one. More vulnerable, yet sophisticated."

Ben swallowed past the knot in his throat. It was worse than he'd feared. Charlton was not going to let the portrait go easily. But if he truly had it hidden away, perhaps it was for the best. Daphne could proceed with her season and find a decent, respectable husband without fear that the painting would surface at an inopportune time.

And if it was someday found, in the back of a wardrobe or in a dusty attic, she'd be a couple of decades older and no one would recognize her. If she, or anyone close to her, did, maybe they'd laugh at the memory of the scandal the portraits had nearly caused. She probably wouldn't even recall the name of the cynical, arrogant bastard who'd volunteered to help her locate it.

Turned out she didn't need him after all.

At least he'd get to tell her the good news. And he'd have a few more days with her at the house party before she returned to the glittering world to which she belonged.

He, on the other hand, would slink into a nice dark cave. Somewhere he wouldn't have to witness some other man living the life *he* might have had with Daphne.

If he were whole.

Chapter Fourteen

There it is," cried Rose, thrusting her arm outside the coach's window. "Biltmore Manor."

"Why, it looks like a palace," Mama said. She gave Daphne a hopeful look, as if to say, *One day, this could all be yours.*

Obviously, Mama had not given up entirely on the idea of Daphne making a match with Lord Biltmore. She took advantage of even the smallest opportunity to praise him. "His penmanship is flawless," she said, examining the invitation for the third time that morning. As if letter formation were a telling indicator of a man's character.

"It *is* beautiful," Daphne agreed. "But judging by the curls at the end of each word, my guess that his housekeeper penned the invitation."

"Do you think so?" Mama looked stricken.

"I must concur with Daphne," Rose said. "However, he did take the time to initial the bottom there. His *H* is exceedingly well formed."

Mama seemed appeased by the observation.

Daphne couldn't deny that Lord Biltmore was a gentleman. His manners were impeccable, his good nature was genuine, and she couldn't imagine him attempting something as improper as kissing her on the stairs of an orphanage.

And therein lay the problem.

Since kissing Benjamin—Ben—she'd been able to think of little else. The firm pressure of his lips, the taste of his tongue, the heat of his body against hers.

In spite of the hasty good-bye he'd said that afternoon— or maybe because of it—she'd hoped that he'd call on her or send a brief note. *Something* to show he was thinking of her. She'd sent the treatment plan to him and in response she'd heard...nothing.

She shouldn't have been surprised or hurt, but it stung that an event that had been so noteworthy in her life—her first real kiss—should seem so insignificant to him.

As the coach pulled up the long, winding drive to Lord Biltmore's estate, Daphne itched to be free of the confines of the cab. Spacious though it was, it seemed considerably less so with five women and all their accompanying hats, reticules, fans, and parasols. Mama, Olivia, and Rose rode on the bench across from Daphne and Hildy—the lady's maid whom Anabelle had insisted they take. Hildy did not tolerate the rocking of the coach very well and was queasy for most of the ride. Only sleeping seemed to ease her misery, so the rest of the women tried to be as quiet as possible, reading books and staring at the countryside outside their windows.

Which had left Daphne with plenty of time to think.

She was desperate to know whether Ben had been able

to talk to Lord Charlton and discover the whereabouts of the second portrait. Each time she glanced across the cab at Rose and Olivia, she *knew* she could not let her indiscretion ruin them. Just as she could not let it devastate Mama and Anabelle. Daphne's stomach clenched at the thought, leaving her as clammy and queasy as poor Hildy.

Knowing she'd soon see Ben only added to Daphne's anxiety. Would he acknowledge what had transpired between them or act as though they were mere acquaintances, at the same house party because of mutual friends? She never knew what to expect with him.

When at last the coach halted and the footman opened the door, Olivia crawled over her sister's lap and bounded out. "What a glorious setting!" She twirled as though she were in a ballroom but almost lost her footing on the gravel drive and bumped into the backside of the footman who was helping Mama step down from the coach.

"Do be careful, Olivia," Mama cried. "We can't have you turning your ankle on the first day of the house party. Such an injury would drastically curtail your participation in the festivities."

Olivia touched her gloved fingertips to her cheeks as though she'd had a sudden epiphany. "James would have to carry me everywhere. Oh, *why* couldn't I have turned my ankle? I have the most horrific luck." She spun again but executed a perfect turn. "Drat!"

Rose and Daphne helped Hildy exit the coach, and the maid seemed vastly relieved to be standing on terra firma. Daphne stretched her legs and squinted into the afternoon sun.

"Welcome!" Lord Biltmore emerged from the shade of a stately portico and descended the front steps with his hands extended. "I am so honored that you've come. While I'm sure you're exhausted from your travels, you don't look wilted in the slightest."

"We're so pleased to be here, Lord Biltmore," Mama said.

"Lord Biltmore sounds too formal to my ears now that we are here in the country. You may call me Hugh if you like."

"We couldn't possibly." Mama was just a hair shy of horrified.

"No?" He looked crestfallen. "Perhaps just Biltmore, then."

"I don't know," said Mama. She looked at Rose and Olivia for guidance. These sorts of social nuances did not come naturally to someone who hadn't spent much time with the elite members of polite society. And they made Mama terribly nervous. She preferred to avoid any possibility of impropriety by adhering strictly to every rule.

Rules Daphne had flagrantly disregarded in posing for the portraits. Her queasiness returned.

Rose stepped forward and, in her usual serene manner, graciously agreed to Biltmore's suggestion.

"Excellent," he replied. "Please, come in, and my housekeeper, Mrs. Norris, will show you to your rooms."

Daphne found the house—which was, as Mama had said, more akin to a palace—both impressive and charming. The black and white tile in the foyer shone like the surface of a lake. A colorful coat of arms hung on the wall beside a richly detailed tapestry depicting some sort of battle scene. But the most striking feature of the foyer was a wide, curved staircase.

Mrs. Norris descended the stairs so gracefully she

might have been a spirit floating down to greet them. "Welcome, ladies. It is a pleasure to have you. Forgive me for not being here when you arrived—I was inspecting your rooms one last time to be certain everything was in order. You are the first guests we've had in some time. We're just delighted you're here."

"Lord Foxburn is here," Biltmore pointed out. "He's a guest."

"Yes," the housekeeper said with a dismissive wave, "but he's more like family. I've known him since he was a lad."

Interesting. Ben must have been closer to Robert than Daphne realized. It seemed they had been more like brothers than friends.

"Foxburn is in the library, where he's been counseling me on some business matters. Don't know what I'd do without his guidance. There's no one more dedicated than he. When he puts his mind to something, it gets done—and heaven help anyone in the way." Biltmore smiled.

The young viscount's confidence in Ben soothed Daphne's frayed nerves.

"Would you like some tea and refreshments before I take you upstairs?" Mrs. Norris offered.

"No, thank you," Mama said. "I'd like to wash up and rest a bit."

"Of course," the housekeeper said. "Please, follow me, ladies. I'll have the footmen bring your things as soon as I get you settled."

She led the way up the grand staircase, pausing once to point out the gilded moldings on the Rococo ceiling and again to name a humorless-looking former Lord Biltmore depicted in a portrait that hung above the handrail. The house was beautiful and furnished almost as exquisitely as Owen's town house in London. For once, even Olivia was speechless.

On the first floor, a large square hall had eight doorways that seemed to lead to various reception rooms and suites. "We've readied rooms for you in the east wing," Mrs. Norris said, gliding through one of the doorways. "You shall each have your own bedchamber. Mrs. Honeycote," she said, opening the door to one room, "you are in the Gold Room." A four-poster bed draped in lush shades of amber velvet dominated the room, and the wooden furniture—which included a wardrobe, a dresser, and a feminine dressing table—shone with a thin layer of polish. A muted gold and blue rug warmed up the gleaming wood floor. The air smelled faintly of lemon wax and the freshly cut flowers that crowned a small round table beneath the window.

"It's lovely. I shall be very comfortable here, thank you," Mama said, her hand fluttering at her throat. Daphne placed an arm around her shoulders to steady her. The room was a far, far cry from their old, dingy apartment.

"The maids will bring up jugs of hot water shortly." The housekeeper walked a little farther into the east wing and opened another door into a similarly appointed room, only slightly smaller and decorated in shades of pink. "I thought the Rose Room would be fitting for you, Lady Rose." Mrs. Norris winked at her.

Rose beamed. "It's perfect. Thank you."

"And for you, Lady Olivia"—the housekeeper opened the door to another chamber—"the Blue Room."

Olivia sighed. "James's favorite color is blue."

Mrs. Norris wrinkled her forehead. "Pardon, my lady?"

"Do not mind my sister," Rose said. "Blue suits her quite nicely."

"Very good, then. Lastly, Miss Honeycote, your room is here. The Violet Room."

The door swung open, revealing light purple drapes, a counterpane of deep plum, and a cream-colored rug. "It's gorgeous," Daphne whispered. "Like something out of a fairy tale."

Mrs. Norris clasped her hands together, delighted. "Please, make yourselves at home. I shall have hot water and refreshments sent up momentarily. Oh, and look, here are your trunks now."

Hildy immediately began unpacking Mama's things, while Rose, Olivia, and Daphne saw to their own. They returned to Mama's room a short time later for a spot of tea and scones, and before long Mama was yawning, declaring the need for a predinner nap. Olivia and Rose seemed similarly inclined, so everyone retreated to their own chambers.

After spending most of the day cramped in a coach, however, Daphne wanted to roam. She gazed out the window of her bedchamber at the well-tended rows of the kitchen garden and beyond to the green, rolling lawn and a line of trees on the horizon. The day was warm, but high clouds kept the sun partially in check. An occasional breeze rustled the leaves on the shrubs and sent rippling waves through the taller grass in the distance.

She had changed out of her traveling clothes earlier and donned an afternoon dress of pale green crepe with short sleeves. It would do nicely for a stroll through the garden. If she brought some writing supplies, she could pen a note to Belle, letting her know that they'd arrived safely.

Daphne ventured out into the square hall and asked a passing maid to direct her to the garden. The young woman escorted her downstairs and through an opulent drawing room. French doors at the rear led to a terrace overlooking a traditional English garden with gravel pathways, symmetrical, box-shaped hedges, conveniently placed benches, sparkling fountains, and a variety of other treasures to explore. Daphne set out in search of a secluded, pretty spot in which to write a letter to her sister.

As she wound her way through shoulder-high hedges, she admired the colorful beds of flowers at her feet. A pond stocked with fish lay beside a trellis covered with flowering vines. In the shade of the trellis sat a small stone bench—a private spot where she could enjoy the sound of water lapping against rocks and the smell of freshly cut grass.

After withdrawing her writing supplies from a small satchel, she kicked off her slippers and tucked her feet beneath her. She touched the feathery end of her quill to her lips and thought for a moment, then began writing. A few lines into the letter, however, her eyes began to droop. The grassy patch in front of the bench seemed to call out to her, and she spread her cloak there and curled up for a short rest. She would shut her eyes for only a moment, to rejuvenate herself after the day of travel. But the splashing of the fish and the chirping of birds in the trees might as well have been a lullaby, and within a few minutes, she dozed off.

Warm lips brushed Daphne's cheek like a whisper. Gentle fingers stroked her hair, traced her ear, and skimmed her neck until she wanted to purr from the pleasure of it. Her entire body tingled and she moaned softly, intent on savoring every second of bliss the dream afforded her. In fact, she would not mind if the stroking continued down her neck a bit, and perhaps across her shoulders...

"Daphne." That voice, so low and raspy, could only belong to Ben.

Ben. She sat straight up and conked her head on the bench. "Ouch."

"Sorry I startled you. Are you all right?" She blinked, and his face—which was level with hers—slowly came into focus. She knew he was waiting for a response, but she was momentarily transfixed by his mouth and, in particular, the fullness of his lower lip. "Daphne?"

"I'm fine. I think." She gingerly felt the back of her head.

"Let me." He was already kneeling on the grass beside her. Gently, he turned her shoulders away from him so that he could search for any bumps or cuts. Tenderly, he speared his fingers through her hair and massaged her scalp.

It was heaven.

"Does that hurt?"

"Mmm, no."

He chuckled. "You like this."

"I suppose it's not proper to admit it, but yes. I do—oooh, that's divine."

He swept aside the tendrils at her nape and gently rubbed small circles at the base of her neck with his thumbs. "How's this?"

"If you must know, it's also quite wonderful."

"Really?"

"Mmm." She desperately wished he'd stop talking and focus on the task at hand.

"Let's see what you think about this, then." He dipped his head close to her ear and brushed his lips along the column of her neck. She was certain she'd melt from the heat between them, and there'd be nothing left of her but the green crepe dress.

His tender touch and playful manner had Daphne's heart tripping in her chest. Perhaps the country air had soothed the beast within him. Or maybe their kiss had. Whatever the reason for the change, she was glad for it—and inordinately pleased that his flirtatious side seemed reserved just for her. If the misses on the marriage mart in London were witness to Ben's charm, he wouldn't stay a bachelor for long.

Wantonly, she turned and leaned into him, welcoming the sweep of his hand down her side and over her hips. In her state of languor, everything seemed pleasantly dream-like and hazy. And miles away from the strictures of society.

That's all this was—an impetuous rebellion to celebrate her escape from civilization. It didn't hurt that Ben was incredibly handsome. His dark hair, which had grown a little longer, gave him a dangerous air. But his intense stare affected her most. One sultry gaze could make her toss common sense out the window—as she quite clearly had now.

He slid an arm around her waist and pulled her close—so close that she could see the dark blue flecks in his eyes. His left leg was bent beside her, while his injured leg was stretched flat on the ground. She clutched at the lapels of his jacket, and just as he leaned in to kiss her, she placed a palm on his right thigh.

He flinched and jerked his leg away, his body seizing as though he were preparing to fight.

What had she done? She gazed up at him and winced at the grim look on his face. "Did I hurt you?"

He pushed himself off the ground and stood, towering over her. "No." He held out a hand and helped her up. The moment their palms pressed together, delicious shivers traveled all the way up her arm. She didn't want to let go of him, but he was clearly agitated, so she sat on the bench and let him pace.

"Did you have a chance to try the treatment I recommended?" she asked.

"No."

"It's very simple, actually. All you need to—"

"Stop," he snapped.

"Stop what?"

He said nothing, but crossed his arms over his chest and scowled.

"Are you sure your leg is all right?"

He stopped in his tracks and faced her, his eyes glinting and cutting like a sword. "Why did you do it?"

"Touch you?" Confusion and inexperience mixed, filled her with shame. "You were touching me. I thought— obviously mistakenly—that you might—"

"Damn it, Daphne."

She hid her face in her hands, utterly humiliated.

"Just...don't touch my leg. Ever. In fact, I'd prefer it if you'd refrain from ever speaking of my bloody leg again. It's like you have some sick fascination with it. Or maybe you enjoy the challenge of trying to fix something that's irreparably broken. Either way, I'd rather *not* be your little medical experiment. You can't cure me and you sure as hell can't change me, so let me be."

Daphne dropped her hands to her lap and stared at

him, dumbfounded. He'd crossed an awful, ugly line, and the way he now avoided her gaze suggested he knew it. The anger that had etched his face during his outburst drained slowly, and he stood there stiffly, gazing at the ground between them.

"I should go." He reached for his cane, which was propped against the bench, and turned as though he'd stroll back to the house and leave her there to ponder what on earth was wrong with him.

And just then, something inside her snapped. "Don't you dare walk away."

He paused but did not face her. After an uncomfortable silence, he said, "I'm not very good company right now."

An understatement if she'd ever heard one. "I don't know what just happened, and I certainly don't understand the source of your ire, but running away will not help matters—it only postpones the inevitable."

He heaved a sigh and slowly turned toward her. "I don't want to argue with you."

"Then, please"—she patted the seat of the bench beside her—"come sit."

"Can we agree to change the subject?"

"Fine," she said reluctantly. "But you might try trusting me sometime. I'm a very good listener. Or so I've been told."

That elicited a wry smile, and he sat.

"I saw you through the window of the library, crossing the terrace and walking in the direction of the garden. I thought it would be a good opportunity for us to talk. When I finally found you and saw you sprawled on the ground, I feared the worst."

"The worst?"

He shrugged, clearly embarrassed. "That you were hurt or sick. When I realized you were only sleeping, I actually said a prayer of thanks."

Warmth filled her chest. "That is very sweet."

"Irrational is more like it." He looked as if he'd swallowed a bad kipper. "Praying to a God who's obviously abandoned me—it makes no sense."

She did not think it wise to engage him into a theological debate, so she said, "You're not irrational."

His dark eyebrows slid up his forehead. "Not usually. But for some reason, when I'm around you, I behave unpredictably. It's . . . disconcerting."

"If it makes you feel any better, I don't act quite like myself when I'm around you either."

"That does help, actually."

They sat without speaking for several moments, listening to the breeze rustling the leaves.

Finally, he spoke. "I have some news about the second portrait."

And he just now thought to mention it? Her stomach sank, and she gripped the edge of the bench, hard. She wanted to know, but then again she didn't. "What is it?"

"I visited with Charlton last night. He has it."

"Did you see it? Do you think anyone else has seen it?"

"No, and probably. But at least he's hidden it for now. He fears someone will try to steal it from him."

Perhaps she hadn't heard him properly. She turned her ear toward him. "He thinks someone will *steal* it?"

"Yes."

"That's odd."

"But it works in our favor."

She warmed again at the way he'd said *our.* "How so?"

She had to get the painting, but it sounded as though Lord Charlton was rather attached to it.

"It buys us some time. He's not going anywhere and neither is the painting. I just need to convince him to sell it to me. And I will."

He sounded utterly confident, as if it were all but done. A huge weight was lifted off her shoulders. And she was suddenly—and quite unexpectedly—perilously close to tears.

"That's wonderful." She wanted to hug him, but the memory of his anger was fresh in her mind, and any sort of touching seemed imprudent. "I'll find a way to repay you."

He pushed himself to his feet. "I don't expect to be recompensed, Miss Honeycote." He looked weary, as though this brief conversation had sapped his strength. "I should return to the house before people notice we're both gone." With that, he hobbled off, leaving Daphne perplexed and curiously bereft.

Chapter Fifteen

Texture: (1) The visual and tactile qualities of a canvas, often achieved through the buildup of paint or application of other materials. (2) The unique feel of a surface, such as the slight prickling of a gentleman's chin beneath one's fingertip.

Ben stared at the plaster ceiling, unable to sleep. Given his behavior in the garden earlier, one might suppose he suffered from a niggling conscience. By all rights, he *should* be guilt-ridden.

He wasn't.

What kept him awake and as alert as a debutante's mother in a roomful of rogues was pain. Of the excruciating variety.

It originated in his thigh but radiated through every bone in his body. Even his teeth hurt.

He began administering treatment—such as it was—at two o'clock in the morning, but the brandy didn't have the desired numbing effect. It merely set the room spinning, compounding his misery. Never had a spell lasted so long. Throughout the night he writhed in pain, cursing himself each time a whimper escaped him.

When the first rays of daylight taunted him, his head pounded in protest.

An insistent knocking added to his agony; he answered with a groan.

The door swung open and Averill stuck his head into the room. "Get up, Foxburn. We're going hunting, remember?"

Hunting had seemed like a good idea the night before. It would have taken him out of the house and away from Daphne. It would have taken his mind off things he'd rather not contemplate.

It now seemed a hellish idea. "Not going." Speaking was a Herculean task. "Leg's acting up. Need to rest." He covered his head with a pillow and waved Averill away. He listened for the sound of the door shutting, but it did not come. "Damn it, Averill. Can't you take a hint?"

"I'm not especially good at inferring meanings, no. Much better with facts, numbers, and the like. You seemed fine yesterday. What happened?"

"I was riding. First time in a while."

"You're in that kind of pain just from riding?"

Ben gritted his teeth. "Yes."

"Shall I send someone up? Call for a doctor perhaps?"

Ben slung the pillow to his side. "Do not summon a doctor. Is that clear enough? Do you get my meaning?"

"I get it," Averill replied grimly. He started to close the door behind him, but hesitated. "You know, Foxburn, sometimes I wonder if you enjoy being miserable."

Ben glared at him, even though the effort hurt his face. "Get the hell out."

Averill left, closing the door softly behind him, when any normal man would have slammed it.

Ben clasped his head in his hands. He hadn't thought it was possible to feel worse.

He was wrong.

The next few hours passed in a haze. He didn't bother drinking more brandy—it wasn't helping anyway. Instead, he lay very still, breathing shallowly, wishing that he could fall asleep. Maybe he'd discover the last twelve hours were a horrible nightmare. He'd wake up, birds would be calling, there'd be a rainbow painted in the sky, and he'd dance a bloody jig.

He didn't have that kind of luck.

He would have to endure the torture for as long as it lasted.

And *that* was the most terrifying part of the ordeal—not knowing how long.

He'd given up counting. And he'd begun to wonder.

What if it never stopped? What if he was sentenced to this pitiful existence for the rest of his sorry life? Sweat covered his body and dampened his sheets. He could hear blood pounding in his ears and above it, occasionally, low, pathetic moans that could only be coming from him.

Anger morphed into something darker. Despair.

Gruesome images flashed in his head. Robert's trampled body; blood sputtering violently from his mouth. The bullet hitting Ben's thighbone; the gaping hole in his flesh. Smoke stinging his eyes; anguished cries echoing across the battlefield.

The dreams, or memories, or whatever they were wouldn't cease. They repeated, over and over, in the same horrifying sequence, until Ben could no longer discern what was real and what was not.

Then a knocking in the distance drove its way into

his consciousness, interrupting the awful rhythm of his visions. He listened, grateful to whoever had given him a short reprieve.

More banging. "Benjamin?" A woman's voice. Pure and sweet, it washed away some of the horror that lurked. But the pain remained.

"Ben, can you hear me?"

He wanted to be near her, needed to answer her. "Yes," he tried to say. It sounded more like a groan.

"I'm coming in."

He vaguely recalled he was in a bedchamber. At Robert's house. Now Hugh's house. He forced his eyes open and looked down at his body. Naked. Not a stitch of clothing, and the sheets were bunched in a ball beneath his feet. Worst of all, his right thigh was completely exposed, in all its grotesque glory, twisted muscle beneath scarred flesh, and a pit the size of a plum where part of his leg was gone.

He scrambled to retrieve the sheets and a quilt. It took every ounce of energy he had left, and he just managed to cover himself before he collapsed back on the mattress. The door cracked open.

Daphne. A very small measure of hope flickered in his soul.

"I hope I'm not disturbing you." She looked like spring and daffodils and lemon cake.

He must look pathetic. Like a sorry, wounded animal. "No," he croaked.

Her pretty blue eyes skittered over him and concern lined her normally smooth forehead. Her gaze lingered on the mostly empty bottle of brandy beside his bed and the clothes and linens on the floor. She placed her hands on her hips and said, "I'm going to help you. First I must ask Mrs. Norris for some supplies, but I'll return shortly. When I do, you will not argue with me but will do as I say. Do you understand?"

He wanted to beg her not to leave, not even for a little while, because he didn't know if he could endure another minute of agony alone. "Yes."

Her eyes widened in surprise and she hurried off. The five minutes she was gone seemed like five hours, but she returned as promised, holding a pitcher in one hand. Several towels were tucked under her arm. "Mrs. Norris is heating some water for us. In the meantime, I'm going to clean you up."

She placed the pitcher on his bedside table and moved the brandy to a far corner of the room. On her way back, she scooped up the clothes and linens and unceremoniously tossed them into the hallway. Then she took the bowl from the washbasin and placed it next to the pitcher.

"Would you like a drink? Of water?" she added quickly.

"Please."

She looked around but could not find a clean glass, so she went to retrieve one. When she returned, she splashed some water into the glass. "Do you think you can sit up, or shall I help you?"

He lifted his head, which was apparently made of stone, about an inch off the pillow. She slipped her arm behind him and put the glass to his lips. He gulped and spilled some on the sheet covering his chest.

She eased him back down and the smell of wildflowers surrounded him. He closed his eyes and took a deep breath.

The next thing he knew, a cool damp cloth rested on his forehead. Daphne moved beside him with brisk efficiency, wringing another towel in the washbasin and humming softly. When she faced him, though, her cheeks were flushed. "You look warm, so I'm going to cool you off. "Are you...ah..." She squeezed her eyes shut as though that would make it easier to finish her question. "Are you wearing any clothes?"

"No."

She opened her eyes but avoided looking directly at him. "Well, then, we shall leave the sheets in place." If he wasn't so miserable, he would have chuckled at her blithe tone. As though she routinely administered baths to naked men.

But any amusement fled the moment she touched him. She removed the cloth from his forehead and pushed back his hair so that she could wipe his face with the fresh, cool one. Anyone could have done it—provided that small relief—but no one else could have even made him think of smiling in his pitiful state.

No one but her.

The soft towel brushed over his forehead, from one cheek to the other, via his nose and around his jaw and mouth. After soaking and wringing out the cloth again, she gently traced his ears and moved on to his neck and shoulders. Her thoroughness was impressive, and after she got over her initial embarrassment, she was all business.

Until she came to his chest.

Her faced turned a deeper shade of pink. "I shall wait until Mrs. Norris returns with the hot water. She can help me bathe the rest of you."

He grunted. Mrs. Norris was not going to get under his

sheets. It wasn't as though he were on his deathbed for Christ's sake.

At least he hoped he wasn't.

"If you bring my robe"—he pointed across the room to where it was hanging over the arm of a chair—"I could put it on and spare you further embarrassment."

"I'm not embarrassed," she lied.

"Well, maybe I am," he lied.

This elicited a small smile from her. "I doubt that. Perhaps we should agree to spare Mrs. Norris the embarrassment."

Daphne glided across the room, returned with his dressing robe, and held it out so that he could slide an arm in.

"I can manage from here," he said.

Her blue eyes twinkled. "I never would have guessed you were so modest, Benjamin."

"Ben," he said. "You promised."

Just before she turned her back, he caught a glimpse of her expression. Surprise . . . and something else. Whatever it was made his heart trip in his chest.

"Let me know if you require assistance . . . Ben."

Even in his sorry state he was sorely tempted to make a suggestive, highly improper remark, but he checked the impulse. It wasn't like him to think before speaking, but when speaking took so much effort, one tended to choose words more carefully.

While he wrestled with his robe, Daphne made pleasant conversation. "All the men are out hunting. The women just left for the village—to shop and see the local sights."

"Why didn't you go?"

"I overheard Mrs. Norris telling a servant that you were not to be disturbed. I thought you might need some company."

"You shouldn't have stayed on my account," he said gruffly. "It's not proper for you to even be in here." He searched in vain for the armhole of his damned robe.

"Perhaps not," she said. "But you shouldn't be alone. Do you mind my company?"

"No. Not exactly. I'm concerned for your reputation. If you stay, Mrs. Norris might mention it to Hugh or one of the guests."

"Very well. When she returns with the water, I'll leave... and then I'll come back later."

"What?"

She shrugged her slender shoulders. "You'll tell Mrs. Norris—in your usual ornery way—that you want to rest and do not wish to be disturbed. Once she is gone I'll sneak back down the hall. No one will know I've been here. You won't have to suffer all alone, and my reputation remains intact—at least for the time being."

He paused in his efforts briefly in order to admire the graceful curve of her back and the smooth expanse of skin below her nape. Under normal circumstances, he wouldn't dream of discouraging a beautiful young woman from sneaking into his bedchamber. "I'm not sure this is a wise plan, Daphne."

"I'm willing to take the risk."

Getting the dressing robe on was more difficult than he'd imagined. The slight twisting of his torso caused his weight to shift and that was enough to make his thigh scream in pain. He must have made some guttural sound.

"Let me help you," she pleaded.

"It's done." His body hit the mattress with a *thud*.

She whirled around and rushed back to his side as though she feared he'd managed to injure himself further in the three minutes while she wasn't watching. Once she was satisfied that he was still in one piece, more or less, she sighed. "Excellent. You shall be more comfortable this way."

No, he wouldn't. But it didn't seem sporting to argue.

Daphne opened her mouth to say something, but Mrs. Norris whisked into the room carrying a steaming bucket. She set it on the floor beside Daphne.

"How is he?" the housekeeper asked.

"Awake and fully conscious," Ben snapped. "But I feel like—"

"He's very uncomfortable," Daphne cut in. "I suspect the excessive physical activity of the last few days is catching up with him."

Excessive physical activity? He'd ridden a horse, walked a bit, and played a game of billiards. It wasn't as though he'd slayed a dragon or rescued a bloody princess from a tower.

"Shall I call for Doctor Sundry?" Mrs. Norris asked.

"No." Ben glowered at the housekeeper, but she wouldn't even acknowledge him. Instead, the question remained in her eyes as she looked pointedly at Daphne.

"Not yet," Daphne replied, although she sounded somewhat unsure. "If he's not vastly improved by the evening, then we shall have to, regardless of his wishes."

Mrs. Norris nodded in full agreement. "What would you like me to do with the hot water?"

"It's fine right here." Daphne picked up a clean cloth, dipped it in the bucket, and squeezed out the excess. "Lord

Foxburn, you can use this as a hot compress if you'd like. I'll just hang it on the side of the pail to let it cool slightly."

"Thank you." Ben sighed and let his eyes droop.

The housekeeper's white brows rose in response. "Is there anything else you require? Tea or porridge?"

"God no. Er, no. I shall be fine, thank you both."

"We'll see that you're not disturbed for the rest of the afternoon," Daphne said, quite the actress.

Mrs. Norris left the room with one last glance of regret—Ben would wager she was more distressed about the state of the room than the state of him. Not that she was unfeeling, but some habits died hard.

Daphne followed the housekeeper and closed the door without looking back.

The moment he was alone, he became more aware of the incessant throbbing in his leg. Pain brought out the pessimist in him, and he began to think of all the things that could go wrong with this ill-conceived plan. If someone discovered Daphne in his bedchamber, her reputation would be in shreds. It might actually be worse than if the portraits were discovered and hung in a public square where all the *ton* could gawk.

But being alone with her was risky in another way. He didn't trust himself to be a gentleman. In his current state he might end up yelling obscenities at her; then again, he might kiss her. There was no way of knowing which, but neither was advisable.

He closed his eyes and inhaled deeply, hoping to smell wildflowers.

The only scents he could detect, however, were desperation, depression, and despair.

Chapter Sixteen

Daphne rummaged through her trunk and in the bottom corner found the small drawstring pouch she was looking for. She tucked it in the waistband of her skirt and grabbed a book from the escritoire to use as cover. If someone discovered her in the bachelors' wing, she'd claim she was looking for the library, and while no one would believe her, the story was at least plausible. She knew the risk she was taking.

Ben was worth it.

Thank goodness she'd forgone the trip into the village. She'd wavered at first, thinking that perhaps all he needed was to rest. One glance at his pallor and the tight lines around his mouth had disabused her of the notion.

He needed her.

The corridor leading to his room was deserted, so she ran lightly all the way to his door. She considered knocking but decided silence was best and simply turned the knob and entered.

The moment she closed the door behind her, the room became smaller, cozier. Although she'd stood in the same spot just minutes before, this visit felt different, more intimate. Like they were two children huddling in a makeshift fort of blankets and chairs. She was very aware that they were alone—and in his bedchamber.

He looked up at her, his blue eyes sober. "Are you sure you want to do this? Someone could return at any moment."

"I'll lock the door. If someone comes, I'll have time to hide."

In spite of his misery, he flashed a wicked grin. "Have you done this before?"

"Nursed patients back to health? Yes."

"I'll wager none as ornery as I."

"Not even close." She smiled. If he could make self-deprecating jokes, surely his condition couldn't be that dire. However, his sunken eyes and sallow complexion were not encouraging signs. She withdrew a small bag from her drawstring pouch and emptied its contents into a glass.

"What in God's name is that?"

"Chopped comfrey leaves. They're for the poultice." After adding a few tablespoons of hot water to the glass, she vigorously mashed the leaves with a spoon. The smell reminded her of the herb garden they'd had at the small cottage where they'd lived before Papa died. It had been a neat, utilitarian garden, filled with plants that could flavor a stew or ease a head cold.

But nothing in their little garden had been able to save Papa. He got sicker and sicker and after he died, weeds choked the plants. When she, Mama, and Belle rode away from the cottage for the final time, the overgrown, neglected garden was the last thing Daphne had seen.

"What are you thinking about? My eulogy?"

"Other patients." She added more water and mashed with renewed energy.

"Like your mother?"

"Yes, and my father."

Ben didn't say anything for a few moments. "You like to take care of people."

It was true. But she wouldn't mind something a little less severe—an ankle sprain or a sore throat would be nice for a change.

She retrieved another small bag from her pouch. Before he could ask, she held it up. "Flour." Little by little, she added flour to the mixture in the glass and it began to thicken nicely. She wished that the glass were a little bigger and that she'd brought more of the comfrey leaves, but the mixture amounted to almost two cups. "There," she said, satisfied at last.

"You're not putting that on my leg."

She'd anticipated this reaction after the incident in the garden, but the nurse in her knew she had to be firm with him. "Yes, I am. But not yet. Why don't you trust me?"

"If you want to know the truth, you're one of the only people in this world I do trust."

"But not when it comes to a poultice?"

"It's complicated."

"Fine." She stooped over the bucket and dipped the cloth in the water, glad to find it was still warm enough. Not scalding, but hot. "You can tell me all about it while I place this cloth on your leg."

"No." The refusal was adamant. Final.

Good heavens. She knew men were awful patients, but this was ridiculous. "It's only *water*. On a towel."

He gave an impressive scowl. "I know that."

"I just want to drape it over your thigh. Please don't tell me you're embarrassed."

"I don't need you to nurse me like I'm some sort of invalid."

"Of course you don't. Pull back the blankets."

He propped himself up on his elbows but made no move to do as she'd asked. "It won't do any good."

"I'd prefer to have you soak the leg in a warm bath, but I thought this would be easier. It should relax the muscles. What have you got to lose?"

"My dignity. Give it to me—I'll put it on myself."

Amazing that such a strong, handsome man could be so infantile. She folded the cloth so that it formed a long rectangle that should cover the length of his thigh and handed it to him.

Curiosity—of a medical nature—niggled. How big had the wound been, and how had it been treated initially? How long had it taken to heal? She stepped closer to the bed.

"Would you turn your back?"

"I've seen a man's leg before." It wasn't exactly a lie. She'd tended to her father, of course, and also to Mr. Coulsen. Who was approximately eighty-two.

"Scandalous. Turn around, please."

She did as he asked, mostly because her cheeks were starting to flame again. "Lay it across your leg so that it wraps around the sides."

He grunted and she could imagine the struggle he was having just to sit up. She should have helped him sit up before she turned around, but perhaps this would make him reconsider the next time he refused her help.

"There."

She turned around to find him reclining and looking even paler than before. She took the cool cloth from the washbasin and dabbed his forehead. He closed his eyes. "Did you know that you are very stubborn?"

"Yes," he said proudly. "That's why I still have my leg."

"The surgeon wanted to remove it?"

He gave a hollow laugh. "*Remove* is the word that he used, too. What he really intended to do was saw it off."

"He was trying to save your life." Daphne sat on the edge of bed and left the cloth on his forehead while she raked her fingers through his hair. She liked the feel of it, thick and slightly wavy.

"I'm still here," he said. "Barely."

"Why don't you want me to see your injury? I'm not squeamish, I promise you. I helped our neighbor Mrs. Munson when her daughter gave birth to twins."

He smiled, opened his eyes. "I'm impressed."

"Then why won't you trust me?"

"My leg is…disfigured. I don't want you to think of me as one of your patients."

"I think of you as a friend, someone who has gone out of his way to help me. I'm not going to think any less of you because you have a scar."

He gave another cynical laugh and looked up at the ceiling. "The scar is the least of my problems."

"How does your leg feel now?"

He blinked and seemed to think about it a moment. "The spasms have subsided, but it still feels like my thigh is in a vise."

"I'd like you to replace the towel with a hot one." She dipped another cloth into the bucket Mrs. Norris had brought and wrung it out. Before he could object, she slipped an arm behind him and helped him sit. She handed him the towel and turned her back once more.

"It's steaming," he said. After he'd shuffled around a few moments, she heard him flop back onto the bed with a sigh.

Daphne turned and took the old towel from his outstretched hand.

"You see?" she said. "No voodoo or witchcraft. So far." She smiled evilly and was rewarded with a slight grin.

"What's next? We sacrifice a small animal?"

"Nothing so dramatic. Just a simple massage."

"No." Emphatic.

"Yes," she said firmly. "I took a risk in coming here. The least you can do is humor me."

"Daphne." It was a plea. "I don't want you to see it."

The fear, the desperation in his voice made her eyes well up. "I know. You can keep it under the blanket if it will make you feel better. But this is going to happen. I am not going to think you any less of a man because you were injured by a bullet. On the contrary, I think you are very brave."

He shook his head, mumbling under his breath.

"It's going to be all right." Slowly, she reached beneath the blanket, removed the warm towel, and hung it on the side of the bucket. Then she took a soft, dry one and eased it under the covers and over his leg. She sat on the edge of the bed beside him. "I'm just going to dry you off."

His other leg was bent at the knee and provided a tented area for her to work. As she rubbed lightly, back and forth, over the towel, his injured leg grew tense and spasmed under her hands. She focused on the task and tried not to dwell on the fact that she was in bed with a very attractive man. Rubbing his bare thigh.

The important thing was to give him some relief— some hope that he wasn't destined for a life of agony.

She turned and scooted closer to him so that she could work with both hands and set up what she hoped was a soothing rhythm. She began with one hand on either side of his knee, and slowly worked her way up his thigh, rubbing small circles with her thumbs. The towel still provided a barrier, but very gradually, Ben seemed to relax. She inched farther up his thigh, noting the irregular bumps and indentations. Even through the towel, the damage to his leg was obvious.

Though her heart was breaking, he did not need her sympathy or pity. He needed someone to stand up to him. "I'm going to massage a bit harder now. It may be uncomfortable at the beginning, but after a few minutes you should notice an improvement."

"Are you sure about this, Daphne? I don't like you risking your reputation for me. I'm not worth it. Ask anybody."

"I'll form my own opinion." It would be much easier if she could see what she was doing, but she had decided to make the one concession of the blanket. The towel, however, had to go. When she slipped it out from under the blanket, Ben's eyes snapped open.

Daphne ignored the signal and pressed on. The feel of his skin beneath her hands was startling, on many levels. He was warm and solid and very...male. Hair tickled her palm, but in some places his leg had icy smooth ridges;

still other parts of his thigh seemed knotted or twisted beneath his skin, as though the wound had healed over, but not everything was quite right under the surface.

She kneaded the flesh as hard as she dared even though Ben's lips were pressed in a thin line and a sheen of perspiration covered his face. As she inched her way up his thigh, she could feel his leg tense until it was as hard as rock. She must be drawing closer to the spot where the bullet had torn into his flesh. Toward the outside of his upper thigh, she felt a depression the size of a large strawberry. She did not avoid it, but instead ran her fingers over and around it, trying to picture what the injury might look like and how it might best be treated.

Ben made a sound in his throat and turned his head away, but she didn't think she was hurting him any more than he already was. Now she began to understand. He didn't want her to see. Didn't want to her to think him weak or, worse, pitiful.

Now that she knew him, she could *never* think of him that way.

"You're doing very well." She hoped she sounded encouraging. "Can you feel the muscles loosening up a bit?"

"I don't know. I'm too mortified by the current situation to notice."

"It feels like the flesh is becoming a little more pliable. That's good. Some of your pain may be caused by the muscles contracting so tightly. The injury probably stretched and damaged them."

He cast a doubtful look her way, but at least he was listening and not discounting her opinion outright. For the next quarter of an hour, she continued massaging his thigh from the knee up to—well, as far as she dared. She worked around the sides of his leg and propped his knee up with a pillow so that she could rub the back as well. By the time she finished, she was breathless and perspiring but satisfied.

She hadn't known if he would let her get this far into the treatment plan. Now she only had to apply the poultice and wrap the leg.

She slid off the bed and set the jar containing the poultice in the pail to warm it. Meanwhile, she prepared another hot towel and draped it over Ben's thigh. While she waited, she gave him some more water to drink and pressed a cool cloth to his brow. Some of the color had returned to his face, and his expression wasn't quite so pinched.

"It was kind of you to come...but foolish, too. The men could return from the woods at any time. I'm surprised they haven't already."

"At dinner last night, Lord Biltmore suggested a trip to the village tavern after hunting." She walked to the window and parted the curtains. The day looked warm but the leaves on the trees beside the house rustled. She opened the window and the curtains billowed slightly behind her. "Can you feel the breeze?" she asked.

"Nice." He'd closed his eyes again.

Perfect.

To apply the comfrey mixture, she would need to see what she was doing, and she didn't anticipate he'd be a cooperative patient. She stirred the poultice and stuck a finger into the center, finding it warm and sticky. Just right.

She took a thin cotton cloth and slid it under Ben's

thigh, then scooped up the jar and eased herself onto the bed beside him. Without asking permission, she folded back the blanket to expose the lower part of his leg.

Ben jerked his head and shoulders off the pillow. "What are you doing?"

"I thought we'd discussed this. I'm putting the comfrey mixture on your leg. See? It doesn't hurt at all."

"Daphne, stop. Please. You don't want to—"

She yanked the blanket completely off.

Ben uttered a curse and threw himself back against the pillow, his eyes squeezed shut. She leaned closer to examine his leg.

Good Lord. Her eyes stung, and she swallowed hard. She would not think about what he must have endured. Not now. She needed to maintain a caring, but professional, demeanor. Or else she'd be of no use to him.

Though she knew nothing about bullet wounds, she guessed this one had been inflicted at close range. His thigh looked like a pack of wolves had feasted on it, leaving gashes, pitting, and jagged scars. On the positive side, the skin had healed over. There was no redness or swelling to indicate infection. Just a mangled mass of muscle and tissue.

"Are you happy now?" His voice was tinged with anger, horror, and something else. Relief.

"I am glad I can properly see what we are dealing with. Did the bullet enter here?" She pointed at the hole in the side of his leg.

He glanced down. "Yes. At least, I think so. My memory of that day isn't very clear."

"What's all the other scarring from?"

"There were bone fragments and other debris lodged

throughout my thigh. The first surgeon to see me when I came off the battlefield wanted to take my leg. I refused. The wound got worse. Another doctor said he might be able to save my leg, but it wouldn't be pretty. He was right."

As he spoke, Daphne gently spread the green paste over his thigh. Now that she could see his bare leg, some of her awkwardness returned. Her cheeks grew hot as she carefully covered every inch, making sure to spread the mixture evenly and to fill in all the indentations left by the bullet and the removal of small pieces of bone. When she'd finished with the top and sides, he raised his leg so that she could apply the poultice to the back as well.

"Do not strain yourself," she scolded. "I won't have you undoing our progress." After setting aside the empty jar, she washed her hands in the basin and returned to Ben's side. "I'm going to loosely wrap the cloth around the poultice and secure it so that you'll be able to rest comfortably while it's working." She gingerly wrapped his leg and used thin strips of linen to keep it in place. "There."

She drew the blanket up to his chest and fluffed his pillow before she began quietly cleaning up her work area. He seemed more peaceful now. His breathing slowed and grew more even. With a little luck, she should be able to leave his bedchamber and sneak back to her own before Mama, Olivia, and Rose returned. She stuck the drawstring pouch back in her waistband and prepared to go. Even though he was resting quietly, she couldn't resist checking on him one last time.

In sleep, he looked younger, like a handsome prince under a witch's spell. His dark lashes brushed the tops of his cheeks and his lips were parted slightly, as if he were waiting for a fair princess to rescue him. Silliness.

She would sit with him for just a moment, to make sure he didn't need anything else. She perched on the edge of the bed and brushed a few locks from his forehead. The corner of his mouth curled in a drowsy smile.

"Feel better," she whispered. Before she knew what she was doing, she leaned over and brushed her lips over his cheek. The prickly feel was surprising, but not nearly as surprising as the hand that reached up and grasped her arm tightly.

"What was that?"

Heat flooded her face. "I'm not sure. I'm sorry—"

He hauled her closer and cupped her cheeks in his hands. "Don't be sorry about that. Ever."

She swallowed hard. "I was just getting ready to return to my room."

"That would be prudent." And yet he made no move to release her. "Thank you, Daphne."

"You should try to rest and let the poultice do its work."

"There's something I need to know."

"What?"

"Are you . . . disgusted by it? By me?"

Now she grasped his wrists. And barely resisted the urge to shake him. "No. But I do hate that you're suffering like this."

"I'm not the same person I was before. I used to work in the fields alongside my tenants during the harvest and help repair cottages damaged by weather or fire. Now I . . . I can't ride a horse without taking to my bed for an entire day afterward. I am, in a word, damaged."

She gasped. "That's ridiculous."

"You should go."

"Listen to me." She leaned over him so that he was forced to look into her eyes. "You lived. You cheated death. That doesn't make you damaged. It makes you a survivor."

He rolled his eyes, clearly unbelieving.

"Ben."

His gaze locked with hers once more, and the intensity of that icy gaze made her shiver.

"If I thought you were damaged, would I do this?" Slowly, she lowered her mouth and touched her lips to his, which were slightly parted. It was the lightest of kisses and lasted only a second. Their breath mingled sweetly in the air between them.

Never before had she done anything so bold, so forbidden.

And she liked it.

Her body had come alive the moment she kissed him. Her skin tingled, her loins pulsed, her nipples hardened.

Ben swallowed. "You feel sorry for me."

She gave a little cry. "Do you really believe that? Because I can show you how mistaken you are." She took his palm and placed it on her breast, over her pounding heart. "One kiss from you did this."

He kept his hand over her heart as though carefully weighing the evidence she'd offered. "You desire me?"

"Heaven help me, I do." She felt like she'd stripped bare before him.

His hand slid slowly up her chest and along the column of her neck. "I don't deserve you, Daphne." His robe gaped open across his chest as he moved, revealing a muscled torso like the ones on statues of Greek gods.

Except his was warm and lightly tanned and sprinkled with springy hair.

"It's not a question of deserving," she said. "Would you deny me another kiss?"

"God, no. Come here."

Chapter Seventeen

Etching: (1) An impression taken from an etched metal plate.
(2) The process of fixing a memory permanently in one's mind,
as in The sweet, soft pressure of her lips on his would be
forever etched in his memory.

Ben pulled Daphne toward him and raked his fingers
through the loosened waves of her hair, as warm and
golden as sunlight. He tasted her, her lips ripe as berries,
her tongue like a tart straight out of the oven.

Daphne kissed him as if imaginary bindings had fallen
away, leaving her free and hungry for passion.

He no longer believed she was humoring him. She
really *did* desire him.

God knew he desired *her*. He could barely breathe for
wanting her.

Somehow, with a few herbs, a bucket of hot water, and
her soothing touch, she'd banished not only the pain, but
the darkness as well. At least for a while.

And that was enough.

Deep inside him the suffocating blackness still lurked,

but as long as she was here, it couldn't touch him. Her goodness acted as armor against it.

So he tried to put all he felt for her into the kiss. Gratitude, certainly. Caring, too. And perhaps...No. He was not capable of that. Even if he were, she deserved better.

But he *could* give her a proper kiss. Or, more precisely, a wicked kiss.

He ran a hand up her rib cage, lingered just beneath the curve of her breast, then made circles around the rigid peak until she was breathless.

"Ben." Her voice, raspy and thick, heated his blood. The little sounds she made in her throat drove him mad.

When he stroked a thumb over her nipple and deepened their kiss, she arched her back and melted into him. Ben could have lain with her like that—cheek to cheek and chest to chest—forever and a day.

Though he'd had no sleep or food in the last twenty-four hours, he suddenly felt like he could take on anything. Anything for her.

He wanted her fiercely, for his own.

Forever.

But today wasn't the right time. And his bedchamber—which felt more like a sickroom at the moment—wasn't the right place. If he were honest with himself, he wasn't the right man. But he didn't want to be quite that honest.

"Daphne."

"Hmm?" She pulled back slightly and blinked as though waking from a pleasant dream.

"If we continue with this, you will end up hating me, and I couldn't bear that, so—"

She shook her head. "I could never hate you."

"You say that now. Trust me, you would."

Her brow furrowed. "Why must you always contradict me?" But she couldn't have been too angry because she slipped her hand inside his robe and across his chest as she kissed the side of his neck. She had no idea what her touch did to him. Or maybe she did. But if he didn't halt her immediately, she was going to be naked in a matter of seconds.

"Stop."

She froze, her warm, smooth palm still splayed over his stomach. Good God.

"It's not that I don't want you to stay," he said. "I doubt I've ever wanted anything more. But we can't risk it."

She sat up. "You don't want to get caught with me."

"Of course I don't. It would ruin you."

"Are you truly concerned about *me* or about the consequences for *you* if we were discovered together?"

"That's not fair. I—"

The clomping of boots down the corridor interrupted his defense. Gruff, loud voices echoed down the hall. Averill had been given the room across from Ben's, and Hugh's two friends from Eton—Neville Edland and Warren Fogg—were also staying in this wing. It sounded like all three men had returned from the fox hunt slightly, er...foxed.

"I don't think I remembered to lock the door," Daphne said, her pale face proof that he wasn't the only one terrified of being caught in a compromising position. She sprang off the bed and spun around, her eyes frantic as she searched for a place to hide. "The wardrobe." She scurried to it and flung open the doors but quickly realized it was too narrow.

"The other side of the desk," he said, pointing. She was

small enough to fit between the desk and the wall in the far corner of the room. As long as no one had the wild urge to scribe a letter, she should be safe there.

A knock sounded at the door. "Foxburn?"

He didn't answer right away, wanting to give Daphne more time to tuck herself into her hiding place.

"Foxburn." It was Averill. More softly, as though he were talking to someone at his side, he said, "Did you hear that? It sounded like he was speaking to someone."

Ben sat up, wincing from the effort. Daphne was mostly hidden, but the white flounce at the bottom of her dress stuck out like a halfhearted surrender flag. He would just have to keep Averill's attention away from that side of the room. "What do you want?" he barked.

Averill swung the door open. Edland and Fogg stood behind him in the doorway, gawking over his shoulders as though they'd slapped down coins to peek in the sideshow tent. "You look marginally better," Averill said. "How are you feeling?"

"Marginally better. Tired."

"I thought I heard voices in here." His gaze swept around the room, and Ben held his breath.

"You caught me. I was reciting poetry."

"I wouldn't have pegged you as a poet, Foxburn," Edland piped. Idiot.

Averill chuckled. "He's jesting. Which means he can't be that bad off." He sniffed the air. "What is that? It smells like a meadow."

"Mrs. Norris opened the window for me. Any other burning questions, or can I get some rest?"

"Glad to see you're improved." Averill grinned. "Think you'll make it down to dinner this evening?"

"That depends on whether I can take a nap before-hand," Ben said dryly.

"Ah, well. Given the number of pints we drank this afternoon, a nap might be in order for all of us," Averill admitted. "We'll leave you be."

And then, because he didn't want Daphne to think he was a complete boor, Ben asked, "How was the hunting this morning?"

"Excellent," Fogg said. "Biltmore's got some fine dogs, he does, and—Say, what's that?"

Ben's stomach dropped as the man sauntered toward the foot of the bed, closer to Daphne. He stooped and picked up a very lacy, very feminine, drawstring pouch.

Fogg held it in front of his face as though it were a rare and mysterious artifact.

"One of the maids must have dropped it," Ben impro-vised, uncomfortably aware how unlikely it was that a maid would possess anything so elegant. "I'll ask Mrs. Norris to check with the staff. Why don't you leave it there." He jerked his thumb toward the table beside his bed.

"I'll just set it here on your desk."

Ben wanted to leap out of bed and tackle him, but of course that was a bad idea for many reasons, the least of which was his half-useless leg. With every step, Fogg drew closer to Daphne. Ben's heart pounded in his chest. He needed to create a distraction, but neither his tongue nor his mind seemed up to the task.

"Bring it here," Averill said. Fogg spun around and plopped the pouch into Averill's outstretched palm.

His gaze flicked to Ben, then to the desk in the cor-ner of the room, and back to Ben. Averill loosened the drawstring and peered inside. "Empty." He looked as though he'd toss it to Ben, but then, apparently changing his mind at the last moment, he raised the pouch to his nose and sniffed.

His eyes narrowed, and he shot Ben a sharp, suspicious look before hurling the bag at him. "There's more mystery surrounding you, Foxburn, than the bloody pyramids. The only difference is, in your case, I'm not sure I want to solve it."

He turned to go, herding the other two men out as well. Ben didn't release the breath he'd been holding until the door latch clicked. Thank God. Even then, he waited until the voices in the hall had quieted before speaking. "You can come out." He threw back his blankets and swung both legs over the edge of the bed.

"What do you think you're doing?" Daphne hissed, her eyes glowing with ire. "Lie back down."

Under different circumstances, he would have obeyed. And he would have hauled her down with him. As it was, he ignored the command. "I don't think they saw you."

She paced before the bed. "I hope not. How shall I ever get out of here?" She might have been Persephone, attempting to escape from the underworld.

"It shouldn't be difficult to sneak down the hall. The men will be in their rooms, changing out of their hunting clothes. I'll check that the hallway is clear." He gingerly lowered his feet to the floor.

"Don't you dare get out of that bed. I'll check myself."

"Too late." He tightened the sash holding his robe in place and hobbled to the door, surprised to find that his leg actually supported his weight. Maybe he shouldn't have scoffed at the comfrey. He cracked the door open and glanced up and down the corridor. Turning back to her, he said, "All clear. Go, before your mother and friends return."

She flitted to the bed and picked up her pouch, then joined him where he stood, leaning against the doorjamb. A slight smile played about her lips as she whispered, "My treatment is working."

He arched a brow. "That's awfully presumptuous. How can you tell?"

"Earlier this morning you were writhing in pain, unable to move. Now you are standing. What further proof do you require?" She leaned closer to him and breathed in his ear, "The poultice works."

"Who says it's the poultice?"

"What else could it be?" Her pretty blue eyes were round with exasperation.

"The kissing," he said matter-of-factly. "Is it time for my next dose?"

She blushed deeply. "I'd better go."

"Yes." He checked the hall once more and waved her out of the room. But before she went, she stood on her toes, leaned into him, and pressed her lips to his in a brief but smoldering kiss.

"For medicinal purposes," she said before darting out the door and down the corridor.

The next day, Ben was much improved. He wasn't quite ready to join the jockey club, but he did venture out of his room for breakfast. Hugh and Averill were the only ones in the breakfast room. Hugh shoveled eggs and ham into his mouth; Averill was absorbed in his paper. Each gave a grunt in Ben's general direction as he entered the room.

After Hugh had cleaned off his plate, he swiped a napkin across his mouth. "Good to see you up and about, Foxburn. Can't have you overdoing it today, though."

Ben objected to his tone, which was the same one might use with a nearsighted, tottering codger who was too stubborn to give up driving his curricle through the crowded streets of town. "I intend to lie low." He gulped strong, hot coffee. "How do you plan to entertain your guests today?"

"I thought we'd have a game of cricket on the lawn. Some of the ladies even expressed an interest. Lady Olivia is keen to 'smack the ball'—her words."

Perfect. He'd be relegated to a shady spot watching cricket and drinking lemonade with the less adventurous ladies. Maybe he and Lady Worsham could play a rousing game of bridge, God help him.

Averill lowered his paper so that only his eyes appeared above it. "Olivia's going to play cricket?"

Hugh smiled. "I offered to teach her the finer points of the game, but she said she'd consult with you."

Averill muttered something under his breath, rustled his paper, and resumed his reading.

"We saw Charlton's son, Rowland Hallows, in the village yesterday," said Hugh. "I invited him to join us for the festivities."

"Let's hope he's sobered up by now," Averill remarked.

A chill crept between Ben's shoulder blades. Charlton's son might have seen the portrait of Daphne. And if he came to the house, he could very well see *Daphne*. It hadn't taken Ben long to identify her; if Rowland Hallows had half a brain, he would, too. Ben's appetite suddenly fled, but he choked down a poached egg and some toast.

He had to warn Daphne to stay away from Charlton's son. Damn it. It had been a mistake for her to come to the house party.

Yesterday, he'd allowed her to nurse him and then thanked her by almost seducing her.

Today he was putting her in the path of one of the few men who could have actually seen the portrait.

He *had* to protect her, and that meant he had to get the painting—and get the hell out of her life.

Chapter Eighteen

Daphne owed Anabelle a letter, so the next morning she dutifully applied pen to paper. She described—in impressive detail—how lovely Biltmore Manor was, how well Mama was doing, and how marvelous the weather had been.

She may have neglected to mention that she'd kissed an earl.

In his bed.

While he wore nothing but a robe.

Ben had just seemed so miserable and hopeless. She'd wanted to prove a point—that he wasn't an object of her pity but of her desire. She'd heard that he'd been out of his room today—a good sign that his leg had improved.

A tiny part of her wondered if yesterday's episode had been a ruse to gain her sympathy, but she'd quickly dismissed the idea. No one, not even Ben, was that superb an actor.

Today she'd awoken with a clear head and an unusual

sense of calm. Miraculously, no one had discovered yesterday's indiscretion. Furthermore, the portrait they'd been looking for was in Lord Charlton's possession, and, at least for the time being, he seemed intent on keeping it hidden.

Her biggest concern this morning had been picking out a dress to wear for the day's festivities. She'd settled on a white gown with blue trim that Anabelle had insisted she purchase last month, saying that the square neckline and delicate sleeves were the perfect frame for Daphne's face. Since she didn't know a festoon from a frog, she always heeded her sister's fashion advice. Hildy had piled her hair high atop her head and freed several strands so that they curled softly about her face.

Today she'd primped more for a cricket match on the lawn than she would for a major ball. She couldn't imagine the reason why.

Well, actually she *could*. But she preferred not to.

A knock on the door snapped her attention away from the mirror. Before she could say "Come in," Olivia burst into the room. Her cheeks were flushed and she wore a pretty yellow gown.

"How lovely you look!" Daphne exclaimed.

"Thank you." Olivia twirled. "Anabelle made this—she said jonquil is my color." She tossed a long dangling curl over her shoulder. "Now, then. It's quite warm this afternoon. Have you a parasol?" She walked to Daphne's armoire, opened the doors, and began rummaging through the items. Over her shoulder she said, "I understand that Lord Biltmore had a tent erected on the lawn so that there will be some shade, but we can't be too careful."

She held up a parasol of blue silk. "Come. Let's fetch your mother and Rose so we may join everyone outside."

Daphne could guess the reason Olivia was so eager and could empathize with her more than ever today. "Looking forward to spending the afternoon with Mr. Averill?"

Olivia beamed. "Of course. I've already seen him once today—he and Lord Foxburn were in the drawing room earlier."

"How did he look?"

Olivia raised her eyebrows wickedly. "Handsome as ever."

"Er, not Mr. Averill—I meant Lord Foxburn. He was not feeling at all well yesterday. Did he seem recovered?"

"He was his typical ornery self," Olivia said. "That must be a good sign, don't you think?" She raised a finger in the air. "I almost forgot. He was asking about you and wondering if you were planning on participating in the outdoor activities today."

Daphne's face warmed. "Was he?"

"He seemed agitated, but then, he always does." Olivia shrugged and held the silk parasol over her shoulder like she was winding up to hit a ball. "Are you ready to play cricket?"

"I suppose I'm as ready as I'll ever be." But a sense of foreboding circled above her like an impatient vulture. She was fairly certain that whatever was agitating Ben had something to do with her. And whether it was the scandalous portrait or their dalliance in his room, it couldn't be good.

Olivia and Daphne found Rose in her room reading a book and still wearing her morning gown. She was therefore subjected to a sound scolding from Olivia.

Daphne attempted to smooth things over between the sisters. "Go on, if you like, Olivia. I'll help Rose dress and we can meet you on the terrace."

"I shall wait," Olivia said, with martyr-like drama. "But she really must not dally or I—*Rose*! Put down the book *this* instant."

Daphne cajoled Rose into her gown, an apple blossom silk, while Olivia rifled through her sister's things in search of another parasol. When at last they were ready, they stopped at Mama's room. Thankfully, Hildy had just finished smoothing her hair into a simple but fetching twist at the nape of her neck.

"I won't be surprised if the teams have already been formed," Olivia muttered, marching down the stairs at an unladylike clip.

The rest of their small party followed after her and were soon spilling out onto the terrace where they joined the group of guests. Mr. Edland and Mr. Fogg stood against the far rail, having a spirited debate related to horses. Lady Worsham and her two daughters, Louise and Jane, sat at a small round table sipping lemonade while Mr. Averill stood beside them, looking predictably dapper and making polite conversation. Olivia made a beeline in his direction. Lord Worsham and Mama listened with rapt attention as Lord Biltmore gestured and pointed at various features of the garden.

And Ben was nowhere to be seen.

"Shall we help ourselves to a glass of lemonade?" Rose asked. A nearly full pitcher and several glasses sat on a table on the side of the terrace.

Daphne nodded and, as she followed Rose, scanned the garden and the nearby paths for any sign of Ben. She had a sudden image of him, holed up in his room and clenching his teeth in pain. If his leg was hurting again, she'd just have to find a way to excuse herself and go to him.

Last evening, she'd given Mrs. Norris a few coins and asked her to purchase some comfrey leaves from the apothecary next time she went to the village. Daphne hoped she received the fresh supply soon. In the meantime, she'd have to look for other methods of easing Ben's misery. The massage had seemed to help a bit—maybe a hot bath would be even more effective than the warm towels. She pictured him lowering himself into a steaming hip bath: the muscles of his arms flexing, his narrow hips sinking into the water, and his—

"Here you are." Rose held out a glass, a concerned look on her face. "Is everything all right? You seemed lost in thought."

"Forgive me, I was woolgathering." Daphne gave her friend an apologetic smile. They filled their glasses and sipped the tepid, lightly sweetened, lip-puckering lemonade. When they joined Olivia, she was in the midst of impressing Mr. Averill with her knowledge of the game of cricket, which she had acquired by reading into the wee hours of the morning.

Mr. Averill would know where Ben was and how he fared. Daphne was debating how best to ask about Ben's condition without sounding too interested when she saw him.

He was walking across the lawn, cane in hand, but otherwise looking agile, fit, and—Lord help her—handsome as sin. Sunlight glinted off his brown hair, which had been freshly cut. She could even detect a slight quirk of his lips that suggested he found the whole affair—from the cricket to the tents to the parasols—rather amusing.

He ambled toward the tent that had been erected on the lawn. Beside him was another gentleman, almost as tall as Ben and considerably stockier, with a shock of blond hair. He wasn't a guest at Lord Biltmore's house party. In fact, Daphne did not think she'd ever met him. She imagined that would soon be rectified.

"Ah, look—there's Foxburn and Hallows." Lord Biltmore pointed in the direction of the tent. To the entire group, he said, "Shall we head for the lawn? If we dally, those two may devour the food without us." Chuckling, he led the way down a garden path, the men following close behind. The women took a bit longer, adjusting their bonnets and opening their parasols to ward off the sun's sinister freckling rays.

Daphne hoped that there would be an opportunity for her to speak privately with Ben at some point during the day, and not just because she wanted to ask about his leg. She had other questions, too. Like, what had happened between them yesterday, and what did it mean, precisely? She would not delude herself into thinking that a few stolen kisses with him would lead to a proposal of marriage. Still. It should mean *something*.

She knew what it meant to *her*. Ben was someone she'd come to care about—and whom she found devilishly attractive. As she walked past the spot by the garden bench where they'd kissed, her pulse quickened. Perhaps in the beginning she'd been drawn to him because she needed his help, but now there was something more. He seemed to respect her, not just in spite of her past, but because of it. And she saw the good in him, too.

The problem was, the good was buried beneath thick layers of cynicism and off-putting behavior. Even if he were inclined to propose—which he most certainly was not—she could never accept.

For one, he had an appalling tendency to be rude to people. She could overlook it, for the most part, because he wasn't vindictive—just brutally honest. So much so that one well-delivered barb from him could make a girl want to throw herself in the Thames. She couldn't subject Mama, Anabelle, and her friends to his cutting remarks. Not to mention her future children, should she be so blessed. No. She needed someone kind and well mannered.

Louise fell into step beside Daphne as they left the pebbled garden path and ventured out onto the broad expanse of soft, green grass. The lawn sloped gradually down to a wooded area. Three round tables dressed with snowy white linens had been placed beneath the shade of the tent. Nearby, a long buffet table bowed under the weight of dishes it held: roasted duck, French beans, asparagus, braised ham, and a selection of pastries, jams, fruit, and sweets. A slight breeze rustled the tablecloths and fluttered the ladies' skirts.

The men had crowded around Ben and the newcomer, so there was little Daphne could do but wait. She turned to Louise, who was wearing a pretty dress of pale pink. "Your performance after dinner last night was wonderful."

Louise sighed. "I would have preferred to leave my violin at home, but Mother wouldn't hear of it. She imagines that by drawing my bow across the strings I will become a pied piper, causing scores of eligible bachelors to trail after me. But the only power my music lords over gentlemen is the uncanny ability to put them to sleep. Did you hear Mr. Edland's snores?"

Daphne winced—everyone had. "Too much after-dinner brandy, perhaps."

"No matter. The violin is not my ally in the campaign to find a husband. If you require further proof, consider the angle at which I must position my chin. It does not make for a very flattering pose. Trust me."

Daphne blinked. "Well, I enjoyed the waltz immensely. I don't know how you manage to move your fingers so nimbly. I am sure the gentlemen were impressed."

"Lord Biltmore was effusive in his praise, but I think he was simply trying to make me feel better about Mr. Edland's snoring. Very kind of him, don't you think?" Louise sighed softly.

"I do. He seems rather taken with you."

"Do you really think so?" Louise's eyes sparkled with hope. "Ever since he came to our musicale, Mama's talked of nothing but his solicitous behavior. She's half convinced that this house party was merely a ruse to get me under the same roof as him—a ridiculous notion."

Daphne wondered about that. "Are you fond of him?"

"He's very handsome." Louise smirked slightly, revealing a dimple at the corner of her mouth. "I must admit, though, that I feared he was courting you."

Daphne shook her head. "No, we are simply friends."

Louise released a breath and gave Daphne's arm an affectionate squeeze. "Well, then, you may be sure that the rest of the men here are besotted with you."

Daphne chuckled. "Despite being two and twenty, this is my first season and foray into polite society. That makes me something of a novelty. If I seem to draw attention it's because everyone is gawking, waiting for me to commit an atrocious faux pas."

"Do you think you might? It would make it ever so much easier for the rest of us who are trying to secure husbands." Louise arched a brow and grinned.

"Never fear. It's only a matter of time. And it may be much worse than anyone ever imagined."

"Very well. Would you do me another favor, then?" Louise gazed in the direction of her mother and Daphne's as the older women filled their plates from the buffet.

"Of course, if I can."

"Mama was adamant that I make an effort to mingle with all the guests, as she's sure this will impress Lord Biltmore. I confess I find the prospect rather daunting—especially when it comes to Lord Foxburn. He's not much for small talk, and when he does say something, I can't help but think that he's mocking me. Look, he's even frowning at that gentleman—I believe Lord Biltmore referred to him as Mr. Hallows."

"Lord Foxburn's bark is worse than his bite. Do you know anything about the other gentleman?"

"No, but I propose we rectify the matter at once." With an elbow, she nudged Daphne toward Ben and the mysterious man with Norse-like features.

Ben glanced up as Daphne approached and turned his back toward her. Rude in the extreme. But she should have expected that. A few stolen kisses didn't change anything—well, not for him.

More determined than ever, she walked directly to him and waited for him to address her and Louise. Mr. Hallows seemed oblivious to their presence, but Ben was deliberately ignoring them. She cleared her throat. Loudly.

Mr. Hallows looked up and raked a bold gaze down Daphne's body. "Forgive us, ladies. I was engrossed in my conversation with—" He halted and narrowed his bloodshot eyes. The hair on the back of her neck stood on end. "I know you."

Chapter Nineteen

Pastels: (1) Drawing sticks made of pigment mixed with oil and wax. (2) The muted rainbow of colored silks and satins used to create gowns for young, marriageable misses.

Daphne had never seen Mr. Hallows before, but he'd seen her, and she knew where. No wonder Ben had avoided her gaze. He'd obviously wanted her to stay away from Mr. Hallows—and with good reason.

Pulling her bonnet forward, she shook her head. "I'm certain we've never met. I'm told, however, that my features are quite common."

"*Common* is not the word I'd use." Mr. Hallows took a step closer, bringing the stench of port and sweat with him. "Exquisite." He reached out as though he meant to take her chin in his beefy hand.

Ben rushed between them and Mr. Hallows's arm dropped like a rock. "Miss Honeycote and Miss Seaton," he said with exaggerated politeness, "allow me to introduce Lord Biltmore's neighbor, Mr. Hallows. His father, Lord Charlton, owns a nearby estate."

Lord Charlton. A low buzzing began in Daphne's ears and the air around her grew thin. No matter what Mr. Hallows said, she knew what she had to do—deny all knowledge of the portrait. Refraining from fainting would be a fine first step, however.

"The pleasure is mine, ladies," Hallows drawled. Chin-length blond hair was slicked back to reveal a pronounced widow's peak.

"Miss Seaton is here with her parents, Lord and Lady Worsham, and her sister," Ben explained.

"And what about you, Miss Honeycote?" A snide smile slashed across Mr. Hallows's broad jaw.

Before Daphne could respond, Ben did. "She is here with her mother, Mrs. Honeycote, and her good friends, Lady Olivia and Lady Rose Sherbourne. Her sister is the Duchess of Huntford. Have you met the duke? He's a formidable sort." Ben dug his cane into the ground, making small pockmarks in the dirt. "Very protective of his family."

Daphne cringed. She was sure Ben meant well, but intimidating Mr. Hallows didn't seem the best tack. He'd know she had something to hide. She would prefer to convince him that her resemblance to the woman in the portrait was nothing more than a peculiar coincidence.

Mr. Hallows rubbed his square chin. "I'm certain I've seen you before, Miss Honeycote. Maybe in our village?"

She attempted her most charming smile. "This is the first time I've had the pleasure of visiting. I've been in London for the last few years, so the country is a welcome change. I understand that after our picnic, there's to be a game of cricket. Have you ever played, Mr. Hallows?"

"What part of town do you live in?" So much for her

attempt to change the subject. It was an impertinent question, and she was debating how to respond when Ben saved her the trouble.

"You do not move in the same circles as Miss Honeycote, Hallows." His blue eyes flashed like a warning flare off a ship's bow. "Let me introduce you to the rest of the guests." He steered Mr. Hallows firmly away from the ladies.

The large man glanced over his shoulder as he walked away, a suspicious smile on his slimy lips. Daphne's stomach lurched.

"Well," Louise said dryly, "that certainly went well."

Daphne suppressed a shudder. "Mr. Hallows makes Lord Foxburn appear positively charming by comparison. I do not believe I care for the gentleman's company."

"No? Well, I would not count on him to take the hint. You look a little pale. Why don't we fill our plates at the buffet and sit for a bit?"

"Excellent idea," Daphne agreed, but she only picked at the food on her plate. The exchange she'd had with Mr. Hallows weighed on her like a sack of stones.

There she sat, using the correct fork, wearing an expensive-but-tastefully-unostentatious gown, mingling with the upper crust of society. To all outward appearances, she was a proper lady with impeccable manners.

On the inside, she was still the woman in her portraits.

Desperate. Indecent. Ashamed.

Which only proved that wearing the right clothes and associating with the right people couldn't help her outrun her past. Today it had caught up with her—in the form of Mr. Hallows.

At least he hadn't mentioned anything about the portrait. He couldn't seem to place precisely where he'd seen her before. If it was true that Mr. Hallows's father, Lord Charlton, had hidden the painting, perhaps she'd be able to keep up the ruse a while longer. Long enough to figure out where to go after she left London, preferably a remote village where no one would think her odd for preferring isolation and spinsterhood to socializing and a family. Long enough for Olivia and Rose to make brilliant matches and for Mama to be firmly embraced by the other matrons of the *ton*. Long enough so that Daphne might at least nuzzle her little niece when she came into the world. She smiled at her own folly—Anabelle's insistence that she was carrying a girl must be contagious.

Ben cast her a pointed look, but if he was trying to send her a message, she couldn't decipher it. The grim lines around his mouth, however, didn't bode well. She needed to speak with him.

For now, though, she had a cricket match to play.

It was the very last thing on earth she felt like doing, but she couldn't possibly let Olivia down. Her friend had carefully chosen the optimal teams the previous evening. After thorough and deliberate consideration, and changing her mind thrice, Olivia had determined that she and Mr. Averill should be on separate teams—an arrangement that would give her a better view of him throughout the match *and* show off her new gown to its best advantage.

That was the plan, anyway.

Olivia made a few last-minute adjustments to account for Mr. Hallows's unexpected arrival. In order to keep the teams even, she'd pressed Ben into service as a batsman. Daphne frowned as he ambled toward the gathering of players. If he did something utterly foolish, such as attempt to run, she would be forced to do something equally as foolish, such as attempt to tackle him. One hoped it wouldn't come to that.

No one besides Olivia had given any thought to the formation of teams—much less devised a plan—so it seemed as though her machinations would not be in vain.

She walked to the center of what was to be the playing area and clapped her hands.

"I have worked out the teams so that they shall be as evenly matched as possible." She withdrew a folded piece of paper from her pocket and snapped it open. "There shall be a Team A and a Team B."

"Not very original, is it?" Lord Worsham teased.

Undaunted, Olivia continued. "Rose and I shall be the respective captains." Rose, clearly uncomfortable with being the captain of anything, gave a weak wave. "Rose's team shall consist of Miss Jane Seaton, Mr. Averill, Mr. Fogg, Lord Foxburn, and Mr. Hallows." Olivia waved the named players toward her sister. "On my team, we shall have Miss Honeycote, Miss Louise Seaton, Lord Biltmore, Mr. Edland, and Lord Worsham. Obviously, our teams are rather small, but I see no reason we cannot follow the proper rules of the game in every other respect."

"But we have no wickets," Mr. Edland pointed out.

"A matter that is easily rectified." Lord Biltmore flourished a few branches whose ends had been whittled into points and stuck a couple into the earth at one end of the playing field, paced to the other side, and repeated the procedure. "I've brought the rest of the equipment as well." He reached into a canvas bag that lay beside the tent and withdrew a paddle and ball.

Under Olivia's direction, the match began, with Lord

Biltmore and Mr. Averill designated as the bowlers. The men shed their jackets and played in their shirtsleeves and waistcoats. Olivia took off her bonnet, but Daphne didn't dare give Mr. Hallows a better look at her face. Players and spectators alike cheered, getting into the competitive spirit—although no one took the game quite seriously enough for Olivia's liking.

She was particularly vexed with Daphne, who proved hopeless when it came to hitting the ball. In her defense, she was not accustomed to standing in one spot while an object came hurtling toward her like some irate bird. Besides, she was preoccupied with more weighty matters than her striker duties. After her fourth attempt at swinging failed to produce any sort of contact with the ball, she decided it was in the best interest of the team to pass the bat to Louise.

But Ben strode off the field, limping slightly without his cane, and stopped her. "You're standing too far away from the wicket. Here." He placed his hands on her shoulders and guided her into position, making her flush. Thank goodness she still wore her bonnet.

"The ball is coming terribly fast. I can scarcely see it."

"That's because you keep closing your eyes."

"How gallant of you to mention it."

His breath warm on her cheek, he said, "I'll help you." He reached around so that his body encased hers like armor and gripped the bat handle just above her hands. "Wait for the pitch. When I say swing, bring the bat around like this. You can do this, Daphne." He demonstrated the motion, which, she had to admit, was infinitely smoother than her own hacking method.

She squared her shoulders. "I'll try."

Ben stayed close but released the bat, leaving the swinging to her.

Mr. Averill wound up and lobbed the ball toward her. She gripped the handle harder, determined not to close her eyes.

The ball bounced once and sailed closer.

She closed her eyes, blast it all. But only for a second.

"Now," Ben called from behind her, and she swung.

She hit the ball. Or, perhaps, it was more accurate to say the ball hit her bat. Olivia squealed and waved her arms, which was clearly a signal for Daphne to run, but she could only stare at the ball, which had rolled approximately two yards in front of her. Not a great distance, true, but she'd done it.

And Ben had known she could. He returned to his spot on the field, a smug, satisfied look on his handsome face.

"Is it time for a break yet?" Louise called. She stood on the side of the playing field, waving her fan with enough force to launch a small sailboat. "I'm parched."

"So am I," Jane chimed in. "Let's have something to drink and sit in the shade." Half the players immediately wandered toward the tent; the rest chatted among themselves.

"But we haven't even finished two innings," Olivia said, hands fisted on her hips.

"Perhaps our level of play will improve after some refreshment," Daphne said, although she had her doubts.

"I suppose. This isn't turning out how I'd hoped."

"I'm sorry. Is there anything I can do?"

"Not unless you have a suggestion for capturing James's attention." Olivia scooped up the ball, tossed it in the air, and caught it with one hand. "I'd hoped to impress him with my knowledge of the game."

Daphne smiled. "It's clear that you're the only female here who knows what she's doing. And you seem more familiar with the rules than most of the men, too."

It was true. Unfortunately, the harder Olivia tried to win Mr. Averill's affection, the more oblivious he seemed. Olivia was slightly mollified by Daphne's response, however, and conceded to a short break.

Daphne and Olivia found a couple of chairs in the shade, where they sipped lemonade. In spite of the drink and the slight breeze, Daphne felt quite wilted. Her once-puffy sleeves clung limply to her shoulders and the jaunty bow she'd tied beneath her chin drooped. She took some consolation from the fact that everyone was similarly afflicted and therefore equally miserable.

"I'm going to see if Mama needs anything," Daphne told Olivia. "I'll be back momentarily." Mama seemed to be tolerating the heat fairly well, but Daphne didn't want her overdoing it. She and Lady Worsham carried on an animated conversation about modistes. Of course, Lady Worsham had no idea that they had an expert dressmaker in the family and that she also happened to be a duchess. Daphne stood a few yards away, patiently awaiting a break in the conversation when someone grasped her upper arm. Hard.

"You're very coy, Miss Honeycote." She turned and found herself face-to-face with Mr. Hallows, her eyes level with his brown-stained teeth.

She jerked her arm away and looked for Ben. Where *was* he?

"Looking for the cripple? He's probably gone to take a nap."

"I don't care for your tone, Mr. Hallows."

"Aren't we high and mighty? There's no need to pretend with me. I know where I've seen you. And let's just say it wasn't church."

"You may *think* you've seen me before, but we have never met."

"I didn't say we had. But I've seen you. I've seen your *portrait*."

Daphne's hand trembled and her drink sloshed in the glass. "I've never had my portrait painted. Now, if you'll excuse me."

"Don't run away," he said, latching on to one of her sleeves. "There's still much for us to discuss."

"I disagree, sir." She shifted her eyes to his hand on her shoulder, and he chuckled before letting her go.

"It would behoove you to treat me with more respect. That painting belongs to my father. The batty old codger might be hiding it somewhere, but I'll find it. It would bring a decent price were I to auction it off at White's or Boodle's. In the meantime, I could host a dinner party and display it for the viewing pleasure of my guests. I do hope you'll be able to attend, Miss Honeycote."

Even as her stomach knotted, she eyed him coldly. "I believe I'll be otherwise engaged."

He laughed, a sharp, barking sound that made Mama and Lady Worsham turn their heads. Daphne smiled as though she found Mr. Hallows a most charming conversationalist. The last thing she wanted was for Mama—or anyone else—to become involved. And the one person she wished *would* materialize was nowhere to be found.

Mr. Hallows licked his lips, a lecherous gleam in his eyes. Daphne's skin itched under his scrutiny, and she wanted nothing so much as a bath and a cloth to scrub herself clean.

"I can imagine all sorts of mutually beneficial arrangements," he said. "When you come to your senses, send word—but don't tarry too long. I'm not a patient man."

Chapter Twenty

$\mathcal{B}$en absently swirled the brandy in his glass as he gazed out one of the tall windows overlooking the front of Biltmore Manor. The late afternoon sun cast distorted shadows across the drive, where Rowland Hallows shouted an order at a coachman before climbing inside his carriage. It rumbled along the road until it disappeared over a hill.

Hallows was an uncivilized brute, and dangerous—not unlike gunpowder near a lit match.

The only way to neutralize him was to get the painting of Daphne, and Ben would.

But from London.

He'd correspond with the baron through letters and make an offer on the portrait. It might take longer that he'd like, but it was the only plan that made sense.

In the meantime, he couldn't bear to be around Daphne. He just couldn't. Her irresistible pull made him do foolish things like putting his arms around her while a small crowd looked on. As long as he stayed in the same house with her, he'd have a hard time keeping his hands off of her, so the best thing for him to do was to leave. She'd taken too great a risk in coming to his bedchamber, and he couldn't let her do that again. Not when her reputation hung in the balance.

He was supposed to be saving her from ruin, for God's sake, not putting her in jeopardy.

So, for a change, he'd do the right thing: return to his town house and continue to mentor Hugh—just until he finished growing into his newly acquired title and found a nice young lady to be his viscountess. Ben would pursue the portrait on Daphne's behalf and send her an update once every month or so. And when both obligations were fulfilled, he would wipe his hands clean of both Hugh and Daphne. Forever. Not because he disliked their company—quite the opposite. But because they'd both be better off without him.

His leg was tenfold better today, but yesterday's agony was too fresh a memory to risk an extended match of cricket. So he'd grabbed the first opportunity to hobble to the drawing room and pour himself a drink.

And now he was about to pour himself another.

The clearing of a throat made him glance at the doorway. Mrs. Norris held up a small folded paper as she approached him. "I was asked to give you this, Lord Foxburn."

Ben set down his glass, lowered himself onto an ottoman, and waited until the housekeeper left before breaking the wax seal on the note.

I must speak with you, in private. If you are able, please meet me in the library after everyone is sleeping.

—D

Ben held the note to his lips and inhaled deeply. Her citrusy scent was barely detectable, but there. Then again, maybe he was so besotted he only imagined it.

Meeting Daphne alone in the library was inadvisable at best.

But he knew, without a doubt, that he'd meet her anyway. It would be the perfect opportunity to say good-bye.

Hugh and his Eton chums stayed up late drinking and playing billiards. God knew Ben didn't begrudge Hugh and his friends a night of carousing and bonding, but did they have to choose *that* particular night to wager on game after game into the wee hours of the morning? Just after two o'clock, Edlund and Fogg stumbled down the corridor looking for their beds, erupting into laughter each time one of them bumped into the wall.

Ben waited another quarter of an hour to make sure that they'd either fallen asleep or passed out, then slipped out of his room and headed for the library. He cruised through the familiar corridors leading to the library, careful not to thump his cane or shatter the silence that blanketed the house.

The door to the library was closed most of the way; only a faint light glowed in the thin crack beside the doorjamb. Ben entered and quickly shut and locked the door behind him.

At first glance the room appeared deserted, but then Daphne peered around the side of a tall wingback chair. "Ben." She stood awkwardly and wrung her hands. "I wondered if you'd come."

Her confidence in him wasn't exactly awe-inspiring. Neither was the welcome. He hadn't expected her to fly into his arms, but she might have looked marginally happy to see him. "Well, here I am."

"I'm sorry to inconvenience you like this." She moved a little closer. Her plain russet-colored cotton dress was old—probably the kind she'd worn before her sister married a duke and she moved to the fashionable part of town, leaving most remnants of her former life behind. He drank it in—this unexpected glimpse of the girl she'd been before.

"Something happened at the picnic after you left." Her hands trembled. "You're the only person I can talk to."

"Let's sit." He took her hand and pulled her to a window seat tucked into a small alcove along the far wall, then retrieved the lantern and her shawl before joining her on the velvet cushion. He leaned his cane against the bench, set the lantern on the floor beside them, and draped the shawl around her shoulders. Everything beyond the small circle of light that the lantern emitted seemed distant and unimportant. At that moment, it was just Daphne and him in the alcove. And, of course, the problem that had brought them together.

"This is better," he said. "Now tell me what happened. Does it involve Rowland Hallows?"

"Yes. He knows, Ben." Her face crumpled.

"Even if he suspects that you're the woman in the painting, he can't prove it at the moment. Charlton has it hidden."

"We *think* it's hidden. We hope it is. But what if Mr. Hallows goes searching for it? He lives in the same house, after all."

Indeed. By talking with members of Hugh's staff and some of the tenants over the past few days, Ben had pieced together a more complete picture of Hallows, and it wasn't flattering. On a recent visit to London, he'd gambled for high stakes—very high stakes. He'd lost everything he had, and then some. As usual, he'd come home to ask his father for money. This time, however, Charlton had refused, and Hallows had gone into a tirade.

From there, things had deteriorated. Hallows maligned his father's name, speaking ill of him to anyone who would listen. Charlton's health declined. Ben didn't think for a moment Hallows was above rummaging through his father's possessions. He was probably to blame for the items Charlton claimed were missing.

"I know the situation seems dire, but I'll figure something out. We just need to think this through."

"He said he was going to host a dinner party and display the portrait."

"He's bluffing," Ben said. With a lot more confidence than he felt.

"That's not all. He said he was going to auction it off at a gentleman's club."

Good God. It was actually a brilliant plan. If the painting proved half as lovely as the one Ben had, it would fetch a pretty sum. And if the gentlemen got wind of the identity of the subject, they'd be willing to spend even more. A member of the Duke of Huntsford's family clad in little more than a chemise? A bidding war would surely erupt. Her mind seemed to be running along the same path. "I don't see any way out of it."

The despair in her voice terrified him. "There's always a way out. Things are never as bad as they seem in the middle of the night."

"All I meant was that I must give up hope of living

in London among polite society. I've resigned myself to leading a simple, secluded life in the country."

His stomach clenched. "You're going to let a bully like Hallows run you out of town? Where's your fighting spirit?"

"There are some things a person can't fight. I willingly posed for those portraits—nobody forced me. And now I must live with the consequences of my actions. But my family and dear friends shouldn't have to. The sooner I can distance myself from everyone, the better off they'll be." She blinked rapidly and turned toward the window, taking a moment to compose herself.

He held his tongue for several seconds, but then all the questions bouncing around in his head spilled out of him. "What about you? Would you deny yourself everything you've dreamed of? I thought you wanted a husband and children. I assumed you wanted to live within shouting distance of your sister so you could see her whenever your heart desired."

"I do. That is, I did. Before."

"Then why would you run away?"

She crossed her arms and raised her chin. Even in the relative darkness, her blue eyes flashed. "I'm not running away. I'm doing what's best for my family and friends. There's a difference."

"Are you *listening* to yourself?" He grasped her shoulders and forced her to look at him. "You're not even making sense. Do you honestly think your family would be happy without you? That your sister would be content to attend lavish balls while you were shriveling up in a godforsaken cottage in the middle of a cow pasture? Do you think your mother would sleep at night knowing that her beautiful, vivacious daughter was hidden away in a one-pub village where the sheep outnumber people seven to one?"

"It wouldn't be as bad as all that."

"No? What about Olivia and Rose? They both need you to help them navigate the social scene. You tone down Olivia's brash nature and nurture Rose's thoughtful one. How will they feel when they learn they've been deserted—again?" He'd heard the stories about the former duchess, their mother, running off to the Continent.

She pulled a hand free and rubbed her forehead. "They'd all adjust to the idea. I'll make them believe it's what I really want."

"They're not stupid, Daphne."

"Of course they're not! But they'll respect my wishes. They don't need to know the reason I'm leaving."

"Maybe not, but you do."

"What are you talking about?"

"You're not being honest with yourself. You don't want to face Hallows or the possibility that your portrait will be seen by London's elite."

She pressed a hand to her chest. "The idea terrifies me."

"Why? Are you ashamed of what you did?"

"Not really. I thought I was helping Mama."

"Then why are you so concerned with what everyone thinks?"

She stared at him incredulously. "And I thought *I* was naïve. Ben, I am a young woman with a questionable past. If the portrait is made public, my reputation will be destroyed beyond repair. I can stay in London and be ostracized or I can leave town of my own accord. I prefer the latter option."

He couldn't believe she was serious. As quickly as she'd come into his life, she was going to leave it. Leave him. Of course, he'd been about to head back to London anyway. Hadn't he? He stood and rifled a hand through his hair. "I'm sure you'd prefer to sneak away quietly. It's more dignified—less messy," he said sharply.

She sighed. "I suppo—"

"But you can't avoid messiness in life. It's complicated and ugly and painful. It has warts. Nobody likes to deal with those parts, but if you try to hide from all that… well, you're not really living."

She sprang off the window seat and stood toe to toe with him. "You have a lot of nerve, suggesting that my life is less full just because I'm not constantly miserable, the way you are."

"That may be overstating things," he said dryly. "I don't recommend having a hole shot in your leg."

"Joke all you like. But you know deep inside that I'm right." She jabbed a finger at his chest. "*You* don't want to let me or anyone try to help you. And do you know why? It's because as long as you're in pain, you don't have to let anyone get close to you. Your cynicism and bitterness might as well be tower walls and a moat. They keep everybody away so that you can wallow to your heart's content. So you never have to risk losing someone again."

She clamped her lips shut immediately after. But the words had already been spoken.

Worst of all, they rang true.

They stood glued to the floor, neither of them speaking, but they were so close that he could feel her breath coming in quick little puffs; he could see the individual lashes on her eyelids.

And the air between them seemed to crackle.

"You may have a point," he admitted.

"You may have one, too." She gave a weak smile. "What are we going to do?"

"Well," he said slowly, "we'll need to come up with a new plan. We'll figure it out together and see it all the way through. Together. There will be no running away from scandal on your part, nor alienating people on mine. Are you game?"

She inhaled deeply. "I think so."

"You *think* so?"

"Yes."

Thank God. "Would you like to hear the first step of this new plan?"

"I would."

"We kiss."

Her face split into a blinding smile that soothed the stinging welts left by their exchange. She circled her arms around his neck, banishing all memory of pain. "I like this plan."

He pulled her against him, and his blood heated instantly. "Wait 'til you hear step two." Slowly, tenderly, he tasted her, lightly sucking the plump flesh of her lower lip. Their mouths melded perfectly, as though each had been specially formed to complement the other. Her breath became his, and vice versa, and Ben knew that if he lived to be one hundred, he would never, ever tire of kissing her, of being near her. Her beauty transcended the visible realm. It was a tangible thing, palpable in every kind word and every thoughtful gesture.

Being near her made him want to be better—worthy of her love.

Not that he ever could be. But he couldn't help wanting her for himself. Forever.

He cradled the back of her head in his palm and trailed kisses down the column of her neck. "Did you ever think that maybe we were meant to be together?"

She pulled back slightly to look at him, her eyelids heavy with passion. "What do you mean?"

"I have the portrait on the sapphire chaise. If not for that twist of fate, I would never have confronted you, asking you to stay away from Hugh."

"Thanks for reminding me of that." A smile played about her lips.

"That connection led to you asking for my help in finding the second portrait."

"Why, my lord," she said teasingly, "that is a most romantic view. It almost sounds as though you believe divine intervention led us both to this moment in time."

Hardly. "I don't believe in that sort of thing."

She narrowed her eyes. "No?"

"I've seen too much pain and suffering to believe in a benevolent supreme being."

She nodded, and he was relieved that she didn't immediately denounce him as the heathen that he was. "It's the question that great philosophers throughout the ages have struggled with. I don't suppose I'll be able to change your mind tonight."

Maybe not. But if anyone could convince him otherwise, it was she.

"Consider this," she continued. "There is good to balance out the bad. And being here with you feels very good. Even though we're being rather wicked."

If she knew a fraction of the wicked thoughts running

through his mind, she'd faint on the spot. He wanted her. Badly. But he didn't want her to make love with him out of gratitude or, worse, a sense of indebtedness.

"I'm going to help you get the portrait from Charlton or Hallows or whoever the hell has it regardless of what happens—or doesn't happen—between us tonight. It's a foregone conclusion." He would get the portrait for her or die trying.

"I believe you." She nodded solemnly.

"But let me tell you what I would *like* to happen tonight. What I've dreamed about in the weeks since I've met you."

She swirled her fingers in the short hair at his nape. "I'm listening."

He pulled her back to the window seat and propped several pillows behind her before she sat. "I want to hold you and kiss you until you're dizzy with desire."

"I like the sound of that."

He traced the demure neckline of her gown, his finger gliding over the smooth skin of her chest. "And then I want to remove this dress and your chemise, and every other stitch of clothing you happen to be wearing."

"Oh? And what next?" Her sultry tone heated his blood even more.

"I would kiss every inch of your skin. Here." He drew an *X* on the curve of her shoulder. "Here." He marked the valley between her breasts. "And here," he said, caressing the curve of her hip. "Only then, after I'd explored to my heart's content, would we make love."

"I see," she said a little breathlessly. "And how would that go?"

"Very slowly at first. But then we would both want

more." He outlined the heart of her face with his hands. "And it would grow more and more powerful until we were both consumed by it."

Her eyes widened. "Just then, you sounded almost... romantic."

"I don't want you to do anything you'll regret, Daphne. I care about you too much to hurt you."

"I made up my mind on the day I came to your bedchamber, maybe even earlier, that I wanted to be with you. We have already connected in so many ways—through pain, fear, longing, and hope—that I can't imagine being with anyone else. Not in this way."

Her words sobered him.

Not because he doubted that he loved her.

But because he *did* love her.

"I cannot make any promises about us," he warned. "I only know that I want you to be happy and would do anything to ensure your happiness."

"I'm happy right now," she purred.

A slow smile spread across Ben's lips. "Bet I can think of a few things that would make you even happier."

Chapter Twenty-One

Stroke: (1) The movement of an artist's paintbrush across a canvas. (2) An affectionate caress that often results in a delicious—if unsettling—sort of tingling throughout one's body.

*B*en held Daphne's face between his palms and kissed her thoroughly, thrusting his tongue into her mouth until her limbs grew heavy and loose. He speared his hands through her hair, and the light pressure of his fingertips on her scalp aroused her, waking her senses from a deep slumber.

And then she knew. She loved him.

She was fairly certain he loved her, too. Every lingering kiss on her lips, every leisurely stroke upon her skin spoke volumes. The heat in his gaze was tempered with a tenderness that made her heart squeeze. If he hadn't yet spoken the actual words, that didn't matter—he would in time.

He brushed his hand up her side, beneath the swell of her breast, and gazed at her like he was committing every inch of her to memory. She hadn't worn a corset—

just thrown the plain, rust-colored gown over her chemise before sneaking out of her room earlier. In retrospect, she wished she'd thought to wear something prettier, more feminine. Ben didn't seem to mind her old dress, though. His hands skimmed the soft, worn fabric, blazing a path over her hips, bottom, and breasts. She squirmed closer to his broad chest, wishing she could shed the wretched layers that separated her skin from his palms.

"I've wanted you since the day I met you, but I never dreamed I'd have you." He stared at her mouth like he wanted to kiss her again, stoking the fire in her belly.

Enough talking. Eager to taste him, she shifted on the window seat cushions and lifted her face to his.

He drew back, his face suddenly serious. "Are you absolutely sure, Daph? Because what we're about to do can't be undone."

She thought about the first time she met him at Anabelle's dinner party and the intense feelings he'd stirred in her even then. With one look, he'd made her insides melt like chocolate. She'd never experienced that kind of desire—the kind that made her want to shed every stitch of clothing and strip Ben of his as well.

But Daphne understood what he was asking. If she gave herself to him, there would be consequences.

In St. Giles, girls routinely fell into bed with men—for love, curiosity, money, or protection. Most of her friends who'd married were already with child on their wedding day, and they'd all teased Daph for her seemingly prudish ways. But Mama had taught her that sex was something to be saved and shared with the man she married—and the belief was deeply ingrained. Any gentleman would expect his bride to be a virgin, of course. Which meant this one night of passion with Ben would prevent her from ever marrying. A frightening thought. No husband, no children, no future. Only decades of growing old...alone.

Ben caressed her arms, making small circles with his thumbs. "You could leave. I'd understand."

She swallowed, more sure than she'd ever been. "I'm not going to leave."

He let out a long, steady breath. "Come here."

He slid his hand up and cupped her breast, gently tweaking her nipple with his thumb. Heat gathered between her legs, and she moaned softly.

Ben reached around to the back of her dress and undid the laces there. She got goose bumps when cooler air tickled her shoulder blades. He tugged at her dress, finally showing a smidgen of the impatience she felt, and in a matter of seconds he'd freed her from restricting seams and made her forget years of cautionary tales. He tossed the gown over his shoulder onto the arm of the wingback chair.

Clad only in her chemise, Daphne shivered. The thin lawn clung to her breasts, which felt ripe and heavy. Her nipples tightened beneath the intensity of his gaze.

He kept his eyes trained on her as he shrugged off his jacket—as though she might disappear if he glanced away. He hadn't bothered with a neckcloth or a waistcoat for their rendezvous, just a plain-fronted cambric shirt. Where the tie at his neck was already loosened, she peeked at the muscled contours of his chest. Her breath caught as he crawled over her, his arms braced on either side.

"You're the loveliest thing I've ever laid eyes upon, Daph." His voice was thick with emotion. "Even now, in the dark, you radiate goodness and light. Everything that's been missing from my life."

Her eyes burned and her nose stung. He *must* love her. "Well, I'm here now." She arched her back toward him, and he eagerly dipped his head toward her breast, capturing a peak in his mouth. The thin lawn of her chemise was a barrier, but not much of one. His wicked tongue soon saturated the fabric and when he moved to her other breast, the cool air kissed her damp nipple like a second lover; her loins pulsed with desire.

She slipped a hand inside his shirt and skimmed the flat, hard plane of his abdomen and the broad expanse of his chest. With every subtle shift of his body, he exuded power, strength, control. For tonight at least, he belonged to her.

He suckled her, nipping lightly at times, until she was writhing beneath him, desperate for something more. As if he knew, he shifted himself so that he lay beside her, and as he stared into her eyes, he slid a warm hand beneath the hem of her chemise. He stroked the sensitive skin behind her knee, then traveled up the inside of her thigh. She resisted the urge to squeeze her legs together and instead let her body respond to him. Her toes curled and her skin flushed; her heart pounded.

He drew small, tantalizing circles on the soft skin of her thighs. When he touched the curls at her entrance, heat flooded her neck and face; she tingled deliciously. His heavy-lidded gaze was still trained upon her, as though he was measuring her reaction to every caress. As though his sole purpose in life was to bring her endless, blissful pleasure.

It was very wanton of her to let him take such liberties,

but she trusted him. His sure, skillful touch filled her with a sweet, burning longing. As he tenderly explored the sensitive folds of her flesh, he whispered titillating things in her ear, driving her mad with desire.

"I want to see all of you. Taste all of you. The chemise has to go."

She sat up, and he peeled it off of her in one smooth motion, leaving her skin exposed to the air and to his appreciative gaze. Any embarrassment she felt melted away when he pulled his shirt off as well, exposing the sinewy muscles in his arms and a torso that tapered to narrow hips.

He was beautiful and scarred and masculine in every respect. Downy hair covered his lower belly, and she reached out to touch the patch just above his waistband to see if it was as soft as it looked.

It was.

"God, Daphne."

Her hand froze. "Is this all right?"

"Yes. Jesus, yes."

Before she knew what he was doing, he pushed her back, the silky pillows cradling her head and neck.

He seemed to be making good on his promise to kiss every inch of her. She should have known he would be very, very thorough.

He did not miss the spot behind her ear. He turned her over in order to attend to the indent at the small of her back and worked his way up her spine to her nape before easing her onto her back once more. Slowly, he kissed a path across her collarbone, between her breasts, down to her navel, and...lower. Her breath caught in her throat, but she opened herself to him.

Instead of moving on as he had with all the other spots, Ben lingered. His dark head nestled between her legs, his soft hair tickling her inner thighs. He flicked his tongue over the most sensitive part of her, teasing her closer and closer to some precipice. A small cry escaped her throat and the muscles of her stomach grew taut. Gradually, he increased the pressure of his tongue, setting up a hypnotic rhythm, until the pulsing down there spread into her ears and...and...

Exploded sweetly. Liquid heat radiated from her core, through her limbs, and out of each finger and toe. She bit her lip to keep from crying out as the tremors blossomed and slowly faded, leaving her sated, sleepy, and limp with contentment.

Through half-closed eyes, she watched him rise and retrieve her shawl from the chair. He sat beside her and pulled her against his warm, musky chest before covering her with the shawl. She idly fingered the fringe on the edge and waited.

For her heartbeat to return to normal.

For Ben to say something.

Or kiss her.

He chose the latter. This time, their tongues joined with a purpose. Each thrust and parry brought them closer to the inevitable conclusion of that night. She would belong to him.

Daphne had no promises from Ben and held no expectation of a proposal.

In spite of her doubts, she was giving herself to him freely because no matter what he felt or did after tonight, there would never be anyone for her but him.

She fumbled with his trousers, he wrestled with his

boots, and they both laughed when he almost kicked over the lantern. But he sobered when he removed his trousers, exposing his leg. He turned to face her, and she could see in his face what it had cost him to reveal his mangled thigh—the part of him that he considered hideous. His biggest weakness.

Frankly, she was too preoccupied with another part of his anatomy to pay much attention.

He must have misinterpreted the look on her face. "Would you like me to put my trousers back on, at least partially? You shouldn't have to look at it or even feel it."

"Come here."

He lay beside her, taking care to keep the injured leg away from her.

"Do you know what I like best about being with you?" she asked.

"My diplomacy and charm?"

"That there are no secrets between us. I don't have to hide anything from you, and you don't have to hide anything from me."

"This is different," he said seriously.

"You're right. It's not a character flaw. It's a scar, and I hate it if you want to know the truth."

He recoiled slightly.

"Not for the reasons you think. I hate it because it represents the suffering you went through and still endure, and because it reminds you of the day you lost your friend, and because it makes you feel inferior when nothing could be farther from the truth." She reached behind him and skimmed her hand over a taut cheek of his buttocks and down over the twisted muscle and ridges that marred his thigh. He tensed but allowed her to continue stroking his leg, and before long, he seemed to relax.

"I have a confession," she said.

"There's a third portrait? And you're completely naked in it?"

"Very funny. No. I didn't notice your leg earlier, because I was too distracted by your…"

He propped himself on an elbow and grinned. "By my what?"

"You know."

"I have no idea what you're talking about. You'll have to be more specific."

She cast her gaze down—at it—and then quickly looked away. Good Lord. Fine. She'd take the challenge. Steeling her resolve, she looked directly into his icy blue eyes and ignored the heat that flooded her face. "I was talking about your, ah…manhood."

"You mean my cock."

"Er, yes."

He leaned closer and rasped in her ear, "Why don't you say it? For me." He kissed her neck and the pulsing between her legs began again; she grew damp with wanting. "Say you were staring at my cock."

"I was"—she gulped—"rather enthralled with your… your…"

He licked his finger and lightly rubbed the tip of an erect nipple. "Say it."

"…cock." She exhaled shakily.

"That's a very good start. I'll have you talking like a sailor in no time."

She grabbed a pillow from beneath her bum and

swatted him on the side of his head. She couldn't recall the last time she'd been so happy.

The swatting led to kissing, which then led to other sorts of wickedness. Ben tortured her exquisitely by trailing the fringe of her shawl over her breasts and across her stomach. Everywhere the fringe traveled, his mouth went, too. And the fringe went *everywhere*.

Her body was both relaxed and aroused when he lowered himself gently onto her, settling between her legs and pressing gently, insistently at her entrance. "Tell me if I hurt you."

"You won't hurt me," she said with more confidence than she felt. She'd just seen him in all of his naked glory, after all, and was now aware of the relative size of things. "I want this," she reassured him. Of that, she was certain.

Slowly, he pushed at her entrance, and while she did her best to accommodate him, she began to despair of them ever fitting together properly. But then he began kissing her deeply and rocking his hips in the most wonderful rhythm. She ran her hands over his chest. His heart thumped wildly—hers did, too. His breath came in quick, hard puffs—just like hers. Their bodies worked together, rising and falling, thrusting and retreating, until at last he eased his way in. Stretching her, filling her. Completely.

He went still then, his entire body tensed. A sheen of moisture appeared on his forehead. "Are you all right?" he asked.

"Yes," she said, smoothing the line between his brows, but her own hand trembled. "More than all right. How are you?"

He closed his eyes briefly and muttered something that might have been a curse. "I want this to be good for you," he said, "but you feel so...right. I don't know if I can last long enough to—"

"Don't worry." She brushed an errant lock from his eyes. His expression was dark and brooding and...hungry. "I want to give you the pleasure you gave me. I suspect I'll like it, too."

He began rocking again, moving slowly within her, stretching her more than she'd ever thought possible. "What makes you so sure?"

"I've liked all the steps leading up to this moment."

"You're amazing, do you know that?" He kissed her like he would die if he did not have her. He thrust harder and deeper. She instinctively wrapped her legs around him to bring him even closer, and he growled as though pleased. So she moved some more, arching her back to take him deeper and he moaned. Or maybe she was the one moaning, because the sweet, insistent pulsing had begun again and she could think of nothing but kindling it and letting it burn to its completion.

Ben lowered his head and kissed her neck and shoulder, the slight stubble on his face abrading her skin. The rocking grew more intense. Faster and faster he pushed, teasing the most sensitive part of her with every thrust.

Her breath came in short pants; little beads of perspiration formed on his brow. "Daphne." It was a plea, but she didn't know what for. "Come. Like before."

She wanted to. Dear God, she wanted to. But how did one go about it? "I'll try," she said seriously.

He smiled. "Close your eyes."

She did, and he touched her where their bodies joined, rubbing little circles until she squirmed with sweet, breathless anticipation. All the while, he continued moving in and out, harder and faster until—

"Oh my God." Pleasure shot through her. Wave after wave overtook her and as soon as the last delicious one passed, Ben withdrew. Chilly air rushed over her as he pulled away, grabbed cloth—a handkerchief perhaps?—and spilled his seed into it.

Suddenly self-conscious, she drew the shawl over her.

Ben returned and sat beside her, so she sat up, too. He laced his fingers through hers but didn't say a word. She wished he would explain what had just happened. Not the physical part—she understood that. For the most part. She was far more curious to know what it had meant to him—or what it hadn't—and why he hadn't spent himself inside of her. Well, obviously, he did not want there to be a babe. Still.

"How are you feeling?" he finally asked.

Glorious. Confused. Like I want to cry. "Fine."

"We've made a mess of things, haven't we?"

It wasn't a mess to her. "How so?"

"I'm supposed to be helping you recover the portrait, not seducing you."

"Can't you do both?"

He grinned. "Yes." He released her hand, stood, and retrieved her clothes, giving her ample opportunity to admire his backside. The hollows on the sides of his buttocks and the muscular lines of his back made her sigh.

"Did you say something?" He handed her the chemise and gown.

"No." Feeling inexplicably modest, she turned away from him as she wiggled her arms into the chemise, pulled it down, and shimmied into her dress. When she faced him again, he wore his trousers and was pulling on his boots, wincing as he struggled with the right one.

"I'll go speak to Charlton tomorrow," he said.

Ah, it was much easier to discuss the portrait than any future plans they might have. Coward. "Thank you," she said.

"I'll let you know what comes of it." His boots on, he stood, favoring his bad leg.

"I brought you some more comfrey." She'd almost forgotten. Deep in the pocket of her gown was the bag that Mrs. Norris had procured from the apothecary. She handed it to him. "I'm happy to make you a poultice any time that you need one, but I thought you should keep some of this with you, in case I'm not available."

He took her hands in his and gave a knee-weakening smile. "I thought you were my round-the-clock nurse."

Lord help her. Any normal girl in her situation would be demanding a proposal of marriage. After one rakish grin, she was on the verge of happily accepting a full-time nursing position. "You are a difficult patient."

"How can I compensate you?" A wicked gleam shone in his eyes.

"Take care of yourself and your leg." She put the bag of comfrey in his palm, matter-of-factly.

He scooped up the lantern and handed it to her. "You go first. Be careful," he said, kissing her forehead.

Her legs wobbled a little as she walked away. "I'll see you tomorrow?"

"Of course." He glanced away, making her doubt the truth of his words. "Good night."

She skulked back to her room, hoping that the night she'd spent with Ben was the beginning of something wonderful . . . and not the end.

Chapter Twenty-Two

"I'm sorry, Lord Foxburn. Lord Charlton is not receiving."

Ben launched a dazzling smile at the housekeeper. At least, he hoped it was dazzling. It might have been desperate. "Receiving? At this time of the morning? I should think not. This isn't a formal call, just a friendly visit. He seemed to respond so well the last time I came by, and I wanted to pay my respects once more before I head back to town. I'm leaving in a few hours, you understand, so it's not as if I plan to set up camp. I just want to say farewell to the good fellow."

Mrs. Parfitt shook her head sadly. "I'm afraid that's impossible. Lord Charlton hasn't been conscious for two days."

Jesus. "What happened?"

"Nothing out of the ordinary. He's been quite ill."

Odd that Hallows hadn't mentioned his father's sudden turn for the worse during his visit yesterday. He'd been drunkenly jovial throughout the game of cricket. "What does the doctor say?"

"There's nothing to be done, except to spoon broth down his throat when we can. I asked my sister to come and care for him. I sit with him when I can, but too many duties call me away from his bedside. I feel better knowing that someone's there in case he wakes. Agnes is keeping him as comfortable as possible."

"Lord Charlton is fortunate to have such a resourceful and thoughtful housekeeper." He stroked his chin idly. "Mr. Hallows must be distraught over his father's condition."

She frowned, puckering her chin like a strawberry. "One would think so, but no. Mr. Hallows is preoccupied with other matters."

"Such as... gambling and drinking?"

Mrs. Parfitt pushed her spectacles up her nose and glanced over her shoulder. "Precisely."

Ben still stood awkwardly in the foyer, neither in the house nor out of it, and his leg was beginning to ache. But he suspected that the housekeeper might be an ally. "Could you spare a moment to sit and chat, Mrs. Parfitt?"

She wrung her small hands. "I am certain Mr. Hallows would not approve."

"He's still sleeping?"

She nodded.

"I won't impose for long. I have an idea about how we might help Lord Charlton."

"Follow me, please." She toddled down the hall to her tiny office in the back of the house and waved him in. "Please, sit."

Jars and tins filled the shelves above the table where

he sat, and the comforting aromas of coffee and peppermint permeated the air. Mrs. Parfitt stuck her head into the hall and looked both ways before closing the door and sitting in the wooden chair across from his, her back as straight as an elm, her hands in her lap. She looked at him expectantly.

"During my last visit, Lord Charlton mentioned that some of his possessions had gone missing—cuff links, a watch, items of that nature."

Her face flushed red. "There's not a member of my staff who would stoop to stealing."

"I didn't mean to imply they would." He paused to let the truth of that sink in. "Mr. Hallows, however, could be responsible."

"I would not dare to make such an accusation."

"Of course you wouldn't." But Ben could tell from the look in her eyes that she had her suspicions about Lord Charlton's reprobate son. "I'm merely suggesting that while the baron is ill, you keep a close eye on Mr. Hallows. Don't give him access to valuable items like jewelry, collectibles, silver... treasured paintings."

Mrs. Parfitt blinked behind the thick lenses of her spectacles. "We cannot dictate where Mr. Hallows goes or what he does. However, I do feel better knowing that Agnes is stationed beside Lord Charlton. She is not a small woman, and it would take a very bold sort of person to waltz into his bedchamber and remove his personal articles."

The problem was that Roland Hallows *was* bold. And stupid. And, very likely, desperate. "You might mention something to the male members of your staff as well. Instruct them to be discreet but watchful."

"I agree that would be prudent." Mrs. Parfitt's gaze flicked to the clock on wall. "Forgive me, Lord Foxburn, but I have a rather forward question to ask you."

"The only kind worth asking. What do you want to know?"

"Why have you taken such an interest in Lord Charlton's well-being?"

By getting directly to the heart of the matter, she'd spared him the trouble. He was prepared to tell her a little about his dilemma...as long as he could protect Daphne's anonymity. A delicate balancing act.

"There are two reasons. The first is that Robert considered him a friend and would have offered to help if he could. The second reason, as I'm sure you have guessed, is infinitely more self-serving. Lord Charlton owns a painting that I wish to purchase—for reasons of a very personal nature. I don't want anything to happen to the painting before I have a chance to speak with him about it."

"The English Beauty portrait."

The small hairs on the back of Ben's neck stood on end. "You've seen it?"

"Indeed. It's one of Lord Charlton's prized possessions. He won't want to part with it."

"When he hears the sum I'm willing to pay, he'll agree to sell it. Do you know where it is?"

The housekeeper stiffened slightly. "Of course I do. Lord Foxburn asked me to have the footmen take it down and move it to a safe location. I confess to being perplexed at the time. However, I now see the wisdom of his request."

"I don't suppose you'd reveal the hiding spot to me?"

"I would not," she said primly. "But you may rest assured that it is secure."

"For now," he added. "Hallows wants it. He said as much when he was at Biltmore Manor yesterday. I wouldn't be surprised if he tore apart the house looking for it."

A serene smile softened her face. "He won't find it."

Her confidence was heartening. Ben hoped that Charlton recovered soon and wasn't so addled that he'd refuse the exorbitant sum he was prepared to offer. "Then I suppose there's nothing more to be done—for now. I appreciate your time, Mrs. Parfitt. Would you keep me informed as to the baron's condition?" He withdrew a calling card from his pocket and handed it to her. It disappeared into the folds of her apron.

"I will notify you if there is any change."

With the help of his cane he heaved himself to his feet, wincing at the stiffness of his leg muscles. "I would prefer to keep my interest in the painting between us."

"I understand, my lord." She cracked open the door and peered into the hallway. "I'll see you out."

And then, because he couldn't resist, he asked another question. "What is it like? The painting, I mean."

"You haven't seen it? And you intend to *buy* it?" she asked, her tone suggesting that she'd never understand the ways of gentry.

"It's for a friend."

Her eyebrows rose as if she were skeptical. After a moment of uncomfortable silence, she inhaled deeply and stared over his shoulder. "The painting is remarkable." If he didn't know better, he'd have thought the portrait hung on the wall behind him. "It's unlike any portrait I've seen—wistful and ethereal and uplifting, all at the same time. The young woman is very beautiful," she said.

"She's not a lady—that much is obvious from her manner of dress." Color gathered in the apples of her cheeks. "And yet, she has a quality about her that is almost... regal." She shook her head slightly and blinked as though the picture had suddenly disappeared, then shifted her focus back to him. "Lord Charlton hung it in his library, along with the other one, which disappeared some months ago. He vowed he'd never have it in his bedchamber, out of respect to his dear, departed wife." The housekeeper's chest swelled a little at that.

"Are there any rumors about the identity of the woman in the portrait?"

"Not that I know of. Lord Charlton seems to think that she is a product of the artist's imagination."

"And are you of the same opinion?"

She seemed to contemplate the question, then shook her head. "The artist may have taken some liberties with her features, but I suspect she is real. Her expression is too complex—too uniquely feminine—to be conjured up in the mind of a man."

"We are a simple lot," Ben admitted.

Her round cheeks dimpled. "I'll see you out now, before Mr. Hallows comes down seeking a cure for last night's overindulgences."

"Have you forgotten how to play chess?" Olivia leaned over Daphne's shoulder, shaking her head with ill-concealed disgust. "You moved directly in the path of Rose's rook."

Sure enough, Rose captured her bishop. Daphne did not expect to win against Rose, but she usually managed to employ *some* feeble strategy.

"It's as though you're in a daze," Olivia said. She narrowed her eyes. "Did you sleep well last night?"

"I'm just a little preoccupied." She hadn't seen Ben all day, and Lord Biltmore said that he'd taken his coach somewhere—probably a drive into the village.

But Daphne knew he'd planned to visit Lord Charlton. She prayed Ben would be able to convince him to part with the painting. Her whole future depended upon it.

And *that* was why she could not play chess to save her life.

"We can postpone the match," Rose offered. "Would you like to take a stroll? There's a lovely path near the lake."

"I'm afraid I wouldn't be good company. Why don't you and Olivia go? I think I'll read until dinner."

"I know what the problem is," Olivia declared.

Daphne swallowed hard. "You do?"

"You're missing Anabelle. I'm sure she's doing just fine. It's only two more days until we return to London; then you shall see for yourself."

Daphne did miss her sister—desperately. She wished she could go to her and tell her everything so that she could somehow fix it. But there were no easy answers to her predicament, and she had the sinking feeling that things were about to get much worse.

"Yes, it will be good to be back in town." *Unless* she returned to find that her portrait was made public and put up for auction.

"Why, good afternoon, Lord Foxburn." Lady Worsham's singsong voice cut through the conversations in the drawing room. "You have been the subject of much speculation. Your ears must have been burning."

"My ears were blissfully unaware," he said dryly.

Daphne's pulse quickened at the sight of him. His buckskin breeches showed off his narrow hips, and his dark green jacket fit snugly across the breadth of his shoulders. Of course, she now knew precisely what lay beneath his expertly tailored clothes, and the memory of his hard body gave her a little jolt. His gaze swept around the room and lingered on her for a moment longer than it should have. She didn't think anyone else noticed, but she had. And she realized just how difficult it was going to be to pretend that there was nothing between them. That he had never stroked her skin or kissed her...everywhere. That she hadn't given herself to him with reckless, adoring abandon.

"Do put an end to the suspense," Lady Worsham pleaded, "and tell us where you have been."

"Nowhere worth mentioning. Besides, I would be remiss if I didn't greet everyone before launching into boring accounts of my day."

He ambled around the drawing room, making polite conversation with Mama and Lady Worsham for a few moments before joining Lord Biltmore and the other gentlemen who were discussing politics. Finally, he made his way toward her, Olivia, and Rose, limping slightly. "Good afternoon, ladies. You're all looking very well today."

His heavy-lidded gaze caused Daphne's heart to beat wildly.

"Thank you, my lord," said Olivia. "This happens to be a new dress, but some people"—she rolled her eyes in Mr. Averill's direction—"have yet to take notice."

"Good God, they must be blind."

"One does begin to wonder," Olivia mused. "And

rather than sit here, unappreciated, my sister and I have decided to go for a stroll around the lake. Would you care to join—Er, forgive me. I forgot about . . . your injury."

"I appreciate the invitation, half-issued though it was. As you predicted, I must decline." He focused stormy eyes on Daphne. "Will you join your friends, Miss Honeycote?"

"I thought I'd take advantage of the cooler weather and read my book in the garden."

"Daphne is missing her sister," Olivia said, as though that explained everything.

Ben raised his dark brows. "Then we must make it our mission to cheer her."

"You may do your best. After dinner," Daphne said. "My book is calling to me now." She dared not look at Ben as she left the drawing room and headed up the stairs to her bedchamber to retrieve a book. She was fairly certain that he would make an appearance in the garden. She hoped he would. They had much to discuss.

And, somehow, she must summon the courage to speak what was in her heart.

Chapter Twenty-Three

Perspective: (1) The technique painters employ to create the illusion of depth and space on a flat canvas. (2) A particular point of view, as in, From the earl's perspective, attempts to reform him were at once pointless and hopeless.

*I*t may have been overly sentimental, but Daphne thought of the stone bench beneath the trellis as *their* spot. He would find her here, she hoped, in order to tell her what had transpired during his visit to Lord Charlton's.

More importantly, she would confess to Ben how she felt about him.

It mattered little that low, grayish clouds had drifted in front of the sun or that a warm breeze portended the distinct possibility of a late afternoon shower. A few raindrops might spot her dress, but nothing could dampen her mood.

During breakfast that morning, she'd had an epiphany. She'd watched as Lord Worsham pushed his wife's chair in and leaned down to whisper in her ear. Lady Worsham blushed and affectionately scolded him, but her eyes had glowed with love.

Daphne wanted *that*.

More specifically, she wanted that with Ben. And it occurred to her that if there was to be any chance of that sort of future actually coming to pass, she would have to convince Ben that he wanted it, too.

It was a daunting prospect, seeing as she was not accustomed to persuading gentlemen to declare their affection for her. She'd never been particularly comfortable pressing others into service if it involved more than passing the jam.

But when doubt slithered into her ear, whispering that Ben would never change his mind, she simply remembered the way he'd held her—like he never wanted to let her go. That had to count for something.

The distinct *step-step-thud*, *step-step-thud* of Ben's feet and cane trodding the path made her shiver in anticipation. She ignored the fat raindrop that plopped on her chest.

"There you are." As he lowered himself onto the bench beside her, his wide smile contorted into a grimace.

Without asking him—without even thinking—she placed her palms on his thigh and began to gently knead the flesh. He stiffened at first but slowly relaxed, and after a minute or two, the muscles seemed more pliant. "Better?"

"Thank you." He lifted one of her hands and pressed his warm lips to the back of it. Her heart tripped in her chest. "I didn't get to see Charlton today. He's not well."

"Oh no. What's wrong?"

"His housekeeper informed me he's been unconscious for a few days."

"It must be serious. Does he have a fever? How is his pallor?"

"I didn't see him, much less have the chance to examine him. The problem, obviously, is that as long as he's in his current state, I can't ask him to sell the painting."

"That *is* vexing, but not nearly as important as the baron's health." She wondered if Lord Biltmore's library contained any medical journals. Of course, she would need to know more about Lord Charlton's condition if she were to have any hope of diagnosing his illness. "I need to visit him."

Ben stared at her like she was touched in the upper works. "Impossible."

"Why?"

"The housekeeper refused to let me see him. Why would she let you?"

Why indeed? "His symptoms sound similar to my mother's—when I cared for her. I might be able to help him."

"He's an old man, Daphne. The list of things that ail him is probably as long as my arm. He has a doctor."

"So do you, I presume. And yet, I was able to help you."

His eyelids lowered a fraction and a corner of his mouth curled. "That is true. I don't doubt your ability to heal people. Just sitting here, next to you, makes me feel better."

She softened. "I may not be able to help Lord Charlton, but it's worth a try."

"We can't risk it."

"Risk what?"

"You being recognized. Mrs. Parfitt, the housekeeper, has seen the painting. She'll identify you as the English Beauty."

Her eyebrows rose. "The English—"

"That's what Charlton dubbed you. I like it," he admitted. "But it's not just Mrs. Parfitt. The staff has seen your portrait, too. Some of the footmen moved it to its current hiding place."

That *was* problematic. The more people who could connect her name to the painting, the more trouble she was in. Still, there had to be a way to avoid detection. "I could hide my hair under a large bonnet and pull the brim low over my face."

"No." It was firm. Final.

Or so he thought. "If there's a chance I can help Lord Charlton, I must. Even if it means I'm discovered. What about your friend Robert? What would he have had you do in this situation?"

She'd struck a nerve. He bit his lower lip and trained his blue eyes upon her. "Lord Charlton could wake. Bonnet or no bonnet, he would recognize you in an instant. Are you willing to risk your reputation and that of your family and friends for the mere possibility that you could aid him?"

Normally, adding her family to the scale tipped it in that direction. But she knew Mama and Anabelle wouldn't want anyone to suffer the way Mama once had. Not if it could be helped. "Yes. I'm willing to risk it."

She braced herself for a string of curses, a scathing glare. But instead he nodded slowly and looked at her as if he were . . . proud. "Hallows will try to prevent you from seeing his father. He thinks he's going to sell the portrait, pay off all his vowels, and have a grand sum left over. He'll be suspicious the moment either one of us sets foot in his home. Actually, he'll be mad as hell. It could get ugly."

"I know."

"We can go tomorrow." The way he said *we*—so casually—made her feel warm inside. Now that the one matter was settled, she summoned the courage to broach the more difficult subject.

"I'd like to talk to you about last night."

Concern wrinkled his forehead. "Of course."

"I…" She swallowed hard. What if the words she'd rehearsed in her head sounded desperate or, worse, trite? Taking a deep breath, she began again. "Last night was special to me. *You* are special to me. I've been doing a lot of thinking, and what I think is that…we should be together." Her traitorous hands trembled, and he clasped them between his steady palms.

"We *are* together. I promised you I would help you get the portrait back. My word is good."

She narrowed her eyes, all but certain he was being purposefully obtuse. "I'm not talking about the painting right now. I'm talking about *us*. We are rather well suited—that is, if last night was any indication."

A wicked smile lit his face. "Indeed."

"I'm relieved to know that we agree on that point." Good Lord, this was ten times more mortifying than she'd imagined. He was going to make her spell it out. "Since we seem to be so compatible—not only in the physical sense, mind you, but in other ways as well—I propose that we take our relationship, as it were, to the next logical step."

He inhaled deeply and rubbed his chin. "You're proposing that I propose?"

Well. That was putting it bluntly. "Yes."

Some of the blue washed out of his eyes, and he refused

to look directly at her, focusing on a spot somewhere over her shoulder.

Every second that he didn't answer was an answer in itself. Her chest ached.

"Daphne. I meant what I said to you last night. I care about you more than I thought possible, but I cannot marry you."

She'd known there was a chance he'd say that, but she wasn't prepared for the way the words cut her—each one was a shard of glass. Her throat constricted. "Why?"

"Look at me." The anger in his voice jarred her. He stood, hoisted his cane, and slammed it against the side of the stone bench with a *crack*, splintering it into ugly, stringy pieces. She flinched. "Why on earth," he choked out, "would you want to be shackled to someone like me?"

She stood and faced him, toe to toe. "That is a very good question, and the answer escapes me at the moment. Perhaps you could tell me why we *shouldn't* be together."

"Fine. I'll tell you." His voice was low, just above a whisper, and then he was silent for the space of a dozen beats of her pounding heart. "You are an amazing young woman with your whole life ahead of you, and I'm not good e—"

"*Stop.*"

He paused midsentence, mouth open.

"Don't presume to tell me what's good for me. I know what I want. I know *who* I want."

"You think you do. But you can't know how you'll feel about me in six months or six years. Dealing with this"—he jabbed a finger at his leg as though she hadn't a clue what he was referring to—"gets very old, very quickly. It's a burden I need to carry myself."

Hot tears welled in her eyes, a sharp contrast to the cool raindrops that splattered on her cheeks. "Why? Why do you think you must endure it on your own? Don't you trust me?"

"That's not it, Daphne."

"Then why?"

He stood, unmoving for several seconds—long enough for her to wonder if he was even going to answer her. "Because," he said softly, "if we married, you would eventually grow weary of me and my ... limitations."

She parted her lips, wanting to ask what on earth he was talking about, but he held up a hand.

"After a couple of years, you'd resent me. After a few more, you'd despise me. And if there's one thing that I absolutely couldn't bear, it's that. I don't want you ... ever ... to despise me."

His confession was heartbreaking and maddening at the same time. "I don't think you give me enough credit. I'm not an ingénue or a sniveling debutante who has a fit of the vapors when she runs her stocking. I know what it's like to wake up hungry and face an empty cupboard." She sighed. "You may not know it to look at me, but I've faced adversity, and I'm not the sort of person who would abandon, in any sense of the word, someone I l—" She caught herself. "Someone I care about."

He shook his head, as if he'd like to rid his ears of the words she'd spoken.

"Just think about it," she pleaded. "What do you want your future to look like? Because it is your choice, you know. You can choose to be miserable and alone, or you can choose ... me."

"You should envision *your* possible futures," he

retorted. "A happy, full life with a man who twirls you around dance floors, indulges your every whim, and gives you a brood of children . . . or me."

"Well, when you put it like that," she said, "the choice is rather obvious."

Confusion clouded his handsome features. "Exactly."

She picked up her book as though the matter was settled. In her mind, it was. Somehow, she'd have to prove to him that love trumped everything. But how? "What time shall we leave tomorrow?"

He planted his hands on his hips. "What?"

"For Lord Charlton's house," she said with exaggerated patience. "You'll recall we planned to visit him. Shall we say the foyer at two o'clock?"

"Fine." Ben looked slightly dazed.

And she left him just so, walking away without looking back.

Little was said during the brief coach ride to Lord Charlton's house the next day. Daphne tried not to dwell on her conversation with Ben in the garden, because each time she thought about it she felt a little ill. No amount of discussion was going to make him change his mind. But action might.

He did not look at her, seeming to prefer the scenery outside the window, which consisted of gray skies and muddy roads. A bit lowering, even if she wasn't looking very stylish this afternoon. Hoping to avoid recognition by Lord Charlton's staff, she'd tucked every last strand of hair beneath her bonnet and donned her plain russet-colored dress. She wasn't as nervous about the staff, however, as she was about Mr. Hallows.

At the picnic, he'd spoken to her as though she were less than a person. As though in posing for the portrait she had surrendered a part of herself, giving him the right to demean her. She knew Ben wouldn't let him harm her, but Daphne would know what Mr. Hallows was thinking. That alone made her skin crawl.

"Mrs. Parfitt might turn us away," Ben said. He still did not look at her.

"Yes."

"You know, it takes more than a dowdy cap and plain dress to disguise your sort of beauty."

It might have been a compliment—if he hadn't spoken as though she were quite simple.

"Thank you, I think."

He glared at her for a long moment before turning back to the window.

As the coach pulled up the circular drive, Daphne took a fortifying breath and reached for the basket she'd prepared. Lord Biltmore's cook had given her a jar of beef broth and his housekeeper provided a variety of tea leaves. Daphne had picked some wildflowers and tied them with a cheerful yellow ribbon. The baron might be too ill to enjoy the gifts, but they certainly couldn't hurt. And when he awoke, it might please him to know that his neighbors were concerned.

Trepidation filled her as she alighted from the coach. Squeezing her hand, Ben said, "You'll be safe with me."

"I know. It's just odd to think that everything's come full circle. I'm going to meet the man who commissioned the portraits."

"You hope you will," he corrected. "First, we must make it past the front door."

"You make it sound as though the house is guarded by Cerberus."

"You haven't met Mrs. Parfitt." Ben knocked on the door.

The butler answered, and upon hearing their request to visit with the baron, he immediately sought out the housekeeper.

She scurried toward them a minute later, wiping her hands on her apron. "Lord Foxburn, I didn't expect to see you back so soon." She looked questioningly at Daphne.

"This is Miss Honeycote. She's a guest at Biltmore Manor, and when I mentioned that Lord Charlton was quite ill, she insisted on visiting him to see if she could help."

"Here are a few things for him." Daphne handed her the basket. "Forgive me for being so forward, but I spent several months nursing my mother back to health and, through trial and error, learned quite a bit. May we visit the baron for a few minutes? I wouldn't disturb him in the slightest, but seeing him would give me an indication as to what troubles him."

The housekeeper's eyes turned to slits in her round face. "The baron is receiving excellent care."

"We do not doubt it, Mrs. Parfitt," Ben assured her. "But Miss Honeycote has something of a gift for healing. I, myself, have been the recipient of her care—for a war injury. Hopeless cases are her specialty."

Daphne could have kissed him—would have, if she could have.

The woman sighed and ushered them farther into the house. "Mr. Hallows is not at home," she said evenly. "I'm certain that he would chastise me for admitting anyone into his father's room, so you must be quick."

"Of course," Daphne assured her.

"My sister is with him." To Ben she said, "You remember the way to his room?"

"Yes. This way, Miss Honeycote." He placed a warm hand at the small of her back and guided her toward the stairs.

They were halfway up the flight when Mrs. Parfitt's voice halted them. "This visit wouldn't have anything to do with the painting, would it?"

A chill slithered down Daphne's spine.

"No," Ben said. "You have my word on that."

The round woman nodded and hurried down the hall carrying the basket.

Daphne preceded Ben up a second set of stairs, impressed by the agility with which he took them. As though he'd read her thoughts, he muttered, "I'll pay for this later."

Daphne was relieved to see the pretty, feminine wallpaper above the chair rail in the hallway and the tasteful, if unimaginative, oil paintings of flowers and fruit that graced the walls. Inconsequential though it seemed, she'd feared that the baron's home might have been a garish monstrosity decorated in an abundance of red and gold and that her portrait—at least, at one time—had been the centerpiece of it all. But it was simply a stately country home that had probably seen generations of children slide down its banisters and grow up within its walls. There was nothing sinister about it; however, it did feel a little sad.

Such a large house should be bustling, but instead, it was hushed. Most of the rooms they passed were unused and sparsely furnished; the curtains were drawn shut.

"Here we are." Ben consulted his pocket watch. "Two-thirty. Let's keep our visit to no more than a quarter of an hour."

A broad-shouldered woman filled the doorway. "May I help you?" she asked—rather insincerely in Daphne's opinion. To her credit, the woman was clearly protective of Lord Charlton.

"Good afternoon," Ben said, flashing a smile. "You must be Mrs. Parfitt's sister. She sent us up for a brief, neighborly visit."

"The baron hasn't opened his eyes in days. When he wakes, I'll be happy to tell him that his neighbors stopped in."

Though Daphne hadn't yet stepped foot in the room, she could feel heat radiating from it. A fire burned on the grate and the windows were shut tight. Mrs. Parfitt's sister's dress was stained with perspiration. "We understand that Lord Charlton is resting and have no intention of disturbing him. Perhaps we could just sit with him for a few moments while you take a well-deserved break?"

Her frown faltered. "Who did you say you were?"

"Forgive us. We didn't properly introduce ourselves. I'm Miss Honeycote, and this is Lord Foxburn."

"I see. Well, if Mary sent you up, I suppose it would be all right."

Daphne exhaled silently. "Thank you."

As the woman lumbered out of the bedchamber, Daphne did a quick assessment. The room was even warmer than she'd imagined, and although Lord Charlton's face was slick with sweat, at least two wool blankets lay over him.

"Stand guard by the door," she told Ben.

"What?"

"Let me know if she returns."

Obligingly, he leaned one broad shoulder against the

doorjamb. An amused smile lit his face. "Let me guess. You're making a poultice."

"No."

"Surgery?"

"Quite amusing. I'm just going to try to make the baron a bit more comfortable." She pulled back the top two blankets, leaving a thin cotton one that covered the patient to his chin. While it might have been Daphne's imagination, she could have sworn that Lord Charlton breathed easier and deeper, like a weight had been lifted off his chest. She eyed the fire with disdain—nothing to be done there. But she could let in some fresh air.

She pushed back the heavy velvet drapes on the window closest to the bed and pulled on the stubborn sash, to no avail.

"I'll do that," Ben offered, and he was at her side in an instant. "This room is on fire. The poor man must be roasting." With one tug, he eased the window open. A damp breeze blew in and Daphne paused at the sill, savoring the slight relief.

"What the devil is going on?"

Dread washed over her. She spun around to find Mr. Hallows stumbling into the room, red-faced and reeking of liquor.

Looking like he was ready to kill.

Chapter Twenty-Four

Ben stepped in front of Daphne, shielding her. "Easy, Hallows. We're just visiting your father."

Hallows seethed, fists clenched at his sides. "He's not exactly fit for visitors. I know the real reason you're here."

Ben felt the gentle touch of Daphne's hand on his back as she spoke over his shoulder. "We were concerned about him."

"What a load of bull. The two of you were opening the window. Drop something outside, did you? A little trinket that might be worth something?"

Ben tucked Daphne farther behind him. Hallows wasn't the type of man you could reason with, even when he was stone sober.

And no one could accuse him of *that*. From the looks of his clothes, he'd been out all night. His soiled shirt peeked through a hole in his jacket where the shoulder seam had split, probably in a brawl. Whoever the other chap had been, Ben felt sorry for him.

"The room was stifling. We wanted to let in some air." A groan sounded from the bed, and before Ben knew it, Daphne had shouldered past him to the baron's side.

"He's stirring," she said hopefully. She took a towel from the washstand, and, with practiced expertise, dipped it in the basin and pressed the damp cloth to Charlton's forehead. She whispered soothing snippets that Ben couldn't make out.

Hallows seemed oblivious to the scene that played out on his father's sickbed. He was probably preoccupied with enumerating the ways he planned to maim Ben. As if he weren't in bad enough shape already.

"We've had a chance to pay our respects," Ben said. "As soon as your father's nurse returns, we'll leave."

Hallows cracked his knuckles, which were cut and bruised. "Like hell, you will."

Ben arched a brow. "The ladies must swoon over your gentlemanly manners."

"Don't act so superior," Hallows slurred. "If you're with her, you're no gentleman."

Damn it. "Call me what you like, but do not besmirch Miss Honeycote's name. Apologize."

"Never mind that," Daphne exclaimed. "Look, Lord Charlton is waking."

Ben turned toward the bed. Bad decision. Hallows's fist plowed into Ben's jaw and he staggered back, grasping the windowsill to keep himself upright. Christ. It felt like his lower jaw had been relocated a full inch to the right of where it was supposed to be. For a drunken slob, Hallows had wickedly good aim.

"Ben!" Daphne screamed, and started toward him.

He held up a hand but this time did not make the mistake of looking at her.

Keeping his eyes trained on Hallows, he said, "Nice punch. Why don't we continue this somewhere else? Someplace where we don't run the risk of breaking a family heirloom or upsetting your very ill father." Someplace where Daphne couldn't get hurt.

"We'll take care of this *now*." Hallows took a couple of steps forward, and Ben circled right, putting the door at his back.

"I thought perhaps we could discuss things, man to man, over a drink."

"My father hid the portrait," Hallows blurted. "Last night I tore this house apart looking for it." His bloodshot eyes narrowed. "I know you're looking for it, too, you greedy son of a bitch. You've got plenty in your coffers, but you're still after my painting."

Ben arched a brow. "I was under the impression it was your *father's*. To do with as he wishes. It seems he does not wish for you to have it."

"Why do *you* want it?" He began to breathe harder; his nostrils flared.

"I haven't the faintest idea what you're talking about."

"The portrait," he began, then shook his blocklike head. "You're playing dumb." He screwed up his face as though he were attempting deep thought—unlikely as that was. "You don't need the blunt. And a toff like you could afford to buy any titillating painting you wanted, so...it must be the girl. You fancy her, eh?"

Ben's ire shot up several notches, but he kept his face impassive and shrugged. "She's a friend."

A lecherous grin unfurled across Hallows's wide face. "A friend," he repeated, sliding his gaze to Daphne—or, more specifically, her backside—as she leaned over the bed ministering to Charlton.

"Have you seen the painting? She's wearing this night-gown and you can almost see her ti—"

Before the word was all the way out of Hallows's mouth, Ben grabbed two fistfuls of his jacket and slammed him into the wall. His head hit the plaster with a satisfying *thud*, but he was hardly fazed. He struggled, trying to squirm to one side. Ben smashed his fist squarely into Hallows's nose. Blood flowed.

Daphne cried out.

Ben tightened his grip on Hallows's lapels and shoved him into the wall once more for good measure.

Another moan came from the bed. "I think he's thirsty," Daphne said, looking to the men for help. Realizing none was forthcoming, she carefully placed an extra pillow beneath her patient's head before bringing a glass to his lips.

"Looks like she can raise the dead," Hallows chuckled. "And that's not all she can raise."

Ben squeezed his throat. "Keep your mouth shut, you bloody idiot."

Hallows didn't. Instead, he had the gall to grin, flashing yellow, crooked teeth. The hairs on the back of Ben's neck stood on end and he realized a split second too late what was coming next.

Hallows braced his boot against Ben's injured thigh, and using the wall as leverage, drove his heel directly into Ben's twisted flesh. If the ape had kicked him in the bollocks it couldn't have hurt more.

Damn his leg and damn Hallows—straight to hell. But Ben had to block out the pain and focus on one thing.

Not. Letting. Go. Who knew what Hallows would do in his drunken rage? Daphne was counting on him and he couldn't let her down. He wouldn't.

Spots danced at the corners of his vision. He broke into a sweat. His arms shook from the strain of holding Hallows in place. He breathed and devoted every ounce of will he possessed into the hand squeezing Hallows's throat. His eyes began to roll back a little and Ben knew he had him, and then—

His leg buckled. Like a tree struck by lightning, it splintered and crashed. Hallows threw him a few yards and Ben hit the floor with a *thump*; he slid until his skull struck a bedpost.

"Ben!" Daphne was at his side, her cool hands on his cheeks.

"Get back." It was all he could manage. He swatted her hands away and gripped the bedpost, intent on hoisting himself upright.

She tried to help him.

"No."

Hallows stomped closer and Daphne cried out. "I'm getting help."

Before Ben could stop her, she tried to dart past Hallows. One shove of his forearm against her chest sent her stumbling back toward the bed.

Ben had heaved himself halfway up the bedpost by the time Hallows reached him. His back was flush with the post, his good leg bent beneath him. The bad leg was like a ship's anchor, weighing him down.

For a brief moment, Hallows loomed over him, savoring the moment like a knight with a lance aimed at his opponent's throat.

Ben felt himself being lifted—so high, both feet left the ground.

Then he was *on* the ground, laid out flat and fighting to catch the breath that had been knocked out of him. Above him, Hallows looked like some sort of Titan—huge and more rock than human. The blood that trickled from his nose dripped to the floor beside Ben, creating odd, inklike splatters.

Hallows's mind was sickeningly predictable, and yet Ben couldn't stop his next assault.

While he lay there like a turtle flipped on its shell, Hallows ground the heel of his boot into Ben's leg.

He stayed conscious long enough to hear Daphne's screams mingle with his own howls. Long enough to wonder if he'd ever see her again.

Dear God, what had she done?

Hallows twisted the heel of his boot into Ben's thigh with nauseating glee.

"Stop it," she shrieked. He didn't.

Ben's face contorted into a mask of pain. Muscles corded in his neck and a deep blue vein throbbed at his temple. She yanked open the desk drawer, desperate to find a letter opener or anything that could improvise as a weapon. She shuffled through the contents—nothing but paper and ink. Blast.

She glanced around. On the washstand was a pitcher half full of water. She grabbed it and hurled it at Hallows. He deflected it like it was a teacup, and it landed on the floor with a crack. Water puddled. She fisted her hands and prepared to launch herself at Hallows.

"Rowland." Daphne spun toward the bed. Lord

Charlton's lips moved as though he were struggling to form more words.

"Your father is stirring," she shouted at Hallows. "He wants to speak with you."

"How convenient. I want to speak to him, too." Finally, Hallows removed his foot from Ben's leg, kicking him aside like a piece of debris on the road. Ben gasped as if starved for air. He struggled to sit up and barely managed to raise his head before he slumped to the floor, limp.

Hot anger flowed through her. Hallows sauntered toward his father as though he were irritated by the interruption.

"My son," Lord Charlton rasped. He stretched out a pale bony hand—a plea.

Hallows looked at the hand with disgust. "Yes. Your son. And yet you refuse to trust me."

The baron's bushy white brows drew together. "Huh?"

Hallows plopped onto the side of the bed, and the mattress sagged under his weight. "I am glad to know you are recovered, Father." Daphne prayed that Lord Charlton's mind was too muddled to detect the obvious lack of sincerity. "I was worried. And spent many a night right here, at your side."

Daphne wanted to scream, but the blatant lie brought a smile to Lord Charlton's wizened face. While Hallows was occupied with his father, she knelt beside Ben and pressed her ear to his chest. His heart beat steadily, and he took shallow breaths. At least he didn't seem to be in pain at the moment. She stroked his hair, wishing she could carry him out of there.

Where was Mrs. Parfitt's sister? Or Mrs. Parfitt for that matter? Could they not hear the ruckus? It seemed as though she and Ben had been here for an hour, although in truth it may have been only minutes.

"There is one small thing I would ask of you, Father— in return for my loyalty."

Daphne's stomach clenched. She stood, feeling an overwhelming sense of powerlessness. And fear.

"What...is it?" Lord Charlton patted his son's thigh.

"The painting."

"Huh?" He squinted, eyes rheumy.

"The painting," Hallows spat.

Lord Charlton's eyes opened wider. "Wh-wh-why?"

Hallows grabbed the old man's shoulders and shook him. "You owe me. I want it."

"What is going on in here?" Mrs. Parfitt's sister stood in the doorway, clearly appalled to see Ben sprawled on the floor and Hallows's rough handling of her patient— not to mention the blood and shards of pottery all over the floor.

"Get help, please," Daphne called out. "I'm afraid he'll hurt his father."

"I'll call for the footmen." She hurried down the hall.

Hallows swiveled his head to look at Daphne. The blood had started to cake beneath his nose and around his mouth. Just the sight of him made her nauseated. "You're not afraid for my father. You're afraid for yourself, *whore*."

"Rowland, stop," Lord Charlton begged.

"I'll stop. Just tell me where the painting is. The English Beauty."

For the briefest of moments, Lord Charlton's eyes focused. "No."

Hallows leaned over him, snarling. "I want it."

The baron closed his eyes, as though doing so could make the whole nightmare end.

But Hallows only shook him again. The old man's jowls flapped and drool trickled out of his mouth. "Look at me," Hallows ordered.

When his father refused to open his eyes, he circled his hand around Lord Charlton's frail neck. "Now you'll tell me."

"Stop! You'll kill him," Daphne cried.

Hallows ignored her. "Where is the portrait of the English Beauty, Father?"

The baron gurgled.

"He's been very ill, and you're hurting him. He needs to rest."

"He'll talk."

Lord Charlton's arms flailed and his face turned a frightening shade of blue.

Hallows sat back slightly and released his father's neck. The old man's chest heaved as he coughed and struggled to fill his sickly lungs.

"Ready to talk?"

A tear slid down the baron's cheek. He nodded and held up a finger.

Hallows looked over his shoulder. "Quickly."

"In the . . . stable."

"Christ. *Where* in the stable?"

"Loft. Under hay."

"You crazy bastard. You wouldn't know the English Beauty if she walked into your bedchamber." Hallows heaved himself off the bed, spat on Ben's still body, and left his father, shaking and crying from shock.

"It's all right." Daphne took his cold hand and warmed

it between her palms. "Your son has been drinking. He didn't mean the awful things he said...or did."

The baron gave her a skeptical but appreciative look. "Who...are you?"

"Daphne Honeycote, a friend of Lord Foxburn. Pleased to meet you, although I do wish it had been under better circumstances."

"Pleasure is mine." His wrinkled face sagged. "Why? Why...my painting?"

She inhaled deeply, untied her bonnet, and pulled it off her head. A few strands drifted to her shoulders, and she smiled weakly.

If it were possible, Lord Charlton grew even paler. "Dear Lord," he whispered. "What have I done?"

Footsteps pounded in the hallway. Thank God, help had arrived. "Don't worry. You need to take care of yourself." She swiftly returned the bonnet to her head, tucking the loose tendrils into it.

On the floor, Ben groaned. "Am I...dreaming?"

Daphne glanced at him and the chaos throughout the room. "No. I'm afraid this is very, very real."

Chapter Twenty-Five

Blocking: (1) The first step in painting, in which general areas of color are applied to the canvas. (2) The act of preventing a young lady from achieving her goal—especially through nefarious methods, such as brutality and threat of ruin.

$\mathcal{M}$rs. Parfitt and her sister charged into the room, followed by two men with rolled up shirtsleeves who might have come directly from the fields or stable.

After one look at the room, the housekeeper pressed a hand to her stomach as though sickened. "Mr. Hallows stormed past us. He did all this?"

Daphne nodded. "Lord Charlton is awake. Will you see to him? I'll tend to Lord Foxburn."

"What should we do about Mr. Hallows?" one of the men asked.

Mrs. Parfitt looked to Daphne, who shrugged. "His tirade is over. I'm afraid he got what he wanted."

"Did he, now?" The housekeeper adjusted her spectacles and planted her hands on her hips. "Shall we send for the magistrate?"

"That is Lord Charlton's decision." Daphne spoke slowly and loudly enough for the old man to hear. "But I do not think there's anything to be gained by involving the authorities. In the end, all of us face the consequences of our actions." And she was about to face hers.

Mrs. Parfitt instructed one of the men to stand guard outside the door and sent the other back to work. She began to return the room to some semblance of order while her sister tried to settle Lord Charlton.

At last, Daphne could focus on Ben. He looked to be sleeping peacefully, and his handsome face showed no sign of the torture he'd suffered minutes before. While she hated to rouse him, she wanted to make sure she could. The housekeeper handed her a blanket, which Daphne folded and tucked under his head. "Ben," she whispered, "can you hear me?"

He mumbled something unintelligible but didn't open his eyes.

"Here's some fresh water and a cloth." Mrs. Parfitt placed the basin and towel beside her. "He'll be all right. He's young and strong."

Daphne laid a damp cloth on his head, and—when the housekeeper was occupied elsewhere—loosened Ben's neckcloth.

His eyelids rose a fraction, and his startling blue gaze sought her out. "Daph?"

Thank God. "I'm here."

"Are you...hurt?"

"I'm fine. You will be, too. Hallows left."

Ben was still and quiet for several moments; then he snorted. "I broke his nose."

"Yes." She smiled. "You were very brave and heroic."

"If you overlook the part where I'm flat on my back."

"I hadn't even noticed."

"Daph?"

"Yes?"

"Can we please get the hell out of here?"

"Of course."

"One more thing."

She quirked a brow and shot him a questioning look.

"I think I'm going to need a poultice. And a drink."

The three-mile coach ride back to Biltmore Manor would be an arduous one. Daphne cajoled Ben into letting the farmhands carry him down the stairs on a makeshift stretcher. Once on ground level, however, he insisted upon walking to the coach using just his cane for support. The exertion etched deep lines on either side of his mouth.

Once they were settled inside the coach, Mrs. Parfitt leaned in and handed Ben a flask. "Something to take the edge off of the pain."

"How'd you know?" His grin made her round cheeks turn pink.

"I wish there were something more we could do."

"I'll take good care of him, Mrs. Parfitt," Daphne said. "I hope that Lord Charlton continues to improve. I'm going to send over some herbs for him. They're thought to sharpen memory."

"Well, in that case, would you kindly send enough for me, too?"

Daphne smiled. Although the afternoon had been disastrous, at least the baron had woken and Ben had survived the brutal torture inflicted by Mr. Hallows. He seemed to take great pleasure in inflicting pain—both physical and mental.

And *she* would likely be his next victim.

The coachman made sure they were situated. Ben's leg was supported by a plank that stretched from one seat to the other. Daphne sat beside him. "I'll take it nice and slow, my lord."

"Just try not to hit every damned rut between here and Biltmore Manor, would you?"

"As you wish, my lord." The coachman smirked as he closed the door of the cab.

The moment they were alone, Daphne threw her arms around Ben. "I'm so glad you're all right. Can you forgive me? I never should have made you bring me here."

He didn't answer but loosened the ribbon beneath her chin, removed her bonnet, and took her face in his hands. "You helped Charlton."

Good Lord, he looked handsome. Dark lashes framed his impossibly blue eyes and the faint stubble on his chin made him look more than a little dangerous. "Not really— *you* opened the window. And he's still very ill. But the human spirit is an amazing thing—the baron is fighting his way back. He just needs a little encouragement."

Ben squinted as if he didn't quite believe her.

"Thank you for defending me," she said. "You didn't have to, you know, but it was very gallant of you. You had Hallows against the wall and then he had the gall to kick you in your wounded leg. I felt so *angry*. Like I wanted to—"

Ben covered her mouth with his and kissed her. Tenderly, as if to savor each touch of their lips, each mingled breath, each taste of her. By the time he stopped, her heart was pounding and she'd quite forgotten what she'd meant to say.

He brushed a thumb across her lower lip. "I wish I'd done a better job of defending you and that I'd succeeded in getting the painting. I haven't given up yet, by the way. But don't you see that you deserve someone who can take better care of you?"

Her eyes burned. "You *did* take care of me."

"No. I tried. And I failed miserably."

"It was his blood that was spilled on the floor."

"I'd gladly exchange it for my own to get the painting back."

"Don't be ridiculous. My reputation isn't worth that sort of sacrifice."

"*You're* worth it, Daphne. You're worth everything."

She'd longed to hear him say something so heartfelt— so romantic—but now the words chilled her...because he'd spoken them like a good-bye.

"When we get back to Biltmore Manor, I'm going to make you a poultice, which I'll give to the housekeeper. Maybe I can sneak into your room this evening and check on you. Massage the muscles a bit. Tomorrow's likely to be worse than to—"

"Daphne."

"What?"

"You cannot risk coming to my room."

"But I'm leaving tomorrow."

"I know. I'll return to London just as soon as I can"— he grimaced at his leg—"and then I'll figure out how Hallows plans to sell the portrait."

Didn't he understand? "I'm not nearly as concerned with the portrait as I am about...*us*."

"I'm sorry if I misled you, Daph. But there's no future for us."

Her throat constricted and convulsed. She opened her mouth but no sound came out.

"I was wrong the other night," he said, "when I told you that life is messy and hard and painful. It doesn't have to be, but if you were to spend it with me...well, it would be all those things. I can't give you all you deserve—"

"I don't care," she sputtered.

"—and even if you *think* you don't care, I do. I couldn't bear it if you grew to resent me. I can't take that chance."

"But the scene back there, in Lord Charlton's bedchamber—it proved that you care about me."

"I won't deny it."

"And now you would walk away from me...because you're afraid that one day I won't love you anymore." She hadn't exactly meant for it to slip out in such a way, but it was true, and it might be her last shot. "I do love you, Ben. And if I can't have you, I don't want anyone."

"Give it a few months. Hell, a few weeks might do it. You'll find someone who will give you a perfect life. Perfect children."

How dare he say such things? She wanted to grab him and shake him. "And what's to become of you?"

He shrugged. "I'll muddle through life the same way I did before I knew you. Alone."

"So, then this is...good-bye?"

He pressed his lips into a thin line and nodded. "I will follow through on my promise to recover the painting— or die trying."

"Please. Don't even joke about such a thing. The painting is...a trifling matter."

"What about your reputation? Your family's good name?"

"What about it?"

"Are you ready to give up?"

She sighed. "I don't know. But I certainly don't want anything to happen to you. Even if you don't feel the same way that I do."

"Daphne, I—"

"I can't make you love me, but I can make sure that you never forget me." She swiveled around on her bottom and leaned across his chest. "After I'm gone," she whispered, "I want you to remember this." With the tip of her tongue, she traced his lower lip, then sucked it gently.

When she pulled back slightly, he said, "I'll remember."

"That's not all. You must also remember this." She kissed the side of his neck, tracing a path from just above his collar to his nape. Meanwhile, she let her hands roam over the hard contours of his chest and the flat plane of his abdomen. Boldly, she crossed the line over his waistband and caressed the front of his trousers. When she touched the length of him, he moaned.

Encouraged, she continued to kiss and stroke him; he kissed and stroked back.

Though they were fully clothed and he was partially immobile, her heartbeat raced and desire coursed through her. He mumbled her name against her lips as though it were a prayer. He cupped her breasts and made small circles around her nipples, driving her mad with wanting. But after a few minutes—or perhaps it had been several— Ben sat back and smoothed her hair away from her face.

"We're almost at Biltmore Manor."

Daphne blinked and glanced out the window, dismayed to see they were already in the front drive. "But I wasn't done."

He picked her bonnet off the seat beside him and carefully placed it atop her head, guiding the smooth ribbons behind her ears. "I promise you, I'll remember and treasure this little coach ride for the rest of my godforsaken life. Possibly even for eternity, if you believe in such things."

The coach stopped, and the driver rattled the cab as he climbed down from his perch.

"If you change your mind—"

He shook his head regretfully. "I won't."

"I'll miss you." And then, because she knew without a doubt that she'd burst into tears if she stayed with him for one more minute, she unlatched the door, jumped to the ground, and fled straight to her room. After locking her door, she flung herself onto her bed and sobbed into her pillow. When the tears would no longer come, she rolled over and stared at the ceiling. For a very long time.

A week later, Daphne was still raw and hurting. The upside of being home was that she got to see Anabelle again; the downside was that even though her sister could sense something was wrong, Daphne couldn't tell her anything—not about the portrait or Ben or any of the heartache she felt. She declined invitations to balls and soirees. The idea of putting on a beautiful gown and pretending to be happy was too daunting. Some mornings, just getting out of bed proved a trial. She went for walks with Mama, assured her everything was fine, and fibbed that she was just having trouble adjusting to the social whirl. Mama knew her too well to believe it but didn't attempt to pry. She'd simply said that she would be there should Daphne ever want to confide in her.

Daphne was tempted. She'd always shared her joys, fears, and heartaches with Mama and Belle. At first she'd kept the portraits a secret because she'd known they'd disapprove of any scheme that could tarnish her reputation. Now, however, she was prevented from confiding about the paintings because they were inextricably tangled up in her relationship with Ben.

And that was too private, too precious, to share just yet. One day, perhaps, she'd reveal the devastating truth—that Ben had chosen a cold, empty life over her. No matter what his reasons, the reality was that he didn't love her enough to give up his self-indulgent bitterness.

Ironically, she desperately missed all his self-indulgent bitterness.

Today, however, she'd decided the moping must stop— at least temporarily. A visit with Caro and the other girls at the orphanage would improve her mood. When she announced her plans to Mama, Anabelle, Olivia, and Rose at breakfast that morning, their delight—or perhaps it was relief—was palpable.

"An outing is just the thing, darling," Mama cried.

"Oh, yes. Just the thing," Olivia echoed.

Daphne arched a brow. "Just the thing for what?"

"Well, for improving one's spirits." Olivia waved her fork like a fairy's wand. "Have you picked out a gown?"

Daphne gazed down at her perfectly suitable, if plain, muslin dress. "I have."

"What a shame that your mother and I have an appointment at the mantua maker's. I should have liked to join you. We could have stopped at Gunter's afterward."

Gunter's was not exactly near the orphanage, and besides, the mere mention of it brought to mind the rainy day when she and Ben had sat in his coach outside the shop. It was the first time she'd seen beyond his crusty exterior to the vulnerability that lay beneath. "I shall be happy just to see the girls. Caro's probably grown an inch since my last visit." She idly pushed the ham around her plate.

At the end of the table, Anabelle eyed her shrewdly. "Caro may not recognize you if you don't start eating a bit more heartily. Soon I shall have to take in all your dresses—a task I would rather not undertake since I am currently in the process of letting out all of mine." She punctuated this announcement by popping a large bite of egg into her mouth. "Thank goodness the nausea has passed."

Daphne smiled. "I'm so glad. You are radiant."

"Do not think to change the subject, Daph. Need I remind you that I have also been working quite industriously on your ball gown? I am putting the finishing touches on it, and if you don't wear it soon, it shall no longer be in the first stare of fashion. Would you like to try it on today?" Her gray eyes shined hopefully.

"Perhaps." She really didn't want to—what was the point?—but Belle had worked so hard on it.

"Excellent. I want to add a bit of beading to the sleeves, and then I think it will be perfect."

"I'm sure it will," Rose said encouragingly. "Daphne, may I join you on your outing today? I found a few books I thought the girls might enjoy."

"Of course. I'd love your company, and the girls are sorely in need of new reading material. Caro confessed that she finds Shakespeare dreadfully boring."

Rose laughed. "Ah. Then the book of fairy tales may be more to her liking."

When Daphne and Rose arrived at the foundling home a few hours later, the girls were finishing up their lessons. Daphne and Rose had tea in Mrs. Middleton's office.

"The books are wonderful," the director said. "Thanks to you and"—she paused before continuing—"another generous donor, we have a rather impressive collection."

"Why, that's remarkable." The last time Daphne visited, the bookshelves had held little more than dust.

"It's four o'clock—the girls should be heading outside just about now." A burst of animated chattering and shuffling from the hallway confirmed her prediction. "Come, I'll show you," the director offered.

She led the way, her skirts swishing over the floor with brisk efficiency. Daphne and Rose had to lengthen their strides in order to keep pace with her. At the doorway to the classroom, she waved them in with a flourish.

Daphne's gaze was immediately drawn to the bookshelves. There had to be one hundred books there—all of them new. Not quite believing her eyes, she walked across the room and trailed a finger along the colorful spines. Books on history, mythology, and science. Volumes of poetry and verse. Atlases and, yes, more Shakespeare.

She turned to face the director. "This collection must have cost a small fortune." Her eyes brimmed. Someone else in the world obviously agreed with her that the girls were worth that small fortune.

"Indeed. The donor provided additional monies for improvements to the dormitory. New mattresses, blankets, and curtains."

"Who?"

Mrs. Middleton blushed slightly. "I'm not at liberty to say, as he wishes to remain anonymous."

Interesting. The director's lips might be tightly sealed, but Daphne knew another potential source of information. She was considerably shorter, with red hair and a riot of freckles on her cheeks.

"Whoever the mysterious gentleman might be, I'm delighted to know that the girls have such a generous and thoughtful benefactor. May Rose and I join them in the courtyard?"

"Of course. You must know your visits are the high point of their week."

Daphne doubted that. In fact, she was almost certain that Caro had mentioned tea cakes were the high point of their week. However, second place to tea cakes was not a bad place to be.

The moment she and Rose walked into the courtyard, a ring of ragamuffins surrounded them.

"Will you braid my hair?"

"I tore the sash on my best dress."

"Watch me do a cartwheel!"

Daphne sighed. Here, at least, she was needed. Between Rose and her, they were able to handle most of the girls' pleas for attention. Eventually, they dispersed and returned to games of hopscotch and blind man's bluff. Only Caro remained on the bench beside Daphne, keeping her company as she mended the sash one of the girls had brought her.

"How is your knee?" Daphne asked.

"Hmm? Oh, it's fine." Caro idly swung her legs, scissors-style, her toes dangling inches above the ground.

"Have you been getting on well with the other girls?"

She bobbed her head quickly and gave her a wide-eyed, innocent look. Daphne chuckled to herself. Caro leaned forward and addressed Rose. "You have the same color hair as me."

"I believe you're quite right, Miss Caroline. Except yours has more fire, like a beautiful sunset."

Pleased with the compliment, Caro smoothed a short lock behind her ear. To Daphne she said, "Where is your other friend? Lord Fox-something?"

Daphne attempted a serene smile. "Lord Foxburn. I'm afraid I don't know."

"He was here a few days ago. I saw him in Mrs. Middleton's office."

"Is that so?"

"He didn't stay long, though. And he didn't visit with me." She pouted prettily. "He probably doesn't even remember me."

Daphne put a finger beneath Caro's pointy chin and looked into her pale blue eyes. "You are not the sort of person one could easily forget."

Caro's wistful smile said she didn't quite believe it. "I think he brought the books."

Daphne's heart squeezed in her chest. Ben cared. "What a kind thing to do."

"I suppose. But visits are better than books." She leaned her head against Daphne's shoulder, and Daphne hugged her tightly.

Visits *were* better than books, she thought.

But books were a start.

Chapter Twenty-Six

$\mathcal{B}$en hadn't been to White's since returning home from the war. In fact, the last time he'd been there, Robert had been with him. They'd toasted the Thoroughbred that Robert purchased at Tattersall's, and Ben ribbed him, saying he paid twice as much as he should have. Robert had just laughed and said life was too short to quibble over a couple thousand pounds.

Too short, indeed.

In any case, he'd been the one who forced Ben to venture out of his dark study and rub shoulders with their peers.

Though Ben had little desire to discuss politics, the weather, or anything else, he'd come to White's this evening with a purpose.

The club looked the same as it had seven months ago. Ben steered away from the side of the room he and Robert used to prefer, opting for a comfortable leather chair near a window. He greeted the gentleman nearby, ordered a drink, picked up a paper, and pretended to read while he listened to snippets of conversations around him.

There was talk of wagers, women, and whiskey, but nothing about the portrait. He supposed he should be relieved that it wasn't the topic on everyone's lips, but how could he help Daphne if he didn't know where Hallows was or what he planned to do?

"Evening, Foxburn." Ben turned toward the commanding voice.

"Huntford. Care to join me?" He waved his glass at the empty wingback chair beside him. Daphne's brother-in-law wore a black jacket and black trousers—formidable, as always. He wasn't scowling, however, which Ben took to be an excellent sign.

The duke signaled to a waiter as he smoothly lowered himself into the chair. Ben noted the effortless way he moved and tried to squash the envy he felt. He wasn't entirely successful, so he tossed back the rest of his drink.

"A pleasant surprise, seeing you here," Huntford said.

"Yes, well, I do venture out on occasion, although I'm never sure why. I trust the duchess is well?"

The corners of Huntford's mouth lifted and the harsh lines of his face softened. "She is much improved. So much so that she insists she is able to resume her normal activities. My wife can be...stubborn."

Ben nodded, intimately familiar with that particular family trait.

"My sisters tell me that Biltmore's house party was an unqualified success."

Ben resisted the urge to shrug. "I'm glad Lady Olivia and Lady Rose enjoyed themselves."

"I've noticed, however, that Anabelle's sister, Miss

Honeycote, seems uncharacteristically despondent since her return from Biltmore Manor."

At the mention of Daphne, Ben's stomach clenched, but he kept his tone light. "You don't say?"

Huntford glared for several seconds, and Ben glared back.

"Miss Honeycote and her mother, as you may know, have been staying with us. Daphne is not her usual, cheerful self. Anabelle is concerned. And when my wife is concerned, so am I."

Ben chose his next words carefully. "Miss Honeycote's sunny disposition will return. She is much like her sister, in that her strong personality cannot be suppressed for long." He hoped to God it was true. She deserved to be happy.

"You wouldn't happen to know the cause of this sudden change, would you?"

"I am no expert on women, Huntford." Truer words were never spoken.

The duke inclined his head, suggesting he, too, found women to be one of the universe's great mysteries. His drink arrived and Ben ordered another.

Ben was searching for a way to broach the topic of the portrait, just in case Huntford had heard anything about it, when the duke sighed. "I just spoke to Lord Foley. He's hosting a ball in a fortnight."

Ben craned his neck in search of the waiter. "Balls hold little interest for me. Dancing's not exactly my strong suit."

Huntford arched a brow. "This ball promises to be... interesting."

Highly doubtful. Where in God's name was his drink? "How so?"

"There's a chap who owes Foley a decent amount of blunt. He doesn't have the coin to pay him back, but he claims to have a valuable painting."

The hair on the back of Ben's neck stood on end; his heart pounded. "What does that have to do with the ball?" He had a good idea of the answer but prayed he was wrong.

"Foley's debtor says the painting is a portrait of 'a proper young miss in a highly improper pose.' He wants Foley to auction it off at the ball and claims it will bring an excellent price—more than enough to cover the debt."

"Who is the woman?"

"It's meant to be a secret. Even Foley doesn't know. He's going to unveil the thing at his bloody ball. He's always had a dramatic streak," the duke said with blatant distaste.

"And he has no qualms about publicly humiliating a young woman or ruining her reputation?"

The duke eyed him suspiciously. "What's this, Foxburn? I would never have taken you for a defender of reputations."

"It just doesn't seem sporting."

"Agreed. However, any well-bred lady who poses for a lewd painting is beyond foolish. She had to have known the risk."

She's your sister-in-law, and she had her reasons, Ben wanted to yell. But any sort of rebuttal would be giving too much away. The waiter hurried over and flourished a tray with Ben's drink in the center. Thank God. "I assume there is plenty of speculation as to the identity of the woman?"

"Wagers are being placed as we speak. Everyone is guessing the name of the English Beauty. Smithson had the gall to write Anabelle's name in the book. I had a word with him."

"A word? Is that what we're calling threat of death these days?"

Huntford grinned. "Suffice it to say that rumor has been squashed. I suspect other names will be bandied about for the next two weeks... until the truth is revealed."

A chill ran the length of Ben's spine. Two weeks to come up with a plan that would prevent Daphne's ruin. With forced casualness, he shrugged. "Sounds like the Foley ball is not to be missed."

The duke raised his glass. "To the English Beauty—whoever she is—for inspiring Foxburn to attend a ball."

Ben drank to that. There wasn't much in this world that he wouldn't do for his English Beauty.

Olivia had convinced Daphne that a trip to the milliner's would be painless, and it appeared that she was correct. The previous night's rain had washed away much of the road dust and the sun glinted off the pristine shop windows. Ladies and their maids scurried about Bond Street, darting in and out of the busy stores, balancing parcels and boxes.

Olivia pulled the brim of her bonnet forward. "I should have brought my parasol. A mere minute in the sun is all it takes to bring out my spots. I do hope they have the trim I'm looking for. It must be just the right color—green, to match James's eyes."

Daphne laughed. "I'm sure they'll have something equally soulful." They'd almost reached the shop when she stopped to check that she hadn't forgotten the list of items Anabelle had asked her to purchase. She peered into her reticule, relieved to see the list there. She secured the drawstring and looked up—to find Miss Starling directly in front of her. The young blonde's mother was just behind her, clucking her tongue and muttering about the potential dangers of failing to look where one is walking.

"Forgive me," Daphne said. "I'm afraid I was a bit distracted. Good afternoon, Miss Starling, Mrs. Starling." She hadn't seen Miss Starling since the Seaton musicale and wished the respite from her company could have lasted another month. Or year.

Olivia greeted the women as well. "What a striking hat, Miss Starling."

It *was* remarkable. The white plumes protruding from the top were so long they brushed the awning above the storefront. Each time she turned her neck to the left, her mother received a mouthful of feathers. But while the hat was a touch ridiculous, Daphne had to admit that Miss Starling looked stunningly beautiful. Every tendril of her golden hair seemed as though it had been trained to curl and cascade perfectly. Her gown clung to her svelte figure without appearing indecent in the least. And while Daphne's day gown was perfectly appropriate for an afternoon shopping trip, she suddenly felt frumpy.

"Imagine," Miss Starling declared, "I was just telling Lord Foxburn that we hadn't seen Lady Olivia, her sister, or Miss Honeycote in an age. And here you are."

"Here we are," Olivia repeated dully.

Daphne glanced down the street. Ben was nearby? She wanted to ask Miss Starling where she'd seen him and how he looked and whether his leg seemed to be bothering him. Instead, she pointed to the shop window and inanely said, "We were just going to get a few supplies."

"Yes," Olivia chimed in. "The right shade of trim can make all the difference in a ball gown."

"Your sister-in-law would know," Miss Starling said snidely. She never could pass up an opportunity to remind others that Anabelle had been her seamstress. The fact that Anabelle was now a duchess was a mite difficult for Miss Starling to swallow. Daphne let her comment pass, hoping to end the encounter as soon as possible. But Miss Starling seemed equally intent on prolonging it. "There are a good number of balls in the next fortnight. Why, four at least! Although none is as anticipated as Lord Foley's. I assume you received an invitation?"

Daphne had not been paying much attention to invitations since her return to London; she shrugged and looked to Olivia.

"Oh, indeed. We shall be there." She elbowed Daphne in the ribs. "Shan't we, Daphne?"

"I suppose."

"Trust me," Miss Starling said, smiling like she had a secret. "You don't want to miss it."

"We don't?" Olivia cried. "Of course we don't. But *why* don't we?"

Miss Starling sighed as though Olivia sorely tested her patience.

Mrs. Starling pushed past her daughter, her very large bosom leading the way like the prow of a ship. "Because some silly chit was foolish enough to pose for a vulgar painting," she announced shrilly. "And on the night of the Foley ball she shall be exposed for all the *ton* to see!"

Daphne's face grew hot and her palms clammy. She swayed slightly, but Olivia righted her without seeming to notice her distress.

"It shall, no doubt, result in a huge scandal," Miss Starling said with obvious glee. She narrowed her eyes at Daphne. "I should think that you would be pleased, Miss Honeycote, that for once you and your sister are not the objects of censure, unless... you *are*."

"What?" Olivia cried. "I am appalled that you would insinuate such a thing. What a ridiculous notion!"

"Is it?" Miss Starling curled a blond ringlet around her finger.

Olivia was indignant. "Imagine how foolish and remorseful you shall feel at Lord Foley's ball when the truth is revealed." She linked arms with Daphne. "We shall be there, of course, so that you may issue your apology."

Miss Starling merely smirked, revealing a perfect dimple.

"Gads!" Mrs. Starling bustled down the sidewalk. "Come along, darling. We don't have time for this nonsense. It's nearly teatime and we still need to stop in the dress shop."

The beautiful young woman cast a smug look over her shoulder as she trailed after her mother. "Until the Foley ball, ladies."

Olivia waited until Miss Starling was out of earshot. "Oh, she is horrid, is she not? I cannot believe that I used to admire her. I actually considered her a friend!" Olivia tossed her head in the same affected way Miss Starling had. "'Until the Foley ball, ladies.' Her snide manner makes me want to pluck each pretty curl right off her head."

"Olivia!" Daphne chided. But her heart wasn't really in it.

"You are quite right. We mustn't let her spoil our outing. Let's go into the shop and see what treasures we may find."

Daphne peered through the large plate-glass window of the milliner's and frowned. Almost every square foot of the shop floor seemed to be stuffed with hats, aprons, hosiery, jewelry, slippers, and more. Customers crowded around the main counter, clamoring for assistance. "Would you mind if I waited out here for a few minutes?" Olivia furrowed her brow, and Daphne rushed to explain. "It looks busy inside and I'm enjoying the fresh air. I'll join you shortly, once the crowd thins."

"Shall I stay with you?"

Daphne shook her head. She needed a moment to herself—a chance to think.

Olivia hesitated. "Well, if you're sure…"

"I am." Daphne forced a smile. "Go, find the trim to match James's eyes."

A dreamy look stole over Olivia's face. "They're the color of moss. But with flecks of gold. Very well, I'll see you inside. Don't linger too long."

"I won't." Daphne stood close to the stone front of the shop, in the shade of the building, and inhaled deeply. For days she'd been tortured by thoughts of what Hallows might do with the painting.

Now she knew.

She was surprised that he hadn't revealed her name. But perhaps he thought the portrait would bring a higher price if there was an air of mystery around it. She hadn't honestly thought Hallows intelligent enough to concoct such a clever scheme, but then, both times that she'd met him he'd been rather inebriated.

Strange as it seemed, there was some comfort in knowing what her fate would be. The painting would be publicly revealed. Mama would be humiliated and utterly aghast at Daphne's wanton behavior. Anabelle would be saddened and disappointed. Daphne would be forever shunned by polite society, and her dream of belonging to that shining, glittering world would be dashed to bits. It was all but done.

"Daphne." She felt Ben's deep voice like a breath over her skin. He stood before her, looking as surprised as she. And more handsome than any man had a right to be. "How are you?"

"Very well," she lied. "How is your leg?"

"I cannot complain." The weary look on his face said he was lying, too. He glanced quickly behind him and in a lower voice asked, "You've heard about the Foley ball?"

Daphne swallowed, determined to be brave. "Miss Starling was kind enough to inform me just now."

Ben made a face like he'd drunk curdled milk, and Daphne adored him for it. "I'm going to try to stop the auction."

"Please, don't do anything that could land you in Old Bailey or the Tower. I'm afraid there's little we can do. Hallows is angry with both of us. He's intent on destroying me, and he has the portrait, which is all the ammunition he needs."

"Don't give up, Daph."

Tears of frustration sprang to her eyes. What a fine thing for him to say. *He* was the one who'd given up. He'd given up on them. "Olivia is inside. I need to go."

"I'm sorry that everything got so complicated and messy."

"But that's the way life is. You taught me that, remember?"

"I remember."

She wiped her eyes and prepared to go inside, then halted. "Thank you for the books."

He shot her a puzzled look.

"Caro told me. Nothing goes on in that orphanage that she doesn't know about. That was a very kind thing to do."

He used the foot of his cane to push a pebble back and forth in front of his boots. "The little urchins need something productive to do. To keep them out of trouble."

"I think it's very nice that you care about them."

He opened his mouth as though he'd deny it, then clamped his lips shut.

Well. If he could change, so could she. "I'll be at the Foley ball."

His gaze snapped up and locked with hers. "Daphne, people can be incredibly cruel. If you think Miss Starling is bad—"

"I'll be there," she repeated. "And I hope you will be, too."

Chapter Twenty-Seven

Varnish: (1) A transparent, protective coating applied to a finished painting. (2) To give a flattering but often deceptive rendition of facts, as in, Try as she might, the beautiful debutante could not varnish the truth about her wanton past.

*B*en might not be a sleuth, but he had a good idea where to find Hallows that night—a gambling hell. The question was, which one?

He wasn't at the hell on Pickering Place or the one on Cleveland Row. But the third one—on Bennett Street—was the charm.

Ben had pressed Averill into service. Naturally, Averill had been curious as to why Ben was so determined to find the infamous painting, so Ben told him the truth: the portrait was of a woman he cared about, and he needed to intercept it before the Foley ball.

Averill's eyebrows had shot up, but he hadn't asked Ben to reveal the identity of the woman—that was the kind of friend he was.

He was also the perfect person to assist with this mission: the rare type of man who could blend in anywhere, as much at ease in a rough tavern near the docks as in the finest drawing rooms. This particular gambling establishment, with its marbled fireplace, ornate paneling, and rich carpet, gave the impression of elegance, but beneath the façade lay desperation and deceit.

Ben and Averill walked through the dimly lit parlor and found two vacant chairs at a table where players bet on the roll of the dice. After a few games, Ben was fairly certain the dice were loaded. He placed a wager, lost, and bet again. All the while, he scanned the room for Hallows's large blocklike head and beefy neck. As he was on the verge of telling Averill it was time to try another house, Hallows sauntered in. A couple of rough-looking men hunkered at his sides.

He had the confident swagger of a man who'd had a few drinks, but not so many that he was stumbling. Ben stayed out of his line of sight. If Hallows recognized him, he'd either run out of the building or beat Ben to a bloody pulp. Neither suited his purposes. He needed information.

Averill might be able to wheedle something out of him, but Hallows had met him briefly at the picnic. If Hallows remembered him, his guard would be up.

An overly rouged woman sidled up beside Ben and laid her bare hand on his shoulder. "Care for a drink? Or something else? She thrust her breasts forward, and they jiggled precariously above her tightly laced corset.

Ben weighed his options. The waitress was young, but her eyes were sharp and intelligent. "See the large man with blond hair who just sat at the faro table?"

"With the bruises around his eyes?"

Ben smiled. "The remnants of a broken nose. If you can get him talking, I'll match your monthly wage."

"What do you want him to talk about?"

"Gambling. Money. His assets."

"That's it?" She looked disappointed at the utter lack of challenge.

"Find out where in town he's staying."

"Shouldn't be too difficult." She pushed the sleeves of her blouse off her shoulders and adjusted her breasts so that they showed to their best advantage.

"I'm going to hang back and listen." Ben twirled his cane beneath the table, debating how much to tell her. He took in her businesslike demeanor and determined expression and decided she was nothing if not enterprising. "There's one more thing. He has a portrait of a young woman. I want to know where it is—but it's going to take a subtle approach. If he suspects you're fishing for information, you won't get anything out of him."

She raised a painted-on brow. "A portrait? It would be easier to find out the color of his drawers."

"If you get him to reveal the location of the painting, I'll triple your wage."

She glared at Hallows as if measuring him up. "Consider it done." She walked toward him, her hips swaying like a boat gliding over waves.

Beside Ben, Averill chuckled. "I almost feel sorry for Hallows."

Ben snorted. "Follow me. I want a good seat for this show."

They found a couple of chairs with a decent vantage point and positioned themselves so that Hallows couldn't see them. They listened as the young waitress presented him with a glass of whiskey. On the house.

She bided her time, perching herself on the arm of Hallows's chair, draping herself over his shoulder, and occasionally whispering in his ear. He gradually became less interested in faro and more interested in the woman.

Nodding toward the high stakes in the center of the table, she said, "Your pockets must be stuffed if you can play that deep."

"My pockets will be stuffed soon enough."

She sniffed, apparently unimpressed. "So, you're like all the other young gents who come in here, thinking they'll make a small fortune off of cards. I'll let you in on a little secret—it don't work that way."

Hallows scoffed. "I don't need winnings. I've got something more valuable than all the stakes in this place."

"No offense, milord, but I seriously doubt that. That gent in the corner just wagered his Thoroughbred."

"I've got a painting—a bloody work of art, it is."

"Is that so?" She examined her fingernails as though unimpressed. "What's so special about it?"

"It's a portrait of a lady. But she ain't acting like one, if you know what I mean."

"Ah. Showing her wares, is she? So you're going to blackmail her?"

"Not exactly. I'm going to auction it off. I'll be rich, and she'll be ruined."

Ben fisted his hand around the top of his cane. Averill placed a firm hand on his arm, warning him to keep a level head.

"Is she pretty?" The waitress wound a curl around her index finger.

Hallows snorted. "Beautiful."

"What have you got against her?"

"You ask a lot of questions."

"I can't help it if I'm curious." She snaked an arm around Hallows's neck and removed imaginary specks of dust from his jacket. "I'd love to see it."

"Why?"

She shrugged. "Maybe *I* could pose for a painting someday. Would you show it to me?" She flicked her tongue at Hallows's ear, and Ben decided right then and there that he was tripling her wages, no matter what. Licking Hallows went above and beyond the call of duty.

Hallows pulled her onto his lap. "Impossible."

The waitress pouted. "I thought it was your painting."

"It is, you little hoyden, but it's not in my possession."

She narrowed her eyes as if she didn't quite believe him. "Why not?"

"For one thing, it's too large to carry with me."

"Then we'll go to your flat," she cooed.

"The idea has promise." Hallows was practically drooling. "But the portrait is not there either."

"Oh." She sat up stiffly, as though miffed. "I can see you are toying with me."

He yanked her closer, and Ben's hackles rose. Hallows better not cross the line.

"I don't play games," he said through clenched teeth. "The painting is in a shop."

A shop? Ben tried to block out the sound of the conversations around him and leaned closer, intent on hearing every word.

"You're selling it?" the waitress asked.

"You're a bit dim-witted, aren't you? I've already explained I mean to auction it." Hallows spoke insultingly slowly. "It's in the shop getting a new frame. Costing me a small fortune, too—I went with the best in town. Mr. Leemore says the right frame can help a painting fetch a much higher price. He'd better be right—or he ain't getting paid." Hallows guffawed at the not-so-subtle irony.

Ben looked at Averill, who nodded. They had what they needed. Now they just had to extricate the waitress from Hallows's sweaty paws. Ben relished the challenge.

The woman glanced over at him and he inclined his head toward the back room.

"My boss is signaling for me. Let me see what he wants and tell him I'm leaving early tonight."

Hallows didn't release her at first. But then he hoisted her off his lap, pinching her bottom as she tried to catch her balance. Charming.

Averill casually followed the waitress as she weaved her way through the crowd, carrying in his pocket a handful of coins that Ben had counted out as payment.

He bided his time, waiting until Hallows became agitated, craning his thick neck and cracking his knuckles. Then Ben walked directly up to him.

"How's your luck tonight, Hallows?"

At the sound of his name, he turned. So did the thugs on either side of him. Just imagining what that rough-looking trio might do to him made Ben's leg ache.

"Foxburn," Hallows growled. He stood and puffed out his chest. To his friends—if the thugs could properly be labeled as such—he said, "This is the bloke who broke my nose."

They stood, too, forming a wall of solid muscle and low intelligence.

"I must admit it's looking better than when last I saw

you." Ben squinted. "Although, it does bend awkwardly to the right."

"Damn you, Foxburn."

Ben shrugged. "Don't fret. It's hardly noticeable with all the bruising."

Hallows fisted his hand. "Funny you should mention bruising."

A small circle of spectators had formed around them. Witnesses were good. Hallows would be less likely to commit murder.

"I didn't expect to see you here in town. Well, not outside of debtor's prison."

"I'm paying off my vowels soon. Of course, I'll have to part with the painting of your mistress."

"Watch yourself," Ben warned.

"It pains me to say good-bye to her. She's got those ripe breasts and an ass that you just want to squeeze. Many a time I've jacked off—"

Bam. Ben slammed his fist into Hallows's nose. Again. Blood splattered. Shouts went up all around him and before Ben knew what was happening, Averill grabbed his arm and hauled him out of the hell.

"Let's go!"

Averill continued to drag Ben toward his coach, which was parked around the corner, but the thugs were in pursuit and his leg was about to buckle. He drew up short, and when Averill looked at him questioningly, Ben said, "I'll take Eyebrow."

"Right. Square Chin is mine."

The words were barely out of Averill's mouth when the men were upon them, fists flying through the air. Ben dropped his cane and ducked below a punch, letting his left leg bear most of his weight. Eyebrow backed up three steps and lowered his shoulder as if he meant to charge and barrel Ben over. He stepped to the left and jabbed his attacker in the stomach. He moaned and leaned over, hands on his knees. Ben could tell the moment Eyebrow spotted the cane on the sidewalk but couldn't beat him to it. The brute snatched it up and tossed it from palm to palm, an evil look in his eyes as he circled Ben.

Behind him, Ben heard Averill scrapping with his opponent. Excellent pugilist that Averill was, he could have knocked him out cold at any time. But what was the fun in that?

"Need a hand, Foxburn?" his friend called out.

"No. But I'll need a drink after this. You almost done there?" He kept a wary eye on his own adversary.

"Aye. I find myself growing bored."

"No lack of excitement here." Eyebrow raised the cane and slashed it through the air in front of Ben, barely missing his neck. Before the oaf had the chance to regain his balance, Ben grabbed the end of the cane and swung it hard, toppling the man to the ground like an ancient tree. His head hit the sidewalk with a *thunk*, leaving him stunned.

Ben leaned over and wrested the cane—which happened to be one of his favorites—from his foe's grip and turned to find Averill waiting, a satisfied smile on his face. "Not a bad ending to the night."

"I must say I prefer it to the alternative—which would have likely involved me being bound and thrown into the Thames."

Much to the relief of Ben's coachman, they hurried into the cab.

Ben sank back into the squabs and stared out the window as he waited for his heartbeat to return to normal. Coming out on the winning end of a brawl wasn't the worst way to spend an evening, but it wasn't the best either.

He missed Daphne.

And he knew how he'd spend the rest of his night.

Drinking a brandy in his study as he stared at her portrait.

And contemplating his next move.

"Your ball gown is finished!" Anabelle waltzed into Daphne's bedchamber, the dress draped over her slender arm, triumphant.

At the ungodly hour of a quarter to seven in the morning.

Daphne flipped onto her stomach and closed her eyes. "Don't you ever sleep?"

"You *must* try it on." She pulled back Daphne's cozy counterpane, and cool air rushed over her neck and arms.

"At this very moment?" Daphne already knew the answer. Her sister was not a particularly patient person.

"It won't take long. I just want to see how the adjustment I made to the sleeves turned out. I would try it on myself, but I'm expanding daily."

Daphne hoisted herself up and took the dress from Anabelle. "Someone who didn't know would never guess you're with child."

"Well then they must be quite perplexed by the sudden and dramatic increase in the size of my breasts."

Daphne lifted the golden gown above her head.

"No." Belle reached for the dress. "Not over your nightgown. It'll ruin the lines."

Though the bedchamber was chilly in the early morning hours, Daphne indulged her sister and removed her night rail. It was the least she could do, especially since Anabelle had likely spent most of the night bent over the dress, scrutinizing every embellishment and seam. It was highly unusual for a duchess to behave in such a manner, of course, but old habits died hard. For a few weeks after they'd married, Owen objected to Anabelle doing any sort of work, which only resulted in her hiding her activities from him. Once he realized she was happier with a needle in her hand, he'd given in. It was difficult for him to refuse his wife anything.

Anabelle slipped the dress over Daphne's head; she shivered as the soft, cool silk cascaded down her arms, back, and legs. Even before Anabelle tightened the laces at the side, Daphne could tell that the fit was perfect. The neckline showed her breasts to advantage without being risqué, and a wide band of beadwork accentuated the narrowest part of her torso. The shimmering fabric flowed from the band all the way to the floor in rippling waves that shone like gold glinting in the sun.

Daphne ran her palms over her ribs and down her hips. For several moments, neither of them spoke. When at last Daphne found her tongue, she said, "It's gorgeous. You've outdone yourself."

Anabelle smiled smugly. "Yes. Yes, I have." She sighed, the sort of contented sigh one exhales after indulging in a positively decadent pastry.

"Thank you. It is the most beautiful thing I have ever owned."

"Well, then, you must start going out again, if only so that you'll have an opportunity to wear it. Perhaps there is a special gentleman you wish to impress," Anabelle fished.

Daphne shook her head. "No one special." Besides Ben. But he'd made himself clear—heartbreakingly so. There was no future for them.

"Well, then, you must wear it to a ball and wait for a special gentleman to come to *you*."

"There *is* a ball coming up, little more than a week from now."

Belle's face brightened. "And you shall go?"

"Yes." The Foley ball would likely be her last. She might as well look her best. And if the dress gave her the confidence to help her do what she must, so much the better.

"Why does it seem as though you're a million miles away?"

Daphne blinked. "Hmm?"

Anabelle took her hand and led her to a small sofa in the cozy sitting area before the dormant fireplace. "Daphne," she said, her pretty gray eyes shining behind her spectacles, "I haven't seen your smile—the real one that lights up an entire room—in days. You can tell me anything, you know. Did something happen at the house party?"

Daphne rested her forehead on the heels of her hands. She couldn't lie to Anabelle. "Yes, although it started much earlier than that if I'm honest with myself."

Anabelle sprang to her feet. "I *knew* it! You must tell me what happened. Is it a man?" She spun to face Daphne and narrowed her eyes. "Whoever he is, he shall rue the day. When Owen finds out about this, he shall—"

"No."

"What do you mean, 'no'? If someone has slighted you or upset you, the offense shall not go unpunished."

"It's not like that. I'm sorry I haven't been myself. The last thing I want is to cast a shadow over what should be a joyful time for you."

"Never fear." Anabelle smiled serenely. "Nothing could dampen my happiness. But we have always faced things together, and the fact that I'm married and starting a family doesn't change that. You were my family before and you always will be, even if I have a brood of a dozen children. Which I very well may, if Owen gets his way."

Daphne chuckled and put her arms around her sister. "I know that I may count on you. In fact, you are more reliable than the stars and moon. But I need to prove that I can count on myself. Lately, I've begun to see things more clearly—a little less naïvely. You've protected me from much unpleasantness over the years, but there are some things that a person must handle on her own. It's not that I don't want to confide in you. I do. But it's time for me to grow up, Belle. And I think that once I face the demons that haunt me, I'll be myself again. Maybe a little wiser and more worldly, but sure of who I am, and…happy."

Anabelle's lip trembled. "Have I told you lately how proud I am of you?"

Daphne shrugged and lifted the skirt of her dress. "You've been otherwise occupied. But some sentiments don't need to be spoken."

"I will let you deal with your troubles in your own way, then. But first you must endure one last lecture from your slightly older and infinitely wiser sister."

With a playful roll of her eyes, Daphne said, "I'm listening."

Belle grasped her shoulders lightly and gazed into her eyes with the fierceness of a lioness. "You have always been strong. When Mama was sick, you were a beacon, never surrendering to sorrow. When all I could see was darkness, you had the courage to sing. It's not because you don't *feel* the pain—it's because you overpower it and refuse to succumb. Your inner light is the source of your strength, and it's much more powerful than you realize."

Daphne swallowed past the knot in her throat. "Thank you. I don't know exactly how things will turn out, and I hope I don't disappoint you or Mama, but whatever happens, I'll know that I acted courageously."

Belle hugged her close. "When did you get to be so smart?"

Daphne breathed in the light flowery fragrance of her sister's hair. She couldn't tell her the truth—that when you feared losing the only man you could ever love, every other worry seemed trivial in comparison. If she lost Ben forever, none of it would really matter anyway. It was like worrying about a hangnail when you were dangling from a cliff.

"I'm going to respect your wish to handle your problem on your own, but if you change your mind, you know I am here."

"I know, Belle. You're my rock."

"Stop it." Anabelle wiped her eyes. "I have an excuse for being maudlin, whereas you—" She blanched. "Dear God, you're not..."

"No!" Daphne blushed furiously. As of a few days ago, she knew for a fact—she wasn't with child.

"Well. I have eliminated one possible source of your melancholy. If I keep guessing, I shall figure out what plagues you in no time at all."

"May I return to bed now?"

"Not while you're wearing that."

"Watch me." She flipped back the covers and raised her knee.

"Daphne!"

"I jest. I adore this gown, and your love is apparent in every small stitch, every shining bead. You're going to be a wonderful mother, you know."

"And you are going to be a wonderful aunt." Belle turned toward the door. "I'm going to leave you to rest now, but promise me you'll hang that gown the moment you take it off."

"Promise. And, Belle?"

"Yes?"

"Thanks for understanding."

She waved a hand dismissively. "It's what sisters are for. And if Owen asks you what I've been doing for the past two hours, *you* must be a good sister and say that I have been lazing abed all morning."

"Agreed."

After Belle left, Daphne walked to the vanity and looked at her reflection in the looking glass. Even with her hair in dishabille, the golden gown gave her an air of confidence. She looked regal and sure of herself.

On the inside, however, she was a cornered mouse— small and trembling. And utterly alone.

The letter from Thomas had arrived yesterday, but Ben had assumed it was simply another ball invitation and therefore didn't open it until breakfast that morning. He'd written to the artist shortly after the party at Vauxhall Gardens, hoping to discover who had commissioned the

English Beauty paintings...and then promptly forgotten about it.

But Thomas, it turned out, was back in town, and the letter gave the address where he was staying.

Ben now knew the location of the painting and of the artist. The question was, what should he do about it? His eggs sat untouched on his plate and his ham grew cold as he ran through several scenarios in his head.

He wanted to send word to Daphne immediately and tell her that he was going to fix everything. But somehow, he didn't think she'd appreciate that. She would have once, but she wasn't the same woman she'd been when he first met her. While speaking to her outside the milliner's shop, he'd seen the resolve in her eyes. She was determined to face her fears on her own.

And he should probably let her.

But surely she wouldn't mind a *little* help.

"Flemings," he bellowed.

The butler shuffled into the dining room. "My lord?"

"I need the coach readied."

Ben was curious to meet the man who had captured Daphne's essence so beautifully. And since Thomas and Daphne had grown up as friends, perhaps he'd be able to predict Daphne's reaction to his scheme—a scheme that was admittedly harebrained. But maybe just harebrained enough to work.

A scant hour later, Ben sat on a wooden chair in a studio across from the artist. Thomas's shirt was untucked and smeared with shades of brown and blue; his sleeves were rolled up to his elbows. Dark smudges above his hollow cheeks suggested he'd been up painting for several hours and that he may have forgotten to eat the previous day. He stared at Ben's cane for several moments and then at his leg. Such a bold perusal from anyone else might have been offensive, but Thomas merely seemed to be studying a subject—putting together all the pieces in order to understand the whole.

Ben took in the ramshackle furnishings, the dust that covered everything but Thomas's easel, and the rat droppings in the corner. The artist seemed oblivious to the squalor.

"Thank you for replying to my inquiry," Ben said. "I have one of the paintings—of Daphne...er, Miss Honeycote."

Thomas narrowed his eyes. "How do you know her? Does she know you're here?"

Impressed by his show of loyalty, Ben decided to answer truthfully, if not fully. "I met her at a dinner party and we became friends. She doesn't know I'm here. In fact, I doubt she knows that you're back from your tour."

He shrugged apologetically. "I've been busy with my painting."

"Well, you certainly haven't been busy cleaning."

Thomas scanned the room like he was seeing it for the first time. "We all have our priorities, Lord Foxburn."

"Indeed. I've already learned that your patron is Lord Charlton. Did you know he's been ill?"

"Nothing serious, I hope?"

"He showed small signs of improvement the last time I saw him." The memory of that day, replete with the stinging sensation of Hallows's boot heel wedged into his flesh, made the muscles of his leg twinge.

"It seems as though you have the answers you originally sought. Forgive me for asking a direct question, but what are you doing here?"

"Daphne is in trouble."

Thomas sat up straighter and tensed. "How so?"

"One of the paintings is about to be sold at auction. When it's revealed in public, her reputation will be destroyed."

"I never thought she would be moving about in polite society. I never thought I would either."

Ben snorted. "You're not. This is about Daphne. Do you want to help her?"

"Of course I do. Just tell me how."

He stroked the stubble he hadn't bothered to shave that morning. "For now, you can simply enlighten me on a couple of painting techniques. The real fun begins tonight—after midnight."

Thomas arched a brow.

"And you're going to need your brushes."

Ben's plans were coming together nicely—a refreshing change from his normal luck. There was, however, one more piece—or rather, one more *person*—he needed to put in place. After returning from the visit with Thomas, Ben sat in his study, debating who would be the right person for the assignment.

It had to be a woman. Someone who was clever, resourceful, and courageous, in a quiet sort of way. Most of all, he needed someone who was good at keeping secrets.

The majority of women he knew were fond of gossip and talking, all except for—

But of *course*. He knew the perfect candidate. She was so shy that he'd almost overlooked her, but he suspected that beneath her reserved demeanor she was more courageous than she let on.

He'd know soon enough.

He withdrew a piece of paper from his desk drawer, dipped the nib of his pen in the ink jar, and hastily scrawled a note to Lady Rose Sherbourne.

In the quietest part of the night, that magical hour or two after the carousers had gone to bed but before even the most industrious souls had awoken, three cloaked figures skulked down Fleet Street. They disappeared into an alley not far from a quaint but highly respected framing shop. If a door was kicked in, no one was there to hear it. And if a light shone from the back room of the little shop, no one was around to see it. The trio stayed as long as they dared and left just as quietly as they had come.

When Mr. Leemore arrived at his shop that morning, he scratched his head over the unlocked door, but a quick glance around the shop revealed nothing was amiss. His cash drawer was secure; his inventory was undisturbed. He would speak to his son about being more careful when closing up. As he donned his work apron, Mr. Leemore sniffed the air. Odd. The smell of oil paints was more pungent than usual today. Must be the humid London weather.

Chapter Twenty-Eight

The evening had arrived.

The Foley ball was by far the most anticipated event of the season and—much to Daphne's chagrin—promised to be huge crush. As she went through the motions of readying herself for the ball, she found it surprisingly easy to forget that she was counting down the minutes until her ruin.

She'd tried to anticipate what she'd feel like the moment the painting was unveiled but couldn't seem to summon the necessary depth of shame and regret. She just couldn't. It was like trying to imagine being shot in the chest. One *knew* it would not be good, but there was no way of knowing what kind of pain it would be or how well one would endure it.

When finally she made her way downstairs to leave, she actually felt a sense of relief, on at least two counts. First, she was able to walk. She'd feared that when the time came, her body would refuse to obey her mind and she'd be frozen. She'd imagined Olivia and Rose carrying her under her stiff elbows and propping her up next to the punch table in the Foley ballroom. Apparently, it wouldn't come to that.

Second, the waiting was over. Whatever was about to happen, at least it would be done with. The aftermath was bound to be messy and ugly . . . and probably lonely. But at least the cleanup could begin.

Since everyone in her household planned to attend, Owen agreed two coaches were needed to transport them the short distance to the Foley residence. Owen, Anabelle, and Mama rode in one; Daphne, Olivia, and Rose rode in the other.

Daphne stared out the window, mentally calculating the minutes that remained before she would be the object of disdain and censure.

One hundred thirty-nine minutes, at least. She reminded herself to breathe and then congratulated herself on accomplishing that small feat.

"Thank goodness Owen let us take a second coach. Had we squeezed ourselves into one, my dress would have had more wrinkles than all our great-aunts combined. Besides," Olivia said, "this way I don't have to endure my brother's scowls."

"He's not scowling at *you*," Rose corrected. "He's scowling at your neckline."

Olivia grinned and thrust her décolletage forward. "It *is* rather daring. James will surely notice these."

"He will notice *you*," Rose said sincerely, "and that would be true with or without the daring gown. You look beautiful, as does Daphne."

Daphne attempted a smile, but her face felt numb. At

least it was fairly dark inside the cab. A couple of lanterns hanging outside the coach allowed them to see outlines and shadows but not much more. Daphne contemplated the chances of her being permitted to stay in the dark coach for the remainder of the evening.

Despite Rose's kind words, Daphne didn't *feel* beautiful. She clenched her teeth to keep them from chattering. Likewise, she crossed her arms to still their trembling. She'd eaten next to nothing that day, and her tea sloshed about in her stomach. Her palms were clammy and a droplet of perspiration trickled between her breasts.

No, *beautiful* was not the word to describe how she felt.

"Would you mind if I opened a window?" she asked, already fumbling with the latch.

Rose leaned across to help. "Are you feeling all right?"

"Just a bit nervous," Daphne confessed. "It's been some time since I've been to a ball."

Olivia clapped her hands. "You both know, of course, who *I'm* excited to see this evening. It's only fair that you two should reveal which gentlemen you are most eager to see."

An alarmed look crossed Rose's face and she shot a sympathetic look at Daphne. "No one in particular. This window is awfully stubborn, is it not?"

Daphne and Rose continued to make a great show of pushing and pulling at the small pane until their coach finally joined the queue that had formed in front of Foley House. As they waited their turn to disembark, Olivia abandoned her line of questioning and began a running commentary on the gowns worn by the women filing up the walk to the front door.

Though Daphne tried very hard to listen to Olivia's opinion on epaulets, she was distracted. What were the chances of Lord Foley's house catching fire and of the ball being canceled? If the portrait went up in flames, her most immediate problem would be solved. Of course, she wouldn't want anyone to be harmed in the blaze. Although, she would not shed a tear if Miss Starling's tresses were singed a little. Just enough to prevent her from tossing her curls over her shoulder in the way that made Daphne dig her fingernails into the heels of her hands.

A jab in Daphne's side snapped her attention back to the grim reality that no inferno was forthcoming.

"You have the best seat for viewing," Olivia said, "and you don't even appreciate it."

"Would you like to switch?"

Olivia frowned. She was probably debating whether shuffling seats was likely to result in a tear. "No. Just tell me about Lady Bonneville's gown—it's sparkling, if I'm not mistaken.

Daphne pressed her forehead to the window. The viscountess was, in fact, surprisingly incandescent. "She must have crystals sewn onto her dress. They're twinkling in the moonlight and catching the light streaming from Lord Foley's windows." Such illumination must take at least a hundred candles. Perhaps not all hope was lost—a small fire was hardly out of the question.

"Ah, here we are at last," said Olivia. "Rose, you go first."

Now that they were alighting from the coach, Daphne's nerves were drawn as tightly as her corset. The smart new-heeled slippers she'd worn felt as heavy as stone. If

Olivia hadn't been behind her, practically pushing her out of the coach, she might have ridden it straight back home.

She, Olivia, and Rose lingered on the walk as the coach carrying Mama, Anabelle, and Owen pulled up and the passengers disembarked. Daphne concentrated on keeping her knees locked and her legs steady. Both coaches rolled away.

There was no going back now.

Anabelle's gaze swept over her, from the delicate sleeves of her amber gown all the way to the flounced hem. "It looks even better than I'd hoped," she whispered in Daphne's ear. "I am a genius."

Daphne forced a smile. "You look beautiful."

"An hour ago I was letting out this gown. I think that must be a sign that the babe's doing well—don't you?"

"Absolutely." She squeezed her arm. Even older sisters needed to be reassured sometimes.

"Are you ready?" From behind her spectacles, Anabelle's gray eyes searched Daphne's face.

Was she?

Was she ready to be ostracized? Ready to speak her mind, and—even more frightening—her heart?

"Ready."

Arm in arm with Belle, she walked into Lord Foley's elegant foyer and followed the meandering stream of guests into the ballroom.

The room, already crowded, buzzed with excitement. The orchestra tuned their instruments, and each discordant note sent a chill down her spine. Anabelle began talking with a lady who was also increasing, and Daphne looked around. At the end of the room opposite the doors through which they'd entered loomed a large, ornate easel. It stood on a rectangular platform. The painting itself was covered, draped in decadent crimson silk brocade.

Daphne swallowed. Drawn to the easel like a sailor lured by sirens to rocky crags, she drifted closer.

"Where are you going?" Olivia scurried to her side. "You walked right past Lady Worsham."

"I'm sorry. I didn't mean to be rude. I just want to see it." She gestured toward the painting.

"Everyone does. It's not to be unveiled until midnight."

"I know." She weaved her way through the crowd, intent on getting as close as she could.

"Wait, I'll go with you," Olivia cried.

The nearer Daphne got to the easel, the thicker the crowd. Footmen stood guard on either side of the painting, their green livery clashing awfully with the fringed red silk covering the painting. Finally, she was as close as she could get without stepping onto the platform. The painting appeared larger than she remembered. Of course, she had never seen it framed. She'd only really looked at it once, after Thomas had declared it finished.

In the last few days, she'd tried to convince herself that perhaps it wasn't so scandalous after all. That it had only *seemed* risqué because she'd been such an innocent at the time. But now that she stood in front of the painting, she could see that it was almost life-sized. Elevated as it was, every detail of her form would be scrutinized.

Dear God.

Maybe she should have prepared Mama and Belle for what was about to take place, warned them of the impending shame. But no, she couldn't have. They would have insisted on shielding her and never would have permitted her to come. And if she hadn't come, she wouldn't have had the chance to do what she needed to.

What she *would* do.

Olivia clucked her tongue. "I feel sorry for the woman. Do you think she's here tonight?"

Daphne's mouth went dry. "She'd have to be very bold to come. Or very stupid."

"I, for one, hope she's here."

"Why?"

Olivia shrugged. "It would make tonight utterly unforgettable."

"I don't think you'll be disappointed."

As they crossed the ballroom to rejoin the rest of their party, Daphne searched for Ben's brown, closely shorn curls. He'd said he'd be here, but his leg could be paining him, or he could have changed his mind. She couldn't really blame him for wanting to avoid the entire scene.

She refused champagne offered by a passing waiter— she needed to keep her wits about her. Olivia took a glass, however, which gave her older brother something besides her neckline to frown about.

Heavens. If Owen was dismayed by Olivia's behavior, what on earth would he think of Daphne after the painting was unveiled? He might forbid her to see his and Anabelle's baby for fear that she'd be a bad influence. A lump lodged in her throat. She couldn't imagine a steeper price.

Just as Daphne and Olivia reached Mama and the others, a shrill voice called out, "Out of the way! These young people have no manners, no respect for their elders."

"Good evening, Lady Bonneville," said Rose.

The white-haired viscountess's lorgnette snapped up with the precision of a soldier raising his bayonet. Her sharp eyes took in Rose, Olivia, Owen, Anabelle, Mama, and Daphne in turn. To Mama, she said, "Marion, you would do well to join me over by the potted palms. It appears Lord Foley has invited all of England to witness the spectacle of the portrait. Personally, I do not understand the fascination. You'd think the *ton* had never seen Aphrodite's breasts or Apollo's dangling bits."

"Henrietta!" Mama cried.

"What? I speak the truth. If you remain here, you run the risk of being trampled by young bucks who have partaken of too many spirits. Come with me. We shall have a better view of the evening's festivities from the gallery anyway." She grabbed Mama's wrist and pulled her along before halting and spinning to face them with impressive agility.

"Where is Lord Foxburn?" she demanded.

Daphne could have kissed the viscountess for asking the question she hadn't dared.

Owen shrugged. "I saw him earlier today. He mentioned that he'd be here. However, he looked rather preoccupied. A bit tired, too."

Daphne nibbled her bottom lip. His leg must be hurting. She wished she could go to him, as she had before. Only to massage his leg or apply a poultice. The mere memory of her visit to his bedchamber made her cheeks flame—a fact that did not go unnoticed by Lady Bonneville.

"Good Lord, gel," she said with obvious distaste. "You needn't pine over him so. If Foxburn said he'd be here, he will. Something tells me that nothing could keep him away from this particular ball." Her gaze traveled the length of Daphne's gown, all the way down to her slippers.

To Anabelle, she said, "This is one of yours?" She inclined her head toward the golden dress.

Anabelle smiled mysteriously.

"It's good. Very good." The viscountess pursed her lips as if she were considering the possibility of hiring the duchess to make a gown for her. If anyone would have the gall to ask, it would be Lady Bonneville. "Come, Marion. Let's leave the young folk to their own devices. They'll have more fun without us, and we shall have infinitely more fun without them."

"Well, if you're sure," Mama waffled. But she really had no choice. Lady Bonneville was quite adamant.

The orchestra began to play.

Guests continued to file in. Mr. Averill arrived, which was a great relief to Olivia and also to Daphne and Rose, who no longer had to endure Olivia's constant angst over his whereabouts.

And still, there was no sign of Ben.

Daphne danced with Lord Biltmore and Mr. Edland.

She deftly avoided Miss Starling on the way to the ladies' retiring room and congratulated herself on that small triumph. The last thing she needed this evening was an ugly confrontation with the beautiful miss.

Once, the sight of a fair-haired, heavy-set man made her suck in her breath. From the back he looked exactly like Mr. Hallows, but he turned out to be a portly, older gent. It may have been too much to hope that Mr. Hallows would stay away from the ball, but she hoped nonetheless. She comforted herself with the knowledge that his brutish behavior wouldn't be tolerated here. As long as she was not alone with him, she would be safe. Physically, at least.

Time continued to slip away. She was acutely aware

of the grandfather clock behind the refreshment tables. It should have been difficult to hear the chimes over the conversation and music, but her ears seemed perfectly attuned to their mournful sound.

With each minute that passed, the chances of Ben showing grew slighter.

And the hour of her ruin drew closer.

By a quarter to midnight, the orchestra ceased their playing, and no one made any pretense of small talk. The crowd converged around the platform holding the easel and painting. Voices hushed and anticipation filled the air like the smoke from the beeswax candles in the chandeliers overhead.

This very moment was the one she'd dreaded for weeks. For longer, actually. She'd known that a day of reckoning would come—she may not have known when or where, but she had known it was inevitable.

She took deep, even breaths and marveled at the steadiness of her hands. Mama sat on the far side of the room with Lady Bonneville, listening raptly while the viscountess appeared to expound on some topic with great vehemence. She waved her lorgnette for added emphasis.

Anabelle stood on the edge of the crowd, with Owen at her side. She seemed to view the unveiling with some distaste, like she hated to stand by and watch while some poor chit was thrown to the lions. And yet, there was no way she could *not* watch. Daphne caught her sister's eye and held it as she smiled. She wanted to apologize to Anabelle for what was about to happen, but mostly she wanted to let her know that she didn't need to worry about her anymore.

No matter what happened, she would be all right. Heartbroken, but all right.

As though she could read Daphne's thoughts, Anabelle opened her mouth and started forward.

Oh no. She couldn't let Belle talk her out of what she must do. She waved her away and began working her way to the front of the crowd.

Olivia, who had been standing next to her, must have suddenly realized that she'd left. "Daph!" she called. Daphne looked back as Olivia began to shoulder her way through the solid ring of spectators. Her unladylike outburst caused a couple of nearby matrons to scowl. Rose reached out and placed a hand on Olivia's arm—as if she sensed Daphne needed to do this alone.

And she did. The farther she was from her family, the better. Her shame should not be theirs.

It took several minutes and all the feminine charm she possessed to make her way to the front of the crowd, directly in front of the easel. A few guests looked at her curiously, then shrugged. Everyone was here for the same reason. To witness the ruin of the English Beauty.

She'd barely caught her breath when the grandfather clock began bonging.

At last, the wait was over.

Chapter Twenty-Nine

Focal Point: (1) The element of a painting that draws the viewer's eye; the primary subject. (2) An object, such as a scandalous portrait, that has captured both the attention and fascination of the ton.

Daphne felt a pang in her chest. Ben had not shown after all.

That didn't change things, however. When it came right down to it, she wasn't doing this for him.

She was doing it for herself.

Lord Foley sauntered into the ballroom through a side door, hard to miss in his bright green coat. Hallows trailed behind him.

Daphne gulped. She'd wanted this unveiling to happen on her own terms, but so many aspects of the evening were beyond her control. She just had to proceed and hope that she had the opportunity to say her piece.

Lord Foley climbed onto the platform. Hallows eyed the makeshift structure doubtfully and kept his large feet planted on the floor in front of it.

"Welcome, ladies and gentlemen," Lord Foley began. "At last, the time has arrived. For weeks you have been wondering about the identity of the English Beauty, as have I. The only one who has known, up until now, is my young friend, Mr. Hallows." He presented the brute with a flourish. Hallows shifted his weight nervously. Although he wore a russet-colored jacket and clean white cravat, he sweated, clearly uncomfortable in the formal setting.

Lord Foley droned on. "His father commissioned this painting and one other—whose whereabouts are unknown. I am assured that while this portrait is an unparalleled work of art, it is also quite scandalous."

Several gasps could be heard throughout the ballroom. As if they didn't already know. Really, the hypocrisy of some people bordered on ridiculous.

"For this reason," Lord Foley continued, "I would advise ladies to turn their heads before the painting is revealed. The last thing I would wish to do is offend any of my esteemed guests."

Several ladies snapped their fans open and shielded their faces from the impending assault on their delicate sensibilities. Most continued to peer over the tops.

"I am pleased to inform you that Mr. Hallows has agreed to sell this masterpiece to the highest bidder. While I have not yet laid eyes upon it myself, I am assured that it would be the crown jewel of any collection. If the young woman in the portrait is half as lovely as Mr. Hallows says she is, I may end up bidding on it myself." Lord Foley paused while several of the gentlemen chuckled at the irony. Daphne barely refrained from rolling her eyes.

"Before I unveil our scandalous miss, there is one more detail that I must impart. The English Beauty is said to be a member of the *ton*, and it is entirely possible that she is *here* tonight. I daresay, there are few souls who aren't." He paused and soaked up the smattering of laughter.

Daphne, who had been staring at the toes of her slippers, looked up and found Mr. Hallows looking directly at her, a triumphant leer on his face. She raised her chin and stared back. He might think he held all the cards—she supposed he did, for now. But in a few minutes, whatever power he held over her would be gone. She was done with hiding. Done with shame.

"Well, then," Lord Foley announced, "I shan't keep you in suspense any longer." He turned toward the easel and reached for the red satin.

"Wait." Daphne's heartbeat pounded in her ears. Lord Foley froze. The ladies and gentlemen who'd been crowded against her a moment before stepped back as though they wanted to distance themselves from whatever spectacle was about to occur. Probably a prudent decision on their parts.

Lord Foley narrowed his eyes and leaned forward like Anabelle did when she wasn't wearing spectacles. "Miss Honeycote? This is not an opportune time for conversation. The painting is about to be revealed."

"I know." Her voice cracked on the second word, so she tried again. Louder. "I know. I have something to say about it. Something I believe your guests will find rather interesting."

"By all means, then." Lord Foley waved her closer, a sour look on his face. He didn't seem pleased about sharing the spotlight.

Hallows bristled at the interruption. Out of one side of his mouth he said, "Why are you letting her up there?"

Lord Foley scowled at him. "Miss Honeycote wishes to say something. We'll get to the auction momentarily."

"You shouldn't trust her," Hallows said, none too softly. Several guests gasped.

"That is a bold assertion." Lord Foley's position on the platform allowed him to look down his nose at Hallows even though the man was nearly a head taller. "Why would you say such a thing?"

Hallows pointed a sausage-like finger at Daphne. "She's the one in the painting."

Daphne swallowed as, all around her, mouths gaped wide. "Mr. Hallows speaks the truth," she said.

Toward the back of the gathering, an older gentleman called, "What did she say?"

She cleared her throat and spoke in a voice that carried throughout the room. "I posed for the painting. And one other. They're not exactly lewd"—she paused and cast a nervous glance at Lady Bonneville—"although I suppose that would depend on one's definition of the word."

"If it's not lewd," Hallows interjected, "what would you call it?"

It was a fair question. "Daring . . . and possibly improper. Scandalous in some circles . . . such as this one."

On the far side of the room, Daphne spied Owen attempting to maneuver his way toward her. He no doubt intended to come to her aid—a gallant gesture, and she adored him for it, but she didn't need to be rescued. Perhaps it was more accurate to say she didn't *wish* to be rescued. When he looked up, she caught his eye, smiled, and gave a firm shake of her head. He went still and nodded in understanding. She loved him even more for that.

"The painting belongs to Lord Charlton, Mr. Hallows's father," she said.

"It's mine. My father gave it to me. I can do what I like with it." Hallows took a menacing step toward her but then retreated as if he'd belatedly remembered that she wasn't a waitress in a tavern but a lady in a ballroom.

"I am not here to challenge your right to sell the portrait. I only want to explain myself before it is revealed." The crowd was so silent that she could hear her own breathing. She swallowed and closed her eyes briefly— just long enough to remember the three points she needed to make.

"The first thing you must know is that no one in my family—not my dear mother nor my lovely sister—knew anything about this painting. Neither did any of my friends, save the artist. The blame lies entirely with me. So, if anyone here objects to my behavior—and I suspect many of you will—please, don't censure my family or friends. I posed for the portrait on my own and was fully aware of the risk to my reputation."

A few of the older matrons pursed their lips. Daphne scanned the room and found Mama near the potted palms looking sad and confused. Lady Bonneville wrapped a plump arm around her shoulder and stared back at Daphne with a bemused expression. Clearly, it was going to take a bit more than her mortifying confession to impress the viscountess.

Well. Daphne wasn't done yet.

"The second thing I need to say is that posing for the paintings was my *choice*. I wasn't forced in any way. I had my reasons, of course, and while they aren't relevant, I freely admit that I'd sacrifice my good name one thousand times over if it would save someone I cared about. You may be shocked to learn that I'm not especially embarrassed about my behavior. I suppose some of you will label me a tart or a lightskirt or…worse. However, I would rather be all of those things than a mean-spirited person—that is, someone who takes pleasure at the misfortune of others." Daphne endeavored not to stare at Miss Starling but couldn't help but notice that her face had turned a ghastly shade of red. "I am not ashamed of the paintings themselves. My only regret is that my actions may end up causing my loved ones pain and humiliation. For that, I'm truly sorry."

Daphne locked eyes with Belle. Her sister looked utterly serene and…proud. That alone gave her the strength to continue.

Because the hardest part was still to come.

She paused, trying to sort through her mishmash of emotions and somehow arrange words into sentences that would begin to explain them.

"She's stalling," Hallows muttered to Lord Foley. "How long are you going to let her go on?"

"For as long as she wishes." Lord Foley's tone was icy. After issuing Hallows a scathing glare, he nodded at her encouragingly.

She could do this. She would pretend that Ben was there, challenging her to finish what she'd started. She drew in a long, deep breath of air. "The last thing I must confess is that this experience, although painful at times, taught me important lessons. A friend helped me to see that it's better to do the right thing than to give the *appearance* of doing the right thing. And he showed me that I cannot run from pain or other unpleasant facts of life. Not for long, anyway. No matter what lies in store for me, I will be forever grateful to him."

Hallows snorted impatiently. "Is that all?"

Lord Foley stepped between him and Daphne. "Miss Honeycote, when I agreed to let Mr. Hallows auction off his painting—or rather his father's painting—I had no inkling of the circumstances." He cast a nervous glance at her brother-in-law, Owen, who looked ready to throttle someone. Anyone. Lord Foley loosened his cravat with an index finger. "All things considered, I think it best to postpone the sale of the portrait."

"I will leave that decision to you and Mr. Hallows," Daphne said, "but with regards to the painting, I must insist that it be revealed. Tonight."

Before she could lose her nerve, she reached over, grabbed a fistful of red silk, and snatched the cover off the painting. It whooshed through the air, snapping like a whip, before it hovered momentarily and floated to the ground, billowing around her feet.

It was done.

And it could never be undone.

The faces before her were an odd mix—powdered, wrinkled, and spectacled. But they all stared raptly at the painting behind her.

She held her chin high, refusing to cower under their disapproval...which would surely manifest itself once they got over the shock of seeing her in a night-gown that was nearly transparent. Although curious to see her image, she dared not turn and look at the painting. If she did, she was sure to blush or blabber or burst into tears.

"What the devil did you do to it?" Hallows roughly

grabbed the frame on both sides and turned the entire easel toward him for a better look. "It's ruined!"

Daphne blinked. Odd. Unless she was mistaken, Hallows was speaking to her. And beneath his anger there was a hint of fear. As if she were some sort of sorceress who could ruin a painting from afar. "I don't understand."

Lord Foley pried Hallows's hands off the gilded frame and repositioned the easel so it faced the crowd.

And Daphne looked.

The portrait was much as she remembered. She stood before a looking glass, a pensive expression on her face. However, there was one significant difference. Instead of the filmy nightgown, she wore a golden ball gown. An exact replica of the one she was currently wearing. The artist had even captured the distinctly unique embroidery around the hem.

She shook her head, trying to reconcile her memories with the painting standing before her. This was the first night she'd worn the dress. And Thomas had painted it well over a year ago. How was it possible?

Lady Bonneville rose from her throne—er, chair—and walked through the crowd like a swan gliding through still water. She stood directly before the platform, which she eyed with undisguised animosity, and held out a gloved arm so that Lord Foley could help her up. Once she'd conquered the step and caught her breath, she raised her lorgnette. Slowly. And examined the painting for a full minute.

It was understood, of course, that the viscountess would take all the time she needed to inspect the portrait and that every other soul in the room would patiently wait for her verdict.

But Daphne's mind reeled. The dress was new. The painting was old. Someone had added to it. And she could guess who.

Ben.

Well, not *him*, per se, because she didn't think painting was among his talents. But there was little doubt that he was the person behind it. He'd found a way to save her from ruin.

His plan almost worked, too.

It was a pity that she couldn't turn back the hands of the grandfather clock to before the rather incriminating monologue she'd just recited.

Lady Bonneville turned with the grace of a woman half her age and cleared her throat with the authority of a woman exactly her age. "This portrait," she proclaimed, "is quite lovely. While I cannot pretend to approve of the indelicate nature of Miss Honeycote's gaze"—her nostrils flared slightly as she motioned to Daphne—"I do not think it will be necessary to exile her. Yet." With that, the viscountess held out her arms and waited for Lord Foley and Owen to escort her back to the potted palms and the comfort of her red tufted footstool.

"You destroyed it," Hallows accused. "To save your reputation. You had no right to—"

Daphne took a step back and would have tumbled off the platform had she not been swept up in a pair of strong arms.

Ben set her on the floor and she spun around to face him. His casual smile and icy blue eyes made her knees go weak.

"You're late," she whispered.

He shrugged guiltily.

"Let me guess. You were delayed by a matter of grave importance."

"Naturally."

"Your valet couldn't tie your neckcloth to your satisfaction?"

"Have you been spying on me?"

She gave him an overly sweet smile. "I have better things to do, my lord."

"I heard what you said."

She felt herself flush. "Which part?"

"The entire soliloquy," he teased. But then his face grew serious. "It was one of the bravest acts I've ever seen. I'm very proud of you, Daph."

A warm glow within curled her toes. "Thank you. I'm pretty proud of me, too."

Up on the platform, Hallows paced, muttering curses under his breath. "I should call the authorities. You had no right to tamper with the portrait."

Ben rolled his eyes. "Mind if I handle this?"

"Not at all." As he headed toward Hallows, she placed a hand on Ben's sleeve and whispered in his ear, "You don't plan to fight him here, do you?"

"No. I'm going to negotiate with him. I *want* that painting."

The utterly determined, possessive note in his voice sent a delicious shiver down her spine.

He joined Lord Foley and Hallows on the platform, and Hallows's face darkened like a thundercloud. He grunted and jabbed his finger at the portrait. Ben's face gave away little—if she didn't know better, she'd have thought he was bored. Lord Foley appeared to play the part of the arbitrator, facilitating the back-and-forth and trying desperately to keep the exchange civil.

Without Ben by her side, Daphne was suddenly bereft. Despite Lady Bonneville's pronouncement, no one seemed quite sure what the appropriate reaction was. Everyone had been prepared for a scandal, and the apparent lack of one was hugely disappointing.

Miss Starling may have been the most disappointed of all. She startled Daphne, who was straining to hear snippets of Ben's conversation, when she approached from behind and hissed in her ear, "You and your sister have an uncanny ability to narrowly escape the clutches of disgrace. You wouldn't be witches, would you?"

Daphne turned and blinked innocently. "If I were, you'd be a toad."

Miss Starling gasped and then smiled with reluctant admiration. "Touché, Miss Honeycote. Under different circumstances, we might have been friends." She drifted back into the crowd, allowing Daphne to turn her attention back to the platform.

Lord Foley raised a palm in the air to quiet the murmurs that bounced restlessly around the ballroom. "I know that many of you attended in the hopes of participating in the auction of this lovely painting. And while tonight's events have been somewhat unexpected, you shall not be disappointed. This portrait would be a lovely addition to any collection. And the bidding shall start...now."

A few shouts went out. Daphne blinked. She hadn't expected to be standing there as gentlemen bid on her portrait. Although it was no longer scandalous, she still felt a bit like a horse at Tattersall's.

The pace of the bidding increased. Certain gentlemen received scathing looks from their wives.

Lord Waldron seemed determined to outbid every

other person there, hushing the competition with a staggering offer of four thousand pounds.

Lord Foley raised his eyebrows. "Going once, going twice—"

"Five thousand!" Lady Bonneville raised her lorgnette in the air like a general charging into battle.

Lord Waldron bowed out gracefully—a wise move, considering his opponent.

All things considered, it was a fitting end to the evening. Nothing had gone quite as Daphne expected, but at least no one had suggested she should be burned at the stake. Yet. Come to think of it, she'd do well to avoid Miss Starling for the rest of the evening.

It looked like Daphne had been very lucky as far as the portrait was concerned.

Whether her luck would extend to Ben remained to be seen.

"Lady Bonneville has bid five thousand pounds. Going once, going twice—"

"Ten thousand." Ben tossed his cane in the air and caught it in one hand.

Lord Foley's jaw dropped, as did every other person's in the room who'd heard the bid. Daphne could barely breathe.

Hallows's eyes went wide, as though he couldn't believe his good fortune. The sum would likely pay off his vowels and allow him to return to a life of gambling and pleasure seeking.

"There is one caveat," Ben said. "I cannot imagine that you would have a problem with it, Mr. Hallows, given the extremely generous offer I am making."

Hallows's eyes narrowed. "We'll see. What's the catch, Foxburn?"

"Half of the money will go directly to the charity of Miss Honeycote's choosing."

"Half?" Hallows was aghast.

"Half."

"I'd rather accept Lady Bonneville's offer."

"I withdraw it," she said.

"Mr. Hallows," Lord Foley said under his breath, "the alternative to Lord Foxburn's offer is debtor's prison. I suggest you accept his terms. Gratefully."

"Fine."

"Foxburn, it looks like you are now the owner of the infamous English Beauty. Er, of the portrait, that is."

The crowd burst into applause.

Ben made an exaggerated bow and stepped off the platform, wearing a knee-weakening smile as he sauntered toward her.

"I told you I'd get it."

"Ten thousand pounds is a lot of money."

"It is. Do you think I might at least have a dance with the real English Beauty?"

"A dance?"

"A small favor to ask after ten thousand pounds."

Daphne frowned. "It's not that. I...I just assumed you would abhor dancing."

"Under normal circumstances, I avoid it like the plague. But it's different with you. Waltz with me."

"I haven't received my vouchers yet. I don't have permission."

"You just stood up in front of God, Lady Bonneville, and everyone and courted scandal. What's one little waltz?"

Daphne cast a glance at Miss Starling, who was

watching her much like a hawk tracking a mouse. She thought about it a moment and shrugged. "I'd be delighted to dance with you, Lord Foxburn. However, do you think we might wait until the orchestra resumes?"

"And here I thought you were no longer a slave to convention."

"Give me time," Daphne said with a saucy smile. "I grow more wanton by the day."

Chapter Thirty

The moment the music began, Ben handed his cane to Hugh, pulled Daphne into his arms, and whirled her onto the dance floor. If he didn't move as fluidly or as quickly as the other men, Daphne didn't seem to mind. They stayed on the periphery where there weren't as many couples and no one cared if they didn't quite keep pace with the music.

The only thing that mattered to him was *her*. When she'd stood up in front of the entire *ton* and confessed to posing for the portrait, he could see her trembling hands and hear the slight quaver in her voice. It had taken every ounce of restraint he had not to jump up on the platform and create a distraction, or simply unveil the portrait and spare her from the whole ordeal. Instead, he'd stood in the wings and watched her face her fear—and conquer it. She'd never looked more beautiful or radiant.

Best of all, she didn't seem overly upset with him for arriving late to the ball. He wasn't so daft that he didn't realize he had some explaining to do.

"I'm sorry I was late."

"I'd just about given up on you."

"But you didn't?" It was more question than statement. She glanced away. "I'm sure you have more pressing matters than balls."

"I do."

She stiffened slightly and gazed at the floor.

"Earlier this evening, for instance, I met with a duke."

"Oh?"

"I believe you know him, in fact—the Duke of Huntford?"

Disappointment and hurt flicked across her face. "Owen came to the ball with us. He's been here all night."

"Of course he has. We met in Lord Foley's library less than an hour ago, before you revealed the painting. You were amazing, by the way. Perfect. I knew you could do it."

She blushed prettily. "I'm glad you were there. I meant what I said about being grateful to you. I don't care what the Miss Starlings of the world think of me. And I don't regret what I did for my family."

God, he wanted to kiss her. And more. But for now he was content to dance with her and bask in her light.

"Look," she said, inclining her head toward the center of the room. "Lord Biltmore is dancing with Louise. They make a lovely couple, do they not?"

Ben glanced over his shoulder at the pair. "Indeed. Not as lovely as you and I, but close."

Daphne arched a golden brow. "So you approve?"

"Miss Seaton makes Hugh happy, and I can tell she truly cares for him. For those reasons alone, I think Robert would have liked her."

"Are you all right?" she asked. "If your leg is hurting, we could go sit on the terrace."

"I'm fine." He'd never been better. "I saw a new physician yesterday. Someone Averill's been nagging me to see. The doctor can't make any promises, but he has a few newer treatments that he thinks might help me."

Her eyes went wide. "And you're willing to try them?"

"Why not? I have nothing to lose and everything to gain."

The smile she gave him—full of promise and hope—made his heart beat wildly.

When the dance ended, he led her back to Huntford. Anabelle, Olivia, and Rose flocked around Daphne and enveloped her in a hug.

"It's been quite an evening," Huntford announced. "I think perhaps we should gather Mrs. Honeycote and go home before we create any more spectacles."

"Owen," Olivia cried, "how can you make light of this? It was a courageous thing that Daphne did."

Huntford inclined his head toward his sister as if to warn that another spectacle was brewing.

Ben cleared his throat. "I agree with Huntford. It's time to go."

Olivia arched a brow at him. "Didn't you just arrive?"

Huntford gave Ben a sympathetic and long-suffering look. "Let's all meet out front in five minutes," he said firmly.

Ben escorted Daphne across the ballroom to where her mother sat with Lady Bonneville. At the sight of her daughter, Mrs. Honeycote leaped to her feet, a worried expression on her face. As Daphne tried to convince her mother that she was truly fine, the viscountess crooked her finger at Ben. Much as he hated to admit it, a chill ran down his spine.

"Good evening, Lady Bonneville. I regret that we were pitted against each other in the auction."

She snorted. "Don't lose any sleep over it, Foxburn. I didn't really want the painting. I knew you'd outbid me. I just wanted to drive up the price."

Of course she did, but she had a softer side, too. "And perhaps spare Miss Honeycote further embarrassment?"

"I thought you knew me better than that. I don't have a kind bone in my body, but I do appreciate a good scandal as much as the next person." She gave a satisfied sigh. "This ball has been the most entertaining of the season."

"Indeed. That is why I think it best that I escort Mrs. Honeycote and her daughter home."

"Good idea."

A few minutes later, the entire party was gathered out front of Lord Foley's house and both of the duke's coaches were brought round. Ben pulled Huntford aside. "Might I be permitted to deliver Miss Honeycote home in my coach?" As he awaited the duke's answer, he was uncharacteristically nervous.

Huntford and Ben glared at each other; they were fairly well matched at issuing withering looks. "You know my intentions are honorable."

"Do I, Foxburn?"

"Of course. But I require some time with Daphne. Alone."

"Be careful. Or the next time you and I meet we'll both be holding dueling pistols."

"That won't be necessary."

Huntford guided Anabelle and the rest of the women—except for Daphne—into his carriages. "We'll see."

Ben took Daphne's hand in his. "Will you ride with me?"

She smiled and stepped up into the cab of his coach.

He instructed the driver to take the circuitous route through the park, climbed in, and sat on the seat beside Daphne. Even in the relative darkness, she shimmered softly, glowing like the goddess of the moon.

"I'm so glad that ordeal is over." She sank into the velvet squabs and sighed happily. "And I'm glad to be here with you."

He took her hand in his and gently tugged at the fingers of her glove. "I suspect anywhere would be preferable to that scandal-hungry ballroom."

"How did you do it?"

"The painting?"

She nodded.

"Thomas is back in town. Rose snuck the dress out of your room."

"*Rose*?"

"She modeled it for Thomas at the frame shop, which we broke in—"

Daphne shook her head. "Maybe you'd better spare me the details."

Slowly, he pulled at her glove, revealing the creamy skin of her forearms, inch by delectable inch. He lowered his head, kissing and lightly nibbling a trail from her elbow to her wrist. She moaned, making his cock go hard.

"Yes, this is definitely preferable to Lord Foley's ball," she breathed.

But seduction was not the first order of business—damn it to hell.

"Daphne . . . I missed you."

She sat up and smiled shyly. "You did?"

"I missed the way you laugh and the way you brighten every room you set foot in. And the way you fuss over me."

"I thought you didn't like me playing nurse."

He grinned wickedly. "I lied."

"Oh."

"That night we spent together at Biltmore Manor...I know I shouldn't have..."

"Do you regret that night?" Daphne asked.

"God no. Do you?"

She was silent for the space of several heartbeats. "No."

Ben exhaled. "That's good. If you'd said yes, this next part would be very awkward."

"Which part?"

"The part where I tell you that earlier tonight I asked your brother-in-law for your hand in marriage."

Daphne made a sound that was half squeak, half cry. "Wait. You asked Owen if you could—"

"Marry you."

She swallowed. "And he said...?"

"That it was up to you. And your mother, of course. And he told me that if you said yes, I was one lucky bastard. Which I already knew."

"I'm lucky, too." Daphne sniffled. "Ben, you saved me—and more importantly, my family and friends—from top billing in the scandal sheets. You bid on the painting and donated more money to the orphanage—you knew I'd say the orphanage, didn't you?"

"I had an inkling."

"If I didn't know better, I'd say you have a soft spot for the girls."

He scoffed at the suggestion. "I don't want to talk about the blasted orphanage."

"All right, then." She pulled him closer, touching her nose to his. "What would you like to talk about?"

He swallowed the knot in his throat. There were very few things he couldn't be glib about. This was one of them. "Our future. Us. Together. That's what I want... because... I love you."

He waited for her to say something. Anything.

Her lips parted and her eyes turned watery. And then she took his face in her hands and kissed him like maybe she loved him, too. That's what he would have liked to think, anyway.

They kissed like lovers who'd been reunited after a decade. She was all light and goodness; he was darkness and pain. And yet, they were so right together. Being with her was like coming home.

Her tongue tangled sweetly with his and he pulled her closer, wanting the moment to last, trying to imprint it upon his soul.

"You haven't answered, Daphne. I know you deserve a hell of a lot better than me. But I love you and *will* love you with every corner of my black heart for the rest of my days. I'll spend every hour trying to be a better man. Please... say you'll marry me."

She swiped at her eyes, took a deep breath, and smiled. "Of course I will. I love you, Ben. Not because of your injury or what you did for me or the orphanage, but because of who you are. You challenge me to grow, make me laugh, and make me feel... incredible. I don't want you to change."

Joy flooded his chest. "I'm going to make you so happy."

"I'm counting on it," she said seductively. "You know, you're saddling yourself with a woman with a rather wanton past."

"If I have anything to say about it, your future will be wanton, too. Can we make a brief detour to my house? There's something I want to show you."

She arched a brow wickedly. "Is there?"

"Not *that*. Well, yes, that." He banged on the roof of the coach. "You'll see."

A few minutes later, they rolled up in front of his town house. He pulled a cloak from beneath the seat and wrapped it around her shoulders so she wouldn't be recognized if someone rode by as they walked to the door. Once they were inside, he dismissed the butler and led Daphne to his bedchamber, whispering naughty things in her ear all the way up the stairs. They arrived at his room, breathless from running and laughing.

He backed her against a wall and kissed her soundly in the hallway before swinging open the door. "This," he said, gesturing to the wall opposite the bed, "is what I wanted to show you."

Daphne froze. There was her portrait—the one on the sapphire chaise. The one she'd posed for in a chilly, abandoned factory. The one that had earned her a few coins to help her family. The one that had brought her and Ben together.

"It's yours," he said. "We had a deal. If you could cure me, it was to be yours."

"But I haven't cured you." Her brow furrowed adorably. "Have I?"

"Not completely. I'll probably always be an ass. But I'd like to think I've made strides. The point is, the portrait belongs to you. No one can ever hold it over your head again. If you want to destroy it, you may. The decision is entirely yours."

Hers. Two months ago, she'd have given anything to hear him say that. And she would have jumped at the chance to erase the evidence of her wanton past. But now...she was rather proud of it. "I don't think we need to destroy it, although, I would prefer to keep it in a private room."

"Here?" he asked, hope evident in his clear blue eyes.

"If it pleases you."

"It does. *Everything* about you does."

"How about this?" She shrugged the cape off her shoulders and let it pool at her feet.

"Definitely."

Slowly, she slid off her remaining glove, removed the pins from her hair, and glided to the bed.

"How shall I please *you*?" he said, laying her across the soft counterpane. He plucked her slippers from her feet and caressed a path from her ankle, to her knee, and up her thigh. Her skin tingled deliciously.

"This is a very good start."

After that, there was very little talking.

Ben removed every stitch of her clothing, and she removed his. He kissed her everywhere. Likewise, he let her explore to her heart's content. He didn't flinch when she lightly traced the scars on his leg and the twisted muscles of his thigh.

They made love slowly at first, but then neither of them was content with the leisurely pace. She arched her back and pulled him closer with her legs. Ben groaned and rocked against her faster, in a rhythm that took over her body like the graceful yet powerful crest of a wave. It carried her higher and higher until there was nowhere left to go and she shattered into beautiful bits of light.

Ben did, too. He held her close and she savored the feel and smell of his skin against hers as the glorious tremors subsided, leaving her content, happy...and rather famished.

Daphne wished they could stay like this all night— assuming a tray was brought up, of course—with their legs entwined and their foreheads touching. Soon, they would be able to spend *every* night like this. She couldn't wait.

"I forgot to tell you," Ben said. "Lord Charlton wrote me. He's much improved and is indebted to you for your kind concern and the herbs you left. He says his memory improves every day."

Daphne preened. She couldn't help it.

"He thinks the English Beauty and I would make a lovely couple."

"I'd have to agree."

"Do you know what I wish?"

"What?"

"That I could paint you just as you are...right now."

Oh no. "I'm done with posing for paintings." Her stomach growled, however, and a thought occurred to her. "We might do a little painting of our own. With melted chocolate perhaps? And strawberries?"

Not surprisingly, Ben was in favor of the suggestion.

Indeed, he showed promising signs of being a *most* indulging husband.

Don't miss

Scandalous Summer Nights

from award-winning
author Anne Barton

Please turn this page
for a preview

Chapter One

London, 1817

$\mathcal{A}$ny girl with a smidgen of good sense would have given up on James Averill years ago.

Olivia Sherbourne's problem was not so much a lack of good sense as it was an abundance of stubbornness. She'd pined after James for ten long years. No matter that he gave her scarce little encouragement; her patience was born out of a love that was deep, abiding, and true.

Also, she'd once seen his naked chest.

It was magnificent. And it had sustained her for the better part of a decade.

The mere memory of his bare, muscled torso glistening in the afternoon haze turned her bones to jelly, and a soft sigh escaped her lips.

"It's your move." Rose, Olivia's younger sister, serenely inclined her head toward the chess board between them.

As Olivia frowned at her precariously positioned rook, the truth of Rose's words struck her. It *was* her move.

And time was running out.

"I was thinking about James," Olivia admitted.

Rose had suffered through scores of one-sided conversations about the handsome solicitor that had begun in precisely this manner. To her credit, however, she didn't roll her eyes or throw up her hands in exasperation. She deserved some sort of sisterly award.

"About his expedition?"

Olivia nodded. At dinner last evening, their brother, Owen, the Duke of Huntford, had casually mentioned that James would travel to Egypt where he'd participate in an archaeological dig—for two years.

Two years.

Which meant Olivia would be four and twenty when he returned. It was too long to wait—even if James did have a chest that rivaled Apollo's.

Olivia looked around the elegant sea-green drawing room to make sure she and Rose were quite alone. "He leaves in three months. That's all the time I have."

"For what?"

"To make him fall in love with me." Of course, she would first have to make him notice her. And treat her as something other than a piece of furniture that one avoided so as not to stub a toe.

Rose's brow furrowed with sympathy. "I know how fond you are of Mr. Averill, but I'm not certain it's possible to *make* someone fall in love."

Blast Rose's inclination toward logic and reason.

"I must try." Olivia sprang to her feet and the skirt of her dress caught the corner of the chessboard, toppling most of the pieces, which was just as well. Rose had been two moves away from trouncing her.

Olivia paced before the dormant fireplace, hands propped on her hips. "If he knew his attentions would not be unwelcome, perhaps he would dare to court me. Is it possible I've been too coy where he's concerned?"

Rose blinked, swallowed and opened her mouth to reply.

"Don't answer that." Hearing Rose recount each time Olivia had worn a daring gown or turned her ankle or read a bit of moving poetry solely with the purpose of capturing James's fancy would only humiliate her further. Because none of her ploys had worked.

"You must remember," Rose said smoothly, "that Mr. Averill is a close friend of Owen's. Our brother can be terribly intimidating."

Olivia raised her chin. "James isn't afraid of Owen. He's one of the best boxers in all of London—and he's blackened our brother's eye more than once."

"True. But Mr. Averill is an honorable gentleman and, as such, would respect Owen's wishes with regard to you. A boxing match is one thing. Sisters are quite another."

"Yes, well, I don't give a fig about Owen's wishes. *My* happiness is at stake." Olivia was vaguely aware that she sounded like a spoiled child and was grateful Rose was the non-judgmental sort.

Rose glided to Olivia's side. "I want you to be happy, and so does Owen." She squeezed the tops of Olivia's arms affectionately. "Now tell me...what do you plan to do about Mr. Averill?"

That was an excellent question. Just thinking of the possibilities made her heart pound in her chest. "I'm not certain yet. But I shall decide before this evening. He's sure to be at the Easton ball."

"You must let me know if there is anything I can do to help you. I'm sure Anabelle would offer her support as well."

Anabelle was their brother's duchess, and she'd been their friend even before she'd become their sister-in-law. "I am lucky to have both of you on my side, but I think I must face this challenge on my own. Wish me luck?"

Rose hugged her. "Of course. Just be careful. I don't want to see you hurt."

Olivia grinned. "Neither do I." But she also knew it was a distinct possibility. "You know, I am feeling rather adventurous at the moment."

"You don't say." Rose's face paled.

"I do indeed. We must celebrate my decision to follow my heart with a drink."

"Tea?" Rose said hopefully.

"Of course not."

"I didn't think so."

Olivia swept her gaze around the drawing room once more before scurrying toward a bookshelf. There, behind the dusty tomes about flora and fauna that no one in the household read, was a half-full decanter of brandy that she'd nicked from her brother's study along with one tumbler.

Rose gasped. "Owen would be furious."

"That's why this is so much fun." Olivia removed the stopper and splashed a healthy dose of liquor into the glass. "To true love," she toasted—only it wasn't a proper toast since they had only the one glass. She swallowed a large gulp of brandy and felt her nostrils flare as the liquid burned a path down her throat and into her chest. Handing the glass to Rose, she said, "Your turn."

Rose's hand trembled as she reached for the drink, but she must have figured that the quicker she drank the less chance they would be discovered. "To true love," she said, before taking the smallest of sips and thrusting the glass back at Olivia.

Olivia narrowed her eyes. "Did you even taste it?"

Rose nodded and the auburn curls at her temples bounced emphatically. "Against my better judgment, yes I did."

"Excellent." Olivia was warmed by her sister's show of loyalty. Or perhaps she was warmed by the brandy.

She drained the glass before returning it and the decanter to their hiding spot.

Rose inhaled deeply, her relief palpable. "I am going to my room to read for a while. But first, Olivia, you must promise me something."

Olivia brushed the dust off her palms, turned to face her sister, and arched a questioning brow.

"Your impulsive nature is one of the things I love best about you," Rose began.

"But...?"

"But you must think carefully about what you will say to Mr. Averill tonight. Your actions could have serious and lasting consequences—for both of you."

"I know." Olivia swallowed, sobered by the truth of her sister's words. "Thank you. I'll think about what you've said."

"I'll see you at dinner."

Olivia smiled and waited until Rose left the drawing room before whirling around and resuming her pacing.

Her unrequited love must seem ridiculous to her sister and her dear friend Anabelle. But Olivia's was not a fleeting infatuation. She had a connection with James, understood him. And she adored everything about him, even the quirks that some might call flaws. She was charmed by the way his lips sometimes moved when he was deep in thought—as though he were talking himself through a difficult problem. She loved the way his eyes lit up when he recounted the latest additions to the British Museum and his passion for math and science—even if she didn't share it. She even loved his infuriating tendency to become distracted by a rare plant when she was endeavoring to show off a smart new pair of slippers.

Rose needn't have worried on one count—Olivia would never stoop to snaring James in a marriage trap. She didn't want to have to trick him into taking her as his wife.

Even if it *would* be ever so much easier.

She paused in front of the settee, took a large silk pillow, and clutched it tightly to her chest.

What she wanted—what she'd dreamed of every single night for the last ten years—was his complete and utter adoration. She wanted him to dance *only* with her, although she supposed he might occasionally take her mother for a turn about the room. Olivia wanted him to go riding with her all afternoon and then find a shady spot where they could eat sliced chicken, crusty bread, and strawberries. She wanted him to pick wildflowers and tuck one behind her ear and look at her as though he couldn't believe how fortunate he was that he'd found her.

Of course, in actuality, *she* had found *him*. But she loved him too much to quibble over such trifling matters.

And that's why the thought of confessing her feelings to James terrified her.

After tonight, she wouldn't be able to delude herself with platitudes like *he simply isn't aware you hold him in such high regard* or *he must believe his attentions would be unwelcome.*

She'd never had to face the very real possibility that he did not return her affections.

A shiver stole through her limbs, but she shook it off. Ten years of dreaming and two and one half seasons of waiting could *not* be for naught.

Their fairytale romance would begin tonight.

She simply refused to believe anything different.

James Averill could be forgiven if he arrived at the Easton ball slightly foxed.

He was celebrating, damn it.

While waiting to greet Lord Easton and his wife, he attempted to straighten his cravat, but feared he'd only made matters worse. He shrugged. Who the bloody hell cared?

When he got to Egypt, he'd never wear cravats.

In three short months he'd be on a ship headed to the land of archaeological wonders.

It had taken years of meticulous planning, but he'd finally realized his dream. He'd saved enough money to ensure his mother and brother would be comfortable. He'd taken on a partner so that his clients wouldn't be left in a lurch.

Before long, he'd be a free man.

And *that's* why he deserved another drink. Damn it.

He swept his gaze around the already bustling ballroom.

Huntford and Foxburn were a head taller than most of the other guests and easy to spot in the crowd. Odds were five to one his friends had already located and partaken of a stash of liquor.

James hoped to hell they'd saved some for him.

He smiled and nodded politely to a viscount and several older ladies as he meandered toward his friends. Thanks to his finely tailored coat and practiced manners, he blended into this privileged world rather well. Like certain species of lizards in the desert, he was capable of mimicking the landscape. However, at times such as this he was acutely aware that ballrooms were *not* his natural environment.

He was a solicitor, someone who worked. For his living. Huntford and Foxburn didn't hold that against him, but then, they both knew he could kick their asses from London to Edinborough and back again.

"Good evening, gentlemen." James had to admit that marriage agreed with both the duke and the earl. Huntford still brooded, but James suspected it was mostly for show. Foxburn now smiled with startling frequency.

"Averill," Huntford replied, welcoming him with a slap on the shoulder. Foxburn signaled to a passing waiter and James deduced that his drink was on its way.

The duke leaned his large frame toward James and lowered his voice. "There's a matter I need to discuss with you."

"Business?" James hoped it was nothing terribly complex. His mind was not at its sharpest at the moment.

Huntford frowned. "Of a sort. Can we meet at your office tomorrow?"

James raised a brow. "Of course."

"Very good. We will deal with it then." The duke

pinched the bridge of his nose, then shook his head—as if to clear his mind of troubling thoughts.

Foxburn idly tapped the foot of his cane on the parquet floor. "I understand congratulations are in order, Averill."

James must have looked mildly confused because the earl narrowed his icy blue eyes and said, "Egypt?"

Right—the expedition. "Yes. I have almost three months to get my affairs in order, and then I'll be off."

Foxburn seemed to consider this as he took a large swig of his drink. "You're giving up all this"—he waved his cane in an arc to indicate the sparkling ballroom—"to ride camels?"

"And unwrap mummies," Huntford added.

"And sleep in a tent." Foxburn was really enjoying himself now. "Be careful you don't get sand in your drawers."

All three men made a face and squirmed at the thought.

"The discomfort will be worth it," James said confidently, "if I unearth one ancient artifact—one clue to the civilizations that came before us."

"What might that be?" Huntford asked. "A bit of broken pottery? Something that *might* have been the tip of a spear, but is more likely a plain old rock?"

"Well, yes." Of course, he hoped to discover something with pictures or writing—a unique piece that had never been seen before—but explaining himself to these two seemed a waste of breath. "If I find some old pottery or rocks, I'll consider the trip a success."

Huntford and Foxburn stared at him as though he were touched in the upper works.

James was about to say the Devil could take them both when the waiter returned with his drink. James tipped it back and found his mood improved almost immediately.

As the strains of a waltz carried through the ballroom, the duke and earl craned their necks in search of their wives. The duchess and countess were sisters—although they didn't resemble one another, each was beautiful in her own right.

"You'd better hurry to your wives' sides," James advised. "There are half a dozen rogues here hoping to claim them for a dance."

Huntford growled. "Anabelle and Daphne are more than capable of fending off advances, aren't they Foxburn?"

The earl snorted. "I feel sorry for the poor bastards."

James had no reason to doubt his friends, but he noticed they practically plowed through the crowd in order to join their lovely wives.

He smiled to himself and looked about for an inconspicuous spot in which to finish his drink and select a couple of beautiful young ladies to later seek out as dance partners.

It was a fine plan. The evening promised to be pleasant—until Olivia Sherbourne waylaid him. "Waylaid" was actually too benign a word; what Olivia did could best be described as "hunting him to ground."

Appearing out of nowhere was an alarming habit of hers. One minute he was relaxed and pondering dance partners; the next he was toe to toe with a brown-haired, doe-eyed force of nature. A hurricane in a pretty blue frock.

"There you are!" she sputtered. "You must follow me."

No greeting, no niceties, just 'You must follow me.' Must he? *Really*? Because he'd been rather content standing there with his drink.

But Olivia was already striding toward the French doors at the back of the room, assuming he was following along at her heels like a well trained pup. She was Huntford's sister, for God's sake. He couldn't *not* follow her.

Bloody hell.

She disappeared briefly behind a trio of matrons before slipping out the doors. James ducked out after her, determined to steer her back into the ballroom as quickly as possible.

He stepped onto the terrace, which spanned the considerable width of the house and was softly illuminated by a few lanterns and the quarter moon in a cloudless sky.

"Over here," she called in a loud whisper. She stood at the corner of the patio, her white gloves waving him over like a beacon on the rocky shore.

Instinct told him he shouldn't do her bidding. Instinct was practically *shouting* at him, in fact, and his feet remained rooted to the flagstone.

Olivia seemed to sense his hesitation, however, and doubled back toward him. "We haven't much time," she explained, dragging him unceremoniously along by his free arm. At least she hadn't spilled his drink.

"Where are we going?" He thought it a fair question and desperately hoped the answer wasn't, oh, Gretna Green.

"Right here." She stopped before a stone bench.

"Why?"

She sat and pulled him down beside her. Her expression was impossible to decipher, but her chest rose and fell as though she were frightened or breathless. Her white teeth nibbled at her lower lip. Now that she had him here, she seemed at a loss for words.

That *never* happened with Olivia.

"Are you in some sort of trouble?"

"No," she said quickly. "Er, that I know of."

He grinned. "How refreshing. Even as a wee lass you always seemed to find trouble. Remember the time you managed to climbed into the stable with the foals and couldn't get—"

"Don't," she snapped.

"Don't *what*?" He'd been trying to put her at ease so she could spit out whatever it was she needed to say. She seemed less than grateful.

"Don't treat me like Owen's little sister."

Holy hell. James drained his glass in one gulp and set it on the bench.

"If you don't want to be treated like a child," he said slowly, "stop acting like one. Start by telling me why you brought me out here."

Olivia moistened her lips with her tongue. It didn't help. Her mouth was as dry as a dust rag. "I needed to speak with you privately."

James's mossy green eyes flashed a challenge. "I'm listening."

Her pulse raced madly. This exchange was not going at all as she'd envisioned while sprawled on her bed that afternoon. James was supposed to have detected the tremor in her voice and taken her hands in his, smoothing the pad of his thumbs over the backs of her gloved hands. By now, he should be gazing at her with concern and a healthy dose of appreciation for the revealing neckline of her gown.

But his strong arms were crossed and his normally full lips were pressed together in a thin line. He had the look of someone who had requested tea an hour ago and was still waiting. Not thirsty so much as . . . exasperated.

Panicked, she considered making up an excuse for her behavior. She could say she wanted to buy a gift for Owen and Anabelle's new baby and was considering a puppy. Surely James must have an opinion on that—

"Olivia." The impatience gave an edge to his voice, but she also heard a hint of compassion, and it propelled her forward.

There would be no dipping of her toe in the water. The only way to proceed was hurl herself in—even if it was way over her head.

She swallowed hard and looked directly into his beautiful eyes. "I love you."

James blinked once. He had the disoriented expression of someone who had been woken in the middle of the night—and was not happy about it. "What do you mean?"

Olivia took a deep breath. "It happened in the summer of 1807, when you visited my brother at Huntford Manor. Owen preferred to spend summers with his friends, but Father insisted he spend at least one week with us, and he always brought you. I was eleven years old that summer, and one day I wanted to fish with you and Owen but he said I couldn't because I would only scare the fish and annoy him. I refused to leave—"

"Of course you did," James mumbled.

"So you remember that day?"

"No. Please, go on." He picked up the glass beside him and looked at the bottom of it forlornly.

"Owen threatened to throw me in the river if I didn't return to the house."

"Let me guess." James dragged a broad hand through

his hair, leaving it charmingly mussed. "I championed your cause—bloodied your brother's nose so you could have your way."

"No. Even better. You gave me a chance to prove myself. You said that if I could bait my own hook with a live worm—without squealing—I should be allowed to stay and fish. Otherwise, I had to go."

"And how did you fare?"

"I succeeded. Well, Owen tried to say that it didn't count because of the retching—"

James cringed. "You didn't."

"A little. But you said that retching had not been prohibited by the agreement and so I must be permitted to stay and fish."

"I see." He looked over his shoulder toward the terrace. "So, I gather you wanted to express your gratitude, and now you have. Excellent. Shall we return to the ballroom?"

With a boldness that was shocking, even for her, she placed her hand on his leg. More precisely, his very hard and muscular thigh. "I haven't told you everything."

His gaze flew to her hand and remained there as he said, "I'm not certain we have time for the entire story, Olivia. We've been out here for a quarter of an hour and you're still in 1807."

She ducked her head so that he was forced to look into her eyes. "I've waited ten years to tell you how I feel. Please, let me finish."

James placed a palm over the back of her hand—the one still on his leg—and a delicious warmth traveled up Olivia's arm and throughout her body, leaving her breathless and tingling all over.

"If someone discovers us alone out here," he said softly, "your reputation will be shattered. Also, your brother will skewer me on the spot. If you feel that there's more you must say, we can arrange another—"

"This won't take long." She could feel him retreating and doubled her resolve. "I didn't fall in love with you that day, but I started to. Every summer I learned more about you, and you always made me feel important—like I was more than Owen's bothersome little sister. I lived for the moments I would see you again."

"You were young," James said. "It was infatuation."

Angry tears sprang to her eyes. "Then why have I waited for you? Why am I devastated at the thought of you leaving for Egypt? Why do I dream of you every single night?

James stood and dragged his hands down his face. "You don't know what you're saying."

Olivia leapt off the bench and stood toe to toe with him. "Look at me, James. I'm not a little girl." She put her hands on her hips for emphasis. "This is not a schoolgirl crush—not anymore."

"Have you been drinking?"

She heaved a sigh—he *would* have to ask that. "Not since four o'clock this afternoon."

"You are incorrigible. Did you know that?"

She fingered the long curl that had been artfully arranged to fall over her right shoulder. "I can see that I have shocked you for the second time this evening, and I'm glad."

He clenched his jaw, and she longed to touch the faint shadow of stubble along his chin.

"I have half a mind to march into that ballroom"—he

pointed behind her—"and inform your brother that he needs to find you a chaperone and tether her to you for the remainder of the season." His broad shoulders strained in the confines of his jacket each time waved his arm for emphasis.

Olivia inched closer to him, so that only a breath separated her chest and his torso. The one she had seen in all its naked glory. He smelled like leather and ink and pure male.

"You won't do that," she said.

A feral smile lit his face. "Oh yes, I will."

Her heartbeat thundered in her chest. She knew what she must do.

Before she could lose her nerve, she threw her arms around his neck and stood on tiptoe.

And she kissed him.

THE DISH

Where Authors Give You the Inside Scoop

♥ ♥ ♥ ♥ ♥ ♥ ♥ ♥ ♥ ♥ ♥ ♥ ♥ ♥ ♥ ♥

From the desk of Roxanne St. Claire

Dear Reader,

Years ago, I picked up a romance novel about a contemporary "marriage of convenience" and I recall being quite skeptical that the idea could work in anything but a historical novel. How wrong I was! I not only enjoyed the book, but *Separate Beds* by LaVyrle Spencer became one of my top ten favorite books of all time. (Do yourself a favor and dig up this classic if you haven't read it!) Since then, I've always wanted to put my own spin on a story about two people who are in a situation where they need to marry for reasons other than love, knowing that their faux marriage is doomed.

I finally found the perfect characters and setup for a marriage of convenience story when I returned to Barefoot Bay to write BAREFOOT BY THE SEA, my most recent release in the series set on an idyllic Gulf Coast island in Florida. I knew that sparks would fly and tears might flow when I paired Tessa Galloway, earth mother longing for a baby, with Ian Browning, a grieving widower in the witness protection program. I suspected that it would be a terrific conflict to give the woman who despises secrets a man who has to keep one in order to stay alive, with the added complication of a situation that can only be resolved with a fake, arranged marriage. However, I never dreamed just how much I would love writing that marriage of convenience! I should have known, since I adored the first one I'd ever read.

Throughout most of BAREFOOT BY THE SEA, hero Ian is forced to hide who he really is and why he's in Barefoot Bay. And that gave me another story twist I love to explore: the build-up to the inevitable revelation of a character's true identity and just how devastating that is for everyone (including the reader!). I had a blast being in Ian's head when he fought off his demons and past to fall hard into Tessa's arms and life. And I ached and grew with Tessa as the truth became crystal clear and shattered her fragile heart.

The best part, for me, was folding that marriage of convenience into a story about a woman who wants a child of her own but has to give up that hope to help, and ultimately lose, a man who needs her in order to be reunited with his own children. If she marries him, he gets what he needs…but he can't give her the one thing she wants most. Will Tessa surrender her lifelong dream to help a man who lost his? She can if she loves him enough, right? Maybe.

Ironically, when the actual marriage of convenience finally took place on the page, that ceremony felt more real than any of the many weddings I've ever written. I hope readers agree. And speaking of weddings, stay tuned for more of them in Barefoot Bay when the Barefoot Brides trilogy launches next year! Nothing like an opportunity to kick off your shoes and fall in love, which is never convenient but always fun!

Happy reading!

Roxanne St. Claire

♥ ♥ ♥ ♥ ♥ ♥ ♥ ♥ ♥ ♥ ♥ ♥ ♥ ♥ ♥

From the desk of Kristen Ashley

Dear Reader,

As it happens when I start a book and the action plays out in my head, characters pop up out of nowhere.

See, I don't plot, or outline. An idea will come to me and *Wham!* My brain just flows with it. Or a character will come to me and all the pieces of his or her puzzle start tumbling quickly into place and the story moves from there. Either way, this all plays in my mind's eye like a movie and I sit at my keyboard doing my darnedest to get it all down as it goes along.

In my Dream Man series, I started it with *Mystery Man* because Hawk and Gwen came to me and I was desperate to get their story out. I'm not even sure that I expected it to be a series. I just *needed* to tell their story.

Very quickly I was introduced to Kane "Tack" Allen and Detective Mitch Lawson. When I met them through Gwen, I knew instantly—with all the hotness that was them—that they both needed their own book. So this one idea I had of Hawk and Gwen finding their happily ever after became a series.

Brock "Slim" Lucas showed up later in *Mystery Man* but when he did, he certainly intrigued me. Most specifically the lengths he'd go to do his job. I wondered why that fire was in his belly. And suddenly I couldn't wait to find out.

In the meantime, my aunt Barb, who reads every one of my books when they come out, mentioned in passing she'd like to see one of my couples *not* struggle before they capitulated to the attraction and emotion swirling around them. Instead, she wanted to see the relationship build and grow, not the hero and heroine fighting it.

This intrigued me, too, especially when it came to Brock, who had seen a lot and done a lot in his mission as a DEA agent. I didn't want him to have another fight on his hands, not like that. But also, I'd never done this, not in all the books I'd written.

I'm a girl who likes a challenge.

But could I weave a tale that was about a man and a woman in love, recognizing and embracing that love relatively early in the story, and then focus the story on how they learn to live with each other, deal with each other's histories, family, and all that life throws at them on a normal basis? Would this even be interesting?

Luckily, life *is* interesting, sometimes in good ways, sometimes not-so-good.

Throwing Elvira and Martha into the mix, along with Tess's hideous ex-husband and Brock's odious ex-wife, and adding children and family, life for Brock and Tess, as well as their story, was indeed interesting (and fun) to write—when I didn't want to wring Olivia's neck, that is.

And I found there's great beauty in telling a tale that isn't about fighting attraction because of past issues or history (or the like) and besting that to find love; instead delving into what makes a man and a woman, and allowing them to let their loved one get close, at the same time learning how to depend on each other to make it through.

I should thank my aunt Barb. Because she had a great idea that led to a beautiful love story.

Kristen Ashley

♥ ♥ ♥ ♥ ♥ ♥ ♥ ♥ ♥ ♥ ♥ ♥ ♥ ♥ ♥

From the desk of Eileen Dreyer

Dear Reader,

The last thing I ever thought I would do was write a series. I thought I was brave putting together a trilogy. Well, as usual, my characters outsmarted me, and I now find myself in the middle of a nine-story series about Drake's Rakes, my handsome gentleman spies. But I don't wait well as a reader myself. How do I ask my own readers to wait nine books for any resolution?

I just couldn't do it. So I've divided up the Rakes into three trilogies based on the heroines. The first was The Three Graces. This one I'm calling Last Chance Academy, where the heroines went to school. I introduced them all in my short e-novel It Begins With A Kiss, and continue in ONCE A RAKE with Sarah Clarke, who has to save Scotsman Colonel Ian Ferguson from gunshot, assassin, and the charges of treason.

I love Sarah. A woman with an unfortunate beginning, she is just trying to save the only home she's ever really had from penury, an estate so small and isolated that her best friend is a six-hundred-pound pig. Enter Ian. Suddenly she's facing off with smugglers, spies, assassins, and possible eviction. I call my Drake's Rakes series Romantic Historical Adventure, and I think there is plenty of each in ONCE A RAKE. Let me know at www .eileendreyer.com, my Facebook page (Eileen Dreyer), or on Twitter @EileenDreyer. Now I need to get back. I have five more Rakes to threaten.

Eileen Dreyer

♥ ♥ ♥ ♥ ♥ ♥ ♥ ♥ ♥ ♥ ♥ ♥ ♥ ♥

From the desk of Anne Barton

Dear Reader,

Regrets. We all have them. Incidents from our distant (or not-so-distant) pasts that we'd like to forget. Photos we'd like to burn, boyfriends we never should have dated, a night or two of partying that got slightly out of control. Ahem.

In short, there are some stories we'd rather our siblings didn't tell in front of Grandma at Thanksgiving dinner.

Luckily for me, I grew up in the pre-Internet era. Back then, a faux pas wasn't instantly posted or tweeted for the world to see. Instead, it was recounted in a note that was ruthlessly passed through a network of tables in the cafeteria—a highly effective means of humiliation, but not nearly as permanent as the digital equivalent, thank goodness.

Even so, I distinctly remember the sinking feeling, the dread of knowing that my deep dark secret could be exposed at any moment. If you've ever had a little indiscretion that you just can't seem to outrun (and who hasn't?), you know how it weighs on you. It can be almost paralyzing.

In ONCE SHE WAS TEMPTED, Miss Daphne Honeycote has such a secret. Actually, she has two of them—a pair of scandalous portraits. She posed for them when she was poor and in dire need of money for her sick mother. But after her mother recovers and Daphne's circumstances improve considerably, the shocking portraits come back to haunt her, threatening to ruin her reputation, her friendships, and her family's good name.

Much to Daphne's horror, Benjamin Elliott, the Earl of Foxburn, possesses one of the paintings—and therefore, the power to destroy her. But he also has the means to help her discover the whereabouts of the second portrait before its unscrupulous owner can make it public. Daphne must decide whether to trust the brooding earl. But even if she does, he can't fully protect her—it's ultimately up to Daphne to come to terms with her scandalous past. Just as we all eventually must.

In the meantime, I suggest seating your siblings on the opposite end of the Thanksgiving table from Grandma.

Happy reading,

Anne Barton

♥ ♥ ♥ ♥ ♥ ♥ ♥ ♥ ♥ ♥ ♥ ♥ ♥ ♥ ♥ ♥

From the desk of Mimi Jean Pamfiloff

Dear Reader,

After living a life filled with nothing but bizarre, Emma Keane just wants normal. Husband, picket fence, vegetable garden, and a voice-free head. Normal. And Mr. Voice happens to agree. He'd like nothing more than to be free from the stubborn, spiteful, spoiled girl he's spent the last twenty-two years listening to day and night. Unfortunately for him, however, escaping his only companion in the universe won't be so easy. You see, there's a damned good reason Emma is the only one who can hear him—though he's not spilling the beans just yet—and there's a damned bad reason he can't leave Emma: He's imprisoned. And to be set free, Mr. Voice is going to have to convince Emma to travel from New York City to the darkest corner of Mexico's most dangerous jungle.

But not only will the perilous journey help Emma become the brave woman she's destined to be, it will also be the single most trying challenge Mr. Voice has ever had to face. In his seventy thousand years, he's never met a mortal he can't live without. Until now. Too bad she's going to die helping him. What's an ancient god to do?

Mimi

CHRISTINE FEEHAN

The Wicked and the Wondrous

POCKET **STAR** BOOKS

New York London Toronto Sydney

A Pocket Star Book published by
POCKET BOOKS, a division of Simon & Schuster, Inc.
1230 Avenue of the Americas, New York, NY 10020

After the Music copyright © 2001 by Christine Feehan
The Twilight Before Christmas copyright © 2003
by Christine Feehan
The Twilight Before Christmas was previously published individu-
ally by Pocket Books. *After the Music* was previously published by
Pocket Books in *A Very Gothic Christmas*.

All rights reserved, including the right to reproduce
this book or portions thereof in any form whatsoever.
For information address Pocket Books, 1230 Avenue
of the Americas, New York, NY 10020

ISBN: 1-4165-0389-7

First Pocket Books printing October 2004

10 9 8 7 6 5 4 3 2 1

POCKET STAR BOOKS and colophon are registered
trademarks of Simon & Schuster, Inc.

Cover design by Lisa Litwack.
Front cover illustration by Alan Ayers.

Manufactured in the United States of America

For information regarding special discounts for bulk purchases,
please contact Simon & Schuster Special Sales at 1-800-456-6798
or business@simonandschuster.com.

❄ contents ❄

THE TWILIGHT BEFORE CHRISTMAS

❄ dedication ❄

This book is dedicated to my sister Lisa, who has a special magic all her own.

❄ acknowledgments ❄

Thank you to Heather King and Rose Brungard for the wonderful chilling Christmas poem they so graciously provided to me to use for this book!

Be sure to write to Christine at Christine@christinefeehan.com to get a FREE exclusive screen saver and join the PRIVATE email list to receive an announcement when Christine's books are released.

The Twilight Before Christmas
by
Heather King and Rose Brungard

'Twas the twilight before Christmas and all through the lands,
Not a thing has occurred that was not of my hand.

The snowglobe they hold has a secret inside,
Where the mist rolls in place of the snow that's outside.

A chill, colder still than the air they will feel,
As I rejoice in release as I slip past the seal

A wreath of holly meant to greet,
Looks much better tossed in the street.

A town dreams of sweet thoughts while nestled in bed,
Until nightmares of me begin to dance in their heads.

The time, it was right, for a present or two,
And the fog on the sand holds a secret, a clue

As lovers meet beneath mistletoe bright,
Terror ignites down below them this night

And the blood runs red on the pristine white snow . . .
While around all the houses the Christmas lights glow.

A star burns hot in the dead of the night,
As the bell tolls it's now midnight

Beneath the star, that shines so bright,
An act unfolds, to my delight

In the stocking hung with gentle care,
A mystery, I know, is hidden there.

A candle burns with an eerie glow,
As it melts, the wax does flow,

My last gift now, is a special one,
A candy cane for a special son,

He watches and tends and knows the land,
But not enough to evade my hand.

All deeds are now done, forgiveness is mine,
As two people share a love for all time.

CRITICS PRAISE CHRISTINE FEEHAN—

"A magnificent storyteller." *(Romantic Times)*

THE TWILIGHT BEFORE CHRISTMAS

"Dark suspense and sensual romance co-exist here in unlikely but perfect harmony."

—Publishers Weekly

"Heart-pounding . . . extraordinary."

—Romantic Times

"Brings together ancient magic and the wonder of romance, creating an exciting drama that builds to a thrilling conclusion."

—A Romance Review

AFTER THE MUSIC

"[A] captivating story. . . . Christine Feehan has written a gothic novella that is not only a page-turner but is highly recommended!"

—Romantic Times

"A modern day gothic tale that will thrill you and chill you . . . plenty of sexual tension and wild romance to heat the blood as well."

—The Belles and Beaux of Romance

"Dark and haunting . . . reminiscent of classic Gothics à la Victoria Holt and Phyllis Whitney."

—Romance Reviews Today

BOOKS BY CHRISTINE FEEHAN

The Shadows of Christmas Past
(with Susan Sizemore)

The Twilight Before Christmas

A Very Gothic Christmas
(with Melanie George)

Published by Pocket Books

chapter

1

'Twas the twilight before Christmas and all through the lands
Not a thing has occurred that was not of my hand

"DON'T SAY IT. DON'T SAY IT. DON'T SAY IT,"
Danny Granite muttered the mantra under his
breath as he sat in the truck watching his older
brother carefully selecting hydro-organic tomatoes from
Old Man Mars's fruit stand. Danny glanced at the keys,
assuring himself the truck was running and all that his
brother had to do was leap in and gun it. He leaned out
the window, gave a halfhearted wave to the elderly man,
and scowled at his brother. "Get a move on, Matt. I'm
starving here."

Matt grimaced at him, then smiled with smooth charm at
the old man. "Merry Christmas, Mr. Mars," he said cheerfully as he handed over several bills and lifted the bag of
tomatoes. "Less than two weeks before Christmas. I'm looking forward to the pageant this year."

Danny groaned. A black scowl settled over Old Man
Mars's face. His craggy brows drew together in a straight,
thick line. He grunted in disgust and spat on the ground.

The smile on Matt's face widened into a boyish grin as
he hurried around the bed of the pickup truck to yank

open the driver-side door. Almost before settling into his seat, he cranked up the radio so that "Jingle Bells" blared loudly from the speakers.

"You'd better move it, Matt," Dan muttered nervously, looking out the window, back toward the fruit stand. "He's arming himself. You just had to wish him a Merry Christmas, didn't you? You know he hates that pageant. And you know very well playing that music is adding insult to injury!"

The first tomato came hurtling toward the back window of the truck as Matt hit the gas and the truck leaped forward, fishtailing, tires throwing dirt into the air. The tomato landed with deadly accuracy, splattering juice, seed, and pulp across the back window. Several more missiles hit the tailgate as the truck tore out of the parking lot and raced down the street.

Danny scowled at his brother. "You just had to wish him Merry Christmas. Everyone knows he hates Christmas. He kicked the shepherd last year during the midnight pageant. Now he'll be more ornery than ever. If you'd just avoided the word, we might have gone unscathed this year, but now he'll have to retaliate."

Matt's massive shoulders shook as he laughed. "As I recall you played the shepherd last year. He didn't hurt you that bad, Danny boy. A little kick on the shin is good for you. It builds character."

"You only think it's funny because it wasn't your shin." Danny rubbed his leg as if it still hurt nearly a year later.

"You need to toughen up," Matt pointed out. He took the highway, a thin ribbon of a road, twisting and turning along the cliffs above the ocean. It was impossible to go fast on the switchbacks although Matt knew the road well. He maneuvered around a sharp curve, setting up for the next sharp turn. It ran uphill and nearly doubled back. The mountain swelled on his right, a high bank grown over with emerald green grasses and breathtaking colors from the explosion of wildflowers. On his left, a narrow ribbon of a trail meandered along the cliffs to drop away to the wide expanse of blue ocean with its whitecaps and booming waves.

"Oh, my God! That's Kate Drake," Danny said gleefully, pointing to a woman on a horse, riding along the narrow trail on the side of the road.

"That can't be her." Matt hastily rolled down his window and craned his neck, gawking unashamedly. He could only see the back of the rider, who was dressed all in white and had thick chestnut hair that flamed red in the sunshine. His heart pounded. His mouth went dry. Only Kate Drake could get away with wearing white and riding a horse so close to the side of the road. It had to be her. He slowed the truck to get a better look as he went by, turning down the radio at the same time.

"Matt! Watch where you're going," Danny yelled, bracing himself as the truck flew off the road and rolled straight into the grass-covered bank. It halted abruptly. Both men were slammed back in their seats and held prisoner by their seat belts.

"Damn!" Matt roared. He turned to his brother. "Are you all right?"

"No, I'm not all right, you big lug, you ran us off the road gawking at Kate Drake again. I hurt everywhere. I need a neck brace, and I think I might have broken my little finger." Danny held up his hand, gripping his wrist and emitting groans loudly.

"Oh shut up," Matt said rudely.

"Matthew Granite. Good heavens, are you hurt? I have a cell phone and can go out to the bluff and call for help."

Kate's voice was everything he remembered. Soft. Melodic. Meant for long nights and satin sheets. Matt turned his head to look at her. To drink her in. It had been four long years since he'd last spoken with her. She stood beside his truck, reins looped in her hand, her large green eyes anxious. He couldn't help but notice she had the most beautiful skin. Flawless. Perfect. It looked so soft, he wanted to stroke his finger down her cheek just to see if she was real.

"I'm fine, Kate." It was a miracle he found his voice. His tongue seemed to stick to the roof of his mouth. "I must have tried to take the turn a little too fast."

A snort of derision came from Danny's side of the truck. "You were driving like a turtle. You just weren't looking where you were going."

The toe of Matt's boot landed solidly against his brother's shin, and Danny let out a hair-raising yowl.

"No wonder Old Man Mars wanted to kick you last year," Matt muttered under his breath.

"Daniel? Are you hurt?" Kate sounded anxious, but her fascinating lower lip quivered as if close to laughter.

Determined to get her away from his brother, Matt hastily shoved the door open with more force than necessary. The door thumped soundly against Kate's legs. She jumped back, the horse half reared, and Danny, damn him, laughed like the hyena he was.

Matt groaned. It never failed. He was a decorated U.S. Army Ranger, had been in the service for years, running covert missions where his life depended on his physical skills and his cool demeanor, yet he always managed to feel clumsy and rough in front of Kate. He unfolded his large frame, towering over her, feeling like a giant. Kate was always perfect. Poised. Articulate. Graceful. There she was, looking beautiful dressed all in white with her hair attractively windblown. She was the only person in the world who could make him lose his cool and raise his temperature at the same time just by smiling.

"Is Danny really hurt?" Kate asked, turning her head slightly while she tried to calm the nervous horse.

It gave Matt a great view of her figure. He drank her in, his hungry gaze drifting over her soft curves. He'd always loved watching her walk away from him. Nobody moved in the same sexy way she did. She looked so proper, yet she had that come-on walk and the bedroom eyes and glorious hair a man would want to feel sliding over his skin all night long. He just managed to stifle a groan. How had he not known, *sensed* that Kate was back in town. His radar must be failing him.

"Danny's fine, Kate," Matt assured her.

She sent him a quick smile over her shoulder, her eyes sparkling at him. "Just how many accidents have you been in, Matt? It seems that on the rare occasions I've seen you, over the last few years, your poor vehicle has been crunched."

It was true, but it was her fault. Kate Drake acted as some sort of catalyst for strange behavior. He was good at everything. *Everything.* Unless Kate was around—then he could barely manage to speak properly.

The horse moved restlessly, demanding Kate's immediate attention, giving Matt time to realize his jeans and blue chambray work shirt were streaked with dirt, sawdust, and a powdery cement mixture in complete contrast to her immaculate white attire. He took the opportunity to slap the dust from his clothing, sending up a gray cloud that enveloped Kate as she turned back toward him. She coughed delicately, fluttering her long feathery lashes to keep the dust from stinging her eyes. Another derisive hoot came from Danny's direction.

Matt sent his brother a look that promised instant death before turning back to Kate. "I had no idea you were in town. The town gossips let me down." Inez at the grocery store had mentioned Sarah was in town, as well as Hannah and Abigail, three of her six sisters, but Inez hadn't said a word about Kate.

"Sarah came back for a visit, and you know how my family is, we get together as often as possible." She shrugged, a simple enough gesture, but on her it was damned sexy. "I've been in London doing research for my latest thriller." She laughed softly. The sound played right down his spine and did interesting things to his body. "London fog is always so perfect for a scary setting. Before that it was Borneo." Kate traveled the world, researching and writing her bestselling novels and murder mysteries. She was so beautiful it hurt to look at her, so sophisticated he felt primitive in her presence. She was so sexy he always had the desire to turn caveman and toss her over his shoulder and carry her off to his private lair. "Sarah's engaged to Damon Wilder." She tilted her head slightly and patted the horse's neck again. "Have you met him?"

"No, but everyone is talking about it. No one expected Sarah to get married."

Matt watched the way the sunlight kissed her hair, turning the silky strands into a blazing mass of temptation. His gaze followed her hand stroking the horse's neck, and he noted the absence of a ring with relief.

Danny cleared his throat. He leaned out the driver's side. "You're drooling, bro." He whispered it in an overloud voice.

Without missing a beat, Matt kicked the door closed. "Are you going to be staying very long this visit?" He held his breath waiting for her answer. To make matters worse, Danny snickered. Matt sent up a silent vow that their parents would have one less child to fuss over before the day was out.

"I've actually decided to stay and make Sea Haven my home base. I bought the old mill up on the cliffs above Sea Lion Cove. I'm planning on renovating the mill into a bookstore and coffee shop, and to modernize the house so I can live in it. I'm tired of wandering. I'm ready to come home again."

Kate smiled. She had perfect teeth to go with her perfect skin. Matt found himself staring at her while the earth shook beneath his feet. He stood there, grinning at the thought of Kate living in their hometown permanently.

A shadow swept across the sky, black threads swirling and boiling, a dark cauldron of clouds blotting out the sun. A seagull shrieked once. Then the entire flock of birds overhead took up the warning cry. Matt was so caught up in Kate's smile, he didn't realize the ground was really rolling, and it wasn't just her amazing effect on him. The horse backed dangerously close to the road, tossing its head in fright, nearly dragging Kate from her feet. Matt swiftly reached past her and gathered the reins in one hand to steady the animal. He swept his other arm around Kate's waist, anchoring her smaller body to his, to keep her from falling as a jagged crack opened several feet from them and spread rapidly along the ground, heading right for Kate's feet. Matt lifted her up and away from the gaping hole, dragging her back several feet, horse in tow, away from the spreading crack. It was only a few inches wide, but it was several inches deep, very long, and ran up the side of the embankment.

"You all right, Danny?" he called to his brother.

"Yeah, I'm fine. That was a big one."

Kate clung to Matt, her small hands clutching at his shoulders. He heard the sharp intake of her breath that belied her calm demeanor, but she didn't cry out. The ground settled, and Matt allowed her feet to touch the path but retained his hold on her. She was incredibly warm and soft and smelled of fresh flowers. He leaned over her, inhaling her fragrance, his chin brushing the top of her head. "You okay, Kate?"

Appearing as serene as ever, Kate murmured soothingly to the horse. Nothing ruffled her. Not earthquakes
and certainly not Matthew Granite. "Yes, of course, it was
just a little earthquake." She glanced up at the boiling
clouds with a small frown of puzzlement.

"It was a fairly good one. And the ground opened
damn near at your feet."

Kate continued to pat the horse's neck, seemingly
unaware that Matt was still holding her, caging her body
between his and the animal. He could see her hands
tremble as she struggled to maintain composure, and it
made him admire her all the more. She lifted her face to
the wind. "I love the sea breeze. The minute I feel it on
my face, I feel as if I'm home."

Matt cleared his throat. Kate had a beautiful profile.
Her hair was swept up in some fancy knot, showing off
her long, graceful neck. When she turned, her breasts
thrust against the thin shirt, full and round and so
enticing it was all he could do to keep from leaning
down and putting his mouth over the clinging white
fabric. He tried to move, to step away from her, but he
was drawn to her. Mesmerized by her. She'd always
reminded him of a ballerina, with her elegant lines and
soft, feminine curves. His lungs burned for air, and
there was a strange roaring in his head. It took three
tries opening his mouth before a coherent word came
out. "If you're really serious about renovation, Kate, it
just so happens my family's in the construction business."

She turned the full power of her huge eyes on him. "I
do recall all of you are builders. That's always struck me

as a wonderful occupation." She reached out and took his hands. He had big hands, rough and callused, whereas her hands were soft and small. "I always loved your hands, Matthew. When I was a young girl I remember wishing I had your capable hands." Her words, as much as her touch, sent little flames licking along his skin.

Matt was certain he heard a snort and probably a snicker coming from the direction of his younger brother.

"I think you've held on to her long enough, bro," Danny called. "The ground stopped pitching a few minutes ago."

Matt was too much of a gentleman to point out to his brother that Kate was holding *his* hands. Looking down at her, he saw faint color steal under her skin. Reluctantly, he stepped away from her. The wind tugged at tendrils of her hair, but it only made her look more alluring. "Sorry, Kate. This is the first time in a while we've had an earthquake shake us up so hard." He raked his fingers through his dark hair in agitation, searching for something brilliant to say to keep her there. His mind was blank. Totally blank. Kate turned back to her horse. He began to feel desperate. He was a grown man, hardworking, some said brilliant when it came to designing, and most women quite frankly threw themselves at him, but Kate calmly gathered the reins of her horse, no weak knees, completely unaffected by his presence. He wiped the sweat suddenly beading on his forehead, leaving a smear of dirt behind.

"Kate." It came out softly.

Danny stuck his head out the window on the driver's side. "Do you want a little help with the old mill, Kate? Matt actually is fairly decent at that sort of thing. He obviously can't drive, and he can't talk, but he's hell on wheels with renovations."

Kate's eyes lit up. "I would love that, Matthew, but I really wouldn't want to presume on our friendship. It would have to be a business arrangement."

Matt hadn't realized she thought of them as friends. Kate rarely spoke to him, other than their strange, brief conversations when they'd run into one another by chance during her high school years. He liked the idea of being friends with her. Every cell in his body went on alert when she was near him, it always happened that way, even when she'd been a teenager and he'd been in his first years of college. Kate had always brought out his protective instincts, but mostly he'd felt he had to protect her from his own attraction to her. That had been distasteful to a man like Matt. He had taken his secret fantasies of her to every foreign country he'd been sent to. She had shared his days and nights in the jungles and deserts, in the worst of situations, and the memory of her had gotten him home. Now, a full-grown man who had fought wars and had more than enough life experience to give him confidence, he found he could speak easily and naturally to any other woman. Only Kate made him tongue-tied. He'd take friendship with her. At least it was a start. "Tell me when you want me to take a look, Kate, and I'll arrange my schedule accordingly. Being my own boss has its advantages."

"Then I'm going to take advantage of your generous

offer and ask if you could go out there with me tomorrow afternoon. Do you think you can manage it that soon? I wouldn't ask, but I'm trying to get this project off the ground as soon as possible."

"It sounds great. I'll pick you up at the cliff house around four. You are staying there with your sisters, aren't you?"

Kate nodded and turned to watch the sheriff cruise up behind the pickup truck. Matt watched her face, mainly because he couldn't tear his gaze away from her. Her smile was gracious, friendly even, but he was aware even before he turned his head that the man getting out of the sheriff's cruiser was Jonas Harrington. It occurred to him that he knew Kate far too well, her every expression. And that meant he had spent too much time watching her. Kate was smiling, but she had stiffened just that little bit. She always did that around Jonas. All of her sisters did. For the first time he wondered why Kate reacted that way.

"Well, Kate, I see you caused another accident," Jonas said in greeting. He shook Matt's hand and clapped him on the back. "The Drake sisters have a tendency to wreak havoc everywhere they go." He winked at Matt.

Kate simply lifted an eyebrow. "You've been saying that since we were children."

Jonas leaned over to brush a casual kiss along Kate's cheek. Something black and lethal, whose existence Matt didn't want to recognize, moved inside of him like a dark shadow. He put a blatantly possessive hand on Kate's back.

Jonas ignored Matt's body language. "I'll still be making the same accusation when you're all in your eighties, Kate. Where is everyone?" He looked around as if expecting her sisters to appear galloping over the mountaintop.

"You look a little nervous, Jonas," Danny observed from the safety of the truck. "What'd you do this time? Arrest Hannah and throw her beautiful butt in jail on some trumped-up charge?"

He subsided when Kate turned the full power of her gaze on him. The wind rushed up from the sea, bringing the scent and feel of the ocean. "I had no idea you were so interested in my sister's anatomy, Danny."

"Come on, Kate, she's gorgeous; every man's interested in Hannah's anatomy," Danny pointed out, unrepentant.

"And if she doesn't want them to look, what is she doing allowing every photographer from here to hell and back to take pictures of her?" Jonas demanded. "And just for your information, I wouldn't have to trump up charges if I wanted to arrest Hannah," he added with a black scowl. "I ought to run her in for indecent exposure. That glitzy magazine in Inez's store has her on the cover . . . naked!"

"She is not naked. She's wearing a swimsuit, Jonas, with a sarong over it." Kate sounded as calm as ever, but Matt noted that her hand tightened on the reins of her horse until her knuckles turned white. He moved even closer to her, inserting himself between her and the sheriff.

"She might try a decent one-piece and maybe a robe that went down to her ankles or something. And does she have to strike that stupid pose just to make everyone stare . . ." Jonas broke off as the wind gusted again, howling this time, bringing whispers in the swirling chaos of leaves and droplets of seawater. His hat was swept from his head and carried away from the group. The wind shifted direction, rushing back to the ocean, retreating in much the same manner as a wave from the shore. The sudden breeze took the hat with it, sailing it over the cliffs and into the choppy water below.

Jonas spun around and looked toward the large house set up on the cliffs in the distance. "Damn it, Hannah. That's the third hat I've lost since you've been home." He shouted the words into the vortex of the wind.

There was a small silence. Matt cleared his throat. "Jonas. I don't think she can hear you from here."

Jonas glared at him. "She can hear me. Can't she, Kate? She knows exactly what I'm saying. You tell her this isn't funny anymore. She can stop with her little wind games."

"You believe all the things people say about the Drake sisters, don't you, Jonas?" Danny said. He imitated the opening theme of *The Twilight Zone*.

Matt stared down at Kate's hand. The reins were trembling. He covered her hand with his own, steadying the leather reins she was clenching. "I'll be happy to come look at the mill tomorrow, Kate. Would you like a leg up?"

"Thanks, Matthew. I'd appreciate it."

He didn't bother with cupping his hands together to assist her into the saddle. He simply lifted her. He was tall and strong, and it was easy to swing her onto the horse. She settled into the saddle as if born there. Elegant. Refined. As close to perfection as any dream he could conjure up and just as far out of reach. "I'll see you then. Say hello to your sisters for me."

"I'll do that, Matthew, and you give my best to your parents. It was nice to see you, Danny." Her cool gaze swept over Jonas. "I'm sure you'll be by the house, Jonas."

Jonas shrugged. "I take my job seriously, Kate."

Matt watched her ride away, waiting until a curve in the road took her out of sight before turning on the sheriff. "What the hell was that all about?"

"You know all seven of the Drake women drive me crazy half the time," Jonas said. "I've told you all the trouble they get up to. You're always grilling me about them. Well—" he grinned evilly as he indicated the truck— "Isn't this the third accident you've had with Kate in the vicinity? You should know what I mean."

Jonas had grown up with Matt Granite, had gone through school, joined the Army, the Rangers, and fought side by side with him. He knew how Matt felt about Kate. It was no secret. Matt wasn't very good at hiding his feelings from his family and friends, especially since Jonas had gotten out of the service two years before Matt and Matt had continually interrogated him about Kate's whereabouts and marital status. Matt had been home three years and he'd been waiting for Kate to come home for good, too.

Danny snickered. "You were there back in his college days, Jonas, when he drove Dad's truck into the creek bed and hung it up on a rock. Wasn't Kate about three at the time?"

Matt took a deep breath. He couldn't kill his brother in front of the sheriff, even if it was Jonas. The time he had wrecked his father's truck, driving it without permission, Kate had been about fifteen, far too young for a college man to be looking at her, and he was still embarrassed that his brothers and Jonas had known why he'd wrecked the vehicle. Of course he'd known the Drake sisters, everyone in town knew them, but he'd never *looked* at them. Not in a fascinated, physical, male way. Until he'd seen Kate standing in a creek bed picking blackberries with the sun kissing her hair and her large sea-green eyes looking back at him. The second time he'd wrecked a vehicle had been four years ago. Matt had been home on leave, and he'd been so busy looking at Kate walking on the sidewalk with her sisters, he'd failed to realize he was parked in front of a cement hump and had hung up his mother's car on it when he'd gone to pull out. Now, ignoring his brother's jibe, he moved around the truck to inspect the damage. "I think I can get the truck out without a tow."

"I see you upset old man Mars." Jonas pointed to the tomato smears on the rear window.

"You know Matt, he just had to wish the old man a Merry Christmas." Danny shoved open the door. "He likes to stir the old geezer up right before the pageant. He does it every year. The time Mom made me play the little drummer boy, Mars broke my drumsticks into ten pieces and threw them on the ground and then jumped up and down on them. All my brothers got a kick out of that, but I've been traumatized ever since. I have nightmares about being stomped by him."

Jonas laughed. "Mars is a strange old man, but he's harmless enough. And he gives away most of his produce to the people who need it. He takes it to some of the single moms in town and some of the elderly couples. And I know he feeds the Ruttermyer boy, the one with Down's syndrome who works at odd jobs for everyone. He persuaded Donna to give the boy a room right next to her gift shop. I know he helps that boy with his bills."

"Yeah, deep down he's a good man," Matt agreed. A slow grin spread over his face. "He just hates Christmas." He nodded toward the other side of the truck, and the other two men went to the front to scrape away the mud and dirt and push until they separated the bumper from the embankment. "I didn't appreciate you saying anything to Kate about her and her sisters being different, Jonas." Matt said it in a low voice, but Jonas and he had been friends since they were boys, and Jonas recognized the warning tone.

"I'm not going to pretend they're like everyone else, Matt, not even for you," Jonas snapped. "The Drakes are special. They have gifts, and they use themselves up for everyone else without a thought for themselves or their own safety. I'm going to watch out for them whether they like or it not. Sarah Drake nearly got herself killed a few weeks ago. Hannah and Kate and Abbey were with her and also might have been killed."

Matt felt the words as a blow somewhere in the vicinity of his gut. His heart did a curious somersaulting dive in his chest. "I heard about Sarah, but I hadn't heard the others were there. What happened?"

"To make a long story short, Wilder had people trail him here. They wanted information only he could give them. He helped design our national defense system, and the government wanted him protected at all costs. With Sarah being from Sea Haven, it was natural enough for the Feds to send her in to guard him. These people had gotten their hands on him once before, killed his assistant right in front of him, and tortured him. That's why he uses a cane when he walks. They broke into the Drakes' house, armed to the teeth when he was there, and were ready to kill Wilder and the Drakes to get what they wanted." The anger in Jonas's voice deepened.

"No one said a word about Kate being in the house at the same time. I knew Sarah was guarding Damon Wilder and that he was a defense expert in some kind of trouble, but . . ." Matt trailed off as he looked back toward the house on the cliff. It was covered with Christmas lights. Beside it was a tall full Douglas fir tree, completely decorated and flashing lights even before the sun went down. When he looked toward the house he felt a sense of peace. Of rightness. The Drake sisters were the town's treasures. He looked away from the cliff toward the old mill. It was farther up the road, built over Sea Lion Cove. A strange cloud formation hung over the small inlet and spread slowly toward land. The shape captured his imagination, a yawning black mouth, jaws opening wide, heading straight for them.

"All of them were nearly murdered," Jonas said. His eyes went flat and cold. "The Drakes take on far too much, and everyone just expects them to do it without thinking of the cost to them."

"I never thought of it like that, Jonas. Now that you mention it, I've seen them all drained of energy after helping out the way they do." Matt didn't take his eyes from the sky. He watched a seagull veer frantically from the path of the slow-moving cloud, braking sharply in midair, wings flapping strongly in agitation. Wisps of fog began to rise from the sea and drift toward shore. "Maybe we all should pay more attention to what's happening with them," he murmured softly, more to himself than to the others.

chapter
2

The snowglobe they hold has a secret inside
Where the mists roll in place of the snow that's outside

INHALING THE MINGLED SCENTS OF CINNA-
MON and pine, Kate wandered into the kitchen
of the cliff house. The sound of Christmas
music filled the air and blended with the aroma of fresh-
baked cookies and the fragrance of richly scented candles. "Is that Joley's voice?" Kate asked, leaning her hip
comfortably against the heavily carved wood cabinet.
"When did she make a Christmas collection?"

Hannah Drake spun around, teakettle in her hands. Her
abundance of blond hair shimmered for a moment in the
last rays of sunshine pouring through the bay window. "Kate,
I didn't hear you get out of the shower. I think I was in my
own little world. Joley sent the CD as a surprise, although she
made a point of saying it was not to go out of the family."

They both laughed affectionately. "Joley and that band
of hers. She can sing just about anything from gospel to
blues, from rock to rap, but she's so careful not to let anyone know. I think she likes her bad girl image. Did she
mention whether she's coming home for Christmas? I
know she was touring."

Hannah's face lit up, her smile brilliant. "She's going to try. I can't wait to see her. We keep missing each other in our travels."

"I hope she gets here soon. Talking on the phone just isn't the same as all of us being together." Kate swept a stray tendril of hair behind her ear. "What about Mom and Dad? Has anyone heard from them? Are they coming here for Christmas?"

Hannah shook her head. "Last I heard they sent kisses and hugs and were snuggling together in their little chalet in the Swiss Alps. Libby got in a quick visit with them before she headed out to the Congo. She said she was coming home for Christmas. Mom and Dad promised next year they'd be here with us."

Kate laughed softly as she leaned over to sniff the canister of loose tea. "Mom and Dad are still such lovebirds. What are you making?"

"I was in the mood for a little lavender, but anything is fine." Hannah scrutinized Kate closely. "But let's go with chamomile. Something soothing."

Kate smiled. "You think I need a little soothing?"

Hannah nodded as she measured the tea into a small pot. "Tell me."

"I ran into Matthew Granite and his brother Danny." Kate tried to sound casual, when her entire body was trembling. Only Matt could do that to her. Only Matt moved her. She'd never understood why.

"Matthew Granite? I thought that might be him." Hannah's huge blue eyes settled on her sister with compassion and interest. "How did he seem?"

Kate shrugged her slender shoulders. "Wonderful.

Helpful. He offered to look at the old mill for me and help with the renovations." She always enjoyed looking at her younger sister. Hannah wasn't just beautiful, she was strikingly so, exotically so, with her bone structure, abundance of pale, almost platinum hair, her enormous, heavily lashed eyes, and sultry lips. Beauty radiated from her. Kate had always thought Hannah's extraordinary beauty came from the inside out. She watched the graceful movements of Hannah's hands as she went about making tea. "Matt's always so helpful." She sighed.

Hannah reached out to her, clasping Kate's hands in a gesture of solidarity. "Was it the same?"

"You mean with his brothers laughing all the time? Well, only one was with him, Danny." Color crept up under Kate's skin. "Yes, of course. Every time I get anywhere near the Granites they all laugh. I have no idea why. It isn't the same way Jonas is with you. Matthew never needles me. He's always perfectly polite, but I seem to have some humorous effect on his family. I try as hard as I can just to be polite and calm, but the brothers laugh until I want to go check a mirror to see if I have spinach in my teeth. Matthew just glares at them, but it really draws attention to all the silly things I do in front of him." She squeezed Hannah's fingers before letting her hand go. "I've showered and changed, but I came home with my clothes covered with dirt. Poor Matthew just came from work, was dusting himself off, and I had to be two steps behind him. When he tried to open his truck door, of course I managed to get too close."

"Oh, Katie, honey, I'm so sorry. What happened?" Hannah's face mirrored her sister's distress.

Kate shrugged. "The door nearly knocked me over, and he had to apologize yet again. The poor man spends every minute apologizing to me. I'll bet he wishes he never had to see me again."

"No he doesn't," Hannah said firmly. "I think he's always been sweet on you."

Kate sighed. "You and I both know Matthew Granite would never look at me twice. He's wild and rough and an adrenaline junkie. He played every sport in high school and college. He joined the Rangers. I researched what they do. Even their creed is a bit frightening. They arrive at the 'cutting edge of battle' and they never fail their comrades and give more than one hundred percent. The creed says things like fight on even if you're the lone survivor, and *surrender* is not a Ranger word." She shuddered delicately. "He's a wild man, and he does very scary wild things. He's going to look at women who climb mountains and scoff in the face of danger. Can you see me doing that?"

"Kate," Hannah said softly, "maybe he's more settled now. He went out and did his save the world thing and now he's come home and he's working the family business. He could have changed."

Kate forced a fleeting smile. "Men like Matthew don't change, Hannah. I was telling you my tale of woe. We were just at the point where Jonas drove up. You know how he has to make his little 'Drake sisters' comments. He implied every time I was around something awful happened. It just made the situation worse." She sighed again. "I tried to look as though it didn't bother me, but I think Matthew knew."

"Jonas Harrington needs to fall into the ocean and have a nice hungry shark come swimming by." Hannah dragged the whistling teakettle from the stove and splashed water into the teapot, a fine fury radiating from her at the thought of Jonas Harrington saying anything to upset Kate. The water boiled in the little china teapot, bubbles roiling and bursting with a steady fury. Steam rose.

Kate covered the top of the teapot with her palm, settling the water back down. "You were out on the captain's walk."

Hannah nodded, unrepentant. "The earthquake bothered me. I felt something rising beneath the earth. I can't explain it, Kate, but it frightened me. I was sitting here listening to Joley's Christmas music, you know how much I love Christmas, then I felt the quake. Almost on the heels of it, something else disturbed the earth. I felt it as a darkness rising upward. I knew you were out riding, so I went out to the walk to make certain you weren't in trouble."

"And you felt the wind come in off the sea," Kate said. She leaned her hip against the counter. "I felt it too." She frowned and drummed her fingers on the tiled counter. "I smelled something, Hannah, something old and bitter in the wind."

"Evil?" Hannah ventured.

Kate shook her head slowly. "It wasn't that exactly. Well," she hedged, "maybe. I don't know. What did you think?"

Hannah leaned against the brightly tiled sink, her body so graceful the casual movement seemed balletic. "I honestly don't know, Kate, but it isn't good. I've felt disturbed ever since the earthquake and when I looked at the mosaic, there was a black shadow beneath the ground. I could barely make it out because it seemed to move and not stay in one place."

Kate glanced at the floor in the house's entryway. Her grandmother, along with her grandmother's six sisters, had made the mosaic, women of power and magic, seven sisters creating a timeless floor of infinite beauty. To most people it was simply a unique floor, but the Drake sisters could read many things in the ever-changing shadows that ran within it. "How very strange that neither of us knows precisely whether the disturbance is evil." She shrugged her shoulders and drew in a deep breath filled with cinnamon and pine. "I love the fragrances of Christmas." She tapped her foot, a small smile hovering on her face.

"You're holding back on me," Hannah guessed, her voice suddenly teasing. "Something else happened, didn't it?"

"When the earthquake started, Matthew put his arm around me to steady me, and we just stood there, even after it was over." She grinned at Hannah. "He is so strong. You have no idea. That man is all muscle. It's a wonder I didn't end up in a puddle at his feet! But I managed to look cool and serene."

Hannah pretended to swoon. "I wish I could have seen it. Matthew is definitely hot, even if he is a Neanderthal. I must have come up on the captain's walk just after that, just in time to see the slimy toad of the world arrive in his little sheriff's car." She smirked. "Too bad the wind came up, and his precious little hat went sailing out to sea."

"Shame on you, Hannah," Kate scolded halfheartedly. "Jonas means well. He's just so used to everyone doing everything he says, and we always seem to be in the middle of any kind of trouble in Sea Haven. You're beginning to enjoy tormenting him."

"Why shouldn't I? He's tormented me for years."

There was so much pain in Hannah's voice that Kate slipped her arm around her sister's waist to comfort her. Jonas had known them all since they were children, and he'd never understood Hannah. She'd been an extraordinarily beautiful, very intelligent child, but she'd been so painfully shy outside of her own home, the sisters had had to work their magic just to get her to school every day. Jonas had been certain she was haughty, when in fact, she'd rarely been able to speak in public. "Well, all in all, it was a good day. You managed to lose another hat for Jonas, and I got to be up close and personal with the hottest man in Sea Haven." Kate hugged Hannah before pouring herself a cup of tea and walking into the living room with it.

Hannah followed her. "Did you get your manuscript mailed off?"

Kate nodded. "Murder and mayhem will prevail in a small coastal town. I forgot to put the tea cozy back on the pot, will you do it?"

Hannah glanced into the kitchen and lifted her arms.

When Kate looked back, the cozy was safely on the teapot. "Thanks, Hannah. I do have to say, Jonas was invaluable to me with the research."

"I know he was, but don't credit him with doing it to be nice or anything." Hannah's large blue eyes reflected her laughter. "He was trying to get on your good side so you'd persuade me to stop messing around with his precious hats."

They both swung around as the front door burst open. Abigail Drake rushed in, a small woman with dark eyes and a wealth of red-gold hair spilling down her back in a thick ponytail. Her face was flushed and her eyes overbright. The moment she glimpsed her sisters, she burst into tears.

"Abbey!" Hannah set her teacup down on the highly polished coffee table. "What is it? You never cry."

"I humiliated myself in front of the entire Christmas pageant committee," Abigail said miserably. She threw herself into the overstuffed armchair, curled her feet under her, and covered her face with her hands. "I can never face any of them again."

Hannah and Kate rushed to her side, both putting their arms around her. "Don't cry, Abbey. What happened? Maybe we can fix it. It can't be that bad."

"It was bad," Abigail muttered from between her fingers. "I accidentally used *the voice*. I wasn't paying attention. There was the earthquake, and I was so distracted because I felt something under us, something moving just below the surface seeking a way out. I *felt* it." Of all the talents gifted to the sisters, Abigail felt hers was the worst. Her voice could be used to extract the truth from people around her. As a child, before she'd learn to control the tone and the wording of her sentences, she'd been very unpopular with her classmates. They would often blurt out the truth of some escapade to their parents or a teacher whenever they were in her presence. Abigail pulled her hands down and stared at them with her sad eyes. "It isn't an excuse. I'm not a teenager. I know I have to be alert all the time."

Hannah and Kate exchanged a long, fearful look. "We felt the shadow too, Abbey. It was very disconcerting to both of us. What happened at the meeting?"

Abbey drew her legs up tighter into her body. "We were all discussing the Christmas pageant." She rubbed her chin on the top of her knees. "I felt the rift in the earth, a blackness welling up, and the next thing I knew I was asking for the truth." She clapped her hands over her ears. "I got the truth too. Everyone did. Bruce Harper is having an affair with Mason Fredrickson's wife. They were all in the room. Bruce and Mason got in a terrible fistfight, and Letty Harper burst into tears and ran out. She's six months pregnant. Sylvia Fredrickson slapped me across the face and walked out, leaving me standing there with everyone looking at me." She burst into tears all over again.

Kate frowned as she rubbed her sister's shoulders. She could feel the waves of distress pouring off of Abigail. "It's all right now, honey. You're home, and you're safe." At once a soothing tranquillity swept into the room, a sense of peace. The wicks on the unlit candles on the mantel leapt to life with bright orange-red flames. Joley's voice poured into the room, uplifting and melodic, bringing with it a sense of home and Christmas cheer. Kate leaned into her sister. "Abigail, your talent is a tremendous gift, and you have always used it for good. This was a distortion of your talent, not something any of us could have foreseen. Let it go. Just breathe and let it go."

Abbey managed a small smile, the sobs fading at the sound of her sister's voice. Kate the peacemaker. Most thought she prevented fights and solved problems, but in truth, she had a magic about her, a tranquillity and inner peace she shared with others just by the way she spoke. "I wish I had your gift, Kate," Abbey said. She pressed her hand to her cheek. "I didn't mind everyone's finding out about Sylvia—she likes to think she can get any man— but poor little Letty, pregnant and loving her stupid unfaithful husband so much. That was heartbreaking. And at Christmas too. What possessed me to be so careless? I'm so ashamed of myself."

"What exactly did you say, Abbey?" Kate asked.

Abbey looked confused. "Everyone had put in a variety of ideas for acting out the play we do every year and someone asked if they really liked the old script and should we keep it as a tradition or should we modernize it. I think I said, now would be a good time to tell the truth if you want to make any major changes. I meant with the script, not in people's lives." She rubbed her temples. "I haven't made a mistake like that since I was a teenager. I'm so careful to avoid the word *truth*." She scrubbed her hand over her face a second time, trying to erase the sting of Sylvia's hand. "You know if I use that word everyone in the immediate vicinity tells the truth about everything."

"It worries me that we all felt the same disturbance," Kate said. "Hannah saw a dark shadow in the mosaic. You said something you would never have normally said, and a crack opened up nearly at my feet and ran all the way up the embankment."

Hannah gasped. "You didn't tell me that. Kate, it could have been an attack on you. You're the most . . ." She broke off, looking at Abbey.

Kate lifted her chin. "I'm the most what?"

Hannah shrugged. "You're the best of us. You don't have a mean bone in your body. You just don't, Katie. I'm sorry, I know you hate our saying that, but you don't even know how to dislike someone. You're just so . . ."

"*Don't* say perfect," Kate warned. "I'm not perfect. And I think that's why Matthew's brothers always laugh at me. They think I want to be perfect and fall short."

Hannah and Abbey exchanged a long, worried look. "I think we should call the others," Hannah said. "Sarah will want to know about this. She must have felt the earthquake too. We can ask her if anything strange happened to her. And we should call Joley, Libby, and Elle. Something's wrong, Kate, I just feel it. It's as if the earthquake unleashed a malicious force. I'm afraid it could be directed at you."

Kate took a long sip of tea. The taste was as soothing as the aroma. "Go ahead, it can't hurt to see what the others have to say. I'm not going to worry about it. I didn't feel a direct threat. I'm not calling Sarah though. She and Damon are probably twined around one another. You can feel the heat right through the telephone line."

"I can go to the captain's walk and signal her," Hannah said wickedly. "Their bedroom window faces us, and for some utterly mysterious reason the curtain keeps opening in that particular room."

"Hannah!" Kate tried not to laugh. "You're impossible."

Hannah did laugh. "And you are perfect whether you want to acknowledge it or not. At least to me."

"And me," Abigail said.

Kate smiled at them. "I'm not all that perfect. I'd like to give Sylvia Fredrickson a piece of mind. She had no right hitting you, Abbey. Even in high school she was nasty."

"I'll take care of Sylvia," Hannah said. "Don't worry, Abbey. She'll spend a long time thinking about how stupid it was to hit you."

"Hannah!" Kate and Abbey chorused her name in protest.

Hannah burst out laughing. "I get the message, Kate. You'll talk to Sylvia, but you don't want me casting in her direction."

Kate grinned. "I should have known you were baiting me."

"Who said I didn't mean it? Sylvia gives women a bad name."

Kate shook her head. "Hannah Drake, you're becoming a bloodthirsty little witch. I think Jonas is having a bad influence on you." She touched Abbey's cheek gently. "Even for this we can't use our gifts for anything other than good."

Hannah made a face. "It's good for Jonas to have to chase his hat. It keeps him from becoming too arrogant and bossy. And who knows what great lesson Sylvia Fredrickson would learn if I tweaked her just a little bit." Before either sister could say anything, she laughed softly. "I'm not going to do anything horrible to her, I just love to see you both get that 'there-goes-Hannah-look' on your faces."

Kate nudged Abbey, ignoring Hannah's mischievous grin. "Guess what I'll be doing tomorrow? Matthew

Granite agreed to look over the mill with me tomorrow. I'm hoping none of his brothers will be around to laugh at me, and maybe he'll notice I'm a grown woman, not a gawky teenager. You'd think the fact that I've traveled all over the world and that I'm a successful author would impress him, but he just looks at me exactly the same way he did when I was in high school."

Hannah and Abbey exchanged a quick, apprehensive look. "Kate, you're going to spend the afternoon with him? Do you really want to do that?" Abigail asked.

Kate nodded. "I like to be with him. Don't ask me why, I just do."

"Kate, you haven't been home in ages. Matthew has a certain reputation," Abigail said hesitantly. "He's always been easygoing with you, and he's very charming, but he's . . ." She trailed off and looked to Hannah for direction.

"What? A ladies' man? I would presume a man his age has dated." Kate walked across the room to touch the first of the seven stockings hung in a row along the mantelpiece. It allowed her to keep her expression hidden from her sisters. "I know he's been in relationships."

"That's just it, Kate. He doesn't have relationships. At best he has one-night stands. Women find him charming and mysterious, and he finds them annoying. Seriously, Kate, don't *really* fall for him. He looks great on the outside, but he has a caveman attitude. He was in the military so long, doing all the secret Special Forces kind of stuff, and he just expects everyone to fall in line with his orders. It's probably why he isn't impressed with your world travels. Please don't fall for him," Hannah pleaded. "I couldn't bear it if he hurt you, Kate."

"You're so certain he wouldn't fall for me? A few minutes ago you were saying you thought he might be sweet on me." Kate tried to guard her voice, to keep her tone strictly neutral when there was a peculiar ache inside. "I really don't need the warning. Men like Matthew don't look at women like me." She shrugged. "It doesn't bother me. I need solitude, I always have. And I don't have a tremendous amount of time to give to a relationship."

"What do you mean, Matthew wouldn't look at a woman like you?" Abbey was outraged. "What are you talking about, Kate?"

Kate took another sip of tea and smiled at her sisters over the rim of her teacup. "Don't worry, I'm not feeling sorry for myself. I know I'm different. I was born the way I am. All of you stand out. Your looks, your personalities, even you, Hannah, with being so painfully shy, you embrace life. You all live it. You don't let your weaknesses or failings stand in your way. I'm an observer. I read about life. I research life. I find a corner in a room and melt into it. I can become invisible. It's an art, and I am a wonderful practitioner."

"You travel all over the world, Kate," Hannah pointed out.

"Yes, and my agent and my publisher smooth the way for me. I don't have to ask for a thing, it's all done for me. Matthew is like all of you. He throws himself into life and lives every moment. He's a born hero, riding to the rescue, carrying out the wounded on his back. He needs someone willing to do the same. I'm a born observer.

Maybe that's why I was given the ability to see into the shadows at times. A part of me is already there."

Hannah's blue eyes filled with tears. "Don't say that, Kate. Don't ever say that." She wrapped her arms around Kate and hugged her close, uncaring that a small amount of tea splashed on her. "I didn't know you felt that way. How could I not have known?"

Kate hugged her hard. "Honey, don't be upset for me. You don't understand. I'm not distressed about it. My world is books. It always has been. I love words. I love living in my imagination. I don't want to go climb a mountain. I love to study how it's done. I love to talk to people who do it, but I don't want the experience of it, the reality of it. My imagination provides a wonderful adventure without the risk or the discomfort."

"Katie," Abbey protested.

"It's the truth. I've always been attracted to Matthew Granite, but I'm far too practical to make the mistake of believing anything could ever work between us. He runs wild. I remember him being right in the middle of every rough play in football both in high school and in college. He's done so many crazy things, from serving as a Ranger to skydiving for the fun of it." She shuddered. "I don't even scuba dive. He goes white-water rafting and rock climbing for relaxation. I read a good book. We aren't in the least compatible, but I can still think he's hot."

"Are you certain you want to spend time with him?" Abbey asked.

Kate shrugged. "What I want to do is to take a look at the mosaic and see if I can make out the shadows in the earth the way Hannah did."

"Maybe all three of us can figure out what is going on," Hannah agreed. She followed Kate to the entryway, glancing over her shoulder at Abigail. "Doesn't Joley sound beautiful? She sent us her Christmas CD. She said she might be able to make it home for Christmas."

"I hope so," Abbey said. "Did Elle or Libby call?"

"Libby is in South America," Hannah said.

"I thought you said she was in the Congo," Kate interrupted.

Hannah laughed. "She *was* in the Congo, but they called her to South America. She phoned right after the quake. Some small tribe in the rain forest has some puzzling disease and they asked Libby to fly there immediately to help and of course she did. She said it will be difficult, but no matter what, she's coming home for Christmas. I think she needs to be with us. She sounded tired. Really tired. I told her we would get together and see if we could send her some energy, but she said no. She told me to conserve our strength and be very careful," Hannah reported.

Abbey and Kate stopped walking abruptly. "Are you certain Libby doesn't need us, Hannah?" Kate asked. "You know what can happen to her. She heals people in the worst of circumstances, and it thoroughly depletes her energy. Traveling those distances on top of it with little sleep won't help."

"She said no," Hannah reiterated. "I heard the weariness in her voice. She obviously needs to come home and regroup and rest, but I didn't feel as if she was in a dangerous state." She knelt on the floor at the foot of the mosaic her grandmother and her grandmother's sisters had worked so hard to make.

Relief swept through Kate. Libby always drove herself too hard, and her health suffered dramatically for it. Libby was too small, too slender, a fragile woman who pushed herself for others. Libby worked for the Center for Disease Control and traveled all over the globe. "We'll have to watch her," Kate said softly, musing aloud.

It was one of the best-loved talents of the sisters, to be able to stay in communication with one another no matter how far apart they were physically. They could 'see' one another and send energy back and forth when it was needed. Kate knelt beside Hannah in the entryway.

Kate always felt a sense of awe when she looked at the artwork on the floor. The mosaic always seemed to her to be alive with energy. Anyone looking into the mosaic felt as if they were falling into another world. The deep blue of the sea was really the ocean in the sky. Stars burst and flared into life. The moon was a shining ball of silver. Kate bent close to the mosaic to examine the greens, browns, and grays that made up mother earth.

Only Joley's voice poured into the room, then melted away on the last notes to leave the room entirely silent. The three sisters linked hands. Small bursts of electricity arced from one to the other. In the dimly lit room the energy appeared as a jagged whip of lightning dancing between the three women. Power filled the room, energy enough to move the drapes at the windows so that the material swayed and bowed.

Kate kept her eyes fixed on the darker earth tones. Something moved, down close to the edge of the mosaic, in the deeper rocks. It moved slowly, a blackened shadow, slipping from one dark area to the next. It had a serpentine, cunning way about it, shifting from the edges up toward the surface as if trying to break through. Kate let her breath out slowly, inhaled deeply to fill her lungs, and let her body go. It was the only way to walk in the shadow world that was invisible to most human eyes.

She felt the malevolence immediately, a twisted sneakiness, shrewd and determined, a being honed by rage and fueled by the need for revenge. The turmoil was overwhelming, spinning and boiling with heat and anger. It crept closer to her, awareness of her presence giving it a kind of malicious glee. She held herself still, trying to discern the dark force in the deeper shadows, but it blended too well.

"Kate!" Hannah shook her hard, catching her by the shoulders and rocking her until her head lolled back on her neck.

Abbey yanked Kate away from the mosaic and into her own body. There was a long silence while they clung to one another, breathing heavily, close to tears. The shrill ringing of the phone startled them.

"Sarah," they said simultaneously, and broke into relieved laughter.

Abbey jumped up to answer the phone. "I'm telling Sarah on you," she warned Kate, "and you're going to be in so much trouble!"

Kate gripped Hannah's hand, trying to smile at Abbey's dire prediction. "Did you feel it, Hannah?" she whispered. "Did you feel it coming after me?"

"You can't go into that world again, Kate. Not with that thing there. I couldn't read what it was, but you have to stay away from it." Hannah held Kate even tighter. "I know what it's like to be afraid all the time, Katie. I can't function in a crowd because the energy of so many people drains me. Their emotions bombard me until I can't think or breathe. You all protect me, you always have. I wish we'd done the same for you."

Kate smiled and leaned over to kiss Hannah's cheek. "I accepted my limitations a long time ago, Hannah, and I've never regretted my choice of lifestyles. I control my environment, and it works for me. I didn't have the need to do all the things you wanted to do with your life. My world is carefully built and has large walls to protect me. You're far more open to the assault. I'll be careful, Hannah. I'm not a risk taker. You don't have to worry that I'll try to find the answers without the rest of you."

"Katie!" Abbey called out. "Sarah has a few things she wants to talk to you about." She held out the phone.

Kate hugged Hannah again. "It will be all right, I promise you, honey. It's Christmas. Most everyone is coming home, and we'll have the best time ever, just like we always do when we're together."

chapter 3

A chill, colder still than the air they will feel
As I rejoice in release, as I slip past the seal

MATT STOOD BESIDE THE ENORMOUS DOUGLAS fir tree decorated with hundreds of ornaments and colorful lights. The tall tree grew in the yard up near the cliffs in front of the house. It was one of the most beautiful sights he'd ever seen, but it paled in comparison to Kate. She stood on her porch, a snowglobe in her hands, smiling at him. Her eyes were as green as the sea, and her long, thick hair was twisted into some kind of intricate knot that made him want to pull out every pin so he could watch it tumble free.

He walked up the porch steps and held out his hand. "Where in the world did you get that snowglobe? The scene inside looks exactly like your house and this Christmas tree."

She put the globe in his hands. Two of her sisters were standing on the porch with her, watching him with serious expressions on their faces. He had been so busy staring at Kate he hadn't even noticed them. His hands closed over the heavy globe, his fingers brushing Kate's. A tingle of electricity sparked its way up his arm. Almost at once the snowglobe grew warm in his hands. "Afternoon, ladies."

"Hi, Matt," Hannah greeted. Abbey nodded to him.

Although he'd made every effort to clean up after work, scrubbing his hands for a good half hour to get the dirt out from under his fingernails, he noticed with dismay that he hadn't been successful. His nails seemed to be spotlighted from the strange glow coming from inside the glass of the globe. The lights of the tree blazed unexpectedly inside the glass, while an eerie white fog began to swirl. Fascinated, he held the globe at every angle, trying to see how he had turned it on, but he couldn't find a battery or a switch anywhere. Peering closer he noticed a strange dark shadow taking shape at the base of the tree and creeping up the path toward the steps of the house. His body reacted, going on alert as he watched the shadow move stealthily.

"This thing is spooky." He handed the snowglobe to Hannah and took Kate's elbow in a deliberate, proprietary action. Staking his claim. Declaring his intentions. His fingers settled around her slender arm, and his heart actually jumped in his chest. She was wearing some lacy white shirt that clung to the shape of her rounded breasts and left her lower arms bare. The pad of his thumb slid over her petal-soft skin just to feel the texture. She shivered, and he moved his body closer to block the breeze coming in off the ocean. They said good-bye to her sisters and headed for his car.

Kate cleared her throat. "I appreciate your coming to pick me up, Matthew. I could have met you there."

"That's silly, Kate, since we're both going to the same

place, and you're on my way. I thought we might discuss the plans for the renovation over dinner when we're finished inspecting the mill." He pulled open the door to his Mustang convertible. The top was securely up. "What were you doing with the globe?"

She smiled up at him and just that easily took his breath away. "We're still putting out our decorations. Hannah just brought the globe down from the attic and was cleaning the glass. It's a Christmas tradition in our family to wish on it."

"What was that strange dark shadow moving in the globe?"

Kate abruptly turned back toward the house. Matt was standing close to her, holding the door open to the Mustang, and she bumped his chest with her nose. For a second she stood there with her eyes closed, then she inhaled deeply. He felt that breath right through his skin, all the way down to his bones. The tips of her breasts brushed his rib cage, sending fire racing through his bloodstream and pooling into a thick heat low in his belly. She smelled of cinnamon and spice. He wanted to pull her into his arms and kiss her right there. Right in front of her sisters.

"Matthew." For the first time that he could remember, Kate sounded breathless. "What are you doing?"

He realized his arms were around her. He was holding her captive against him, and his body was growing hard and making urgent demands. He cursed silently and let her go, turning away from her. "I thought you were getting into the car." His voice was rough, even to his own ears. He had never wanted a woman the way he wanted

Kate. He didn't feel gentle when he wanted to be gentle. He didn't feel nice and charming when it was usually so easy for him to be charming. He felt edgy and restless and achy as hell. He had a mad desire to scoop her up and lock her in his vehicle, a primitive, out-of-character urge when she looked on the verge of flight.

"You really saw a shadow in the globe?" she asked. "What was it doing?"

It was the last thing he expected her to say, and it sent a chill skittering down his spine. "I couldn't tell what it was. The dark shadow went from the base of the tree up the path toward the porch of the house. It is your house in the globe, isn't it? There's fog or mist instead of snowflakes swirling around. It gives the globe a very eerie effect."

Kate glanced back at her sisters. Hannah set the snowglobe very carefully on the wide banister and stepped away from it. Inside the glass, heavy fog swirled. The lights from the tiny Christmas tree glowed a strange orange and red through the mist, almost as if on fire. Matt watched Kate's sister closely. He had lived in Sea Haven all of his life. He had heard strange things about the Drake sisters. Up close to them, he *felt* power and energy crackling in the air, and it emanated from them. The power filled the space around them until he breathed it. Hannah lifted her arms, and the wind swept in from the sea. With it came soft voices, whose words were impossible to distinguish, but the chant was melodious and in harmony with the things of the earth. The strange light in the snowglobe faded and diminished until it was a soft, faint glow. The voices on the wind continued until the lights behind the glass flickered and vanished, leaving the globe a perfectly ordinary Christmas ornament.

The wind swirled cool air around them. Matt tasted the salt from the sea. He looked down at his fingers curled around Kate's arm. He had pulled her protectively to him without thought or reason. He knew he should release her, but he couldn't let go. Her slender body trembled, with power or with fear, Matt wasn't certain which, but it didn't matter to him.

Kate looked up at him. "I can't explain what just happened with the snowglobe."

"I'm not asking for an explanation. I just want you to get in my car."

She smiled up at him. "Thank you, Matthew. I really appreciate it." She relaxed visibly and allowed him to help her into the warm leather seats.

Kate felt very small beside Matt. Inside the car, he appeared enormous and powerful. His shoulders were wide enough to brush against her in the confines of the Mustang. When she inhaled, she took the masculine scent of him deep into her lungs. For a moment she felt dizzy. It made her want to laugh aloud at the thought. Kate Drake dizzy from the scent of a man. None of her sisters would believe it. The car handled the tight turns along the coastal highway with precision and ease, flowing around the corners so that she relaxed a little. Being around Matt always made her feel safe. She didn't know why, but she no longer questioned it.

He glanced over at her. "Does it bother you, the way people are always talking about your family?"

"They talk in a nice way," Kate pointed out.

"I know they do. You're the town's treasures, but does it bother you?"

Kate smiled at him. "Only you would ask me that question." She sighed. "It shouldn't bother me. We are different. We can't exactly hide it, and of course people are going to talk about our strange ways. We grew up here, so everyone knows us and to some extent they protect us from outsiders, but yes, it does bother me that people are always so aware of us when we're around." She'd never voiced that aloud to anyone, not even her sisters.

"I miss you when you're gallivanting around the world, Kate. I'm glad you've decided to come home."

Her smile widened. "You're such a flirt, Matthew, even with me, and I've known you all of my life. You haven't calmed down much since your wild college days. When I was in high school, all the girls said you were legendary at Stanford."

"Well, I wasn't. I should have gone to a college far away from here instead of only a couple of hours. It might have cut down on the talk. And I don't flirt," he said firmly. He wanted to park the car and just look at her. Touch her soft skin and kiss her for hours. The moment the thoughts crept into his head his body hardened into a dull, painful ache. He couldn't get near her without it happening. He was a grown man, and his body responded to her as if he were an adolescent.

"Matthew, you flirt with everyone. And your reputation is terrible. If I wasn't already so talked about, I'd be worried."

"No one talks about me."

She laughed softly. "I can relate the story of you and Janice Carlton by heart, I've heard it so many times."

He groaned. "Is that still going around? That happened long ago. I was on leave, it must have been what? Six years ago? I did pick her up in the bar, she was drunk, Kate. I couldn't just leave her there."

"And how did her blouse get on the bushes outside the grocery store?"

Matt glanced sideways at her. "All right, I'll admit it was her blouse, but come on, Kate, I wasn't in high school. Give me a little credit for growing up. She was as drunk as a skunk and began peeling off her clothes the minute we were driving down the street. She threw her blouse out the window and would have thrown her bra but I told her I'd put her out on the sidewalk if she did. I took her straight home. And in case you want to know why my version was never told, I don't like talking about women who throw themselves at me when they're drunk. In spite of what you've heard, my mother raised me to be a gentleman. We may be a little rough around the edges, but the Granites have a code of honor."

The Mustang swung fluidly into the driveway leading to the old mill on the cliff above Sea Lion Cove. Matt drove straight up the dirt driveway to the long, wooden building and parked. He turned off the engine and slid his arm along the back of her seat. The ocean boomed below the cliffs, a timeless rhythm that seemed to echo the beat of his heart. "Most of the stories about me aren't true, Kate."

Kate stared straight ahead at the old building. Much of the wood was pitted from sea salt. The paint had long since worn away from the steady assault of the wind. She loved the look of the mill, the way it fit there on the cliff, a part of the past she wanted to bring with her into the future. She took a deep breath, composed herself, and turned to take Matt in.

Up close, Matthew Granite was a giant of a man with rippling, defined muscles and a strong, stubborn jaw. His mouth was something she spent far too much time staring at and dreaming about, and the shape of it had managed to slip into her bestselling novels on several heroes. His eyes were amazing. They should have been gray but they were more silver, a startling color that made her heart do triple time. He had the kind of thick, dark hair that made her want to run her fingers in it, and he wore it longer than most men. Kate felt a bit faint looking at his heavily muscled chest, then up into his glinting silver eyes. "Well, darn it, Matthew, all this time I thought I was in the presence of greatness." She managed to conjure up a lighthearted laugh. "It's not nice to destroy a woman's illusions."

He frowned. "I didn't say I *wasn't* the bad boy of Sea Haven."

"I thought Jonas Harrington was the bad boy of Sea Haven."

Matt looked affronted. "I never come in second place." His hand came up, unexpectedly spanning her throat.

Kate was certain her heart skipped a beat. His palm was large, and his fingers wrapped easily around her neck, his thumb tipping her head up so she was forced to meet the sudden hunger blazing in his eyes. It was the last thing Kate expected to see, and his intensity shocked her.

"Matthew." She breathed his name in a small protest. It wasn't a good idea. They weren't a good idea.

He simply lowered his head and took possession of her mouth. His kiss was anything but gentle. He dragged her close, a starving man devouring her with hot, urgent kisses. The breath slammed out of her lungs, and every nerve ending in her body screamed at her. Electricity crackled between them, arcing from Matt to Kate and back again. Fire raced over her skin, melting her insides. He took the lead, kissing her hungrily, hotly, his tongue dueling with hers, demanding a response she found herself giving.

Her arms crept around his neck, her body pressing close to the heat of his. She felt so much heat, so much magic she couldn't think straight.

The blare of a horn made Kate jump away from him. Matt cursed and glanced at the highway in time to see his brothers waving, hooting, and honking as they drove by. "Damned idiots," he said, but there was a wealth of affection in his voice impossible to miss.

Kate pressed a trembling hand to her swollen mouth. Her skin felt raw and burned from the dark shadow on his jaw. She didn't dare look in the mirror, but she knew she looked thoroughly kissed. "They saved us."

"They may have saved you, but I'm in dire straits here, woman." And dammit all, he was. What was it about this woman that made him lose control whenever he was around her? Was she really a witch? He was going to have a few things to say to his brothers when he got his hands on them. He wasn't looking forward to the ribbing he was going to get after being caught necking like a teenager with Kate Drake. It didn't help matters that he saw Jonas Harrington cruising by very slowly, obviously looking for them. Damn Danny and his radio. It would be all over Sea Haven if they weren't more careful, and the last thing he wanted was for Kate to run from him because of gossip.

He touched Kate's red face. Her soft skin was raw from his whiskers. "I should have shaved, Katie, I'm sorry. I wasn't planning on kissing you." So, okay, he wanted to kiss her. He'd hoped to kiss her. He'd actually gotten down on his knees briefly last night when no one was around and asked for a Christmas miracle, but she didn't need to know how badly he wanted her.

The way he said Katie, turned her heart over, sending a million butterfly wings brushing at her stomach. "I don't mind."

He caught her face in his hands. "I mind. I need to be more careful with you." Abruptly he let her go and opened the door. It was the only safe thing to do when she looked so tempting. The chill from the sea rushed in to displace the heat of their bodies inside the car.

Kate didn't wait for him to come around and open her door. She was too shaken, too shocked by her reactions to him. It was so un-Kate-like of her. Kate the practical had just made a terrible mistake, and she couldn't take it back. She could still taste him, still had his scent clinging to her body, still felt a tremendous, edgy pressure, a need as elemental as hunger and thirst. She stood in the wind and lifted her face, hoping her skin would cool and that the raging need that was always inside of her would once again find rest.

Matt took her hand and led her up the broken and uneven path to the building. She didn't resist or pull away.

"The structure's sound," she assured him as she unlocked the door. "I want to be able to incorporate as much of the original building as possible when I expand. I was thinking decks outside with some protection against the wind for the sunnier days, and indoors, a large area with chairs and small tables for reading and drinking coffee or chocolate or whatever. There's a large stone fireplace in what must have been an office, and I'd like to keep that too if possible."

Kate covered her anxiety with talk, pointing out the rustic features she wanted to save and as many of the problem areas as she knew about. She was very aware of Matt's hand holding hers securely. Twice she tried to casually disengage, but he tugged her across the room to examine a rotted section of wood near the foundation.

"Where do the stairs lead?" He opened the sagging door and peered down into the dark interior. The stairs appeared to be very steep and halfway down he was certain the walls were dirt. "Is there a light?"

"Of sorts," Kate said. "It's over the second stair down. I can't reach the chain."

"Why wouldn't it be up here?" He pulled the chain gingerly, half-expecting the light to explode. It came on, but it was a dim yellow and made a strange humming sound. "What is that?"

"I don't know, but the fire marshal assured me it was safe in here." She smiled at him. "Isn't one of your brothers an electrician?"

"It will be a while before we need him," Matt said, starting down the stairs. The staircase was solid enough, but he didn't like the look of the wall. Several cracks spread out from the center of the wall in all directions like spiderwebs. He glanced at Kate, his eyebrow raised.

She shook her head. "The earthquake must have damaged it. It wasn't like that when I came down here with the Realtor. I actually came down twice just to make certain the entire place wasn't going to sink into the ocean. I know it's in bad shape, but it's such a perfect location. If I have to, I can pull down the mill and start from scratch. If you think that's the best thing to do, I'll take your advice, but I really want to save as much of the original building as possible."

"It's going to cost more money than it might be worth, Kate," he warned.

Kate shivered as they went down the stairs to the dimly lit basement. It was far colder than she remembered. Always sensitive to energy, she felt an icy malevolence that hadn't been there before. She looked around cautiously, moving closer to Matt for protection. The atmosphere vibrated with unrestrained malicious amusement. "Matthew, let's leave." She tugged at his arm.

He looked down at her quickly. "What is it, Katie?" There was a caress to his voice, one that warmed her in spite of the icy chill in the basement. "You can wait upstairs while I look around." He felt her shiver and took the jacket she was holding from her to help her into it. "It won't take me very long." He pulled the edges of the jacket together and buttoned it up, his fingers lingering on the lapels, just holding her there, close to him.

Kate shook her head. "It feels unhealthy down here. I

don't want to leave you alone. Matthew," she hesitated, searching for the right words. "This doesn't feel right to me, not the way it did before."

His silver eyes moved over her face. He suddenly winked, a quick, sexy gesture that sent her heart thudding. "I'll make it quick, I promise."

Kate trailed after him, reluctant to be too far from him in the gloomy basement. It was long and wide and had a dirt floor. "I think this was used as the smugglers' storehouse. There's a stairway leading to the cove through a narrow tunnel. Part of the tunnel collapsed some years ago, but I read in my grandmother's diary that the mill was used to store supplies and weapons and spices coming in off the boats." She pressed her lips together, determined not to distract him as he studied the walls and the floor of the basement.

"What's this?" Matt halted next to a strange covering in the dirt. It was at least two inches thick and looked almost like the lid of a coffin, except it was oval in shape. The surface was rough and covered with symbols, which were impossible to read with the dirt and grime over them. Running straight through the middle of the lid was a large crack.

Kate frowned. "I didn't notice it before. It must have been covered by the dirt. Could the earthquake have shifted that much dirt?" She moved closer to it reluctantly. The icy cold air was coming from the deep crack. "I don't like this, Matthew."

"It isn't a grave, Kate," he pointed out, crouching beside it and brushing at the dirt along the edges. "It's more like a seal of some kind."

She hunkered down beside him. A blast of cold air touched her palm as she passed it above the crumbling rock. She brushed the dirt away from the symbols, trying to decipher the old hieroglyphics. The language was an ancient one, but it was all too familiar to her. Her ancestors, generations of powerful witches, had used such symbols to communicate privately. Her mother had urged them to learn the language, and Kate knew a few of the symbols, but not all. "It says something about rage. The symbols are chipped and worn away. I can make out the words, 'sealed until the day one is born'—" She broke off in frustration, leaning closer to try to figure out the meaning of the words.

"Where did you learn those symbols? Are they Egyptian?" Matt asked.

Kate shook her head. "No, it's a family thing. We were all supposed to have learned. Do you think this is a well of some kind?"

Matt continued to dig around the edges of the thick lid. "It can't be a well, Kate. Maybe some kind of memorial?" He pushed at the heavy slab. It crumbled around the edges but slid slightly.

"No!" Kate caught Matt's arm, tugging hard. "We don't know what's inside. Something about this doesn't feel right to me. Can't you feel the malevolence pouring out of the crack?" She stumbled back, taking him with her, nearly sprawling on the ground so that he had to catch her as a noxious gas poured from the slit that had opened.

"It's just gas created from decomposed matter that's been trapped for a long time," Matt said, dragging her as far from the crevice as he could get them. He pushed her toward the stairs. "Sometimes the gases can make you sick or worse, Kate. Don't breathe it in." She looked pale, her eyes wide with horror. She stared at the lid without moving, one hand pressed to her mouth. Matt could see that her entire body was trembling.

At once he wrapped his arms around her and drew her close to him. He practically enveloped her entire body, yet she never looked away from the oddity in the basement, mesmerized by the yellow-black vapor streaming from the crack. "It's nothing Kate, just a hole in the ground. It's probably a couple of hundred years old." He remained calm in order to reassure her, but all of his senses had gone on alert.

Matthew obviously couldn't feel the malicious triumph pouring out of the ground, a welling-up of victory, a coup of sorts. She couldn't identify it, had no idea what it was, but she was terrified they might have unleashed something dangerous. Horrified, she watched the dark, ugly vapor swirl around the room, then stream up the stairs toward freedom, leaving behind an icy cold that chilled her to her bones.

"Stop shaking, Kate. It's gas. It happens all the time in these old vents." Matt couldn't bear that she was so frightened. "We find pockets all over the place. You haven't gone into the tunnel, have you? That could have all sorts of gas pockets as well as cave-ins."

"Have you ever seen gas do that? Travel around the room?"

"We're getting some kind of wind off the ocean, Kate. Can't you feel the draft in here? It's very strong."

"I have to take a look at those symbols, Matthew. I think something was sealed beneath that lid, and the earthquake disturbed it." She knew she sounded utterly ridiculous. She probably appeared a crackpot to him, but she was certain she was right. Something had slid out of that vent, something not meant to inhabit the world.

Matt studied her serious face, the fear in her eyes. "Let me make certain it's safe, Kate." He gently set her aside and made his way across the uneven dirt floor to the crumbling rock lid.

"Be careful, Matthew." When he looked at her, she wished she'd kept her mouth shut. She was sounding more and more paranoid.

He sniffed the air cautiously. The odor was foul, but he could breathe easily without coughing. "I think it's safe enough, Kate. I'm not keeling over, and I don't feel faint. I don't know what the hell you think just happened, but if it has you so afraid, I'm going to believe it. Jonas says never to doubt any of you Drakes."

She was grateful that he was trying to understand, but she knew he couldn't. Kate ducked her head, avoiding his gaze, afraid to see the way he was looking at her. She sank down beside the lid and dusted lightly with her fingers, afraid of crumbling the old rock even more.

Matt waited silently as long as he could. There was the sound of the sea booming in the background. The echo of it pounded off the walls eerily. "Does it mean anything to you?" He tried to keep impatience from his voice when all he wanted to do was snatch Kate up and carry her out of the place.

Kate peered closer to decipher the words. Seven sisters. Seven Drake sisters. Her ancestors. They had bound something to earth, committed its spirit to the vent hole to protect something. She couldn't read it exactly as parts of the letters were smashed and worn away, but she was afraid it was the townspeople who needed to be protected. She could also make out something to do with Christmas and fire and one who would be born who could bring peace. Kate looked up at Matt. There was no way to hide the terror in her eyes, and she didn't bother to try. "I need to go home right now."

chapter
4

A wreath of holly meant to greet
Looks much better tossed in the street

 MATT SAT IN HIS CAR WITH THE HEATER RUN-
ning and his favorite CD playing low. Joley
Drake's unique, sultry voice had taken her up
the charts fast. He loved this particular collection, usually
finding it soothing, but it wasn't doing him any good
now. He gripped the steering wheel and stared up at the
blazing lights of the Christmas tree in front of the cliff
house. The fog was beginning to roll in off the sea,
stretching white fingers toward land and the house he
was watching. There were no electric lights in the windows, yet he could see the flicker of candlelight and an
occasional shadow as one of the Drake sisters moved past
the glass.

The passenger door jerked open, and Jonas Harrington
slid into the seat beside Matt, shutting the door against
the cold.

"Dammit, Jonas, you scared the hell out of me!" Matt
snapped. He hadn't realized just how jumpy he was until
Jonas had pulled the door open.

"Sorry about that." Jonas sounded as pleasant as ever.

Too pleasant. Matt turned his head to look at his childhood friend. "What are you doing out here? It's cold, and the fog's coming in. You aren't stalking our Kate, are you?"

Matt studied his friend's face. He was smiling, looking amicable, but his eyes were ice-cold. "Of course I'm stalking Kate. Do you think I've lost my mind? That woman belongs with me." He grinned to relieve the tension gathering between them. "I just have to figure out how to convince her of that. What are you doing here? And why didn't I see the headlights of your car?" He glanced in the rearview mirror and noted Jonas had cruised silently up behind him.

"I ran without headlights, didn't want to scare you away. What happened tonight? Why are they all upset?" There was no obvious accusation in the voice, but Matt had been around Jonas his entire life, and he recognized the underlying note of suspicion.

"What the hell are you trying to say, Jonas? Spit it out and quit beating around the bush." Temper was beginning to flare. "I've had a hell of an evening, and you aren't helping."

Jonas shrugged. "I did just spit it out. They're upset. I can feel it. All of them, every single sister. Does it have something to do with you and Kate?"

"What kind of question is that? Hell, yes, I want Kate. And yes, I'd do just about anything to get her, but I sure wouldn't lay a finger on her if she didn't want me to, and I wouldn't *ever* hurt her. Is that what you want to know?"

Jonas nodded. "That's about what I was looking for. I'd hate to have to kick your ass, but if you hurt that girl, I'd have to do it."

"As if you could." Matt tapped his finger against the steering wheel, frowning while his temper settled. "What do you mean, you can feel they're all upset?"

"I've always been able to feel when something's wrong with the Drakes. And right now, something's very wrong." Jonas continued to look at him with cool, assessing eyes.

Matt shook his head. "It wasn't me, Jonas. Something weird happened at the old mill, and Kate was very distressed. She asked me to take her home, and I did." He raked his fingers through his hair, not once, but twice. "I didn't even have a chance to ask her out again. I was just sitting here, trying to figure out whether I should go up to the house and ask her what happened, or go back to the mill and try to figure it out."

"There they are!" Jonas muttered an ugly word beneath his breath. "What the hell do they think they're doing going out in the middle of the night with the fog rolling in?"

Matt could just make out the three Drake sisters swirling dark, hooded cloaks around them as they hurried down the steps. The fog was heavy and thick, an invasion of white mist that hid the women effectively as they rushed down the worn pathway that wound down the hill toward the road. Matt leaped out of his car, losing sight of them in the curtain of fog. He was aware of Jonas swearing under his breath, keeping pace as they angled to cut off the Drakes before they could reach the highway.

Jonas beat him to the women, catching Hannah's arm and yanking her around to face him. "Are you out of your mind?"

Kate's expression went from startled to troubled when she caught sight of them. "Matthew, I thought you went home." She looked uneasily around her at the fog. "You shouldn't be out here. I don't think it's safe. And neither should you, Jonas."

Hannah glared at the sheriff. "Has anyone ever told you you have bad manners?"

"Has anyone ever turned you over their knee?" Jonas countered. "If you don't think it's safe out here, what are you doing running around in the dark?"

Kate indicated the heavy wall of fog. "It isn't like we're going to get very far in this stuff. We have an errand, Jonas, an important one."

"Then you should have called me," Jonas snapped impatiently. Hannah stirred as if to say something but Jonas's fingers tightened around her arm. "I'm really, really angry right now, Hannah. Don't make it worse."

"Jonas," Kate's voice was placating. "You don't understand."

"Then make me understand, Kate," he snarled.

Matt immediately stepped between Jonas and Kate. "I don't think you need to talk to her like that, Jonas. Let her explain."

Kate's fingers curled around Matt's arm. "Jonas worries about us, Matthew. We probably should have called him."

Matt didn't want her calling Jonas; he wanted her to call him when something was wrong. And something was obviously wrong. Before she could pull her hand away from his arm, he covered her fingers with his. "We're already here, Kate. Tell us what you need to do."

Her sea-green eyes moved over his face. He had the feeling she could see more deeply into him than most people, but it was always like that with Kate. He tightened his hold on her hand. "Kate. You trust Jonas. He can vouch for me."

Kate closed her eyes briefly. Matthew Granite was her dream man, and after he witnessed what really went on around the Drake sisters she wouldn't even be able to sustain the fantasy of a relationship with him. She sighed but she squared her shoulders. Some things were just more important than romantic dreams. She took a deep breath. "Something was unleashed today, something malevolent. We think." She looked at her sisters for courage before continuing. "We think the earthquake may have awakened it or at least provided it with the opportunity to rise. It was the shadow you saw in the globe, Matt, and my sisters and I saw in the mosaic. It's very real, and it feels dangerous to us." She stared up at him, clearly expecting him to laugh.

Matt kept his face completely expressionless. He knew the Drakes were different; some said they performed miracles, some said they were genuine witches. Sea Haven was a hotbed of gossip, and the Drake sisters were always at the forefront. But not Kate. Never Kate.

"So it felt dangerous to you, and the first thing you do is rush out into the night in the middle of one of the worst fogs we've ever had," Jonas snapped. "Dammit, Kate, Abbey and Hannah might rush headlong into danger, but you usually show some trace of sense." He hauled Hannah back against him when she tried to squirm away. "I'm not playing around with you, Hannah. Keep it up, and I'll lock you away for the night."

Hannah's beautiful face radiated fury, but instead of taking Jonas to task as Matt expected, she was gasping for breath.

Abbey leaped to her side. "Breathe, Hannah, very slow."

Hannah shook her head, fear filling her eyes. Abbey extracted a paper bag from her purse and handed it to her sister. "Breathe into this."

Looking alarmed, Jonas wrapped his arm around Hannah's waist to support her as she doubled over, clearly unable to breathe adequately. "What the hell is wrong with her? Should we get an ambulance?"

"Would you please stop swearing at her?" Abbey snapped. "Be very careful, Jonas, or I'll ask you questions you don't want to answer."

"Shut up, Abbey, don't you dare threaten me," Jonas growled back.

"Stop it, all of you, stop it," Kate pleaded.

Seeing the anxiety on Kate's face, Matt stepped closer to her and put his arm around her. Hannah breathed into the paper bag for a couple of minutes and lifted her head. She looked ready to cry. "Abbey, if you want to take Hannah back to the house, I'll go with Kate to do whatever it is you all think is so important." He made the offer before he could stop himself. Kate was shivering in the cold fog. She didn't need to be out on such a night. He wanted just to pick her up and take her home and lie down with her by the fireplace.

Jonas pushed back Hannah's wealth of blond hair. "Are you all right, baby doll?" His choice of words should have been insulting, but the gentle concern in his voice made them an endearment.

Hannah nodded but didn't look at any of them, still clearly fighting for air.

"Maybe that's a good idea, Hannah. I'll go with Matt and just look around a little, and you and Abbey pull out the diaries and see if you can find anything that might help us figure this out," Kate said. "Matthew, are you certain you don't mind? I want to walk around town and just get a feel for what's going on."

"I don't mind. Are you going to be warm enough?"

"Just how dangerous is this, Kate?" Jonas asked.

"I honestly don't know," she replied. "I wish I knew. We thought if we went out together, all of us might be able to pick something up, but I already feel it. I think I can track it."

Matt cleared his throat. "Track a shadow?" If they weren't all so serious, he would be thinking it was a Halloween prank. He glanced up at the house. The fog was a heavy shroud, almost obliterating the house. He could see the lights of the Christmas tree, but only as pale, orange-glowing haloes distorted by the blanket of grayish white. He went still. The fog was changing color, darkening from white to a charcoal gray. Just as the fog had done in the snowglobe when he'd picked it up to examine it.

"The fog is bad, Kate. I've never seen it like this," Jonas said. "Stay close to Matt. I'll take Hannah and Abbey back to the house."

Hannah stiffened and looked at Abbey. Abbey smiled. "We'll make it home fine, Jonas. It's just up the hill. We know the path."

"I'm coming with you, Abbey, so don't argue." Jonas

turned resolutely toward the house. "Matt, if it feels wrong to you, or you think Kate's in any danger at all, get her back here and don't let her give you any nonsense."

Kate smiled at Jonas. "I never talk nonsense. You take care of my sisters because if anything happens to them . . ."

"I know, I've heard it all before." Jonas waved at her, and the fog swallowed them up, even muffling the sound of their footsteps on the path, leaving Kate alone with Matt.

She looked up at him. "You don't have to do this, you know. I'm capable of walking up and down the streets of Sea Haven."

Matthew stared down into her beautiful sea-green eyes. "But I'm not capable of leaving your side when there's even a hint of danger near you." He lowered his head slowly to hers, drawn as if by a magnet, expecting her to pull away, giving her plenty of time to think about it.

Kate watched his eyes change, go dark with desire, right before his mouth took possession of hers. It didn't matter that the air was cold, and the wind chilled them, their bodies produced a remarkable heat, their mouths fused with fire. He dragged her against his body, his muscular arms enveloping her, holding her as if she were the most precious person in the world to him. He was exquisitely rough, yet impossibly gentle, voraciously hungry, nearly devouring her mouth, yet so tender he brought tears to her eyes. She had no idea how he did it, but she wanted more.

"You're not good for me," she whispered against his mouth.

His tongue slid along the seam of her lips, teased her tongue into another brief, but heated tango. "I'm absolutely perfect for you." He tugged at her cape until her body was pressed tightly against his. "I was born to be with you, Kate. You're supposed to be some kind of a magical woman, filled with the second sight, yet you don't see what's right in front of you. Why is that?" He didn't give her the opportunity to debate, he just kissed her long and thoroughly.

Kate felt her insides melting, turning to a warm puddle and settling somewhere in her lower region as a frustrating and unrelenting ache. Her knees actually went weak. "I can't think straight when we're kissing, Matthew."

"That's a good thing, Kate, because neither can I," he answered, his lips drifting into the hollow of her neck and back up to find her ear.

Heat pulsed through her, but she forced herself to pull away from him. He wasn't for her. She knew that, and once he found out what she was really was like, he'd know it too. She might seem courageous and strong, but when it came to losing him, she knew she'd be very fragile. Starting up with Matthew Granite was a decidedly ridiculous thing for her to do. "Matthew, really, I have to find this malevolent shadow and hopefully help it find some peace or get my sisters to help me seal it back up."

Matt silently cursed dark shadows and evil entities and every other thing that went bump in the night. She obviously believed they had let something harmful loose on the small town of Sea Haven. He was certain it was a pocket of gas; but if it meant walking around town with her at night, holding hands and kissing her every chance he got, well, hell, he was her man. He could do that. And he would even try to keep an open mind.

"Then let's go." He wrapped his arm around her. "I've got a flashlight in my car. This fog is really thick."

"We won't need a flashlight, Matthew. I have a couple of glow sticks. My sister Elle makes them. They work very well in the fog." She pulled several thin tubes from the inside pocket of her cape and handed him one. "Just shake it."

"I forgot about little Elle and her chemistry set. She blew up more missiles on the beach than any other kid at Sea Haven. Didn't she get a full scholarship to Columbia or MIT or some other very prestigious school? One very brave to take her on?"

Kate laughed, warmth spreading through her. "They were very brave, but fortunately they turned out a remarkable physicist able to do just about anything she wants to do. Elle is a genius and utterly fearless. She's not afraid to crawl around in caves looking at strange rock formations, and she's not afraid of taking apart a bomb when she's needed. Unlike me."

"What do you mean?" Matt tightened his fingers around hers.

"My sisters do incredible things and people expect it of us, but I wouldn't want you to think I'm capable of climbing mountains or jumping out of planes because you've heard of all of their exploits." She was feeling her way in the fog rather than following the glow stick. She lifted her face to the droplets of sea moisture, inhaling to try to catch the scent of something foul. "We have to cross the highway."

With the fog so thick there was virtually no traffic. Matt moved with her across the coastal highway and took the shortcut that led to the center of town. She was so serious all of a sudden, so distant from him, that he was actually beginning to believe she was on the trail of something evil. He could sense the stillness in her, the gathering of energy.

The survival instincts he'd honed during his years as a Ranger kicked in. His skin prickled as he went onto alert status. Adrenaline surged, and his senses grew keener. He felt the need for complete silence and wondered if he was beginning to believe in supernatural nonsense. Matt eased the glow stick inside his jacket without activating it. The fog muffled the sound of Kate's footsteps. He was aware of her breathing, of the eerie feel of the fog itself, of everything.

By mutual consent they were silent as they walked along the street. He became aware of a slight noise. A puffing. It was distant and hushed, barely audible in the murky blanket of mist. Matt found himself straining to listen. There was a rhythm to the sound, reminding him of a bull drawing air in and out of its lungs hard before a charge. Breathing. Someone was breathing, and the sound was moving, changing directions each time they changed directions.

Matt pressed his lips to her ear. "There's someone in the fog with us." He was certain someone was watching them, someone quite close.

Kate tipped her head back. "Some*thing*, not someone."

Kate turned toward the residential area. The town looked strange shrouded in the gray-white fog. Heavily decorated for Christmas, the multicolored lights on the stores and office buildings, the houses and trees gave off the peculiar glow of a fire in the strange vapor, giving the town a disturbing infernal appearance rather than a festive one. Matt wished he had brought a weapon with him. He was a good hand-to-hand fighter because he was a big man, strong, with quick reflexes and extensive training, but he had no idea what kind of adversary they faced.

Something hit him in the back, skittered down his jeans, and fell to the street. Matt whirled around to face the enemy and found nothing but fog.

"What is it?" Kate asked. Her voice was steady, but her hand, on the small of his back, was shaking.

Matt hunkered down to look at the object at his feet. "It's a Christmas wreath, Kate. A damned Christmas wreath." He looked around carefully, trying to penetrate the fog and see what was moving in it. He could feel the presence now, real, not imagined. He could hear the strange, labored breathing, but he couldn't find the source.

As he stood, a second object came hurtling out of the fog to hit him in the chest. He heard the smash of glass and knew immediately that the wreath had been decorated with glass ornaments. "Let's get out of here, off the street at least," he said.

Kate was stubborn, shaking her head. "No, I have to face it here."

Matt pulled Kate to him, shielding her smaller body

with his own as more wreaths came flying through the air, hurled with deadly accuracy at them from every direction. He wrapped his arms around her head, pressing her face against his chest. "It's kids," he muttered, brushing a kiss on top of her head to reassure her. "Always playing pranks; it's dangerous in this fog, not to mention destructive."

He hoped it was kids. It had to be an army of kids, tearing wreaths off the doors of the houses and throwing them at passersby as a prank. He heard no laughter, not even running footsteps. He heard nothing but the rough breathing. It seemed to come out of the fog itself. The nape of his neck prickled with unease.

"It isn't children playing a prank, Matt." Kate sounded close to tears. "It's much, much worse."

"Kate." He stroked a caress down the back of her head. Her hair was inside the hood of the cape, but his palm lingered anyway. "It isn't the first time a group of kids decided to play around, and it won't be the last."

The Christmas wreaths lay around them in a circle, some smashed or crushed and others in reasonably good shape. Kate lifted her face away from his chest and took a breath. "I can smell it, can't you?"

Matt inhaled deeply. He recognized the foul, noxious odor of the gases in the old mill. His heart jumped. "Dammit, Kate. I'm beginning to believe you. Let's get the hell out of here before I decide I'm crazy."

She pulled free of his arms. "Is that what you think about me? That I'm crazy?"

"Of course not. This is all just so damned odd."

Her sea-green eyes moved over his face, a little moody,

a little fey. "Well, brace yourself, it's going to get damned odder. Stay still."

The fog swirled around them, their faces, their feet, and bodies, spinning webs of charcoal gray matter. As at the cliff house, Matt got the impression of bony fingers, and this time they were trying to grab at Kate. Without thinking, he caught her up and started to run, the urge strong to get her away from the long gray tentacles, but the blanket of fog was thick around them.

Kate pressed her lips to his ear. "Stop! I have to try to stop it, Matthew; it's what I do. We can't outrun the fog, it's everywhere."

"Dammit, Kate, I don't like this." When she didn't respond, he reluctantly put her down and stayed very close to her, ready for action.

She turned in the direction of her home, her face serene, thoughtful, yet determined. She radiated beauty, an inner fire and strength. She whispered, a soft, melodic chant that became part of the night, of the air surrounding them. She wasn't speaking English but a language he didn't recognize. Her voice was soothing, tranquil, a soft invitation to a place of peace and harmony with the earth.

The fog itself breathed harder, in and out, a burst of air sounding like a predatory animal with teeth and claws. The mist seemed to vibrate with anger, roiling and spinning and growing darker. Gray fog whirled around the Christmas wreaths at Matt's feet, spinning fast enough to lift them into the air. Bright green wreaths withered and blackened as if all the life was being sucked out of them. The objects reminded Matt of the garlands at funerals rather than the cheery decorations for a holiday, and each of them seemed to be aimed straight toward Kate.

His breath caught in his throat, and his heart pounded. Kate looked small and fragile under the onslaught of the vicious gray-black vapor. He moved, a fluid glide that took him into the path of the blackened garlands so that they smashed into his larger frame. Kate ignored the fog and the wreaths, concentrating on something inside of herself. She stared toward the house on the cliffs and abruptly lifted her arms straight up into the air. The wind rushed in from the ocean with wild force. It carried the crisp scent of the sea, the taste and feel of the waves, and a spray of salt. It also carried voices, soft and melodious and very feminine. The wind swept through the fogbank, the voices swelling in strength, Kate's voice joining theirs until they were in perfect harmony, in total command.

The spinning Christmas wreaths dropped to the road. The fog receded, heading inland, blanketing the residential homes; but the wind was persistent, shifting directions and herding the fog back toward the ocean. Kate looked translucent, her skin pale and beaded with moisture, wisps of hair clinging to her face, but she didn't falter. Her voice brought a sense of peace, of tranquillity, of something beautiful and satisfying. It filled Matt with longing for a home and a family of his own. It filled him with a deep sense of pride and respect for Kate Drake.

He watched the fog reluctantly retreat until it was far out over the ocean, dissipated by the force of the wind.

There was a silence left behind in the vacuum of the tempest. Kate dropped her arms as if they were leaden. She staggered. He leaped forward to catch her before she collapsed, swinging her into his arms and cradling her against his chest.

"It's growing in strength. I couldn't have sent it away if my sisters hadn't helped." Kate looked up at him with frightened eyes.

Matt kissed her. It was the only thing he could think to do. She seemed weightless in his arms. He kissed her eyes and the tip of her nose and settled his mouth, feather-light over hers. "It's all right now, Kate. Rest. You sent it away. Tell me what you need." He could see that every drop of her strength had been used up in fighting the unseen enemy in the fog. She'd made a believer out of him. He was a man of action, having spent several years in the service training to protect his countrymen, yet there had been nothing he could do to stop the evil shadow in the mist. "What is it?"

She rubbed her face tiredly against his jacket. "I don't know, Matthew, I honestly don't know."

"How did you know what to say to it? What language it would understand?"

"I didn't know. I was using a healing chant my family has passed down from generation to generation. I was attempting to heal its spirit."

He stared at her, trying not to look shocked. The dark shadow seemed beyond any sort of redemption to him, something dark and dangerous, looking for a chance to strike out at anything or anyone around it.

Kate looked at the wreaths strewn all over the road.

"Strange that he would choose to attack us with the wreaths."

"Strange that it could use them at all. Do you think it's a he?"

She shrugged. "It felt male to me."

The adrenaline was beginning to subside, but he continued to eye the cliffs warily. "I'm never going to look at fog again in the same way."

"A wreath is a continuous circle, Matthew, and it symbolizes real love, unconditional, true affection that never ceases." Her voice was thoughtful.

"I didn't feel love flowing out of the fog," he answered. He began walking back in the direction of her house, Kate in his arms.

"But he tore the Christmas wreaths off every door on the street and threw them."

"At *us*," he said grimly. "I'm used to looking my enemy in the eye, Katie, fighting him with weapons or my bare hands. I couldn't exactly grab the fog and throttle it, although I wanted to."

"Put me down, Matthew, I'm too heavy for you to carry all that way."

"I was a Ranger for ten years, Katie, I think I can pack your weight with no problem."

She wasn't going to argue, she was just too drained. "Ten years. That's right, you joined right out of college. I've been wandering around so much, and I knew you didn't live here, but your family always made it seem as if you were here."

"I spent my leave here, every chance I could. I picked up my life here again immediately after I got out of the service because the family business was waiting for me. My father and brothers kept me a part of it, even though they did all the work."

"Why did you join the Rangers, Matthew? As soon as I heard, I researched what they were all about. It was very—" she hesitated, searching for the right word— "intense. And frightening. Why would you want to do something like that?"

"I've always needed to push myself to find out my limits. And I believe in my country, so it seemed a perfect fit for me. The Rangers embody everything I believe in. Move farther and faster and fight harder than any other soldier. Never surrender, never leave a fallen comrade, survive and carry out the mission under any conditions."

Kate sighed heavily and turned her face into his shoulder, hiding her expression from him. Something about that sigh gave Matt a sick feeling in the pit of his stomach. He wanted to ask her about it, but by the time he reached the path leading to the house, Kate was asleep.

chapter
5

A town dreams of sweet thoughts while nestled in bed,
Until nightmares of me begin to dance in their heads.

"KATE. KATIE. WAKE UP, HON." THE SOFT VOICE beckoned Kate from layers of sleep. "You need to eat now, wake up."

Kate opened her eyes and stretched, blinking drowsily up at her sister. "Sarah. What are you doing here?" She pushed at the heavy fall of hair tumbling around her face. She always braided her hair before she went to bed, yet it was everywhere. She turned her head and went still. Matthew Granite was sprawled in a chair beside her bed, his silver gaze trained intently on her face. Her stomach did a funny little flip.

A slow smile softened his tough features, lit his gray eyes, and stole her heart. "You're finally awake. I was getting worried."

"You slept in the chair?" Kate couldn't imagine his large body finding a relaxing position in her bedroom chair.

"Well, I did want to share your bed, but I was worried about your sisters giving me the evil eye." His smile widened into a teasing grin. "Jonas slunk out of here a couple of hours ago afraid even to drink a cup of coffee. He warned me one of you might slip an eye of newt into my coffee, so I thought it best to stay in everyone's good graces."

"You like coffee that much, do you? Enough to stay in our good graces?" She couldn't stop looking at him. There was a blue-black shadow along his jaw, and his clothes were rumpled, but it didn't make him any less attractive to her. "Just so I'm not the one slipping the eye of newt to you, why are you sleeping in my room?" She glared at Sarah rather than at Matt.

Sarah held her hands up, palm out. "We all tried to get him to leave last night, Kate, but he wouldn't go. Granite might be his last name, but it's also what he's made of. No one could budge him. Jonas tried scaring him off, but that didn't work either."

Kate tried not to be pleased. She tried to frown at Matt, to pretend displeasure, but there was no way she could carry it off, so she gave up. He just winked at her anyway, looking sexier than ever with the dark stubble shadowing his jaw.

Sarah sat on the edge of the bed. "I hate interrupting, but you have to eat. You expended far too much energy last night. Even Joley called and was feeling drained." She waved a hand toward the drapes, and, to Matt's astonishment, the curtain slid open to allow the morning light to pour in. "I know you don't feel hungry, you never do afterward, but you have to eat for all of us."

Neither Kate nor Sarah seemed to think anything

was unusual. Matt blinked several times to test his eyesight.

"How's Hannah?" Kate sat up, thankful she was still wearing her clothes. Matt and her sisters must have removed her cape and her shoes and socks before putting her in her bed, but at least she was safely clad in her slacks and blouse. "I couldn't believe with all of us working on her, she still had an attack. That's the first time I can remember that our joining together failed her."

Sarah glanced at Matt and hesitated. He raised his hands. "If you need to be alone with Kate, I'll go on down to the kitchen and see what kind of trouble I can get into." He stretched out his hand to Kate, resting it palm down on the bed.

"It's just that Hannah is such a private person, Matthew." Kate placed her hand over his. "She was embarrassed that it happened in front of you and Jonas. Especially Jonas."

"It? You mean her asthma attack?" He turned his hand to circle hers with his fingers, knowing she was trusting him with something private. "It was an asthma attack, wasn't it?"

"Not exactly." Kate sighed. "I wish Jonas would let up on her a little bit."

"She seems to be able to dish it right back to him." Matt leaned over to brush strands of hair from her face. "I don't quite get your relationship with Jonas, but I served with him in the Rangers. Jonas, me, and Jackson Deveau. Jonas is a good man."

"Jackson Deveau is the deputy who scares the hell out of everyone," Sarah informed Kate when she frowned.

"You must have seen him a few times. He doesn't ever say much, but he looks lethal. He came to Sea Haven with Jonas when he returned from the Army."

"Jackson's a good man too," Matt said.

Kate hadn't met the deputy because she hadn't been back long, and she tended to wrap herself up in the cocoon of her own world. "I take it Jackson isn't from here originally."

"No, but he often came to Sea Haven on leave with us. He had no family and nowhere else to go when he left the service, so we asked him to come back with us. This town is friendly and tolerant, and Jackson needs tolerance. He's family to us. As for Jonas, you have to understand him. I saw him go in under heavy fire to drag a wounded man out of a battle zone. He carried that man for miles on his back. And Jackson . . ." He broke off, shaking his head. "I know Jonas watches over you all."

"Like a hawk," Sarah interjected dryly.

Matt shrugged. "Maybe it's because he really cares about all of you."

"Don't worry about our relationship with Jonas," Kate said. "We all love him dearly, even when we want to conjure up a spell to turn him into a toad."

Matt cleared his throat, rubbed the bridge of his nose, and sat back in his chair. "Can you really do that?"

Kate exchanged a mischievous grin with Sarah. "You never know about the Drake sisters. Really, Matthew, Jonas is intertwined deeply with our family. He always seems to know when something is wrong. He's sensitive to things not seen with the human eye."

Sarah leaned toward Matt. "You felt it last night, didn't you, when you were in the fog with Kate, and we joined with her? You knew something was wrong."

Matt sighed. "I don't know what happened last night, but I sure as hell don't want Kate facing anything like that again." His gray eyes smoldered with something dangerous as he looked at Kate. "I didn't like the way the fog seemed to be attacking you."

Sarah gasped. "What do you mean attacking her?"

"Nothing came at me," Kate denied hastily. "Really, Sarah, it was just throwing Christmas decorations around and Matthew was actually hit a few times. I was never touched."

Sarah looked at Matt steadily. "Why did you think it was after Kate?"

"I stepped in front of her to protect her. The wreaths were thrown, but not very hard in the beginning, yet when Katie began to talk to it, whatever it is, the Christmas wreaths were thrown much more forcefully and with greater accuracy."

"Were you hurt?" Kate looked suddenly anxious, coming up on her knees on the bed to look at him. "Libby's the best at healing, but Sarah. . . ."

"I'm fine," Matt said, but wished he didn't have to admit it. She looked incredibly beautiful leaning toward him with her hair tousled and her eyes enormous with concern for him.

"Kate—" Abbey stuck her head in the room— "Gina over at the preschool says something's wrong, and she needs you. I could hear the children crying in the background. I told her you weren't well, but she said it was an emergency. She said she needed your help. I'll go if I absolutely have to go."

Abbey was clearly apprehensive about going in Kate's place. Matt looked at Sarah. "What does Kate have to do with the preschool?"

"Haven't you noticed Kate has a gift for calming people with her voice? She's able to bring peace to even the most distressed person or situation," Sarah answered.

"Is that what your lives are like? People need you, and it doesn't matter if you're tired or not, you just go to them."

"We were born with certain gifts, Matt," Kate said. "We've always known we were meant to serve others. Yes, it isn't always easy, and all of us have to have ways of protecting ourselves but when we can help, we have to go."

"How do they know to call you?"

Sarah smiled. "You were older than us, Matthew, ahead of us in school, so you really weren't around when our talents began to develop. I'm sure you've heard the rumors, but you didn't witness what we could do the way other people in town did. Jonas has always connected with us in some way, so it was easy enough for him to believe."

"Kate?" Abbey prompted.

"I'll go. Give me a few minutes to shower and have a cup of tea."

Matt followed her to the bathroom door. "I don't like this, Kate. You look fragile to me. I think Sarah's right. You need to stay home."

Sarah's eyebrow shot up. "Did I say that?"

Kate rubbed a caress along Matt's stubbly jaw right in front of her sisters, then closed the bathroom door on his startled expression. When he turned around, Sarah and Abbey were grinning at him. "She doesn't listen, does she?" he asked.

"Not very well," Sarah agreed. "Kate may be quiet about it, but she goes her own way and does what she thinks is right."

"Do you have another bathroom so I can clean up really fast?"

Sarah grinned at him. "I even have an extra toothbrush. You've got that look in your eye when you look at her."

He followed her down the hall. "What look?"

"You look at her like you can't wait to kiss her," Sarah said. "A toothbrush is definitely in order."

"Does she have something against the Rangers?" Matt asked, remembering the small sigh from the night before. It had haunted him most of the night.

Sarah pushed open a door to a powder blue bathroom. "Of course not. Why would you think that?"

"No reason. Thanks, Sarah." Matt didn't want to think about that strange little sigh of Kate's. She wasn't the type of woman to react that way unless she had a reason. He'd ask her about it later. He hurried through his shower wanting to get back to her.

Kate was still in the bathroom when he returned to her room. He rested his palm on the door, the exact level as her head. "Come out of there, Katie, you're beautiful enough without working at it."

From behind the door she laughed. "How do you know? You took a terrible chance staying. You could have woken up and my mask could have slipped off in the middle of the night."

"I didn't go to sleep. I watched over you."

There was a small shocked silence. Kate jerked the door open and stared up at him. "You must be exhausted. Go home and go to bed."

"I'd rather go with you." He reached out and pulled her to him. Her body fit perfectly against his, as if made to be there.

"Matthew." There was hesitation in Kate's voice.

He kissed her. He didn't want her to voice her reservations. Kissing her was a much better and far more enjoyable idea. It was magic, if there was such a thing, and he was beginning to believe there was. He meant for it to be a brief, good morning kiss, a gentle shut-up-and-just-kiss-me kiss, but she caught fire, or he did, and they both just went up in flames. He wanted more than to kiss her, he wanted to touch her, to claim her soft body, to feel her moving beneath him, her hands clinging . . .

"Stop!"

Matt and Kate drew apart, their hearts racing, and blinked at each other, then looked around in surprise to see Sarah, Hannah, and Abbey in the doorway glaring at them.

"Kate," Sarah said, taking a deep breath. "You know we're all connected in some way. You can't be in such close proximity to us and carry on like that. We're all in overdrive, thank you very much."

Unrepentant, Matt grinned at them as he pulled Kate tight against him. "Sorry about that. We're off to see some preschoolers." Kate hid her face in his shoulder, trying not to laugh. He did the gentlemanly thing and got her out of there quickly, waving at Damon, Sarah's fiancé, as they hurried past him.

"The man should thank us," he whispered, and pretended to wince when Kate smacked his arm.

Kate stared out the window of the Mustang at the white-capped ocean as they drove along the highway toward the exit to the street where the preschool was located. "The fogbank is very thick out over the ocean," she said, a note of apprehension in her voice. "See how dark it is, more gray than white, and it seems to be churning." She turned her gaze on Matt. "I should have been more careful. Somewhere in the diaries there has to be something about this strange phenomenon."

"What diaries? You've mentioned the diaries before. How can they help?"

"My family keeps a history, books handed down generation to generation. Somewhere this event had to be recorded. The problem is, all of us were supposed to learn the earlier languages used, but we gave it a half-hearted attempt. All of us know a little, but Elle really can read it. We have to decipher the books."

Matt turned the car onto the exit. "You think this thing is coming back."

"I know it is. Can't you feel it on the wind?"

He could only feel how close he was to her. How just out of his reach she always seemed to be. Matt parked the car in the lot at the preschool, and they sat for a moment, absorbing the unnatural silence. There were no children playing in the small yard.

Kate squared her shoulders. "Do you want to wait out here?"

For an answer, he got out of the car and went around to open her door. He wasn't about to miss his opportunity to see more clearly what Kate's life was all about.

Gina Farley greeted them with obvious relief as they entered. Many of the children were sobbing and sniffling as if they'd been crying a long time. Some of the children stared silently at Kate and Matt with large, frightened eyes. Others hid their faces. In the room were several adults, many of whom Matt recognized and nodded to.

There was tension and fear in the room, but Kate smiled at everyone and went directly to the children. "Hello, everyone. I'm Kate Drake." She sat down in the circle and looked at the little ones in invitation.

Matt stood back and watched her. She looked utterly serene, a center of calm in the midst of a violent storm. Immediately the children were drawn to her, pushing and shoving to sit as close to her as they could get. She began talking to them, and a hush fell over the room so that only Kate's magical voice could be heard, bringing a sense of peace and contentment.

"So most of you had a bad dream last night?" Kate's smile was a starburst, radiating light and warmth. "Dreams can be very frightening. All of us have had them. Haley, would you tell us about your dream?" She asked the little girl who had been sobbing the hardest. "Dreams are like stories we make up in our imaginations. I make up stories and write them down for people to read. My stories can be very frightening sometimes. Was your dream scary, Haley?"

It wasn't so much her actual words that were magic as it was her voice. It became apparent to Matt that somehow Kate drew the intensity of the children's emotions out of them. As the room grew calm, and the children quieter, the tension dropped dramatically. It was only Matt who could see the effect on Kate. How draining it was to accept the backlash of emotion not only from the children but their parents as well.

Haley revealed her dream in halting sentences. A skeleton-like man in a long coat and old hat with glowing eyes and bony fingers came out of the fog. He burned the Christmas tree and stole the gifts, and he did something awful to the shepherd in the Christmas pageant. Matt stood up straight when the shepherd was mentioned. His brother, Danny, always played the shepherd in the Christmas pageant. His alarm grew as child after child revealed they'd had a similar dream.

Kate didn't seem the least bit alarmed. Her smile never wavered, and her voice continued to dispel the trauma the nightmares had caused. She told several Christmas stories and soon had the children laughing. As she stood up to leave, Matt saw her sway with weariness. Without a word, Matt waded through the children and slipped his arm around her. She leaned heavily into him as they spent the next ten minutes trying to leave gracefully.

"You look a bit on the fierce and forbidding side," she said once they were back in the car. "I've never quite seen that expression before."

"I was contemplating picking you up and carting you out of there."

Kate laughed softly. "That would have given everyone something to talk about, wouldn't it?" She pressed her fingers to her temples. "Where are you taking me?"

"To the Salt Bar and Grill. You need to eat. Danny's been dating the waitress there, Trudy Garret, so we've spent quite a bit of time sampling the food. It's not bad." He glanced at her and noted that her hands were shaking. "You were using some sort of magic, weren't you? With your voice, and it drained your strength."

"There's always a cost to everything, Matthew." She shrugged without looking at him, closing her eyes and leaning back against the leather seat. "I'm not certain I'll be able to eat, but I'll try."

"You're already too thin, Katie."

She laughed. "A woman can never be too thin, Matthew, don't you know that?"

"That's what women like to think, but men think differently." He parked the car. "I don't mind carrying you."

She opened her eyes then. "Don't you have work to do?"

"I am working. I'm courting you the old-fashioned way. Showing you what a great guy I am and impressing you." He opened the car door for Kate and helped her out, happy to see her laughing. Some of the shadows had disappeared from her eyes.

"You think you're impressing me?"

"I know I'm impressing you."

"Only when you kiss me. I'm really impressed when

you kiss me," she admitted, deliberately tempting him. She needed the comfort of his arms more than she needed anything else.

Matt didn't need a second invitation. He pulled Kate's slender body into the shelter of his and lowered his mouth to hers. He brushed her lips gently, back and forth, giving her teasing little kisses meant to prolong the moment. Then his mouth settled over hers, and he kissed her hungrily, like a man starving for more.

Kate's slender arms circled his neck, and her body pressed tightly against his. He knew she couldn't help but feel his body's stark reaction to her, but she didn't seem to mind, burrowing even closer to him so that he felt the warmth of her breasts and the cradle of her hips beckoning with heat.

Tendrils of fog floated in from the sea, ghostly gray strands drifting past them as they stood together on the steps of the restaurant. Kate stiffened, her fingers gripping Matt's shoulders. "Did you hear the weather report? Did they say there would be fog?"

Matt scowled at the mist floating lazily into the parking lot. "We get fog all the time here in Sea Haven, Kate." But it didn't make the hair on his arms rise or his reflexes leap into survivor mode as it had the night before. "I don't smell that noxious odor, do you?"

She shook her head. "But the sun should have burned this fog off. The sky isn't that overcast, Matthew."

"Let's go inside." He held the door open for her to precede him. At once they could hear the wailing of a child in terror. The tension in the restaurant was tangible.

"Oh, Kate! I'm so glad you're here." Trudy Garret beckoned to them from behind the counter, her expression anxious. She was tall and pretty even with the apron she was wearing. Her youthful face was lined with worry.

Danny Granite stood behind her, his arm wrapped around her. He looked relieved to see them. There were a few people in the Salt Bar and Grill, but they were obviously tense and upset over the continual unrestrained sobs coming from somewhere in the back.

"Danny, why aren't you at work?" Matt asked. "Is everything all right at home?"

"Trudy's son had a bad nightmare last night. She can't seem to calm him down, so I offered to come over and see what I could do for him. He's only four years old, a cute little tyke, and I could hear him crying when I called her. I couldn't stand it."

"We haven't been able to calm him down," Trudy said. She was wringing her hands and looking imploringly at Kate. "I'm so glad you came in. Would you talk to him, Kate? Please?"

The cook stuck his head out of the kitchen. "Kate, thank heaven you're here!"

A few of the local patrons broke into applause.

Matt looked at Kate. Her face was pale, her eyes too big for her face, and there were shadows under her eyes. He stirred protectively but didn't speak when Kate put a light, restraining hand on his forearm. She smiled at Trudy. "Of course, I'll be happy to talk to him, Trudy. He isn't alone, many of the children at the preschool had nightmares last night."

Matt slid his hand down her arm, circling her wrist with his fingers. Her pulse was very fast, her skin cool. "While Kate talks to your son, Trudy, maybe you can heat a bowl of soup for her."

"Of course, be happy to," Trudy said. "Right this way, Kate, he's in the back."

Matt followed Kate behind the counter to the back room. The wails grew louder as they approached the small room. Kate opened the door. Matt winced at the high-pitched shrieks, but he stepped inside with her. It was the same scenario as at the preschool. Little Davy Garret sat in Kate's lap, telling her the details of a skeleton in a long coat and old hat in between gulping and tears, finally listening to the sound of her magical voice. Kate replaced the boy's memory of the terrifying nightmare with several funny Christmas stories. She rocked him while she talked, using her talent, her gift, to bring him peace, to soothe him, and make him feel that his world was right again.

After Kate spent twenty minutes sitting on the floor with the boy, Matt reached down and took the child from her arms and set him aside to play happily with his toys. "Danny can take over, Kate. Come eat the soup, then I'll take you home. You're exhausted." He pulled her gently to her feet.

Kate nodded. "I am tired. I wish I knew what was going on, though. I've never seen anything like this. How could all these children have the same dream? At the preschool, at first I thought maybe Haley told her dream to the others, and they all became upset because she was; but the parents said, no, the children had woken up that way. And Davy certainly didn't have contact with any of them. I don't like it at all." She slipped into a booth near the window and peered out. "The fog seems to be rolling in again, Matthew." She couldn't keep the apprehension she felt out of her voice.

"I noticed," he said grimly. The bright, blinking Christmas lights and cheerful music couldn't quite dispel the tension in the air. "Tell me more about the diaries."

Kate sipped at the hot tea Trudy brought her and stared out the window, avoiding his gaze. "Each generation in our family records our activities in journals, or diaries as we sometimes call them. They're considered the history of the Drake family. The earlier journals were recorded using a language or code of symbols like the ones we saw in the mill. I could read part of what was written on the seal. Someone in my family sealed that malevolent force in there. If it was that dangerous that they decided to seal it without laying it to rest, it was because they couldn't give it peace. And that's very frightening."

"And Elle's the only one who can read the language?"

"Sarah knows a little, just as I do. The others have some working knowledge as well, but there's a lot of history to go through when you don't have a good understanding of the language. We need Elle, but I'm certain Sarah and the others will keep trying to find the proper entry and hopefully decipher it."

The wind whirled through the room as the door to the restaurant was thrust open and Jonas strode in, coming directly to them, his face etched with deep lines.

Without asking, he slid into the booth beside Kate. "It's Jackson, Kate. I've never seen him like this. I need you to come and talk to him."

A chill went down Matt's spine. "What's wrong with him?"

At Matt's tone, Kate looked up quickly and caught an expression passing between the two men. "What is it? Why are you both so worried?"

There was a small, uncomfortable silence. "You know how you said Hannah was a private person and wouldn't want people to find out what happened the other night? Jackson is the same way," Matt said.

Jonas sat up straight. "What doesn't Hannah want talked about?"

"We're talking about Jackson," Kate reminded him. "What's wrong with him, and why are you both so worried?"

The two men exchanged another long look. Jonas sighed and shrugged in resignation. "I need your help or I wouldn't be telling you this, Kate. I expect you to keep it confidential."

She nodded because he had actually waited for her answer.

"Jackson is—was—is a specialist for the Rangers."

There was another silence. Kate watched their eyes. They looked grave, more than a little worried. When neither was more forthcoming she took a guess. "He's trained in things I don't want to know about, and you don't want to talk about. Right now he's in a bad way and both of you are concerned for his mental well-being. And what do you mean by is—was—is?"

"That about sums it up, Kate. Let's go," Jonas said.

"Once a Ranger always a Ranger," Matt added. "And she needs to eat her soup. Give her a few minutes."

"Do you have any idea what's going on, Kate?" Jonas asked. "Your sisters are all upset, and whatever happened last night to you and Matt sounds bizarre. You were so drained, even I could feel it."

She shook her head. "My sisters are still looking in the old family diaries for an explanation, but I don't have any answers, Jonas. I wish I did."

chapter 6

The time, it was right, for a present or two,
And the fog on the sand holds a secret, a clue.

 JACKSON DEVEAU PACED BACK AND FORTH IN complete silence. That was the first thing Kate noticed, how very silent he was. His clothes didn't rustle, and the soles of his shoes didn't make any noise. His eyes were as cold as ice, as bleak and as dead as she had ever seen in a human being. She sat down in the one good armchair and tried to repress a shiver. If the man had any gentleness in him, she couldn't detect it.

"I told you I didn't need a damned psychiatrist, Jonas," Jackson snapped, without looking at her. "Get her out of here. You think I want anyone to see me like this?" Sweat beaded on his forehead, dampened his dark, unruly hair.

"I'm not a psychiatrist, Mr. Deveau," Kate said. "I'm simply a friend of both Jonas and Matthew. I have a gift, and they thought it might help you in some way. Neither meant to upset you."

"Stop growling like a Neanderthal, Jackson, and let her talk," Matthew said. "You'd think you didn't have a civilized bone in your body."

"How strange that you would choose that particular

description when my sisters said the same thing about you, Matthew," Kate replied. "Did you have a particularly disturbing dream, Mr. Deveau?"

Jackson whirled around and stalked toward her from across the room, his body moving like a large predatory cat's. "What'd they tell you about me? That I'm crazy? That I have nightmares and can't sleep? What the hell do you want me to say?"

Kate noted both Jonas and Matt were close to her, ready to defend her if necessary. In spite of the shiver of fear, she calmly looked up at the deputy. "They didn't say anything. They've told me next to nothing about you. Most of the children in town seem to have had a collective nightmare. So far, none of the adults have admitted to it, but everywhere we've been today, there's unexpected tension. I thought maybe you would be able to tell me about it. I'm getting garbled accounts from the children, and so far no adult has been courageous enough to admit they had the dream too."

Jackson raked both hands through his dark hair, the muscles rippling under his thin, tight tee shirt. He looked from Jonas to Matthew as if expecting a trap. "Kids have been having nightmares?"

Kate nodded. "Last night, after the fog rolled in, something bizarre happened. This morning, children from all over town were distressed and in tears, some traumatized by a dream they all seem to have shared."

"About what?" For the first time since she'd entered the room, Jackson sat down, his hands still gripping his head as if he had a violent headache.

"They described a skeleton man in a long coat and old hat."

Jackson hesitated, clearly reluctant to discuss his problem with her. He looked from Jonas to Matt and finally capitulated. "The coat and hat were old-fashioned, a heavy wool, maybe. There was no real face, just white-gray bones. There was a woman and a baby and a shepherd, or at least someone with a shepherd's staff." He scrubbed his hand over his face. "I go after real people, real threats, but this thing, this was from a place I can't get to, and I sense that everyone is in danger." He looked at Kate. "More than the actual dream, it was the feeling the dream left me with that's disturbing. The danger was real. I know it sounds crazy, but dammit, it was real!"

Matt stiffened. Jackson Deveau had never feared very much, certainly not his own mortality, yet he was deeply shaken by the nightmare.

"Then you felt it too. That the threat is real," Kate said, leaning toward Jackson.

Jackson drew back. Matt had forgotten to tell Kate the deputy didn't like physical contact. "I know it is." He looked at Jonas and Matt. "You two probably think I've finally gone around the bend, but I swear, whatever that thing was in my dream, he's looking for a way to walk among us."

"He uses the fog," Kate explained. He was no child to be soothed with Christmas stories and loving smiles. He was a grown man, a warrior, and what he needed was the naked truth. It was the only thing he would accept. He needed facts to assure him he was not losing his mind. "Whatever he or it is, he's growing stronger. I think the earthquake cracked a seal locking him deep in the earth, and he managed to escape. Matthew and I found a broken lid in the basement of the old mill. Something came out of a crack in the form of a noxious vapor. I've smelled the same odor in the fog." She met Jackson's gaze steadily. "If you're losing your mind, so am I. So is Matthew. And so are all the children of Sea Haven."

Matthew heard it then, that magical note that brought absolute peace to a troubled mind. He had become attuned to it, aware of the surge of energy in the room, going from Kate to the person she was speaking with. He was also aware of her absorbing the negative energy, taking it in and holding it away from its victim.

"That's a relief. I thought this time I was really losing my mind. I have nightmares, and I can deal with them, but this was something out of a horror film." Jackson shook his head. "I'm not going into an institution."

"You're the only one who ever thinks that way," Jonas said quietly. "So do your sisters have any ideas, Kate? This is more your field than ours." He nodded toward the other two Rangers. "We can be your soldiers, but you're going to have to give us a direction."

Kate leaned back in the chair, fatigue in every line of her body. "We're working on it. Abbey and Sarah and Damon were going through the diaries this morning. We'll find the reference and at least have a starting point."

"I notice you didn't mention Hannah," Jonas observed. There was a challenge in his voice. "Is she ill? Is that what's wrong with her?" When Kate didn't answer, Jonas swore. "Dammit, Kate, if she's ill, you owe it to me to tell me. Something's wrong with her."

"Something's always been wrong with her, Jonas, you just never noticed before." Kate folded her arms. "I'm not going to be bullied into telling you something that is Hannah's private business. Ask her."

Jonas swore again and stormed out. Kate rolled her eyes. "His temper hasn't improved much with age."

"Come on, Kate, I'm taking you to dinner at my house. I'm a great cook." Matt reached down and drew her up from the chair. "I think it's the only sanctuary left to us."

"I should go home and help the others."

Jackson stood up too. "You made me feel better. How did you do it?"

Kate smiled at him and offered her hand. "It was a pleasure finally to meet you, Mr. Deveau. Jonas and Matthew speak so highly of you."

He hesitated but took her hand. "Please call me Jackson."

Kate felt the jolt of his heavy burden go up her arm. It was difficult to maintain her smile when she felt the brooding darkness in the man. She wasn't Libby. She couldn't heal the sick, and in any case, she didn't sense that Jackson Deveau was physically ill so much as spiritually so. "I wish you peace, Jackson," she murmured softly, and allowed Matthew to draw her from the house out into the cool air.

"He didn't have a Christmas tree up, or any decorations at all," she said sadly. "If anyone needs Christmas, it's that man."

"He'll work it out, Kate," Matthew assured her. "He has his demons, but the bottom line is, honor and integrity rule his life. He would never do any of the things he's afraid he will, and, just like Jonas, he would protect this town and the people in it with his last breath."

"I'm glad you brought him to Sea Haven. You were right about this place. There's just something about the way the people are here—they're welcoming to outsiders." The interior of his car was warm after the chilling wind blowing in off the ocean.

"Did your sisters really call me a Neanderthal?"

She burst out laughing. "Well, yes, but in a good way. I think they could easily picture you beating your chest and tossing your woman over your shoulder to carry her off to somewhere private."

He nodded. "I can understand that. I do have those urges. Often." He looked at her, his hand still around the key. "I really want to take you back to my house, Kate." He waited a heartbeat before starting the engine.

"Are your brothers going to be there? Because, honestly, I think I'm too tired to have them all laughing at me today. I'd probably burst into tears."

He pressed a hand to his heart. "Don't even say that. I think I'd rather take a bullet than see you cry. And my brothers don't laugh at you." He glanced at her to see if she was serious.

"They *always* laugh at me," she said. "I'm always doing these idiotic things whenever I'm around you. Like the other day when you had that accident and you tried to get out of the truck and I was standing too close." She looked down at her hands. "Danny just about fell out of the truck laughing."

"At *me,* Katie, never at you. My entire family knows

how I feel about you, and they think it's a riot that I can make such a complete fool of myself every time you're near."

Kate sat very still, her gaze fixed on his face. "How do you feel about me?"

"I've made that pretty damn clear, Kate."

"Have you? I know you're attracted to me physically."

He gave a small snort of derision. "Is that what you call it? I haven't had a good night's sleep since I looked at you when you were fifteen years old. I hate admitting that. I shouldn't have been looking at you, but I did, and I just knew. I've had more dreams about you, more fantasies, than any man should admit to having." He pulled the car into the driveway of his yard and turned off the engine before facing her. "Hell, Kate, if you didn't know, you're the only person in this town who didn't. Jonas asked me last night if I was stalking you."

"He wouldn't do that. You're his friend. He must have been kidding."

"With his hand on his gun. Afraid not, and here you are, at my house, all alone with me. Are you coming in?"

"Am I supposed to be afraid now?"

"I thought my fantasies might scare you off."

"Did you?" Kate slid out of the car. The wind whipped her hair around and tugged at her clothes. "Actually I'm intrigued."

His entire body reacted to her sultry tone. Maybe she didn't mean it the way it sounded, but he was going to take her words as an invitation to love her every way a man could love a woman.

Kate smiled to herself as she went up the stairs to his

home. It was situated on the bluff above the ocean, his deck wrapping around the house providing a view from every direction. The house itself was obviously built for a man of Matt's size. The ceilings were vaulted, there were few walls, so the space seemed enormous, one room running directly into the next. His furniture suited the house, casual, yet overstuffed to go with the dimensions of the house.

"It's so beautiful, Matthew. I love all the bay windows and the alcoves and the way everything is so spacious. Did you design it?"

He felt a little glow of pleasure. "Yes, I wanted a home I was comfortable living in day in and day out. I need space. Even the doorways are wider and taller than normal, so I don't always feel as if I might have to duck."

"I love the open beams and the rock fireplace. This is what I had in mind for my house, or at least something very similar. I love the beams and the natural-looking fireplace in the mill." She turned to smile at him. "We do have very similar taste."

His heart did a curious somersault in his chest. He gripped the edge of the door. "I think so. It should be easy to come up with a design you'll really fall in love with." He said the words deliberately.

Kate stilled and turned her head to look at him. The movement was graceful and elegant. So Kate. He ached, just looking at her. Color swept her face. She glanced from him to the tall Christmas tree in his front room. It was a silver tip, beautiful and decorated with lights and a few ornaments. "Did you put up your tree?"

"I brought in the tree and hung the lights. Mom

insisted I get ornaments. She said I was supposed to have a theme, but I just picked up ones I liked."

Kate wandered around the tree. One of the ornaments was a wooden house carved by a local artist. She was surprised and pleased to see it was her cliff house. She didn't comment on the ornament, but she hoped it meant he'd been thinking of her when he'd bought the miniature replica of her home.

"This is my favorite room. I spend a lot of time in here. My office is straight ahead, and I have a large library. I call it a library; Danny and Jonas call it my den." He grinned at her. "They talked me into a pool table."

She laughed. "Of course they did. I'll bet they had to twist your arm."

Matt hastily gathered up a few shirts he'd tossed aside earlier in the week. There was an old pizza box on the coffee table along with an empty doughnut box overturned beside a half-full coffee cup.

Kate grinned at him. "I see you're into health food."

"I actually like to cook. I used to cook all the time for the men in my unit." He opened a door, tossed his shirts inside without looking where they landed, and hastily closed the door to gather up the dirty boxes and coffee cup. "I haven't been home much. Dad's running a big job, and all of us have been working to bring it in on time."

"Matthew." Kate put her hand lightly on his arm. "Are you nervous?"

He stood there looking down at her upturned face. Her enormous soft eyes. Her tempting mouth. Could she be any more beautiful? "Hell, yes, I'm nervous. I don't even know what a woman like you would be doing in the same house with a man like me."

"A woman like me?" She looked genuinely puzzled.

Matt groaned. "Come on, Kate. Are you telling me you haven't known I've been wild about you for years? I can't even have a good time with another woman. I've tried dating numerous women. We have one date, and I know it isn't going to work."

"You're wild about me?" she echoed.

He tossed the boxes on the couch and pulled her into his arms. Hard. Possessive. Commanding Ranger style. "I can't even think straight around you."

There was no way to think when his mouth took hers, hot and hungry and devouring her. Her body melted into his, her arms sliding around his neck, her fingers brushing the nape of his neck intimately, creeping into his hair while she met his ravenous hunger with her own.

He couldn't kiss her and not touch her soft, tempting skin. Without conscious thought, he slid his hand beneath her blouse to move up the soft expanse of skin. Just that slight contact brought him such deep pleasure it bordered on pain. He trembled, his hand actually shaking as he brushed the pads of his fingers over her rib cage, and up to cup the soft weight of her breast in his palm. His body went into overdrive, his heart slamming in his chest and his jeans growing uncomfortably tight.

"Aren't you going to stop me, Kate? One of us should know what we're doing." He wanted to be fair with her. She was exhausted and obviously not thinking straight, arching into his hand, pushing closer, rubbing her body against his. Soft little moans came from her throat, driving him right over the edge. He found himself kissing her again and again, long hot kisses that pushed their temperatures even higher.

Her lips smiled under the assault of his. "I know exactly what I'm doing, Matthew, you're the one who's unclear." Her hands dropped to the buttons of her blouse.

There was a strange roaring in his ears. He had waited years for this moment. Kate Drake in his home. In his arms. Kate's body open to his exploration. It would take a lifetime to satisfy him. More than that. Much more. Her blouse fell open, exposing the creamy swell of her breasts. White lace cupped her skin lovingly.

Matt stared down at her body, mesmerized by the sight of his large hand holding her, his thumb brushing her nipple through the white lace. For one moment, it occurred to him he was making the entire thing up. Kate Drake. His Christmas present. He bent his head to her breast, his mouth closing around soft flesh and lace. His tongue teased and danced over her nipple while his arms enfolded her closer.

The pounding on the front door was abrupt, loud, and unexpected. Kate cried out, and he felt her heart beneath her skin jump with fear.

Matt lifted his head, his gray eyes appearing silver as they smoldered with a mixture of anger and desire. "Don't worry, Katie." He pulled the edges of her blouse together. Why couldn't the world leave them alone for one damned hour? Was that too much to ask?

Kate buttoned her blouse and tried to finger comb her

hair. He caught her wrist and brought her hand to his mouth. "You look beautiful. Whoever it is can just go away."

She waited in the middle of his living room while he yanked the door open. The sheriff stood there, his fist poised for another assault. "Jonas, I'm beginning to think our friendship is going to suffer," Matt greeted with a scowl.

Jonas pushed right past him. "Come on out here and take a look at this." His voice was grim. He stalked through the house to the ocean side, pushing open the double doors leading to the deck overlooking the sea. "What the hell is going on, Kate?"

The fog whirled around the house as if alive. Dark and gray and gloomy, the mist was thick, almost oily. It crept up the walls and swirled around the chimney. Jonas glared at the fog. "No one can drive anywhere. Car accidents are happening all over town. Your sister Elle called. She's in the islands and yet she had *the exact same dream as Jackson and the children.* How could she have the same dream? She said to tell you the symbols meant something. When I asked her what they meant she said you would know."

Both men looked at Kate. She hesitated, trying to remember, but there was nothing that seemed to be of great significance. "There were symbols on the seal, but the only thing of importance I could read was that a locking spell had been placed on the lid to hold something in the ground. I'll call Elle and ask her to give me details. Is she on her way home? She was going to try to make it back for Christmas."

"She said she'd be catching a late flight." Jonas stared at the thick gray blanket of mist, frowning as he did so. "The worst of the fog seems to be centered here. It's much heavier around your house, Matt. People are going to start dying if we don't figure out what's going on. We've been lucky, most people pulled their cars over to wait it out and the accidents that have occurred have been minor. But it would be very easy to drive off the cliff in this dense fog. We've asked the radio stations to alert everyone to the driving hazards."

"I'm guessing you called the weather station and the meteorologists there told you this fog is unnatural," Matt said with a small sigh. The supernatural wasn't his realm of expertise, but he had the feeling he was going to have to learn more about it very fast. A part of him had hoped it would all go away. Instead, the fog was wrapped tightly around his house. He glanced at Kate. She stood very still, her hand to her throat, staring out into the dark gray mist. There was fear on her face.

Anger began to smolder in the pit of his belly, not hot and fiery, but ice-cold and clear, dangerous and deadly, an emotion he recognized from his combat days. Matthew took Kate by the shoulders and pulled her back, away from the deck and into the safety of the house. "Did Sarah say whether or not they found anything in the diaries, Jonas? They were all looking, hoping to find an explanation."

Jonas shook his head. "Sarah said she doesn't have a clue as to what's going on, but she thought with all the sisters concentrating, they might be able to drive this fog back to sea to give us more time to figure it out."

Matt's hands tightened on Kate's shoulders. "I don't want you to do it again, Katie. I think you're making it angry, and it's striking back at you. Why else would it have followed us to my house and stayed here?" He couldn't articulate the emotions the fog gave off, but there was something dark and ugly about it that reeked of pitiless hostility. He didn't want Kate anywhere near it.

"We can't take chances, Matthew," Kate said, her voice trembling. She pressed her lips together. Instinctively she moved back toward Matt as if for protection. "Jonas said there have already been traffic accidents."

Matt could feel her reluctance. Whatever was in the fog had grown in strength and intensity. The previous night it had been an eerie annoyance; now it seemed darker . . . more aggressive and dangerous.

"The fog swept through town, Kate, right after the two of you left Jackson's house," Jonas explained. "People came out of their houses to stand there and watch it. The sheriff's office logged well over a hundred calls. When it receded, it left behind a mess. All over town gifts left outside, everything from bicycles and ATVs to garden furniture, were smashed and covered with sea trash—sand, kelp, driftwood, smashed seashells, you name it. Even crabs crawling around." Jonas pushed back his hat and rested his gaze on Kate's face. "The worst damage was done to the town square. The three wise men statues were all but destroyed, and the gifts they carried were ground into the lawn. The statues had kelp wrapped around their necks and wrists and ankles. It was bizarre and ugly and it scared everyone enough that the folks on the committee are concerned about the safety of the men playing the parts of the wise men in the pageant. Do you think it was a warning?"

Kate rubbed at her throbbing temples. She was already so tired. She felt drained and just wanted to lie down for a few hours. "I honestly don't know, Jonas, but the entity is accelerating its destructive behavior."

"Dammit, Kate, what the hell could be alive in the fog?" Matt burst out, wanting to throttle the thing. "I don't want you anywhere near this stuff. Why do you have to be the one to face it?"

"My voice. The others can channel through me. And Hannah can call up the wind to drive it back to sea."

He wasn't touching that. It sounded like witches and spells and things he saw in movies, not in real life.

Matt began a slow massage at the nape of Kate's neck to help ease the tension out of her. "Katie, why would this thing smash gifts? If it's capable of destroying things and moving objects as it did with the wreaths on the doors, why such a silly, almost petty display? Why do the gifts bother it? What would be the significance?"

Jonas followed them back to the sliding glass door. "That's a good question. Is that all it can do? When the calls started coming in I thought it was kids and childish pranks. Smashing gifts and outdoor ornaments and leaving behind dead fish are relatively harmless acts of vandalism a kid might do. Well, at least I thought a kid might be the culprit until I saw the three kings smashed to pieces. Jackson came out to the square to take a look at the damage, and he said the scene was reminiscent of his nightmare."

Kate shook her head. "I think it's growing stronger, testing its abilities. It doesn't feel childish to me. It used wreaths, a symbol often associated with Christmas, and now gifts. Elle said the symbols matter. Gifts obviously are another symbol of Christmas." She sighed and rubbed at her temples. "Obviously this thing does not like Christmas at all. Any guesses as to why?"

"I have no idea," Matt said. He used his body to gently shepherd her farther back into the room, wanting to close the doors against the fog.

She turned in his arms and pressed her body close to his for strength and comfort. "My sisters are waiting. Even Libby. It isn't easy to sustain a channeling for any great length of time."

Matt tightened his arms around her, holding her captive, holding her safe. He buried his face against her neck. "I hate this, Kate. You have no idea how much. I want to pack you up and take you far away from this place. I know you're in danger."

"If I don't do this, Matthew, one of my sisters will try, and they don't have my voice." She hugged him hard and slowly pulled away from him.

Matt allowed her to slip from his arms, taut with fear for her when she stepped onto the deck. He stepped beside her. Close. Protective. Daring the thing to come through him to get to her. Jonas took up a position on her other side. Kate closed her eyes and raised her face to the sky.

A breeze from the sea fluttered against her face. She felt the cooling touch. She felt the joining of her sisters. All seven, together yet apart. Strength flowed into her, through her. She lifted her arms and knew Hannah stood on the battlement of their ancestral home and simultaneously did the same.

Matt heard the moaning of the wind. Out on the ocean, the caps on the waves reached high and foamed white. The fog became frenzied, whirling and spinning madly, winding around Kate so that for a moment it obscured Matt's vision of her. He reached out blindly, instinctively, and yanked her into the protection of his body. "This is bullshit, Kate." He pressed her face against his chest and wrapped his arms around her head to keep the fog from getting at her.

Kate didn't struggle. She didn't act in any way as if she noticed. Her voice was soft, barely above a whisper, yet the wind carried it into the bank of mist, and it vibrated through the vapor, taking on a life of its own. Kate remained against him, her eyes closed but her chanting continuing, a gift of harmony and peace, of contentment and solidarity. She called on the elements of the earth. Matt heard that clearly.

Voices rose on the wind. Seawater leaped in response to the chant, waves rising high, bursting through the fogbank and breaking it into tendrils out over the ocean. The wind howled, gathering strength, rushing at them, bringing the taste of salt and droplets of water to brush over their faces. Thunder crashed, shaking the deck. Still the voices continued, and the tempest built.

"Hannah." Jonas said her name softly, slightly awed by the raw power forged and controlled between the sisters.

Kate took a deep breath and let go. Let go of her sisters and her body and the physical world she lived in to enter the shadow world. Far off, she heard the echo of Hannah's frightened cry. The world wasn't silent as one would expect. She never got used to that. There were noises, moans and cries, not quite human, unidentifiable. Static, the sound of a radio not tuned properly. And the terrible howl of the wind endlessly blowing. It was cold and bleak and barren. A world of darkness and despair. She looked around carefully, trying to find the one she was seeking.

She wasn't alone. She could feel others watching her. Some were merely curious, others hostile. None were friendly. She was a living being, and they were long gone. Something slithered close to her feet. She felt the touch of something slimy against her arm. Kate took another breath and called out softly. At once she saw it. A terrifying sight. Tall, bare white bones, the skull ghastly with a gaping mouth and empty sockets for eyes. It wasn't fully formed. A great hole was in the chest cavity. The ribs were missing. It came striding toward her, and she noticed that the skeleton wore old-fashioned boots stuck at the end of the sticklike bones of its legs. She might have laughed had it not been so frightening. The bones rattled as it rushed toward her, deadly purpose in every bone.

"Kate!" Abigail's cry echoed Hannah's and Sarah's.

Kate held up her hand to ward the thing off as it reached her.

Matt felt Kate's energy crackling in the air around them, a fierce force never wavering, yet her slender body shook with the effort, or maybe with fear, crumbling beneath the strain. Without warning he felt every hair on his body stand up. Kate went sickly pale. Afraid for her, he swept her up into his arms and held her tight against his chest, the only thing he could do to shelter her from the onslaught of the wind and the menace of the fog.

Kate wrenched herself from the shadow world, opened her eyes, expecting to see Matt. Empty sockets stared back at her. The skull's mouth gaped wide, the jaw loose, bony fingers wrapping around her throat. She screamed and pulled away, trying to run when there was nowhere to go. The pressure on her throat increased. She choked.

The wind rose to a howl. Feminine voices became commanding. The bony fingers slid from Kate's throat. She fell to the ground and stared in horror as the voices of the Drake women forced the skeleton away from her one dragging step at a time. Those pitiless empty eye sockets stared at her with malice. Kate tried to scoot crab-like in the opposite direction, feeling sick as the entity clacked white bones together in a dark, ugly promise of retaliation.

The wind blew sand into the air, obscuring Kate's vision. She squeezed her eyes closed tightly against the new assault. At once she felt Matt's body pressed close to hers. Afraid to look, she lifted her lashes, hands out in front of her for protection. Matt's reassuring face was there, the planes and angles familiar to her. She buried her face against his throat, felt the warmth of his body leeching some of the icy cold from hers.

The fog crept back toward the ocean slowly, almost grudgingly, retreating from around the house and deck to the beach, with obvious reluctance. With Kate safely in his arms, Matt stared in horror at the wet sand. Distinct footprints were left behind, as if someone had backed toward the ocean with short, dragging steps, a man's boots with run-down heels. A cold chill swept down his spine. His gaze went from the prints in the sand to Jonas. "What the hell are we dealing with here?"

chapter

7

As lovers meet beneath mistletoe bright,
Terror ignites down below them this night.

MATT STARED DOWN AT KATE'S FACE. SHE LAY in his bed, sound asleep, the signs of exhaustion present even as she slept. She looked more fragile than ever, as if fighting back the entity in the fog had taken most of her spirit and drained all of her strength. The curtains over his sliding glass door were pulled back to allow him a clear view of the ocean. He had always enjoyed the sight and sound of the waves pounding, but now he searched the horizon for signs of the fog. Kate was worn out. He worried that if the entity returned, she wouldn't have the strength to fight it, even though she'd slept for hours. The day had disappeared, and night had fallen.

He rubbed his hands over his face to wipe away his own exhaustion. He hadn't slept the night before, standing watch at Kate's bedside, and he was feeling the effects. He had stripped her of her clothes and wrapped her in one of his shirts. It was far too big for her and covered every curve. He'd tucked her in his bed and all the while she lay passively, making little effort to do anything but close her eyes. He had the feeling she'd faced something far worse than the fog, but she hadn't been ready to talk about it with him. Recognizing the signs of exhaustion, he hadn't pushed her.

Matt removed his shirt and shoes and socks and stretched out beside her. He had built his home in the hopes of finding a wife when he returned from serving his country, but no matter how many women he had dated, there had been only one woman for him. Kate had been in his dreams from the moment he'd first laid eyes on her. He would never forget that moment, driving his father's truck, his rowdy brothers cranking up the music and laughing happily. He had glanced casually to his right not realizing that his life was about to change forever. Kate was standing in the creek bed with her six sisters, her head thrown back, laughing, her eyes dancing, totally oblivious to his gaze. A jolt of electricity had sizzled through his entire body. In that one moment, Kate Drake had managed to burn her brand into his very bones, and no other woman would do for him.

"Matthew?" Her voice was drowsy. Sexy. It poured into his body with the force of a bolt of lightning, heating his blood and bringing every nerve ending alive.

"I'm here, Katie," he answered, wrapping his body around hers as he slipped his arm around her waist.

"Didn't Sea Haven always seem like home to you? When you were far away, in another country, in danger, didn't you dream of this place?"

"I dreamed of you. You were home to me, Kate." There in the darkness with the ocean pounding outside his bedroom he could admit the truth to her. "You got me through the gunfire, and the ugliness, and it was the thought of you that brought me back to Sea Haven. My family always kept track of you for me."

Kate turned her face into his shoulder, snuggling closer to him. "I heard you were doing things that seemed so scary to me. I have such an imagination, and I would wake up in the middle of night picturing you rising up out of the desert sand in your camouflage fatigues with your rifle and enemies all around you. Sometimes the dreams were so vivid I'd actually get sick. I've never told that to anyone, not even my sisters. They saw the differences in us and knew we weren't right for each other."

"Kate." He said her name tenderly. With an aching need in it. "How can you say that? Or even think it? I was made for you. To be with you. I feel it so strongly, the rightness of it. You feel it too. I know you do." He held her possessively, his arms locking her to him. Matt buried his face in the soft warmth of her neck. "Katie, you can't hand a man his dream, then take it away. Especially not a man like me. I stood back and gave you all the room in the world when you were too young for me. Later, when you were grown, you were busy and happy with your life, traveling around the world doing what you do. I never once made a move on you. I knew you needed your freedom to pursue your writing. But now you're home, telling me you're ready to settle down, and I can't just step back and pretend we don't feel anything for one another. Every time you looked at me, you had to know we belonged. You should never have kissed me if you weren't willing to give a relationship between us a try."

Kate closed her eyes, feeling tears welling up. His lips

moved over her neck, drifted lower to nudge the collar of the shirt aside. Her pulse pounded frantically. Her heart went into overdrive. "I'm not brave the way you are, Matthew," she admitted in a small voice. "I can't be like you. I'm not at all a person of action. In a few months when you realize that, you'll be so disappointed in me, and you'll have too much honor to tell me."

Matt lifted his head and looked down at her. Tears shimmered in her eyes, and his heart nearly stopped beating in his chest. "What the hell are you talking about, Kate?" He bent his head to kiss the tears away. He tasted grief. Fear. An aching longing. "Dammit." He muttered the words in sheer frustration, then kissed her hard, his mouth claiming hers. A ravenous hunger burst through him, over him. There was a strange roaring in his head. His chest was tight, his heart pounding with the force of thunder. He had faced enemy fire without flinching, but he couldn't bear the idea of Kate walking away from him.

He poured everything he felt into his kiss. Everything he was. His hands framed her face, held her to him while he ravaged her mouth. Heat spread like a wildfire, through him, through her, catching them both on fire until he thought he might ignite. She melted into him, her arms sliding around him, nearly as possessive as he was. He lifted his head to look at her, memorizing every beloved line and angle of her face. He was gentle, his fingertips stroking caresses and tracing her cheekbones, the shape of her eyes, the curve of her eyebrows. The pad of his thumb slid back and forth over the softness of her lips. He loved her mouth, loved everything about her. "Kate." He kissed her gently. Once. Twice. "How could you think I don't know you? We've lived in the same town practically all our lives. I've watched you. I've listened to you. Do you know how many times I've dreamed of you?"

"Dreams aren't the same as reality, Matt," Kate said sadly.

Her gaze moved over his face, examining every inch of his features. Matt waited, holding his breath. He was rough and she was elegant. He was a man who protected the ones he loved. And he loved Kate Drake.

"Matthew . . ." There was that catch in her voice again. Need. Caution.

Matt couldn't imagine why Kate would fear a relationship with him, a life with him, but the thought that she might pull away had him bending his head. His teeth tugged at her delicate ear. His tongue made a foray along the small shape. She shivered in reaction. He grew harder. Thicker. His body was heavy and painful, straining against the confines of his jeans. "Katie, unzip my jeans." He breathed the words into her ear, his lips drifting lower to find her neck. Her soft, sensitive neck.

Kate closed her eyes as his teeth nipped her chin, her throat, as his lips found her collarbone, his chin nudging aside the shirt collar again. She ached with wanting him, her body hot and sensitive. Her breasts felt swollen, begging for his attention. What was so wrong with reaching for something, just this one time? He was everything she'd ever wanted, yet was always out of her reach. Matthew Granite was a fighter, larger-than-life. He'd done things she would never comprehend, never experience. He felt like a hero from one of her novels, not quite real and too good to be true. She knew she'd thought of him when she'd written each and every one of her books. She'd used him as her role model because, to her, he was everything a man should be. Why would he ever choose to be with a woman who looked at life, wrote about life, but refused to participate in it?

Kate was certain she was going to leap from the bed and run, but her body had a mind of its own. She was already working on the button at the waistband of his jeans, finding the zipper and dragging it down. The air left his lungs in a rush when her hand shaped the thick, heavy bulge, caressed and stroked with loving fingers. "You're wearing too many clothes, Matthew," she pointed out, determined to have her time with him, even if it couldn't be forever.

"So are you." His hands dropped to the buttons of her shirt, sliding them open so that the edges gaped apart. He raised his upper body in order to stare down at her, to drink in the sight of Kate Drake in his bed. She shrugged out of the shirt and allowed it fall to the floor before lying back. His mouth went dry.

Outside, the continual booming of the sea seemed to match the pounding of his heart. In the soft light, her skin was flawless, inviting. Her breasts were full and round, her nipples taut inviting peaks. Kate's long hair spilled around the pillows, just as he'd always fantasized. For a moment he was caught and held by the sight of her, unable to believe she was real. "There was more than one night out in the desert when I was lying half-buried in the sand, surrounded by the enemy. It was important to get in and out without being seen. The enemy showed up and set up camp virtually on top of us. It was the fantasy of you lying just like this in my bed, waiting for me at home, that got me through it."

"Then I'm very glad, Matthew." She tugged on the loop at the waistband of his jeans. "Get rid of those things."

He didn't wait for a second invitation. "I've always loved you, Kate. Always." She would never know how often he thought of her, in the hot arid desert and the freezing nights, in the painful sandstorms. Lying in a field with the enemy not ten feet from him. He had been all over the world, performing high-risk covert missions in places no American leader would ever admit to sending troops, and Kate had gone with him every single time.

He stroked his hand down her leg, more to ensure she was real than for any other reason. He felt her shiver in response. Her lips parted slightly. Her sea-green eyes watched his every move. Matt knelt on the bed, tugging on her ankles, a silent command to open her legs. She complied, parting her thighs wide enough to allow him to slide between her legs.

Matt was a big man. At once Kate felt vulnerable, the cool night air teasing the tiny curls at the junction of her legs. His hands, sliding up her thighs, were gentle, removing her anxiety as fast as it rose. She loved the way he looked at her, almost worshiping her skin, her body, his hot gaze exploring in the same thorough way as his hands. A wave of heat rushed through her, of anticipation. Matt took his time caressing every curve along her slender leg, even the back of her knee as if memorizing the texture of every inch of her was terribly important.

His touch sent darts of fire racing over her skin, penetrating every nerve ending until she could hardly lie still beneath his touch. Her breath was coming in a gasp, and heat coiled deep inside her, a terrible pressure beginning to build.

Matt couldn't contain himself another moment. She lay there like a beautiful offering. He bent over her, kissed her enticing navel, his tongue swirling in the small, sexy dip, his hands continuing their foray lower. He felt her reaction, a warm, moist welcoming against his palm as he pushed against her. He kissed his way up her smooth body to the underside of her breast. Kate gasped and arched her body, her hips moving restlessly. She flushed, her luminous skin taking on a faint peach-colored glow.

He groaned. His body reacted with another swelling surge. Fire raced through his veins. His tongue flicked her nipple, once, twice, and his mouth settled over her breast. Kate cried out, her hands grasping handfuls of his hair, tugging him closer to her. She was magic. He could think of no other word to describe her. His body pressed into the softness of hers, while he lavished attention on her breasts. He'd dreamed of her skin, of the feel and shape of her every curve, and his imagination hadn't come close to the real thing. He cupped her other breast, teasing her nipple, feeling the response in Kate. She was very sensitive to his touch, to his mouth, to every caressing stroke. And she showed him she loved his touch.

Her soft moans heightened Matt's pleasure. He hungered for the sounds and responses Kate showed him. He needed them. She was generous in her reception, her hands moving over him, her body restless with the same hunger. He flicked her nipple one more time with his tongue and took possession of her lips, swallowing her moan, robbing her of breath.

Matt kissed her mouth over and over because no amount of kissing Kate would ever be enough. He trailed kisses down her throat, in the valley between her breasts. Her fingers dug into his hips, urging a union, but he took his time. He rained kisses across her stomach, pausing to dip again into her fascinating belly button.

"Matthew, really, I don't think I'm going to live through this." Her breath came in a series of ragged gasps.

"I waited a long time, Kate. I'm not rushing things." He ducked his head, his tongue sliding wickedly over her wet, hot sheath. She nearly jumped out of her skin. He grinned at her. "I may only have this one chance to prove my worth to you. I'm not about to blow my chances by charging the battlefield." He bent his head and blew softly against her sensitive body. He caught her hips more firmly, dragged her closer to him, and bent his head to taste her.

Kate screamed and nearly rose off the bed. He held her hips firmly, locking her to him while he feasted. She was hotter than he had ever imagined, a well of passion, and he had just begun to tap into it. He felt the first strong ripple of her muscles rushing to overtake her, and his body swelled even larger in response.

"I think you're ready for me, Kate." He didn't bother to hide the satisfaction in his voice. It was still a miracle to him that she chose to be with him. He pushed her thighs a little wider to accommodate his hips, pressing against her so that the sensitive tip of his penis slipped into her hot, welcoming body. The breath slammed out of his lungs. He pushed deeper so that she swallowed the tip, her tight muscles gripping with soft relentless pressure that sent violent waves of pleasure shooting through his body.

Kate gasped and clutched at the bedsheets. Matt froze, understanding dawning. He bit back a string of swear words, took a deep breath, and let it out. "Relax, honey, just relax. I swear, we fit together perfectly."

She smiled at him. "I'm not afraid, you idiot, I've never felt this before, and it's amazing. I want more, Matthew, all of you. Stop being so careful." If he didn't quit moving so slowly, she was going to spontaneously combust. She wanted to push her body over his. It was difficult to hold back when every instinct demanded she lift her body to receive his.

"Dammit, Kate, you're not experienced." He was sweating now. It was impossible to hold back. She was squirming, her hips pushing hard into his, and he was inching his way deeper into the hot core of her. Pleasure was building at such a ferocious rate he was losing all control just when he needed it the most. She was so damned tight, squeezing and gripping him, the friction like a hot velvet fist pumping him dry. Matt thrust deeper because he had no other choice. It was that or risk death. He was certain of it. She took him in, gasping with pleasure, when he'd been so worried.

Matt let go of his fears and took the ride, thrusting deep, tilting her body until she could take all of him. He moved the way he wanted, the way he needed, hard and fast and deep, joining them together in a rush of heat. The ocean pounded the shore just outside the glass door. Matt was unaware of it, unaware of anything but Kate and her body and the way she gave herself so completely to him. She came over and over, crying out, clutching his arms, lifting up to meet him as eagerly as he surged into her. The explosion started somewhere near his toes and blew through his entire body. His voice was hoarse, a roar of joy, as he emptied himself into her.

He sank on top of her, completely spent, completely sated, his lungs burning for air and his heart pounding out of his chest. And it was a perfect moment in time. Her body was soft and welcoming beneath his. He turned his head to capture her breast in his mouth, to lie there in contentment, to have her with him. He had been in hell many times in his life. But he had never been in paradise until now. His arms tightened around her possessively. "Dammit, Katie, don't ask me to give you up." He said the words around her tantalizing breast.

Kate combed her fingers through his hair, lying back with her eyes closed, savoring every aftershock while his mouth pulled strongly at her breast, and his tongue did delicious things to cause fiery sparks zinging in her deepest core. "Silly man," she murmured, clearly amused by his reaction. "I'm right here. Did you think I was going to grab my clothes and go slinking off?" The smile faded from her mind. There was a small part of her that wanted to do just that, run while she still had the chance. Self-preservation was strong in her. Everything about Matthew appealed to her. His lovemaking dazzled her, but she wasn't so far gone that she couldn't look ahead to the future and realize they couldn't spend every moment in bed.

Matt shifted position enough to take most of his weight off of her smaller body, but his arms held her in place and he turned her so he could keep access to the temptation of her breasts. His tongue flicked her nipple. "I want you forever, Kate. I want to grow old and have you here in my arms. I want children. I've wanted you for so long. I don't think that's about to change." He noticed that when he drew her breast into his mouth her hips moved restlessly. It was a wonderful find and one he intended to spend time exploring. He stroked her stomach and moved his hand between her thighs to cup her heat. She jumped but pushed against his hand. His thumb caressed her, his finger pushed deep to find the one spot that could give her another release.

Kate was Kate. She didn't try to pull away or pretend she wasn't ready for another orgasm, she rode his hand, gasping with pleasure, her fingers digging into his shoulder with one hand and the other curled in his hair directing his mouth. He wanted this every damn day of his life. Not just a Christmas present. He wanted to go to sleep with her breast in his mouth. He wanted to wake up with his body buried deep in hers. He wanted to be the man to bring her pleasure in every way possible.

"Marry me, Kate. Stay with me."

She heard him through a haze of piercing fulfillment, so sated with contentment, with the throbbing fire spreading through her like a storm, she could only lay there dazed by the gift he was holding out to her. The temptation.

Matt lifted his head to look at her, his fingers still buried deep inside of her. "Kate. I'm serious. Marry me. I'll make you happy."

"I am happy, Matthew," she said. "I lead a relatively quiet life. I work hard, meet my deadlines, and I'm looking forward to renovating the old mill."

Sensing her withdrawal, he turned to lie over the top of her, his head resting on her stomach. He pressed a series of kisses along her sensitive skin and flicked her enticing navel with his tongue. "We can renovate the old mill together, Katie."

"You're moving a little too fast for me, Matthew."

His Kate was becoming cautious again. He should have known she would. He nibbled his way down her body to her thigh. "We don't have to move fast. We don't have to go for the wedding and children and the entire package if that's too much for you right now." His teeth nipped as his fingers moved deep inside of her. He wasn't above a little persuasion. "We can keep it to great sex. Incredible sex."

She heard the note of pain in his voice, and it upset her. "Matthew, I'm not normal. I'll never be normal. You think you know me, but you don't. You can't. My sisters and I inherited a legacy that we have no choice but to use. It comes with a price. Sarah has phenomenal athletic abilities, and she can sense things before they happen. Abigail can demand the truth. I can bring peace to people in need. Libby heals people. Joley has incredible powers, and so does Hannah. Both command the wind and the sea. And our Elle." Kate shook her head. "Elle's legacy is tremendous and important and very frightening. She has it all, along with the responsibility to bring the next generation into the world. We each have gifts, but when we're together, we are very powerful. We try to lead our own lives, but we keep the cliff house so we always can be together."

He lifted his head, his silver eyes darkening to smoldering charcoal. "You think I can't understand honor and commitment? You live by a code the same as I do. I understand codes. You have a way of life that's important to you. Why would you think it would be any less important to me? I don't mind sharing you with your sisters, Kate."

She sighed. "I'm sorry. I didn't mean to upset you, Matthew. I just want you to know what we do isn't going to go away, even if we wanted it to. And it isn't only sharing me with my sisters, but with a lot of other people as well." But it was more than that. She wasn't like her sisters, embracing life in the way they did. In the way he did.

"I know a lot of ways to be happy with you," he promised, dipping his head to her breasts, not wanting her to see his face. "We'll take it slow if that's what you need, Katie. Just don't shut me out because you're afraid."

She tried not to react to his words. Of course she was afraid. She was afraid of everything, and that was *exactly* why she couldn't agree to marry him.

He kissed her ribs, her belly button. The phone rang, startling them both. He ignored it, dropping kisses over her stomach. The shrill ringing of the telephone persisted. Matthew sighed heavily and reached lazily across her small body, deliberately brushing across her bare breasts. "Hello." It was the middle of the night. He didn't have to be polite. He didn't want to waste a single moment of his time with Kate, especially when she needed persuasion to stay with him.

"This is Elle Drake. I need to speak with Kate." It was Kate's youngest sister, reputed to be traveling home for Christmas. There was anxiety in her voice. Without a word, Matt passed the phone to Kate.

She sat up, dragging the sheet over her breasts. "Elle? What's wrong, hon?"

"Something's there, Kate. Something's where you are. Below you. It's dangerous, and it's below you."

"Are you certain?" Kate leaned over the bed to examine the floor. Matt could clearly hear the terrified voice on the other end of the phone. "Calm down, Elle, I'm fine. We're both fine."

"Kate, I'm really afraid for you. What's going on? I saw you clearly. You were kissing Matthew Granite. There was mistletoe very close to you, but not directly over your head. And then something bright burst out from under you, a flash and flames and it was truly frightening. What is it?"

"I don't know, but we'll find out."

Matt was already out of the bed, pulling on his jeans, his eyes searching every inch of the floor. Moonlight pouring through the sliding glass door provided enough light for him to search every corner of the room. With his training ingrained in him, Matt chose not to turn on the light and give their position away to the enemy. He might have dismissed the phone call as hysteria or a nightmare, but he had been around the Drake sisters long enough now to see the strange things Jonas sometimes spoke of and to know to take them seriously.

"I'll call you later, Elle," Kate said, her eyes mirroring her fright. "Thank you for the warning." She placed the receiver in its cradle and looked up at Matt. "She's never wrong, Matthew. Do you have a basement? Maybe whatever it is has found a way to get in through the basement."

He shook his head. "There is no actual basement. I did take the space beneath the deck and create storage rooms and a lab to develop photographs." Their eyes met in sudden silence.

Kate slid out of bed and caught up his shirt, the nearest article of clothing she could wrap herself in. "Do you have mistletoe in the house, Matthew?"

"No, but it grows in several of the trees outside near the deck. I've stood on my deck to knock it out of the branches a few times."

Quickly buttoning the shirt, she followed him on bare feet. He didn't like her exposed to danger, but at least he could keep an eye on her if she were with him. He reached back to take her hand. She looked small and vulnerable in his too-large shirt with her hair tousled from their lovemaking. He bent his head and kissed her, a brief hard kiss of reassurance. Kate's public image was always neat and elegant. He liked that Kate very much. He loved the one with him now. His sexy, passionate, private Kate, with her hair mussed and her delicate skin red from his five o'clock shadow. Nothing was going to harm her. *Nothing.*

Kate felt her heart beating wildly in her chest. She tightened her fingers around Matt's hand. Matt slid open the glass door leading outside. The wind rushed in, bringing a cold chill and the scent of the salty air. The roar of the ocean was loud, whereas before the walls of the house had muffled it. She glanced nervously out toward the open sea, afraid of seeing the gray fog, but the ocean's surface was clear.

"Kate." Matt said her name as a warning.

Kate froze and dropped her gaze to the sand below them. It was wet from the continual pounding of the waves, rolling up onto the beach and receding according to the tide. There was a clear trail of boot prints, coming out of the ocean, and marks alongside them that indicated something heavy had been dragged. Kelp lay in tangles along the path toward the stairs leading up to Matthew's home. There was a heavy dark stain, much like oil in several spots in the sand. Kate wanted a closer look and stepped out onto the deck.

Matt pulled her back and thrust her behind him. "It doesn't feel right to me." He had long ago learned to rely on his survival instincts when something wasn't right. "Stay in the house, Kate."

"The fog isn't out there anymore," she pointed out, but she stayed behind him, holding tight to his hand. "Should we call Jonas?"

Matt sighed. "I imagine Elle called him. Don't all your sisters call him when something supernatural happens? I don't think the poor man's had a night's sleep since Sarah came home."

"Supernatural? I never thought of it like that. We've always had certain gifts. We were born with them, and using them seems as natural as breathing. Some people call us witches, and others just think we're able to use magic, but it's different. More. And less. I wish I could explain it." Kate frowned up at him. "It's natural to us."

Matt pushed her hair from her face, his fingers lingering in the silky strands. He tucked her hair behind her ear, the gesture tender. "You don't have to explain it. I'm a believer, Kate." He paused and drew in a deep breath. "Something's wrong. We're not going out on the deck. Come through the house with me." Matt silently slid the glass door closed, lifting his gaze to the night sky, where patches of dark, ominous clouds floated lazily.

Deliberately he didn't turn on any lights as he led her through the house. He paused long enough to slip a leather sheath around his calf. Kate's eyes widened as he shoved a long knife down into it. "Do you think that's necessary?"

"I believe in being safe. You're with me, Kate. Nothing's going to take you away from me. I don't care if it's a monster in the fog or something crawling out of the ocean." He pushed open the door to his house and stepped outside. His eyes searched the terrain restlessly, never stopping. "Do you smell something burning?"

The breeze shifted again, but Kate caught the peculiar pungent odor. "Oily rags?"

Matt hurried over the stepping-stones leading around to the back of the house. He had a good ocean view on three sides, but the bedroom was to the back. The dark stains led from the beach to the stairs and straight to the small photography laboratory he had built. The door was closed and appeared locked, but there were oily smudges all over the door, the same oily smudges they'd seen on the beach.

Kate's heart began to pound. She felt the danger swamping her. Glancing up, she could see the branches of the tree spread over the top of the deck, reaching over the bedroom where she and Matt had been kissing. In the branches were nests of mistletoe and the base of the tree was covered in the oily substance. "Matthew, let's wait for Jonas."

"I have photo-developing chemicals in there, Kate. I'm not losing my house to this thing." He set her away from him. "You stay back. I mean it, Kate. If I have to run, I'll need the way clear. Drag the hose over here for me, but don't get too close."

Matt felt the door. It wasn't hot to the touch. He opened it cautiously. The stench was overpowering, smelling of the sea, dead fish, and heavy oil. Black smoke seeped from a pile of photo paper and rags piled with smashed glass and a mixture of what he knew was lethal chemicals. He dragged some of the papers from the pile, trying to stop the inevitable. Tiny flames licked up the sides of the pile. There was a flash of white and a popping sound.

Kate thrust the hose into his hands. The water was running full out. He turned it on the greedy flames. "Get out of here, Kate," he ordered.

Kate stifled a scream when Jonas emerged out of nowhere and pulled her back, away from the deck. "Call the fire department," he snapped. "Use my car radio and stay out of the house." He pointed to the driveway, where he'd pulled in and left the door on the driver's side open. "I have a jacket it in the car, put it on, you aren't wearing very much."

Kate heard the wail of a siren and saw the deputy's car tear up the driveway. She ran to Jackson as he stepped out of his car. "Jonas says to call the fire department."

He made the call from his radio, pointing silently to the car, as if that was enough to make her stay, then he quickly joined Jonas and Matt. Kate dragged on Jonas's jacket, nearly sagging with relief. There was something utterly reassuring about the three men being together. They exuded complete confidence and worked as a team, almost as if each knew what the others were thinking. They had the fire out before the fire trucks even arrived. It took longer to go through the mess in the photo lab, searching for evidence. She was grateful to be able to return to the house where it was warm. Kate curled up in a chair and waited for Matt to return to her.

chapter 8

And the blood runs red on the pristine white snow . . .
While around all the houses the Christmas lights glow.

MATT STARED OUT THE LARGE BAY WINDOW OF his kitchen at the pounding sea. He frowned at the foaming waves, peering toward the darkness far out in the distance, almost at the horizon where a mass seemed to be congealing. Dark clouds had spread across the entire sky by the time the three men had sifted through the mess in his photography lab. Matt had taken calls from his parents and his brothers making certain he was alive and well and the house was still standing. Kate had received calls from her sisters.

Kate, fresh from her shower and wrapped in his robe, sat in the chair nearest him. "It's out there, isn't it?" she asked quietly. "I'm sorry about all your equipment."

He spun around to look at her. "Do you think I blame you for this?"

She hesitated. "I don't think he would have come here if I hadn't been here. I don't know why I draw him," she said, shaking her head. "Maybe he got my scent in the old mill, or maybe he perceives me as a threat."

"So it's definitely a he. I think it's taking shape, gaining a form," Matt said.

"I need to go home and help find the appropriate entry in the diaries. There are quite a few written in the symbols, and my sisters will need help. I don't think we have a lot of time to figure this out, Matthew. It's only a few days until Christmas, and I think this thing means to stop the town from having a Christmas." It sounded melodramatic even to her own ears. How could she expect to have any kind of a relationship with Matthew Granite and still be who and what she was?

"Time enough, Kate. We'll go right after we take care of things here. I promise."

She lifted an eyebrow. "What things? I thought you and Jonas and Jackson took care of everything."

Matt padded over to her on his bare feet and simply lifted her in his arms. "It takes some getting used to."

Kate clasped her fingers at the nape of his neck. "I'll admit I've never faced anything like this before." She wanted him. Suited or not, for just this space of time, Matthew belonged to her.

"I wasn't referring to our foggy fiend. I was referring to you. Having you in my house. Having you right here where I can look at you or touch you." He set her on the tiled counter and slid his hand inside the warmth of the robe.

He loved her instant response, the way she pushed into his hand. Welcoming him. "Remind me to thank your sister for the warning." Matt leaned forward to take her offering into the warmth of his mouth.

"I think you're a breast man," she teased.

"Mmmm, maybe," he agreed, his hands sliding down her waist and over her hips inside the robe. "But you also have a beautiful butt, Kate. I absolutely love the way you walk. I used to get behind you just to breathe a little life into my fantasies."

He was wedging himself between her legs, and Kate opened her thighs wider to accommodate him. "You've had fantasies about my rear end?"

"More than you'll ever know." He leaned in to capture her mouth. To spread heat and fire. Her fingers tangled in his hair. His fingers tangled in hers. Their mouths welded together so that they breathed for one another. He pulled her bottom closer to the edge of the counter and yanked her robe all the way open. "I've had fantasies about every separate part of you." Very gently he slid her legs apart.

"Matthew." There was a gasp in her voice. Kate stared at the long bank of windows, her hands still in his hair. "What are you doing?"

"Having you for breakfast. I've always wanted you for breakfast."

If Kate had thought to protest, it was far too late. He was already devouring her, and she was too far gone to care where they were. It was a deliciously decadent moment, and she reveled in it as wave after wave of pleasure crashed over her and rushed through her. The room spun dizzily, and colors mixed together, while his tongue and his fingers worked magic on her body. Her hands grabbed the edge of the smooth-tiled counter to keep herself anchored when she was flying so high, but then he was lifting her and laying her on the table, his body buried deep inside of hers, and there was no room for thought. No room for anything but feeling. The sound of his body joining with hers, their pounding hearts and heavy breathing, was a kind of music accompanying the strong orgasms as they broke over her and through her. His heat was so deep inside of her, she felt as though she were melting from the inside out.

She stared up into his face, the hard angles and planes, the rough shadow on his jaw. His eyes held secrets, things he had seen that should never have been witnessed. She realized how alone he seemed, even in the midst of his family. Like Jonas. Or Jackson. A man apart, not by choice, but by experiences. Kate framed his face with her palms, her thumb sliding in a caress over his faint whiskers. "You're a very wonderful man, Matthew Granite. I hope you know how special you are."

He gathered her to him as if she were the most precious being on the face of the earth, carrying her tenderly to the bathroom so they could shower. He said little, but he watched her all the time, would reach out and touch her body, her face, his fingers lingering against her skin, almost as if he couldn't believe she was real.

"My clothes are dirty," she said, pulling them on. At least she managed to tame her hair, braiding the long length and swirling the braid around the back of her head in an intricate knot.

He smiled at her. "Your clothes are never dirty, you just think they are." He dragged out a fresh pair of jeans from his drawer. "How can we find out what this thing is, Katie? I need to know what we're facing."

"My sisters are poring over the diaries, and I think

Damon is helping them. I can try as well, and Elle's on her way home. We should be able to find some clue."

"What's your gut telling you?"

She pressed her lips together to keep from smiling. There was something raw about the way Matt talked, something that always intrigued her. "I think it has to do with the history of our town, possibly an event that happened around Christmas, maybe the pageant itself. I think whatever is in the fog is gaining strength and becoming more destructive, but I'm not entirely certain why. The tree beside the deck with the mistletoe in it is a fir tree, and you had lights strung in it. You didn't have them on, but the dark stain, which seemed to be oil of some kind, was all around the bottom of the tree and going partially up the trunk."

"I noticed that," he agreed. "But there was nothing to ignite it."

"If Elle hadn't called and warned us, we never would have gone outside, Matthew. We would have been above the room when the fire took off, and it might have exploded. I think the fire would have raced to the tree, and he was hoping it would go up in flames as well."

"Strange way to kill us."

"Maybe not just us. Maybe it was the fir tree." She sat on the edge of the bed to watch him dress. He moved with such power, so fluidly, with a masculine grace he didn't seem aware of having. "Each symbol attacked so far has been attached to the Christian belief. There were ancient beliefs far before Christianity ever celebrated Christmas. It's widely believed the birth of Christ was in April, not December."

He paused in the act of buttoning his shirt. "I didn't know that."

She nodded. "I'm not Elle, or the others who sometimes are able to see things clearly, but I *feel* it's connected in some way."

"I get feelings when there's danger near." He suddenly grinned, transforming his face from man to boy. "Unless I'm otherwise occupied."

Kate couldn't help smiling back. In spite of everything, he looked more relaxed than she'd ever seen him. She always thought of him as a great tiger prowling through town. "We can forgive you that." She stood up. "The fir tree's needles rise toward the sky, and the fir tree stays green all year round."

"And that means something?"

"Everlasting hope, and, of course, the raised needles are reputed to represent man's thoughts turning toward heaven. If I were right, why would he want to destroy those symbols? He's not attacking Santa Claus. He isn't someone thinking Christmas is too commercial, he's actually destroying the symbols themselves." She looked up at him, rubbed her temple, and smiled a bit tiredly. "Or not. I could be way off base."

"I doubt it, Katie. I think your guess is as close as we can get right now." Matt looked across the room at her, still astonished that she was in his bedroom. "Let's go shopping for groceries. We can take them to your house and spend the day going over those diaries until we find something."

"Sounds good. I want to get home and put some decent clothes on."

She wandered out of the room while he pulled on his socks and boots. The house was so open, it beckoned her to walk the length of it. Entering the kitchen, she found herself smiling. In her wildest dreams she had never considered making love on a tabletop. A character in one of her novels might do such a thing, but not Kate Drake, with her every hair in place and her need for order. She'd never be able to look at a kitchen counter or table in quite the same way again.

Matt listened to Kate moving around his home. He liked the scent of her, the soft footfalls, the way her breath would catch when she looked at something she liked.

"Matthew?" Kate called out to him. "You have a very interesting kitchen. I wanted to put the cups in the dishwasher, and it seems to be a bread bin."

There was a small silence. Matt cleared his throat. "I've never actually used the dishwasher, Kate. I just do dishes by hand."

"I see. I guess that makes sense. But why would you put all the fruit in the microwave?"

He hurried into the kitchen. "It's convenient. What are you looking for?"

She grinned at him. "You don't really cook much, do you?"

He rubbed the bridge of his nose. "I do a mean barbecue."

"I'll just bet you do. Are you ready?"

Matt took her hand and drew her close to him as they went out into the morning air. She fit with him, belonged with him. She didn't believe it. He could see the reservations in her eyes, but he was determined to change her mind.

All the regulars considered the grocery store the center of town. Inez Nelson had a way with people. She didn't know the meaning of the word *stranger* and nearly everyone shopped at the local market, more to catch up on all the news and see Inez than for any other reason. She had known every one of the Drake sisters since their births and considered them akin to family.

Matt parked his car in front of the town square just to the left of Inez's store. "The Christmas pageant is growing, so many people want to participate that I think we're going to **have** to get a larger town square. The actors can barely get through the crowd as they walk up the street to the manger."

"I love the fact that everyone participates. It's so fun for the children afterward, when Santa shows up with his reindeer and gives out candy canes." Kate took the hand Matt held out to her. They stood together looking at the nativity scene in the town square, astonished that the statues, minus the wise men, had already been cleaned and the scene put back together. It would be reenacted with humans Christmas Eve, but a local sculptor had created the beautiful statues and several artists had done woodwork for the manger and life-size stable, and others had painted the entire backdrop. This year, Inez had managed to find a powdery substance that looked exactly like snow and had sprinkled it on the roof of the stable and on the surrounding ground, to the townspeople's delight and amusement. Snow was rarely seen in their coastal town.

"How many kids do you think have snuck into the square for a snowball fight?" Matt lowered his voice and looked around, half-expecting Inez to hear him even though she was a safe distance away inside the store.

Kate turned her laughing gaze on him. "You would have, wouldn't you?"

Fast-moving shadows slid across the ground, blocking out the sun's rays. "Damn right. Jonas and I would have made a snow fort and pelted everyone within throwing distance." His smile faded even as he finished his sentence. His hand gripped her arm to draw her attention. He nodded toward the sky. Seagulls filled the air overhead, winging their way fast inland. The birds were eerily silent, their great wings flapping as they hurried away from the ocean.

Kate shook her head and looked out toward the sea. The gray fog was rolling in fast. It roiled and churned, a turbulent mass, displaying raw energy. Lightning arced, chains of red-orange flashing within the center of the gray mist.

Matt swore and tugged her toward the store. "Let's get inside."

"It's growing stronger," Kate said.

Matt could feel her trembling against him. He pulled her closer to him. "We knew he would get stronger, Kate. You'd think the damned thing would take a vacation and give us a break. We'll figure this out."

"I know." She walked with him to the store. The entity was growing stronger and she felt stretched and tired and breakable. She couldn't very well tell Matt. He was already worried about her. She could read it in his eyes. How had she never managed to see the stark loneliness in him before? The aching desire? It was deep and intense and swamped her sometimes when he looked at her. Yet still, as he walked beside her, a tall, formidable man with wide shoulders and a thick chest and eyes that were never still, she could barely take in that he loved her.

Matt slid his arm around Kate's shoulders as they entered the building. As always, the small store had more than its share of customers. Inez greeted them loudly, gazing at them speculatively with bright eyes and a cheerful smile. "Kate, how lovely to see you, dear. And with Matt. I swear you grow taller every day, Matt."

Her comments effectively turned him into a boy again. Only Inez could manage to do that. "I feel a little taller today, Inez." He winked at Kate.

"Are you two coming to the pageant practice?" Inez asked. "I organized another one after the big fiasco the other night. No one blames Abbey, Kate. It certainly wasn't her fault that rat Bruce Harper is having an affair with little miss hot pants Sylvia Fredrickson."

"Abbey felt terrible, Inez," Kate said. "I'm sure it must have caused problems."

"Well, Bruce's wife left him. You know she's due to give birth any day now. They all dropped out of the production, and I had to find replacements." Inez glared at Matt. "Danny was in a fine snit saying he wasn't certain he could work with *amateur* actors. I told him he was an amateur actor."

"Inez," Kate protested. "You probably broke his heart."

For a moment Inez pursed her lips, looking repentant. "Well, he deserves it. I've got enough trouble without that boy complaining about his part. The three wise men are nervous, and I'm afraid they're fixing to drop out. I don't want to cancel the pageant. It's been put on every year since this town was founded."

"Danny won't drop out. He likes to herd those sheep around," Matt said.

Inez scowled. "He likes to chase them toward the kids and get a huge reaction."

"That is the truth." Matt grinned at her, but his eyes were on the wisps of gray-white fog slipping into town. He moved away from the women toward the plate-glass window, where he studied the fog. The enemy. It was strange to think of the fog, a nearly everyday occurrence on the coast, as the enemy.

The dark tendrils stretched toward houses, reached with long, spiny arms and bony fingers. The image was so strong Matt took a step closer to the window, narrowing his eyes to peer into the fog. "Katie, come here for a minute," he said softly, and held out his hand without taking his eyes from the fog. Something was moving inside of it.

Kate immediately put her hand into his and stepped up beside him. "What is it?"

"Look into the fog and tell me what you see."

Kate studied the rapidly moving vapor. It was darkening and spinning, almost boiling with turbulence. She shivered as long streaks stretched across the highway and began to surround the residences. It made her think of a predator hunting something, sniffing for the right scent. She thought something moved in the middle of the thick fogbank, something shaped vaguely like a tall man in a long, flowing coat and an old hat. She glimpsed a form, then it disappeared in the seething mass, only to reappear moments later, fading into the edges of the whirling mists. It was tall with bare white bones, pitiless eyes, and a wide, gaping mouth. She stepped back, gasping. The skeleton had more than taken shape. This time the entire chest was intact, and small pieces of flesh hung on the body, making it more grotesque than ever.

Kate put a hand protectively to her throat to stifle the scream welling up as she backed completely away from the window. She realized the store was eerily silent. Inez and the patrons stared out the window fearfully.

"It's taking shape, isn't it?" Matt asked.

Jonas and Jackson stalked into the store, Jonas's expression grim. "Kate, get out there and get rid of this before we start having fatalities," Jonas snapped without preamble, ignoring everyone else. "No one can see to drive the highway. I issued a warning on the radio, but we're going to have people not only driving over cliffs but also walking over them. Unfortunately, not everyone listens to the radio."

"Go to hell, Jonas." Matt was furious. *Furious.* At the thing in the fog. At Jonas, and at his own inability to stop the entity. "You're not sending Kate out there to battle that damned thing alone again. She's scared and tired, and I'll be damned if you bully her into thinking she's responsible for taking this thing on by herself. You want someone to fight it, be my guest."

"Dammit, Matt, don't start with me. You know I would if I had a chance in hell, but I don't. This is the Drakes' territory, not mine," Jonas bristled.

Kate put a restraining hand on both men's arms. "The last thing we need is to fight among ourselves. Jonas, I can't manage it alone. I really can't. I need Hannah." She leaned her head against Matt's chest. "I don't bring the wind, Hannah does. She's exhausted with fighting this thing. My sisters have been working with me the entire time. Without Hannah, we can't do anything."

Matt glanced down at her face, saw the lines of weariness there, the look of far too much energy expended, and for the first time, uncertainty. He wrapped his arms more tightly around her, and addressed Jonas. "How bad is it out there? Can they pass on this one and get some rest?"

"I'm getting damned sick of this secrecy where Hannah's concerned," Jonas said, obviously trying to get his temper under control. He felt every bit as impotent against the entity as Matt did, and it was clearly wearing on him. "We may have a running battle going; but if she's ill, it matters to me, Kate. You've been my family for as long as I can remember."

Kate felt Matt stirring, a fine tremor of anger rippling through his body at the tone Jonas used with her. She rubbed her head against his chest. "I know that, Jonas. Hannah is aware you're angry too. You know we all have a difficult time after we use our gifts. Hannah has to expend a tremendous amount of energy controlling something as capricious as the wind. Using our gifts is very draining. And whatever is in the fog has been growing in strength and resisting us, so we're having to expend more effort to contain it."

"Can you get rid of it, Kate?" Inez asked.

Everyone in the store seemed to hold their breath, waiting for her answer. Kate could feel the hope. The fear. All eyes were on her. "I honestly don't know." But she had to try. She could already hear the feminine voices whispering in the soft breeze heading inland from the sea. She felt her sisters calling to her to join with them. Hannah was already on the battlement, drooping with weariness, but facing the fog, waiting for Kate. Sarah and Abbey stood with her, and Joley had arrived. She'd been traveling for two days, yet she stood shoulder to shoulder with her sisters, waiting for Kate.

Kate closed her eyes and drew in a deep breath in an effort to summon her strength. Her courage. A paralyzing fear was beginning to grip her, one she recognized and was familiar with. Like Hannah, she suffered from severe panic attacks. Unlike Hannah, she was not a public figure. As a writer, her name might be known, but not her face. She could blend into the background easily, yet now everyone was watching. Waiting. Expecting Kate to work some kind of magic when she didn't even know what she was dealing with.

Matt felt the fine tremors that ran through Kate's body and turned her away from everyone in the store, his larger body shielding her. "You don't have to do this, Katie." He whispered the words, his forehead pressed against hers.

"Yes, I do," she whispered back.

Jonas instinctively stepped in front of her to protect her from prying eyes. Jackson spoke. His voice was utterly low, so soft one felt they had to strain to hear his words, yet his voice carried complete authority. "Inez, move everyone to the center of the store away from the windows, and let's give Kate some room to work. We have no idea what's going to happen, and we don't want to take chances with injuries."

Kate was grateful to the three men. She took another breath and pulled away from Matt, deliberately yanking open the door and slipping outside before her courage failed her. At once she felt the malevolence, a bitter, twisted emotion beating at her. The dark fog wrapped around her body, and twice she actually felt the brush of something alive sliding over her skin. She pressed her teeth together to keep them from chattering. Strength was already flowing into her—her sisters, reaching out from a distance, calling to her with encouraging words.

Matt joined her outside, slipping behind her, circling her waist with his arms, drawing her back against his hard, comforting body so that she had an anchor. Jonas took up a position on her right side, and Jackson was at her left. Three big men, all seasoned warriors, all ready to defend her with their lives. It was impossible not to find the courage and the strength she needed when it was pouring into her from every direction.

Kate faced the dark, boiling fog, lifting her arms to signal to Hannah, to signal to bring in the wind. She began to speak softly, calmly, using the gift of her soothing voice in an attempt to bring peace to the swelling malevolence in the fog. She spoke of peace, of love, of redemption and forgiveness. Gathering every vestige of courage she possessed, Kate made no attempt to drive it away. Rather she summoned it to her, trying to find a way to pierce the veil between reality and the shadow world where she could see into the soul of what was left behind and, hopefully, find a way to heal the broken spirit.

The fog spun and roiled in a terrible frenzy, a reaction to the sound of her voice. Her sisters protested for a moment, frightened by what she was trying, but joining with her when they recognized her determination. Jonas made a small sound of dissent and moved closer to her, ready to jerk her back into reality.

Moans assaulted her ears. The shadow world was vague and gray, a bleak hazy place where nothing was what it seemed. She chanted softly, her voice spreading through the world with little effort, stilling the moans and alerting whatever lived there to her presence. Kate felt the impact when the entity realized she'd once again joined him in his world. She could feel his blazing rage, the fierce anger, and the intensity of his guilt and sorrow. The thing turned toward her, a tall skeleton of a man, blurred so that he was nearly indistinct in the gray vapors surrounding him. He wore a long coat and shapeless hat, and he shook his head and pressed his bony hands over his ears to stop the enchantment of her voice. Flesh sagged from the bones, a loose fit in some places, stretched tight in others.

Kate whispered softly to him, calling, beckoning, trying to coax him to reveal the pain he suffered, the torment of his existence. She used her voice shamelessly, cajoling him to find peace. The shadowy figure took a few steps toward her. Kate held out her hand to him, a gesture of camaraderie. *There is peace. Let yourself feel it surround you.*

The being took another cautious step toward her. Her

heart pounded. Her mouth was dry, but she kept whispering. Speaking to him. Promising him rest. He was only a few feet from her, his arm stretching out toward her hand. The bony fingers were close. Inches away from her flesh. She remembered the feel of the finger bones closing around her throat, but she stood her ground and kept enticing him.

Something slithered around his boots. Snakelike vines wrapped around bony ankles. Out of the barren rocks bounded a huge creature with matted fur and yellow eyes. In the cold of the shadow world, she could see the creature's vaporous breath mingling with the fog. The eyes fixed on her, an intruder in their world.

The tips of her fingers touched the bony ends of the skeleton as it reached toward her. The creature howled, sending a shiver of fear down Kate's spine. Her sisters held their collective breath. Jonas stiffened, communicating his apprehension to Matt and Jackson.

Kate continued to whisper of peace, of aid, of a place to rest. The being took more shape, the pitiless eyes swimming with tears, extending its hand as far as the snakelike vines allowed. Abruptly the skeleton threw back its head and roared, rejecting her. Rejecting the idea of redemption and forgiveness. She glimpsed a raging hatred of self, of everything symbolizing Christmas, of peace itself. There can be no peace. She caught that as the being began to whirl around, furious, using the vortex of its wild spinning to hurl objects at her. The moans rose to shrieks. The huge creature bounded toward Kate, breathing as loudly as any bull. Kate made one last grab for the hand of the skeleton, but it had turned on her completely, rushing at her along with the beast.

"Get her out of there!" Jonas shouted, catching the collective fear that ran through the Drake family. He gripped Kate's arm hard, shaking her. "Matt, pull her back to us!"

"Kate," her sisters cried out, "leave him, leave him there."

"Hannah!" Jonas cried the name desperately. "The wind, Hannah, bring in the wind."

Kate stared at the terrible figure coming straight at her, fury in its every line. The eyes glowed red through the dark fog; the face was made of bones, not flesh. The mouth gaped open in a silent scream. She was trapped there in the world of shadows, real, yet not, unable to find her way back. The worst of it was, she caught sight of a second insubstantial figure coming at her from the left.

"Kate." Matt whispered her name, lifted her into his arms. Her body was an empty shell, her mind caught somewhere else.

"Kate, darling, go with the other one, he'll lead you out." Elle's soft voice pushed everything else away.

The dark demon was almost upon her. Kate felt a hand on her arm. She looked down and saw Jackson's fingers circling her wrist like a vise. She didn't have time to go voluntarily; he yanked her out of the shadows, back into the light. She heard a roar of rage, shuddered when she felt bones brush against her skin. Matt was real and solid, and she gripped him hard, needing to feel grounded. She felt physically ill, her stomach a churning knot. She closed eyes, sliding into a dead faint.

The wind swept in from the sea, a strong tempest of retaliation. Hannah's fear added to the strength of the storm. Rain burst down on them. The dark fog swirled and fought, not wanting to give ground. For a brief moment there was a confrontation between the entity and the Drake sisters, sticks and debris flying in the wind. The three men could hear the desperate cries of seagulls. And then it was over, the fog retreating to the sea, leaving behind silence and the rushing wind and rain. Matt stood there on the sidewalk, Kate, safe in his arms, staring in shock at the mess left behind.

Clouds overhead obscured the sun, the day overcast and gloomy. Christmas lights twinkled on and off where they hung over the buildings in rows of vivid colors, a terrible contrast to the scene left behind in the town square. Feathers were everywhere and in the pristine white snow by the manger there was a bright red pool of blood.

chapter 9

A star burns hot in the dead of the night,
As the bell tolls it's now midnight

"NEVER AGAIN. NEVER AGAIN." MATT SHOVED both hands through his hair and glared at the Drake sisters. "I swear, Kate, you are never doing that again." He paced restlessly back and forth across the living room floor.

Sarah, Kate's older sister, rested her head against her fiancé's knee, and watched Matt in silence. Abbey sat on the couch, Joley's head resting in her lap. Joley lay stretched out, her eyes closed, appearing to be asleep in spite of his tirade. Hannah lay on the couch closest to the window, lines of exhaustion visible on her young face.

"It doesn't do any good to get upset," Jonas said. "They do whatever they want to do without a thought for the consequences."

Sarah sighed loudly. "Don't start, Jonas. That's not true, and you know it. If you were the one trying to get rid of this thing, you wouldn't worry about your own safety, and you know it. You'd just do whatever had to be done."

"That's different, Sarah," Jonas snarled back. "Dammit anyway. Look at Hannah. She can't even move. I think she needs a doctor. Where the hell is Libby when we need her?"

"Are you ever going to stop swearing at us?" Sarah asked. She rubbed her face against Damon's knee. "Hannah needs rest and maybe some tea."

"I'll make tea," Damon offered. "I think all of you could use it."

"Damon, you are a darling," Sarah said. "The kettle's boiling."

Matt glanced into the kitchen, and, sure enough, the kettle was steaming. He knew very well it hadn't even been turned on minutes earlier.

Damon leaned down to brush a kiss across Sarah's temple before making his way into the kitchen. "This feels like old times," he called out, reaching for the tea kept for just such occasions.

"We could use a little more festive atmosphere," Abigail decided. She stared at the row of candles on the mantel until they spluttered to life, flames leaping and flickering for a moment, then taking hold. At once the aroma of cinnamon and spice scented the air.

"Good idea," Sarah agreed and focused on the CD player. Instantly Joley's voice filled the room with a popular Christmas carol.

"Not that one," Joley protested. "Something else."

"Are you all insane?" Jonas demanded. "Kate could have been killed. Are we going to pretend it didn't happen and have a little Christmas get-together?"

"Jonas, it does no good yelling at them. What do you

want them to do?" Damon returned, carrying a tray with several cups of tea on it. He distributed them among the Drake sisters.

"And you were the one asking me, no, telling me to get out there and stop the fog," Kate pointed out.

Jonas muttered something ugly under his breath and reached down for Hannah's limp wrist to take her pulse. As he did a breeze swirled around the room, and his hat sailed from the chair where he'd placed it and landed in the middle of the room. Jonas straightened and glared down at Hannah, who didn't stir.

"Jonas, we didn't know the entity was going to try to hurt Kate," Abbey pointed out. "We have to know what his motivation is."

Sarah shoved a heavy book across the floor. "Trying to read this thing without Elle is impossible. She's the only one that can read the language our ancestors used. The writing is in that strange hieroglyphic language we were all supposed to study back when we were teens. Mom told us to learn it, but we kept putting it off, wondering why we needed to delve that far back into the past. With the little bit we know, it's impossible to find a single entry in all of this."

Matt stopped pacing, coming to a halt beside Kate, his hand resting on the nape of her neck. "Elle's on the way home, isn't she? It shouldn't be long. How come she learned the language when the rest of you only know a little?"

Abbey blew on her tea. "She learned it in order to teach the next generation, just as our mother did."

"Speaking of Elle, how did she connect with you,

Jackson? How did she know you were able to go into the shadows and bring Kate out?" Sarah asked.

There was a sudden silence, and all eyes turned to regard the man sitting in absolute stillness just to the side of the window. His cool dark eyes moved over their faces, a brooding perusal. "I don't know what you're talking about. I don't even know Elle."

Abbey sat up straighter. "That's not the truth, Jackson."

Jonas sucked in his breath sharply. "Don't, Abbey!" His warning came a heartbeat too late. She'd already said it, her voice pitched perfectly to turn people inside out, to reach into their darkest depths and pull the truth from them.

Jackson stood up slowly, his eyes hard steel. He walked across the floor without a single sound. Joley sat up and blinked at him. Matt moved in on one side of Abbey, Jonas on the other. Ignoring the two men, Jackson bent down until he was eye level with Abbey. "You don't ever want to ask me for the truth, Abbey. Not about me and not about Elle." He hadn't raised his voice, but Abbey shivered. Joley put her arm around her sister.

"I'll be outside," Jackson said.

"He's never met Elle," Sarah said, after the door closed behind the deputy. "Jonas, he hasn't, has he?"

Jonas shook his head. "Not to my knowledge. And he's never mentioned her. They both had the same nightmare, but so did half the kids in Sea Haven."

"He scares me," Abbey said. "I don't want Elle near him. She's so tiny and fragile and so sweet. And he's . . ."

"My friend," Jonas said. "He saved my life twice, Abbey."

"And mine too," Matt added. "You shouldn't have done that."

Abbey looked down. "I know. I don't know why I did. It's just that he's so frightening, and the thought that Elle was out there in the shadow world too . . ."

"But she wasn't," Kate interrupted. "She wasn't there. I heard her voice, but she wasn't in the world, she was in my head." Her voice trailed off in sudden speculation. The sisters exchanged a long look. "Jonas, is Jackson telepathic?"

"How the hell would I know?" Jonas asked.

"Well, because you are. Sort of." The sisters looked at one another again and burst out laughing. Their bright laughter dispelled the air of gloom in the room.

Jonas made a face at Matt. "See what I have to put up with?" He stomped across the room to reach down and retrieve his hat. Before his fingers could close around the rim, the flames on the candles flared from a sudden gust of wind, and the hat leaped away from him to land dangerously close to the fireplace. Jonas straightened slowly, his hands on his hips, glancing suspiciously around the room at the Drake sisters. They all wore innocent expressions. "You are not going to get me to believe that the wind is in the house without a little help."

Unexpectedly the logs in the fireplace burst into flame. Jonas took a step toward his hat. It went up on the rim and rolled a few inches toward the burning logs. "My hat had better not go into that fire," Jonas warned.

"Really, Jonas." Joley didn't open her eyes. "You're becoming paranoid. Hannah's already asleep."

He continued to study their faces and finally crossed to the couch where Hannah lay asleep, looking almost a child. "I'm taking the baby doll to bed. It's the only safe thing to do." He simply lifted her in one quick movement and, before anyone could protest, started out of the room.

"The tower," Sarah called after him.

"What a surprise there. I can see Hannah as the princess in her tower," Jonas called back.

The sisters looked at one another and burst out laughing. Matt shook his head. "You all are downright scary."

Joley leaned her head back and grinned at him. "I'd like to know what's going on with my sister and you all alone up in that house of yours. I was going to help Hannah whip up a little love potion and stick it in your drink the next time I saw you, but they tell me you've been playing fast and loose with her already."

Kate turned a particularly fetching shade of crimson. "Joley Drake, that will certainly be the last we hear on that subject."

Joley didn't look impressed with the stern tone. "In case anyone is interested, I took a good look at Kate's neck, and she has a particularly impressive love bite."

Kate clapped her hand over her neck and shook her head. "I most certainly do not. Drink your tea."

"What's even more impressive," Joley continued, "is that Matt seems to be sporting one of his own."

A collective gasp went up. "We want to see, Matt," Abigail pleaded.

"Only if I get to make a wish on the snowglobe," he bargained.

There was instant silence. Sarah sat up straighter. "Matt," she paused and glanced at Kate. "Wishing on our snowglobe is not like making a silly, frivolous wish. It's very serious business. You have to know what you want and really mean it. You have to have weighed your decision very carefully."

"I can assure you I have. If you want to see the love bite, you can produce the snowglobe." Matt folded his arms across his chest.

"Matt," Kate cautioned, "if you're thinking about wishing for anything we already discussed—don't. It wouldn't work."

Joley lifted her head off the back of the couch and eyed them both. "This sounds very interesting. Does anyone else want Christmas snacks to go with the tea, because I really could go for those little decorated sugar cookies." She waggled her fingers in the direction of the kitchen. "Tell us more, Matt. The snowglobe is right over there by the fireplace. Please do step on Jonas's hat. It always livens things up when he does his sheriff he-man routine." She turned her head to glance at the stairs. "He's been up there a long time. You don't suppose he's taking advantage while Hannah is asleep, do you?"

Sarah nudged Joley with her foot. "You're terrible, Joley."

Matt skirted around Jonas's hat and reached for the snowglobe. It felt solid in his hands. He glanced at Kate. She shook her head, looking fearful. The globe warmed in his hands. He stared at the scene, the snowflakes whirling around the house until they all blended together to become fog. The lights on the tree sprang to life.

"You activated it," Sarah said. "That's nearly impossible."

"Not unless he's . . ."

"Joley!" Kate interrupted her sister sharply. "Matt, really, it isn't something to play with."

"I've never been more serious. Tell me what to do." He looked at Sarah.

She glanced at Kate, then shrugged. "It's relatively easy, Matt, but be sure. You look into the fog and picture what you want most in the world and wish for it. If you meet the criteria, the globe will grant your wish."

"And it works?"

"According to tradition. Family is allowed one wish a year, no more. And you can't wish for harm to anyone."

"That's why we don't allow Jonas access to it," Joley said.

Matt inhaled the fragrance of the candles and fresh-baked cookies wafting from the kitchen. He didn't question who made the cookies. He wasn't even surprised by the fact that there were cookies. He stared into the fog inside the snowglobe and conjured up the exact image of Kate. With everything in him, body, soul, heart, and mind, he made his wish. The fog was still for a moment, then swirled faster, dissipating until the globe was once more clear and the lights on the tree dimmed. He placed the globe back on the shelf carefully and grinned at Kate.

"Let's hope you know what you're doing," Joley said.

Suddenly in a much better mood, Matt flashed her a smile. "At the risk of sounding like an adoring fan, I love your collection of blues. You have the perfect voice for blues." He grinned at her. "Or Christmas music."

Joley winced. "I just sent that to my family for fun."

"It's beautiful," Abbey said. "Are you having fun on your tour?"

Joley frowned. "Yes, it's tiring, and there are always the freaks out there, but there's nothing quite like the energy of forty thousand people at a concert."

"What freaks?" Jonas demanded, walking back into the room. "Hannah didn't even wake up, not even when I called her Barbie doll. Are you certain she's okay, Sarah?"

Sarah paused for a moment, seeking inside herself, reaching out to her sister. "She's exhausted, Jonas, and needs sleep. We'll have to find a way to get some food into her soon."

Jonas rolled his eyes. "We can't have Miss Anorexic gaining an ounce. She's probably worried the camera won't love her, and she won't be able to parade around half-naked on the cover of a magazine for the entire world to see."

Kate tossed her napkin at Jonas. "Go away, you're annoying me. We have to have clear heads to decide how to handle this, and you just stir everyone up."

Jonas shrugged, in no way perturbed. "I have to go back to work anyway. But I want to hear about these freaks of yours, Joley. You haven't been getting any nutcases stalking you, have you?"

Joley took a sip of tea and looked up at Jonas. "I don't know. I hired a couple of bodyguards, bouncers really, just to protect the stage. Each concert hall has a security force, of course, but I thought if these two traveled with us, we'd have a little extra protection. Stalkers come with the territory, you know that. The more famous you get, the more crazies you attract."

Matt sat down beside Kate. "Do writers have that kind of problem?"

Before Kate had a chance to deny it, Jonas answered. "Of course they do. Anyone in the public eye does, Matt. Writers, musicians, politicians, and—" he glanced toward the stairs—"supermodels."

Joley laughed. "You worry so much, Jonas, you ought to go into law enforcement. It's right up your alley."

"Ha-ha, very funny. I'll call you later to see if anything new has happened." Jonas glanced out the window. "I never thought I'd dread nightfall."

Matthew looked out the window to the pounding sea. "Is Elle expected tonight?"

"She said around midnight. She's flying into San Francisco and renting a car to drive here. I offered to pick her up," Abbey said, "but she didn't want any of us on the road with the fog. She promised she'd check the weather station before she came into Sea Haven."

Jonas scooped up his hat. "I'll keep an eye out for her. You all rest and stay out of trouble." He left, banging the door behind him.

At Sarah's urging, Damon nodded toward the kitchen and Matt obliged.

Abbey waited until the men were out of the room. "I didn't mean to challenge Jackson like that." She pressed her hand to her mouth, her eyes enormous. "That's twice now. And the house should have protected me. How could that happen in our home?"

"You were relaxed," Sarah said. "You let your guard down."

Abbey shook her head. "I haven't let my guard down

since I caused such a problem during the committee meeting. Poor Inez called me this afternoon and told me no one realized it was me, but Sylvia knew."

"She went to school with us," Joley pointed out.

Hannah walked back into the room. Tall and blond and beautiful, she looked so fragile she could have been made of porcelain. "Don't worry about Sylvia. I'm certain she's very sorry she hit Abbey."

Joley held out her arms. "Come here, baby, sit by me. You look done in. You were very bad teasing poor Jonas that way and making him think you were sleeping." Joley kissed Hannah. "You really should be in bed."

"I couldn't sleep," Hannah admitted. "I needed to be with all of you."

Joley stroked back her hair. "You didn't do anything awful to Sylvia, did you?"

Hannah's eyes widened in a semblance of innocence. "You all think I'm so bent on revenge all the time."

Sarah paused in the doorway to the kitchen. "That's not an answer, you bloodthirsty little witch. Exactly what did you do to Sylvia?"

Hannah leaned against Joley. "I'm glad you're home. You don't give me that stern face like Sarah does."

"Hannah Drake, what did you do to Sylvia?"

Hannah shrugged. "I *heard* from a reliable source . . ."

"Inez at the grocery store," Abbey supplied.

"Well, she's reliable," Hannah pointed out. "I heard Sylvia developed a bright red rash on the left side of her face. It appears to be in the shape of a hand. I couldn't help but think it was fitting."

Sarah rubbed her hand over her face, trying to stare

down her younger sister without smiling. "You know very well you can't use our gifts for anything other than good, Hannah. You're risking reprisal."

Hannah stretched her legs out in front of her and gave Sarah a sweet smile. "You never know what a humbling experience can do for someone's character."

"I'm getting your tea for you, but I hope this is a big joke, and I won't hear about it later at the store." Sarah turned away quickly to keep Hannah from seeing her laughter.

Abbey squeezed Hannah's hand. "You didn't really do anything to Sylvia, did you?" There was a hopeful note in her voice she couldn't quite hide.

"Drink your tea," Sarah said. "And eat some cookies. You're too pale. Matt and Damon are making us dinner tonight."

"Did I miss anything important while I was making Jonas carry my deadweight up those long and winding stairs?"

"Only Matt wishing on the snowglobe," Joley said. "And we're all fairly certain what he wished for."

"You're so brave, Kate," Hannah said. "I could never be with a man so absolutely frightening. They have those cold eyes and those scary voices, and I just want to curl up and fade away." For a moment tears shimmered in her eyes. She looked over the rim of her teacup at Kate. "You thought I was so brave to go out into the world and be seen, while you chose to stay out of sight and share your wonderful stories with the world, but you're willing to try with a man to have a real life with him."

"I haven't made up my mind yet," Kate admitted. "I'm

afraid he'll wake up one day and realize what a coward I am. You'll find someone though, Hannah."

Hannah shook her head. "No, I won't. I don't want some man snarling at me because I forgot to put the dishes in the dishwasher, or angry because I had to fly to Egypt to do a photo shoot. And I could never live with a man who always seemed on the edge of violence, or even capable of violence. I'd be so afraid I'd be paralyzed."

Kate laid her hand on Hannah's knee. "Matt isn't capable of violence against a woman. He's protective, there's a difference."

"That's how everyone describes Jonas, as protective, but he's really a bully. He'll order his wife around day and night."

"If Jonas ever falls in love with a woman, I think he would move heaven and earth to make her happy," Kate said. "He looks after all of us, and we're sometimes very aggravating. He has a job to do, and he works hard at it. We often make his job much more difficult. And it must be very disconcerting to be so connected emotionally to us. He senses when we're in trouble or hurt, and unfortunately we're in trouble quite often."

Hannah sighed. "I know. He's just so annoying all the time. I closed the window in the entryway; too much fog was drifting in, and it scared me." She forced an uneasy laugh. "I never thought I'd be afraid of the fog."

Kate stood up and looked around the house. "What do you mean too much fog was drifting in?" She stared out the window toward the sea. "You *saw* it? You weren't dreaming? What did it look like?"

Sarah stood up too and began to move uneasily about the room, checking the windows.

"It looked like fog," Hannah said. "I came down the stairs and, to be honest, was a little unsteady, so I sat on the floor in the entryway for a couple of minutes. I could see fog drifting in through the open window. It appeared to be normal fog, a long wisp of it, but the fact that I could see it in the house upset me. So I closed the window."

"Nothing can get into the house, Sarah," Abbey said. "It's protected. You know that the house has always protected us."

Sarah shook her head. "Mom told us we needed to know the ancient language of the Drake sisters, and we all shrugged it off with the exception of Elle. She also told us we needed to renew our safeguards every single time we came home, but did we do that? No, of course not—we've become complacent. Mom has precog, we all know it. It was a foreshadowing, but we didn't take her instructions seriously."

Abbey put a hand to her throat. "Do you think the entity was influencing me to use my voice on Jackson as well as at the committee meeting?"

Sarah nodded. "There's a good chance of it. We have to be very careful. None of us are handling this very well. We've never faced such a thing before."

"And I never want to again," Kate said fervently.

"Dinner," Matt called from the kitchen. "Come eat. And bring Hannah with you. Jonas said she had to eat something."

Hannah rolled her eyes. "There's my point exactly, Kate. Men always try bossing women around. It's their nature, they can't help themselves. We know the thing in the fog is a male, and I'll bet he's seriously upset with a woman."

They all started into the kitchen. Sarah and Kate helped steady Hannah. "Actually, I felt guilt and sorrow and rage coming from him," Kate said. "I could feel the connection, but he tossed it away because he feels he doesn't deserve forgiveness. Something terrible happened, and he believes he's to blame for it."

"Why is he causing terrible things to happen now?" Hannah asked.

"I don't know," Kate admitted. "But it has something to do with Christmas. Sarah's right. We have to really pay attention to every detail now. He can't get any stronger, or we won't be able to stop him."

Matt spent the rest of the day poring over the entries in the diaries and listening to the easy teasing back and forth between the sisters. The women slept on and off throughout the day. Damon and Sarah spent a lot of time kissing every chance they could steal away, and he was a bit jealous that he didn't have the right to be as openly demonstrative with Kate. As the hours slipped by, all he could think about was Kate and being alone with her.

He slipped his arm around her shoulders. "It's late, let's go back to my house."

"Elle's driving in tonight. I'd like to wait for her. She's supposed to be here any minute, and we slept most of the day after that horrible encounter this morning," Kate replied.

"The fog is coming in," Matt announced. He opened the door and wandered out to the wide, wraparound veranda to stare out over the ocean.

"Elle should be here any minute; she told us midnight," Kate said, studying the wisps of fog as they drifted toward land. "She'll make it before the fog hits the highway."

"Who decorated your Christmas tree?" Matt indicated the huge tree covered in lights and adorned with a variety of ornaments.

Kate went down the porch stairs to stand in front of the tree. She touched a small wooden elf. "Isn't it beautiful? Frank, one of the local artists, did this carving. Many of these ornaments have been handed down from generation to generation."

"Don't you worry about them out in the weather?" The tree was inside the yard, and two large dogs protected the area. Sarah's dogs. No one would sneak in and steal the ornaments, even the more precious ones, but the sea air and the continual rain could ruin the decorations.

"We never worry about weather," Kate said simply. "The Drakes have always decorated a tree outside and, hopefully, we always will."

The fog burst over them in a rolling swirl, wrapped around the tree, and filled the yard, streaming in from the ocean as if pushed by an unseen hand.

"I think our old nemesis is attacking another Christmas symbol," Matt said, pointing to the top of the huge Christmas tree in the front yard. "What does the star stand for? There has to be a meaning."

The fog tangled around the branches, amplifying the glow of the lights through the vapor. Kate looked up at the star as it shorted out, sparks raining down through the fog. It brightened momentarily, then faded completely. She was looking up and saw through the wisps of clouds a hot, bright star streaking across the sky, plunging toward Earth. She went still, the color draining from her face. "Elle." She whispered her sister's name. "He's coming for Elle. That's what he was doing in the house. He's after Elle." The fog was choking the road, making it impossible to see.

"What the hell do you mean, it was in the house?" Matt raced back inside the house just as her sisters hurried outside to join Kate. He caught up the phone and called Jonas. He had no idea what Jonas could do. No one could see in the fog. They didn't know exactly where Elle was, only that she was close. She had said she'd arrive sometime around midnight. It was close to that now. She might be on the worst section of narrow, twisting highway leading to Sea Haven.

Kate whirled around, facing toward the town as a bell began to ring loudly. The sound reverberated through the night. "The bell is the symbol for guidance, for return. She's here now. She's coming up the highway now, returning to us. Returning to the fold. Sarah—" she caught her sister by the hand—"she's nearing the cliffs right now. Even if Hannah had the strength to bring in the wind, it's too late. He's warning us, telling us what he's going to do. Why would he do that?"

Kate reached for her youngest sister, mind to mind. She wasn't the most telepathic of her siblings, but Elle was a strong telepathic. Kate heard music, Joley's voice filling the car with her rich, warm tones. Elle's voice joining in. Elle drove slowly, crawling through the thick fog, knowing she was only a mile from her home. It was impossible to see in front of the car; she had no choice but to pull off the road and park until the fog lifted.

Elle peered at the side of the road, trying to see where the shoulder was wide enough to get her car off the highway in case another vehicle came along. She steered slowly over, aware the cliff was high above the pounding sea. Joley's voice was comforting, a sultry heat that kept the chilling cold from entering the car. Elle turned off the engine and pushed open the door, needing to get her bearings. If she could see the lights from any direction, she would know where she was. She knew she had to be close to her home. The fog surrounded her, a thick, congealed mass that was utterly cold.

Kate drew in her breath, tried to touch Elle, tried to warn her of the impending danger. Elle kept her hand on the car. *What is it, Kate?*

Kate cursed the fact that she couldn't form an answer and send it to her sister. She could only send the impression of danger very close. They all knew when their siblings were in danger, or tired or upset. But Kate didn't have the ability to actually tell Elle something was in the fog, something that was taking enough of a form that it could cause bodily harm. She didn't even know whether to tell her to stay in the car or to get away from it. She could only hope that Elle was sufficiently tapped in to all of her sisters and would know what was transpiring. Elle turned in the direction of their home and began to walk along the narrow path.

Matt rushed past Kate, heading toward the highway. The fog swallowed him immediately. "Try to clear it out, Kate," he called back. His voice sounded muffled in the thick mist, even to his own ears. He knew the trail; he'd walked it enough times over the years and was certain Elle would do the same.

Jonas and Jackson were converging from their locations as well, all of them running to Elle's aid from three different directions, but Matt had no idea if any of them would be in time. He only knew that his heart was in his throat, and he had such an overwhelming sense of imminent danger, he wanted to run flat out instead of carefully jogging his way along the steep, uneven path.

chapter
10

Beneath the star, that shines so bright,
An act unfolds, to my delight.

 MATT HEARD VOICES, THE RISE AND FALL OF feminine voices. He knew Kate and her sisters were doing their best to fight against the wall of fog crouched so malevolently on the highway. He picked his way as fast and as carefully as he could. The ocean pounded and roared beneath him, waves slapping against the cliff and leaping high so that every now and then, as he jogged, he could feel the spray on his face. Rocks and the uneven ground impeded his progress. The wind picked up, blowing fiercely against the fog, taking chunks out over the roiling sea.

"Matt!" Jackson's disembodied voice called to him from deep inside the fog, somewhere ahead of him. "She's gone over the cliff. She's not in the water, but she's not going to be able to last much longer. Search along the edges." The voice was muffled and distorted by the fog.

"Watch yourself, Jackson, the cliff is crumbling in places," Matt cautioned. He didn't ask how Jackson knew Elle had gone over. Hell, he was beginning to believe he was the only person in the world without some kind of psychic talent. "Dammit, dammit, dammit." He couldn't return to Kate and tell her Elle was dead, that they'd been too late. He'd never be able to face her sorrow.

Matt inched toward the cliff, testing the ground every step of the way, making certain it would hold his weight. "Elle!" He shouted her name, heard Jackson, then Jonas echo his call. The ocean answered with another greedy roar, lifting higher, seeking prey. "Dammit, Elle, answer me." He felt desperation. Rage. Fear for Elle was beginning to swirl in the pit of his stomach. He detested inaction. He was a man who took charge, got the job done. He could have endless patience when needed, but he had to know what he was doing.

It seemed a hundred years until Jackson called out. "Found! I'll keep calling out so you both can get a direction. She's not going to be able to hang on, so I'm going down after her. I've tied off a safety rope."

Even with the fog distorting the voice, Matt got a sense of Jackson's direction and moved toward him. Jackson's voice was far more distant the second time he called out, and Matt knew he'd gone over the side of the cliff to try to get to Elle before she plunged into the sea. He'd been in combat with Jackson, had served on many covert missions with him. He wasn't a man to rush headlong into anything. If he was already going over the cliff to get to Elle, she needed the help. He was counting on Jonas and Matt to rescue them both. He knew they'd come for him.

Matt felt the crushed grass with his hand and flattened his body, belly down, reaching along the crumbling edge of the cliff until he found the rope. Jackson had tied off the end, using an old fence post. Matt sucked in his breath.

The fence post was rotted and already coming out of the ground. "I'm tying off again, Jackson, give me a minute," Matt called down to him. He peered over the cliff.

Jackson was climbing down almost blind, feeling with his hands and toes for a grip. Elle lay sprawled out on a small ledge, clinging to a flimsy tree. He caught only glimpses of her as the fog was pushed out toward the sea. The heavy mist crawled down below the cliff line, hovering stubbornly in the more protected pocket to obscure the vision of the rescuers.

"Pass the rope back to me," Jonas said, coming up behind Matt.

Matt did so immediately, not taking his eyes from the scene unfolding below him. The fog was thick and churning, but the wind kept attacking it, driving it out in feathery clumps. It was the only thing that provided him with glimpses of the action. Jackson made his way, with painstaking care, down the sheer side of the cliff. Jonas tied off the rope to a much more secure anchor behind them, where Matt couldn't see.

"We're ready up here, Jackson, say the word," Matt called when Jonas signaled him the rope was safe to use. "Elle, I'm not hearing anything from you." He hadn't. Not a moan, not a call for help. It was alarming. He thought he could see her actively holding on to the small tree growing out of the side of the cliff, but the more he tried to pierce the veil of the fog, the more he was certain Elle wasn't moving.

As Jackson reached her, Matt held his breath, waiting. Afraid to hear, afraid not to hear. His heart beat loudly over the sound of the sea.

"She's alive," Jackson called up. "She has a nasty bump on the head, and she's bruised from head to toe, but she's alive."

Matt leaned farther over the cliff to hear the conversation below him. Jackson's voice drifted up to him. "Lie still, let me examine you for broken bones. I'm Jackson Deveau, the deputy sheriff."

"This ledge is crumbling." Elle's voice trembled. "Someone pushed me. I didn't hear them, but they pushed me."

"It's all right. Don't move. You're safe now." Jackson's voice was soothing. "Do you remember me? We met once a long time ago."

Matt recognized instantly the calming quality to Jackson's voice. He was talking to keep her from being agitated. "Jonas, I think Elle's injured. I can tell by the way Jackson's acting." Keeping his voice low, he gave the news to the sheriff, aware that Jonas was anxious to know Elle's condition.

"I heard your voice, in a dream," Elle said. Her words blurred around the edges, sending Matt's heart tripping. "You were in pain. Terrible pain. Someone was torturing you. You were in a small closet of a room. I remember."

Matt went still. Jonas froze behind him, obviously hearing Elle's response.

"Then you know you're safe with me. You helped me when I needed it. I'll get you out of this. That's the way the buddy system works."

It was the most Matt had ever heard Jackson say to anyone. He glanced back to look at Jonas's face. The fog along the highway was clearing. The wind gusted, careening off the cliff face in order to push the heavy mist away from Elle and Jackson. Jackson never talked about being captured. Never talked about the treatment he'd endured. He never spoke of the escape that followed or how difficult it had been as he led a small ragtag group of prisoners back through enemy lines to join their forces.

That a Drake sister might be aware of details Matt and Jonas weren't privy to no longer surprised either of them.

"Can you hold on to me as I climb up?" Jackson asked. "I can send you up by the rope. Matthew Granite and Jonas Harrington are up top waiting for you. You're bound to accumulate a few more bruises being hauled up that way."

"I'd feel safer going up with you, but I seem to keep fading in and out. Things sort of drift away," Elle answered.

Matt felt the tug of the rope, knew Jackson was tying the safety line around Elle.

"Then we'll go up together," Jackson said. "I'm not going to let anything happen to you."

"I know you won't." Elle circled his neck with her arms and crawled carefully onto his back. Matt felt more tugs with the rope and knew Jackson was tying her body to his.

"Your arm is broken. Can you hold on?"

"I don't exactly like the alternative, and Libby is blocking the pain for me."

Matt shook his head. Libby Drake, the doctor. A woman reputed to have a gift for healing the impossible. "Did you know Libby was anywhere near here?" he asked Jonas.

Jonas shook his head. "I knew she was coming home for Christmas, but not that she was on the way. But that isn't unusual for the Drakes. They're all connected somehow, and they tend to do things together."

Jackson's voice drifted up to them. "Good. I'm going to start climbing, Elle. It's going to hurt."

Elle pressed her face against Jackson's broad back. Matt watched Jackson start up the cliff, testing each finger- and toehold carefully before committing to the climb. Matt and Jonas kept the rope just taut enough to allow him to scale the vertical rock face. When Jackson was halfway to the top, the fog simply gave up, retreating before the onslaught of the wind. Matt leaned down to grasp Elle, as Jackson gained the top of the cliff.

Matt untied the rope and gently laid Elle on the ground. "I'll get to a car and radio for an ambulance," Jonas said.

Elle shook her head. "Libby's on her way. She'll fix me up." She turned her head to look at Jackson. "Thank you for coming for me. I didn't think anyone would find me." She touched the bump on her forehead. "I know the fall knocked me out."

Jackson shrugged and glanced at Matt and Jonas, shook his head, and remained silent. A car pulled up beside them and Libby Drake leaped out, dragging a black leather case with her. "How bad is she hurt, Jonas?"

"I'm fine, Libby," Elle protested.

Libby ignored her, looking to Jonas for the truth as she knelt beside her sister. Jackson answered her. "I think her left arm is broken. She definitely has a concussion, and she's either bruised her ribs or possibly fractured them. She's very tender on the left side. There's one laceration on her left leg that looks as if it could use a few stitches. Other than that, she's a mass of bruises."

"I don't want to go to the hospital, Libby," Elle protested.

"Too bad, baby, I think we're going to go and check you out."

Libby's word was obviously law. Elle protested repeatedly, but no one paid any attention to her. Matthew found himself holding Kate's hand in the waiting room while Libby went through all the required tests with Elle and finally settled her in a hospital bed for the remainder of the night.

Kate leaned into Matt's hard frame, looking up at him. "Thank you. I don't know what we would have done if you, Jonas, and Jackson hadn't found her. She looks all cut up." There was a little catch in her voice.

Matt immediately put his arms around her. "I'm taking you home. To my home, where you can get some rest, Kate. Elle's in good hands, you've kissed her ten times, and Libby's going to stay overnight with her. She can't be safer than that. Jackson brought her car to your house and left it for her, so everything's taken care of. Come home with me, Katie. Let me take care of you."

"You need a shave," she observed, her hungry gaze drinking him in.

They walked together to his car, their steps in perfect harmony. Matt smiled because he loved being with her more than anything else. He rubbed his jaw. "You're right, I do. You're not only going to have whisker burn on your face, but if I'm not more careful, you'll have it other places too."

She blushed beautifully. "I already do."

He opened the door for her, caught her chin before she could slide in. "Seriously?" Just the idea of it made his body hard.

Kate nodded. "It's nice to have a constant reminder." It was more than nice. Just the thought of how the marks had gotten there made her hot with need.

Matt dragged her close to him, his mouth taking command of hers. It seemed far too long since he'd been able to kiss her. To have her all to himself. "I want to get you home where I can put you into my bed. I still have such a hard time believing you're with me."

She laughed. "Imagine how I feel."

Kate leaned her head back against the seat of his car and looked at him, the smile fading from her face. "Matt, you shouldn't have wished on the snowglobe. It isn't an ordinary Christmas globe."

He glanced at her, then back at the road, his expression settling into serious lines. "Nothing about you or your family is ordinary, Katie. I knew what I was doing."

She opened her mouth to speak, shook her head, and stared out the window into the night.

Matt searched for something to say to reassure her. Or maybe it was he that needed the reassurance. Kate was still resistant to the idea of a long-term relationship, and he wasn't certain he could change her mind. He couldn't begin to explain the sense of rightness he felt when he drove up to his house with Kate beside him. He sat in his car, looking up at the house with its bank of windows for the view, and the wide, inviting decks going in every direction. "I built this house for you. I even put in a library and two offices, just in case you wanted your own office. I asked Sarah a few years ago, when I first came back, if you had a preference where you wrote, and she said you preferred a room with a view and soft music. I added a fireplace just in case you needed the ambience."

Kate blinked back tears, leaned over, and kissed him. What could she say? Everyone in town knew Sarah. Sarah was magic. She could scale cliff walls and she knew things before they happened. She could leap out of airplanes and climb tall buildings. Sarah lived her life. She didn't dream the way Kate did or live in her imagination.

Matt took her hand and pulled her out of the car. "I soundproofed your office so the noise wouldn't bother you."

"What noise?" She knew better than to ask, but she couldn't stop herself.

"Our kids. You do want kids, don't you? I'm afraid the Granites tend to throw males. I don't have a single female cousin. You do like boys, don't you?"

Kate looked away from him, out to the booming sea. Sarah would have children. All of her sisters would have them. She'd probably tell them all stories. Maybe she should have been the one to wish on the snowglobe. Maybe she should have wished for the courage to do the right thing.

"Katie, if you don't want children, I'll be happy with it being just the two of us. You know that, don't you?" He unlocked the door to the house and stepped back to let her in. "Children would be wonderful, but not necessary. If we can have them. Sometime in the future, after I've spent endless time making love to you all over the house."

Kate went straight to the Christmas tree. She wanted him. She wanted him for as long as she could have him. She swallowed her tears and lifted her chin, smiling at him. "I like that idea. Making love to you all over the house. Would you turn on the Christmas lights? I love miniature lights like these."

Matt plugged in the lights for her. His house was dark and quiet and a bit on the cool side. He'd never bothered with heavy curtains in the living room because he had no close neighbors, and the bank of windows faced the sea. Kate dropped her purse on the nearest chair and kicked off her shoes. "It's nice to come home. Just for tonight, I want to think about Christmas and not some awful thing coming out of the fog to hurt everyone." She looked up at him, her large eyes sad. "Do you think we'll manage to get one night together, Matthew?"

"I don't know, Katie. I hope so. I'm going to check the house and downstairs, and I'll be right back." He didn't think he could sleep, not even holding her in his arms, until he checked the sand outside for any peculiar footprints.

"That's a good idea. I'll make us up a bed. You don't mind if we sleep out here by the tree do you?"

Matt looked around the huge, spacious living room. The miniature lights winked on and off, colors flickering along the walls and the high ceiling. "I'd like that, Kate."

He circled the house, checked the rooms beneath the

deck and the beach for any signs of intrusion. He had the feeling the enemy was as fatigued as they were. He glanced out to sea. "How about giving us a break, buddy," he murmured softly. "Whatever has you all upset, Kate had nothing to do with it."

Above his head the skies opened up and poured down rain. Matt grinned wryly and hurried back to the house. Back to Kate. The gas fireplace was lit, the "logs" burning cheerfully. On the mantel were several lighted candles. The scent of berry permeated the air. In the flickering lights, he saw Kate, lying naked on the sheets, her body beautiful, sprawled lazily on the covers while she watched the lights of the Christmas tree. His breath rushed from his lungs, so that he burned for air, just standing there in the doorway staring in surprise at the most incredible Christmas present he could imagine. That was how he thought of her. His Christmas present. He would love this time of year forever.

"Matthew." She turned over, smiled at him. "Come lie down with me."

He could see the real Kate Drake. On the outside, she seemed flawless, perfect, out of reach, yet she was really vulnerable, and as fragile as she was courageous. Kate needed a shield and he was more than happy to be that shield, for her. He could stand between her and the rest of the world. "Give me a minute, Kate."

Kate turned back to the tree, watching the lights blinking on and off, so many colors flickering across the wall. It was heaven just to lie down and rest. To relax. More than anything she loved to feel Matt's heated gaze on her. He made her feel beautiful and incredibly special. He was a large man, and the feel of his hands on her body, the way his body came alive at the sight of her, was a gift. A treasure.

Kate lay with the sheets cool on her skin and the lights playing over her body. She imagined his hands on her. His eyes on her. Thinking about him made her grow hot with need. A small sound alerted her, and she looked up to see him towering over her. For a moment she couldn't breathe. She drank him in. His strong legs and muscular thighs. His amazing erection. His flat stomach and heavily muscled chest. Finally, his eyes. His eyes had turned smoky, seductive, and now they smoldered with intensity and heat. "You take my breath away." It was a silly thing to say, but it was true. She patted the blanket beside her. She wanted to touch him, to know he was real. To feel him solid and strong beneath her fingertips.

"I'm supposed to say that to you." He stretched out beside her, gathered her into his arms to hold her to him. "I want to lie here with you for a very long time."

She rested her head on his shoulder, fitting her body more closely to his. "I wouldn't mind staying here for the rest of the winter, locked away in our own private world." She stretched languidly, pleased to be able to relax. To have him holding her with such gentleness.

Matt knew she was tired, and it was enough to hold her in his arms, even with his body raging at him and her body so soft and inviting and open to his. His mouth drifted down the side of her neck. She snuggled closer, turning her head toward the Christmas tree, giving him even better access.

"I love the way you smell," he said. Because he couldn't resist, he slid his palm over her skin. He'd never felt anything so soft. He traced her ribs, a gentle exploration, not in the least demanding, simply wanting to touch her. Her soft belly called to him, a mystery for a breast man, but he loved the way she reacted each time he caressed her there.

Kate smiled. "I love the feel of your hands."

"I've always hated my hands. Workingman hands, rough and big and meant for manual labor."

"Meant to bring pleasure to a woman, you mean," she contradicted, and caught his hand to bring it to her lips. She kissed the pads of his fingers, nibbled on the tips, and drew one into her mouth.

He caught his breath, aching with love, burning up with need. "Everything about you is so damned feminine, Kate. Sometimes I'm afraid if I touch you, I'm going to break you." He measured her wrist loosely by circling it with his thumb and index finger.

She laughed and rubbed her body against his affectionately, almost like a contented cat. "I doubt you have to worry about breaking me. This thing with the fog is draining, but I recover quickly." She frowned, even as she ran her fingertips along the hard column of his thigh. "I am a little worried about Hannah though, and now Elle."

He was very much aware of her fingers so close to his throbbing erection. She was tapping out a little rhythm on his upper thigh. His stomach constricted, and his blood thickened. The lights on the Christmas tree blinked on and off in harmony with the drumming of her fingers. Every tap brought a surge of heat through his body. "The doctors said Elle was going to be fine. She'll have a whale of a headache, though, and Jackson was right about her ribs and arm, but she'll heal fast with Libby around."

Matt cupped her breast in his hands, his thumbs teasing her nipples into taut pebbles. He felt her response, the swift intake of breath. The flush that covered her body. "It seems such a miracle to me to be able to touch you like this. I wonder if every other man knows what a miracle a woman's body is."

"And all this time, I thought the miracle was a man's body." Kate ran her fingernails lightly along his belly.

"Maybe the miracle is just that I finally managed to stop you from hiding from me," Matt decided. He bent his head, flickered her nipple with his tongue, made a lazy foray around the areola. She moved slightly, turning to give him better access.

"I've been thinking about the fog. Something isn't quite right."

"Quite right?" He lifted his head to look at her, arching his eyebrow. The Christmas lights were playing red and green and blue over her stomach. A bright red light glowed across the small triangle of curls at the junction of her legs. It was distracting and made it hard to concentrate on conversation. He slipped his hand in the middle of the flashing light, watched his fingers stroke the nest of curls, felt Kate shiver, and pushed his fingers deep into her warm wet sheath. She pushed back against him, a soft moan escaping. He dipped his head to find her breast, suckling strongly. "What are you thinking, Kate?" His tongue swirled over her nipple, and he pushed deeper inside her until her hips began a helpless ride.

"He isn't going after Hannah. Why attack me? Or Elle? Or even Abbey? He should go after Hannah. She summons the wind to drive him out to sea. She stops him." Her words came in little short bursts. She gasped as she pushed against his hand, as her body tightened with alarming pressure, with the pure magic of passion shared with Matthew.

"Take the pins out of your hair," he whispered, his voice raw. "I love your hair down. You look very sexy with your hair down."

"You think I look sexy no matter what," she pointed out.

His teeth teased her nipple, nibbled over her breast. "True, but I love the hair."

"You won't love it when it's falling all over you." But she was lifting her arms, pulling out pins and scattering them in every direction while he shifted her, lowering his body into the cradle of her hips, thrusting deep inside her.

She cried out when he surged forward. Whips of lightning danced through her blood. "Matthew." There was a plea for mercy, and he hadn't even gotten started.

"We have all the time in the world, Katie," he whispered, his lips sliding over her throat, her chin, and up to her mouth. His strong hips paused, waiting. She held her breath. He thrust hard, a long stroke surging deep to bury himself completely within her. A coming home. She was velvet soft and tight and fiery hot. He wanted a long slow night with her. His hands shaped her body, stroking and caressing every inch of her.

"I don't feel like we have all the time in the world." She protested, breathless, arching her hips to meet the impact of his. "I feel like I'm going to go up in flames."

"Then do it," he encouraged. "Come for me a hundred times. Over and over. Scream for me, Kate. I love you so much. I love watching you come for me. And I love your body, every square inch of it. I want to spend the night worshiping you."

Kate wanted the same thing. She did scream, clutching at the bedcovers for an anchor as her body fragmented, and she went spinning off into space. She couldn't tell if the whirling colors were behind her eyes or from the Christmas tree lights. She found it didn't matter when he caught her hips firmly, held her still, and began surging into her once more with his slow, deep strokes.

chapter 11

In the stocking hung with gentle care,
A mystery, I know, is hidden there.

MATT WOKE ALREADY AROUSED. HE WAS thick and aching, so tight he thought he'd burst through his own skin. The blankets had fallen onto the floor as if he had spent a long, restless night. His body was stark naked and mercilessly aroused. He looked down at Kate. She smiled up at him, her sea-green eyes sultry, her hands moving gently over his flat stomach. Her long hair spilled over his hips and thighs, teasing every nerve ending. He knotted a long strand around his fist. "I dreamed of you, Kate."

Her smile was that of a temptress. "I hope it was a good dream." She bent her head to her task, lovingly stroking her tongue over the thick inviting length of him, sliding the velvet knob into the heated tightness of her mouth.

Matt gasped as the pleasure/pain of it rocked him. "How could it not be?" he asked when he got his breath back. Her tongue made a teasing foray along the rigid length and stroked over him before she once again slid her mouth around him.

He closed his eyes, his hips surging forward, wanting more, needing more, as waves of heat spread through his body, as every muscle clenched and tightened. Kate's fist wrapped him up while her mouth performed miracles. "I don't know if I'll survive this, Kate."

Her answer was muffled, her breath warm and enticing, her mouth hot and tight. He was certain he felt her laughter vibrate through his entire body. There was joy in Kate. That was her secret, he decided. Joy in everything she did with him. She didn't pretend not to enjoy his body, she reveled in exploring him, teasing him, driving him to the very edge of his control.

Kate kissed her way up his belly and over his chest. She mounted him, the way an accomplished horseback rider smoothly slides aboard a horse, settling her body over his with exquisite slowness. She put up her hands and he took them so she could use leverage as her body rose and fell, stroking his. Her hair spilled around her, adding to her allure as her full breasts bounced and beckoned with every movement. She threw her head back, arched back, moving differently, tightening muscles until he was certain he would explode.

"Kate." Her name was a husky, almost hoarse sound, escaping from his constricted throat. His lungs burned. A fire spread through his belly, centered in his groin, and gathered into a wild conflagration. He couldn't take his gaze from her. There was a sheen to her skin, a flush over her body. She moved with a woman's sensuous grace and mystery. "The feel of your hair on my legs and belly makes me crazy." It should have tickled his skin, but the silky fall brushed over sensitive nerve endings and added to the heat and fire building in the deep within him. He felt as if every part of his body was being pulled in that direction.

Kate moved with exquisite slowness, undulating her body, sending him right out of his mind. The erotic visual only increased his raging hunger for her. In the soft morning sunlight, her hair flashed red streaks, and her pale skin seemed made of dewy petals. Most of all, the expression on her face, deeply absorbed in the ride of lust and love and passion, shook his entire being. He could read the way her body began to build pressure, her muscles clenching tightly, gripping him strongly. He could see it on her face, the rapture, the passion, the intensity of the orgasm as it overtook her. He watched her ride it out, watched the excitement and pleasure on her face, in her body. Seeing her like that heightened his own pleasure, and he wanted more, wanted her flushed body to feel it again and again and bring his body to his own explosive orgasm.

He caught her hips in his hands, taking control, guiding her ride, thrusting upward hard as she slid down over him, encasing him in a fist of hot velvet. He shuddered with pleasure, feeling the pressure building relentlessly. He could feel her body preparing for a second shock, the muscles tightening around him, adding to the intensity of his explosion. It shook him, a volcano going off, detonating from the inside out, taking everything in its path. He caught her to him, fighting for air, fighting to regain some sense of where he was, of a time and place, not fantasyland, where his every dream came true. It seemed impossible to be lying on his living room floor, his heart raging at him, his body in ecstasy, and the love of his life in his arms. His world had been guns and sand and jungles and an enemy fighting to kill him. Women like Kate were not real and they didn't wind their arms around his neck and rain kisses all over his face and tell him he was too sexy to be alive.

They lay together just holding one another, trying to get their heart rates back to normal and to push air through their lungs. Kate lay stretched out on top of Matt, pressing her soft body tightly against his. Beneath her, he suddenly stiffened.

"What the hell is that?" he growled, hearing a noise outside the house.

Kate gasped and rolled off of him, landing on the pile of blankets. "We have company, Matthew," she whispered, gathering the sheets around her.

He sat up abruptly, his breath hissing through his teeth. He'd asked for a night with Kate, he should have asked for the entire damned week. He was never going to get enough of her, never be sated. "I thought I'd at least get you for a few more hours," he groused as he padded naked across the floor. He suddenly halted halfway to the door and uttered a string of curses. "It's my parents."

Kate's eyes widened. She clutched the sheet to her naked breasts. "What?"

"My parents," he announced. He reached down to help her up. "Why is it that even when you're grown, parents can make you feel like a teenager caught in the act?"

Kate wrapped the sheet around her and hurried toward his bedroom while Matt scooped up the blankets and followed her. "Did you get caught in the act often?"

"Are you laughing at me?" he asked, a dangerous glint in his silver eyes.

"Only because I'm disappearing into the bathroom to leave you to face the music alone. You might get dressed." She grinned mischievously at him as she gathered up her clothes and retreated behind a securely locked door.

Matt caught sight of the wisp of peach-colored lace that lay on the floor and found a wicked smile stealing over his face. He stooped down and picked it up, bunching it into his hand before shoving it into the pocket of his jacket, which was lying on the back of a chair. He dragged on clothes as fast as he could, combing his hair with his fingers just as the polite knock on his door came.

He could hear Kate laughing, and it was contagious. He couldn't wipe the grin off his face as he opened the front door. Victoria Granite threw her arms around her son and hugged him hard. "You frightened us, Matt! We called and called and you never answered. First there was a fire here and Danny told us about that horrible incident at the store and then a call went out and . . ."

"Victoria, take a breath," Harold Granite advised. He smiled lovingly at his wife, used to her run-on sentences. "We heard the fog came in last night, and Elle Drake went over the cliff. Victoria was worried."

Matt's mother made a face. "Really, Harold, I knew he was perfectly fine; you were the one who spent the entire morning trying to call him and pacing back and forth like a wild tiger. I was fine!"

Matt met his father's gaze over the top of his mother's head. They both stifled a knowing grin. "I'm sorry, Dad. I should have remembered after all these years, how you worry."

Victoria smiled and patted Harold's arm. "There, dear, you see there was nothing at all to worry about. All that pacing." She shook her head, stopping in midsentence as she looked up at the mantel and the candles that had burned down to the holders. "Oh my goodness." She looked around carefully. "Matthew Granite, you had a woman here last night, didn't you?"

"Mom, once I turned thirty, I thought we agreed I didn't have to talk about women with you."

From the bedroom came the sound of a door closing. His parents exchanged a long, satisfied look. Victoria arched her eyebrow at her son. "She's still here?"

"As a matter of fact, yes. And don't start on her, Mom. I don't want her scared off. This is the one."

There was another startled silence. "Kate's here?" Harold asked, clearly astonished. "Kate Drake?"

"Of course it's Kate," Victoria said.

Kate came out of the bedroom with a bright smile and desperation in her eyes. She was wearing one of his shirts over her thin white blouse. Matthew was instantly mortified. He thought he would tease her, and at the same time, he'd have the added pleasure of knowing she was sitting beside him in the warmth of his car without a bra. He'd planned to slip his hand inside the white silk of her blouse and caress her soft creamy skin. The idea alone had made him as hard as a rock. It hadn't occurred to him that her blouse was sheer enough that her darker nipples would show so alluringly.

Kate always presented a near flawless appearance to

the world, and he realized immediately when he saw the desperation in her eyes that it was her armor. She wore her clothes and hair and makeup to keep people from seeing the real Kate. The vulnerable Kate. The Kate she shared only with her sisters, and now with him.

"Hello Mrs. Granite, Mr. Granite," she greeted.

Matthew drew the edges of his shirt together around her, sliding several buttons in place. He bent to kiss her, shielding her from his parents' scrutiny for a brief moment. When he was certain she was sufficiently covered, he circled her waist with his arms and held her in front of him. He could feel her soft unbound breasts pushing against his arms. Instantly his body reacted, thickening, hardening, an ache pounding through his blood. He held her close to him, covering the painful bulge stretching the material of his jeans. Kate was without mercy, slowly and sensuously rubbing her round bottom over the hard ridge. "I would very much like to visit, but Elle's in the hospital, and we have to go by Kate's house before we go to see her." Was that his voice? It sounded thick and husky to his ears. He was even afraid color burned in his face. His palms itched to cup Kate's breasts in his hands. The soft weight on his arms was driving him crazy. His mouth had actually gone dry. And if she didn't stop the way she was rubbing against him, he was going to shock everyone right then and there. "Let's have dinner tonight," he suggested, in desperation making eye contact with his father.

Harold, taking the cue, caught Victoria's elbow firmly. "Danny will be spending the evening with Trudy

Garret and her little boy at the Grange. Santa Claus is stuffing stockings and delivering presents around seven. We were going to watch," Victoria said. "Can we plan for another night?"

"Tomorrow is the pageant rehearsal," Matt said. "You all are in that. Maybe we can grab dinner afterward."

"There's never time." Harold shook his head, but headed across the living room to the front door. "The pageant rehearsal never runs smoothly, and we're always there until midnight."

"Good point," Matt agreed. "Don't worry, Mom, we'll have dinner together soon." He walked them to the door. "Who's playing Santa Claus this year?"

Harold grinned. "No one's supposed to know, Matt." He went out into the light drizzle and paused. "Jeff Burley broke his leg a couple of weeks ago. He's done it every year, and we had a bit of trouble finding a replacement. Everyone's afraid of the fog. Some of the townspeople think it's some kind of alien invasion."

Victoria put up her umbrella and made a little face. "People are so silly sometimes."

"I hope you're not trying to ask me to be Santa Claus this year, I'm more afraid of the kids than I am of aliens." Matt sounded as stern as he dared with his mother.

Kate made a move to retreat back into the house, but Matt held her firmly as if she were his only refuge. The cold air hardened Kate's nipples into tight buds, and she was acutely aware she wore no bra beneath Matt's shirt. The drizzle was penetrating straight through the material and turning the silk blouse beneath it transparent.

She crossed her arms over her chest and kept her smile firmly in place.

"There aren't any aliens," Victoria said, exasperated. "And no, you don't have to play Santa. I know better than to ask any of you boys. You'd frighten the children with your nonsense."

"Not Dad!" Matt suddenly sounded authoritative, and Kate looked up. "Dad, the doctor told you not to overdo."

"Playing Santa Claus wouldn't overdo anything." Harold was clearly annoyed. "And no, it isn't me. We had someone come forward, but he wishes to remain anonymous. It would ruin all of his fun if I revealed his identity."

Matt followed his parents to their car, taking Kate with him. "I'm not going to tell anyone."

"The last man you'd ever expect," Victoria said primly.

"The last man I'd ever expect to play Santa would be Old Man Mars." Matt laughed. "Can't you see Danny's face? He'd run from Santa."

Victoria and Harold looked at one another and burst out laughing. Victoria waved gaily at Kate. Matt stared after them. "You don't think they meant that mean old man is going to play Santa."

"I can't imagine it. I think they were teasing you. Do you have the car keys? I'm getting cold, and I have to stop by my house to pick up some clothes before we go to the hospital."

"I've got them. Come on. Let's get you out of the rain." Matt drew her bra from his jacket pocket and held it out to her. "I'm sorry, Katie. I couldn't stop thinking about playing out my little fantasy of being able to touch you when I was taking you home. It was childish of me."

Kate merely looked at the peach-colored bra in his outstretched hand, but made no move to take it. "And you wanted to be able to touch me how?" She walked past him to the car. There was a distinct sway to her beautiful rear, one he couldn't resist. Kate settled into his car, slowly unbuttoned the wet overshirt, and allowed the edges to gape open to reveal the transparent silk blouse underneath. She leaned back against the seat.

Matt drove slowly along the coastal highway, fighting for air when there was none in the car. The shape of her breasts was not only outlined beneath the see-through material, but highlighted. "Kate, you're an incredible woman."

"I'm a lucky woman. I rather like your fantasies. By all means, tell me whenever you get one."

He couldn't resist. Matt slipped his hand inside her blouse, cupped the soft, creamy flesh in his palm. His knuckle rubbed gently over her breast, the pads of his fingers possessive as he caressed her body. Right at that moment he could think of a hundred fantasies. He turned the car onto the drive leading to the bluff overlooking the sea. The moment he parked, he caught the back of her head and held her still while he devoured her mouth.

They spent an hour in the car, laughing like children, necking like teenagers, wildly happy as they held hands, touched and kissed and whispered of dreams and hopes and erotic fantasies.

When they arrived at the Drake house, no one was

home; the sisters were all at the hospital. There was a note for Kate telling her Elle was doing much better and instructing her to join them when she could. Kate took the time to shower. Matt joined her and spent a long while leisurely lathering soap over her and rinsing her off. He made love to her under the spray of water, then dried her off with large towels. He couldn't take his eyes off of her while she dressed. "I've never been happier, Kate," he admitted, as she pinned the thick length of hair on top of her head into her "perfect Kate" style.

"Me either," she answered, and leaned over to kiss him.

Matt caught her hand and dragged her through the house into the living room. "Kate, do you love me? You know I love you. I tell you. I show you. I want to spend my life with you, and I've made no secret about that. Do you love me?"

Kate nearly stopped breathing. She touched his face. "How could you not know, Matthew? I love you so much I ache with it sometimes."

"Then why won't you agree to marry me? I don't think your family objects to me, and obviously my family would welcome it."

She let her breath out slowly. "I have some things to work out, Matt. I want to marry you. I do. But I have to be certain it's right for you. That I'm right for you."

"Katie. Honey. I know you're right for me." He looked around the room. "Where's that damned snow-globe anyway?" He retrieved it from the shelf.

Kate took it out of his hands. "You only get one wish, Matt, and you've had yours." She went to place the globe back on the shelf, but it came alive in her hands, the fog swirling. Waiting. Kate closed her eyes and made her wish. She couldn't stop herself. She wanted Matthew Granite more than she'd ever wanted anything in her life.

Matt said nothing, asking her no questions. He simply took her hand in a gesture of solidarity.

Kate and Matt spent most of the afternoon in the hospital with Kate's sisters in Elle's room. Matt and Damon played a game of chess while the seven sisters caught up on news. Joley helped Damon, and when Matt expressed disapproval, Abbey immediately took Matt's side. They did their best to entertain Elle, who looked bruised and very young. Her bright red hair tumbled around her white face and heightened her pale skin and deepened the purple in the bruises. She was in good spirits but weak and still had a headache.

Matt and Kate left the hospital in the evening to meet the Granites at the Grange, where most of the townspeople were bringing their children for photos with Santa and a small party.

The Grange hall was packed with parents and children. "Jingle Bells" blared through the building, mistletoe was hung in every conceivable place, and holly decorated the tables laden with cookies and punch. A fake mantel went along the entire length of one wall with holly, candles, and tiny sleighs filled with candy canes adorning the top. Rows of stockings hung on gleaming hooks. The silver-tipped fir tree nearly reached the ceiling and was covered in lights, ornaments, and a multitude of white angels with silver wings.

"The ladies at the arts and crafts shop have been busy," Matt whispered.

Kate shushed him, but her eyes were laughing. Several elves hurried past them, bells tinkling from their hats and ankles. Kate and Matt followed the elves through the crowd to the back of the building, where Santa Claus sat in a high-backed chair surrounded by more elves and a reindeer that looked suspiciously like a dog with plastic antlers attached to his head. The line to visit Santa was long, small children clutching parents' hands and staring with large round eyes at the jolly old man. The Santa suit fit perfectly, and the white beard and mustache seemed natural, both bushy enough to hide the face successfully. Matt tried to get close enough to get a good look at the Santa. Several preteenagers rushed past him laughing loudly, tossing popcorn at each other.

"Do you think it's Old Man Mars?" Matt whispered.

"How could it be?" Kate asked. "He hates Christmas."

"Right height. I could tell if he were talking loud or maybe even by the way he walks." Matt weaved his way through the small children.

"Hey!" A young boy with red hair protested. "No cutting in."

"I just wanted to ask Santa if he'd give me Kate for Christmas," Matt explained.

Unimpressed, the boy wrinkled his nose, and all of his friends made faces. "Well, you got to stand in line like everyone else."

Kate laughed and dragged Matt away from Santa Claus. He spotted Inez and pulled Kate toward her. "If anyone knows who Santa Claus is, it'll be Inez. She knows everything."

"Doesn't that come under the heading of gossip?"

"News, Katie. How can you even use the word *gossip?*" Matt stopped moving abruptly and brought her up short, staring out the window. He bit out a string of curses. "The damned fog is rolling in, Kate. It's coming right this way."

Kate looked at him, then looked around at the children. "I don't want people to panic and run for their cars to get away from here. No one would be able to drive in the fog. I'll find a way to distract the kids." She hurried toward Santa Claus, whispering softly to the children so that the throng parted like the Red Sea to give her access to the jolly old man sitting with a child on his lap. She leaned in and spoke to him.

From a distance, Matt watched Santa stiffen, listen some more, and nod. Kate straightened up and directed the children into a large circle. Santa gave out candy canes, patting heads and laughing as he did so. Several mothers began distributing cookies and punch while Kate started an enthralling Christmas story. Matt had never seen anyone hold an entire room in her hand, but there was no sound other than the faint background of Christmas music and Kate's spellbinding voice. He found himself caught up in the sheer beauty of the magical tone, even when the fog began to seep through the cracks of the doors and windows.

There was no way to keep the fog out. It was only the magic of Kate's voice, the anonymous Santa Claus's cheerful punctuation of ho, ho, ho woven cleverly into the storyline, and the Granite reputation in the community that kept panic from spreading as the gray-white vapor filled the room, bringing with it the scent and feel of the sea. Kate smoothly incorporated the fog into the storyline, having the children hold hands and interact with Santa's ho, ho, ho. The children did so with enthusiasm, laughing wildly at the antics of Kate's characters in the fog. Matt realized she was creating the illusion that the fog was deliberate, a part of the story she was telling, used for effect. He could see parents relaxing, thinking Kate had found a way to keep the children from fearing the incoming fog, a part of life for anyone who lived on the coast.

It seemed hours to Matt, watching the fog churning, swirling in deeper shades of gray, spinning when there was no breeze to create the effect, yet it was only a few minutes before the fog began a hasty retreat . . . almost as if it couldn't take the sound of Kate's voice. It was a silly notion. Fog had no ears to listen, but it also shouldn't have been able to leave footprints in sand or do damage to property. He made his way closer to Kate, knowing she would pay a steep price using her energy to keep such a large crowd under the spell of her voice. As he moved toward her, he felt something in the fog, something tangible brush against his arm.

Matt whirled toward it, hands going up in a fighter's defensive position, but there were only coils of vapor surrounding him. He heard a sound, a growling voice muttering a warning. A chill went down his spine. He felt the touch of death on him, bony fingers reaching for him, or someone who belonged to him. The hair on his body stood up in reaction to the half moan, half growl that could have been wind, but there was no wind to generate the sound. Matt knew it was a warning, but the words made no sense.

Anger was impotent against fog. He couldn't fight it, couldn't wrestle it; he couldn't even shoot it. How could he protect Kate when he couldn't see or get his hands on the culprit? He stood very still as the vapor simply rolled from the building, leaving behind the soft Christmas music and the laughter of the children. He looked around the room, at the sunny faces, at the tree and decorations. Why had the fog come, only to recede without incident?

He made his way to Kate's side, slipping his arm around her waist to lend her strength. She sent the children to the tables of food, a smile on her face, shadows in her eyes. Laughter picked up as if the fog had never been; but Matt continued to survey the room, inch by inch, concerned there had to more, something they were all missing.

Kate leaned into him as they looked out the window. "It's heading out to sea on its own. Why would it do that? Why would it come here and leave?"

Matt watched the children eating. Santa Claus was eating. "Could it have poisoned the food some way?" he asked, his heart in his throat at the thought. His parents were seated at a table with Danny, Trudy Garrett, and her young son.

"I doubt it, Matthew, how could it?"

"How could he do any of the things he's been doing?" His hands tightened on her shoulders. "Santa

Claus is a symbol of Christmas, right? What does he represent?"

"You don't think he came to attack the man playing the part of Santa, then decided against it, do you?" Her anxious gaze followed the burly man in the red-and-white suit.

Matt shook his head. "I feel danger, Katie. When I feel it this strong, it's here, close by. Tell me what Santa represents."

She rubbed her throbbing temples. "Goodwill, I suppose. He represents goodwill and generosity. He gives presents, stuffs stockings, eats the children's milk and cookies."

"He spreads goodwill among the people and is generous, teaching by example to be generous." Matt tugged on her hand, moved toward the tree where Santa's pack lay. He peered inside. There were a few netted candy cane stockings holding small toys, candy, and various small personal items the town always generously donated for the event. Santa had slipped most of the candy cane net stockings into the children's stockings hanging from the fake mantel earlier when he'd first arrived, so that each child would have something to take home after the party.

Matt went to the brightly colored stockings, each with a child's name stitched in bold letters across the top. Kate's fingers tightened around his. She already knew, just as he did. They peered inside. She drew back, stifling a cry, looking at him with fear. Inside each stocking, the fog had added to Santa's generous gift. A mass of sand and sea bugs writhed in hideous black balls in the toes of the stockings. All were damp with seawater and smelled faintly of the noxious odor the fog seemed to leave behind. Crushed shells and spiny sea anemone, kelp and small crabs were mixed with the wiggling insects.

Santa Claus joined them, staring at the mess while all around them children ate and laughed and played. "We have to get rid of these. Some of these creatures are venomous."

Matt glanced quickly at the man, recognizing the voice. Old Man Mars was indeed playing Santa. "You're right. I'll get a couple of the men, and we'll get the stockings out of here before the children start trying to collect them. Kate." He pulled out a chair for her. "Sit down before you fall down. I'll take you home when we're through here."

"To my house," she said in a weary voice. "I need to go to my house."

He nodded, his gut knotting tightly.

chapter

12

A candle burns with an eerie glow,
As it melts, the wax does flow

 "THE THING IN THE FOG SPOKE TO ME." MATT made the announcement after the Drake sisters had settled Elle firmly in the living room. It was late afternoon before the doctors let her go home, and her family had been so anxious, Matt had steered clear of the subject of the danger in the fog. He and Kate had gone to the mill earlier in the morning to reexamine the seal and see if she could find anything new about the spirit. He hadn't wanted to bring up the subject at the very source of the trouble.

There was a sudden silence. He had their attention immediately. Kate set down her teacup. "You didn't say anything to me about it."

"You were exhausted and worried about Elle last night, Katie, and again this morning. I didn't want to bring it up. Now that she's home and safe, I thought it was a good time to discuss it." En masse, the Drake sisters were difficult to contend with. He could feel every eye on him. There was power in the room, intangible, feminine, but a steady flow of it. An energy he couldn't begin to explain, but he knew it moved from sister to sister.

"What did it say?" Sarah asked. Her voice was gentle, nonjudgmental. Practical, magical Sarah. She was the oldest and the most influential.

"It made no sense. It was a moan and a growl mixed together. The syntax was old-fashioned, but from what I got, it was a warning to keep my loved ones away from one with the staff."

"The staff? He used the word *staff*?" Kate asked.

Matt nodded. "I've thought a lot about it, and maybe it all ties up with Christianity and the staff of life or something. Anything to do with the Christian beliefs of Christmas is under attack?" He made it a question.

Elle lifted the old journal Sarah handed to her. "I'll do my best to try to find a reference to a staff in here," she said. "I don't think I thanked you for coming to my rescue the other night, Matt. One minute I was making my way home, and the next I felt something shove me over the side of cliff. I broke every fingernail on the way down, grabbing at dirt and rocks. I have no idea how Jackson climbed down to get me. I couldn't even call out with a strong enough voice for help, and I was afraid to move. The ledge was literally crumbling under me."

"I know it was frightening, Elle, but we have you, you're safe now," Joley soothed.

"Kate said something the other evening about how the entity didn't go after Hannah. It's strange because Hannah's the one providing the wind to drive him out to sea and away from the town," Matt said. "Do any of you have any idea why he's chosen not to try to harm her?"

Sarah frowned. "It really only went after Elle."

Kate shook her head. "It definitely tried for me, Sarah. And I think it tried to use Sylvia and her amorous ways to get to Abbey, then made a second attempt here in the house, pitting her against Jackson. Jackson's a mercurial man, and Sylvia's unpredictable. I think it wanted Abbey out of the way too. Of all of us, wouldn't Hannah be its main obstacle?"

"What do you all have in common?" Matt asked. He watched as Sarah moved through the living room lighting tall, thick candles at each entranceway. The candles each had three wicks and sat in wrought-iron holders. She murmured something he couldn't hear as she lit each candle. He realized the windows had arrangements of colorful flowers and herbs tied in bundles on either side of the sills and above the window frames. The bundles of dried arrangements hadn't been there before. The fragrance was a blend of outdoors and strong scents of rosemary, jasmine, and something else he couldn't quite identify. The lights of the candles flickered on the walls, dancing and leaping with every movement of the sisters, as if tuned to them.

"Abbey, Kate, and Joley all have special gifts involving their voices," Sarah answered, bending over a tall cranberry candle near the bay window. She glanced over at her youngest sister before lighting the round candle. "Elle has many talents, but she doesn't share their voice. She is, however, a strong telepath, and she can share the shadow world with Kate. Neither Joley nor Abbey have has that ability."

"But nothing happened to Joley," Matt said. He sighed. "So much for my great detective work."

Joley made a small dissenting sound. "That's not exactly true." Immediately, she had the attention of all of her sisters.

"Something happened that you didn't tell us," Kate asked.

"I didn't want to worry anyone," Joley admitted. "I get all kinds of silly threats on the road, and in light of the threat to Kate, I didn't want to worry anyone."

Joley stretched, a sensuous flow of feminine muscle. Everything Joley did, every way she moved or even spoke was sultry. It was as natural to her as breathing. Matt found he could appreciate her looks and voice, yet not react in the least. It was a further revelation to him just how deeply in love he was with Kate. He sank onto the floor in front of Kate and leaned against her knees. At once her fingers tunneled into his thick hair, a connection between them.

"What happened, Joley?" Sarah prompted.

"I went up to my room after we all talked the other day. Hannah said she closed the window because the fog was slipping into the house, and it made her uncomfortable. I was so tired I just crashed on the bed, and I didn't think to pay attention to the feel of the room. I woke up choking, strangling really. At first I thought I'd wrapped a scarf around my neck in my sleep and somehow pulled it tight. But the fog was everywhere, layers of it. I could barely see. I pulled the scarf away from my throat and turned on the fan. My throat hurt and . . ." She hesitated, sighed softly, and dragged the turtleneck sweater away from her throat. Distinct round bruises marred her skin.

"And you didn't think it was important to tell us?" Sarah turned on her younger sister. "That we shouldn't know this thing has advanced to such a sophisticated level of violence? Joley! You weren't thinking."

"I know." Joley rubbed her palm over her thigh. "At first I was terrified, and I went through the house and began to gather the herbs and flowers for the windows, but the entire time I wondered why it just didn't kill me. If it could partially strangle me, why didn't it just do it all the way?"

"Maybe he isn't strong enough," Abbey ventured.

Sarah glanced toward the sea. "He's strong enough. He managed to take shape and, from what Matt says, even find a voice."

"Are you saying he didn't try to kill Joley? He certainly tried to kill Elle," Abbey argued. "Maybe he wasn't prepared for how hard she fought."

"*I'm* saying it didn't try to kill me," Joley said.

"Then what was it doing?" Sarah asked.

"I think it was trying to silence my voice."

Kate put a protective hand to her throat. "In the shadow world, he went for my throat as well."

Something deep inside of Matt went very still. Kate had an incredible voice. "If he wants to still the voices capable of enthrallment, Joley, Abbey, and Kate are definitely on the hit list." He looked at Elle. "But why you?"

She smiled, her green eyes bright. "Maybe he doesn't like redheads."

"I think he doesn't want to be saved," Kate announced. "When I touched him, I felt rage, yes, but it wasn't his primary emotion." She leaned towards Elle. "Didn't you feel sorrow and guilt? You were there, you had to have felt it."

Elle looked down at the journal, her expression sorrowful. "I felt it," she said in a small voice.

Matt raised his head sharply. "Elle shares emotions, doesn't she? You connected with Jackson when he was taken prisoner."

Elle refused to meet his eyes. "Yes."

"But he was halfway around the world," Matt protested.

Libby put her hand out to her youngest sister, and Elle took it immediately. "It's very difficult sometimes, Matthew," Libby explained. "We're different. We look the same and try to act the same, but we're not normal and sometimes the overload is . . ." She searched for the right word, looking helplessly at her sisters.

"Dangerous," Sarah supplied. "Using our talents is very draining. Each of us has to overcome by-products of her gift."

"I've seen it in Kate," Matt agreed. "Is there any way to minimize it?"

The seven women looked at one another. As usual, it was Sarah who answered. "We all handle it in different ways. Most of us find our own space and live there, as shielded as we can manage to be." She smiled at Matt. "I know it will help Kate to have you. Damon helps me."

"So far I haven't managed to keep her from wearing herself out. Every time I think we're going to get a little respite, the fog comes in again," Matt pointed out. He was extraordinarily happy that Sarah had accepted his relationship with Kate.

"You've helped enormously," Kate acknowledged.

Elle leafed through the journal. "You said there were symbols on the seal, Kate? Could you read it at all?"

"The first Drake settlers must have been the ones to seal the restless spirit, Elle. It was definitely formed around the time the town was settled. From what I could read, it was something about rage and sealing until one is born who could do something. I went back to take another look, but most of the seal was crushed and the actual writing lost," Kate admitted.

"Until one is born who can do something," Sarah repeated aloud. "Something to do with a voice."

"Here it is," Elle said triumphantly. "'He who will not receive forgiveness shall remain sealed until one is born who can give him peace.'"

There was a long silence. Matt stared at the cranberry candle as the three flames leaped and burned. Hot wax poured over the side like a lava flow, forming a thick pool around the holder. It was a fascinating sight, deep purple wax flowing almost like dark blood. "Why would he need peace?"

Elle pushed a pair of glasses on her nose and studied the faded writing. "One of the sisters who helped to seal the spirit must have had precognition the way Mom does. If that's the case, it means we should be able to find a way to allow him to rest."

"Unless the earthquake opened the crack in the ground and allowed him to escape before his time," Matt said.

"I doubt it," Sarah said seriously. "Things usually happen the way they're supposed to happen, Matthew. It's obviously our time. We have no choice but to figure this out. It's our destiny."

Matt wiped his hand over his mouth. He wasn't certain he believed in destiny. He felt Kate's hand in his hair and changed his mind. "Hannah, are you feeling any better?" She didn't look better. Without her, he wasn't positive they could have managed to get Elle back up the cliff in the midst of the thick fog or drive the entity out to sea and away from the townspeople time after time.

"I've been resting. Libby's helped."

Libby Drake. Matt looked at her. She was legendary in the small town. She was the only Drake with midnight black hair and pale, almost translucent skin. She was a natural-born healer, the real thing. He smiled at her. "It's good to see you again, Libby. Maybe you better hide out while you're home. If word gets out you're back, you'll have everyone in town lining up for a cure."

"I do want to visit Irene's son while I'm home. My sisters went to see him and did what they could to make him comfortable, but I promised I'd go see him."

"Libby—" Matt shook his head—"you know he has terminal cancer. Even you can't get rid of that." He waited. When no one said anything he looked at her. "Can you?" The idea was unsettling.

"I won't know until I visit him," Libby admitted.

"What would be the price?" Matt couldn't imagine what it would cost Libby to actually cure someone sent home to die.

Libby smiled at him. "I can see why Kate loves you so

much, Matt. You're very discerning. It's a trade-off. I might save one person, but while I'm recovering, I might lose a hundred others."

"That bad?" He reached his hand for Kate. The thought of what the women had to go through on a daily basis moved him. In their own way, they were warriors, and he had a deep respect for them.

"Does anyone want more tea? I'm getting another cup," Hannah volunteered.

"I can get it," Matt offered. He felt a little useless.

Hannah paused just a few feet from the entrance to the kitchen. "I'm already up, but thank you," she said, and took two steps, halting abruptly, staring at the flickering candle in the bay window facing the sea. "Sarah, you need to come look at this."

Matt got to his feet, pulled Kate up beside him. Apprehensively, he glanced out the large window to the sea. He already knew what he would see. Anytime anything strange happened, the fog was back, settling over the town like a smoky monster crouched and waiting.

"What is it, Sarah?" Elle asked from her position on the couch. She had pillows piled around her, a comforter over her, and strict orders to remain where she was.

"The wax is forming something as it runs down the sides," Sarah explained. "It looks like a hook to me."

"Or a candy cane." Matt was more pragmatic.

"It's a staff," Hannah corrected. "A long staff, or maybe a cane. Something used to walk with."

"This is getting more bizarre by the minute," Abbey said, rubbing her hands up and down her arms. "And while we're on the subject of bizarre, Joley, I'm sorry, but there was no excuse for your not telling the rest of us what happened. You take shielding all of us way too far."

Sarah's smile at Joley was gentle. "She's right, hon. You should have told us what happened. Do you have any other bad news you don't want to worry us with?"

Joley hesitated for a brief moment, then shrugged. "I'm sorry, I should have mentioned the strangling fog. Do you have any idea how ridiculous that sounds?" She burst out laughing.

Kate joined her. "I have to admit, it threw Christmas wreaths at me."

"And no one is going to believe the fog *pushed* me over the cliff," Elle said with a small grin. "This one will go into our journal and nowhere else!"

"I plan on telling our children," Matt announced. "It's a great story for around the campfire, and they aren't going to believe us anyway. They'll think I'm a brilliant storyteller."

"Children?" Joley raised her eyebrow. "I love the idea of Kate having children. Don't the Granites produce boys? Very large hungry boys?" Her sisters erupted into laughter while Kate covered her face and groaned.

"You aren't helping, Joley," Matt said, putting his arms protectively around Kate so she could hide her face against his shoulder. "She hasn't even agreed to marry me yet. Don't be scaring her off with the idea of little boys running around."

Sarah continued to study the wax flow over the sides of the candle. "Do you see anything else that could be helpful in that book, Elle?"

Elle rubbed at the bump on her head and frowned at

the thin pages. "There was no single predominant religion in the town at the time people first settled here. A faction celebrated the birthday of a pagan god. This is very interesting." Elle looked up at her sisters. "Many of the settlers here came together to celebrate their differences, unable to live anywhere else. The founding fathers wanted a safe haven by the sea, a place they envisioned would one day have a port for supplies. It actually says a lot about the town's founders and perhaps gives us insight to why the people here are so tolerant of others."

"And it explains why our own people settled here."

Kate nuzzled Matt's throat. "If I remember my grandmother and her history lessons correctly, she said Christmas was slow to catch on in America, that the colonists didn't celebrate it, and in some instances actually banned it."

"That's right." Joley snapped her fingers. "It was considered a pagan ritual in some places. But that was a long while before this town was settled, wasn't it?" She swept Elle's hair away from her face and fashioned it into a ponytail. "Does that have anything to do with all of this?"

"Thanks, Joley," Elle said. She smoothed the worn pages. "The townspeople wanted to celebrate the Christmas season and settled on a pageant. They asked everyone to participate regardless of their beliefs, just for the fun of it. They treated it more as a play, a production that included all town members, meant to be fun rather than religious." She looked up with a small smile. "Libby, our however-many-greats-grandmother has your very interesting handwriting. Aside from the language, I have to decipher the worst handwriting on the face of the earth."

"I do not have the worst handwriting on the face of the earth." Libby tossed a small pillow at her sister, missing by a great distance.

"There's something else in the wax," Sarah said. "All of you, look at this! Tell me what you see."

The sisters crowded around the cranberry candle. Kate tilted her head, studying it from every angle. "Where did you get this candle, Sarah? Is this one Mom made?"

"Yes, but I didn't know it would do this."

"Is a candle a symbol of Christmas?" Matt asked.

"Yes; some people say the light of the candle relieves the unrelenting darkness," Kate answered. "My mother makes incredible candles."

"I can imagine. Do they all do this?" Matt indicated the flowing wax.

"It's a face, I think," Sarah said. "Look, Abbey, don't you think it's a face?"

"That wouldn't surprise me." Matt peered at the thick pool of wax. "The spirit found feet, a coat and hat, and bones, why not get himself a face, even if it's made of wax. Does it have eyes? Maybe he wants to get a good look at us."

"Ugh." Kate made a face. "That's a horrible idea. It could never use one of Mom's candles for that. Mom instills a healing, soothing magic in each of them. We were the ones who forgot to guard our home. She insisted we make certain every time, but we just got complacent. I'm not forgetting this lesson for a very long time."

"Me either," Joley agreed.

"I think I found it now," Elle said in excitement. "Most

everyone wanted to participate with the exception of a small group of believers in the gods of the earth. They considered the pageant a Christian holiday celebration and felt it was wrong to participate. One of the most out-spoken said the pageant was evil and those participating would be punished. His brother-in-law, Abram Lynchman, went against his advice and allowed his wife and child to take part. Because he stood up to Johann, the rest of the group also decided to join the town in the pageant."

"Is this Johann angry because his flock was out of his control?" Joley asked.

Elle held up her hand for silence. Her hand went to her throat. Matt noticed that her hand was trembling. "Everyone helped with the production, bringing home-made candles and lanterns. The shepherd herded several sheep with his staff, and the sheep got away and ran through the crowd."

None of the sisters laughed. They were watching Elle's face intently. Matt glanced out the window to see the fog solidly in place. For some reason, his heart began to pound. The strange radar that always told him dan-ger was near was shrieking at him, even there in the warmth and safety of the Drakes' home.

"The people were having fun, laughing as the sheep rushed through the crowd with the shepherd running after them. The sheep panicked and ran straight into the small shelter the town had erected to use as the stable for the play. The shelter crumpled, knocking several candles into the dry straw. Fire spread along the ground and across the wooden planks used to make the shelter. Several participants were trapped under the debris, including Abram's wife and child." Elle had a sob in her voice. She shook her head. "I can't read this. I can't read the words. Anastasia, the one writing the journal, was there, she saw the entire thing, heard the cries, saw them die. Her emotions are trapped in the book. I can't read it, Sarah." She sounded as if she were pleading.

Matt wanted to comfort her. The feeling was so strong he actually stepped toward her before he realized he was feeling the emotions of Elle's sisters. They rushed to her side, Sarah pulling the book from her hands, Kate putting her arms around Elle. The others touched her, helping to absorb the long ago, very strong emotions still clinging to the pages of the journal.

"I'm sorry, honey," Sarah said gently, "I should have thought of that. You've been through so much already. Kate, do you think you can get an idea of what happened next? I wouldn't ask, but it's important." She held the book out to Kate.

Matt wanted to yank the book out of her hands and throw it. "Kate's been through enough with this thing, Sarah. You can't ask her to do anymore." He was furious. Enough was enough. "Elle almost died out there. Without Jackson, she would have. You have no idea what a miracle it was that she didn't end up at the bottom of the ocean."

Kate put a restraining hand on his arm. Sarah simply nodded. "I do realize what I'm asking, Matthew, and I don't blame you for being angry. I don't want Kate to touch the journal, but the truth is, if we don't know why this spirit is doing the things he's doing, someone very well could die. We have to know."

Kate took the book from Sarah's hand. Matt muttered a string of curses and turned away from them, feeling impotent. All of his training, his every survival skill, seemed utterly useless in the unfamiliar situation. Not wanting to look at Kate, not wanting to witness the strain and weariness on her face, he stared hard at the cranberry candle and the eerie flow of wax. He stared and stared, his heart suddenly in his throat. He took a step closer, stared down in a kind of terror. "Katie." He whispered her name because she was his world, his talisman. Because he needed her.

Kate put her arm around him, held him. He couldn't take his eyes from the face in the wax, praying he was wrong. Knowing he was right. She looked down and gasped. "Danny. It's Danny."

chapter

13

My last gift now, is a special one,
A candy cane for a special son,

He watches and tends and knows the land,
But not enough to evade my hand.

MATT TOOK KATE BY THE SHOULDERS AND SET her aside. She made a grab for him, but he was already moving swiftly for the front door.

"Danny's at the pageant rehearsal," Kate reminded him. She ran after him, tossing the journal onto the floor, trying to keep up with him. Hannah grabbed Kate's coat and hurried after both of them.

The fog obstructed Matt's vision, but he could hear the women. "Go back, stay in the house, Kate. It's too dangerous." His voice was grim. Authoritative. It made Kate shiver. He didn't sound at all like her Matthew.

"I'm coming with you. Stay to the left. The path leads down the hill to the highway. If we cross right beside the three redwood trees, like we did the other night, we'll end up quite close to the shortcut to town." Kate followed the sound of his voice. Hannah took her hand and held on tightly.

"Kate, dammit, this one time, listen to me. I have to find Danny, and I don't want to have to worry about what's happening to you."

Kate wished he sounded angry, but Matt's tone was chillingly cold. Ice-cold. She tightened her fingers around Hannah's hand but continued hurrying along the narrow path. "Hannah's with me, Matthew, and you're going to need us." She kept her voice very calm, very even. She ached for him and shared his rising alarm for the safety of his brother. The features in the wax had definitely been Daniel Granite. She had a strong feeling of impending doom.

Hannah pressed closer to her. "It's going to happen tonight, Katie." Her voice shook. "Should we try to clear the fog now?"

Matt loomed up in front of them, startling both of them, catching Kate by the shoulders. "It has never gone after me. Only you. Go with your sisters and work your magic. Clear the fog out of town, and this time get rid of it. I'll do what I can to keep Danny alive. I'm safe, Kate." His gray eyes had turned to steel. "I need to know you're as safe as possible in this mess."

She clung to him for just one moment, then nodded. "We'll be up on the captain's walk, where we can better bring in the wind."

Matt dropped a hard kiss on her upturned mouth, turned, and hurried down the narrow, well-worn trail. His mind was racing, working out the route the actors in the pageant used. Had they noticed the fog rolling in and taken shelter in one of the businesses along the parade route, or had they gone ahead with the rehearsal plans? Matt made it to the highway and stood listening for a moment in silence. He couldn't hear a car, but the fog seemed capable of muffling every sound. Still, he didn't want to wait. He felt a terrible sense of urgency, of his brother in acute danger. He cursed as he ran, nearly blind in the fog. It was only his training that kept him from being completely disoriented. He moved more from instinct than from sight, making his way toward the town square. Most of the committee meetings were held at the chamber of commerce building near the grocery store. The players were supposed to be rehearsing, though, and he doubted whether Inez would let a heavy fog and some entity she couldn't see change her plans.

He heard a shrill scream, the sounds of panic, and his heart stuttered. "Danny!" He called his brother's name, using the sheer volume of his voice to penetrate the cries coming out of the fog. He followed the sound of the voices, not toward the square, but away from it, back toward the park on the edge of town, where the river roared down through a canyon to meet the sea. The wall along the river was only about three feet high, made of stone and mortar. He nearly ran into it in his haste to reach Danny. At the last moment he sensed the obstruction and veered away, running parallel with it toward the cries.

He was getting closer to the sounds of the screams and calls. He heard Inez trying to calm everyone. He heard someone shout for a rope. The river, rushing over the rocks, added to the chaos in the heavy fog. "Danny!" Matt called again, trying to beat down his fear for his brother. Danny would have heard him, would have answered.

Right in front of him, Donna, the owner of the local gift shop, suddenly appeared. Her face was white and strained. He caught her shoulders. "What happened, Donna? Tell me!"

She grabbed both of his arms to steady herself. "The wall gave way. A group of the men were sitting on it. Your brother, the young Granger boy, Jeff's son, I don't know, more maybe. They just disappeared down the embankment, and all the rocks followed like a mini-avalanche. We can't see to help them. There were some groans, and we heard cries for help, but we can't see them at all. We tried to form a human chain, but the bank is too steep. Jackson went over the side by himself. He was crawling. I heard a terrible crack, now he's silent. I was going to try to find a telephone to call for help. The cell phones just won't work here."

"What was Jackson doing here?" He knew the deputy never participated in the town pageant. "Is Jonas here?" As he talked he was moving along the wall, feeling with his hands for breaks, taking Donna with him.

"Jackson happened to be driving by when the fog thickened. He was worried about us, I think, so he stayed. I haven't seen Jonas."

"Don't wander around in this fog. Hopefully, Kate and her sisters will move it out of here for us." He patted her arm in reassurance and left her, continuing the search for the break in the wall with an outstretched hand. When he found it, he swore softly. He knew the section of wall was over a steep drop and the river below had a fast-moving current running over several sub-merged boulders. The bank was littered with rocks of every size, with little to hold them in place should something start them rolling.

"Danny! Jackson!" His call was met with eerie silence. He began to crawl down the bank, distributing his weight, on his belly, searching with his hands before slid-ing forward. It was painstakingly slow. He didn't want to displace any more of the rocks in case his brother or any of the others were still alive and in the path of an avalanche.

Matt's fingertips encountered a leg. He forced himself to remain calm and used his hands to identify the man. Jackson was unconscious, and there was blood seeping from his head. In the near-blind conditions, it was impossible to assess how badly he was injured, but his breathing seemed shallow to Matt.

Something moved an arm's length below Jackson. Matt followed the outstretched arm and found another body. The Granger boy. Matt knew him to be sixteen or seventeen. A good kid. The boy moved again, and Matt cautioned him to stay still, afraid he would disturb the rocks.

"You okay, kid?" he asked.

"My arm's broken, and I feel like I've been run over by a truck, but I'm all right. The deputy told me not to move, and the next thing I knew he was somersaulting and smashed hard into the rock right there. He hasn't moved. Is he dead?"

"No, he's alive. What about the others? What about Danny?" He crawled around Jackson to get to the boy, to take his pulse and run his hands over him to examine him for other injuries.

"Tommy Dockins fell too. Danny tried to push him clear when the slide started. We didn't really have any time. I didn't see either of them, but Tommy's yelled for help a couple of times. I couldn't tell from which direction though."

The kid sounded tinny and distorted in the fog, and his voice shook, but he lay quietly and didn't panic. "Your name's Pete, right? Pete Granger?" Matt asked.

"Yes, sir."

"Well, I'm going to slide on around you and see if I can locate Danny and Tommy. Don't move. The fog will be gone soon, and Jonas is on the way with the rescue squad. If you move, you'll send the rest of those rocks right down on top of the others and me. Got it?"

"Yes, sir."

"I'll be back as quick as I can." Matt glanced in the direction of the cliff house, where the Drake family had lived for over a hundred years. He needed the modern-day women to work their magic, to remove the fog so he had a semblance of a chance to save his brother and Tommy and to get Jackson and Pete to safety.

"Come on, baby," he whispered, hoping the swirling clouds would take his voice to her. "Do this for me. Clear this mess out of here."

As if they could hear his words, the seven Drake sisters moved together out onto the battlement and faced the sea. Libby and Sarah both had their arms wrapped around Elle to aid her as they stood in the midst of the swirling fog.

Sarah looked up at the sky, to the roiling clouds gathered over Sea Haven and back to her sisters. "This troubled spirit is in terrible pain and does not believe there can be forgiveness for his mistake. He cannot forgive himself for what he believes to be bad judgment. I am certain his motive was to save others his sorrow. He believes that by halting the pageant, history will not repeat itself. He has lived this unbelievable nightmare repeatedly and needs to be able to forgive himself and go to his rest." She looked at Kate. "Your gift has always been your voice, Kate. I think the journal is referring to you. One born who can bring peace."

Kate could think only of Matt, somewhere out in the fog. She didn't want to be up on the captain's walk facing another struggle, she wanted to be with him. It was the first time in her life she had ever felt so divided around her sisters. She knew at that moment that she belonged with Matthew Granite. It didn't matter that she was an observer and he was a doer, she loved him, and she belonged with him.

As if reading her mind, Hannah took her hand, squeezed it tightly. "He's counting on you to do this, Kate. He's counting on all of us."

Kate took a steadying breath and nodded. She stepped away from Hannah, knowing Hannah would need room. Facing the small town invaded with the fog, Kate began to chant softly. An inquiry, no more, a soft plea to be heard. Her voice was carried on the smallest of breezes as Hannah faced the sea and lifted her arms, directing the wind as she might an orchestra.

Behind Kate, Joley and Abbey began to sing, a soft

melody of love and peace, harmonizing with Kate's incredible voice so they produced a symphony of hope. Power began to build in the wind itself, in the sky overhead. Lightning forked in the spinning clouds. Kate spoke of forgiveness, of unconditional love. Of a love of family that transcended time. She beckoned and cajoled. She pleaded for a hearing.

"You've touched him," Elle reported. "He's fighting the call. He's determined to keep the accident from happening. There is no past life or future life as he understands it, only watching his wife and child die a horrible death over and over, year after year." She staggered under the burden of the man's guilt, of his loss.

Kate didn't falter. Matt was out there somewhere in the fog, and she felt him reaching for her, counting on her. And she knew he was in danger. She talked of the townspeople coming together with every belief represented. Of the elderly and the young given the same respect. She spoke of a place that was a true haven for tolerance. And she spoke of forgiveness. Of letting go.

Power spread with the building wind. The ocean leaped in response. A pod of whales surfaced, flipping their tails, almost in unison, as if creating a giant fan. Joley's voice, a sultry purity that couldn't be ignored, swelled in volume, taking over the lead, while Abbey's voice joined in perfect harmony.

Hannah's voice called on the elements she knew and loved. Earth. Wind. Fire. Rain. Lightning flashed. The wind blew. Rain poured from the clouds. And still the power continued to build. Her hands moved in a graceful pattern as if conducting a symphony of magic.

Kate lured the spirit to her with promises of peace. Rest. A family waiting with open arms, holding him dear, not placing blame. An accident, not the hand of an ancient god angry that he had allowed his loved ones to participate in something different. Simply an unfortunate accident. Joley sang of Christmas, past, present, and future. Of a town committed to all the members celebrating together in a variety of ways. Of festivals for ancient gods and a gala for those who didn't believe. The two voices blended, one in song, one in storytelling, weaving a seamless creation to draw the lost soul back home.

Abbey lifted her voice finally, a call for those lost to welcome loved ones. As she could draw truth, so did she speak truth. She added her voice to the tapestry, promising peace and rest and final sleep in the arms with those he loved most.

"He's coming. He's beginning to believe, to want to take the chance," Elle said. "He's hesitant, but he's so utterly weary, and the idea of seeing his wife and child and resting in their arms is irresistible."

Libby raised her arms with Hannah, sending the promise of healing, not the body, but mind and soul. She added her power to the force of the wind, added her healing energy to Kate's soothing peace.

The wind increased in strength, blowing with the force of a small gale, tearing through Sea Haven, herding the fog, guiding it toward the sea. Toward the house on the cliff and the seven women who stood on the battlement, hand in hand. The feminine voices carried unbelievable power throughout the air, land, and sea. Rising on the wind. Calling. Promising. Leading.

And the fog answered. The thick gray vapor turned toward the sea, drifting reluctantly at first, tendrils feeling the way, hesitant and fearful. The voices swelled in strength. The wind blew through the fog.

Elle reached for Kate. "Now, Kate. Go to him now."

Kate never stopped talking in her beguiling voice, but she closed her eyes and deliberately entered the world of shadows. He was there. A tall, gaunt man with sorrow weighing him down. He looked at her and shook his head sadly. She held out her hand to him. Beside her, Elle stiffened as a beastly creature with glowing eyes and fur stared down at Kate with hate. As the snakelike vines slithered and coiled and hissed as if alive, wanting to get to her sister. Elle moved them, holding them back with the sheer force of her power, giving Kate the necessary time to lure the spirit of Abram to her.

Kate told a story of the love of a man for his wife and children. A man who made a courageous decision to go against what others said was right and allowed his family to participate in a production designed to bring people together. She spoke of laughter and fun and his pride in his family as he watched them. And the horror of a terrible accident. The candles and dry straw, the heavy planks coming down on so many. The man watching his loved ones die. The guilt and horror. The need to blame someone . . . to blame himself.

Joley and Abbey sang softly, the voice of a woman and child calling for the one they loved to join them. Kate used the purity of her voice, silver tones to draw him closer. The woman and child waited. Loved. Longed for him. His only job was to go to them, to forgive himself. There was no one to save but himself.

Kate kept her hand extended and pointed behind him. Clouds of dark gray fog drifted aside. He turned to see the shadows there. A woman. A child. Far off in the distance waiting.

There was a sharp cry like that of a seagull. The waves crashed against the cliff, rose high and frothed white. Lightning veined the clouds, forked into the very center of the fog. The flash lit up the shadows, throwing Kate out of that world and back into the reality of her own. She landed heavily on the wet surface of the captain's walk, in the middle of her sisters. Libby held her close.

"You're all right. It's all right now. You did it, Kate. You gave him peace," Sarah said.

"We did it," Kate corrected with a wan smile.

They sat together, too weary to move, the rain lashing down at them. Sarah turned her head to calculate the distance to the door. "Damon will be here with tea, but I don't think he can carry us back inside."

Elle draped herself over Abbey. "Who cares about going inside? I want to just lie here and look up at the sky."

"I want to know Matt's safe and that he was able to get to Danny," Kate said. "When Damon comes up, please have him call Jonas."

Matt scooted carefully down the steep bank, skirting rocks until it became impossible to go farther. He had no choice but to go over them.

"I'm Tommy, not Kate," a voice called weakly from his right side.

Matt didn't realize until that moment that he was whispering her name over and over like a prayer. He glanced up at the sky, felt the wind in his face, the first few drops of real rain. He felt power and energy crackling in the air around him. "Thank you, Katie, you are unbelievable." He said it fervently, meaning it. Already the fog was beginning to thin so that he could make out the boy lying a few feet from him. "Are you hurt?"

"I don't think so. I don't know what happened though. One minute I was falling off the fence and rolling, and the next Danny shoved me. I woke up a few minutes ago and when I tried to move, I dislodged several rocks. I didn't know where anyone was, so I thought I'd better just wait until help came."

Matt remained lying flat, searching carefully for Danny. The wind drove down through the canyon and shifted abruptly, coming back off the river. He caught sight of his brother a few yards away. Danny was lying facedown on the cliff over the water's edge, partially buried under debris. He wasn't moving. The pulse pounded in Matt's temples. He forced himself to go to the boy and examine him first. "You'll be fine. Just stay down until we can get help to you. I'm checking on Danny."

He took a deep breath and called toward the top. "Donna? Is Jonas here yet?"

"He's on his way along with the rescue squad," She yelled back.

"I'm working my way down to Danny. Everyone else is alive. Jackson looks the worst. Could be a concussion.

The entire mountainside is unstable. Tell them to be careful moving around up there until I can get Danny out of the avalanche zone."

Matt patted the teenage boy and proceeded to make painfully slow progress through the rocks. The smallest trickle of pebbles could bring down a tremendous storm of boulders on his brother. He inched his way through the rubble until he reached Danny's side.

Danny was precariously balanced at the edge of the bank. It was actually the rocks that saved his life, holding him pinned in the dirt. Matt was very gentle as he examined his brother. He couldn't find a single broken bone, but there were several lacerations, particularly on Danny's hands. His face was pushed hard into the dirt. He carefully turned Danny's head, scooping dirt from his mouth. Danny coughed, and the rocks slid. Some dislodged and one fell to the river below. "Don't move, Danny, don't even cough if you can help it," Matt instructed.

"Tell us what you need, Matt," Jonas shouted down to him.

"I've got to move Danny. When I do, everything above him is going to slide. You'll have to get Pete out of there and Jackson. When you move them, Jonas, don't disturb the rocks. If I take Danny now, there's a chance we'll lose those two. I'll shield my brother, just work fast."

Matt knew Jonas wouldn't bother to argue with him. There was no way Matt would leave his younger brother hanging out over the edge of the fast-moving river with an avalanche of boulders poised to slide. The Drake sisters had managed a miracle removing the fog, but there was still dangerous work to be done.

"Don't forget about me," Tommy called.

"We'll get you," Jonas promised.

"You're going to be just fine, Danny boy," Matt said, brushing more dirt from the lacerated face.

"Get out of here, Matt," Danny barely mouthed the words. "Breathing moves the rocks. If they're working up above, the boulders will smash us both."

"Have a little faith, bro, that's Jonas up there. Are you hurt?"

"What does it look like?"

Matt heard the ominous rumble above him. "Incoming," Jonas yelled from above them. Matt shifted so his upper body protected Danny's head. He put his arms over his own head and tried to shrink as rocks bounced down, knocking a few more loose. The rocks rained down and splashed into the river below. One glanced off his calf and rolled away, dislodging more rocks before it hit the water.

"Dammit, be careful." Matt could hear Jonas snarling at the rescue team. "If you can't move them without setting off a landslide, get the hell back up here and let someone else do that! You all right down there, Matt?"

"We're fine. Just be careful," he called back.

"You weigh more than the rocks do," Danny complained.

"You deserve it, scaring the hell out of me like this. Anything broken?"

"Naw. I'm a Granite. We're tough."

Matt rubbed his brother's head in a rough, affectionate gesture. He glanced up. "They've got Jackson and the boys out, and they're on the way to us. When we move you, Danny, the entire side of the bank is going to come down. I won't be able to be very gentle, but I'm not going to let anything happen to you."

"Just get me the hell out of here."

It was not an easy task. The rescuers inched their way down and worked out a coordinated plan to move Danny, knowing once they pulled him from under the pile of rocks it would set off an avalanche. Matt stayed beside his brother, joking, keeping Danny's spirits up. The men cleared as many of the rocks from Danny as they could without triggering the landslide. It was only the soft damp dirt that saved Danny from terrible injury or death. His body was pressed deep into the muck. They dug around him with painstaking slowness, careful not to disturb the precarious balance of boulders poised over their heads.

"Ready, Danny boy?" It was Matt who locked arms with his brother.

"More than ready." There was fear in Danny's eyes, but he winked at his older brother and managed a weak smile.

Matt didn't wait. They had cleared as much of the ground as possible out of the way of the landslide path so that Matt had a clear trail on the steep embankment to drag Danny quickly out of harm's way. He exerted his great strength, pulling his brother out from under the rocks, moving as fast as humanly possible. The rocks immediately crashed into the river, starting the avalanche. The boulders above, with nothing to hold them, rolled down, taking most of the embankment with it. Matt covered Danny's body a second time, waiting until the debris had cleared.

Danny tried to stand, but his brother held him down. "You made me come down here and play mud-cakes with you, you can just get on the stretcher and let the medics carry your butt to the hospital and check you out."

"I'm fine," Danny protested, as they strapped him into a litter. "I feel like an idiot," he said.

"That's good, Danny. You are an idiot." Matt took up a position at the head of the stretcher to help carry him up the steep bank. They were still cautious, worried about the unstable conditions, but managed to get him to the top without incident.

Danny protested more when they put him in the ambulance, but no one paid him any attention. Matt jumped in beside him, keeping one hand on his brother's shoulder. It wasn't until the doctors pronounced Danny bruised, but fine that Matt left him to go check on Jackson and the teens.

By the time he returned to the cliff house, he was tired and only wanting to hold Kate to him. The Drake sisters were sprawled in every chair of the living room, pale and drawn, all greeting him with their brilliant smiles.

Matt gathered Kate to him, holding her close. All he wanted to do was take her home with him where she belonged. She looked exhausted and in need of a hot meal and two or three days of sleep. Kate clung to him, turning her face up for his kiss, burrowing against him.

"I heard there was an accident on the river wall," she greeted.

"Everyone's fine. Shook up, but fine. Did Jonas stop by?"

She shook her head. "Inez called to make certain we

were all right. She knew we must have cleared out the fog and that we would be exhausted. She told us what happened. Jackson's in the hospital, but the two boys were treated and released. She said Jackson's going to be fine." Her smile was slow coming but bright. "I have a feeling he'll make a terrible patient."

"Somehow I think you're right. Danny was treated and released also. He's bruised from head to toe, but he didn't have a single major injury." There was elation in Matt's voice. "He's hoping Inez will upgrade his part next year in the pageant due to his, quote, 'heroism.' It was pretty dicey, Kate. Thanks for all you did."

"We all did it. I could never have managed without my sisters. I'm so glad your brother is fine. The pageant just wouldn't be the same without him in his annual role as the shepherd. Speaking of the pageant—" She broke off as her sisters burst out laughing.

Matt's head went up suspiciously. He was beginning to know the Drake sisters, and their laughter heralded trouble for him. He was certain of it.

"Inez sent over a costume she made for the third wise man. A king," Kate said brightly. "She asked if you would be willing to fill the role at the last minute and of course, with Inez being so distressed, we said we were certain you'd want to help out."

He stiffened. "I'd rather be boiled in oil."

"Acting runs in your family," she pointed out.

He held up his hand. "You can't look at me with those eyes while you're weak and tired, it's unfair tactics."

"I know, Matthew," she said. "I'm trying not to, but Inez is such a good friend, and I couldn't bear her being so upset. The pageant is important to the town after all the near accidents. We need to get our confidence back."

"And I have to be in the pageant in order for our town to do that?" He raised one eyebrow skeptically.

"All you have to do is walk through the town. No lines, nothing awful. You don't mind, do you?"

"Does wanting to be boiled in oil instead sound like I want to do this?"

She turned her face into his chest. Pressed her lips against his skin.

He growled, deep in his throat. The growl turned into a groan. "I can see what my life's going to be like. I'll do it. This one time. Never again."

"Thank you." She kissed him again. "I just want to go home with you and sleep in your arms," she said, uncaring that her family could hear her. "Let's go home, Matthew."

Matt kissed her gently, her lips, her throat, bringing her hand to his mouth as elation swept through him. She had said, "Let's go home." He lifted her with ease. "I'll take good care of her," he promised her family.

Sarah nodded. "We have every confidence that you will, Matt."

chapter
14

All deeds are now done, forgiveness is mine,
As two people share a love for all time.

"WE'RE GOING TO BE LATE," KATE SAID, EVADing Matt's outstretched hand. "We promised the committee you'd be on time. We didn't make rehearsals, and everyone's worried you're going to mess up their play."

"I wasn't the one who agreed to wear that silly-looking robe Inez made. *You* agreed I'd wear it! Is it my fault they lost a couple of their stars to a scandalous affair?" He stalked her through the house, one slow step at a time.

Kate laughed and dodged around the table, putting a chair between them. "You theater people are always involved in scandals."

He moved the chair out of the way and proceeded to back her into a corner. "I'd be more than willing to cause a scandal. Just let me get my hands on you."

"I don't think so. Inez is probably watching her clock and tapping her foot. I'm not about to get a lecture about the benefits of being on time. Put on your costume!"

"I am in my costume. What king travels by starlight from one country to another and wears a satin bathrobe with cheesy lightning bolts sewn all over it? And I doubt very much if he sat on that camel naked under the robe."

Kate held her stomach, laughing so hard she could barely manage to squeak through a small opening he'd left beside the counter. "Somehow I think Inez might object to the idea that you were running around naked in her kingly robes. I, however, am rather intrigued by the idea." She backed down the hallway, holding her hand palm out. "Seriously, Matthew, she'll reprimand you in front of the entire town if you're late."

She was nearing the entrance to the bedroom. His silver eyes gleamed with anticipation. "If you think that's more humiliating than wearing this damned robe, which, by the way, is two sizes too small, you're sadly mistaken. I think Bruce had the affair with Sylvia just to get out of wearing it."

She pressed her hand to her mouth to keep an undignified giggle from emerging. "I think it looks dashing on you." He was right; the robe looked utterly ridiculous on him. His huge muscles strained the material so that it stretched tight over his wide shoulders and back. Instead of reaching the ground, it was halfway up his calves, and the front gaped open to reveal . . . She laughed. "I think it has interesting possibilities."

He spread his arms wide and rushed her, using an old football tackle. She screamed and turned to run, but he caught her up and carried her across the floor to the bed, where he unceremoniously dropped her. The kingly robe made its way to the floor. "I'm the king, and I demand my rights."

Kate pushed one hand against his chest to fend him off. "You have no rights. Inez has you under contract, and you're supposed to be *on time*. Do you want the entire town waiting for you?"

"I wouldn't mind in the least." He caught her legs, pinning her to the bed, stopping her from scooting away from him. "I think everyone should wait on me. I have this tremendous need to see your breasts. Why don't you unbutton your blouse for me?"

"It doesn't have buttons, oh mighty King."

"Who the hell cares," he growled. "Get rid of the shirt."

"I think that robe went to your head." Excitement raced through her, curled heat in her deepest core. She drew the blouse obediently over her head so that her full breasts spilled over the fine white cups of her bra. "Is this what you're looking for?" She slid her hand over her skin, drawing his attention to the taut peaks.

Matt reached to draw the zipper of her jeans down. "Exactly like that." There was a husky catch to his voice, the playfulness slipping away as he tugged the material from her body. He left her sexy little thong. "Every time I see that thing, I want to take it off with my teeth," he admitted, and bent to the task.

Kate enjoyed the feel of his hands on her body. Big hands. Capable. Nearly covering her buttocks as he lifted her hips and teased her skin with his teeth. Just that fast she was swamped with heat, her body flushed and alive and in desperate need. The thought of the Christmas pageant went out of her head, and much more erotic thoughts took its place. His mouth was everywhere, his tongue teasing and dancing, his teeth pulling at the only barrier between him and his goal.

She felt the sudden release as the material parted, the cool air mingling with her own heat, then the plunging of his tongue going deep while she nearly came off the bed, air bursting from her lungs in a wild rush. It was only his hands holding her down that kept her open to him while he made certain she not only was prepared for him, but that she hungered for him. Laughing, he slid his body over hers, settling over her soft form, gripping her hips to pull her to meet the hard thrust as he joined them together.

"I think that kingly robe works just fine," Kate managed to say, in between gasps of pleasure.

"Maybe I'll keep it if it gets this kind of results," he teased. He began to move, a slow assault on her senses, driving deep, needing her body, needing to feel the way she welcomed him. The heat and fire. Flames licking over his skin. "I love watching you when we make love," he admitted. She was so completely abandoned in the way she gave herself to him.

Kate loved the way he watched her. There was desire etched into the lines of his face. There was hunger in the depths of his eyes. There was steel in his body and a fine hot heat that made her flame, catch fire, and burn with passion. "I love making love with you," she told him, sliding her arms around his neck to draw his head down to hers.

"That's a good thing, Katie." His teeth nibbled at her

chin, her full bottom lip. "Because I think we're going to be spending a lot of time doing just that."

Kate gave herself up to the sheer glory of his body driving so deeply into hers. The pressure built and built, and she dug her fingers into his shoulders, holding on as they soared together in perfect unison.

He lay over her, fighting for his breath, trying to slow his heart rate.

"You're laughing," she observed. "I told you, your entire family laughs at me."

"I can't help it, Kate. And I'm laughing at me. I feel like one of those sappy men who run around with a big grin on his face all the time. I feel like grinning all the time around you, and it's so idiotic."

Kate's answering smile was slow. She rubbed her face against his chest. "I'm just beginning to realize how much I mean to you, Matthew."

He kissed her tenderly, his hands framing her face. "I adore you. Why else would I ever put that horrible robe on in front of the entire town?"

Kate looked smug. "And you know what I'll be thinking about when you come walking down the street looking sexy and kingly."

"I'll tell you what you'd better be thinking, Katie." He took a deep breath. "You'd better be thinking, 'here comes the man I intend to marry.'" He feathered kisses along the corners of her mouth. "Marry me, Kate. Spend your life with me."

She looked up at his beloved face. Her fingers slid through his hair in a loving caress. "I don't climb mountains or swim seas, Matthew. I sit in the corner and read books. I'm not at all brave. You have to be very sure that it's me you want."

"More than anything in the world, Kate. You. With you I have everything."

"Well, I guess that kingly robe is lucky after all." She kissed his throat, his chin. Found his mouth with hers and poured heat and fire and promises into her kiss.

He responded just the way she knew he would, his arms wrapping her close, his body coming alive, growing hard and thick deep inside her. He made love to her slowly, leisurely, as if they had all the time in the world and the entire town wasn't waiting on them. He made a thorough job of it. Kate felt like the most important person in the world. And the happiest.

They lay on the bed in a tangle of arms and legs, fighting to breathe. She turned her head to look at him. "I'm thinking you should wear that robe more often, Matthew."

He snorted his derision and glanced at his watch. "Kate! We're late."

"I told you we were late."

"Not this late, we're holding up the parade." He hastily leaped off her, looking around for his clothes. Kate laughed at him through the entire drive to the park where the members of the production were assembling. He caught Kate by the hand and ran across the lawn to the pavilion.

"Where have you been?" Inez demanded, gesturing toward the huge crowd assembled along the streets. "We've all been waiting for you."

"*And,*" Danny added, "you didn't answer your cell

phone." He shook his head, hands on his hips, clucking like an old hen. "You aren't even in that lovely costume Inez made for you. What have you been doing?" He wiggled his eyebrows at Kate.

"Are you feeling all right, Danny," Kate asked.

He tugged her hair affectionately. "I'm fine, but don't tell Trudy, she's babying me. And Mom's worse."

Inez all but stamped her foot. "Why are you late?"

"Kate made me late," Matt told Inez, and the interested group of actors crushed together to see the fireworks when Inez told Matt off. Matt exchanged a long, slow smile with Kate while he listened to Inez politely.

"I believe him," Jonas said. "You know how the Drake sisters are. Barbie doll alone takes three hours to get ready for anything. Put them all together, it could take days."

Kate glared at both former Rangers and took Hannah's hand. "Why aren't you participating this year, Jonas?" she asked sweetly. "Inez, didn't he promise you last year? I could have sworn Sarah told me Jonas really wanted to play a major role."

"He likes to stand out," Hannah added, smiling at Inez. "If you don't offer him a lead, he won't cooperate. You know Jonas. He has to be the star."

Inez turned to the sheriff. "Why didn't you sign up this year?"

"I didn't sign up," Matt pointed out.

"We don't have time for this argument," Jonas said, glaring at Kate. "Traffic is going to be backed up from here to hell and back. Get this show on the road, Inez, or we'll have to shut it down."

Inez began barking orders like a drill sergeant. Hannah nudged Jonas. "Don't look so smug. I'm putting your name in for the role of donkey next year. I'm certain Inez will come up with a suitable costume."

Deliberately the sheriff leaned into her, so close her body was pressed up against his. "That's great, baby doll, as long as you're the one riding me." He breathed the words against her ear, then stalked away from her.

The wind rushed over him and sent his hat sailing toward the river. He glanced back, his grin wide. "You have such a bad temper, Hannah. Merry Christmas."

Matt tried to cling to Kate but was dragged firmly away and forced into his satin costume. He did his best not to notice the other actors hiding their smiles behind their hands as they looked at him, or that Inez and Donna looked horrified. The streets were lined with townspeople, from the oldest to the youngest. Even Sylvia had turned up, with one side of her face covered in a red rash.

The parade began, and Matt was forced to endure trudging through the streets where everyone could see Inez's bizarre creation. The other two wise men went before him. He thought they looked somewhat ridiculous in their robes of velvet, but if he squinted enough, he could use the word *regal*. Cursing the fact that his costume looked more like a woman's bathrobe than a king's robe, Matt thought it took an eternity to get through town, with everyone singing slightly off-key, and to finally catch sight of the town square. Worse, he couldn't prevent the silly grin from breaking out on his face. It just wouldn't go away, and he knew it had to look like he was enjoying parading through town in a woman's bathrobe. He knew Kate and her sisters had grabbed a spot near the makeshift stables to wait for him, and he kept a sharp eye out for them. He let out a sigh of relief when he finally spotted them.

"You look really good in that satin robe, bro," Danny declared, nudging his brother with the hooked end of his staff.

"Shut up, Danny, or I'm going to kick your butt," Matt threatened out of the side of his mouth. He kept his eyes straight ahead, trudging like a man doomed, carrying his gift of frankincense on a white satin pillow out in front of him. He'd argued the wise men hadn't had white satin pillows to use carrying the foul-smelling stuff, but not a single person had listened, and his protests had earned him a black scowl from Inez. He kept his eyes straight ahead, not looking at the waving townspeople as he marched stoically onward to the town square with his silly grin on his face.

Danny whistled at him. "That robe manages to show your butt off nicely, Matt." He tapped the offending part of Matt's anatomy with the staff again. "Sorry, little accident, couldn't help myself."

"I hope you have life insurance," Matt said in his most menacing voice. He made the mistake of looking up to judge the distance to the square. He had to know the exact amount of time he would have to suffer further humiliation. Kate stood there with her sisters. Every last one of them had a huge smile on her face. Matt entertained the idea of throwing the frankincense at their feet and hauling Kate over his shoulder like the Neanderthal they all thought he was. He'd keep the robe, it might come in handy.

Danny poked him with the staff again. "Get along there little dogie," he teased.

Matt's furious gaze settled on Old Man Mars. He stood slightly apart, watching the pageant with a peculiar look on his face, somewhere between mortification and shock. It was obvious he shared Matt's view of the idiotic robes. The old man caught his eye, read the pain on Matt's face, and stepped closer to commiserate. He walked alongside Matt.

"She made you do this, didn't she?" Mars asked.

"Damn right. Otherwise, I wouldn't be caught dead in this getup," Matt replied, hope beginning to stir.

Mars nodded as if he understood Matt's total misery and stepped back away from him with his arms folded. Behind him, Danny began the mantra. "Don't say it. Don't say it. Don't say it." He glanced nervously at the old man as he approached him.

"Merry Christmas." Matt turned back with a cheerful grin. "Merry Christmas, Mr. Mars," he said happily.

A black scowl settled over Old Man Mars's face. His craggy brows drew together in a straight thick line. He made a single sound of disgust and spat on the ground. The old man delivered his yearly kick right to Danny's shin and shuffled off, muttering something about tomatoes. Danny howled and jumped around, holding his injured shin. The staff swung around in a wide circle so that the participants had to break ranks and run for safety. Matt kept walking straight past Inez and the outraged look on her face. Kate met him at the stable, lifting her face for his kiss, while Inez followed Danny, giving him her annual Christmas lecture on behavior.

"All in all, Katie," Matt said, holding her close, "I'd say this was a very satisfactory pageant."

epilogue

"So, did your wish come true?" Sarah asked.

Matt reached out to take the snow-globe from her, turning it over and over in his hands. He looked across the room at Kate. His Kate. The flames leaped and danced in the fireplace. The Drake sisters were decorating a live tree they'd brought in for Christmas Day. The next day they would plant it on their property near the many other trees that marked the passing of the years.

The house smelled of cedar and pine and cinnamon and spice. Berry candles adorned the mantel and the aroma of fresh-baked cookies drifted from the kitchen. Jonas appeared in the doorway of the kitchen. Red and green frosting smeared his face and fingers, and an apron covered his clothes. "No one asked me if my wish came true," he complained.

"You're such a baby, Jonas," Joley informed him with a little sniff. She caught the apron strings and dragged him backward. "You were the one who said there was nothing to baking cookies, and we should try our hand at doing it the old-fashioned way."

Jonas escaped and raced back into the living room.

"*You! You!*" he protested. "*Women* bake cookies. That's what they do. They sit around the house looking pretty and hand their man a plate of cookies and a drink when he comes home."

Jonas grinned at the women tauntingly. Matt groaned and covered his face with his hands, looking between his fingers. He already felt power moving in the air. Curtains swayed. Hair stood up. Crackles of electricity snapped and sizzled. The flames on the candles and in the fireplace leaped and danced. Jonas watched the sisters, clearly expecting reprisal. It came from behind him. The small fish tank lifted into the air and tilted part of the contents over Jonas's head. Water rushed over his head. He stiffened, but he didn't turn around, nor did he attempt to wipe it off.

"I just want to point out that this is Christmas Day," he said. "And you all just came back from church."

Joley sat down at the upright, perfectly tuned piano. "And we're all feeling full of love and goodwill, Jonas. Which is why you aren't swimming in the sea with the sharks right now. Shall I play something cheerful?"

"Oh, please do, Joley," Hannah entreated wickedly. "I'm feeling *very* cheerful."

"You would be," Jonas muttered. He took the towel Libby handed him and wiped off his face and hair.

Hannah blew him a kiss.

"Matt didn't answer my question," Sarah persisted.

"The globe only works for family," Abbey said.

Music swelled in volume, filling every corner of the house with joy. Matt heard the sound of feminine laughter, felt his heart respond. Kate walked around the tree, an ornament in her hand. She moved with grace and elegance, his perfect Kate. Feeling the weight of his gaze, she looked across the room at him and smiled.

"Yes, that's true, Abbey," Sarah said. "It only works for family. Matt? Did the globe grant your wish?"

He cleared his throat. "Yes." The affirmation came out on a husky note.

Joley's fingers stilled on the piano. She turned to look at him. Libby put her hand out to Hannah. Abbey put her arm around Elle. All of the Drakes looked at Matt. Kate's sisters. The magical witches of Sea Haven. He thought he fit in rather nicely.

"What did you wish for, Matthew?" Sarah asked. She sat down in Damon's lap, wrapping her arms around his neck.

"I wished for Katie, of course," he answered honestly.

Kate walked over to him, leaning down to kiss him. "I wished for you," she whispered aloud.

"So that little jewelry box in your jacket pocket means something?" Elle asked.

"It means Kate said yes," Matt said. He believed his grin was a permanent fixture on his face.

Jonas shook his head, still mopping up the water. "You got her to say yes just by wishing on that snowglobe?"

"That's what it took," Matt said. "But they say it only works for family. I guess it acknowledged that Katie belonged with me."

"Really? It can reason all that out, can it?" Jonas stared at the snowglobe sitting so innocently on the shelf. "Family, huh? Well, I've been family for about as long as I can remember."

A collective gasp went up from the seven Drake sisters as Jonas reached for the snowglobe.

"No! Jonas, don't touch that." Hannah sounded frightened.

"You can't, Jonas," Sarah said.

His hand hovered over it. Matt could swear he heard hearts beating loudly in the sudden silence. Jonas picked up the globe. Almost at once it sprang to life, the tiny lights on the tree glowing, the fog beginning to swirl.

"Jonas, put it down right now and step away from it," Joley warned.

"You can't play with things in this house," Elle added. "They can be dangerous."

"Jonas," Abbey said, "it isn't funny."

Jonas turned toward the women, his hands absently cradling the globe. "Aren't you all supposed to be cooking dinner for us? Jackson's going to be here any minute, expecting the full Christmas fare, and all he's going to get is some cookies I made." As he spoke, he kept his gaze on Hannah. All the while his palm rubbed the globe as if he could conjure up a genie.

"Don't you *dare* wish on that globe, Jonas Harrington," Hannah hissed. She actually backed a step away from him. "I'm sorry about the fish tank. And the silly hat thing as well. Just put the globe down and keep your mind blank. We'll call it even."

"Are you watching this, Matt?" Jonas asked, clearly taunting Hannah. "This is called power."

"Not for long," Kate said. She held out her hand for the globe. "Hand it over and stop tormenting Hannah. We're liable to serve you up dragon's liver for dinner."

"All right," Jonas agreed. He looked into the glass. "It's certainly beautiful." Instead of giving it to her, he stared into it for a long moment. The fog swirled into a frenzy, obliterating the house until only the lights on the tree blazed, then it slowly subsided, leaving the glass clear and the lights fading away. Only then did he hand it over to Kate.

There was a long silence. Jonas grinned at them. "I'm teasing. You all take things so seriously." He nudged Matt. "I'm not a dreamer like my friend here. I wouldn't let a snowglobe decide my fate. Come on, let's get that turkey carved."

Kate accepted Matt's kiss and watched him go into the kitchen with Damon and Jonas. She joined her sisters as she did each year in surrounding the tree, hands connecting them in a continuous circle. The overhead lights went off, leaving them in the shadows with the flickering candles and Christmas lights. She felt the familiar power running up and down her arms. Running through her. Tiny sparks leaped into the air like little fireflies. Electricity crackled around them. She could feel the minuscule threads in the tapestry of power that wove them together. Energy sprang from one to the other.

Matt stood in the doorway with Damon and Jonas and Jackson, who had come in through the kitchen, and watched the seven women as they stood hand in hand circling the Christmas tree. The women looked beautiful and fey, with their heads thrown back and the sparks leaping around them like miniature fireworks.

Jonas nudged him. "Welcome to the world of the Drake sisters, Matt. And Merry Christmas."

Matt couldn't imagine a better one.

AFTER THE MUSIC

❄ dedication ❄

For Manda and Christina, may you always be survivors.
Much love.

❄ acknowledgments ❄

Special thanks to Dr. Mathew King for all of his help with
the research needed for this book. Also to Burn Survivors
online. Thank you for your courtesy and patience and all
the offers of help. And of course, to Bobbi and Mark
Smith of the Holy Smoke Band, who gave me their time
and help with my persistent questions.

chapter 1

JESSICA FITZPATRICK WOKE UP screaming, her heart pounding out a rhythm of terror. Fear was a living, breathing entity in the darkness of her room. The weight of it crushed her, held her helpless; she was unable to move. She could taste it in her mouth, and feel it coursing through her bloodstream. Around her, the air seemed so thick that her lungs burned for oxygen. She knew something monstrous was stirring deep in the bowels of the earth. For a moment she lay frozen, her ears straining to hear the murmur of voices rising and falling, chanting words in an ancient tongue that should never be spoken. Red, glowing eyes searched through the darkness, summoning her, beckoning her closer. She felt the power of those eyes as they neared, focused on her, and came ever closer. Her own eyes flew open; the need to flee was paramount in her mind.

The entire room lurched, flinging her from the narrow bunk to the floor. At once the cold air brought her out of her nightmare and into the realization that they were not safe in their beds at home, but in the cabin of a wildly pitching boat in the middle of a ferocious storm. The craft, tossed from wave to powerful wave, was taking a pounding.

Jessica scrambled to her feet, gripping the edge of the bunk as she dragged herself toward the two children, Tara and Trevor Wentworth, who clung together, their faces pale and frightened. Tara screamed, her terrified gaze locked on Jessica. Jessica managed to make it halfway to the twins before the next wild bucking sent her to floor again.

"Trevor, get your life jacket back on this minute!" She reached them by crawling on her hands and knees, and then curled a supporting arm around each of them. "Don't be afraid, we'll be fine."

The boat rose on a wave, teetered and slid fast, tossing the three of them in all directions. Salt water poured in a torrent onto the deck and raced down the steps into the cabin, covering the floor with an inch of ice-cold water. Tara screamed, and clutched at her brother's arm, desperately trying to help him buckle his life jacket. "It's him. He's doing this, he's trying to kill us."

Jessica gasped, horrified. "Tara! Nobody controls the weather. It's a storm. Plain and simple, just a storm. Captain Long will get us safely to the island."

"He's hideous. A monster. And I don't want to go." Tara covered her face with her hands and sobbed. "I want to go home. Please take me home, Jessie."

Jessica tested Trevor's life jacket to make certain he was safe. "Don't talk that way, Tara. Trev, stay here with Tara while I go see what I can do to help." She had to shout to make herself heard in the howling wind and booming sea.

Tara flung herself into Jessica's arms. "Don't leave me—we'll die. I just know it—we're all going to die just like Mama Rita did."

Trevor wrapped his arms around his twin sister. "No, we're not, sis, don't cry. Captain Long has been in terrible storms before, lots of them," he assured. He looked up at Jessica with his piercing blue eyes. "Right, Jessie?"

"You're exactly right, Trevor," she agreed. Jessica had a firm hold on the banister and began to make her way up the stairs to the deck.

Rain fell in sheets; black clouds churned and boiled in the sky. The wind rose to an eerie shriek. Jessica held her breath, watched as Long struggled to navigate the boat through the heavier waves, taking them ever closer to the island. It seemed the age-old struggle between man and nature. Slowly, through the sheets of rain, the solid mass of the island began to take shape. Salt water sprayed and foamed off the rocks but the sea was calmer as they approached the shore. She knew it was only the captain's knowledge of the region and his expertise that allowed him to guide the craft to the dock in the terrible storm.

The rain was pouring from the sky. The clouds were so black and heavy overhead that the night seemed unrelentingly dark. Yet Jessica caught glimpses of the moon, an eerie sight with the swirling black of the clouds veiling its light.

"Let's go, Jessie," Captain Long yelled. "Bring up the

kids and your luggage. I want you off this boat now." The words were nearly lost in the ferocity of the storm, but his frantic beckoning was plain.

She hurried, tossing Trevor most of the packs while she helped Tara up the stairs and across the slippery deck. Captain Long lifted Tara to the dock before aiding Trevor to shore. He caught Jessica's arm in a tight grip and pulled her close so he could be heard. "I don't like this—Jess, I hope he's expecting you. Once I leave you, you're stuck. You know he isn't the most pleasant man."

"Don't worry." She patted his arm, her stomach churning. "I'll call if we need you. Are you certain you don't want to stay overnight?"

"I'll feel safer out there," he gestured toward the water.

Jessica waved him off and turned to look up at the island while she waited to get her land legs back. It had been seven years since she'd last been to the island. Her memories of it were the things of nightmares. Looking up toward the ridge, she half expected to see a fiery inferno, with red and orange flames towering to the skies, but there was only the black night and the rain. The house that once had sat at the top of the cliff overlooking the ocean was long gone, reduced to a pile of ashes.

In the dark, the vegetation was daunting, a foreboding sight. The weak rays of light from the cloud-covered moon were mottled as they fell across the ground, creating a strange, unnatural pattern. The island was wild with heavy timber and thick with brush; the wind set the trees and bushes dancing in a macabre fashion. Naked branches bowed and scraped together with a grating sound. Heavy evergreens whirled madly, sending sharp needles flying through the air.

Resolutely, Jessica took a deep breath and picked up her pack, handing Trevor a flashlight to lead the way. "Come on, kids, let's go see your father."

The rain slashed down at them, drenching them, drops piercing like sharp icicles right through their clothes to their skin. Heads down, they began to trudge their way up the steep stone steps leading away from the sea toward the interior of the island where Dillon Wentworth hid from the world.

Returning to the island brought back a flood of memories of the good times—her mother, Rita Fitzpatrick, landing the job as housekeeper and nanny to the famous Dillon Wentworth. Jessica had been so thrilled. She had been nearly thirteen, already old enough to appreciate the rising star, a musician who would take his place among the greatest recording legends. Dillon spent a great deal of his time on the road, touring, or in the studio, recording, but when he was home, he was usually with his children or hanging out in the kitchen with Rita and Jessica. She had known Dillon in the good times, during five years of incredible magic.

"Jessie?" Trevor's young voice interrupted her reflection. "Does he know we're coming?"

Jessica met the boy's steady gaze. At thirteen, Trevor had to be well aware that if they had been expected, they wouldn't be walking by themselves in the dead of night in the middle of a storm. Someone would have met them by car on the road at the boathouse.

"He's your father, Trevor, and it's coming up on Christmas. He spends far too much time alone." Jessica slicked back her rain-wet hair and squared her shoulders. "It isn't good for him." And Dillon Wentworth had a responsibility to his children. He needed to look after them, to protect them.

The twins didn't remember their father the way she did. He had been so alive. So handsome. So everything. His life had been magical. His good looks, his talent, his ready laugh and famous blue eyes. Everyone had wanted him. Dillon had lived his life in the spotlight, a white-hot glare of tabloids and television. Of stadiums and clubs. The energy, the power of Dillon Wentworth were astonishing, indescribable, when he was performing. He burned hot and bright on stage, a man with a poet's heart and a devil's talent when he played his guitar and sang with his edgy, smoky voice.

But at home . . . Jessica also remembered Vivian Wentworth with her brittle laugh and red, talon-tipped fingers. The glaze in her eyes when she was cloudy with drugs, when she was staggering under the effects of alcohol, when she flew into a rage and smashed glass and ripped pictures out of frames. The slow, terrible descent into the madness of drugs and the occult. Jessica would never forget Vivian's friends who visited when Dillon wasn't there. The candles, the orgies, the chanting, always the chanting. And men. Lots of men in the Wentworth bed.

Without warning, Tara screamed, turning to fling herself at Jessica, nearly knocking her off the stairs. Jessica caught her firmly, wrapping her arms around the girl and holding her close. They were both so cold they were shivering uncontrollably. "What is it, honey?" Jessica whispered into the child's ear, soothing her, rocking her, there on the steep stairs with the wind slashing them to ribbons.

"I saw something, eyes glowing, staring at us. They were red eyes, Jess. Red, like a monster . . . or a devil." The girl shuddered and gripped Jessica harder.

"Where, Tara?" Jessica sounded calm even though her stomach was knotted with tension. Red eyes. She had seen those eyes.

"There." Tara pointed without looking, keeping her face hidden against Jessica. "Through the trees, something was staring at us."

"There are animals on the island, honey," Jessica soothed, but she was straining to see into the darkness. Trevor valiantly tried to shine the small circle of light toward the spot his twin had indicated, but the light couldn't penetrate the pouring rain.

"It wasn't a dog, it wasn't, Jessie, it was some kind of demon. Please take me home, I don't want to be here. I'm so afraid of him. He's so hideous."

Jessica took a deep breath and let it out slowly, hoping to stay calm when she suddenly wanted to turn and run herself. There were too many memories here, crowding in, reaching for her with greedy claws. "He was scarred terribly in a fire, Tara, you know that." It took effort to keep her voice steady.

"I know he hates us. He hates us so much he doesn't ever want to see us. And I don't want to see him. He *murdered* people." Tara flung the bitter accusation at

Jessica. The howling wind caught the words and took them out over the island, spreading them like a disease.

Jessica tightened her grip on Tara, gave her a short, impatient shake. "I *never* want to hear you say such a terrible thing again, not *ever*, do you understand me? Do you know why your father went into the house that night? Tara, you're too intelligent to listen to gossip and anonymous phone callers."

"I saw the papers. It was in all the papers!" Tara wailed.

Jessica was furious. *Furious.* Why would someone suddenly, after seven years, send old newspapers and tabloids to the twins? Tara had innocently opened the package wrapped in a plain brown paper. The tabloids had been brutal, filled with accusations of drugs, jealousy, and the occult. The speculation that Dillon had caught his wife in bed with another man, that there had been an orgy of sex, drugs, devil worship, and murder, had been far too titillating for the scandal sheets not to play it up long before the actual facts could come out. Jessica had found Tara sobbing pitifully in her room. Whoever had seen fit to enlighten the twins about their father's past had called the house repeatedly whispering horrible things to Trevor and Tara, insisting their father had murdered several people including their mother.

"Your father went into a burning house to save you kids. He thought you were both inside. Everyone who had gotten out tried to stop him, but he fought them, got away, and went into a burning inferno for you. That isn't hate, Tara. That's love. I remember that day, every detail." She pressed her fingers to her pounding temples. "I can't ever forget it no matter how much I try."

And she had tried. She had tried desperately to drown out the sounds of chanting. The vision of the black lights and candles. The scent of the incense. She remembered the shouting, the raised voices, the sound of the gun. And the flames. The terrible greedy flames. The blanket of smoke, so thick one couldn't see. And the smells never went away. Sometimes she still woke up to the smell of burning flesh.

Trevor put his arm around her. "Don't cry, Jessica. We're already here, we're all freezing, let's just go. Let's have Christmas with Dad, make a new beginning, try to get along with him this time."

Jessica smiled at him through the rain and the tears. Trevor. So much like his father and he didn't even realize it. "We're going to have a wonderful Christmas, Tara, you wait and see."

They continued up the stairs until the ground leveled out and Jessica found the familiar path winding through the thick timber to the estate. As islands went, in the surrounding sea between Washington and Canada, it was small and remote, no ferry even traveled to it. That was the way Dillon had preferred it, wanting privacy for his family on his own personal island. In the old days, there had been guards and dogs. Now there were shadows and haunting memories that tore at her soul.

In the old days the island had been alive with people, bustling with activities; now it was silent, only a caretaker lived somewhere on the island in one of the smaller houses. Jessica's mother had told her that Dillon tolerated only one older man on his island on a regular basis. Even in the wind and rain, Jessica couldn't help noticing the boathouse was ill-kept and the road leading around and up toward the house was overgrown, showing little use. Where there had always been several boats docked at the pier, none were in sight, although Dillon must still have had one in the boathouse.

The path led through the thick trees. The wind was whipping branches so that overhead the canopy of trees swayed precariously. The rain had a much more difficult time penetrating through the treetops to reach them, but drops hitting the pathway plopped loudly. Small animals rustled in the bushes as they passed.

"I don't think we're in Kansas anymore," Trevor quipped, with a shaky smile.

Jessica immediately hugged him to her. "Lions and tigers and bears, oh, my," she quoted just to watch the grin spread across his face.

"I can't believe he lives here." Tara sniffed.

"It's beautiful during the day," Jessica insisted, "give it a chance. It's such a wonderful place. The island's small, but it has everything."

They followed a bend, stumbling a little over the uneven ground. Trevor's flashlight cast a meager circle of light on the ground in front of them, which only served to make the forest darker and more frightening as it surrounded them. "Are you certain you know the way, Jess? You haven't been here in years," he said.

"I know this path with my eyes closed," Jessica assured

him. Which wasn't exactly the truth. In the old days, the path had been well manicured and had veered off toward the cliff. This one was overgrown and led through the thick part of the forest toward the interior of the island, rising steadily uphill. "If you listen, you can hear the water rushing off to our left. The stream is large right now, but in the summer it isn't so strong or deep. There are ferns all along the bank." She wanted to keep talking, hoping it would keep fear at bay.

All three of them were breathing hard from the climb, and they paused to catch their breath under a particularly large tree that helped to shelter them from the driving rain. Trevor shined the light up the massive tree trunk and into the canopy, making light patterns to amuse Tara. As he whirled the light back down the trunk, the small circle illuminated the ground a few feet beyond where they were standing.

Jessica stiffened, jammed a fist in her mouth to keep from screaming, and yanked the flashlight from Trevor to shine it back to the spot he had accidentally lit up. For one terrible moment she could hardly breathe. She was certain she had seen someone staring at them. Someone in a heavily hooded long black cloak that swirled around the shadowy figure as if he were a vampire from one of the movies the twins were always watching. Whoever it was had been staring malevolently at them. He had been holding something in his hands that glinted in the flash of light.

Her hand was shaking badly but she managed to find the place where he had been with the flashlight's small circle of light. It was empty. There was nothing, no humans, no vampires in hooded cloaks. She continued to search through the trees, but there was nothing.

Trevor reached out and caught her wrist, pulling her hand gently to him, taking the flashlight. "What did you see, Jess?" He sounded very calm.

She looked at them then, ashamed of showing such naked fear, ashamed the island could reduce to her to that terrified teenager she once had been. She had hoped for so much: to bring them all together, to find a way to bring Dillon back to the world. But instead she was hallucinating. That shadowy figure belonged in her nightmares, not in the middle of a terrible rainstorm.

The twins were staring up at her for direction. Jessica shook her head. "I don't know, a shadow maybe. Let's just get to the house." She pushed them ahead of her, trying to guard their backs, trying to see in front of them, on both sides.

With every step she took, she was more convinced she hadn't seen a shadow. She hadn't been hallucinating. She was certain something, *someone* had been watching them. "Hurry, Trevor, I'm cold," she urged.

As they topped the rise, the sight of the house took her breath away. It was huge, rambling, several stories high with round turrets and great chimneys. The original house had been completely destroyed in the fire and here, at the top of the rise, surrounded by timber, Dillon had built the house of his boyhood dreams. He had loved the Gothic architecture, the lines and carvings, the vaulted ceilings, and intricate passageways. She remembered him talking with such enthusiasm, spreading pictures on the counter in the kitchen for her and her mother to admire. Jessica had teased him unmercifully about being a frustrated architect and he had always laughed and replied he belonged in a castle or a palace, or that he was a Renaissance man. He would chase her around with an imaginary sword and talk of terrible traps in secret passageways.

Rita Fitzpatrick had cried over this house, telling Jessica how Dillon had clung to his dreams of music and how he had claimed that having the house built was symbolic of his rise from the ashes. But at some point during Dillon's months at the hospital, after he'd endured the pain and agony of such terrible burns and after he realized that his life would never return to normal, the house had become for him, and all who knew him, a symbol of the darkness that had crept into his soul. Looking at it, Jessica felt fear welling inside her, a foreboding that Dillon was a very changed man.

They stared at the great hulk, half expecting to see a ghost push open one of the shutters and warn them off. The house was dark with the exception of two windows on the third story facing them, giving the effect of two eyes staring back at them. Winged creatures seemed to be swarming up its sides. The mottled light from the moon lent the stone carvings a certain animation.

"I don't want to go in there," Tara said, backing away. "It looks . . ." she trailed off, slipping her hand into her brother's.

"Evil," Trevor supplied. "It does, Jess, like one of those haunted houses in the old movies. It looks like it's staring at us."

Jessica bit at her lower lip, glancing behind them, her

gaze searching, wary. "You two have seen too many scary movies. No more for either of you." The house looked far worse than anything she had ever seen in a movie. It looked like a brooding hulk, waiting silently for unsuspecting prey. Gargoyles crouched in the eaves, staring with blank eyes at them. She shook her head to clear the image. "No more movies, you're making me see it that way." She forced a small, uneasy laugh. "Mass hallucination."

"We're a small mass, but it works for me." There was a trace of humor in Trevor's voice. "I'm freezing; we may as well go inside."

No one moved. They continued to stare up at the house in silence, at the strange animating effect of the wind and the moon on the carvings. Only the sound of the relentless rain filled the night. Jessica could feel her heart slamming hard in her chest. They couldn't go back. There was something in the woods. There was no boat to go back to, only the wind and piercing rain. But the house seemed to stare at them with that same malevolence as the figure in the woods.

Dillon had no inkling they were near. She thought it would be a relief to reach him, that she would feel safe, but instead, she was frightened of his anger. Frightened of what he would say in front of the twins. He wouldn't be pleased that she hadn't warned him of their arrival, but if she had called, he would have told her not to come. He always told her not to come. Although she tried to console herself with the fact that his last few letters had been more cheerful and more interested in the twins, she couldn't deceive herself into believing he would welcome them.

Trevor was the first to move, patting Jessica on the back in reassurance as he took a step around her toward the house. Tara followed him, and Jessica brought up the rear. At some point the area around the house had been landscaped, the bushes shaped, and beds of flowers planted, but it looked as though it hadn't been tended in quite a while. A large sculpture of leaping dolphins rose up out of a pond on the far side of the front yard. There were statues of fierce jungle cats strewn about the wild edges of the yard, peering out of the heavier brush.

Tara moved closer to Jessica, a small sound of alarm escaping her as they gained the slate walkway. All of them were violently shivering, their teeth were chattering, and Jessica told herself it was the rain and cold. They made it to within yards of the wraparound porch with its long thick columns when they heard it. A low, fierce growl welled up. It came out of the wind and rain, impossible to pinpoint but swelling in volume.

Tara's fingers dug into Jessica's arms. "What do we do?" she whimpered.

Jessica could feel the child shivering convulsively. "We keep walking. Trevor, have your flashlight handy—you may need it to hit the thing over the head if it attacks us." She continued walking toward the house, taking the twins with her, moving slowly but steadily, not wanting to trigger a guard dog's aggressive behavior by running.

The growl rose to a roar of warning. Lights unexpectedly flooded the lawn and porch, revealing the large German shepherd, head down, teeth bared, snarling at them. He stood in the thick brush just off the porch, his gaze focused on them as they gained the steps. The dog took a step toward them just as the front door was flung open.

Tara burst into tears. Jessica couldn't tell if they were tears of relief or fear. She embraced the girl protectively.

"What the hell?" A slender man with shaggy blond hair greeted them from the doorway. "Shut up, Toby," he commanded the dog.

"Get them the hell off my property," another voice roared from inside the house.

Jessica stared at the man in the doorway. "Paul?" There was utter relief in her voice. Her shoulders sagged and suddenly tears burned in her own eyes. "Thank God you're here! I need to get the kids into a hot shower and warm them up immediately. We're freezing."

Paul Ritter, a former band member and long-time friend of Dillon Wentworth, gaped at her and the twins. "My God, Jess, it's you, all grown up. And these are Dillon's children?" He hastily stepped back to allow them entrance. "Dillon, we have more company. We need heat, hot showers, and hot chocolate!" As wet as she was, Paul gathered Jessica in his arms. "I can't believe you three are here. It's so good to see you. Dillon didn't say a word to me that you were coming. I would have met you at the dock." He shut the door on the wind and rain. The sudden stillness silenced him.

Jessica stared up at the shadowy figure on the staircase. For a moment she stopped breathing. Dillon always had that effect on her. He lounged against the wall, looking elegant and lazy, classic Dillon. The light spilled across his face, his angel's face. Thick blue-black hair fell in waves to his shoulders, as shiny as a raven's wing. His sculptured face, masculine and strong, had that hint of five o'clock shadow along his jaw. His mouth was so sensual, his teeth amazingly white. But it was his eyes, vivid blue, stunningly blue, burning with intensity that always mesmerized everyone, including Jessica.

Jessica felt Tara stir beside her, staring up in awe at her father. Trevor made a soft sound, almost of distress. The blue eyes stared down at the three of them. She saw joy, a welcoming expression of surprise dawning on Dillon's face. He stepped forward and gripped the banister with both hands, a heart-stopping grin on his face. He was wearing a short-sleeved shirt and his bare hands and arms were starkly revealed as if the spotlight had picked up and magnified every detail. Webs of scarred flesh covered his arms, wrists, and hands. His fingers were also scarred and misshapen. The contrast between his face and his body was so great it was shocking. That angel's face and the twisted, ridged arms and hands.

Tara shuddered visibly and flung herself into Jessica's arms. At once Dillon slipped back into the shadows, the welcoming smile fading as if it had never been. The burning blue eyes had gone from joyful to ice-cold instantly. His gaze raked Jessica's upturned face, slid over the twins, and came back to her. His sensual mouth tightened ominously. "They're freezing, Paul; explanations can wait. Please show them to the bathrooms so they can get out of those wet clothes. You'll need to prepare a couple more bedrooms." He started up the darkened stairway, taking care to stay well in the shadows. "And send Jess up to me the minute she's warm enough." His voice was still that perfect blend of smoke and edginess, a lethal combination that could brush over her skin like the touch of fingers.

Her heart beating in her throat, Jessica stared after him. She turned to look at Paul. "Why didn't you tell me? He can't play, can he? My God, he can't play his music." She knew what music meant to Dillon. It was his life. His soul. "I didn't know. My mother never brought me back. She came the one time with the twins, but I was ill. When I tried to see him on my own, he refused."

"I'm sorry." Tara was crying again. "I didn't mean to do that. I couldn't stop looking at his hands. They didn't look human. It was *repulsive*. I didn't mean to do that, I didn't. I'm sorry Jessie."

Jessica knew the child needed comfort badly. Tara felt guilty and was tired, frightened, and very cold. Shaken by what she had discovered, Jessica had to fight back her own tears. "It's all right, honey, we'll find a way to fix this. You need a hot shower and a bed. Everything will be better in the morning." She looked at Trevor. He was staring up the stairway after his father as if mesmerized. "Trev? You okay?"

He nodded, clearing his throat. "I'm fine, but I don't think he is."

"That's why we're here," she pointed out. Jessica looked at Paul over Tara's bent head. She didn't believe for a minute that they'd find a way to fix the damage Tara had done, and looking at Paul's face, she guessed, neither did he. She forced a smile. "Tara, you might not remember him, you were just a little girl, but this is Paul Ritter.

He was one of the original members of the *HereAfter* band, right from the very beginning. He's a very good friend of your family."

Paul grinned at the girl. "The last time I saw you, you were five years old with a mop of curly black hair." He held out his hand to Trevor. "You had the same mop and the same curls."

"Still do," Trevor said, grinning back.

chapter
2

 THICK STEAM CURLED through the bathroom, filling every corner like an unnatural
fog. The tiled bathroom was large and beautiful with its deep bathtub and hanging plants. After
her long, hot shower, Jessica was feeling more human,
but it was impossible to see much with the steam so
thick. She towel-dried the mirror, staring at the reflection of her pale face. She was exhausted, wanting only
to sleep.

The last thing she wanted to do was face Dillon
Wentworth looking like a frightened child. Her green
eyes were too big for her face, her mouth too generous,
her hair too red. She had always wished for the sophisticated, elegant look, but instead, she got the girl-next-
door look. She peered closer at her reflection, hoping she
seemed more mature. Without make-up she appeared
younger than her twenty-five years. Jessica sighed, and
shook her head in exasperation. She was no longer a child
of eighteen, but a grown woman who had helped to raise
Tara and Trevor. She wanted Dillon to take her seriously,

to listen to what she had to say and not dismiss her as he might a teenager.

"Don't be dramatic, Jess," she cautioned aloud, "don't use words like 'life and death'. Just be matter-of-fact." She was trembling as she pulled on a dry pair of jeans, her hands shaking in spite of the hot shower. "Don't give him a chance to call you hysterical or imaginative." She hated those words. The police had used them freely when she'd consulted them after the twins had been sent the old tabloids and the phone calls had started. She was certain the police thought her a publicity-seeker.

Before she did anything else, she needed to assure herself the twins were being taken care of. Paul had shown her to a room on the second floor, a large suite with a bathroom and sitting room much like in a hotel. Jessica knew why Dillon had his private home built that way. In the beginning, he would have clung to the idea that he would play again. He would compose and record, and his home would be filled with guests. She ached for him, ached for the talent, the musical genius in him that must tear at his soul night and day. She couldn't imagine Dillon without his music.

She wandered down the wide hallway to the curving staircase. The stairs led up another story or down to the main floor. Jessica was certain she would find the twins in the kitchen and Dillon up on the third floor so she went downstairs, delaying the inevitable. The house was beautiful, all wood and high ceilings and stained glass. It had endless rooms that invited her to explore, but the sound of Tara's laughter caught at her and she hurried into the kitchen.

Paul grinned at her in greeting. "Did you follow the smell of chocolate?" He was still as she remembered him, too thin, too bleached, with a quick, engaging smile that always made her want to smile with him.

"No, the sound of laughter." Jessica kissed Tara and ruffled her hair. "I love to hear you laugh. Are you feeling better, honey?" She looked better, not so pale and cold.

Tara nodded. "Much. Chocolate always helps, doesn't it?"

"They're both chocolate freaks," Trevor informed Paul. "You have no idea how scary it gets if there's no chocolate in the house."

"Don't listen to him, Mr. Ritter," Tara scoffed. "He loves chocolate, too."

Paul burst out laughing. "I haven't had anyone call me Mr. Ritter in years, Tara. Call me Paul." He leaned companionably against the counter next to Jessica. "I had the distinct feeling Dillon had no idea you were coming. What brought you?"

"Christmas, of course," Jessica said brightly. "We wanted a family Christmas."

Paul smiled, but it didn't chase the shadows from his dark eyes. He glanced at the twins and bit off what he might have said. "We have more company now than we've had in years. The house is full, sort of old home week. Everyone must have had the same idea. Christmas, huh?" He rubbed his jaw and winked at Tara. "You want a tree and decorations and the works?"

Tara nodded solemnly. "I want a big tree and all of us decorating it like we did when Mama Rita was alive."

Jessica looked around the large kitchen, closer to tears

than she would have liked. "It looks the same in here, Paul. It's the same kitchen that was in the old house." She smiled at the twins. "Do you remember?" The thought that Dillon had had her mother's domain reproduced exactly warmed her heart. They had spent five happy years in the kitchen. Vivian had never once entered it. They had often joked that she probably didn't even know the way. But Tara, Trevor, and Jessica had spent most of their time in or near that sanctuary. It was a place of safety, of peace. A refuge when Dillon was on the road and the house was no longer a home.

Trevor nodded. "Tara and I were just talking about it with Paul. It feels like home in here. I expected to find the cupboard I scratched my name into."

Paul caught Jessica's elbow, indicating with a jerk of his head to follow him out of the room. "You don't want to keep him waiting too long, Jessie."

With a falsely cheery wave at the twins, she went with him reluctantly, somersaults beginning in the pit of her stomach. Dillon. She was going to face him after all this time. "What did you mean, old home week? Who's here, Paul?"

"The band. Even though Dillon can't play the way he used to, he still composes. You know how he is with his music. Someone got the idea to record a few songs in his studio. He has an awesome studio, of course. The sound is perfect in it, all the latest equipment, and who could resist a Dillon Wentworth song?"

"He's composing again?" Joy surged through her. "That's wonderful, just what he needs. He's been alone far too long."

Paul matched her shorter strides on the stairs. "He's having a difficult time being around anyone. He doesn't like to be seen. And his temper . . . He's used to having his own way, Jessica. He isn't the Dillon you remember."

She heard something in his voice, something that sent alarm bells ringing in her head. She looked sideways at him. "I don't expect him to be. I know you're warning me off, trying to protect him, but Trevor and Tara need a father. He may have gone through a lot, but so did they. They lost their home and parents. Vivian might not have counted, they barely knew her and what they remember isn't pleasant, but he abandoned them. Add it up any way you like, he retreated and left them behind."

Paul stopped on the second floor landing, looking up the staircase. "He went through hell. Over a year in the hospital, so they could do what they could for his burns, all those surgeries, the skin grafts, and through it all, the reporters hounding him. And, of course, the trial. He went to court covered in bandages like a damned mummy. It was a media circus. Television cameras in his face, people staring at him like he was some freak. They wanted to believe he murdered Vivian and her lover. They wanted him to be guilty. Vivian wasn't the only one who died that night. Seven people died in that fire. They made him out to be a monster."

"I was here," Jessica reminded him softly, her stomach revolting at the memories. "I crawled through the house on my hands and knees with two five-year-olds, Paul. I pushed them out a window and followed them. Tara rolled down the side of the cliff and nearly drowned in the ocean. I didn't get her out of the sea and make my way around to the other side of the house in time to let Dillon know we were safe." She had been so exhausted after battling to save Tara who could barely stay afloat. She had wasted precious time lying on the shore with the children, her heart racing and her lungs burning. While she'd been lying there, Dillon had fought past the others and run back into the burning house to save the children. She pressed a hand to her head. "You think I don't think of it every day of my life? What I should have done? I can't change it, I can't go back and do it over." Guilt washed over her, through her, so that she felt sick with it.

"Jessica." Dillon's voice floated down the stairs. No one had a voice like Dillon Wentworth's. The way he said her name conjured up night fantasies, vivid impressions of black velvet brushing over exposed skin. He could weave spells with that voice, mesmerize, hold thousands of people enthralled. His voice was a potent weapon and she had always been very susceptible.

Jessica grasped the banister and went up to him. He waited at the top of the stairs. It saddened her to see that he had changed and was wearing a long-sleeved white shirt that concealed his scarred arms. A pair of thin black leather gloves covered his hands. He was thinner than in the old days, but still gave the impression of immense power that she remembered so vividly. He moved with grace, a sense of rhythm. His body didn't just walk across a stage, it flowed. He was only nine years older than she, but lines of suffering were etched into his face, and his eyes reflected a deep inner pain.

"Dillon." She said his name. There was so much more, so many words, so many emotions rising up out of the ashes of their past. She wanted to hold him close, gather him into her arms. She wanted him to reach for her, but she knew he wouldn't touch her. Jessica smiled instead, hoping he would see how she felt. "I'm so glad to see you again."

There was no answering smile on his face. "What in the world are you doing here, Jessica? What were you thinking, bringing the children here?"

His face was a mask she couldn't penetrate. Paul was right. Dillon wasn't the same man any longer. This man was a stranger to her. He looked like Dillon, he even moved like Dillon, but there was a cruel edge to his mouth where before there had been a ready smile and a certain sensuality. His blue eyes had always burned with his intensity, his drive, his wild passions, his joy of life. Now they burned a piercing ice-blue.

"Are you taking a good look?" He had a way of twisting his words right at the end, a different accent that was all his own. His words were bitter but his voice was even, cool. "Look your fill, Jess, get it out of your system."

"I'm looking, Dillon. Why not? I haven't seen you in seven years. Not since the accident." She kept her voice strictly neutral when a part of her wanted to weep for him. Not for the scars on his body, but the ones far worse, the ones on his soul. And he was looking at her, his gaze like a rapier as it moved over her, taking in every detail. Jessica would not allow him to rattle her. This was too important for all of them. Tara and Trevor had no one else to fight for them, for their rights. For their protection. And neither, it seemed, did Dillon.

"Is that what you believe, Jessica? That it was an accident?" A small, humorless smile softened the edge of his mouth but made his eyes glitter like icy crystals. He turned away from her and led the way to his study. Dillon stepped back, gestured for her to precede him. "You're much more naive than I ever gave you credit for being."

Jessica's body brushed up against his as she stepped past him to enter his private domain. At once she became aware of him as a man, her every nerve ending leaping to life. Electricity seemed to arc between them. He drew in his breath sharply and his eyes went smoky before he turned away from her.

She looked around his study, away from him and his virility, and found it to be comforting. It was more like the Dillon she remembered. All warm leather, golds and browns, warm colors. Books were in floor-to-ceiling shelves, glass doors guarding treasures. "The fire was an accident," she ventured, feeling her way carefully with him.

The ground seemed to be shifting out from under her feet. This house was different, and yet the same as the one she remembered. There were places of comfort that could quickly disappear. Dillon was a stranger, and there was something threatening in his glittering gaze. He watched her with the same unblinking menace of a predator. Uneasily, Jessica seated herself across from him with the huge mahogany desk between them, feeling she was facing a foe, not a friend.

"That's the official verdict, isn't it? Funny word, official. You can make almost anything official if you write it up on paper and repeat it often enough."

Jessica was uncertain how to reply. She had no idea

what he was implying. She twisted her fingers together, her green eyes watching him intently. "What are you saying, Dillon? Do you think Vivian started the fire on purpose?"

"Poor neglected Vivian." He sighed. "You bring back too many memories, Jess, ones I can do without."

In her lap, her fingers twisted together tightly. "I'm sorry for that, Dillon. Most of my memories of you are wonderful and I cherish them."

He leaned back in his chair, carefully positioned to keep his body in the deeper shadows. "Tell me about yourself. What have you been doing lately?"

Her green gaze met his blue one squarely. "I have a degree in music and I work at Eternity Studios as a sound engineer. But I think you know that."

He nodded. "They say you're brilliant at it, Jess." He watched her mouth curve and his body tightened in reaction. Actually hardened, in a heavy, throbbing ache. He was fascinated by her mouth and his fascination disgusted him. It brought up too many sins he didn't want to think about. Jessica Fitzpatrick should never have walked back into his life.

"You moved the house away from the cliffs," she said.

"I never liked it there. It wasn't safe." His blue eyes slid over her figure, deliberately appraising. Almost insulting. "Tell me about the men in your life. I presume you have one or two? Did you come here to tell me you've found someone and you're dumping the kids?" The idea of it enraged him. A volcanic heat that erupted into his bloodstream to swirl thick and hot and dangerous.

There was an edge to him, one she couldn't quite nail down. As soon as she focused on something, he shifted and moved so that she was thrown off balance. Their conversation seemed more like one of the chess matches they'd often played in her mother's kitchen so many years earlier. She was no match for him in sparring and she knew it. Dillon could cut the heart out of someone with a smile on his face. She'd seen him do it, charming, edgy, saying the one thing that would shatter his opponent like glass.

"Are we at war, Dillon?" Jessica asked. "Because if we are, you should lay out the rules for me. We came here to spend Christmas with you."

"Christmas?" He nearly spat the word. "I don't do Christmas."

"Well, we do Christmas, your children, your family, Dillon. You remember family, don't you? We haven't seen you in years; I thought you might be pleased."

His eyebrow shot up. "Pleased, Jess? You thought I'd be pleased? You didn't think that for a minute. Let's have a little honesty between us."

Her temper was beginning a slow smolder. "I doubt if you know the meaning of honesty, Dillon. You lie to yourself so much it's become a habit." She was appalled at her own lack of control. The accusation slipped out before she could censor it.

He leaned back in his leather chair, his body sprawled out, lazy and amused, still in the shadows. "I wondered when your temper would start to surface. I remember the old days when you would go up in flames if someone pushed you hard enough. It's still there, hidden deep, but you burn, don't you, Jess?"

Dillon remembered it all too vividly. He'd been a

grown man, for God's sake, nearly twenty-seven with two children and an insane drug addict for a wife. And he'd been obsessed with an eighteen-year-old girl. It was sick, disgusting. Beyond his every understanding. Jessica had always been so alive, so passionate about life. She was intelligent; she had a mind that was like a hungry sponge. She shared his love of music, old buildings, and nature. She loved his children. He'd never touched her, never allowed himself to think of her sexually, but he had noticed every detail about her and he detested himself for that weakness.

"Are you purposely goading me to see what I'll do?" She tried not to sound hurt, but was afraid it showed on her face. He always noticed the smallest detail about everyone.

"Damn right I am," he suddenly admitted, his blue eyes glittering at her, his lazy, indolent manner gone in a flash. "Why the hell did you bring my children all this way, scaring the hell out of them, risking their lives . . ." He wanted to strangle her. Wrap his hands around her slender neck and strangle her for wreaking havoc with his life again. He couldn't afford to have Jessica around. Not now. Not ever.

"I did not risk their lives." Her green eyes glared at him as she denied the charge.

"You risked them in that kind of weather. You didn't even call me first."

Jessica took a deep breath and let it out slowly. "No, I didn't call. You would have said not to come. They belong here, Dillon."

"Jessica, all grown up. It's hard to stop thinking of you

as a wild teen and accept that you're a grown woman." His tone was sheer insult.

Her chin lifted. "Really, Dillon, I would have thought you would have preferred to think of me as a much older woman. You certainly were willing to leave Trevor and Tara with me after Mama's death, no matter what my age."

He rose from his chair, moving quickly across the room, putting distance between them. "Is that what this is about? You want more money?"

Jessica remained silent, simply watching him. It took a great deal of self-control not to get up and walk out. She allowed the silence to stretch out between them, a taut, tension-filled moment. Dillon finally turned to look at her.

"That was beneath even you, Dillon," she said softly. "Someone should have slapped your face a long time ago. Are you expecting me to feel sorry for you? Is that what you're looking for from me? Pity? Sympathy? You're going to have a long wait."

He leaned against the bookcase, his blue eyes fixed on her face. "I suppose I deserved that." His gloved fingers slid along the spine of a book. Back and forth. Whispered over the leather. "Money has never held much allure for you or your mother. I was sorry to hear of her death."

"Were you? How kind of you, Dillon, to be sorry to hear. She was my mother and the mother of your children, whether you want to acknowledge that or not. My mother took care of Tara and Trevor almost from the day they were born. They never knew any other mother. They were devastated at losing her. I was devastated. Your kind gesture of flowers and seeing to all the arrangements . . . lacked something."

He straightened, pulled himself up to his full height, his blue eyes ice-cold. "My God, you're reprimanding me, questioning my actions."

"What actions, Dillon? You made a few phone calls. I doubt that took more than a few minutes of your precious time. More likely you asked Paul to make the phone calls for you."

His dark brow shot up. "What did you expect me to do, Jessica? Show up at the funeral? Cause another media circus? Do you really think the press would have left it alone? The unsolved *murders* and the fire were a high profile case."

"It wasn't about you, Dillon, was it? Not everything is about you. All that mattered to you was that your life didn't change. It's been eleven months since my mother's death and it didn't change, did it? Not at all. You made certain of that. I just stepped right into my mother's shoes, didn't I? You knew I'd never give them up or let them go into foster care. The minute you suggested hiring a stranger, maybe breaking them up, you knew I'd keep them together."

He shrugged, in no way remorseful. "They belonged with you. They've been with you their entire life. Who better than you, Jessica? I already knew you loved them, that you would risk your life for them. Tell me why I was wrong not to want the best for my children?"

"They belong with you, Dillon. Here, with you. They need a father."

His laughter was bitter, without a trace of humor. "A

father? Is that what I'm supposed to be, Jessica? I seem to recall my earlier parenting skills. I left them with their mother in a house on an island with no fire department. Do you remember that as vividly as I do? Because, believe me, it's etched in my brain. I left them with a mother who I knew was out of her mind. I knew she was flying on drugs, that she was unstable and violent. I knew she brought her friends here. And worse, I knew she was fooling around with people who were occultists. I let them into my home with my children, with you." He raked gloved fingers through his black hair, tousling the unruly curls so that his hair fell in waves around the perfection of his face.

He pushed away from the bookcase, a quicksilver movement of impatience, then stalked across the floor with all the grace of a ballet dancer and all the stealth of a leopard. When had his obsession started? He only remembered longing to get home, to sit in the kitchen and watch the expressions chasing across Jessica's face. He wrote his songs about her. Found peace in her presence. Jessica had a gift for silences, for laughter. He watched her all the time, and yet, in the end, he had failed her, too.

"Dillon, you're being way too hard on yourself," Jessica said softly. "You were so young back then, and everything came at once—the fame and fortune. The world was upside down. You used to say you didn't know reality, what was up or what was down. And you were working, making it all come together for everyone. You had so many others who needed the money you generated. Everyone depended on you. Why should you expect that you would have handled everything so perfectly? You weren't responsible for Vivian's decisions to use drugs nor were you responsible for any of the things she did."

"Really? She was clearly ill, Jess. Whose responsibility was she if not mine?"

"You put her in countless rehabs. We all heard her threaten to commit suicide if you left her. She threatened to take the kids." She threatened a lot more than that. More than once Vivian had rushed to the nursery, shouting she would throw the twins in the foaming sea. Jessica pressed a hand to her mouth as the memory rose up to haunt her. He had tried to get her committed, to put her in a psychiatric hospital, but Vivian was adept at fooling the doctors, and they believed her tales of a philandering husband who wanted her out of the way while he did drugs and slept with groupies. The tabloids certainly supported her accusations.

"I took the easy way out. I left. I went on the road and I left my children, and you, and Rita, to her insanity."

"The tour had been booked for a long time," Jessica pointed out. "Dillon, it's all water under the bridge. We can't change the things that happened, we can only go forward. Tara and Trevor need you now. I'm not saying they should live with you, but they should have a relationship with you. You're missing so much by not knowing them, and they're missing so much by not knowing you."

"You don't even know who I am anymore, Jess," Dillon said quietly.

"Exactly my point. We're staying through Christmas.

That's nearly three weeks and it should give us plenty of time to get to know each other again."

"Tara finds me repulsive to look at. Do you think I would subject a child of mine to my own nightmare?" He paced across the hardwood floor, a quick restless movement, graceful and fluid, so reminiscent of the old Dillon. There was so much passion in him, so much emotion, he could never contain it. It flowed out of him, warmed those around him so that they wanted to bask in his presence.

Jessica was sensitive to his every emotion, she always had been. She could practically see his soul bleeding, cut so deeply the gash was nearly impossible to heal. But agreeing with his twisted logic wouldn't help him. Dillon had given up on life. He had locked his heart from the world and was determined to keep it that way. "Tara is only thirteen years old, Dillon. You're doing her an injustice. It was a shock to her, but it's unfair to keep her out of your life because she had a childish reaction to your scars."

"It will be better for her if you take her away from here."

Jessica shook her head. "It'll be better for you, you mean. You aren't thinking of her at all. You've become selfish, Dillon, living here, feeling sorry for yourself."

He whipped around, taking her breath away with his speed. He was on her before she had a chance to run, catching her arm, his fingers wrapping around it so tightly she could feel the thick ridges of his scars against her skin, despite the leather of his glove. He dragged her close to him, right up against his chest, pulled her tight so that every soft curve of her body was pressed relentlessly against him. "How dare you say that to me." His blue eyes glared at her, icy cold, *burning* with cold.

Jessica refused to flinch. She locked her gaze with his. "Someone should have said it a long time ago, Dillon. I don't know what you're doing here all alone in this big house, on your wild island, but it certainly isn't living. You dropped out and you don't have the right to do that. You *chose* to have children. You brought them into this world and you are responsible for them."

His eyes blazed down into hers, his mouth hardened into a cruel line. She felt the change in him. The male aggression. The savage hostility. His hand tangled in the wealth of hair at the nape of her neck, hauled her head back. He fastened his mouth to hers hungrily. Angrily. Greedily. It was supposed to frighten her, to punish her. To drive her away. He used a bruising force, demanded submission, in a primitive retaliation designed to send her running from him.

Jessica tasted the hot anger, the fierce need to conquer and control, but she also tasted dark passion, as elemental as time. She felt the passion flood his body, harden his every muscle to iron, soften his lips when they would have been brutal. Jessica remained passive beneath the onslaught, her heart racing, her body coming alive. She didn't fight him, she didn't resist, but she didn't participate either.

Dillon lifted his head abruptly, swore foully, dropped his hands as if she had burned him. "Get out of here, Jessica. Get out before I take what I want. I'm damned selfish enough to do it. Get out and take the kids with you, I won't have them here. Sleep here tonight and stay the hell out of my way, then go when the storm passes. I'll have Paul take you home."

She stood there, one hand pressed to her swollen lips, shocked at the way her body throbbed and clenched in reaction to his. "You don't have a choice in the matter, Dillon. You are perfectly within your rights to send me away, but not Tara and Trevor. Someone is trying to kill them."

chapter
3

 "WHAT THE HELL are you talking about?" All at once Dillon looked so menacing, that Jessica actually stepped back.

She held up her hand, more frightened of him than she had ever conceived she could be. There was something merciless in his eyes. Something terrifying. And for the first time, she recognized him as a dangerous man. That had never been a part of Dillon's makeup, but events had twisted him, shaped him, just as they had shaped her. She had to stop persisting in seeing him as the man she had loved so much. He was different. She could feel the explosive violence in him swirling close to the surface.

Had she made a terrible mistake in coming to Dillon? In bringing the children to him? Her first duty was to Trevor and Tara. She loved them as a mother would, or, at the very least, an older sister.

"What the hell are you up to?" he snapped.

"What am I . . ." Her voice broke off in astonishment. Fear gave way to a sudden wave of fury. She stopped backing away and even took a step toward him, her fingers curling into fists. "You think I'm making up a story, Dillon? Do you think I dragged the children out of a home they're familiar with, away from their friends, in secret, in the dead of night, to see a man they have no reason to love, who *obviously* doesn't want them here, on a whim? Because I felt like it? For what? Your stupid, pitiful money?" She sneered it at him, throwing his anger right back in his face. "It always comes back to that, doesn't it?"

"If I *obviously* don't want to have them here, why would you bring them?" His blue eyes burned with a matching fury, her words obviously stinging.

"You're right, we shouldn't have come here, it was stupid to think you had enough humanity left in you to care about your own children."

Their gazes were locked, two combatants, two strong, passionate personalities. There was a silence while Jessica's heart hammered out her fury and her eyes blazed at him. Dillon regarded her for a long time. He moved first, sighing audibly, breaking the tension, walking back to his desk with his easy, flowing grace. "I see you have a high opinion of me, Jessica."

"You're the one accusing me of being a greedy, grasping, money-hungry witch," she pointed out. "I'd say you were the one with a pretty poor opinion of me." Her chin jutted at him, her face stiff with pride. "I must say, while you're throwing out accusations, you didn't even have the courtesy to answer my letter suggesting the children come live with you after my mother died."

"There was no letter."

"There was a letter, Dillon. You ignored it like you

ignored us. If I'm so money-hungry, why did you leave your children with me for all these months? Mom was dead, you knew that, yet you made no attempt to bring the children back here with you and you didn't respond to my letter."

"You might remember when you're stating things you know nothing about that you are in my home. I didn't turn you out, despite the fact that you didn't have the courtesy to phone ahead."

Her eyebrow shot up. "Is that a threat? What? You're going to kick me out into the storm or even better, send me to the boathouse or the caretaker's cottage? Give me a break, Dillon. I know you better than that!"

"I'm not that man you once knew, Jess, I never will be again." He fell silent for a moment watching the expressions chase across her face. When she stirred, as if to speak, he held up his hand. "Did you know your mother came to see me just two days before she died?" His voice was very quiet.

A chill went down her spine as she realized what he was saying. Her mother had gone to see Dillon and two days later she was dead in what certainly wasn't an accident. Jessica didn't move. She couldn't move as she assimilated the information. She knew the two incidents had to be connected. She could feel his eyes on her, but there was a strange roaring in her ears. Her legs were all at once rubbery and the room tilted crazily. *She had brought Trevor and Tara to him.*

"Jessica!" He said her name sharply, "Don't faint on me. What's wrong?" He dragged a chair out and forced her into it, pushing her head down, the leather covering his palm feeling strange on the nape of her neck. "Breathe. Just breathe."

She inhaled deeply, taking in great gulps of air, fighting off dizziness. "I'm just tired, Dillon, I'm all right, really I am." She sounded unconvincing even to her own ears.

"Something about your mother's coming here upset you, Jess. Why should that bother you? She often wrote or called to update me on the progress of the kids."

"Why would she come here?" Jessica forced air into her lungs and waited for the dizziness to subside completely. Dillon's hand was strong on her nape; he wasn't going to allow her to sit up unless she was fully recovered. "I'm fine, really." She pushed at his arm, not wanting the contact with him. He was too close. Too charismatic. And he had too many dark secrets.

Dillon abruptly let her go, almost as if he could read her thoughts. He moved away from her, back around the desk, back into the shadows, and hid his gloved hands below the desk, out of her sight. Jessica was certain his hands had been trembling.

"Why should it upset you that your mother came to see me? And why would you think someone might want to harm the twins?" The anger between them had dissipated as if it had never been, leaving his voice soft again, persuasive, so gentle it turned her heart over. "Does it hurt to talk about her? Is it too soon?"

Jessica gritted her teeth against his effect on her. They had been so close at one time. He had filled her life with his presence, his laughter, and warmth. He had made the entire household feel safe when he was home. It was difficult to sit across from him, thrown back to those days of camaraderie by his smoky voice, when she knew he was a different person now.

"My mother's car had been tampered with." Jessica blurted it out in a rush. She held up her hand to stop his inevitable protest. "Just hear me out before you tell me I'm crazy. I know what the police report said. Her brakes failed. She went over a cliff." She was choosing her words carefully. "I accepted that it was an accident but then other accidents started happening. Little disturbing things at first, things like the fan on a motor ripping loose and tearing through the hood and windshield of *my* car."

"What?" He sat up straight. "Was anyone hurt?"

She shook her head. "Tara had just gotten into the backseat. Trevor wasn't in the car. I had a few scratches, nothing serious. A mechanic explained the entire thing away, but it worried me. And then there was the horse. Trevor and Tara ride every Thursday at a local stable. Same time, every week. Trev's horse went crazy, bucking, spinning, squealing, it was awful. The horse nearly fell over backward. They discovered a drug in the horse's system." She looked straight at him. "I also found this in the horse's stall, sticking out of the straw." Watching his face she handed him the guitar pick with the distinctive design made for Dillon Wentworth as a gift so many years ago. "Trevor admitted that it might have been in his pocket and fallen out. That and other things were sent anonymously to the kids."

"I see." He sounded grim.

"The stable owners believe it was a prank on the horse, that it happens sometimes. The police thought Trevor did it, and grilled him until I called an attorney. Trevor would never do such a thing. But it felt wrong to me, two accidents so close together and only a few months after my mother's car went out of control." Jessica tapped her fingernail on the edge of his desk, a nervous habit when she was worried. "I might have accepted the accidents had that been the end of it, but it wasn't." She watched him very, very closely, trying to see past the impassive expression on his face. "Of course, the incidents didn't happen one on top of the other, a couple of weeks elapsed between them." She wanted desperately to read his blue eyes, but she saw only ice.

Jessica shivered again, experiencing a frisson of fear at being alone in the shadowy room with a man who wore a mask and guarded the darkness in his soul as if it were treasure.

"What is it, Jess?" He asked the question quietly.

What could she say? He was a stranger she no longer trusted completely. "Why did my mother come here and when?"

"Two days before her death. I asked her to come."

Her throat tightened. "In seven years you never asked us here. Why would you suddenly ask my mother to travel all the way out here to see you?"

One dark brow shot up. "Obviously because I couldn't go to see her."

The alarm bells were ringing in her mind again. He was sidestepping the question, not wanting to answer her. It was too much of a coincidence, her mother's visiting Dillon at his island home and two days later her brakes mysteriously failing. The two events had to be connected.

She remained silent, suspicion finding its way into her heart.

"What else has happened? There must be more."

"Three days ago the brakes on my car failed, too. It was a miracle we all lived through it. The car was totaled. Someone also has been phoning the house and sent old newspaper accounts of the fire to the children. That's when the guitar pick was sent. The phone calls were frightening. That, along with the other incidents over the last few months, made me decide to bring them here to you. I knew they would be safe here." She injected a note of confidence into her voice which she no longer felt. Her instincts were on alert. "Christmas was a natural, a perfect excuse should anyone question why we decided to visit you." She had been so certain he would be softer at Christmastime, more vulnerable and much more likely to let them into his life again. She had run to him for protection, for healing, and she was very much afraid she had made an enormous mistake.

Dillon leaned toward her, his blue eyes vivid and sharp. "Tell me about these phone calls."

"The voice was recorded like a robot's voice. Whoever was calling must have prerecorded it and then played it when one of the twins answered. They said terrible things about you, accused you of murdering Vivian and her lover. Of locking everyone inside the room and starting the fire. Once he said you might kill them, too." She could hear her own heart beating as she confessed. "I stopped allowing the twins to answer the phone and I made plans to come here."

"Have you told anyone else about this?"

"Only the police," she admitted. She looked away from him, afraid of seeing something she couldn't face. "The minute they realized Trevor and Tara were your children, they seemed to think I was looking to grab headlines. They asked if I was planning to sell my story to the tabloids. The incidents, other than the car, were minor things easily explained away. In the end they said they would look into it, and they took a report, but I think they thought I was either a publicity-seeker or the hysterical type."

"I'm sorry, Jess, that must have been painful for you." There was a quiet sincerity in the pure sensuality of his voice. "I've known you all of your life. You've never been one to panic."

The moment he said the words aloud, her heart slammed hard in her chest. Both of them froze, completely still while the disturbing memories invaded, crowding in, filling the room like insidious demons crawling along the floor and the walls. A sneak attack, uninvited, unexpected, but all-invasive. The air seemed to thicken with the heavy weight of memory. Evil had come with the mere mention of a single word and both of them felt its presence.

Jessica did indeed know panic intimately. She knew complete and utter hysteria. She knew the feeling of being so helpless, so vulnerable, so stripped of power she had wanted to scream until her throat was raw. Humiliation brought color sweeping up her face and her green gaze skittered away from Dillon's. No one else knew. No one. Not even her mother. She had never told her mother the entire truth. The nightmare was too real, too ugly, and she couldn't look at it.

"I'm sorry, Jess, I didn't mean to bring it up." His voice was ultra soft, soothing.

She managed to get her shaky legs under her, managed to keep from trembling visibly, although her insides were jelly as she pushed away from his desk. "I don't think about it." But she dreamt about it. Night after night, she dreamt about it. Her stomach lurched crazily. She needed air, needed to get away from him, away from the intensity of his burning, all-seeing eyes. For a moment she detested him, detested that he saw her so naked and vulnerable.

"Jessica." He said her name. Breathed her name.

She backed away from him, raw and exposed. "I *never* think about it." Jessica took the coward's way out and retreated, whirling around and fleeing the room. Tears welled up, swimming in her eyes, blurring her vision, but somehow, she made her way down the stairs.

She could feel Dillon's eyes on her, knew he followed her descent down the stairs but she didn't turn around, didn't look at him. She kept moving, her head high, counting in her head to keep the echo of the long ago voices, of the ancient, hideous chanting from stealing its way into her mind.

When she reached her room, Jessica shut the door firmly, and threw herself, face down, onto the bed, breathing deeply, fighting for control. She was no child, but a grown woman. She had responsibilities. She had confidence in herself. She would not, *could* not let anything or anyone shake her. She knew she should get up, check on Tara and Trevor, make certain they were comfortable in the rooms Paul had provided for them, on either side of her room, but she was too tired, too drained to move. She lay there, not altogether asleep, not altogether awake, but drifting, somewhere in between.

And the memories came to take her back in time.

There was always the chanting when Vivian and her friends were together. Jessica forced herself to walk down the hallway, hating to go near them, but needing to find Tara's favorite blanket. Tara would never go to sleep otherwise. Her heart was pounding, her mouth dry. Vivian's friends frightened her with their sly, leering smiles, their black candles, and wild orgies. Jessica knew they pretended to worship Satan, they talked continually of pleasures and religious practices, but none of them really knew what they were talking about. They made it up as they went along, doing whatever they pleased, each trying to outdo the other in whatever outrageous perverted sexual ritual they could envision.

As Jessica moved past the living room, she glanced inside. Black heavy drapes darkened the windows, candles were lit in every conceivable space. Vivian looked up from where she sat on the couch, naked from the waist up, sipping her wine while a man lapped greedily at her breasts. Another woman was naked while several men surrounded her, touching and grunting eagerly. The sight sickened and embarrassed Jessica and she looked away quickly.

"Jessica!" Vivian's voice was imperious, that of a queen speaking to a peasant. "Come in here."

Jessica could see the madness on Vivian's flushed face, in her hard, over-bright eyes, and hear it in her loud, brittle laugh. She made herself smile vaguely. "I'm sorry, Mrs.

Wentworth, I have to get back to Tara immediately." She kept moving.

A hard hand fell on her shoulder, another hand clapped over her mouth hard enough to sting. Jessica was dragged into the living room. She couldn't see her captor, but he was big and very strong. She struggled wildly, but he held her, laughing, calling out to Vivian to lock the door.

Hot breath hit her ear. "Are you the sweet little virgin Vivian is always teasing us with? Is this your little prize, Viv?"

Vivian's giggle was high-pitched, insane. "Dillon's little princess." Her words slurred and she circled Jessica and her captor several times. "Do you think he's had her yet?" A long-tipped fingernail traced a path down Jessica's cheek. "You're going to have such fun with us, little Jessica." She made a ceremony of lighting more candles and incense, taking her time, humming softly. "Tape her mouth, she'll scream if you don't." She gave the order and resumed her humming, stopping to kiss one of the men who was staring at Jessica with hot, greedy eyes. Jessica fought, biting at the hand covering her mouth, a terrified cry welling up. She could hear herself, screaming in her head, over and over, but no sound emerged.

She struggled, rolled over, the sound of ugly laughter fading into terrified weeping. She woke completely, sobbing wildly. She pushed the pillow harder against her face, muffling the sound, relieved it was a nightmare, relieved she had managed to wake herself up.

Very slowly she sat up and looked around the large, pleasant room. It was very cold, surprisingly so when Paul had turned on the heater to take the chill off.

Pushing at her long hair, she sat on the edge of the bed with tears running down her face and the taste of terror in her mouth. She hadn't come back to the island with the sole purpose of keeping the children safe. She had come back in the hopes of healing herself, Dillon, and the children, of finding peace for all of them. Jessica rubbed her hand over her face, resolutely wiping the tears away. Instead the nightmares were getting worse. Dillon wasn't the same man she had known seven years ago. She wasn't the same hero-worshipping girl.

She had to think clearly, think everything through. Tara and Trevor were her greatest concern. Jessica flicked on the lamp beside the bed. She couldn't bear to sit in the dark when her memories were so raw. The curtains fluttered, danced gently, gracefully in the breeze. She stared at the window. It was wide open, fog and rain and wind creeping into her room. The window had been closed when she'd left the room. She was absolutely certain of it. A chill crept down her spine, unease prickling her skin.

Jessica looked quickly around the room, her gaze seeking the corners, peeking beneath the bed. She couldn't stop herself from looking in the closet, the bathroom, and the shower. It would be difficult for anyone to enter her room through the open window, especially in a rainstorm, because it was on the second floor. She tried to convince herself one of the twins must have come into her room to say goodnight and opened the window to let in some air. She couldn't imagine why, it didn't make any sense, but she preferred this explanation to the alternative.

She crossed the room to the window, stared out into

the forest, and watched the wind as it played roughly in the trees. There was something elemental, powerful about storms that fascinated her. She watched the rain for a while, allowing a certain peace to settle back over her. Then, abruptly, she closed the window and went to check on Tara.

The bedside lamp was on in Tara's room, spilling a soft circle of light across it. To Jessica's surprise, Trevor lay on the floor wrapped in a heap of blankets, while Tara lay on the bed beneath a thick quilt. They were talking in low tones and neither looked at all astonished to see her.

"We thought you'd never come," Tara greeted, moving over, obviously expecting Jessica to share her bed.

"I thought I was going to have to go rescue you," Trevor added. "We were just discussing how to go about it since we didn't exactly know which room you were in."

Warmth drove out the cold in her soul, pushing away her nameless fears and the disturbing remnants of old horrors. She smiled at them and rushed to the bed, jumping beneath the covers and snuggling into the pillow. "Were you really worried?"

"Of course we were," Tara confirmed. She reached for Jessica's hand. "Did he yell at you?"

Trevor snorted. "We didn't see any fireworks, did we? If he yelled at her we would have seen the Fourth of July."

"Hey, now," Jessica objected. "I'm not that bad."

Trevor made a rude noise. "Flames fly off you, Jess, if someone gets you angry enough. I can't see you being all mealymouthed if our own father didn't want us for Christmas. You'd read him the riot act, probably knock

him on his butt and march us out of his house. You'd
make us swim back to the nearest city."

Tara giggled, nodding her head. "We call you Mama
Tiger behind your back."

"What?" Jessica found herself laughing. "Total exaggeration. Total!"

"You're worse. You grow fangs and claws if someone is
mean to us," Trevor pointed out complacently. "Justice
for the children." He grinned at her. "Unless you're the
one getting after us."

Jessica threw her pillow at him with perfect aim. "You
little punk, I never get after you. What are you doing
awake, it's four-thirty in the morning."

The twins erupted into laughter, pointing at her and
mimicking her question. "That's called getting after us,
Jess," Tara said. "You're worse than Mama Rita was."

"She spoiled you rotten," Jessica told them haughtily,
laughter brimming over in her green eyes. "All right, fine,
but nobody in their right mind is up at four-thirty in the
morning. It's silly. *And* it was a perfectly *reasonable* question."

"Yeah, because we're not in some spooky old house
with total strangers and a man who might want to throw
us out on our butts or anything like that," Trevor said.

"Taking you off upstairs to do some dastardly deed
we've never heard of," Tara said, adding her two cents.

"When did you two become such smart alecks?"
Jessica wanted to know.

"We talked to Paul for a while downstairs," Trevor said
when the laughter had subsided. "He's really nice. He said
he knew us when we were little."

Jessica was aware of both pairs of eyes on her. She caught the pillow Trevor tossed to her and slipped it behind her back as she sat up, drawing up her knees. "He and your father were best friends long before the band was put together. Paul actually was the original singer for their band. Dillon wrote most of the songs and played lead guitar. He could play almost any instrument. Paul played bass guitar, but he sang the songs when they first started out. Brian Phillips was the drummer and I think it was his idea to form the band. They started out in a garage and played all the clubs and made the rounds. Eventually they became very famous."

"There were a couple of other band members, Robert something," Trevor interrupted. "He was on keyboard and for some reason I thought Don Ford was the bass player. He's on all the CD covers and in the old magazine articles written on *HereAfter*." There was a note of pride when he said the band's name.

Jessica nodded. "Robert Berg. Robert's awesome on the keyboard. And yes, Don was brought in to play bass. Somewhere along the line, Paul picked up a big drug habit."

Tara wrinkled her nose. "He seemed so nice."

Jessica pushed back her hair. "He is nice, Tara. People make mistakes, they get into things without thinking and then it's too late to get out. Paul told me he began using all the time and couldn't remember the lyrics to the songs during their live performances. Your father would step up and sing. Paul said the crowds went wild. Paul was on a downward spiral and eventually the band members wanted him out. He was doing crazy things, tearing places up, not showing up for scheduled events, that sort of thing, and they said enough."

"Just like you read in the tabloids," Trevor pointed out.

There was a small silence while both children looked at her. "Yes, that's true. But it doesn't make the things they wrote about your father true. Remember, this was all a long time ago. Sometimes when people become famous too fast, have too much money, they have a hard time handling it all. I think Paul was one of those people. It overwhelmed him. Girls were throwing themselves at him all the time, there was just too much of everything. Anyway, Dillon wouldn't give up on him. He made him go into rehab and helped him recover."

"Is that when they picked up another bass player?" Trevor guessed.

Jessica nodded. "The band really took off while Paul was cleaning himself up and they had to have another bass player, so Don was brought in. Dillon's voice rocketed them into stardom. But he wouldn't leave Paul behind. Your father gave Paul a job working in the studio and eventually made a place for him in the band. And when Dillon needed him most, Paul came through."

"Did Paul know Vivian?" Tara's question was hesitant.

Jessica realized Vivian still managed to bring tension into a room years after her death. "Yes he did, honey," she confirmed gently. "All of the members of the band knew Vivian. Paul didn't do all the tours with them so he often stayed here, seeing to things at home. He knew her better than most." And despised her. Jessica remembered the terrible arguments and Vivian's endless tirades. Paul had tried to keep her under control, tried to help Rita and Jessica keep the twins safe when she brought her friends in.

"Does he think my father murdered Vivian and that man she was with, like the newspaper said?"

Jessica swung her head around, her temper rising until she saw Tara's bent head. Slowly she let her breath out. How else was Tara going to learn the truth about her father if she couldn't ask questions? "Honey, you know most of those tabloids don't tell the truth, right? They sensationalize things, write misleading headlines and articles to grab people's attention. It wasn't any different when your father was at the height of his career. The tabloids twisted all the facts, made it sound as if Dillon found your mother in bed with another man. They made it sound like he shot them both and then burned down his own house to cover the murders. It didn't happen like that at all." Jessica curved her arm around Tara's shoulders and pulled her close, hugging her. "Your father was acquitted at the trial. He had nothing to do with the shooting or the fire. He wasn't even in the house when it all happened."

"What did happen, Jess?" Trevor asked, his piercing blue gaze meeting hers steadily. "Why wouldn't you ever tell us?"

"We're not babies," Tara pointed out, but she cuddled closer to Jessica's warmth, clearly for comfort.

Jessica shook her head. "I would prefer your father tell you about that night, not me."

"We'll believe you, Jess," Trevor said. "You turn beet red if you try to lie. We don't know our father. We don't know Paul. Mama Rita wouldn't say a word about it. You know it's time you told us the truth if someone is sending us newspapers filled with lies and calling us on the phone telling more lies."

"It's the three of us, Jessie," Tara added. "It's always been the three of us. We're a family. We want you to tell us."

Jessica was proud of them, proud of the way they were attempting to handle a volatile and frightening situation. And she heard the love in their voices, felt the answering emotion welling up in her. They weren't babies anymore, and they were right, they deserved to know the truth. She didn't know if Dillon would ever tell them.

Jessica took a deep breath, then she began. "There was a party at the house that night. Your father had been gone for months on a world tour and Vivian often invited her friends over. I didn't know her very well." The fact was, Jessica had never understood Dillon's relationship with his wife. Vivian had left the twins with Rita from almost the moment they were born so she could tour with the band. She rarely returned home the first three years of their lives. Yet during the last year of her life she had stayed home, the band's manager refusing to allow her to travel with them due to her violent mood swings and psychotic behavior.

"You've gone quiet again, Jessica," Trevor prompted.

"The fact is, Vivian drank too much and partied very heavily. Your father knew about her drinking, but she threatened him with you. She said she'd leave him, take you with her, and get a restraining order so he couldn't see you. She knew people who would take money in return for testimony against Dillon. He was often on the road, and bands, especially successful ones, always have reputations."

"You're saying he was afraid to risk a court fight," Trevor said, summing it up.

Jessica smiled at him. "Exactly. He was afraid the court would say you had to live with Vivian and he wouldn't be able to control what was happening to you if he didn't have custody. By staying with her, he hoped he could keep her contained. It worked for a while." Vivian didn't want to be home, she preferred the nightlife and the clubs of the cities. It was only during the last year, when the twins were five, that Vivian had returned home, unable to keep up appearances.

"That night, Jess," Trevor prompted.

Jessica sighed. There was no getting around telling them what they wanted to know. The twins were very persistent. "There was a party going on." She chose her words very carefully. "Your father came home early. There was a terrible fight between him and your mother, and he left the house to cool off. He made up his mind that he would leave Vivian and she knew it. There were candles everywhere. The fire inspector said the drapes caught fire and it spread fast, because there was alcohol on the furniture and the walls. The party was very wild. No one knows for certain where the gun came from or who shot whom first. But witnesses, including me, testified that Dillon had left the house. He ran back when he saw the flames and he rushed inside because he couldn't find you."

Jessica looked down at her hands. "I had taken you out a window on the cliff side of the house and he didn't know. He thought you were still inside so he went into the burning house."

Tara gasped, one hand covering her mouth to stop any sound but her eyes were glistening with tears.

"How did he get out?" Trevor asked, a lump in his throat. He couldn't get the sight of his father's terrible scars out of his mind. "And how could he make himself go into a burning house?"

Jessica leaned close to them. "Because that's how courageous your father is, how absolutely dependable, and that's how much he loves both of you."

"Did the house fall down on him?" Tara asked.

"They said he came out on fire, that Paul and Brian tackled him and put out the flames with their own hands. There were people on the island then, guards and groundskeepers who had all come to help. The helicopters had arrived I think. I just remember it being so loud, so angry . . ." her voice trailed off.

Trevor reached up and caught her hand. "I hate that sad look you get sometimes, Jess. You're always there for us. You always have been."

Tara kissed her cheek. "Me, too, I feel the same way."

"So no one really knows who shot our mother and her friends," Trevor concluded. "It's still a big mystery. But you saved our lives, Jess. And our father was willing to risk his life to save us. Did you see him after he came out of the house?"

Jessica closed her eyes, turned her head away from them. "Yes, I saw him." Her voice was barely audible.

The twins exchanged a long look. Tara took the initiative, wanting to wipe away the sorrow Jessica was so clearly feeling. "Now, tell us the story of the Christmas miracle. The one Mama Rita always told us. I love that story."

"Me, too. You said we were coming here for our miracle, Jess," Trevor said, "tell us the story so we can believe."

"We're all going to be too tired to get up tomorrow," Jessica pointed out. She slipped beneath the covers and flicked off the light. "You already believe in miracles, I helped raise you right. It's your father who doesn't know what can happen at Christmas, but we're going to teach him a lesson. I'll tell the story another time, when I'm not so darned sleepy. Goodnight you two."

Trevor laughed softly. "Cluck cluck. Jessica hates it when we get sappy."

The pillow found him even in the dark.

chapter
4

BRIAN PHILLIPS WAS FLIPPING pancakes in the kitchen when Jessica entered the room with Tara and Trevor early the next evening. She grinned at him in greeting. "Brian! How wonderful to see you again!"

Brian spun around, and missed a pancake as it came flying down to splat on the counter. "Jessica!" He swooped her up, hugged her hard. He was a big man, the drummer for *HereAfter*. She had forgotten how strong he was until he nearly broke her ribs with his hard, good-natured squeeze. With his reddish hair and stocky body, he always had reminded Jessica of a boxer fresh from Ireland. At times she even heard the lilt in his voice. "My God, girl, you look beautiful. How long has it been?" There was a moment of silence as both of them remembered the last time they had seen one another.

Jessica resolutely forced a smile. "Brian, you must remember Tara and Trevor, Dillon's children. We were so exhausted we slept the day away. I see you're serving breakfast for dinner." She was still in the circle of Brian's arms as she turned to include the twins in the greeting. Her smile faltered as she met a pair of ice-cold eyes over the heads of the children.

Dillon lounged in the doorway, his body posture deceptively lazy and casual. His eyes were intent, watchful, focused on her, and there was a hint of something dangerous to the edge of his mouth. Jessica's green gaze locked with his. Her breathing was instantly impaired, her breath catching in her lungs. He had that effect on her. Dillon was wearing faded blue jeans, a long-sleeved turtleneck shirt, and thin leather gloves. He looked unmercifully handsome. His hair was damp from his shower and he was barefoot. She had forgotten that about him, how he liked to be without shoes in the house. Butterfly wings fluttered in the pit of her stomach. "Dillon."

Jessica ripped out his heart, whatever heart he had left, with her mere presence in his home. Dillon could hardly bear to look at her, to see her beauty, to see the woman she had become. Her hair was a blend of red and gold silk, falling around her face. A man could lose himself in her eyes. And her mouth . . . If Brian didn't take his hands off of her very, very soon Dillon feared he might give in to the terrible violence that always seemed to be swirling so close to the surface. Her green eyes met his across the room and she murmured his name again. Softly. Barely audible, yet the way she whispered his name tightened every muscle in his body.

The twins whirled around, Tara reaching out to take Trevor's arm for support as she faced her father.

Dillon's gaze reluctantly left Jessica's face to move

broodingly over the twins. He didn't smile, didn't change expression. "Trevor and Tara, you've certainly grown." A muscle jerked along his jaw but otherwise he gave no indication of the emotions he was feeling. He wasn't certain he could do this, look at them, see the look in their eyes, face up to his past failures, face the utter and total revulsion that he had seen in Tara's eyes the night before.

Trevor's gaze flickered uncertainly toward Jessica before he stepped forward, thrusting out his hand toward his father. "It's good to see you, sir."

Jessica watched Dillon closely, willing him to pull his son into a hug. To at least smile at the boy. Instead, he shook hands briefly. "It's good to see you, too. I understand you're here to celebrate Christmas with me." Dillon glanced at Tara. "I guess that means you'll be wanting a tree."

Tara smiled shyly. "It's sort of an accepted practice."

He nodded. "I can't remember the last time I celebrated Christmas. I'm a little rusty when it comes to holiday festivities." His gaze had strayed back to Jessica and he silently damned himself for his lack of control.

"Tara will make sure you remember every little detail about Christmas," Trevor said with a laugh, nudging his sister. "It's her favorite holiday."

"I'll count on you, then, Tara," Dillon said with his customary charm, still watching Jessica intently. A smile slipped out. Menacing. Threatening. "If you can manage to take your hands off Jess, Brian, maybe we can all share those pancakes." There was a distinct edge to his voice. "We keep strange hours here, especially now that we're recording. I prefer to work at night and sleep during the day."

Tara glanced at her brother and mouthed, "Vampire."

Trevor grinned at her, covering for his twin with a diversion. "I take it we get pancakes for dinner."

"You'll grow to love them," Brian assured. He laughed heartily and squeezed Jessica's shoulders quickly before dropping his arms. "She's turned into a real beauty, Dillon." He leered at Jessica. "I don't know if I mentioned to you or not, that I'm recently divorced."

"Ever the lady's man," Jessica patted his cheek, determined not to let Dillon shake her confidence. "What was that, your third or fourth wife?"

"Oh, the pain of the arrows you sling, Jessica girl." Brian clutched his heart and winked at Trevor. "She never lets anything slip by, I'll bet."

Trevor grinned at him, wide and engaging, that famous Wentworth smile that Jessica knew so well. "Not a single thing, so be careful around her," he cautioned. "I'm a fairly good cook. I can help you with the pancakes. Don't let Jessie, even if she offers. The mere thought of her cooking anything is scary." He shuddered dramatically.

Jessica rolled her eyes. "He should be in acting." She was aware of Tara inching closer to her for comfort, aware of the tension in the room despite the banter. Trying to ignore Dillon, she drew the child to her and hugged her encouragingly as her father should have done. "Trevor turns traitor when he's in the company of other men, have you noticed?"

"I'm stating a fact," Trevor denied. "She sets the

popcorn on fire in the microwave whenever we let her pop it."

"It's not my fault the popcorn behaves unpredictably when it's my turn to pop it," Jessica pointed out.

She stole a glance at Dillon. He was watching her intently, just as she suspected he was. When she inhaled, she took his clean, masculine scent into her lungs. He dominated the room simply by standing there, wrapped in his silence. Awareness spread through her body, an unfamiliar heat that thickened her blood and left her strangely restless.

"Can anyone join in the fun?"

The blood drained out of Jessica's face. She felt it, felt herself go pale as she turned slowly to face that strident voice. Vivian's voice. The woman was tall and model thin. Platinum blond hair was swept up onto her head and she wore scarlet lipstick. Jessica noticed her long nails were polished the exact same shade. Jessica swallowed the sudden lump in her throat and looked to Dillon for help.

"Brenda." Dillon said the woman's name deliberately, needing to wipe the fear out of Jessica's eyes. "Jess, I don't believe you ever had the chance to meet Vivian's sister. Brenda, this is Jessica Fitzpatrick and these are my children, Trevor and Tara."

The twins looked at one another and then at Jessica. Trevor put his arm around Tara. "We have an aunt, Jessie?"

"Apparently," Jessica said, her gaze on Dillon. She had never seen Brenda in her life. She had a vague recollection of someone mentioning her, but Brenda certainly had never come to see the children.

"Of course I'm your aunt," Brenda announced, waving her hand airily. "But I travel quite a bit and just haven't gotten around to visiting. No pancakes for me, Brian, just coffee." She walked across the kitchen and threw herself into a chair as if she were exhausted. "I had no idea the little darlings were coming, Dillon." She blew him a kiss. "You should have told me. They certainly take after you, don't they?"

"Must have been a lot of traveling," Trevor muttered, leaning into Jessica. He quirked an eyebrow at her, half amused, half annoyed, in a way that was very reminiscent of his father.

Jessica felt Tara tremble and immediately brushed the top of her head with a kiss. "It isn't quite dark yet, honey, would you like to go for a short walk? The storm's passed over us and it would be fun to show you how beautiful the island is."

"Don't leave on my account," Brenda said, "I don't get along with kiddies. I make no apologies for it. I need coffee, for heaven's sake, can't one of you manage to bring me a cup?" Her voice rose, a familiar pitch that was etched for all time in Jessica's memory. "Robert, the lazy slug, is still in bed." She yawned and leveled her gaze at Dillon. "You've turned us all around so we don't know whether it's morning or night anymore. My poor husband can't get out of bed."

"Are you here for Christmas?" Trevor ventured, uncertain what to say, but instinctively wanting to find a way to smooth out the situation.

"Christmas?" It was Brian who answered derisively. "Brenda doesn't know what Christmas is, besides a day she expects to be showered with gifts. She's here for more money, aren't you, my dear? She's gone through Robert's money and the insurance money, so she dropped by with her hand out."

"So true." Brenda shrugged her shoulders, unconcerned with Brian's harsh assessment of her. "Money is the bane of all existence."

"She has an insurance policy on everyone, don't you, Brenda," Brian accused. "Me, Dillon," he indicated the twins with his jaw, his eyes glittering at her, "the kids. Poor Robert is probably worth far more dead than alive. What do you have on him, a cool million?"

Brenda raised one eyebrow, blew another kiss at him. "Of course, darling, it's just good sense. I figured you'd go first with your horrendous driving abilities, but, alas, no luck so far."

Brian glared at her. "You're a cold woman, Brenda."

"You didn't used to think so, babe."

Jessica stared at her. *Insurance policy on the kids. On Dillon.* She didn't dare look at Dillon; he would know exactly the suspicion going through her mind.

Brenda gave a tinkling laugh. "Don't look so shocked, Jessica, dear. Brian and I are old friends. It ended badly and he can't forgive me." She inspected her long nails. "He actually adores me and still wants me. I adore him, but choosing Robert was a good decision. He balances me." She lifted her head, moaning pathetically, her eyes pleading. "I could *kill* for a cup of coffee."

Jessica turned over the information in her mind. Insurance money. It had never occurred to her that someone other than Dillon or the children might have

profited monetarily from Vivian's death. She remembered her mother talking about it with Dillon's lawyer
after the fire. The lawyer had said it was good that Dillon
didn't have a policy on his wife because an insurance policy was often considered a reason for murder.

Reason for murder. Could an insurance policy on
Tara's and Trevor's lives be the motive behind the accidents? Jessica looked at Brenda, trying to see past her perfect makeup to the woman beneath.

"How could you have an insurance policy on Vivian,
Brenda?" Jessica asked curiously. "Or on Brian or Dillon
or the twins? That's not legal."

"Oh please." Brenda waved her hand. "I'm dying for
coffee and you want to talk legalities. Fine, a little lesson,
kiddies, in grown-up reality. Viv and I went together to
get insurance on each other years ago. With consent it
can be done. Dillon gave his consent," she blew him
another kiss, "because we're family. Brian gave consent
when we were together and Robert's my husband, so *of
course* I have insurance on him."

"And you're so good at persuading people to let you
have those policies, aren't you, Brenda," Brian snapped.

"Of course I am." Brenda smiled at him, in no way
perturbed by his accusations. "You're becoming so
tedious with your jealousy. Really, darling, you need
help."

"You're going broke paying your insurance premi-
ums," Brian sniped.

Brenda shrugged and waved airily. "I just call Dillon
and he pays them for me. Now, stop being so mean,
Brian, and bring me coffee; it won't hurt you to be nice

for a change," Brenda wheedled, slumping dramatically over the table.

"Yes, it would," he said stubbornly. "Doing anything for you is bad karma."

"But how would you manage to take out a policy on the twins?" The very idea of it repulsed Jessica.

Brenda didn't lift her head from the tabletop. "My sister and Dillon gave me permission of course. I'm not talking anymore, without coffee! I'm fading here, people."

Jessica glared accusingly at Dillon across the room. He flashed a heart-stopping, rather sheepish smile and shrugged his broad shoulders. Brenda groaned loudly. Jessica gave in. It was clear that Brian wasn't going to get Vivian a cup of coffee and Dillon looked unconcerned. She found the mugs in a cupboard and did the honors. "Cream or sugar?"

"You don't have to do that, Jess," Dillon snapped suddenly, his mouth tightening ominously. "Brenda, get your own damn coffee."

"It's no big deal." Jessica handed the cup to Brenda.

"Thank you, my dear, you are a true lifesaver." Her eyes wandered over Jessica's figure, an indifferent, blasé appraisal, then she turned her attention to Tara. "You look nothing like your mother, but fortunately you inherited Dillon's good looks. It should take you far in life."

"Tara is at the top of her class," Jessica informed the woman, "her brains are going to take her far in life."

Trevor wolfed down a pancake without syrup. "Watch yourself now, Jessica's got that militant look in her eye."

His voice changed, a perfect mimic of Jessica's. "School is important and if you mess around thinking you can get by on good looks or charm, or think you're going to make it big in the arts, think again buddy, you're going nowhere if you don't have a decent education." He grinned at them. "Word for word, I swear, you opened a can a worms."

"Looks have gotten me what I want in life," Brenda muttered into her coffee cup.

"Maybe you weren't aspiring high enough," Jessica said, looking Brenda in the eye.

Brenda shuddered, surrendering. "I don't have the energy for this conversation. I told you I wasn't good with kiddies or animals."

"Tara," Jessica said, as she handed the girl a plate of pancakes, "you are the kiddie and that brother of yours is the animal."

Trevor grinned at her. "Too true, and all the girls know it."

Dillon watched them bantering back and forth so easily. *His* children. *His* Jessica. They were a family, basking in each other's love. He was the outsider. The circle was tight, the bond strong between the three of them. He watched the expressions chasing across Jessica's face as she snapped a tea towel at Trevor, laughing at him, teasing him. The way it should have been. The way it was supposed to be.

Jessica was aware of Dillon every moment that they stayed in the same room. Her wayward gaze kept straying to him. Her pulse raced and he affected her breathing. It was aggravating and made her feel like a teenager with a crush. "We want to go for that walk before it gets dark, don't we, Tara?" Now *she* wanted to escape. Needed to escape. She couldn't stay in the same room with him much longer.

"The grounds haven't been kept up, Jess," Dillon informed her. "It might be better if you amuse yourselves inside while we work."

Her eyebrow shot up. "Amuse ourselves?" She ignored Trevor's little warning nudge. "What did you have in mind? Playing hopscotch in the hall?"

Dillon looked at his son's face, the quick, appreciative grin the boy couldn't hide fast enough. Something warm stirred in him that he didn't want to think about or examine too closely. "Hopscotch is fine, Jess, as long as you draw the boxes with something we can erase easily." He said it blandly, watching the boy's reaction.

Trevor threw his head back and laughed. Brian joined in. Even Brenda managed a faint smile, more, Jessica suspected, because Trevor's laugh was infectious than because Brenda found anything humorous in Dillon's reply.

Jessica didn't want to look up and see Dillon smiling but she couldn't stop herself. She didn't want to notice the way his face lit up, or that his eyes were so blue. Or that his mouth was perfectly sculpted. Kissable. She nearly groaned, blushing faintly at the wild thought. The memory of his lips, velvet soft, yet firm, pressing against hers was all too vivid in her mind.

She had to say something, the twins would expect her to hold her own in a verbal sparring match, but she couldn't think, not when his blue eyes were laughing at her. Really laughing at her. For one brief moment, he looked happy, the terrible weight off his shoulders. Jessica glanced at the twins. They were observing her hopefully. She took a deep breath and deliberately leaned close to Dillon, close enough that she could feel electricity arcing between them. She put her mouth against Dillon's ear so that he could feel the softness of her lips as she spoke. "You cheat, Dillon." She whispered the three words, allowing her warm breath to play over his neck, heat his skin. To make him as aware of her as she was of him.

It was a silly, dangerous thing to do, and the moment she did it, she knew she'd made a mistake. The air stilled, the world receded until there was only the two of them. Desire flared in the depths of his eyes, burning hot, immediate. He shifted, a subtle movement but it brought his body in contact with hers. Hunger pulsed between them, deep, elemental, so strong it was nearly tangible. He bent his dark head to hers.

No one breathed. No one moved. Jessica stared into the deep blue of his eyes, mesmerized, held captive there, his perfect mouth only a scant inch from hers. "I play to win," he murmured softly, for her ears alone.

The sound of a creaking chair, as someone shifted restlessly, broke the enchantment. Jessica blinked, came out of her trance, and hastily stepped away from the beckoning heat of Dillon's body, from the magnetic pull of his sexual web. She didn't dare look at either of the children. Her heart was doing strange somersaults and the butterflies were having a field day in the pit of her stomach.

Dillon ran his gloved hand down the length of her hair

in a gentle caress. "Were you and the children comfortable last night?"

Tara and Trevor looked at each other, then at Jessica. "Very comfortable," they said in unison.

Jessica was too wrapped up in the sound of his voice to answer. There was that smoky quality to it, the black velvet that was so sexy, but it was so much more. Sometimes the gentleness, the tenderness that came out of nowhere threw her completely off balance. Dillon was a mixture of old and new to her, and she was desperately trying to feel her way with him.

"That's good. If you need anything, don't hesitate to say so." Dillon poured the rest of his coffee down the sink and rinsed the cup out. "We're all pitching in with the chores as the housekeeping staff is gone on vacation this month. So I'll expect you kids to do the same. Just clean up after yourselves. You can have the run of the house with the exception of the rooms where the others are staying, my private rooms and the studio. That's invitation only." He leaned his back against the sink and pinned the twins with his brilliant gaze. "We keep odd hours and if you get up before late afternoon, please keep quiet because most of us will be sleeping. The band is here to try recording some music, just to see what we can come up with. If it works, we hope to have a product to pitch again to one of the labels. It requires a great deal of time and effort on our part. We're *working*, not playing."

Trevor nodded. "We understand, we won't get in the way."

"If you're interested, you can watch later, after we've

worked out a few kinks. I'm heading to the studio now, so if you need anything, say so now."

"We'll be fine," Trevor said. "Getting up at four or five o'clock in the afternoon and staying up all night is an experience in itself!" His white teeth flashed, an engaging smile, showing all the promise of his father's charisma. "Don't worry about us, Jess will keep us in line."

Dillon's blue gaze flicked to Jessica. Drank her in. She made his kitchen seem a home. He had forgotten that feeling. Forgotten what it was like to wake up and look forward to getting out of bed. He heard the murmur of voices around him, heard Robert Berg and Don Ford laughing in the hall as they made their way together to the kitchen. It was all so familiar yet completely different.

"Well, we have a houseful." Robert Berg, the keyboard player for the band, entered and crossed the kitchen to plant a kiss on the nape of Brenda's neck. Robert was short and compact with dark thinning hair and a small trim goatee gracing his chin. "This can't be the twins, they're all grown up."

Trevor nodded solemnly. "That happens to people. An unusual phenomenon. Time goes by and we just get older. I'm Trevor." He held out his hand.

"With the smart mouth," Jessica supplied, frowning at the boy as he shook hands with Robert. "Good to see you again, it has been a while." She dropped her hands onto Tara's shoulders. "This is Tara."

Robert smiled at the girl, saluted her as he snagged a plate and piled it high with pancakes. "Brian's been doing the cooking, Jessica, but maybe now that you're here we can have something besides pancakes."

Trevor choked, went into a coughing fit, and Tara burst out laughing. Dillon's heart turned over as he watched Jessica tug gently on Tara's hair, then mock strangle Trevor. The three of them were so easy with one another, playfully teasing, sharing a close camaraderie he had always wanted, but had never found. He had been so desperate for a home, for a family, and now when it was in front of him, when he knew what was important, what it was all about, it was too late for him.

"*Men* are the supreme chefs of the world," Jessica replied haughtily, "why would I want to infringe on their domain?"

"Here, here," Brenda applauded. "Well said."

"You coming, Brian." Dillon made it a command, not a question. "I'll expect the rest of you in ten minutes and someone get Paul up."

There was a small silence after Dillon left. It had always been that way, he dominated a room with his presence, the passion and energy in it had flowed from him. Now that he was gone there seemed to be a void.

Don Ford hurried in, his short brown hair spiked and tipped with blond and his clothes the latest fashion. "Had to get in my morning smoke. Dillon won't let us smoke in the house. Man, it's cold out there tonight." He shivered, rubbing his hands together for warmth as he looked around and caught sight of the twins and Jessica. He shoved small wire rim glasses on his nose to peer at them. "Whoa! You weren't here when I went to bed or I'm giving up liquor for all time."

"We snuck in when you weren't looking," Jessica

admitted with a smile. She accepted his kiss and made the introductions.

"Am I the last one up?"

"That would be Paul," Robert said, shoving cream and sugar across the counter toward Don.

Paul sauntered in, bent to kiss Jessica's cheek. "You're a sight for sore eyes," he greeted. "I'm here, I'm awake, you can cancel the firing squad." He winked at Tara. "Have you already made plans to go hunting for the perfect Christmas tree? We won't have time to go hunting one on the mainland so we'll have to do it the old-fashioned way and chop one down."

Brenda yawned. "I hate the sound of that. What a mess. There might be bugs, Paul. You aren't really going to get one from the wilds, are you?"

Tara looked alarmed. "We are going to have a Christmas tree, aren't we, Jessica?"

"*Jessica* doesn't have a say in the matter," Robert pointed out, "Dillon does. It's his house and we're here to work, not play. Brenda's right, a tree from out there," he said, gesturing toward the window, "would have bugs and it would be utterly unsanitary. Not to mention a fire hazard."

Tara flinched visibly. Trevor stood up, squared his shoulders, and walked straight over to Robert. "I don't think you needed to say that to my sister. And I don't like the way you said Jessica's name."

Jessica gently rested her hand on Trevor's shoulder. "Robert, that was uncalled for. None of us need reminders of the fire, we were all here when it happened." She tugged on Trevor's resistant body urging him away from Robert. "Tara, of course you'll have a tree. Your father has already agreed to one. We can't very well have Christmas without one."

Brenda sighed as she stood up. "As long as I'm not the one dealing with all of those needles that will fall off it. You need such energy to cope with the kiddies. I'm glad it's you and not me, dear. I'm off to the studio. Robert, are you coming?"

Robert obediently followed her out without looking at any of them. Don drained his coffee cup, rinsed it carefully and waved to them. "Duty calls."

"I'm sorry about that, Jessie," Paul said. "Robert lives in his own little world. Brenda goes through money like water. Everything they had is gone. Dillon was the only one of us who was smart. He invested his share and tripled his money. The royalties on his songs keep pouring in. And because he had the kids he carried medical and fire insurance and all those grown-up things the rest of us didn't think about. The worst of it is, he tried to get us to do the same but we wouldn't listen to him. Robert needs this album to come about. If Dillon composes it and sings and produces it, you know it will go straight to the top. Robert is between a rock and hard place. Without money, he can't keep Brenda, and he loves her." Paul shrugged and ruffled Tara's hair. "Don't let them ruin your Christmas, Tara."

"Whose idea was it to put the band back together?" Jessica asked. "I had the impression that Dillon wanted to do this, that it was his idea."

Paul shook his head. "Not a chance. He's always composing, music lives in him, he hears it in his head all the time, but up until last week, he hadn't worked with anyone but me since the fire. He can't play instruments anymore. Well, he plays, but not anything like he used to play. He doesn't have the dexterity, although he tries when he's alone. It's too painful for him. I think Robert talked to the others first and then they all came to me to see what I thought. I think they believed I could persuade him." His dark eyes held a hint of worry. "I hope I did the right thing. He's doing it for the others, you know, hoping to make them some money. That was the pitch I used and it worked. He wouldn't have done it for himself, but he's always felt responsible for the others. I thought it might be good for him but now, I don't know. If he fails . . ."

"He won't fail," Jessica said. "We'll clean up in here. You'd better go."

"Thanks, Jess." He bent and dropped a kiss on the top of her head. "I'm glad you're all here."

Trevor grinned at her the moment they were alone. "You're getting kissed a lot, Jess. I was thinking there for a few minutes when you were . . . er . . . *talking* with my dad, I might even get my first lesson in sex education." He took off running as Jessica madly snapped a tea towel at him. His taunting laughter floated back to her from up the stairs.

chapter
5

❄ JESSICA SLOWED MIDWAY up the staircase, the smile fading from her face. It was the smell. She would never forget the smell of that particular incense. Cedarwood and alum. She inhaled and knew there was no mistake. The odor seeped from beneath the door to her room and crept out into the hallway. Jessica paused for just a moment, allowing herself to feel the edginess creep back into her mind. It seemed to be there whenever she was alone, a warning shimmering in her brain, settling in the pit of her stomach.

"Jess?" Trevor stood at the top of the stairs, puzzlement on his face. "What is it?"

She shook her head as she walked past him to stand in front of the door to her room. Very carefully she pushed it open. Ice-cold air rushed out at her, and with it, the overpowering odor of incense. Jessica stood in the doorway of her room, unmoving, her gaze going immediately to the window. The curtains fluttered, floating on the breeze as if they were white, papery thin ghosts. For one moment there was vapor, a thick white fog permeating her room. She blinked and it seemed to dissolve, or merge with the heavy fog outside the house.

"It's freezing in here, why did you open the window?" Trevor hurried across the room to slam it closed. "What is that disgusting smell?"

Jessica had remained motionless in the doorway, but when she saw his shoulders stiffen, it galvanized her into action. She hurried to his side. "Trev?"

"What is that?" Trevor pointed to the symbol ground into the throw rug near the window.

Jessica took a deep breath. "Some people believe that they can invoke the aid of spirits, Trevor, by using certain ceremonies. What you're looking at is a crude magician's ring." She stared, mesmerized, at the two circles, one within the other, made from the ash of several sticks of incense.

"What does it mean?"

"Nothing at this point, there's nothing in it." Jessica's teeth tugged at her bottom lip. Two circles meant nothing. It was simply a starting point. "Some people believe that you can't make contact with spirits without a magic circle drawn and consecrated. The symbols invoking the spirit and also for protection would be inside." She sighed softly. "Let's check Tara's room and then yours, just to be on the safe side."

"You're shaking," Trevor pointed out.

"Am I?" Jessica rubbed her hands up and down her arms, determined not to scream. "It must be the cold." She wanted to run to Dillon, to have him hold her, to comfort her, but she knew the minute he saw that symbol he would throw each and every one of the band members out. And he would never try to make his music again.

"I want to go get Dad," Trevor said, as they entered Tara's room. "I don't like this at all."

Jessica shook her head. "Neither do I, but we can't tell your father just yet. You don't know him the way I do. He has an incredible sense of responsibility." She took his arm as they entered Tara's room. "Don't shake your head—he does. He didn't leave you alone because he didn't love you. He left you alone because he believed it was the right thing to do for you."

"Baloney!" Trevor poked around the room, making certain the window was securely closed and that no one had disturbed his sister's things. "How could he believe that leaving was the right thing to do, Jessie?"

"After the fire he spent a year in the hospital, and then he had over a year of physical therapy. You have no idea how painful it is to recover from the type of burns your father suffered. The kinds of things he had to endure. And then the trial dragged on for nearly two years. Not the actual trial, but the entire legal process. No one actually found the murderer so Dillon wasn't freed from suspicion. You had to know him. He took responsibility for everyone. He took the blame for everything that happened. He's his own worst enemy. In his mind he failed Vivian, the band, you kids, even my mother and me. I don't want to take a chance that he might quit his music. Someone wants us to go away and they know what frightens me. But they directed this prank at me, not at you."

"I knew you thought someone was trying to hurt us." Trevor shook his head as they walked into his room. "You should have told me. That's why you brought us to him."

She nodded. "He would never allow anything to happen to you. Never."

They finished the examination of Trevor's room. It was immaculate; he hadn't even pretended to be using it. "What was all that business about insurance money? Does Brenda really have a policy on us? Can she do that? It freaks me out."

"Unfortunately, it sounds as if she has. I intend to talk to your father about it at the earliest opportunity." Jessica sighed again. "I don't understand any of this. Why would someone want us gone enough to try to scare us with a magic circle? They all know Dillon, they must realize he'd throw off the island whoever is trying to scare me. If the music is so important to them, why risk it?"

"I think it's Brenda," Trevor said. "Robert doesn't have any more money and she's looking at my dad. You come along and Dad's looking at you. Jealousy rears its ugly head. Case solved. It's the cold-hearted woman looking for the cash every time."

"Thank you, Sherlock, blame it on the woman, why don't you. Let's go back downstairs and find Tara. She's probably already cleaned the kitchen."

"Why do you think I'm stalling up here?"

Jessica was glad the tea towel was still in her hand. She snapped it at him as she followed him downstairs.

To Trevor's delight, Tara had tidied the kitchen so the three of them spent the next couple of hours exploring the house. It was fun discovering the various rooms. Dillon had antique and brand-new musical instruments of all kinds. There was a game room consisting of all the

latest video and DVD equipment. Jessica had to drag
Trevor out of a poolroom. The weight room caught her
interest, but the twins dragged her out. Eventually they
settled in the library, curled up together on the deep
couch surrounded by books and antiques. Jessica found
the Dickens Christmas classic and began to read it aloud
to the twins.

"Jess! Damn it, Jess, where are you?" The voice came
roaring out of the basement. Clipped. Angry. Frustrated.

Jessica slowly put the book aside as Dillon called for
her a second time.

Tara looked frightened and reached for Jessica's hand.
Trevor burst out laughing. "You're being yelled at, Jessie.
I've never heard anyone yell at you before."

Jessica rolled her eyes heavenward. "I guess I'd better
go answer the royal command."

"We'll just go along with you," Trevor decided, striving
to sound casual as Dillon roared for her again.

Jessica hid her smile. Trevor was determined to protect
her. She loved him all the more for it. "Let's go then,
before he has a stroke."

"What did you do to make him so angry?" Tara asked.

"I certainly didn't do anything," Jessica replied indignantly. "How could I possibly make him angry?"

Trevor flicked her red-gold hair. "You could make the
Pope angry, Jessie. And you bait him."

"I do not!" Jessica chased him along the hall leading to
the stairs. "Punky boy. An alien took you over in your
sleep one night. You were good and sweet until then."

Trevor was running backward, dancing just out of her
reach, laughing as he neared the top of the stairway. "I'm

still good and sweet, Jessie, you just can't take hearing the truth."

"I'll show you truth," Jessica warned, making a playful grab for him.

Trevor stepped backward onto the first stair and unexpectedly slipped, his foot going out from under him. For a moment he teetered precariously, his hands flailing wildly as he tried to catch the banister. Jessica could see the fear on his young face and lunged forward to grab him, choking on stark, mind-numbing terror. Her fingers skimmed the material of his shirt, but missed. Tara, holding out both hands to her twin, screamed loudly as Trevor fell away from them.

Dillon rushed up the stairs, taking two at a time, furious that Jessica hadn't answered him when he knew *damn* well she'd heard him. Strangling her might not be a bad idea *after* she explained to that idiot Don what he was looking for. What was so difficult about hearing the right beat? The right pause? As Tara's scream registered, he glanced up to see Trevor falling backward. For one moment time stood still, his heart lodged in his throat. The boy hit him hard, squarely in the chest, driving the air out of his lungs in one blast. Protectively he wrapped his arms around his son as they both tumbled down the stairs to land heavily on the basement floor.

Jessica started down the stairs, Tara in her wake. The moment her foot touched the first stair, she felt herself slide. Clutching the banister, she caught Tara. "Careful, baby, there's something slippery on the stair." They both clung to the banister as they rushed down.

"Are they dead?" Tara asked fearfully.

Jessica could hear muffled swearing and Trevor's yelp of pain as Dillon ran his hands none too gently over his son to check for damage. "Doesn't sound like it," she observed. She knelt beside Trevor, her fingers pushing his hair from his forehead tenderly. "Are you all right, honey?"

"I don't know." Trevor managed a wry grin, still lying on top of his father.

Dillon caught Jessica's hand, his thumb sliding over her inner wrist, feeling her frantic heartbeat. "He's fine, he fell on top of me. I'm the one with all the bruises." Fear, mixed with anger, pulsed through his body. He hadn't experienced such panic and dread in years. The sight of Trevor falling from the top of the stairs was utterly terrifying. "I can't breathe, the kid weighs a ton." Dillon didn't know whether to hug Trevor or to shake him until his teeth rattled.

Jessica pushed back the unruly waves of hair falling into the center of Dillon's forehead. "You're breathing. Thanks for catching him."

Her touch shook him. Dillon's blue gaze burned over her face hungrily. It was painful to be jealous of his son, of the tender looks she gave him, the way she loved him. The way she was so at ease with him. Dillon wanted to drag her to him right there in front of everybody and kiss her. Devour her. Consume her. She was wreaking havoc with his body, breaking his heart and reopening every gaping laceration in his soul. She was making him feel things again, forcing him to live when it was so much better to be numb.

"And it was a great catch," Trevor agreed.

Dillon shoved the boy to one side, glaring at him, furious that he had been so terrified, furious that his life was being turned upside down. "Stop fooling around, kid, you could have really been hurt. You're too old to be playing so carelessly on the stairway. Roughhousing belongs outside, that way you don't break things that don't belong to you or injure innocent parties with your stupidity."

The smile faded from Trevor's face and color crept up his neck into his face. Tara gasped, outraged. "Trevor didn't hurt your stupid staircase."

"And you need to learn how to speak to adults, young lady," Dillon concluded, switching his glare to her furious little face.

Jessica stood up, drawing Tara up with her. She reached down to help Trevor to his feet. "Trevor slipped on something on the stairs, just as I did, Dillon," she informed him icily. "Perhaps, instead of jumping to conclusions about Trevor's behavior, you should ask your other guests to be more careful and not spill things on the stairs that will send people flying."

Dillon climbed to his feet slowly, his face an expressionless mask. "What's on the stairs?"

"I didn't stop and check," Jessica answered.

"Well, let's go see." He started up the stairs with Jessica following him closely.

The top stair was shiny, a clear, oily substance covering it. Dillon hunkered down and studied it. "Looks like cooking oil, right out of the kitchen." He glanced down at the twins who were waiting at the bottom of the stairs as if suspecting them.

"They didn't spill oil here. They were with me," Jessica snapped. She reached past him, touched the oil with a fingertip, and brought it to her mouth. "Vegetable oil. Someone must have poured this oil onto the stair." Oil was used in magical ceremonies to invoke spirits. She remembered that piece of information all too well.

"Or accidentally spilled some and didn't realize it." Dillon's blue gaze slid over her. "And I wasn't accusing the kids, it didn't occur to me they did this. Don't jump to conclusions, Jess."

"Let's go ask the others," she challenged him.

He sighed. "You're angry with me." He held out his leather-covered hand to her, an instinctive gesture. The moment he realized what he'd done, he dropped his hand to his side.

"Of course I'm angry with you, Dillon, what did you expect?" Jessica tilted her head to look up at him. "Don't treat me like a child, and don't use that infuriating patronizing voice on me either. I told you the accidents that have been happening at home could easily be explained away. I'll guarantee you, no one in this house is going to admit to spilling cooking oil on the stairs."

He shrugged. "So what if they don't? This wasn't directed at Trevor and Tara—how could it be? We're recording down there. Why would anyone think the kids would come down? No one could possibly have predicted that I would be calling for you."

"I disagree. I love music and I'm a sound engineer, and everyone here knows it. And you mentioned earlier in the kitchen that the twins could come down later and watch."

He raised his eyebrow at her. "Everyone, including Brenda, is in the studio. How do you explain that?"

"The twins were with me the entire time, Dillon," Jessica countered, her green eyes beginning to smolder, "how do you explain that? And speaking of Brenda, why in the world would you give your consent to allow that woman to hold an insurance policy on you and your children?"

"She's family, Jessie, it's harmless enough, although costly," he shrugged carelessly, "and it makes her feel a part of something."

"It makes me feel like a vulture is circling overhead," Jessica muttered. She followed him back down the stairs to where the twins waited expectantly.

"Hey, we're wasting time," Brian called. "Are you two going to come and work or are you going to discuss the positive versus the negative flow of the universe around us? What's going on out there?"

"We fell down the stairs," Dillon said grimly. "We'll be right there." He leaned close to Jessica. "Take a breath, Mama Tiger, don't rip my head off," Dillon teased, searching for a way to ease the tension between them. "Pull in the claws." Her instant, fierce defense of his children amused and pleased him.

Jessica glared at the twins. Both backed away innocently, shaking their heads in unison, awed that their father knew their secret pet name for Jessica. "I didn't tell him. Honest," Trevor added, when she kept glaring. "And he didn't mention fangs."

"Does she have fangs?" Dillon asked his son, his eyebrow shooting up. He was so relieved the boy hadn't hurt himself in the fall.

"Oh, yeah," Trevor answered, "absolutely. In a heart-beat. Fear for your life if you mess with us."

Dillon grinned suddenly, his face lighting up, mischief flickering for a brief moment in the deep blue of his eyes. "Believe me, son, I would."

Trevor stood absolutely still, shaken at the emotion pouring into him at his father's words. Jessica's hand briefly touched his shoulder in silent understanding.

"Come on, Jessica, we could use a little help." Dillon caught her arm and marched her down the hall as if she were his prisoner. He leaned close to her as they walked, his breath warm against her ear. "And I am *not* volatile." He glanced back at the twins, beckoning to them. "If you two can keep quiet, you can come and watch. Brenda! I have a job for you."

Jessica made a face at Trevor behind Dillon's back that set the children laughing as Dillon dragged her into the sound room.

"A job?" Brenda stretched languidly as she stood up. "Surely not, Dillon. I haven't actually worked in years. The idea is a bit on the daunting side."

"I think you'll find it easy enough. There's oil on the stairway, a large amount of it. It makes the stairs danger-ous and it needs to be cleaned up. My household staff is gone, we're all pitching in, so this is your task for the day."

Brenda widened her eyes in shocked dismay. "You can't possibly be serious, Dillon. It was a terrible decision to allow your staff to leave. What were you thinking to do such a crazy thing?"

"That it was Christmastime and they might want to be with their families," Dillon lied. The truth was he hadn't wanted anyone to witness him falling flat on his face while he worked with the band. It was terrifying to think of the enormity of what he was doing. "You knew there was no staff, that we would be working. You agreed to help with the everyday chores if I allowed you to come."

"Well, chores, of course. Fluffing the towels in the bathroom, not cleaning up a mess on the stairs. You," she pointed to Tara, "surely you could do this little job."

Before Tara could reply Dillon shook his head. "You, Brenda, get to it. Tara and Trevor, sit over there. Jessica, take a look at my notations and listen to the tracks and see if it makes any sense to you. I'm ready to pull out my hair here." He pulled Jessica over to a chair, pressing down on her shoulders until she sat. "It's a nightmare."

Jessica waited until he was safely in the studio before muttering her reply. "It is now. Working with Dillon Wentworth is going to be pure hell." She winked at the twins. "Wait until you see him. He's all passion and energy. Quicksilver. And he yells when he doesn't get *exactly* what he wants."

"Big surprise there," Trevor said drolly.

Brenda threw a pencil onto the floor, a small rebellion. "That man is an overbearing, dominating madman when he's working. I don't know where he gets the mistaken idea he can boss me around."

"True, but he's a musical genius and he makes lots and lots of money for everyone," Jessica reminded, frowning down at the sheets of music. It was obvious Dillon's smaller motor skills were lacking, his musical notations were barely legible scratches.

Brenda sighed. "Fine then, it's true, we need our wonderful cash machine, so I'll do my part to make him happy. One of you kiddies should take a picture of me scrubbing the stairs like Cinderella. It might be worth a fortune." She gave her tinkling laugh. "I know Robert would certainly love to see such a thing, but then, it would ruin his image of me and I can't let him think I'm capable of working." She winked at Trevor. "I'm trusting you not to say a word to him. If you both want to come with me, I'll even pass on smoking, which the master has decreed I can't do in his house."

"Well, you shouldn't smoke. It's not good for you," Tara pointed out judiciously.

Brenda made a face at her. "Fine, stay here and listen to your father yell at everyone, but it won't be nearly as entertaining as watching me." Her high heels tapped out her annoyance as she left.

Jessica spent an hour deciphering Dillon's musical notations then listening through the tracks he had already recorded, trying to find the mix Dillon was looking for. The problem was, the band members weren't hearing the same thing in their heads that Dillon was hearing. Don was no lead guitarist; his gift lay in his skill with the bass. It was apparent to Jessica that the band needed a lead, but she wasn't altogether certain who could play Dillon's music the way he wanted it to be played. Most musicians had egos. No one was going to allow Dillon to tell him how to play.

She saw that the band had once more ground to a halt. Brian grimaced at her through the glass. Paul shook his head at her, worry plain on his face. She leaned over to flip the switch to flood the room with sound. Dillon paced back and forth, energy pouring out of him, filling the studio, flashes of brilliance, of pure genius mixed with building frustration and impatience.

"Why can't any of you hear it?" Dillon smacked his palm to his head, stormed over to the guitar leaning against the wall. "What's so difficult about anticipating the beat? Slow the melody down, you're rushing the riff. It isn't to show what an awesome player you are alone, it's a harmony, a blending so that it smokes." He cradled the guitar, held it lovingly, almost tenderly. The need to play what he heard in his head was so strong his body trembled.

Watching him through the glass, Jessica felt her heart shatter. She could read him, and his need to bring the music to life, so easily. Dillon had always been exacting, a perfectionist when it came to his music. His passion came through in his composing, in his lyrics, in his playing. It was what had shot the band to the top and all of them knew it. They wanted it again, and they were banking on him to find it for them.

Dillon glared at Don. "Try again and this time get it right."

Visibly sweating, Don glanced uneasily at the others. "I'm not going to play it any differently than I did the last time, Dillon. I'm not you. I'll never be you. I can't hear what you want me to hear just by you telling me about blending and smoke and strings. I'm not you."

Dillon swore, his blue eyes burning with such intensity Don stepped away from him and held up his hand. "I want this, I do. I'm telling you, we need to find someone else to play lead guitar because it's not going to be me.

And no matter who we get, Dillon, it still won't be you. You aren't ever going to be satisfied."

Dillon winced as if Don had struck him. The two men stared at one another for a long moment and then Dillon turned and abruptly stalked out of the room. He stood in the sound room, head down, breathing deeply, trying to push down despair. He never should have tried, never should have thought he could do it. Aloud, he cursed his hands, cursed his scarred, useless body, cursed his passion for music.

Tears swam in Tara's eyes and she buried her face against her brother's shoulder. Trevor put his arm around his sister and looked at Jessica.

The movement snapped Dillon back to reality. Jessica was fiddling with a row of keys, concentrating intently, not looking at him. "Jess!" The sight of her was inspiring, a gift! He stalked across the room like a prowling panther, caught her arm, and pulled her to him. "You do it, Jess, I know you hear what I hear. It's there inside of you, it's always been there. We've always shared that connection. Get in there and play that song the way it's meant to be played." He was dragging her toward the door. "You've been playing guitar since you were five."

"What are thinking? I can't play with your band!" Jessica was appalled. "Don will get it right, stop yelling at him and give him time."

"He'll never get it right, he doesn't love the melody. You have to love it, Jessica. Remember all those nights we sat up playing in the kitchen? The music's in you, you live it and breathe it. It's alive to you the same way it is for me."

"But that was different, it was just the two of us."

"I know you play guitar brilliantly, I've heard you. I know you would never give up playing, you hear it the same way I hear it." He was shoving her, actually pushing her as she mulishly tried to dig in her heels.

Jessica looked to the twins for support but they were wearing identical grins. "She plays every day, sometimes for hours," Tara volunteered helpfully.

"Little traitor," Jessica hissed, "you've been hanging around with your brother too long. Both of you have dish duty for the next week."

"*Both* of us?" Trevor squeaked. "I'm innocent in this. Come on, Tara, let's leave them to it. We can explore that game room a little more."

"Deserters," Jessica added. "Rats off the sinking ship. I'll remember this." She was holding the door to the studio closed with her foot.

"Actually, I think it will be fun to catch Aunt Brenda cleaning the goop off the stairs," Tara said mischievously. She flounced out with a little wave and Trevor sauntered after her, grinning from ear to ear.

"It's obvious that you raised them," Dillon said, his lips against her ear, his arm hard around her waist. "They both have smart mouths on them."

"Stop making such a spectacle! You have the entire band grinning at us like apes!" Jessica pushed away from him, made a show of straightening her clothes and smoothing her hair. Her chin went up. "I'll do this, Dillon. I think I have an idea of what you're looking for, but it will take some time to pull it out of my head. Don't yell at me while I'm working. Not once, do you understand? Do not raise your voice to me or I will walk out of that room so fast you won't know what hit you."

"I'd like to get away with saying that," Brian observed.

"You all can take a break. Jessica is going to save the day for us."

"I am *not*." She glared at Dillon. "I'm just going to see if I can figure it out and if I can get it, I'll play it for you. Do you mind, Don?"

"I'm grateful, Jess." Don smiled for the first time since entering the studio. "Yell very loud if you need help and we'll all come running."

"Great, the place is soundproof." Jessica picked up the guitar and idly began to play a blues riff, allowing her fingers to wander over the strings, her ear tuning itself to the tones of the instrument, familiarizing herself with the feel of it. "You're leaving me with Dillon, just remember that."

chapter

6

JESSICA CLOSED HER EYES as she played, allowing the music to move through her body. Her heart and soul. It wasn't right, there was something missing, something she wasn't quite hitting. It was so close, so very close, but she couldn't quite reach it. She shook her head, listening with her heart. "It's not quite what it should be. It's almost there, but it isn't perfect."

There was frustration in her voice, enough that Dillon checked what he would have said and waited a heartbeat so that his own frustration wouldn't betray him. She didn't need him raging at her. What she needed was complete harmony between them. Unlike Don, Jessica was aware of what he wanted, she heard a similar sound in her own head, but it wasn't coming through her fingers. "Let's try something else, Jess. Pull it back a bit. Hold the notes longer, let the music breathe."

She nodded without looking at him, intense concentration on her face as her fingers lovingly moved over the strings. She listened to the flow, the pitch, a moody, introspective score, opening slowly, building, until the pain and heartbreak swelled, spilled over, filling the room until her heart was breaking and there were tears in her eyes. Her fingers stopped moving abruptly. "It's not the guitar, Dillon. The sound is there, haunting and vivid, the emotions pouring out of the music. Listen, right here, it's right here." She played the notes once, twice, her fingers lingering, drawing out the sounds. "This isn't a piece where we can just lay a track and have bass and drums doing their thing. It isn't ever going to be enough."

He snapped his fingers, indicating for her to play again, his head cocked to one side, his eyes closed. "A saxophone? Something soft and melancholy? Right there, cutting into that passage, lonely, something lonely."

Jessica nodded and she smiled, her entire face lighting up. "Exactly, that's it exactly. The sax has to cut in right there and take the spotlight for just a few bars, the guitar fading a bit into the background. This melody is too much for just bass and drums. We just aren't looking at the entire picture. When we mix it, we can try a few things, but I'd like to hear what it would sound like with Robert giving us synthesized orchestra sounds on the keyboard. This song should have more texture to it. The vocal will add the depth we need."

Dillon paced across the room, once, twice, then stopped in front of her. "I can hear the saxophone perfectly. It has to come in right on the beat in the middle of the buildup."

She nodded. "I'm excited—I think it will work. I've got the ideas for mixing. Don can come in and play it . . ."

"No!" He nearly bit her head off, his blue eyes burning at her.

He looked moody, dark. Intriguing. Jessica nearly groaned. She looked away from him, wishing she didn't find him so attractive. Wishing it was only chemistry sizzling between them and not so many other things.

"Don will never have your passion, Jess. He knows that, he as much as said so. He told me to find another lead."

She leaned the guitar very carefully against the wall. "Well, it isn't going to be me. I can't play the way you want—I don't have enough experience. And even if I did, this is a men's club. Very few musicians want to admit that a woman can handle a guitar."

"You'll have the experience when we need it. I'll help you," he promised. "And the band wants this to work. They'll try anything to keep it going forward."

She shook her head, backing away from him as if he were stalking her.

Dillon's grin transformed his face. He looked boyish, charming, altogether irresistible. "Want to go for a walk with me?"

It was late, already dark outside. She had been away from the twins for a long while but the temptation of spending more time alone with him was too much to resist. She nodded her head.

"There's a door over here." He picked up one of the sweaters he'd thrown aside days earlier and dragged it over her head. Shrugging into his jacket, Dillon opened the door and stepped back to allow her to go first. He whistled softly and the German shepherd who had greeted Jessica and twins so rudely when they had arrived, came running to them, a blur of dark fur.

The night was crisp, cold, the air coming off the ocean, misty with salt and tendrils of fog. They found a narrow path winding through the trees and took it, side by side, their hands occasionally brushing. Jessica didn't know how it happened but somehow her hand ended up snugly in his.

She glanced up at him, drawing in her breath, her heart fluttering, racing. Happy. But it was now or never. She either cleared the air between them or he would be lost to her. "How did you happen to end up with Vivian? She didn't seem to fit you."

For a long moment she thought he wouldn't answer her. They walked in silence for several yards and then he let out his breath in a long, slow exhale.

"Vivian." Dillon swept his free hand through his black hair and glanced down at her. "Why did I marry Vivian? That's a good question, Jess, and one I've asked myself hundreds of times."

They walked together beneath the canopy of trees, surrounded by thick forest and heavy brush. The wind rustled through the leaves gently, softly, a light breeze that seemed to follow them as they followed a deer path through the timber. "Dillon, I never understood how you chose her, you two were so different."

"I knew Vivian all of my life, we grew up in the same trailer park. We had nothing. None of us did, not Brian, or Robert, or Paul. Certainly not Viv. We all hung out together, playing our music and dreaming big dreams. She had a hard life, she and Brenda both. Their mother was a drunk with a new man every week. You can imagine what life was like for two little girls living unprotected in that environment."

"You felt sorry for her." Jessica made it a statement.

Dillon winced. "No, that would make me appear noble. I'm not noble in this, Jess, no matter how much you want me to be. I cared a great deal for her, I thought I loved her. Hell, I was eighteen when we got together. I certainly wanted to protect her, to take care of her. I knew she didn't want kids. She and Brenda were terrified of losing their figures and being left behind. Their mother drilled it into them that it was their fault the men always left because they had ruined her figure. She even told them, when her boyfriends came on to them, that it was their fault, that of course the men preferred them to her." He raked his hand through his hair again, a quick, impatient gesture. "I'd heard it from the time we were kids. I heard Vivian say she would never have a baby, but I guess I didn't listen."

They continued along the deer path for several more minutes in silence. Jessica realized they were moving toward the cliffs almost by mutual consent. "So many old ghosts," she observed, "and neither one of us has managed to lay them to rest."

Dillon brought her hand to the warmth of his chest, right over his heart. "You didn't have the kind of life we lived, Jess, you can't understand. She never had a childhood. I was all Vivian had—me and the band and Brenda, when she wasn't fighting her own demons. When Vivian found out she was pregnant, she freaked. Totally freaked. Couldn't handle it. She begged me to give her permission to get rid of them, but I wanted a family. I thought she'd come around after they were born. I married her and promised we'd hire a nanny to take care of the kids while we worked the band."

Dillon led the way out of the timberline onto the bare cliffs overlooking the sea. At once the wind whipped his hair across his face. Instinctively he turned so that his larger body sheltered hers. "I hired Rita to take care of the children and we left. We just left." He stared down at her, his blue eyes brooding as he brought her hand to the warmth of his mouth. His teeth scraped gently, his tongue swirled over her skin.

Jessica shivered in response, her body clenching, molten fire suddenly pooling low in her belly. She could hear the guilt in his voice, the regret, and she forced herself to stay focused. "The band was making it big."

"Not right away, but we were on the upswing." He reached out, because he couldn't stop himself, and crushed strands of bright red-gold hair in his fist. "I wanted it so bad, Jess, the money, the good life. I never wanted to have to worry about a roof over our heads or where the next meal was coming from. We worked hard over the next three years. When we would go home, Vivian would bring the twins bags of presents but she would never touch them, or talk to them." He allowed the silky strands to slide through his fingers. "By the time the twins were four, the band was a wild success but we were all falling apart." Abruptly he let go of her.

"I remember her coming in with gifts," Jessica acknowledged, shivering a little as the wind blew in from the sea. All at once she felt alone. Bereft. "Vivian stayed away from us, away from the twins. She didn't come home very often." Dillon had visited without her, but Vivian had preferred to stay in the city most of the time with the other band members.

A peculiar fog was drifting in on the wind from the sea. It was heavy, almost oppressive. The dog looked out toward the pounding waves and a growl rumbled low in his throat. The sound sent a chill down Jessica's spine but Dillon snapped his fingers and the animal fell silent.

"No, she didn't." Dillon shrugged out of his jacket and helped her into it. "She was always so fragile, so suscepti- ble to fanatical thinking. I knew she was drinking. Hell, we were all drinking. Partying was a way of life back then. Brian was into some strange practices, not devil worship, but calling on spirits and gods and mother earth. You know how he can be, he runs a line of bull all the time. The problem was, he had Vivian believing all of it. I didn't pay attention, I just laughed at them. I didn't real- ize then that she was seriously ill. Later, the doctors told me she was bipolar, but at the time, I just thought it was all part of the business we were in. The drinking, even the drugs, I thought she'd tame down when she got it out of her system. I didn't realize she was self-medicating. But I should have, Jess, I should have seen it. She had the signs, the intense mood swings, the highs and lows and the abrupt changes in her thinking and behavior. I should have known."

His hands suddenly framed her face, holding her still. "I laughed, Jess, and while I was laughing about their silly ceremonies, she was going downhill, straight into mad- ness. The drugs pushed her over the edge and she had a schizophrenic break. By the time I realized just how bad she really was, it was too late and she tried to hurt you."

"You put her in rehabs—how could you have known what bipolar even was?" She remembered that clearly. "No one told you that last year while you were on the world tour just how bad she'd gotten. You were in Europe. I heard them all discussing it; the decision was made not to say anything to you because you would have thrown it all away. The band knew. Paul, Robert, especially Brian, he called several times to talk to her. Your manager, Eddie Malone, was adamant that everyone stay quiet. He arranged for her to stay here, on the island. He thought with all the security she would be safe."

Dillon let go of her again, his blue gaze sliding out to sea. "I knew, Jess. I knew she had slipped past sanity, but I was so wrapped up in the tour, in the music, in myself, I didn't check on her. I left it to Eddie. When I'd talk to her on the phone she was always so hysterical, so demanding. She'd sob and threaten me. I was a thousand miles away and feeling so much pressure, and I was tired of her tantrums. At the time I listened to everyone telling me she would pull out of it. I let her down. My God, she trusted me to take care of her and I let her down."

"You were barely twenty-seven, Dillon—cut yourself some slack."

He laughed softly, bitterly. "You always persist in thinking the best of me. Do you think she started out the way she ended up? She was far too fragile for the life I took her into. I wanted everything. The family. The success. My music. It was all about what I wanted, not what she needed." He shook his head. "I did try to understand her at first, but she was so needy and my time was stretched so thin. And the kids. I blamed her for not wanting them, not wanting to be with them."

"That's natural, Dillon," Jessica said softly. She tucked her hand into the crook of his arm, wanting to connect herself to him, wanting the terrible pain, the utter loneliness etched so deeply into his face, to be gone.

The fog thickened, a heavy blanket that carried within it the whisper of something moving, of muffled sounds and veiled memories. It bothered her that the dog stared at the fog as if it held an enemy within its midst. She tried to ignore the animal's occasional growl. Dillon, too engrossed in their conversation, didn't appear to notice.

"Is it natural, Jess?" His eyebrow shot up as he looked down into her wide green eyes. "You're so willing to forgive my mistakes. I left the kids. I put my career first, my own needs first, what I wanted, first. Why was it okay for me, but unforgivable for her? She was ill. She knew she had something wrong with her; she was terrified of hurting the kids. She didn't need rehab, she needed help with mental illness." He rubbed his hand over his face, his breath coming in hard gasps. "I didn't come home much that year because of you, Jessica. Because I was feeling things for you I shouldn't have been feeling. Rita knew, God help me. I talked to her about it and we agreed the best thing to do was for me to stay away from you. It wasn't sex, Jess, I swear to you, it was never about sex."

There was so much pain in his voice her heart was breaking. She looked up at him and saw tears shimmering in his eyes. At once she put her arms around his waist, laid her head on his chest, holding him to her without words, seeking to comfort him. He had never touched her, never said a word that might be deemed improper to her, nor had she to him. But it was true they'd sought each other's company, talked endlessly, *needed* to be close. She could feel his body tremble, with emotion rising like a long dormant volcano come to life.

Dillon was all about responsibility; he always had been. She had always known that. His failure was eating him from the inside out. Jessica felt helpless to stop it. She drew back cautiously, putting a step between them so she could look up at his face. "Did you know she was into séances and calling up demons?" She had to ask him and her heart pounded in time to the rhythm of the sea as she waited for his answer.

"She and Brian would burn candles to spirits but there had been nothing remotely like devil worship, sacrifices, or the occult. I didn't know she had hooked up with some lunatic who preached orgies and drugs and demon gods. I had no idea until I walked into that room and saw you." He closed his eyes, his fist clenching.

"You got me out of there, Dillon," she reminded gently.

Rage. He tasted it again, just as it had swirled up in him that night, a violence he hadn't known himself capable of. He had wanted to destroy them all. Every single person in that room. He had beat Vivian's lover to a bloody pulp, satisfying some of his rage in that direction. He had vented on Vivian, his wrath nearly out of control, calling her every name he could think of, allowing her to see his disgust, ordering her out of his home. He had sworn she would never see the children, never be allowed into his life again. Vivian had stood there, naked, sobbing, and hanging on him, the musty smell of other men clinging to her as she begged him not to send her away.

Dillon looked down to meet Jessica's vivid gaze. They both recalled the scene clearly. How could they not remember every detail? The heavy fog carried a strange phosphorescence within, a shimmering of color that floated inland.

Dillon looked away from the innocence on Jessica's face. Staring at the white breakers he made his confession. "I wanted to kill her. I didn't feel pity, Jessica. I wanted to break her neck. And I wanted to kill her friends. Every last one of them."

There was honesty in his voice. Truth. She heard the echo of rage in his voice, and the memories washed over her, shook her. He had learned there was a demon hidden deep within him and Jessica had certainly witnessed it.

"You didn't kill them, Dillon." She said it with complete conviction.

"How do you know, Jess? How can you be so certain I didn't go back into that room after I carried you upstairs? How can you be so certain, after I laid you on the bed with your heart torn out, after I knew that she had encouraged some lecherous pervert to put his hands on you, to write symbols of evil all over your body? When I saw you like that, so frightened—" His fist clenched tightly. "You were everything good and innocent that they weren't. They wanted to destroy you. Why would you believe that I didn't walk back up the stairs, shoot both of them, lock them all in that room, start the fire, and leave the house?"

"Because I know you. Because the twins, the band members, my mother, and I were all in that house."

"Everyone is capable of murder, Jess, and believe me, I wanted them dead." He sighed heavily. "You need to know the truth. I did go back into the house that night."

A silence fell between them, stretching out endlessly while the wind rose on a moan and shrieked eerily out to sea. Jessica stood on the cliffs and stared down into the dark foaming waves. So beautiful, so deadly. She remembered vividly the feeling of the water closing over her head as she went after Tara who had tumbled down the steep embankment. She felt exactly the same way now, as if she were being submersed in ice-cold water and dragged down to the very bottom of the sea. Jessica looked up at the moon. The clouds, heavy with moisture, were sliding through the sky to streak the silver orb with shades of gray. The fog formed tendrils, long thin arms that stretched out as greedily as the waves leapt and crashed against the rocky shore.

"Everyone knows you went back. The house was on fire and you ran in." Her voice was very low. There was sudden awareness, a knowledge growing inside of her.

Dillon caught her chin, looked into her eyes, forcing her to meet his gaze, to see the truth. "After I left your room I went outside. Everyone saw me. Everyone knew I was furious at Vivian. I was crying, Jess, after seeing you like that, knowing what you'd been through. I couldn't stop ranting, couldn't hide the tears. The band thought I'd caught Viv with a lover. I stalked out, huddled in the forest, walked around the house a couple of times. But then I went to find your mother. I felt she ought to know what Vivian, her friends, and that madman had done to you."

"She never said a word to me."

"I told her what happened. All of it. How I found you with them. What they were doing. I was crazy that night," he admitted. "Rita was the only person I could talk to and I knew you wouldn't tell her about it, you kept begging me not to, you couldn't bear for her to know." He raked a hand through his hair again in agitation, the memories choking him. "Rita blamed herself. She knew what Vivian was doing, had known for some time. I yelled at her when she admitted it, I was so angry, so out of control, wanting vengeance for what had happened to you. Looking back, I can see that it was my fault, all of it. I blamed everyone else for what happened to you, and I hated them and wanted them dead, but I was the one that allowed it to happen."

Dillon studied her face as she stared up at him with her wide eyes. He reached out, brushed her face with his gloved hand, his touch lingering long after he dropped his hand. "I went back into the house, angry and determined to avenge you. Rita knew I went back. Your mother believed I murdered Vivian and her lover. She thought the fire was an accident, caused by the candles being knocked over while we were fighting. She knew I went back into the house and she believed I shot them but she never told anyone."

Jessica's green gaze jumped to his face. "She didn't believe you killed them." She shook her head adamantly. "Mom would never believe that of you."

"She knew my state of mind. There was so much rage

in me that night. I didn't even recognize myself. I had no idea I was capable of such violence. It consumed me. I couldn't even think straight."

Jessica shook her head. "I won't listen to this. I won't believe you." She turned away from him, away from the pounding sea and the heartache, away from the thick, beckoning fog, back toward the safety of the house.

Dillon caught her arms, held her still, his blue eyes raking her face. "You have to know the truth. You have to know why I stayed away all those years. Why your mother came to see me."

"I don't care what you say to me, Dillon, I'm not going to believe this. Seven people died in that fire. *Seven.* My mother may have kept quiet to save you because of what Vivian did to me, but she would never stay quiet if she thought you'd killed seven people."

"But then, if the fire was an accident, it wouldn't have been murder, and those seven people who died were having an orgy upstairs in my home, using Rita's daughter as the virginal sacrifice for their priests to enjoy." He said it harshly, his face a mask of anger. "Believe me, honey, she understood hatred and rage. She felt it herself."

Jessica stared up at him for a long while. "Dillon." She reached up to lay her hand along his shadowed jaw. "You will never get me to believe you shot Vivian. Never. I know your soul. I've always known it. You can't hide who you are from me. It's there each time you write a song." Her arms slid around his neck, her fingers twining in the silk of his hair. "You were different enough at first that I was afraid of who you had become, but you can't hide yourself from me when you compose music."

Dillon's arms stole around her. It was amazing to him, a miracle that she could believe in him the way she did. He held her tightly, burying his face in her soft hair, stealing moments of pleasure and comfort that didn't belong to him.

"My mother never said a word to me, Dillon, about what happened to me that night. Why didn't she talk to me about it all those years? The nightmares. I wanted someone to talk to." She had wanted him.

"She told me she waited for you to come to her, but you never did."

Jessica sighed softly as she pulled away from him. "I could never bring myself to tell her what happened. I felt guilty. I still go over every move I made, wondering what I should have done differently to avoid the situation." Her hand rubbed up and down his arms. She felt the raised ridges of his scars beneath her palm, the evidence of his heroism. A badge of love and honor he hid from the world. "How could Mom have thought you were guilty?"

"I told her what went on and the entire time I was breaking things, threatening them, swearing like a madman. She was sobbing; she sat on the floor in the kitchen with her hands over her face, sobbing. I went back upstairs. I didn't know what I was going to do. I think I was going to physically throw Vivian and her friends out of the house, one by one, into the ocean. Your mother saw me go up the stairs. I stood on the landing and could hear Vivian weeping, shrieking to the others to get out, and I knew I couldn't look at her again. I just couldn't. I went back downstairs and out through the courtyard. I didn't want to face your mother, or the band. I needed to be alone. I walked into the forest and sat down and cried."

She could breathe again. Really breathe again. He wasn't going to do anything silly such as try to convince her that he had actually shot Vivian. "I've always known you were innocent, Dillon. And I still don't think my mother believed you killed them."

"Oh, she believed it, Jessica. She stayed silent at the trial, but she made it abundantly clear that I wasn't to go near you or the children. I owed her that much. For what happened to you, I owed her my life if she asked for it."

Jessica felt as if he'd knocked her legs out from under her. "She never said anything but good things about you, Dillon."

"She knew I wanted you, Jess. There was no way I would ever be able to be around you and not make you mine." He admitted it without looking at her.

His tone was so casual, so matter-of-fact, she wasn't certain she heard him correctly. He was looking out to sea, into the thick veil of mist, not at her.

"And I would have let you." She confessed it in the same casual tone, following his example, looking out at the crashing waves.

His throat worked convulsively; a muscle jerked along his jaw at her honest admission. He waited a heartbeat. Two. Struggled for control of his emotions. "Someone has been attempting to blackmail me. They sent a threatening letter, telling me that they knew I had gone back into the house that night and that if I didn't give them ten thousand dollars a month, they would go to the police. I was supposed to transfer the money to a Swiss account on a certain day each month. They used words cut out of a newspaper and pasted onto paper. To my knowledge Rita was the only person who saw me go back into the house that night before the shots were fired. That was the reason I asked her to come here, to discuss the matter with me."

"You thought my mother was blackmailing you?" Jessica was shocked.

"No, of course not, but I thought she may have seen someone else that night, someone who saw me go back into the house."

"You mean one of the security people? The staff? One of the groundskeepers? There were so many people around back then. Do you think it was one of them?"

"It had to be someone familiar with the inside of the house, Jessie." He raked a hand through his hair, his gloved fingers tunneling deep, tousling the strands in his wake.

Jessica glanced back toward the house. "Then it has to be one of them. A member of the band. They lived there on and off. They all survived the fire. Robert? He and Brenda need the cash and it's a plan she's capable of coming up with. I doubt if blackmailing someone would bother her in the least."

Dillon had to laugh. "That's true—Brenda would think she was perfectly within her rights." His smile faded, leaving his blue eyes bleak. "But they all need money, every last one of them."

"Then it's possible one of the band members killed my mother. She must have seen someone, maybe she confronted them about it."

Dillon shook his head. "That's just not possible. I thought about it until I thought I'd go out of my mind—it just isn't possible. I've known them all, with the exception of Don, all of my life. We were babies together, went through school, went through hard times together. We were family, more than family."

Her hand went to her throat, a curiously vulnerable gesture. "I can't imagine someone we know killing Mom."

"Maybe it really was an accident, Jessie," he said softly.

She just stood there looking up at him with that look of utter fragility on her face, tugging at his heartstrings. Unable to stop himself, Dillon reached out, pulled her to him, and bent his dark head to hers. There was time for a single heartbeat before his lips drifted over hers. Tasting. Coaxing. Tempting. Kissing Jessica seemed as natural to him as breathing. The moment he touched her, he was lost.

Dillon drew her into his arms and she fit perfectly, her body molding to his. Soft. Pliant. Made for him. His tongue skimmed gently along the seam of her lips, asking for entrance. His teeth tugged at her lower lip, a teasing nip, causing her to gasp. At once he took possession, sweeping inside, claiming her, exploring the heated magic of her. Where she might have wanted to be cautious, with him she was all passion, a sweet eruption of hunger that built with his insistence.

Her mouth was addicting and he fed there while the wind whipped their hair around them and tugged at their clothing. The sea breeze cooled the heat of their skin as the temperature rose. His body was full, heavy, and painful. The hunger raged through his body for her, a dark craving he dared not satisfy. Abruptly he lifted his head, a soft curse escaping him.

"You don't have an ounce of self-preservation in you," he snapped at her, his blue eyes hot with an emotion she dared not name.

Jessica stared up at his beloved face. "And you have too much of it," she told him softly, her mouth curving into a teasing smile.

He swore again. She looked bemused, her eyes cloudy, sensual, her mouth sexy, provocative. Kissable. Dillon shook his head, determined to break free of her spell. She was so beautiful to him. So innocent of the vicious things people were capable of doing to one another. "Never, Jess. I'm not doing this with you. If you have some crazy idea of saving the pitiful musician, you can think again." He sounded fierce, angry even.

Jessica lifted her chin. "Do I look the type of woman who would feel pity for a man who has so much? You don't need pity, Dillon, you never have. I didn't run away from life, you did. You had a choice. No matter what my mother said to you about staying away from me and the children, you still had a choice to come back to us." She couldn't quite keep the hurt out of her voice.

His expression hardened perceptibly. "It was my choices that brought us all to this point, Jess. My wants. My needs. That isn't going to happen again. Have you forgotten what they did to you? Because if you haven't, I can tell you in vivid detail. I remember everything. It's etched into my memories, burned into my soul. When I close my eyes at night I see you lying there helpless and frightened. Damn it, we aren't doing this!" Abruptly he turned his back on her, turned away from the turbulent sea and stalked back toward the house.

Jessica stared after him, her heart pounding in rhythm with the foaming waves, the memories crowding so close that for a moment madness swirled up to consume her. The fog slid between them, thick and dangerous, obscuring her vision of Dillon. She swayed, heard chanting carried on the ocean breeze. Beside her, the German shepherd snarled, his growl rumbling low and ominous as he stared at the moving vapor.

"Jess!" Dillon's impatient tone cut through the strange illusion, dispelling it instantly. "Hurry up, I'm not leaving you out here alone."

Jessica found herself smiling. He sounded gruff, but she heard the inadvertent tenderness he tried so hard to keep from her, to keep from himself. She went to him without a word, the dog racing with her. There was time. It wasn't Christmas yet and miracles always happened on Christmas.

"COME ON, JESSIE," Trevor wheedled, stuffing a third pancake in his mouth. "We've been here a week. Nothing's happened to us. There's no weird stuff happening and we haven't even had a chance to explore the island."

Jessica shook her head adamantly. "If you two want to explore, I'll go with you. It's dangerous."

"What's dangerous?" Trevor glared at her as he picked up a huge glass of orange juice. "If Tara and I are in any danger, it's of being sucked into one of those video games we're playing so much. Come on, you and the others have been locked in the studio and we're always alone. We can only watch so many movies and play so many games. We're living like zombies, sleeping all day and staying up all night."

"No." Jessica didn't dare look at the band members. She knew they thought she was overly protective when it came to the twins.

Brenda snickered. "It's none of my business but if you ask me, they're old enough to go outside all by themselves."

"I have to agree with her," Brian seconded, "and that's plain scary. Trevor's a responsible kid, he's not going to do anything silly."

Tara glared at Brian. "I am *very* responsible. I said we'd *look* for a Christmas tree. Trevor wants to find one and chop it down."

Jessica paled visibly. "*Trevor!* Chopping involves an axe. You certainly aren't going to go chopping down trees." The thought was truly frightening.

"They aren't babies." Brenda sounded bored with the entire conversation. "Why shouldn't they go outside to play? All that fresh air is supposed to be good for kiddies, isn't it?"

Jessica glared at the twins' aunt as she sipped her morning coffee. "Stop calling them kiddies, Brenda," she snapped irritably. "They have names and like it or not you are related to them."

Brenda slowly lowered her coffee mug and peered intently at Jessica. "Do us all a favor, hon, just have sex with him. Get it over with and out of your system so we can all live in peace around here. Dillon's walking around like a bear with a sore tooth and you're so edgy you exhaust me."

Trevor spewed orange juice across the counter, nearly choking. Tara gasped audibly, spinning around to glare accusingly at Jessica.

"Oh dear," Brenda sighed dramatically. "Another huge gaffe. I suppose I shouldn't have said 'sex' in front of them. One must learn to censor oneself around kid . . ." she paused, rolled her eyes, and continued. "*Children.*"

"Don't worry, Brenda," Trevor said good-naturedly,

"we *kiddies* learn all about sex at an early age nowadays. I think we were a little more shocked at your mentioning Jessica and our dad doing the a . . ." he glanced at his sister.

"Dastardly deed," Tara supplied without missing a beat.

Brian mopped up the orange juice with a wet cloth, winking at Jessica. "It would be dastardly if you decided to hop in the sack with Dillon. All his wonderful angst and creativity might evaporate in a single night."

"Shut up," Jessica snapped, placing her hands on her hips. "This conversation is not appropriate and it never will be. And we aren't doing anything, dastardly or otherwise, not that it's any of your business."

Tara tugged at the pocket of Jessica's jeans. "You're blushing, Jessie, is that why you're irritable all the time?"

"I am certainly *not* irritable." Jessica was outraged at the suggestion. "I've been working my you-know-what off with a madman perfectionist and his group of comedy club wannabes. If I've been a teensy little bit *edgy,* that would be the reason."

"Teensy?" Brenda sniffed disdainfully. "That doesn't begin to describe you, dear. Robert, rub my shoulders. Having to watch my every word is making me tense."

Robert obediently massaged his wife's shoulders while Brian circled around Jessica completely, peering at her with discerning eyes. "Your you-know-what is definitely intact and looking delicious, Jess, no need to worry about that."

"Thank you very much, you pervert," Jessica replied, trying not to laugh.

Dillon paused in the doorway to watch her with hungry eyes. To drink in the sight of her. The sound of her laughter and her natural warmth drew him like a magnet.

He had spent the last week avoiding brushing up against her soft skin, avoiding looking at her, but he couldn't avoid the scent of her or the sound of her voice. He couldn't avoid the way his blood surged hotly and little jackhammers pounded fiercely in his head when she was in the same room with him. He couldn't stop the urgent demands of his body. The relentless craving. She haunted his dreams and when he was awake she became an obsession he had no way to combat.

Thoughtfully, Dillon leaned one hip against the door. The intensity of his sexual hunger surprised him. He had always felt that Jessica was a part of him, even in the old days when it was simply companionship he had sought from her. They merged minds. Her voice blended perfectly with his. Her quick wit always brought him out of his brooding introspections and pulled him into passionate battles in every aspect of music. Jessica was well versed in music history and had strong opinions about composers and musicians. His conversations with her inspired him, animated him.

There was so much more. He felt alive again after a long interminable prison sentence. It wasn't at all comfortable, but along with bringing him to life, Jessica was putting the soul back into his music. He swore to himself, each time the moment he opened his eyes that he wouldn't give in to the whispers of temptation, but it seemed to him that he had gone from a barren, frozen existence straight into the fires of hell.

He couldn't help loving his children, being proud of

them. He couldn't help seeing the way Jessica loved them and the way they loved her back. And he couldn't help the desperate longing to be part of that bond, that intense love. Dillon had no idea how much longer he could keep his hands to himself, how much longer he could resist the lure of a family. Or even if he wanted to resist. Did he have the right to allow them into his world? He had failed once and it had changed the course of so many people's lives. Death and destruction had followed him. Did he dare reach out again, risk harming the ones he loved? He swept a hand through his thick hair and Jessica immediately turned, her vivid eyes meeting his.

Jessica could feel her heart thundering at the sight of him. A faint blush stole into her face as she wondered if he had overheard the conversation. She could only imagine what he must be thinking. Looking at him nearly took her breath away. There had always been such a casual masculine beauty to Dillon. Now, it seemed more careless, a sensual allure against which she had no resistance. One look from his smoldering eyes sent her body into meltdown. He was looking at her now, his blue eyes burning over her, intense, hungry, beyond her ability to resist.

Jessica tilted her chin at him in challenge. She had no reason to resist the strong pull between them. She wanted him to belong to her, body and soul. She saw no reason to deny it. As if knowing her thoughts, he lowered his gaze which drifted over her body, nearly a physical touch that left her aching and restless and all too aware of his presence.

"Dad?" Tara's voice instantly stopped all conversation

in the room. It was the first time she had addressed Dillon that way. "Trevor and I want to go looking for a Christmas tree." She glared at Jessica. "We aren't going to chop one down, only look for one."

Dillon smiled unexpectedly, looking like a mischievous, charming boy, so much like Trevor. "Is Mama Tiger showing her fangs?"

"Her claws anyway," Brenda muttered into her coffee mug.

"The weather's good, so we'll be perfectly safe," Trevor added, a glimmer of hope in his eyes. "Someone has to get this Christmas thing off the ground. We have less than two weeks to go. You're busy, we don't have that much time left, so Tara and I can handle the decorations while you work."

Dillon didn't look at Jessica. He *couldn't* look at her. The boy's face was hopeful and eager and trusting. Tara had called him 'Dad'. It tugged at his heartstrings as nothing else could have. His gaze shifted to his daughter's face. She wore an expression identical to her brother's. Trust was a delicate thing. It was the first time he'd come close to believing in miracles, that there might be second chances given out in life, even when he didn't deserve it. "You think you can find the perfect tree? Do you know how to choose one?"

Jessica blinked, her teeth sinking into her lower lip to keep from protesting. Dillon's tone had been casual, but there was nothing casual in the vivid blue of his eyes, or the set of his mouth. His gloved hand rubbed along his denim-clad thigh, betraying his uncharacteristic show of nerves. The gesture disarmed her, stole her heart. She wanted to put her arms around him, hold him close, protectively, to her.

Tara nodded eagerly. She grinned at Trevor. "I have a long list of requirements. I know exactly what we want."

Don had been sitting quietly in a chair by the window but he turned with a quick frown. "You don't just arbitrarily chop down trees because you want a momentary pleasure. In case you're not aware of it, when you chop the tree down, it dies." The frown deepened into a fierce scowl when Dillon turned to face him. "Hey, it's just my opinion, but then that doesn't count for much around here, does it?"

"I'm well aware of your environmentalist concerns, Don," Dillon said gently. "I share your views, but there's no harm in topping a tree or taking one that's growing too close to another and has no chance of survival."

"We're supposed to be working here, Dillon, not celebrating some commercialized holiday so the privileged little rich kids can get a bunch of presents from their rich daddy." There was unexpected venom in Don's voice.

Tara slid close to Jessica for comfort. Immediately Jessica pulled the girl into her arms, stroking the dark, wavy hair with gentle fingers. Beside her, Trevor shifted, but Jessica caught his wrist in a silent signal and he remained silent. His arms went around both Jessica and Tara, holding them close to him. The silence stretched to apprehension.

Dillon stirred then, straightening from where he had been leaning lazily against the doorframe. Dillon walked over to stand in front of his children. Very gently he caught Tara's chin in the palm of his gloved hand and lifted her face so that her blue eyes met his. "I'm looking forward to Christmas this year, Tara, it's been far too long for me without laughter and fun. Thank you for giving the holiday back to me." He bent his head and kissed her forehead. "I apologize for my friend's rudeness. He's obviously forgotten, in his old age, how fun holidays can be."

He touched his son then, his hand on the boy's shoulder. "I would greatly appreciate it if you and your sister would go out this evening before it gets too dark and find us the best tree you can. If we weren't in the middle of working this song I'd go with you. You find it and we'll go together to get it tomorrow evening." His fingers tightened momentarily as his heart leapt with joy. His son. His daughter. The terrible darkness that had consumed him for so long was slowly receding. His body actually trembled with the intensity of his emotions. He had never dared to dream of the two beloved faces staring up at him with such confidence and faith. "I'm trusting you to take care of your sister, Trevor."

Trevor swelled visibly. He glanced at Jessica, a tremor running through him, his hands tightening until his fingers dug into Jessica's arm. She smiled up at him with reassurance. With understanding. She could not allow her fears to take the pleasure from all of them. Especially when she didn't even know if her fears were grounded in reality. When she looked back at Dillon her feelings were naked on her face.

Dillon's breath caught in his chest. There was raw love on Jessica's face, in her eyes. She looked up at him as no other in his life ever had. Complete confidence, unconditional love. There was never a hidden agenda with Jessica. She loved his children completely, fiercely, protectively. And she was beginning to love him the same way. "You and Tara go now before it gets dark. I have some business matters to discuss."

Trevor nodded his understanding, grinning triumphantly at Don. He led Tara out of the room, urging her to hurry to get her jacket so they wouldn't lose the light they needed.

Dillon reached down and took Jessica's hand, raised it to the warmth of his mouth. His blue gaze burned into her green one. Mesmerizing her. Holding her captive with his sensual spell, in front of all the band members, he slowly pressed a kiss into the exact center of her palm, blatantly branding her. Staking his claim.

Jessica could feel hot tears burning behind her eyes, clogging her throat. Dillon. Her Dillon. He was coming back to life. The miracle of Christmas. The story her mother had so often told her at night. There was a special power at Christmas, a shimmering, translucent, positive, force that flowed steadily, that was there for the taking. One had only to believe in it, to reach for it. Jessica reached with both hands, with her heart and soul. Dillon needed her, needed his children. He had only to open his heart again and believe with her.

Dillon tugged on her hand, drew her to him so that her soft curves fit against the hard strength of his body. Then he turned his head above hers toward Don, pinning the man with a gaze of icy cold fury. "Don't you ever speak that way to my children again. Not ever, Don. If you have a gripe with me, feel free to tear into me, but never try to get to me through my children." There was a promise of swift and brutal retaliation in his voice.

Jessica looked up into his face and shivered. Dillon was different now, no matter how many glimpses she caught of the person she had once known.

"You want me out, don't you, Wentworth? You've always wanted me out. It's always been about 'Precious Paul' with you. You're loyal to him no matter what he does," Don snarled. "I worked hard, but I never got the recognition. You've always resented me being in the band. Paul," he gestured toward the man sitting ramrod stiff in the chair by the window. "He can do anything and you forgive him."

"You're not so innocent, Don." Brenda yawned and lazily waved a dismissing hand. "You musicians are so dramatic. Who cares who loves whom best? At least Paul didn't use his lover to get him into the band."

Dillon's head snapped up, his eyes glittering. "What the hell are you talking about, Brenda?"

Jessica glanced around the room. Everyone had gone still, looking nervous, guilty, even Paul. Don flushed a dull red. His eyes shifted away from Dillon.

Brenda winced. "Ouch. How was I to know you were kept in the dark?" Dillon's relentless blue gaze continued to bore into her. "Fine, blame me, I'm always in trouble. I thought you knew; everyone else certainly knew."

Dillon's fingers tightened around Jessica's hand. She could feel the tension running through his body. He was trembling slightly. She shifted closer to him, silently offering support.

"Tell me now, Brenda."

For the first time, Jessica saw Brenda hesitate. For a moment she looked uncertain and vulnerable. Then her expression changed and she shrugged her shoulders carelessly, her tinkling laugh a little forced. "Oh for heaven's sake, what's the big deal? It was a million years ago. It's not as if you thought Vivian had been faithful."

Jessica felt him take the blow in his heart. It was a gut-wrenching jolt that shook him, turned his stomach so that for a moment he had to fight to breathe, to keep from being sick. She felt his struggle as clearly as if she were experiencing it herself. Dillon's face never changed expression, he didn't so much as blink. He could have been carved from stone, but Jessica felt the turmoil raging in him.

"So Viv had an affair with Don, no big deal," Brenda shrugged again. "She got him into the band. You needed a bass player—it all worked out."

"Viv and I weren't having problems when Don joined the band," Dillon said. His voice held no expression and he didn't look at Don.

Brenda inspected her long nails. "You know Viv, she had problems, she always had to be with someone. You were working on songs for the band, trying to help Paul. If you weren't with her every minute, she felt neglected."

Dillon waited a heartbeat of time. A second. A third. He was aware of Jessica, of her hand, of her body, but there was a strange roaring in his head. His gaze shifted, settled on Don. "You were sleeping with my wife and playing in my band, allowing me to believe you were my friend?" He remembered how hard he had tried to make Don feel a part of the band.

Don's mouth tightened perceptibly. "You knew, everyone knew. It was no secret Viv liked to pick up a man now and then. And you got what you wanted. A bass player to kick around, someone to put up with your wife's tantrums when you didn't have the time or inclination to put up with her yourself. I won't even mention the extra money you saved because she was always wanting me to buy her things. I'd say we were more than even."

Dillon remained silent, only a muscle jerked along his jaw, betraying his inner turmoil.

"She was a bloodsucker," Don continued, looking around the room for support.

"She was ill," Dillon corrected softly.

"She had no loyalty and she was as cold as ice," Don insisted. "Damn it, Dillon, you had to have known about us."

When Dillon continued to look at him, Don dropped his gaze again. "I thought that was why you didn't want me in the band."

"Your own guilt made you think I didn't want you in the band." Dillon's voice was very soft, yet deep inside he was screaming at Jessica to help him. To stop him from saying or doing anything crazy. To save him. There had been such a surge of hope in him. A spreading warmth, a belief that he might reclaim his life. In a blink it was gone. He felt ice-cold inside. Emotionless. His heart and soul had been torn out. Everything he had built or cared about had been destroyed. He thought it had all been taken from him, but there was more, gouging old wounds to deepen them, to reopen them. He was shattering, crumbling, piece by piece until there was nothing left of who he had been.

"Damn it, Dillon, you had to have known," Don was almost pleading.

Dillon shook his head slowly. "I can't discuss this right now. No, I didn't know, I had no idea. I always thought of you as my friend. I did my best to understand you. I trusted you. I thought our friendship was genuine."

Jessica reached up and touched his face. Gently. Lovingly. "Take me out of here, Dillon. Right now. I want to be away from here." More than anything she wanted to get him away from treachery and betrayal. He had just begun to emerge into the sun after a long, bleak, cold winter. She could feel hands pulling him away from her, back into the deeper shadows. She kept her voice soft, persuasive. Her hands stroked his jaw, the pad of her thumb caressed his lips, a brush of a caress that centered his attention on her. His vivid blue gaze met hers. She saw the dangerous emotions swirling in the depths of his eyes.

Jessica tugged at him, forced him to move away from the others, out of the kitchen. She guided him through the house up to his private floor. He went with her willingly enough, but she could still feel the edge of violence in him, roiling and swirling all too close to the surface.

"I learned a lot of things about myself when I was at the burn center," Dillon said, as he pushed open the door to his study and stepped back to allow her to precede him. "There's so much pain, Jess, unbelievable pain. You think you can't bear any more, but there's always more.

Every minute, every second, it's a matter of endurance. You have no choice but to endure it because it never goes away. There's no way to sleep through it, you have to persevere."

The room was dark with the shadows of the late afternoon but he didn't turn on the light. Outside, the wind set the tree branches in motion so that they brushed gently against the sides of the house, producing an eerie music. Inside the room the silence stretched between them as they faced one another. Jessica could feel the turbulence of his emotions, wild, chaotic, yet on the surface he was as still as a hunter. She knew his strength of will, knew why he had survived such a terrible injury. Dillon was a man of deep passions. He sounded as if he was describing his physical pain, but she knew he was telling her about the other kinds of pain he'd also endured. The emotional scars were every bit as painful and deep as the physical ones.

"Don't look at me like that, Jess, it's too dangerous." He warned her softly, even as he moved to close the distance between them. "I don't want to hurt you. You can't look at me with your beautiful eyes so damn trusting. I'm not the man you think I am and I never will be." Even as he uttered the words aloud, meaning every one of them, his hands, of their own volition, were framing her face.

Electricity arced and crackled, a sizzling whip dancing with white-hot heat through their blood. The heat from his body seeped into hers, warming her, drawing her like a magnet. His head was bending toward her, his dark silky hair spilling around her angel's face like a cloud. Jessica's breath caught in her lungs. There was no air to breathe, no life other than his perfectly sculpted lips. His mouth settled over hers, velvet soft and firm. The touch was tantalizing. She opened her mouth as his teeth tugged teasingly at her lips to give him entrance to her sweetness, to the dark secrets of passion and promise.

Dillon closed his eyes to savor the taste of her, the hot silk of her. There was sheer magic in Jessica's kiss. It was madness to indulge his craving for her, but he couldn't stop, taking his time, leisurely exploring, swept away from the gray bleakness of his nightmare world into one of vivid colorful fireworks, bursting around him, in him. The need was instantaneous and elemental, the hunger, voracious. His body was all at once savagely alive, thick and hard and pounding with an edgy, greedy lust that shook him to the foundations of his soul. He'd never experienced it before, but now, it surged through his body, primitive and hot, demanding that he make her his.

Jessica felt his mouth harden, change, felt the passion flair between them, hot and exciting, a rush that dazzled her every sense. Her body melted into his, pliant and soft and inviting. His mouth raged with hunger, devoured hers, dominating and persuasive and commanding her response. She gave herself up to the blazing world of sheer sensation, allowed him to take her far from reality.

The earth seemed to shift and move out from under her feet as his palms slid over her back, down to her bottom, where they settled to align her body more firmly with his. His touch was slow and languorous, at odds with his assaulting mouth. His tongue plundered, his hands coaxed. His mouth was aggressive, his hands gentle.

Dillon's body was a hard, painful ache, his jeans

stretched tight, cutting into him. The feel of her, so soft and pliant, was driving him slowly out of his mind. There was a strange roaring in his head; his blood felt thick and molten like lava. She tasted hot and sweet. He couldn't get close enough to her, wanting her clothes gone so that he could press himself against her, skin to skin.

His mouth left hers to travel along her throat, with playful little kisses and bites, his tongue swirling to find shadows and hollows, to reach little trigger points of sheer pleasure. When he found them, she rewarded him with a little gasp of bliss. The sound was music to him, a soft note that drowned out his every sane thought. He didn't want sanity, he didn't want to know that what he was doing was wrong. He wanted to bury his body deep inside of her, to lose himself forever in a firestorm of mindless feeling.

His mouth found the hollow of her throat, the pulse beating so frantically there. He nudged aside the neckline of her blouse to find the swell of her breasts. She was soft, a miracle of satin skin. His hand closed over her breast, her taut nipple pushing into his palm through her blouse, through his glove. Beckoning. Urging him on. He bent his head to temptation.

The door to Dillon's study burst open and Tara stood there, her face white, her hair wildly disheveled. There was sheer panic on her face. "You have to come right now. *Right now!* Jessica! Hurry, oh, God, I think he's crushed under the logs and dirt. Hurry, you have to hurry!"

chapter
8

 PANIC SENT ADRENALINE coursing through Jessica's body. She looked up at Dillon, sheer terror in her eyes. His eyes mirrored her fear. He circled Jessica's waist with one strong arm, pulling her tight against him so that, briefly, they leaned into one another, comforting them both.

"Take a deep breath, Tara, we need to know what happened." Dillon's voice was calm and authoritative. He pulled the child into the circle of his arms, up against Jessica where she felt safe.

Tara gulped back her tears, buried her face against Jessica's shoulder. "I don't know what happened. One minute we were walking along and then Trevor said something weird, it didn't make sense, something about a magic circle and he ran ahead of me. I heard him yell and then there was a huge noise. The side of a hill gave way, rocks and dirt and logs rolling down. His yell was cut off and when I got to where I thought he was, the air was all dirty and cloudy. I couldn't find him and when I called and called, he didn't answer me. I think he was buried under all of it. The dog started digging and barking and growling and I ran to get you."

"Show me, Tara," Dillon commanded. "Jessica, you'll have to find the others, tell Paul we'll need shovels just in case." He was already pushing his daughter ahead of him.

They ran down the stairs, Dillon calling for the band members. As he jerked open the front door and raced across the front verandah, he nearly knocked Brian back down the front steps. They steadied one another. "It's Trevor. It sounds bad, Brian, come with me," Dillon said.

Brian nodded. "Where are the others?"

"Jess is rounding them up," Dillon replied. Tara ran ahead of him, but he kept pace easily, swearing under his breath. Night was falling all too fast and it would be very dark in a matter of minutes. He prayed his daughter didn't get lost, that she could lead them straight to his son.

Tara ran fast, keeping to the main path, her heart pounding loudly in her ears, but terror had subsided now that her father was taking command. He seemed so calm, so completely in control, that she felt her panic fading. She was afraid she wouldn't be able to find the exact location in the dark so she ran as fast as she could in an attempt to outrun the nightfall. It was even more of a relief when the large German shepherd came bounding out of the timberline to pace beside her. He knew the way to Trevor.

Jessica took several deep breaths as she hurried through the large house calling for the others. She found

Brenda outside the kitchen, in the courtyard, smoking. "What is it now? I swear there's no rest for the wicked around this place."

"Where are the others?" Jessica demanded. Brenda's chic hiking boots were covered in mud. Pine needles were stuck to the bottom and Brenda was trying to remove them without getting her fingernails dirty. "There's been an accident and we need everyone to help."

"Oh good heavens, it's those kids again, isn't it?" Brenda sounded annoyed. She backed up a step holding up a placating hand as Jessica advanced on her. "Really, darling, you wear me out with your agonizing over those *children*. See? I'm learning. Tell me what's wrong and I'll do my part to help, although I hope you send them both to their rooms and punish them suitably for disrupting my day."

"Where are the others?" Jessica spit each word out distinctly. "This is an emergency, Brenda. I think Trevor is trapped under a landslide, under dirt and rocks. We need to dig him out fast."

"Surely not!" Brenda's hand fluttered to her throat and she paled visibly. Her throat worked as if she was struggling to speak but no words would come. When they did, it was a choked whisper. "This place really is cursed, or maybe just Dillon is."

Jessica was surprised to see the woman was close to tears. "Brenda," she said desperately. "Help me!"

"I'm sorry, of course." Brenda straightened her shoulders. "I'll find Robert, he'll know what to do. Paul's around back playing horseshoes, at least he was when I walked up. I think Don was going to the beach, but I'm not certain. You get Paul and I'll find the others and send them to you. Which way did they go?"

"Thanks." Jessica put a hand on Brenda's arm, touching her to offer comfort. There was something very vulnerable on Brenda's face when her mask slipped. "I think they took the main trail heading into the forest."

"I just came back from that way," Brenda frowned. "I didn't see the kids."

Jessica didn't wait to hear any more; she raced around to the back of the house. Paul was idly tossing horseshoes. He paused in mid-swing when he spotted her. "What is it?" He tossed the horseshoe aside and hurried to her.

Feeling desperate, Jessica blurted out what she knew. Time seemed to be going by while she was getting nowhere. She wanted to race to Trevor, dig him out with her bare hands, not rely on the others.

"I'll get the lights," Paul told her, pulling open the door to a small shed. "There are shovels in here. I'll meet you around in the front." He was gone quickly.

Jessica pressed a hand to her churning stomach as she looked frantically through the potting shed for the shovels. All the larger tools were at the back of the shed. She felt sick, *sick* with fear for Trevor. How many minutes had gone by? Not many, her conversation with Brenda had taken only seconds, but it seemed an eternity. It was dark in the shed, the waning light insufficient to light the interior. She felt her way to the back, placing her hand on first a rake, a pry bar, and two sharper tools before she found the shovels. Triumphantly she caught up all three and rushed out of the small building.

Don was waiting impatiently for her. "Paul's gone on ahead." He grabbed the shovels from her, frowning as he did so. "What the hell did you do to your hand?"

Jessica blinked in surprise. Her palm was muddy and a single long slash in the center mingled blood with the dirt. A few stray pine needles stuck in the mixture as if it were artwork. "It doesn't matter," she muttered, and hurried past him to take the trail.

Darkness had fallen in the forest, the heavier canopy blocking out what little light remained. Jessica ran fast, uncaring of her burning lungs. She had to get to Trevor and Tara. To Dillon. It couldn't be that bad. She consoled herself with the thought that someone would have come for her if the news were the worst. She could hear Don running beside her, and was vaguely aware of her throbbing palm. She wiped it on her thigh as they spotted lights off to her left.

Tara threw herself at Jessica, nearly knocking her over. "He's under all those big rocks and dirt. That big log fell on him, too! Dad's been trying to dig him out with his bare hands and Robert's been helping."

"They'll get him out quickly," Jessica reassured, holding the little girl close, "the soil is soft enough for them to dig him out very fast."

"Take her up there, out of the way," Dillon directed. His gaze met Jessica's over Tara's head as he caught in midair the shovel that Don tossed to him. "It's going to be okay, baby, I promise. He's talking, so he's alive and conscious. He's got air to breathe, we just have to get him out to see the damage."

Jessica nodded. Hugging Tara closer to her, she bent

down to the child's ear. "Let's move out of the way, honey. We'll go up there." She pointed to a small embankment off to the side but up above where the men were frantically digging.

The dog nudged her legs as she walked and Jessica absently patted his head. "Are you all right, Tara?" The girl was trembling.

Tara shook her head. "I shouldn't have insisted we keep looking. We found two trees we thought you and Dad might like, but I wanted to keep looking. Trevor said it was getting dark and wanted to go back to the house." She rubbed her face against Jessica's jacket. "I knew if I hadn't been with him he would have kept looking. I hate that, the way he always treats me like I'm a baby."

"Trevor looks out for you," Jessica corrected gently. "That's a good thing, Tara. He loves you very much. And this wasn't your fault." She stroked the girl's hair soothingly. "It just happened. Sometimes things just happen."

Tara shivered again. She looked up at Jessica, her eyes too large for her face. "I saw something," she whispered softly and looked around quickly. "I saw a shadow back in the trees, over there." She pointed toward the left in the deeper timber. "It looked like someone with a long cape and hood, very dark. I couldn't see the face, but he was watching us; he watched it all happen. I know he was there, it wasn't my imagination."

If it was possible, Jessica's heart began to pound even harder. "He was watching you while the rocks and dirt crumbled down on Trevor?" Jessica struggled to get the timing right. She believed Tara, she'd seen a cloaked figure in the woods the night they'd arrived, but she couldn't imagine any of the band members not rushing to aid the twins. Whoever had been in that cloak really might want to cause harm to one of them. Could someone other than the band members be on the island? The groundskeeper was an older, kindly man. The island was large enough that someone could hide out, camping, but surely the dog would have alerted the children to a stranger's presence. The twins had been spending time with the animal and she knew the German shepherd had guard instincts.

Tara nodded. "I yelled and yelled for help. I couldn't see Trev, he was buried under everything and when I looked back, the person was gone." She wiped her face, smearing dirt across her chin and cheek. "I'm telling the truth, Jessie."

Jessica brushed the top of the girl's head with a kiss. "I know you are, honey. I can't imagine why whoever it was didn't come to help you." She was determined to find out, though. She had been lulled into a false sense of security, but if the cloaked figure was a band member, and it had to be, then one of them was behind the accidents and the death of her mother. Which one? "Stay here, honey, away from the edge."

She couldn't stand still, pacing back and forth restlessly, her fist jammed in her mouth to keep from screaming at them to hurry. Don and Robert pried a rather large rock loose and it took all of the men to move it carefully away from the site.

Brenda joined Tara a little hesitantly. "He'll be all right, honey," she offered, placing her hand on her niece's shoulder in an attempt to offer comfort.

"He hasn't moved," Tara told her tearfully. "He hasn't moved at all."

"He's breathing though," Brenda encouraged. "Robert said Trevor told them he dove into a small space, a depression against the hillside."

"He was talking? Dillon said he spoke, but I haven't heard anything." And Jessica wanted the reassurance of the sound of his voice. She continued to pace, rubbing her arms as she did so, shivering in the night air. "Are you certain he spoke?"

"I'm pretty sure," Brenda answered.

Jessica stared up at the sky. She could hear the pounding of the sea in the distance. The wind rustling through the trees. The chink of the shovels against rock. Even the heavy breathing of the men as they worked. She could not hear Trevor's voice. She listened. She prayed. There was not even a murmur.

"He'll be all right." Brenda tried again to be reassuring. She tapped her foot, drawing Jessica's attention to the muddy ground strewn with pine needles and vegetation. A few fallen trees crisscrossed the area from the violent storm. Most had been there for some time but two smaller ones were fairly fresh.

She couldn't help the terrible suspicion that slid into her mind. Another accident. Could it have been rigged? Almost without even being aware of it, she examined the ground, the position of the logs, searching for clues, searching for anything that might provide an answer for what had happened. There was nothing she could see, nothing that would make Dillon listen to her that something wasn't quite right. Maybe she was paranoid, she didn't know, only that she had to find a way to make the children safe.

"I won't be able to take it if anything's happened to him," Jessica murmured to no one in particular. She meant it. Her heart was breaking. She was white-faced, sick to her stomach, and moving to keep from being sick in front of everyone. "I shouldn't have let him go off like that. I should have been with him."

"Jessica, you couldn't have prevented this," Brenda said firmly. "They'll get him out." Awkwardly she hugged Tara to her as a muffled sob escaped the child. "Neither one of you could have stopped this. After a storm, sometimes the land is soft and it just shifts. You both would have been hurt had you been with him."

Jessica crouched down, peering at the men as they frantically dug away the dirt and rocks to free Trevor. She could see his legs and part of one shoe. "Dillon?" Her voice wavered. Trevor wasn't moving. "Why is he so still?" She could barely breathe, her lungs burning for air.

"Don't go getting all sappy," Trevor's disembodied voice floated up to her. He sounded thin and reedy, but it was his usual cocky humor. "You'll just be mad at me later if everyone sees you all teary-eyed."

Jessica slowly attempted to stand, her body trembling with relief. Her legs felt rubbery, and for a moment she was afraid she might faint. Brenda shoved her head down, held her there until the earth stopped spinning so crazily. Robert came up on the other side of her, holding her arm as she swayed. Jessica bit down hard on her fist to keep from crying as she straightened. Tears glittered in her eyes, on her lashes. Her gaze met Dillon's in complete understanding. For a moment there was no one else, just the two of them and the sheer relief only a parent could feel after such a frightening experience.

Tara hugged her, relief in the vivid blue of her eyes. Jessica barely registered it. She couldn't remember ever being so shaky but she managed a tentative smile at Brenda and Robert. "Thanks for keeping me from landing on my face in the dirt."

Brenda shrugged with her casual eloquence. "I can't let anything happen to you. I'd be stuck with the kiddies." She winked at Tara even as she went into her husband's arms. She seemed to fit there, to belong.

Tara grinned back at her. "We grow on you."

"No they don't," Jessica replied firmly, "they take years off your life. I think you have the right idea, Brenda, no kiddies or animals." Her eyes remained on Trevor as they slowly freed him. He was stretching his legs cautiously. She could hear him talking with Dillon. His voice was still shaking, but he was holding his own, laughing softly at something his father said to him.

"Brenda, would you mind taking Tara back to the house? It's already so dark. She should take a hot bath, and when I come in I'll fix hot chocolate. She's muddy and wet and shaking whether she knows it or not," Jessica said.

"So are you," Brenda pointed out with unexpected gentleness.

"I'll be right in," Jessica promised. She squeezed Tara's hand. "Thank you for getting everyone here so quickly, honey, you were wonderful."

"We'll get her to the house safely," Robert assured

Jessica, and with an arm around Brenda and one around Tara, he started back toward the house.

Jessica had to touch Trevor, to make certain he had not suffered a single injury. She made her way down to the site and knelt beside Dillon next to Trevor. Dillon examined every inch of the boy, testing for broken bones, lacerations, even bruises. His hands were unbelievably gentle as he ran them over his son.

Trevor was filthy, but grinning at them. "It's a good thing I'm skinny," he quipped, patting Jessica's shoulder, knowing if he hugged her she'd burst into tears in front of everyone and then he'd really be in trouble.

"He's fine, a few bumps and bruises. Tomorrow he's going to be sore," Dillon announced to the others. "Thank you all for helping." He sat back, wiped his hand across his forehead, leaving behind a smear of dirt. His hand was trembling. "You took a couple of years off my life, son. I can't afford it."

Paul gathered up the shovels. "None of us can afford it."

"Don't feel alone," Trevor said. "It felt like the entire hillside came down on top of me. For a few minutes there, all I could think about was being buried alive. Not a pleasant thought."

Jessica stepped back to allow Paul room. Dillon and Paul lifted Trevor to his feet. The boy swayed slightly but stood upright, his familiar grin on his face. "Jess, I'm really okay, you know?"

Dillon watched her face crumble, her composure gone as she circled Trevor's neck with her slender arms and hugged him fiercely, protectively, to her. There was no awkwardness in the boy's manner as he tightened his arms around her and buried his face on her shoulder. They were easy, natural, loving with one another. Dillon felt a burning in his chest, behind his eyes, as he watched them. A terrible longing welled up, nearly blindsided him. The layers of insulation were being stripped away, exposing his heart, so that he was raw and vulnerable.

Part of him wanted to lash out at them like a wounded animal. Part of him wanted to embrace them, to hold them safely to him. *Safe.* The word shimmered bitterly in his mind. He tasted bitterness in his mouth. For a heartbeat of time he stared at them, his heart pounding, adrenaline surging. His blue eyes glittered with the violence that always seemed to be swirling just below the surface.

Before Dillon could turn away from them, Jessica lifted her head, her gaze colliding with his. At once he was lost in the joy on her face. Her smile was radiant, like a burst of sunshine. She held out her hand to him. An invitation to a place he couldn't go. He stared down at her hand. Delicate. Small. A bridge back to living.

He didn't move. Dillon later swore to himself he hadn't moved, but there he was, taking her hand in his. His gloves were filthy but she didn't seem to notice, her fingers tightening around his. Touching her, he was lost in her spell, a web of enchantment, losing all touch with reality, with sanity. He found himself drawn up against the soft invitation of her body. Her head nuzzled his chest, her silky hair catching in the shadow along his jaw.

Without thought, without hesitation, his hand circled her vulnerable throat, tipping her head back. Her green eyes were large, haunting, cloudy with emotion. He swore softly, a surrender, a defeat, as he bent his dark head to hers. Her mouth was perfection, velvet soft, yielding, hot and moist and filled with tenderness. With the taste of love. The smoldering ember buried deep in his gut flared to life, flooded his system with such craving he fed on her, devoured her, swept away by the addicting taste of her. By the rich promise of passion, of laughter, of life itself.

She found a way past his every barricade, past his every defense. She wrapped herself around his heart, his soul, until he couldn't breathe without her. The loneliness that had consumed him for so long, and the bleak endless existence, vanished when she was near him. Need slammed into his body, hard and urgent, a demand that threatened to steal his control. The sheer force of their chemistry alarmed him. His body trembled, his mouth hardened, his tongue thrusting and probing, a hot mating dance his body desperately needed to perform.

Trevor cleared his throat loudly, dragging Dillon back to reality. Startled, he lifted his head and blinked, slowly coming back into his own scarred body and soul.

Trevor grinned up at him. "Don't look so shell-shocked, Dad, it's kind of embarrassing when I had this image of you all suave with the ladies."

"Suave isn't the word for it," Don muttered acidly under his breath.

Dillon heard him and turned the weight of his stare in Don's direction. The others attacked from all directions, diverting him.

"Boyo," Brian let out his breath in a slow whistle. "What the hell was that?"

"I'd like to see that on rewind," Paul said, nudging

Dillon with his elbow. "A little vicarious experience goes a long way around here."

Jessica hid her scarlet face against Dillon's shoulder. "All of you go away."

"We don't dare, Jessie girl, no telling what you might do to our beloved leader," Brian teased. "We want the boyo suffering angst and melancholy. Haven't you heard that makes for the best songs?"

"Frustration's good for that, too," Paul chimed in.

Jessica reached up to frame Dillon's face with her hand. "I don't think it matters what state he's in," she objected, "he manages to compose beautiful music."

Dillon caught her hand and turned up her palm, his eyes narrowing. "What the hell did you do to your hand? It's bleeding."

He sounded so accusatory Jessica couldn't help smiling. "I was feeling around in the tool shed for the shovels and cut my hand on something sharp." Now that he'd pointed it out, the wound was beginning to burn.

"We have to wash that. I don't want you picking up an infection." Dillon indicated the path, retaining possession of Jessica's hand. "Are you steady enough to walk back, Trevor?"

Trevor nodded, hiding his smile as he turned onto the trail, following Paul closely. Don and Brian gathered up the lights. Dillon brought Jessica's hand up for another, much closer inspection. "I don't like the look of this, honey—you clean it the moment you get to the house." He was fighting to breathe, to stay sane. What the hell was he doing? He raked a hand through his hair, breathing hard, feeling as if he'd run miles. Emotions were crowding in so fast, so overwhelming he couldn't sort them out.

Jessica couldn't suppress the small surge of joy rushing through her. Dillon sounded so worried about such a trivial cut. They walked close together, his hand holding hers. Above their heads the stars tried valiantly to shine for them despite the gray clouds stretching out into thin veils covering the tiny lights.

Dillon deliberately slowed his pace to allow the others to get ahead of them. "I'm sorry, Jess, I shouldn't have kissed you like that in front of the others."

"Because they're going to tease us? They've already been doing that," she pointed out. She tilted her chin at him, a clear challenge to deny what was between them.

He sighed. "Because I wanted to tear your clothes off and take you right there, right then. I think I made it damned obvious to the band. You aren't some groupie and I don't want them looking at you that way—to ever see you in that light. You always think the best of everyone. Has it occurred to you, that their seeing me kissing you like that, they might consider you fair game?"

Jessica shrugged her shoulders, feigning a casualness she didn't feel. A heat wave spread through her body at his words. The thought of Dillon so out of control left her breathless. She managed to keep her voice even. "I doubt that I'll faint if one of them makes an attempt. This might shock you, Dillon, but other men have actually found me attractive and some of them have even asked me out. Believe it or not, you're not the only man who has ever kissed me." She felt him stiffen, felt the sudden tension in him.

A hint of danger crept into the deep blue of his eyes. "I don't think now is the best time to talk to me about other men, Jess." His voice was rougher than she'd ever heard it, that smoky, edgy tone very much in evidence. He halted abruptly, dragging her into the deeper shelter of the trees. "Do you have any idea what you're doing to me? Any idea at all?" He pulled her uninjured hand between his legs, rubbed her palm along the front of his jeans where the material was stretched taut, where he was thick and hard and she could feel heat right through the fabric. "I haven't been with a woman in a very long time, honey, and if you keep this up, you're going to get a hell of a lot more than you bargained for. I'm not some teenager looking for a quick feel. You keep looking at me the way you've been doing and I'm going to take you up on the invitation."

For one moment Jessica thought about slapping his handsome face, outraged that he would try to reduce her to a teen with a crush. That he would try to frighten her, or that he would think that he ever could frighten her. If there was one man on earth she trusted implicitly with her body, it was Dillon Wentworth. It took a heartbeat to realize he had captured her uninjured palm, that he was still cradling her wounded hand against his chest. Carefully. Tenderly. The pad of his thumb was rubbing gently along the edge of her hand and he wasn't even aware of it. But she was.

Deliberately provocative, she rubbed the stretched material at the front of his jeans. "You aren't very well suited to the role of big bad wolf, Dillon, but if it's some fantasy you have, I guess I can play along." Her tone was seductive, an invitation. Her fingers danced and teased, stroking and caressing, feeling him respond, thicken more, harden more.

His eyes glittered down at her like two burning gemstones. "You don't have a clue about fantasies, Jessie."

"You're in the wrong century, Dillon." Her tongue slid provocatively along her lush bottom lip and, damn her, she was laughing at him. "I certainly wouldn't mind unzipping your jeans and wrapping my hand around you, feeling you, *watching* you grow even harder. And I did consider not wearing my bra so that the next time you kissed me and started working your way along my throat, you would feel my body is ready for you. The thought of your mouth on . . ."

"Damn it." A little desperately he bent his head and stopped her nonsense the only way he could think of. He took possession of her mouth and instantly was lost in her answering hunger. She was too sexy, too hot, too everything. Magic. Jessica was sheer magic. He caught her shoulders and resolutely set her away from him before he lost his mind completely.

She smiled up at him. "Are you ever going to kiss me without swearing first?"

"Are you ever going to learn self-preservation?" he countered.

"I don't have to learn," Jessica pointed out, "you watch out for me very nicely."

chapter

9

✳ JESSICA TOOK HER TIME in the shower, allowing the hot water to soak into her skin. *Dillon.* He filled her thoughts and kept her mind from dwelling on the possibility that she could have lost Trevor. She had never experienced such a powerful attraction. They had always belonged together. Always. Best friends when it hadn't made sense. She had always found him magnetic, but it had never occurred to her that one day the sexual chemistry between them would be so explosive. She shook with her need for him.

She closed her eyes as she dried her body with a thick towel, the material sliding over her sensitive skin, heightening her awareness of unfamiliar sexual hunger. She didn't feel like herself at all around him. His blue gaze burned over her and made her feel a wanton seductress. Jessica shook her head as she dressed with care. She wanted to look her best to face him.

By the time she was back downstairs, everyone was already in the kitchen ahead of her. Dillon looked handsome in clean black jeans and a long-sleeved sweater. It bothered her that he still felt the need to wear gloves in front of his family and friends, in front of her. His hair was still damp from his shower, curling in unruly waves to his shoulders. As always he was barefoot, and for some strange reason, it made her blush. She found it amazingly sexy and intimate. He looked up the moment she appeared in the doorway as if he had built-in radar where she was concerned.

Dillon almost groaned when he turned his head. He knew she was there, how could he not know the moment she was close to him? She was so beautiful she took his breath away. Her jeans rode low on her hips showing a little too much skin for his liking. Her top was an inch too short, and the material lovingly hugged her full breasts the way his hands might. Her red-gold hair looked wine-red, still wet from her shower and pulled back away from her face, exposing the column of her neck. He blinked, looking closer. She damn well had better be wearing a bra under that thin almost nonexistent top. When she moved, he thought he saw the darker outline of her nipples, but then, he wasn't certain.

Just looking at her made him so hard he didn't want to take a step. "Did you put something on that cut?" His voice was harsh enough that even he winced at his tone.

Brian caught her wrist as she swept past him and turned up her palm for his inspection, halting her before she could make her way to Dillon's side. "It's still bleeding a bit, Jessie girl," he observed. "She needs to cover it with a bandage, Dillon," he added helpfully, tugging until Jessica followed him around the counter.

Dillon grit his teeth together, watching them. Brian

was a large bear of a man and Jessica looked small and delicate beside him. His scowl deepened as he watched the drummer span her waist and lift her onto the counter, wedging himself between her legs as he bent forward to examine her palm. His forehead nearly brushed her breasts. Brian said something that made Jessica laugh.

"What the hell are you doing?" Dillon burst out, stalking around the counter to jerk the bandage out of Brian's hand. "It doesn't take a rocket scientist to put a Band-Aid on her hand." He just managed to restrain himself from pushing Brian out of the way. Her thighs were open and she looked sexy as hell sitting there with her large green eyes silently reprimanding him. "Move," he said rudely.

Grinning broadly, Brian held his hands up in surrender and strode back around to the other side of the counter. "The man's like a bear with a sore tooth," he confided to Trevor in an overloud whisper.

"I noticed," Trevor replied in the same exaggerated whisper.

Dillon didn't care. He slipped into the spot Brian had vacated, nudging Jessica's thighs apart and moving close enough to catch that fresh elusive scent that stirred his senses. At once the heat of her body beckoned. And damn her, she wasn't wearing a bra, he was certain of it. He bent over her palm, examining the laceration.

The smile faded from Jessica's mouth. She nearly snatched her hand back. His breath was warm on the center of her palm sending tiny whips of lightning dancing up her arm. His hips were wedged tight between her legs. The smallest movement caused a heated friction along the inside of her thighs and spread fire to her deepest core. Her body clenched unexpectedly as he moved closer, his head brushing her breasts. She bit down on her lip to keep a small moan from escaping. Her breasts were achy and tender, so sensitive she could barely stand the lightest touch. He moved again, his forehead skimming against her blouse as he examined her palm. Right over her taut nipple. Tongues of fire lapped at her breasts, her body clenched again, throbbed and burned for release. All he had to do was turn his head slightly to pull her aching flesh into his hot, moist mouth. Her breath hitched in her throat.

His blue gaze found hers. Both of them stopped breathing.

"Well, is she going to live?" Paul asked, breaking the web of sexual tension between them. "Because if you don't finish up over there, the rest of us might not make it through the night."

"Holy cow, Jess," Trevor began.

"You don't need to say a word, young man," Jessica stopped him. She kept her eyes averted from Dillon; it was the only safe thing to do. She noticed it was awkward for him to manipulate the bandage into place. The brush of his fingers was like a caress against her skin, the glove stroked across her hand as he worked. Her body clenched more with each graze. She trembled. His hand tightened around hers, brought her injured palm to his chest, right over his heart.

"I think that should protect it, baby," he said gently. He caught her waist, only his gloves preventing him from touching her bare skin as he helped her to the floor. "It doesn't hurt, does it?"

She shook her head. "Thanks, Dillon, I appreciate it."

"How long is the darned thing going to take to heal?" Don demanded. "We need her to play. We're not nearly finished."

"I laid down several different guitar tracks earlier today, before you were up," Jessica said. "I wanted to try a few things, so at least you have something to work with." She moved cautiously around Dillon's large frame, careful not to touch his body with hers. She curled her fingers in Trevor's hair, needing to touch him, but not wanting to injure his boyish pride by making too big a fuss now that he was safe.

"What things?" Robert asked curiously, a hint of eagerness in his voice. "I thought bringing in the sax was a perfect touch. The orchestral background worked like magic. You have some great ideas, Jess."

Jessica gave him a quick grin of thanks. "I wanted to record a few different guitar sounds. I used the progression we started with yesterday but enhanced it with some melodic embellishments. I wanted an edgy sound to go with the lyrics so I used the *Les Paul* for rhythm. I still would like to do a little more layering. You should listen to it, Robert, and see what you think. I thought we might use the *Strat* for lead over the rhythm. The different sounds layered might really add to the piece."

"Or make it too busy," Don objected. "Dillon has a hell of voice, we can't just blast over the top of him."

"But that's the beauty of it, Don," Jessica countered. "We're still sticking to basic sounds. Very simple. Layering allows us to do that."

Brenda slumped over the tabletop dramatically. "Just

one night I'd like to talk about something other than music."

"I thought they were talking in a foreign language," Tara said. She pulled out the chair beside her aunt. "Boring."

Jessica laughed at her. "You just want that hot chocolate I promised you. I'll get it for you. Trevor? Anyone else?"

"You shouldn't be so careless, Jessie," Don reprimanded. "We only have a short time to get this together. You can't afford to damage your hands."

She paused in the act of removing mugs from the cupboard. "I don't honestly remember you being such a jerk, Don. Have you always been this way, or just recently?" If he took one more potshot at Dillon she was afraid she might throw a mug at his head. She didn't look at Dillon as she took the milk and chocolate from the refrigerator. There were wounds that went deep and Don seemed to want to rake at them. Jessica set everything very carefully on the counter and smiled sweetly, expectantly, at Don.

Trevor and Tara exchanged a long, amused glance. They'd heard Jessica use that tone before and it didn't bode well for Don. Tara nudged Brenda to include her, and was rewarded with a small smirk and a raised eyebrow.

"I didn't mean anything by it, Jess—everyone's too sensitive," Don replied defensively.

"I suppose we'll all overlook it this time but you need to work on your social skills. Some things are acceptable and some things aren't." Without turning her head she raised her voice. "You'd better not be mimicking me, Trev."

The twins exchanged another quick grin. Trevor had been mouthing the words, having heard them said numerous times. "Wouldn't think of it," he said cheekily.

"Dillon, would you like me to make you a cup of hot chocolate?" Jessica offered.

Dillon shook his head adamantly, shuddering at the mere thought of it. "I can't bear to look at the stuff. I had enough of that at the burn center."

"Why do you keep it then?" Jessica asked curiously.

"For Paul, of course." Dillon grinned boyishly at his friend. "He practically lives on the stuff. I think it's his one vice."

Jessica held up a mug. "How about you then, Paul?"

"Not tonight, I've had enough excitement. It might keep me up." He ruffled Tara's hair. "I figure we can share it until Christmas, then I expect it to be replaced by gift certificates and Hershey bonuses."

"I write lovely I.O.U.'s," Tara announced. "Just ask Trev."

"And you'll be old before you can cash them in," Trevor warned Paul. "But her handwriting is beautiful."

"So true, I'm vain about my handwriting. I need to be famous so I can sign autographs." Tara took a sip of the chocolate. "Why did you have too much chocolate at the burn center, Dad?"

There was a small silence. Brenda casually draped her arm around Tara. "Good question. What did they do, make you live on the stuff?"

"Actually, yes." Dillon looked across the room at Paul,

a vulnerable, almost helpless look on his handsome face. It was so at odds with his usual commanding presence, his expression tugged at Jessica's heartstrings.

It was Paul who answered very matter-of-factly. "Burn patients need calories, Tara, lots and lots of calories. Where your father was, they made drinks using chocolate. You'd think they would taste good, but they didn't—the mixture was awful, and he was forced to drink them all the time."

"They ruined chocolate for you?" Tara was outraged. "That's terrible."

Dillon gave her his heart-stopping, lopsided grin. "I guess it was a small price to pay for surviving."

"Chocolate is my comfort drink," Tara admitted. "What's yours?"

"I never really thought about it," he admitted. His blue gaze was drawn to Jessica. There had been no comfort in his life since he'd lost his family, lost his music, lost everything that mattered to him. Until Jessica. He felt a sense of peace when he was with her. In spite of the overwhelming emotions, the explosive chemistry, in spite of all of it, when she was near him, he felt comforted. He could hardly say that to his thirteen-year-old daughter. If he didn't understand it, how could anyone else?

"I like that thought, Tara," Paul said, "I use chocolate for my comfort drink, too."

"Coffee, black as can be," Brenda chimed in. "Robert likes a martini." She smiled up at him. "I drive him to drink."

"You drive everyone to drink," Brian pointed out.

"You were swilling six-packs of beer long before I ever

came on the scene," Brenda said, looking bored. "Your sins are all your own."

"We went to kindergarten together," Brian reminded everyone.

"And you were already beyond salvation."

"Give it a rest," Don begged.

Jessica thought it a perfect time to change the subject. "By the way, who owns the long, hooded cape?" She asked with feigned indifference. "It's quite dramatic."

"I have one," Dillon said. "I used it onstage years ago. I haven't thought of it in years. What in the world made you ask?"

"I've seen it a couple of times," Jessica said, her eyes meeting Tara's as they sipped their chocolate. "It was so different, I wanted to get a look at it up close."

"It has to be here somewhere," Dillon said, "I'll look around for it."

A chill seemed to creep into the room with her question. Jessica shivered. Once again the terrible suspicion found its way into her mind. Had someone deliberately lured Trevor to that exact spot? It wasn't possible. No one could actually predict a rockslide closely enough to set a trap. She was really becoming paranoid. Dillon couldn't have been the one wearing the cape when the rockslide had buried Trevor because Dillon had been with her. She glanced around the room surreptitiously, realizing she really knew very little about the other band members.

"I remember that cape!" Brenda sat up very straight with a wide smile. "Do you remember, Robert? Viv loved it. She was always swirling it around her and pretending to be a vampire. Dillon, we borrowed it from you for that

Hollywood Halloween thing, Robert wore it, remember hon?" She looked up at her husband, patting his hands as he gently massaged her shoulders.

"I remember it," Paul said. "It was hanging in your closet, Dillon, at least it was a month ago. I hung your shirts up when they came back from the laundry service. Viv thought vampire and you thought magician."

"I thought women," Brian said. "You know how many women wanted to see me in that cape and nothing else?" He puffed out his chest.

"Ugh," Tara wrinkled her nose. "That's totally gross."

"That's beyond gross, Brian," Brenda protested, "I'll never get the picture out of my mind." She covered her face with her hands.

"You loved it," Brian pounced immediately. "You begged me."

"Way too much information," Jessica cautioned.

"I did not, you idiot!" Brenda was outraged. "I may be many things, Brian, but I have taste. Seeing you prance around naked in a vampire cape is not my idea of sexy."

"You know, Brian," Robert said conversationally, "I actually like you. But I may have to shove your teeth down your throat if you aren't more careful in the way you choose to taunt my wife."

"Wow! That's so cool," Tara said, her blue eyes shining up at him. "He's pretty cool, after all, Brenda."

Brenda grinned at her in complete agreement. "He is, isn't he?"

Dillon leaned against Jessica, trapping her body between his large frame and the counter. "That cape might have possibilities," he whispered wickedly against her bare neck. His teeth skimmed very close to her pulse as if he might bite into her exposed skin.

"Not with knowing what Brian was doing in it," she whispered back. She pushed back against him, resting her bottom very casually against him. With the counter between their bodies and the rest of the room, no one could see her blatantly tempting him. She ached for him, her body heavy and needful. She wanted to turn into his arms, be held by him, and lie beside him, under him. She wanted to see his blue eyes blazing, burning for her alone.

Dillon savored the feel of her small, curved bottom pressed tightly against him. He was becoming used to walking around in a continual state of arousal. At least, he knew he was alive. She had the softest skin, and smelled so enticing he couldn't think of too much else when she was near. He cleared his throat, trying to pull his mind away from the thought of her body.

"Are you going to tell us about your Christmas trees?" Dillon wanted to find a way to connect with the children. They always seemed just out of his grasp. He reached around Jessica to remove the mug of chocolate from her hand. The smell was making him feel slightly sick and he wanted to inhale her delicate scent. To think about the possibility of a future, not remember the agony of where he had been. Jessica gave him such hope. His arms caged her, brought his chest in contact with the sweeping line of her back. She was the bridge between Dillon and the children. She was the bridge that led from merely existing to living life.

"We found two that might work," Trevor said, "but neither was perfect."

"Does a Christmas tree have to be perfect?" Don asked.

"Perfect for us," Trevor answered before Jessica could draw a breath and breathe fire. "We know what we're looking for, don't we, Tara?"

"Well, next time you'd better be a little more careful and stay on the trails," Dillon cautioned, using his most authoritative voice.

"There isn't going to be a next time," Jessica muttered rebelliously, "my heart couldn't stand it."

Trevor looked mutinous. "I knew you were going to be like that, Jess. It could have happened to anybody. You always get so crazy, even when we fall off a bike."

"Watch your tone." Dillon's mouth settled in an ominous line. "I think Jessica and the rest of us are entitled to feel protective. You were completely buried, Trevor, we didn't know if you were alive or dead or whether you were able to breathe or were broken into a million pieces." His arms tightened around Jessica, holding her close, feeling the tremor go through her body. His chin nuzzled the top of her head in sympathy. "Have the decency to let us be shaken up. But don't worry, we'll get a Christmas tree."

Jessica wanted to protest. She didn't want Trevor going anywhere outside, but Dillon was his father. There was no sense in dissenting, but she was *not* letting the twins go anywhere outside by themselves, father or no father.

Dillon felt her instant reaction, her body stiffening, but she remained silent. He pressed a quick kiss against the tempting nape of her neck. "Good girl." Her skin was so soft he wanted to rub his face against her. His palms itched to hold the soft weight of her breasts. His mind was becoming cloudy with erotic fantasies right there in the kitchen with everyone standing around.

"Sorry, Jessie," Trevor mumbled. "I saw that circle. The one with two rings, one inside of the other. The one you said was used to invoke spirits or something. It was drawn on a flat rock. It was really bright. I went off the trail to check it out."

There was a sudden silence in the room. Only the wind outside could be heard, a low mournful howl through the trees. A chill went down Jessica's spine. She felt the difference in Dillon immediately. His body was nearly blanketing hers as they both leaned against the counter, so it was impossible to miss the sudden tension in him. His body actually trembled with some sudden overwhelming emotion.

"Are you certain you saw a double circle, Trevor?" Dillon's face was an expressionless mask, but his eyes were blazing.

"Yes, sir," Trevor answered, "it was very distinct. I didn't get close enough to see what it was made out of before everything came down on me. It wasn't drawn or painted onto the rock. The circles were made of something and set on the rock. That's all I saw before I tripped on a log and everything crashed on top of me. I fit into the little opening against the hill so I wasn't crushed. I covered my mouth and nose and as soon as everything settled, I breathed shallowly, hoping you'd hurry. I knew Tara would get you fast."

Dillon continued to look at his son. "Brian, have you brought that filth into my home? Did you dare to do that after all that happened?"

No one moved. No one spoke. No one looked at the drummer. Brian sighed softly. "Dillon, I have my faith and I practice it, yes, wherever I am."

Dillon turned his head slowly to pin Brian with his steely glare. "You are practicing that garbage here? In my home?" He straightened up unhurriedly and there was something very dangerous, very lethal in his body posture as he rose to his full height.

Dillon was vaguely aware of Jessica laying a restraining hand very gently on his arm, but he didn't even glance down at her. The anger always simmering far too close to the surface rose in a vicious surge. The memories, dark and hideous, welled up to devour him. Screams. Chanting. The smell of incense mingled with the musty smell of sexual lust. Jessica's terror-stricken face. Her nude body painted with disgusting symbols. A man's hand violating her innocent curves while others crowded around her breathing heavily, obscenely. Watching. Stroking and pumping to bring their own bodies to a fever pitch of excitement while they urged their leader on.

Bile rose, threatening to choke him. Dillon suppressed the urge to coil his hands around Brian's throat and squeeze. Instead he held himself utterly still, curling his fingers into fists. "You dared to bring that abomination back to my home after all the damage that was done here?" His tone was soft, menacing, a spine-chilling threat.

"Trevor and Tara go upstairs right now." Jessica stood up straight, too, very afraid of what might happen. "Go, right now and don't argue with me."

Jessica rarely used that particular tone of voice. The

twins looked from their father to Brian and obediently left the room. Trevor glanced back once, worried about Jessica, but she wasn't looking at him and he had no choice but to go with Tara.

"I want you off this island, Brian, and don't ever come back," Dillon bit out each word distinctly.

"I'll go, Dillon," Brian's dark eyes betrayed his own rising anger, "but you're going to listen to me first. I do not now, nor have I ever had anything to do with the occult. I don't worship the devil. I never turned Viv on to that scene, someone else did. I did my best to talk to her, to influence her away from it."

Jessica rubbed her hand soothingly up and down Dillon's stiff arm, feeling the ridges of his skin, the raised scars, reminders of that horror-filled night that were forever etched into his flesh.

"Go on," Dillon said, his voice rough.

"My religion is old, yes, but it is the worshiping of things of the earth, spirits that live in harmony with the earth. I use the magic circles, but I don't invoke evil. That would be against everything I believe. I did my best with Viv to make her understand the difference. She was so vulnerable to anything destructive." Tears glittered in his eyes, his mouth trembled slightly. "You aren't the only one who loved her, we all did. And we all lost her. I watched her go downhill just like you did. I did my best to stop her, I really did, the minute I found out she was involved with that Satanic crowd."

Dillon raked a hand through his hair. "They weren't even the real thing," he said softly, sighing heavily.

"She went nuts when she hooked up with Phillip

Trent," Brian said. "She listened to everything he said as if it was gospel. I swear to you, Dillon, I tried to stop her, but I couldn't counteract his influence." He looked as if he were breaking apart, his face crumbling under the memories.

Dillon felt his rage subsiding. He had known Brian nearly all of his life. He knew the truth when he heard it. "Trent dragged her down into a world of drugs and manic delusion so fast I don't think any of us could have stopped her. I had him investigated. He had his own little religious practices, looking for money, drugs, and sex, kicks maybe, but not based on anything he didn't make up."

Jessica stepped away from him, her lungs burning. She needed to be alone. Away from them all. Even Dillon. The memories were crowding far too close. None of the others knew what had happened to her and the discussion was skimming the edges of where she did not want to go.

"I'm sorry, Brian, I guess it just seems so much easier to blame someone else. I thought I'd gotten over that. I should have tried harder to put her into a hospital."

"I don't worship in your house," Brian said. "I know how you feel. I know you keep battery-powered lights rather than candles in case your generator breaks down because you can't stand to see an open flame. I know you don't want incense or any reminders of the occult here and I don't blame you, so I take it outside away from your home. I'm sorry—I didn't mean to upset you, Dillon."

"I shouldn't have accused you. Next time, get rid of the circle so the kids don't get curious. I don't want to have to explain all that to them."

Brian looked confused. "I didn't set up for a ceremony

anywhere near the trail, or that area." His protest was a low murmur.

Dillon's gaze and attention was on Jessica. She was very pale. Her hands were trembling and she put them behind her as she backed toward the door. "Jess." It was a protest.

She shook her head, her eyes begging him for understanding. "I'm turning in, I want to spend some time with the twins."

Dillon let her go, watched her take his heart with her as she hurried out of the room.

chapter
10

Tara held the covers back to allow Jessica to leap beneath the quilt. Clad in her drawstring pajama bottoms and a spaghetti strap top, Jessica's hair spilled loosely down her back in preparation for bed. She hopped over Trevor's makeshift bed and slid in beside Tara. "Why is the room so cold?"

"Your mysterious window-opener has struck in Tara's room," Trevor said. "It was wide open and the curtains were wet from the rain. The room was all foggy, Jess." He deliberately didn't tell her about the magic circle made of incense ash on the floor beside the bed which both he and Tara had worked to clean. She would never let them out of her sight if she found out about it.

Jessica sighed. "How silly. Someone has a fetish for open windows. How about your room, Trev, anything out of place?"

"No, but then I set up the video camera in my room," he said with a cheeky grin. "I thought someone had come in and gone through my things so I wanted to catch them in the act if they came back." He wiggled his eyebrows at her.

"And just who did you suspect and what did you think they were looking for?" Jessica demanded.

"I figured I'd catch Brenda looking for the cash," he admitted.

"Brenda's nice now," Tara objected. "She's not going to go through your smelly old socks looking for the money everyone knows you stash in them."

"Only you know that." Trevor glared at her.

"Now I do," Jessica pointed out with an evil smirk.

Tara wrinkled her nose. "He puts the money in his dirtiest, smelliest pair."

"That is so disgusting, Trevor. Put your dirty socks in the clothes hamper," Jessica lectured, "they aren't a money bank."

"So are you going to tell us whether or not Dad killed Brian?" Trevor tried to sound very casual, but there was an underlying hint of worry in his voice. "The suspense is doing me in."

"Of course he didn't. Brian's religion is a very old one, the worshipping of the earth and deities that are in harmony with the earth. He does not worship the devil, nor is he into the occult." She hesitated, looked at the two identical faces. "Your mother followed his example for a while but during the last year of her life, when she became so ill, she met a man named Phillip Trent. He was truly evil." Just saying his name sickened her. She felt it then, that terrible coldness that could creep into a room. Unnatural. Unbidden. Beneath the covers she pressed her hand to her stomach, terrified she would be sick.

"What's wrong, Jess?" Trevor sat up very straight.

She shook her head. It was a long time ago. A different house. That evil man was dead and nothing that he had brought to life remained behind. It was impossible. Everything had burnt to the ground, reduced to a pile of ashes. It was only her imagination that the curtain stirred slightly on a cold air current when the window was closed. It was only her imagination that she felt eyes watching her. Listening. To think that if she spoke of that time, something evil would triumph, would be set free.

"Your father knows the difference. Brian explained that he worships outside, rather than in the house, out of respect for Dillon's feelings. I didn't ask him about the circle in my room because I want to ask him about it in private. Dillon is protective of all of us. They're good friends and they've talked it out." Jessica shivered again, her gaze darting around the room to the corners hidden in shadows. She felt uneasy. Memories were far too close to the surface. She knotted her fist in the quilt.

Tara leaned close to her, studying her face. She glanced at her brother, and then put her hand over Jessica's, rubbing lovingly. "Tell us the Christmas story, Jessie. It always makes us feel better."

Jessica slipped deeper into the bed, snuggling into the pillow, wanting to hide beneath the covers like a frightened child. "I'm not certain I remember it exactly."

Trevor snorted his disbelief but gamely opened the familiar tale. "Once upon a time there were two beautiful children. Twins, a boy and a girl. The boy was smart and handsome and everyone loved him, especially all the girls in the neighborhood, and the girl was a punky little thing but he generously tolerated her."

"The true story is just the opposite," Tara declared with a sniff.

"The true story is, they were both wonderful," Jessica corrected, falling in with their all too obvious ploy. "The children were good and kind and very loving, and they deserved much happiness. Alas, they both suffered broken hearts. They hid it well, but the evil, wicked Sorcerer had stolen their father. The Sorcerer had locked him away in a tower far from the children, in a bitter, cold land where there was no sun, where he never saw the light of day. He had no laughter, no love, and no music. His world was bleak and his suffering great. He missed his children and his one true love."

"You know, Jess," Trevor piped up, "that whole one true love thing used to make me gag when I was little, but I think I like it now."

"That's the best part," Tara objected, appalled at her brother's lack of romance. "If you can't see that, Trev, there's no hope you're ever going to get the girl."

He laughed softly. "It's all in the genes, little sister."

Tara rolled her eyes. "He's so weird, Jessie, is there hope for him? Don't answer, just tell us why the evil Sorcerer took him away and put him in the tower."

"He was a beautiful man with an angel's face and a poet's heart. He sang with a voice like a gift from the gods and wherever he went, people loved him. He was kind and good and did his best to help everyone. He brought joy to their hard lives with his music and his wonderful voice. The Sorcerer grew jealous because the people loved him so very much. The Sorcerer didn't want him to be happy. He wanted the father to be ugly and mean inside, to be cruel the way he was. So the Sorcerer took away everything that the father loved. His children. His music. His one true love. The Sorcerer wanted him to be bitter and to grow hateful and twisted. He had the father tortured, a painful, hideous cruelty in the dungeons of the tower. The Sorcerer's evil minions hurt him, disfigured him and then they threw him in the tower, sentenced to an eternity of darkness. He was left alone without anyone to talk to, to comfort him, and his heart wept."

There was a catch in Jessica's voice. They would never know completely what life had done to him, taken from him. The twins had been five at the time of the fire and they had only vague memories of Dillon as he was in the old days, the charismatic, joyful poet who brought such happiness to everyone with his very existence.

"The children, Jess," Trevor prompted, "tell us about them."

"They loved their father dearly, so much so that they cried so many tears the river swelled and flooded the banks. Their father's one true love comforted them and reminded them that he would want his children to be strong, to be examples of how he had always lived his life. Helping people. Loving people. Taking responsibility when others would not. And the children carried on his legacy of service to the people, of loyalty and love even as their hearts wept in tune with his.

"One night, when it was cold and the rain poured down, when it was dark and the stars couldn't shine, a white dove landed on their windowsill. It was tired and hungry. The children immediately fed it their bread and gave it their water. The father's one true love warmed the shivering bird in her hands. To their amazement the dove spoke to them saying that Christmas was near. That they should find the perfect tree and bring it into their home, and decorate it with small symbols of love. Because of their kindness, a miracle would be granted them. The dove said they could have riches untold, they could have life immortal. But the children and the father's one true love said they wanted only one thing. They wanted their father returned to them."

"The dove said he wouldn't be the same, that he would be different," Tara chimed in eagerly with the detail.

"Yes, that's true, but the children and the father's one true love didn't care, they wanted him back any way they could have him. They knew that what was in his heart would never be changed."

Outside Tara's room, Dillon leaned against the door, listening to the sound of Jessica's beautiful voice telling her Christmas tale. He had come looking for her, hating the sorrow he'd seen on her face, needing to remove the swirling nightmares from her eyes. He should have known she would be with the twins. His children. His family. They were on the other side of the door. Waiting for him. Waiting for a miracle. Tears burned in his eyes, ran down his cheeks unchecked, and clogged his throat, threatening to choke him as he listened to the story of his life.

"Did they find the perfect tree?" Tara prompted. There was such a hopeful note in her voice that Dillon closed his eyes against another fresh flood of tears. They were wrenched from the deepest gouge in his soul. Enough to overflow the banks of the mythical river.

"At first they thought the dove meant perfection, as in physical beauty." Jessica's voice was so low he had to strain to hear. "But eventually, as they looked through the forest, they realized it was something far different. They found a small, bushy tree in the shadow of much larger ones. The branches were straggly and there were gaps but they knew at once it was the perfect giving tree. Everyone else had overlooked it. They asked the tree if it would like to celebrate Christmas with them and the tree agreed. They made wonderful ornaments and carefully decorated the tree and the three of them sat up on Christmas Eve waiting for the miracle. They knew they had chosen the perfect tree when the dove settled happily in the branches."

There was a long silence. The bed creaked as someone turned over. "Jessie. Aren't you going to tell us the end of the story?" Trevor asked.

"I don't know the end of the story yet," Jessica answered. Was she crying? Dillon couldn't bear it if she were crying.

"Of course you do," Tara complained.

"Leave her alone, Tara," Trevor advised. "Let's just go to sleep."

"I'll tell you on Christmas morning," Jessica promised.

Dillon listened to the sound of silence in the next room. The tightness in his chest was agony. He stumbled away from the pain, back up the stairs, back into the darkness of his lonely tower.

Jessica lay listening to the sounds of the twins sleeping.

It was comforting to hear the steady breathing. Outside the house, the wind was knocking at the windows like a giant hand, shaking the sills until the panes rattled alarmingly. The rain hit the glass with force, a steady rhythm that was soothing. She loved the rain, the fresh clean scent it brought, the way it cleared the air of any lingering smell of smoke. She inhaled, drifting, half in and half out of sleep. Fog poured into the room carrying with it an odor she recognized. She smelled incense and a frown flitted across her face. She tried to move. Her arms and legs were too heavy to lift. Alarmed, she fought to wake herself, recognizing she had moved beyond drifting, past dreams to her all too familiar nightmare.

She wouldn't look at them. Any of them. She had gone beyond terror to someplace numb. She tried not to breathe. She didn't want to smell them, or the incense, or hear the chanting, or to think about what was happening to her body. She felt the hand on her, deliberately rough, cruelly touching her while she lay helplessly under the assault. She had fought until she had no strength. Nothing would stop this demented behavior and she would endure it because she had no other choice.

The hand squeezed her hard, probed in tender, secret places. She would not feel, would not scream again. She couldn't stop the tears; they ran down her face and fell onto the floor. Without warning the door burst open, kicked in so that it splintered and hung at an angle from broken hinges. He looked like an avenging angel, his face twisted with fury, his blue eyes blazing with rage.

She cringed when he looked at her, when he saw the obscenity of what they were doing to her. She didn't want

*him to see her naked and painted with something evil
touching her body. He moved so fast she wasn't certain he
was real, ripping Phillip Trent away from her. There was
the sound of fist meeting flesh, the spray of blood in the
air. She was helpless, unable to move, unable to see what
was happening. There were screams, grunts, a bone
cracked. Shouted obscenities. The smell of alcohol. She
was certain she would never be able to bear the odor
again.*

*And then he was wrapping her in his shirt, loosening the
ties that bound her hands and feet. He lifted her, with tears
streaming down his face. "I'm sorry, baby, I'm sorry," he
whispered against her neck as he carried her from the room.
She caught glimpses of broken furniture, of glass and scat-
tered objects. Bodies writhing and moaning on the floor as
he carried her out. His hands were bloody but gentle as he
placed her in her bed, rocked her gently while she cried and
wept until both their hearts were broken. She begged him
not to tell anyone how he found her.*

*She had no idea how much time passed. He was filled
with fury, his rage was still lethal. He was arguing she
needed her mother, stalking from her room to cool off outside where he couldn't hurt anyone. She scrubbed herself in
the shower until her skin was raw, until there were no tears
left. She was dressing, her hands shaking so badly she
couldn't button her blouse, when she heard the volley of
shots ring out. The sound of the gun was distinctive. The
smell of smoke was overwhelming. It took a few moments to
realize it wasn't steam from the bathroom that was making
the room hazy, it was clouds of thick smoke. She had to
crawl through the hall to the twins' room. They were crying,*

hiding under the bed. Flames ate greedily at the hall, up the curtains. There was no getting to the others.

She dragged the children to the large window, shoved them through, following, dropping to earth, skidding on the slick dirt. Tara crawled forward blindly, tears streaming from her swollen eyes that prevented her from seeing. She screamed as she slipped over the edge. Jessica lunged after her. They rolled, bounced, sliding all the way to the sea. Tara disappeared beneath the waves, Jessica hurtled after her. Down. Into darkness. The salt water stung. It was icy cold. Her fingers brushed the child's shirt, slipped off, she grabbed again, caught a handful of material and held on. Kicking strongly. Surfacing. Struggling through the pounding waves with her burden. They lay together on the rocks, gasping for breath, the child in her arms. Her world in ruins.

Black smoke. Noise. Orange flames reaching the clouds. Screams. Wearily she pulled Trevor into her arms when he joined them. Together they slowly made their way back up the path leading to the front of the house. She saw Dillon lying there. He was motionless. His body was black, his arms outstretched. He was utterly silent but his eyes were screaming as he looked down in shock at the blackened ruin of his body. He looked up at her. Looked past her to the children. She understood then. Understood why he had entered a burning inferno. His gaze met hers as he stared helplessly up at her, in much the same way she must have stared up at him when he'd rescued her. As long as she lived, she would never forget the look on his face, the horror in his eyes. Jessica watched his blackened fingers turn to ash, watched the ash fall to the ground. She heard herself screaming in denial. Over and over. The sound was pure anguish.

"Jessie," Trevor called her name softly, his arm around Tara. They helplessly watched as Jessica pressed herself against the wall near the window and screamed and screamed, her face a mask of terror. Her eyes were open, but they knew she wasn't seeing them, but something else, something vivid and real to her, that they couldn't see. Night terrors were eerie. Jessica was caught up in the web of a nightmare and anything they did often made it worse.

The door to the bedroom was flung open and their father rushed in, still buttoning his jeans. He wore no shirt, he was barefoot. His hair was wild and disheveled, falling around his perfectly sculpted face like dark silk. His chest and arms were a mass of rigid scars and whorls of raised red skin. The scars streaked down his arms and spread down his chest to his belly fading into normal skin.

"What the hell is going on?" Dillon demanded but his frantic gaze had already found Jessica pressed against the wall. He glanced at his children. "Are you all right?"

Tara was staring at the mass of scars. She pulled her gaze up to his face with an effort. "Yes, she has nightmares. This is a bad one."

"I'm sorry, I forgot my shirt," Dillon told her softly before turning his attention back to Jessica. "Wake up, baby, it's over," he crooned softly. His voice was low and compelling, almost hypnotic. "It's me, sweetheart, you're safe here. I'm not going to let anyone hurt you."

Tara turned her head as more people crowded into the doorway of her room. She had to blink tears out of her eyes in order to focus on them. Trevor put his arm around her, offering comfort, and she took it.

"Good heavens," Brenda said, "what happened now?"

"Get them out of here, Trevor," Dillon ordered, "get out and close the door."

Trevor acted at once. He didn't want anyone staring at Jessica, seeing her in such a vulnerable state. And he didn't like the way they were staring at his father's body, either. He took Tara with him, pushing through the group, closing the door firmly and leaving Dillon alone with Jessica. "Show's over," he said gruffly, "you all might as well go back to bed."

Brenda glared at him. "I was actually trying to be help-ful. If Jessie needs me, I don't mind sitting up with her."

To everyone's astonishment, Tara wrapped her arms around Brenda's waist and looked up at her. "I need you," she confided. "I hurt him again."

Trevor cleared his throat. "No you didn't, Tara." He was happy to see the band members dispersing, leaving only Brenda and Robert behind.

"Yes I did, I was staring at his scars and he noticed," Tara confessed, looking up at Brenda. "Even with Jessie screaming and how much he wanted to help her, he noticed. And he said he was sorry." Tears welled up and spilled over. "I didn't mean to stare at him, I should have looked away. It must have hurt him so much."

It was Robert who dropped his hand on her head in a clumsy effort to comfort her. "We couldn't stop him. The house was completely engulfed in flames. He was calling for you and your brother, for Jessica. He ran toward the house. I caught him, so did Paul. He knocked us both down." There was sorrow in his voice, guilt, a ragged edge. Robert paused, rubbed the bridge of his nose, frowning slightly.

Brenda put her hand on his arm. Casually. As if it didn't matter, but Trevor saw that it did. That it steadied Robert. Robert smiled down at Brenda's hand and leaned forward to kiss her fingertips. "He ran inside the house, right through a wall of flames. Paul tried to go in after him, but Brian and I tackled him and held him down. We should have done that to Dillon. We should have." He shook his head at the memories.

Trevor found himself reaching out to his uncle, touching him for the first time. "No one could have stopped him. If I know anything about my father, it's that no one could have stopped him from trying to get to us." He glanced back at the closed door. Jessica's screams had stopped. He could hear the soft murmur of Dillon's voice. "No one could have stopped him from trying to get to Jess."

Robert blinked and focused on Trevor. "You're so like him, like he was back in the old days. Tara, what I'm trying to say to you is, don't be afraid of looking at your father's scars. Don't ever be ashamed of the way he looks. Those scars are evidence of how much he loves you, what you mean to him. He's a great man, someone you should be proud of, and he'll always put you first. Few people have that and I think it's important for you to know that you do have it. I could never have entered that house, none of the rest of us could go in, even when we heard the screams."

"Don't, Robert," Brenda said sharply. "No one could

have saved those people. You didn't even know they were up there."

"I know, I know." He rubbed a hand over his face, wiping away old horrors and determinedly forcing a smile to his face, needing to change the subject. "Anyone up for one of Brenda's silly board games? She's obsessed with them."

"I always win," Brenda pointed out smugly.

Trevor glanced at the closed door anxiously, then switched his attention back to his aunt. "I always win," he countered.

Tara slipped her hand into Robert's. "He does," she confided.

"Then it's all-out war," Brenda decided, leading the way back to her rooms. "I detest losing at *anything*."

"Do you really have an insurance policy on us?" Trevor asked curiously as he followed her down the hall.

"Of course, silly, you're a boy, the odds are much higher that you'll do something stupid," Brenda remarked complacently. "All that lovely lollie," she added, grinning back at him over her shoulder.

Trevor shook his head. "I'm not buying your act any more, *Auntie*. You're not the bad girl you want the world to believe you are."

Brenda flinched visibly. "Don't even say that, it's sacrilegious. And by the way, your cute little pranks aren't scaring me in the least, so you may as well stop."

"I don't pull cute little pranks," Trevor objected strenuously to her choice of words. "If I was pulling off a prank, it wouldn't be cute or little. And it would scare you. I'm a master at practical jokes."

Brenda pushed open the door to her room, raising one

eyebrow artfully as he preceded her into the suite. "Oh, really? So what is with the hooded face appearing in the window, and the mysterious messages written on my makeup mirror? *Get out while there's still time.*" She rolled her eyes. "Really! Perfectly childish. And just how do you explain the water running in the bathtub with the stopper in the drain and the room always filled with steam? If I didn't know it was you, it would give me the creeps. The open window and Brian's magic circle is such a clever touch, throwing suspicion his way. We've all talked about it, we know it's you two. Even that motley dog is in cahoots with you, growling at the steam and staring at nothing just to scare us."

There was a small silence. Tara and Trevor exchanged a long look. "Is your window open when you come into your room?" Tara ventured, her voice tight. "And fog or steam all through the room?"

Robert looked at her sharply. "Are you saying you kids haven't been pulling these pranks?" He poured them both a soda from the small ice chest they had stashed in their room.

Trevor shook his head, took a long grateful drink of the cold liquid, nearly draining the glass. He hadn't realized how thirsty he was. "No, sir, we haven't. And Jessica's window is open all the time." A chill crept into the room with his denial. "Tara's window was open this evening. And there was burned incense and one of those circles on the floor of both Jessie's and Tara's rooms. Jess didn't tell Dillon because she was afraid he would quit recording with everyone, and she thinks it's important for him and everyone else to make the music."

Robert and Brenda exchanged a long look. "If you kids have been playing tricks, it's all right to say so," Robert persisted. "We know kids do that sort of thing." He pulled a *Clue* game from the closet, carried it to the table.

"How perfectly apropos, a murder game on a dark and stormy night just when we're discussing mysterious occurrences," Brenda quipped as they spread the game board out on the small table.

"We didn't do any of those things," Trevor insisted. "I don't know who it is or why, but something wants us out of here."

"Why do you say that?" Robert asked sharply as he separated the cards.

Trevor noticed his clue sheet was filled and he crumpled it, looking around for a wastebasket. He couldn't toss it, practicing his technique, because the basket was filled with newspaper. With a sigh he got up and walked over to it. For some reason his stomach was beginning to cramp uncomfortably and his skin felt clammy. The conversation was bothering him a lot more than he realized. "I don't know, I always feel like something's watching us. We've been letting the dog in and sometimes we're in a room alone and it starts growling, looking at the door. All the hair rises up on its back. It's freaky. But when I go look, no one's there."

"I'd think you were making it up," Robert said, "but there have been some strange things happening in here, too. We thought it was you kids, so we didn't say anything either, but I don't like the sound of that. Have you told Jessie?"

Trevor bent down to press the sheet of paper into the wastebasket. The newspaper caught his eye. It had tiny little holes in it where words were cut out. He glanced back at his aunt and uncle. They were putting the game pieces on the board. Tara looked pale, a frown on her face. She was holding her stomach as if she had cramps, too. Trevor lifted the newspaper slightly. It reminded him of movies where ransom notes had been concocted from printed words pasted on paper. The glass in front of Tara was empty. A frisson of fear went down his spine. Very slowly he straightened, moved casually away from the evidence in the wastebasket.

"No, I haven't told Jessie much at all. She's been busy with the recording and she's so darned overprotective." He looked directly at his aunt. "I'm feeling a little sick. It wasn't the soda, was it?"

"I'm not feeling very well either," Tara admitted.

Brenda bent over Tara solicitously. "Is it the flu?"

"You tell me," Trevor challenged. A wave of nausea hit him. "We need Jessie."

Brenda sniffed. "I think I'm quite capable of taking care of a couple of little kiddies with the flu."

"I hope so," Tara said, "because I'm going to throw up." She ran to the bathroom, holding her stomach.

Brenda looked harassed for a moment, then rushed after her.

"JESS, BABY, CAN YOU hear me now? Do you know who I am?" Dillon used his voice shamelessly, a velvet blend of heat and smoke. He didn't make the mistake of trying to approach her, knowing he could become part of her frightening world. Instead, he flicked on the light, bathing the room in a soft glow. He hunkered down across from her, his movements slow and graceful. "Honey, come back to me now. You don't need to be in that place, you don't belong there."

She was staring, focused on something beyond his shoulder. There was so much terror and horror in her eyes that he actually turned his head, expecting to see something. It was icy cold in the room. The window behind her was fully open, the curtains fluttering like twin white flags. It made him uneasy. She was pressed up against the wall, her hands restlessly searching the surface, seeking a place of refuge. His breath hitched in his throat when her fingers skimmed the windowsill and she inched toward it.

"Jess, it's Dillon. See me, baby, know I'm here with you." He slowly straightened, shifted to the balls of his feet. His heart was hammering out his own fright. Her screams had stopped but she was staring at something he couldn't see, couldn't fight.

With a small moan of terror, Jessica flung herself at the open window, crawling out as quickly as she could pull herself through. Dillon was on top of her in an instant, his hands wrapping securely around her waist, dragging her backward into the room. She fought like a wild thing, tearing at the windowsill, the curtains, her fingernails digging into wood as she desperately tried to make her escape.

"You're two stories up, Jess," Dillon said, twisting to avoid her scissoring legs. He managed to wrestle her to the floor without hurting her, holding her down, straddling her, pinning her there so she couldn't harm herself. "Wake up. Look at me."

Her gaze persisted in going beyond him, caught in a web he couldn't break through. When she stopped fighting, he pulled her onto his lap, his arms still holding her tightly there on the floor, and he sang softly to her. It had been her favorite song as long as he could remember. His voice filled the room with a warmth, a soothing comfort, a promise of love and commitment. He had written it in the days of hope and belief, when he believed in love and miracles. When he believed in himself.

Jessica blinked, looked around her, focused on Dillon's angel's face. It took a few moments to realize she was on his lap, his arms binding her tightly to him. She turned her head to search for the twins. The room was empty.

She shivered, relaxed completely into Dillon, allowing his voice to drive away the remnants of terror.

"Are you back, baby?" His voice was a wealth of tenderness. "Look at me." He brought both of her hands to his mouth, kissed her fingers. "Tell me you know who I am. I swear I won't let anything happen to you." With Jessica on his lap, only thin cloth separated them, and the knowledge was awakening his body. Her breasts were spilling out of her thin top giving him a generous view of soft skin. The temptation to lean down and taste her was strong.

A small smile managed to find its way to her trembling mouth. "I know that, Dillon. I've always known that. Did I frighten Tara and Trevor?"

"Tara and Trevor?" he echoed, astonished. "You frightened *me.*" He brought her palm to his bare chest, straight over his pounding heart. "I can't take much more of this. I really can't." He traced her trembling lips with a scarred fingertip. The raised whorls rasped sensually over her soft mouth. "What in the hell am I supposed to do with you? If I had a heart left, I'd have to tell you, you're breaking it." He had been so afraid for her that he had left his room with his body uncovered. He had turned on the light to help dispel her dream world, not thinking what it would reveal of him. He held her in his lap, his scarred body exposed to her gaze when it was the last thing he ever intended.

"I'm sorry, Dillon." Tears shimmered in her vivid green eyes, threatened to spill over onto her long lashes. Her lips were still trembling, tearing at his heart even more. "I didn't mean for this to happen. I didn't know it would be like this."

He groaned, a sound of surrender. The last thing he wanted was for her to be sorry. He helped her from his lap, rose and hauled her up beside him, his arm curling around her waist, clamping her to his side. "Don't cry, Jess, I swear to God if you cry you'll destroy me."

She buried her face against his chest, against the scars of his past life. She didn't wince, she didn't even stare in utter disgust. His Jessica. His one light in the darkness. He could feel her tears wet against his skin. With an oath he lifted her, cradled her slight weight to him. There was only one place to take her, the only place she belonged. He took the stairs fast, climbing to the third story, his refuge, his sanctuary, the lair of the wounded beast. He kicked the door closed behind him.

"Are you afraid of me, Jess?" he asked softly. "Tell me if you're afraid of how I look." He strode to the large bed and laid her down on his sheets. "Tell me if you're afraid I went back into that house and did what most people think I did."

She rested her head on the pillow, met the hypnotic blue of his eyes, was lost instantly, drowning in the deep turbulent sea. "I've never been afraid of you, Dillon," she answered honestly. "You know I don't believe you shot anyone that night. I've never believed it. Knowing you went back into the house before the gun was fired doesn't change what I know about you." She reached up, framed his face with one hand while the other skimmed lightly over his chest. How could he ever think his scars would repulse her? He had gone into a burning inferno to save his children. The scars were as much a part of him now as his angel's face. Her fingertips traced a whorl of ridged flesh. His badge of courage, of love—she could never think of his scars any other way. "And you've always been beautiful to me. Always. You were the one who kept me away from you. I tried so many times to see you in the burn center and you wouldn't give your consent." There was hurt in her voice, pain in her eyes. "You cut yourself off from me and you left me struggling on my own. For so long I couldn't breathe without you. I couldn't talk to anyone. I didn't know how to go on."

"You deserve something better than this, Jess," he said grimly.

"What's better, Dillon? Being without you? The pain doesn't go away. Neither does the loneliness, not for me or the children."

"I always knew exactly what I was doing, what I was worth." Confusion slipped across his face. "My music was my measure of who I was, what I could offer. Now I don't know what I can give you. But you have to be certain being with me is what you really want. I can't have you and then lose you. I have to know it means the same thing to you as it does to me."

Jessica smiled at him as she stood up. Deliberately she moved in front of the large sliding glass door leading to the balcony. She wanted what light there was to fall on her, so there would be no mistake. For her answer, she simply caught the hem of her tank top and pulled it over her head.

Standing there, facing him with the glass framing her, she looked like an exotic beauty, ethereal, out of reach. Her skin gleamed at him, a satin sheen, beckoning his touch. Her breasts were full, firm, jutting toward him, so perfect he felt his heart slam hard in his chest and his mouth go dry. His body tightened painfully, his need so urgent his body was straining against the fabric of his jeans.

He reached out to the offering, his palm skimming along her soft skin. She felt exactly as she looked and the texture was mesmerizing. Jessica's breath hitched in her throat, her body trembled as he cupped her breasts in his hands. His thumbs found taut buds and stroked as he leaned into her to settle his mouth over hers.

Jessica was aware of so many sensations. Her breasts achingly alive, wanting his touch, his thumbs sending bolts of lightning whipping through her bloodstream until her lower body was heavy and needy. Every nerve ending was alive, so that his silken hair brushing her skin sent tiny darts of pleasure coursing through her. His mouth was hard and dominant, moving over and into hers with male expertise and hot, silken passion.

Outside the wind began to moan, shifting back from the sea, rattling at the glass doors as if seeking entrance. Dillon's mouth left hers to follow the line of her shoulder, the hollow of her throat, to close, hot and hungry, around her breast. Jessica's body jerked with reaction, her arms coming up to cradle his head. His mouth was fiery hot, suckling strongly, a starving man let loose on a feast. His hands skimmed her narrow rib cage, tugged impatiently at the drawstring of her pajamas.

Her body wound tighter and tighter, a spiral of heat she couldn't hope to control. The pajama bottoms dropped to the floor and she kicked them aside, reveling in the way his hands glided possessively over her.

"I've wanted you for so long," he breathed the words against her satin skin, moving to her other breast, his fingers stroking the curve of her bottom, finding every intriguing indentation, every shadow. "I can't believe you're really here with me."

"I can't believe it either," she admitted, closing her eyes, throwing back her head to arch more fully into his greedy mouth. She felt a wildness rising in him, skating the edge of his control. It gave her a sense of power that she might not have had otherwise. He wanted her with the same force of need as she did him which allowed her a boldness she might never have managed. Her hands found the waistband of his jeans. She deliberately rubbed her palm over his bulging hardness, just as she'd done in the woods. She felt the breath slam out of his lungs. He lifted his head, his blue gaze burning into her like a brand.

Jessica smiled at him as she unfastened his jeans. "I've wanted to do this," she confided as he burst free. Thick and long and ready for her, pulsing with heat and life. Her fingers wrapped around the length of him, a proprietary gesture. Her thumb stroked the velvet head until he groaned aloud.

Very gently he exerted pressure on her, forcing her back toward the bed. "I don't want to wait any longer, I don't think I can."

Jessica knelt on the bed, still stroking him, leaning forward to kiss his sculpted mouth, loving the hunger in his gaze. He was more intimidating than she had expected so she took her time getting used to the feel and size of him. She fed on his mouth, trailed kisses over his scarred chest, experimentally swirled her tongue over the head of his shaft. He jumped beneath her ministrations, sucked in his breath audibly.

"Not yet, baby, I'll explode if you do that. Lie back for me." His hands were already assisting her, pushing her into the mattress so she lay naked and waiting for his touch. His hand stroked a caress down her body, over her breast, lingering for a moment until she shivered, over her belly, down to the thatch of curls, glided to her thighs.

He sat up, his blue eyes moving over every inch of her. She was so beautiful, moving restlessly on the bed beneath him. Wanting him. Needing him. Hungry for him alone. He loved the way the muted light skimmed lovingly over her body, touching her here and there along the curves and shadows he was familiarizing himself with.

"Dillon." It was a soft protest, that he had stopped when she was burning for him, her body heavy and throbbing with need.

"I love to look at you, Jess." His hands parted her thighs just a little wider, his fingers stroking a long caress in the damp folds between her legs. She jumped when he touched her, pushed forward against his palm, a small cry of pleasure escaping her. Dillon smiled at her, leaned down to swirl his tongue around her intriguing belly button. Those little tops she wore that didn't quite cover her flat belly were enough to drive him mad. His hair brushed her sensitive skin and he pushed his finger slowly, deep inside her tight, hot sheath. At once her muscles clenched around him, velvet soft, firm, moist, and hot. His own body throbbed and swelled in response.

Her hips pushed forward wantonly. Jessica had no inhibitions with Dillon. She wanted his body, wanted every single erotic dance with him. She had no intention of holding back; she was determined to get every last gasp of pleasure she could. She had learned the hard way that life is precarious and she wasn't going to let an opportunity slip by because of modesty, pride, or shyness. Jessica lifted her hips to meet the thrusting of his finger, the friction triggering a rippling effect deep in her hottest core.

Dillon nipped her flat belly with a string of teasing kisses, distracting her while he stretched her a little more, sinking two fingers into her soft, hot body. More than anything else, her pleasure mattered to him. He was large and thick and he could tell she was small. Her velvet folds pulsed for him, wanting, and he fed that hunger, pushing deep, retreating, entering again so that her hips followed his lead. "That's what I want, honey, just like that. I want you ready for me."

"I am ready for you," she pleaded softly, her fingers tangling in his hair.

"Not yet, you're not," he answered. His breath was warm against the curve of her hip. She felt his tongue stroke a caress in the crease along her thigh. His mouth found the triangle of fiery curls at the junction of her legs. Her breath hissed out of her as his tongue tasted her moist heat. His name was a whispered plea. He lifted his head to look at her face. Very slowly he withdrew his fingers to bring them to his mouth. She shivered, her gaze fascinated as he licked her juices from his hand. "Open your thighs wider, baby." It was a whispered enticement. "Give yourself to me."

She was lost in the pulsing hunger; the fire was racing through her body. She opened her legs wider to him, a clear invitation. She was hot and wet and slick with her passion. Dillon pressed his palm once against her heated entrance, so that she shivered in anticipation. Then he slowly lowered his head once more.

She nearly screamed, drowning in the sensation of pure pleasure. His tongue caressed, probed deep, stabbed into hot folds, swirled and teased and sucked at her until she was mindlessly sobbing his name, writhing beneath him, her hips thrusting helplessly for the relief only he could bring her. He took her up the path several times, pushing higher each time so that her body shuddered and rippled with pleasure over and over. Until he knew she was hot and slick and needed him enough to accept him buried deep within her body.

Dillon knelt between her legs, and watched his body probe desperately for the slick entrance to hers. He wanted to see them come together, in a miracle of passion. His engorged head pushed into her. At once he felt her sheath, tight and hot, grip him, close around him. The sensation shook him so that he had to hang on to his control. "Jess." Her name burst from between his teeth. He slid in another inch, pushing his way through the tight folds. If it was possible, she grew even hotter. His hands tightened on her hips. "Tell me you're okay, baby."

"Yes, more," she gasped. He was invading her body, a thick, hard fullness, stretching her immeasurably, but at the same time, the craving for him grew and grew.

His hands tightened and he surged forward, past her barrier, and buried himself deeper. Sweat broke out on his forehead. He had never felt such a sensation of pure ecstasy. It was difficult to keep from plunging his body madly into hers. "Tell me what it feels like." He bit the words out huskily, and lowered his head to flick his tongue over her taut nipple. The action tightened her body even more around his.

"It's everything, Dillon. You're big and you're stretching me so it burns a little, but at the same time, I want more, I want all of you deep inside me," she answered honestly. "More than anything, that's what I want right now."

"Me, too," he admitted and surged forward. The sensation shook him. Her muscles were slick and hot and velvet soft, so tight he could barely stand it. He buried himself deep, withdrew, and thrust hard again. He watched her face carefully for signs of discomfort, but her body was flushed, her eyes glazed, her breath coming in little needy pants.

Satisfied that she was feeling the same pleasure he was feeling, Dillon began to move in a gentle rhythm. Long and slow, gliding in and out of her, stretching, pushing deeper with each stroke. He tilted her hips, held her body so he could thrust even deeper, wanting her to accept every last inch of him, almost as if her body could accept his, she would see who he really was and love him anyway. He buried himself to the hilt, sliding so deep he felt her womb, felt her contractions beginning, a spiraling that began to increase in strength. "Jess, I've never felt like this. Never." He wanted her to know what she meant, how much a part of him she was.

His rhythm became faster, harder, his hips surging forward into her, his body beyond any pretense of control. Jessica cried out softly as her body fragmented, as the room rocked and the earth simply melted away. Dillon could feel how strong her muscles were, milking him, gripping him in the strength of her orgasm, taking him with her right over the edge. He pumped into her frantically, helplessly, unable to control the wildness in him, the explosion ripping through his body from his toes up to the top of his head.

Dillon didn't have enough energy to roll over, so he lay on top of her, his body still locked to hers. His heart was beating hard. He buried his face against her breast, tears burning at the back of his eyes and throat. He had never been so emotional in the old days. He had never felt like this, sated and at peace. He had never thought it possible.

Jessica wrapped her arms around Dillon, holding him close, feeling the emotions swirling so deeply in him. She knew he was struggling. Part of him wanted to remain a recluse, hidden from the past and the future, and part of him desperately wanted what she was holding out to him. It was all tied up in his music. In his perception that he had failed everyone he loved. He wanted her to love him as he saw himself, a man without anything to offer. She didn't see him that way and never could. She could only offer him what she had, her honesty, her belief in him, her trust.

She felt his tongue flick her nipple, a lazy back and forth swirl that sent shock waves through her body. Her muscles rippled with the aftershock and gripped his. He exhaled, his breath warm against her skin.

"Tell me I didn't hurt you, Jess," he asked. He lifted himself up to his elbows, his hands framing her face.

"Dillon! I was practically yelling your name shamelessly for the entire household to hear." She smiled as he leaned down to kiss her. The touch of his mouth sent a series of shocks through her body so that she once more rippled with pleasure. "I think I'm hypersensitive to you," she admitted.

His eyebrow shot up. "That appeals to me on a purely primitive level," he said as he buried his face in the valley between her breasts. "I love how you smell, especially now after we've made love." His mouth nuzzled her skin, his tongue teasing along her ribs. He allowed his sated body to slide away from hers, but his hand slipped along the path of her belly to rest in her triangle of curls. "I want to just explore every inch of you for the rest of the night. I want to know you, what brings you pleasure, what gets you hot fast and what takes a little longer. Mostly, I just want to be with you." His silky hair played over her aching breasts as he lifted his head high enough to look at her. "Do you mind?"

There was a curious vulnerability about him. Jessica stretched languidly beneath him, offering up her body to him. "I want to be with you, too."

She lay listening to the rain on the roof while his hands skimmed her body, framed every curve, touched every inch of her with tenderness. She felt as if she were drifting in a sea of pure pleasure. He made love to her a second time, a slow, leisurely joining that stole her heart along with her breath.

Jessica realized she must have fallen asleep a while

ago when she woke to feel Dillon's hands gliding over her once again. She lay in the dark, smiling as he brought her body to life. His hands and mouth were skillful, teasing, tempting. He shifted to pull her closer to him, his knowledge of her body growing with every exploration.

His tongue was busy at her nipple, his mouth hot with passion and Jessica closed her eyes, willing to give herself up to the incredible sensation. Her hands in his hair, she tried to relax, tried to ignore the shiver of awareness moving down her spine. She felt eyes on them. Watching them. Watching Dillon suckling at her breast, his fingers delving deeply into her wet core. Her eyes flew open and she looked wildly around the room, trying to see into every shadow.

Dillon felt her sudden resistance. "What is it, baby?" he asked, his mouth still busy between words. "Have I made you sore?"

"Someone is outside the door, Dillon," Jessica whispered against his ear, "listening to us." It was difficult to think when his mouth was pulling so strongly at her breast, sending white-hot streaks of lightning dancing through her bloodstream. When he pushed two fingers deep and stroked her with such expertise.

Dillon's body was hard and hot and wanting hers. His tongue flicked over the tight bud of her nipple, did a long, slow lazy swirl. He lifted his head away from the lush pleasures of her body when she tugged at his hair. His blue eyes burned over her face hungrily. "I didn't hear anything."

"I'm not kidding, Dillon," Jessica insisted, "someone is

listening to us, or watching us. I can feel them." She stiffened, pushing at him, looking toward the glass balcony half expecting to see a hooded figure standing there.

Sighing with regret, Dillon left the pleasures of her body and looked around for his jeans. She had already slipped into his robe, cinching it around her slender body. Her face was pale and her red-gold hair spilled around her like a waterfall of silk. He didn't understand her. She was always a miracle of good sense, but when it came to certain things, she lost every bit of it, she was so positive that forces were conspiring to harm those she loved. He couldn't really blame her for worrying. Dillon stalked to the door and jerked it open wide to show her no one was there.

His heart nearly stopped when he came face-to-face with his bass player. They stood so close their noses were nearly touching.

Don stared for a moment at Dillon's exposed chest, then glanced past him to see Jessica huddled in Dillon's robe. Dillon stepped instantly to block Don's view of her. "What the hell are you doing, Don?" Dillon snapped, angrily.

Don flushed, glanced past him to Jessica's pale face, and half turned to leave. "Forget it, I didn't realize you were busy. I saw the light and knew you were up."

Dillon swallowed his annoyance. Don never sought him out. It was a rare chance to clear the air between them, even if it was untimely. "No, don't go, it must have been something important that brought you here this late." He raked a hand through his thick black hair, tossed Jessica a pleading smile. She responded exactly the way he knew she would, nodding slightly and drawing his robe more closely around her. "Hell, it must be close to five in the morning." He stepped back and gestured for Don to enter. "Whatever it is, let's deal with it." Don looked rumpled and Dillon smelled alcohol on his breath.

Don took a deep breath, stepped inside. "I'm sorry Jessie." His gaze found her, then slid away. "I didn't know you were here."

She shrugged. It was far too late to hide anything that had been going on. The bed was rumpled, the pillows on the floor. Her hair was disheveled and she wore nothing under Dillon's robe. "Would you like me to leave?" She asked it politely. Don seemed terribly nervous, his apprehension adding to her own discomfort. Her stomach rolled ominously, a wave of nausea swamping her for a moment.

"I don't know if I have the courage to say to Dillon what I need to say, let alone in front of anyone, but on the other hand, you're always a calming influence." He paced across the room several times while they waited.

"Have you been drinking?" Dillon asked, curious. "I've never seen you drink, Don, not more than one beer."

"I thought it would give me courage." Don gave him a half hearted humorless grin. "You need to call the police and have me arrested." The words tumbled out fast, in a single rushed breath. The moment he said them, he looked for a place to collapse.

Dillon led him to one of the two chairs positioned on either side of a small reading table. "Would you like a glass of water?"

Jessica had already hurried to get a glass from the large master bathroom. "Here, Don, drink this."

He took the glass, gulped the water down, wiped his mouth with the back of his hand, and looked up at Dillon. "I swear to God I thought you knew about Vivian and me. All this time I thought you were waiting for a chance to get rid of me and replace me with Paul. I kept waiting for it to happen. I tried so hard never to give you a reason."

"Before anything else, Don, I'm a musician. I love Paul. He's my best friend. We've stood together through the best and worst of times, but he doesn't have your talent. I *wanted* you in the band. From the first time I heard you play, I knew you were right. Paul doesn't have your versatility. He helped start the band, and I had no intention of leaving him along the wayside, but once you signed on with us, you were as much a part of the band as I was." Dillon shook his head regretfully. "I'm sorry you thought differently, that I never told you how valuable you were to me."

"Great. I didn't need to hear you say that." Don heaved a sigh. "This isn't easy, Dillon. I don't deserve you to be civil to me."

"I'll admit I was shocked and upset about you and Vivian," Dillon said. He reached for Jessica, unable to help himself, needing to touch her. Needing her real and solid beside him. At once she was there, her small body fitting beneath his shoulder, her arm slipping around his waist. "It was a rotten thing to do, Don, but it hardly warrants calling the police."

"I tried to blackmail you." Don didn't look at either of

them as he made the confession. He stared down at his hands, a lost expression on his face. "I saw you go into the forest that night. We all heard the yelling upstairs, and the pounding. We figured you caught Viv with one of her lovers. No one wanted to embarrass you so they all went to the studio to be out of the way, but I went to the kitchen for something to drink and I saw you go out. You had tears on your face and you were so shaken, I followed you, thinking I could offer to help. But you were more distraught than anyone I'd ever seen before and I figured, since it involved Vivian, you wouldn't want to talk to me. I walked around, undecided, and then just when I was going back, I saw you go in through the kitchen. Rita was in there and I heard you talking, telling her what happened. You were so angry, you were wrecking the place. I didn't dare approach you or Rita. I saw you start up the stairs and I headed for the studio. Then I heard the shots." As proof of his crime he pulled a plain sheet of paper from his pocket. Words cut from the headline of a newspaper were pasted on it. "This was one I was going to send you."

"Why didn't you testify to that at the trial?" Dillon's voice was very low, impossible to read. He snatched the paper from Don's hand and crumpled it without glancing at it.

"Because I was already on the basement staircase, looking out through the glass doors, and I saw you when the shots were fired. I knew you didn't do it. You had gone back outside a second time and you were heading toward the forest."

"Yet you decided blackmail was a good alternative?"

"I don't know why. I don't know why I did any of the things I've done since then," Don admitted. "All I cared about was the band. I wanted it back. You sat up here in this house with Paul, no one else could get near you. You had all that talent just going to waste, a musical genius, and you locked yourself up with Paul as the warden. He never wanted me anywhere near the place. I had this stupid idea that if you had to pay out a lot of money, you'd have go back to work and we'd all be back on the ride."

"Why didn't you just talk to me?" Dillon asked in the same quiet voice.

"Who could talk to you?" Don demanded bitterly. "Your watchdog wouldn't let anyone near you. You have him so well trained he practically has the Great Wall of China surrounding the island." He held up his hand to prevent Dillon from speaking. "You don't have to defend him, I know he's protective and even why. I needed the band back and I felt hopeless so I sent you a stupid letter and followed it with a couple of others. Obviously you weren't very worried because you didn't respond."

"I didn't give a damn," Dillon admitted.

"There's no excuse for what I've done," Don announced, "so I'm ready to go to jail. I'll confess everything to the cops."

Dillon looked so helpless, Jessica put her arms around him. "Did you talk to my mother about this?" She couldn't see Don sneaking around her mother's car, fraying the brake lines. Nothing seemed to make sense anymore. If she felt so lost, with the ground shifting out from under her, how must Dillon feel?

"Hell no, she would have boxed my ears," Don said emphatically. "Why would I do a dumb thing like that?"

"You're drunker than you think you are, Don," Dillon said, "go sleep it off. We'll talk about this later." He had absolutely no idea what he was going to say when they talked. He almost felt like laughing hysterically.

Jessica pressed her hand to her stomach as Dillon closed the door. "I feel sick," she announced before he could speak and raced for the bathroom.

chapter
12

"COME ON, BRENDA, you have to come with us," Tara wheedled. "It will be fun."

"Are you certain you're feeling better? You were so sick this morning. I almost made Robert get Paul to bring in a helicopter to transport you to the hospital. And now you're jumping around like nothing happened."

Jessica looked up alertly. Everyone had gathered in the kitchen, sleeping late as usual so that it was early evening. "Tara was sick this morning? Why didn't someone come and get me?"

"*Both* the children were sick this morning and I handled it just fine, thank you very much," Brenda announced. "Some kind of stomach flu. You know, Jessie, you aren't the only one with maternal instinct. I was a miracle of comfort to them. Not to mention I was being wonderfully helpful and discreet to give you and Dillon time to . . . er . . . work things out."

Trevor made a rude noise, somewhere between a raspberry and a choking cough. "A miracle of comfort? Brenda, you were hanging out the window gagging and calling for smelling salts. Robert didn't know whether to run to you, Tara, or me. The poor guy was cleaning up the floor half the day."

"Robert, you are a true prince." Jessica flashed him a grateful smile. "Thank you for cleaning up after them."

"Just remember it was my good sense to notice him," Brenda took the credit.

Don made a face. "I thought we were working today. I want to finish the recording and see what we have. Do we have to do this now?"

"We're staying up all night working," Paul pointed out. "By the time we get up, most the day is gone and we lose the light we need hunting for the Christmas tree. I say we go now."

Don muttered softly beneath his breath, his gaze studiously avoiding Dillon's.

Jessica frowned, studying the twins. "You *both* had the stomach flu? I was feeling a bit queasy this morning myself. Did anyone else? Maybe we all ate something bad."

"Brian's pancakes," Brenda said instantly, "ghastly things designed to drive us all mad with monotony. Devoid of all nutrition and basically the worst meal on the face of the earth. And if you ask me, he's trying to poison me." She blew him a kiss, pure glee on her face. "The heinous plot won't work, genius though it might be, because I have a cast-iron stomach."

Brian leapt up out of his chair, nearly knocking it over. "I make pancakes that are works of art, Brenda," he snapped, as if goaded beyond endurance. "I don't see you slaving away in the kitchen for all of us."

"And you won't ever, darling—the very idea makes me shudder," she said complacently. "Trivial things should be left to trivial people."

"The children are fighting again," Jessica pointed out with a soft sigh, leaning into the comfort of Dillon's body. "And as usual, it isn't the twins."

"Tara, are you certain you're feeling well enough to go traipsing around in the woods? It's cold out and the wind is really blowing. There's another storm on the way. If you'd rather curl up here where it's warm, we'll go look and bring you back a tree," Dillon offered. He wrapped his arms around Jessica, uncaring that anyone saw them.

For the first time in years, he felt at peace with himself. There was hope in his life, a reason for his existence. "Jess and Trevor can stay with you, if you'd like."

"No way," Trevor objected. "I'm feeling fine. No one else can pick our tree. We know what we're looking for, don't we, Tara?"

Tara nodded solemnly, wrapping her arm around her brother's waist, her eyes on Jessica. All three smiled in perfect understanding. "We all go," she announced. "We'll know the right tree."

Dillon shrugged. "Sounds fine to me—let's do it then. Anyone who would like to find the tree with us is welcome to come. We can get the tools out of the shed and meet you on the trail." He tugged at Jessica, determined to take her with him. A few minutes alone in the shed was looking good. He hadn't had two minutes to steal a kiss from her.

"Whoa there." Trevor held up his hand. "I'm not

sure how safe it is to let our Jessica go to a *shed* with you, Dad. You have a certain reputation as a Casanova type."

Dillon's eyebrow shot up. "And where would I get a rep like that?"

"Well, for one thing, look at this house. I've been meaning to talk to you about this place. You have weird carvings and things hanging off the eaves. What's that all about? This place looks like something out of an Edgar Allen Poe novel. The men in those books were always up to no good with the ladies." He wriggled his eyebrows suggestively.

"Weird carvings?" Dillon was horrified. "This house is a perfect example of early Gothic and Renaissance architecture combined. You, son, are a cretin. It's a *perfect* house. Look at the carvings on the corners: winged gargoyles scaling the south side, lions clawing their way up the east side. The detail is fantastic. And every true Gothic and Renaissance man has his secret passageways and moving walls. Where's the fun in a stately mansion? Everyone has one."

"Dad," Tara stated firmly, "it's creepy. Have you ever looked at it at night from the outside? It looks haunted and it looks as if it's staring at you. You're a little bit out there, even if you are my father."

"Treacherous children," Dillon said. "You've been spending far too much time with your aunt. She shares your opinion of my home."

Brenda rolled her eyes heavenward. "Dillon, you have things crawling up your house and watching every move one makes outside. I shudder every time I'm in the garden or walking through the grounds. I look up and there something is, staring at me."

"Technically," Brian interrupted, "they watch over the house and the people in it. If you're afraid, it's probably because you have good reason to be." He hitched closer. "Like maybe you're harboring ill will toward those inside."

Jessica crumbled a napkin and pitched it at Brian. "Back off, drummer boy, since Brenda was such a miracle of comfort to my babies, I can't very well let you spout your nonsense. I've always loved Gothic architecture, too. We used to look at all the books together and Dillon would bring home photos from Europe." She winked at Trevor. "I would think those hidden passageways would intrigue you."

Dillon captured her hand and pulled her toward the double doors leading toward the courtyard. "Dress warm you two—we'll meet you on the trail."

Jessica followed him out into the courtyard, ignoring Trevor's taunting whistle. "I don't like it that both of the kids were sick this morning, Dillon," she said. "Yesterday, Tara saw someone watching them when the landslide occurred. She couldn't tell who it was, he or she was wearing a long hooded cape. I saw the same person the night we arrived."

Dillon slowed his pace, pulling her closer to him so that she was beneath the protection of his shoulder. "What are you saying, Jess?" He was very careful to keep his tone without expression. "Do you think the landslide was rigged in some way? And the kids didn't have the flu, that someone somehow poisoned them?"

When he said the words, they did sound absurd. Oil on a staircase anyone could slip on. How could one rig a landslide and know the children would be in that exact spot? And she had been sick, too. People got the flu all the time. She sighed. How could she explain the uneasiness she felt? The continual worry that never went away? "Why wouldn't the person wearing the hooded cape help them? Clearly they were in trouble, Tara was screaming her head off."

"I don't know the answer to that, baby, but we'll find out," he assured. "Everyone certainly pitched in and helped to free Trevor. I didn't notice anyone holding back, not even Don."

"Don." Jessica shook her head. "It's hard to like that man. Even after last night, and I did feel sorry for him, I've been struggling to find something good about him."

"I did like him," Dillon answered, frowning slightly. "He was always reserved with me but he always worked hard. There was no looking around for him at the end of the night; he pulled his share of the work and then some. He was steady and I counted on him heavily at times. I had no idea he disliked me so intensely. And I sure didn't know Vivian was sleeping with him. She suggested I go hear him play, but I brought him into the band because he's so talented, not because she asked me." He sighed, raked his hand through his hair. "I don't know anymore, Jess. In the old days, it was all so easy. I never opened my eyes. I just lived my life in blissful ignorance until it all came crashing down." He looked at her, his fingers tightening around hers. "I was so arrogant, so sure that I could make it all work out. The truth is, how can I condemn Don when I've made so many mistakes myself?"

"Do you think it was a member of the band who killed Vivian and Phillip?" she asked carefully.

"No, of course not. They had five nutcases up there with them that night. All of them were mixing drugs and alcohol. For all I know, one of them brought a gun in. Someone shot Viv and Trent and maybe the others jumped the shooter, tried to wrestle the gun away, and knocked over the drinks and candles. I hope it happened that way. I hope the fire didn't start while I was beating up Trent. It was pretty wild. We knocked tables and lamps over. Maybe a candle hit the floor and no one noticed. I'll never know. The band had no idea what was going on up there. We'd just arrived."

"Why did you come upstairs?" she asked curiously.

"I wanted to check on the kids. Tara was asleep but she didn't have her blanket. I hadn't seen you in so long and I knew you must have gone looking for the thing. I was looking for you," he admitted. "I couldn't wait until morning to see you."

Pleasure rushed through her at his words. "I'm grateful you came looking for me, Dillon," she said softly.

Dillon threw open the door to the shed, flicked on a switch to flood the room with light. "So am I, honey." He couldn't look at her, knowing the fury of that moment was etched into his face. He couldn't look back and not feel it.

Jessica laughed, the sound of her joy dispelling old memories. "I would like to have known about the lights in here yesterday."

"Really." His eyebrow shot up. His voice softened into seduction. "I was just thinking it would have been smarter to keep it dark."

Jessica quirked an eyebrow at him and took a step backward. "You have that wicked look on your face like you're up to something." His expression alone sent heat coursing through her body.

"Wicked? I like that." His hand curled around the nape of her neck, drew her to him. He bent his head to claim her mouth. His lips were firm, soft, tempting. His tongue teased her lower lip, tracing the outline, probing and dancing until she opened to him.

His hand slipped under her jacket and blouse to find bare skin. Her breast pushed into his palm. He tasted the same hunger in her mouth. "Take off your jacket, Jess," he whispered as he reached once more for the light switch, plunging the shed into a murky gray. "Hurry, baby, we don't have much time."

"You can't think we're doing anything in this little shed, outdoors where anyone could find us," she said, but she was shedding her jacket, tossing it aside, wanting the searing heat of his mouth on her breast. Wanting her hands on him. It already seemed far too long.

Dillon watched her unbutton her blouse with breathless anticipation. He watched the richness of her breasts spill into his sight and he slowly let out his breath, his lungs burning for air. She did that to him with her exquisite skin and haunting eyes. "I thought about you while I showered this evening," he confided. "You should have been there with me. I thought about how you tasted and how you feel and how you sound when

I'm inside of you." He bent his head to draw her breast into his mouth.

Her body rippled with instant need, with hunger. She laughed softly. "I was with you. As I recall, you did a lot of tasting."

"Are you certain? It wasn't enough, I need more." His hands slipped over her jeans, fumbled with the zipper. "Get rid of these things, you need them off." His teeth nipped at the underside of her breast, returned to the heat of her mouth, kissing her senseless. "I need them off."

"Do you think we have time?" She was already complying, wanting him so much that the stolen moments were as precious as the long all-night session of lovemaking.

"Not for all the things I want to do with you," he whispered against her ear, his tongue probing her frantic pulse. "But enough for what I have in mind. Push my jeans off my hips." The instant his body was free of the confining cloth he breathed a sigh of relief. "Much better. I'm going to lift you up. Put your arms around my neck and wrap your legs around my waist. Are you ready for me?" His fingers were already seeking his answer, probing deep, slipping into her body to find her damp with need.

He buried his face in her neck. "You are so hot, Jess. I love how you want me the same way I want you." Just feeling her dampness hardened his body even more. He took her weight as she put her arms around his neck and lifted her legs to wrap them around his waist. The engorged head of his shaft was pressed tightly to her. Very slowly he lowered her body over his. There was the familiar resistance, her body stretching to receive his fullness. The impression of sliding a sword into a tight sheath left every nerve ending raw. The sensation was building like a firestorm, spreading wilder, hotter, more explosive than ever. It roared through his body like a freight train, through his mind, a crescendo of notes and promises, of half-formed thoughts and needs.

He loved the little anxious sounds escaping her throat, the way she moved her hips to meet his, in a perfect rhythm. Jessica, the completion of his heart.

Jessica lost herself in the hard thrusts of his body into hers, in the fiery heat and sizzling passion that rose up and engulfed her entirely. She threw her head back, riding fast, tightening her muscles around him, gripping and sliding with a friction designed to drive them both up and over the edge quickly.

She couldn't believe herself, the wild wanton ride she took, there in the shed with their disheveled clothes half on and half off. But it didn't matter, nothing mattered but the burst of light and color as she broke into fragments and dissolved, her body rippling with a life of its own. She hung on tightly to Dillon as he thrust hard, repeatedly, his hoarse cry muffled by her shoulder.

They clung, their laughter coming together, a soft, pleased melding as their heart rates slowed to normal and Dillon slowly lowered her feet to the floor. The stolen moments were as precious as gold to both of them. It took a little scrambling and fumbling to adjust their clothing. Jessica couldn't find her slip-on shoes. Dillon distracted her often while she searched, kissing her neck, her fingers, swirling his tongue in her ear. She found one shoe among the pots and the other upside down on top of a bag of potting soil. She picked it up and idly picked out the seaweed caught in the sole.

"I haven't worn these shoes anywhere near the ocean bank. Where did I pick up seaweed?" She slipped the shoes back on her feet and went back into his arms again, turning up her mouth for his kiss. There was a long silence, while they simply got lost in each other. Dillon trailed kisses down her chin to her throat.

Jessica tilted her head to give him better access and caught a movement outside the small window.

"What's wrong?" Dillon asked, lifting his head reluctantly as he felt her stiffen. "Your neck is so perfect to nibble on—soft and tempting. I could stay here forever. Are you certain we have to get the Christmas tree today?"

"Something moved out there. I think someone is watching us," Jessica whispered. A shiver crept down her spine. Looking through the small window, she strained to see but couldn't spot anyone. It didn't matter. Someone watched them.

Dillon groaned. "Not again. Don had better not make another confession or I might pitch him off the cliff." He stepped past her to the small square window, looked around carefully. "I don't see anyone, baby, maybe it's the gargoyles on the roof."

Jessica could hear the amusement in his voice. Soft, gentle, teasing. She tried to respond, going into his arms, but she couldn't shake the feeling of something sinister staring at them.

"Come on, Jessie," Trevor shouted, breaking them

apart immediately. "You two better not be doing anything I don't want to know about, because I'm coming in." There was the briefest of hesitations and then the door was thrust open. Trevor glared at them. "Everyone else was too chicken to come see what you were up to."

"We're looking for the axe," Jessica improvised lamely.

"Oh, really?" Trevor's eyebrow went up, in just the same way as his father's did sometimes. He fit the role of the chastising father figure perfectly. "Do you think this might help?" He flicked the switch so that light permeated every inch of the small building. He glared at his father in disapproval. "In a tool shed?"

"Trevor!" Blushing, Jessica hurried to the back of the shed where she knew the larger tools were kept. As she reached for the axe, she knocked over the large pry bar. Muttering, she picked it up and started to replace it. The dried mud and pine needles stuck on the edge of it caught her eye. She frowned at the tool.

Trevor took up the axe. "Come on, Jessie, everyone's waiting. Stop mooning around, it's embarrassing. At least you have the good sense to fall for my dad."

"You don't mind?" Dillon asked, his eyes very serious as he studied his son's face.

"Who else would we want for Jessie?" Trevor asked matter-of-factly. "She's our family. We don't want someone else stealing her away from us."

"As if that could happen," Jessica leaned over to kiss his cheek. "Come on, we'd better hurry or the others will be looking for us." She led the way out of the shed.

"And, by the way, we had kitchen duty this afternoon," Trevor added righteously.

She turned to look at him skeptically. "*You* cleaned up or your sister did? I can't imagine you remembering."

"Well, Brenda remembered and I would have cleaned up but Tara's mothering me again because I suffered trauma yesterday." He put on his most pathetic face.

"Trauma?" Dillon interrupted. "*We* suffered the trauma, Jess, your sister, and I, not you. You ate it up. Don't think we didn't notice your sister waiting on you hand and foot. Is that a normal, everyday thing?"

"Absolutely." Trevor was grinning with unabashed glee. "And I love it, too!"

"He has no shame," Jessica pointed out to Dillon.

"Not when it comes to *domestic* chores," Trevor admitted. "Hey! I'm beginning to sound like Brenda and that's scary!" He waved to Tara and the group huddled together under the trees waiting for them. "I told you I'd get them," he called.

There was no time for anything but finding the all-important Christmas tree. Tara and Trevor had an idea where to look and they set off immediately. Paul kept pace with them, laughing, punching Trevor's arm good-naturedly and occasionally tousling Tara's hair. Brenda and Robert walked together at a much more sedate pace, whispering with their heads together. Brian and Don argued loudly over the best way to save the rain forest and the ozone layer and whether or not the taking of one small Christmas tree was going to have global effects.

Dillon walked along the trail, his hand firmly anchored in Jessica's. His life had changed dramatically. Everyone who was important to him was with him, sharing his home. He glanced down at the woman walking so close to him. Jessica had somehow changed his entire world in the blink of an eye. His children were with him, trust was slowly beginning to develop among them. He could see such potential, his mind awakening to all the possibilities of life. It was exhilarating, yet frightening.

Dillon knew his self-esteem had always been wrapped up in his music, in his ability to shoulder enormous responsibility. His childhood had been difficult, a struggle just to feel as if he counted for something. What did he have to offer them all if he could no longer play the music pounding in his head?

The fine mist began to turn into a steady drizzle as they walked along the trail. The band members pointed out tree after tree, big fir trees with full branches. The twins adamantly shook their heads, looking to Jessica for support. She agreed and followed them to the small, thin tree with gaps between the branches they had chosen the night before. The tree was growing at a strange angle out from under two larger trees at the edge of a bluff overlooking a smaller hill. The rain was making the ground slick.

"Stay away from that edge, Tara," Dillon commanded, scowling as he walked around the sad little tree. "This is your perfect Christmas tree?"

Trevor and Tara exchanged a grin. "That's the one. It wants to come home with us. We asked it," Tara said solemnly.

"I tramped through the forest in the pouring rain for that little mongrel of a tree?" Brenda demanded. "Good heavens, look around, there are fantastic trees everywhere."

"I like it," Don said, clapping his hands on the twins' shoulders. "It hasn't a hope of surviving here—I say we take it in, show it a good time, and let it have some fun."

Jessica nodded. "It looks perfect to me." She skirted the forlorn little tree, touched one of the longer branches that reached out toward the sea. "This is the one."

Dillon raised his eyebrow at Robert, who shrugged helplessly. "Whatever makes them happy, I guess."

Brian stepped forward to take the axe out of Dillon's hands. "I like the darned thing—it needs a home and some cheering up." He sent the axe sweeping toward the narrow trunk. He was strong and the first bite cut deep.

Tara hugged her brother, her eyes shining. "This is *exactly* how I imagined it, Dad." She wrapped her other arm around her father.

Dillon stood very still while pleasure coursed through him at his daughter's affectionate gesture.

Paul laughed and began removing his jacket. "Did you imagine the rain, too, Tara? We could have done without that."

The gray drizzle was beginning to fall a little faster. Brian took another swipe at the tree trunk, sinking the blade in solidly. He repeated the action again and again with a steady rhythm that matched the drone of the rain. Robert put his arm around his wife to help protect her from the rising wind. The tree shivered, beginning to tilt.

"Hey!" Paul was shaking out his jacket, reaching across Jessica, holding it out toward Tara. "Put this on."

Tara grinned happily at him through the gray mist. "Thanks, Paul." Her fingers closed around the material just as there was an ominous crack.

The branches wavered, then rushed at them. Paul yelled a warning, stepping back in an attempt to stay out of reach. His elbow cracked into Jessica's shoulder, sending her flying backward as his feet slipped out from under him in the thick mud.

Dillon shoved Tara hard, sending her sprawling into Trevor's arms, even as he dove across the muddy ground for Jessica. To his horror, Jessica went down hard, skidding precariously close to the edge of the bluff. He saw her make a grab for the wavering tree branches but Paul's larger frame crashed into hers in a tangle of arms and legs. They both went sliding over the edge of the crumbling cliff. Paul's fingers made thick tracks in the mud as he attempted to find a purchase.

Dillon skidded in the mud, lying flat out on the ground, catching Jessica's ankle as she plummeted over the edge. He realized he was yelling hoarsely, a mind-numbing terror invading him. The Christmas tree lay beside him, inches to his left. Don threw himself across Dillon's legs, pinning him to the ground to prevent him sliding over the edge after Jessica and Robert leapt to catch Paul's wrists as he clung to the rocks. There was a moment of silence broken only by the moaning wind, the pounding sea, the sound of rain, and heavy breathing.

"Daddy?" Tara's voice was thin and frightened.

Trevor dropped into the mud beside his father, looking down over the edge at Jessica. She was upside down, straining to turn her head to look up at them. Other than her head, she was very still, aware that the only thing preventing her from falling was Dillon's fingers circling her ankle. Trevor reached out with both hands and caught her calf. Together they began to pull her up.

"It's all right, honey," Dillon soothed his daughter. "Jess is fine, aren't you, baby?" He could pretend his hands weren't shaking and his mind wasn't numb with terror. "Robert, can you hold Paul?"

"I've got him." Robert was straining back. Brenda and Tara caught his belt and pulled as hard as they could. Brian simply reached past them and added his strength to Robert's, pulling Paul straight up. He immediately turned his attention to helping Trevor and Dillon with Jessica.

All of them sat in the mud, Dillon, Tara, and Trevor holding Jessica tight. The rain poured down harder. Jessica could hear her heart thundering in her chest. Dillon's face was buried against her throbbing shoulder. Tara and Trevor clung to her, their grip so tight she thought they might break her in two. She looked at the others. Paul looked absolutely stunned, his face a mask of shock. Brenda's face was white. Robert, Don, and Brian looked frightened.

Another accident. This time Jessica was in the middle of it. She couldn't imagine that it had been anything other than an accident. Had all of the other accidents that had occurred recently really just been flukes and coincidence? Had she become paranoid after her mother's death? Certainly with Trevor's accident, she had carefully examined the ground, yet she had seen no signs that the landslide had been anything more than a natural shift in the land after a storm. But what about the hooded figure Trevor and Tara had seen yesterday and the one she'd seen the night they'd arrived on the island? Who could that be? Perhaps it was the groundskeeper and his eyesight was so poor he didn't notice anyone or anything around him. It was a poor explanation, but other than someone hiding on the island, she couldn't think of anything else.

"I saved your jacket, Paul," Tara said in a small voice, holding up the precious item for everyone to see.

Everyone burst out laughing in relief. Except Paul. He shook his head, the stunned disbelief still on his face. Jessica was certain it was on her face, too.

"Let's get back to the house," Dillon suggested. "In case no one's noticed, it's really raining out here. Are you okay, Paul?"

Paul didn't answer, his body shaking in reaction, but he allowed Brian and Dillon to help him to his feet.

Jessica mulled the idea over that she could be wrong about the accidents. Even about the brakes on her mother's car being tampered with. About her own car. All the other trivial things could be something altogether different. She swept a shaky hand through her hair. She just didn't know.

chapter
13

❄ IT TOOK A SURPRISINGLY short time for everyone to reconvene in the kitchen, freshly showered and once more warm after the outdoor adventures. Upset by another near tragedy, Jessica kept a close eye on the twins. The string of accidents was just too much for her to believe they were all coincidences. Yet nothing ever added up.

She looked around the room at the other occupants of the house. She liked them. That was the problem. She really liked them. Some more than others, but she couldn't conceive of any of them deliberately harming the twins.

"Jessie, you aren't listening to me," Tara's voice penetrated her thoughts. "I don't know what kinds of ornaments we can make." Tara added sadly, "Mama Rita had beautiful ornaments for our trees." She stood very close to her brother, her gaze seeking reassurance from Jessica. Obviously she was as shaken by the accident as Jessica was.

"We're supposed to *make* them, Tara," Trevor pointed out. "That's the way it works, right, Jessie?"

Jessica nodded. "I have a great recipe for a dough. We can roll it out, cut out whatever shapes we want, bake them and then paint them. It will be fun." She set two mugs of chocolate in front of the twins and held up a third mug toward Paul. He shook his head and she set it down in front of her, reaching for a towel to clean the counter.

Brenda yawned. "Susie Homemaker strikes again. Do you know how to do *everything*, dear? Have you any idea how utterly tiring that can be?"

Jessica threw the wadded up tea towel at her, hitting the perfectly fashionable head and draping the Kelly green towel over the chic chignon. "No one believes your little heartless wench act, Brenda—you've blown it, so start thinking up ideas. And I didn't say I was going to do the mixing and baking. I'm the *supervisor*. You and the twins are the worker bees."

"Robert, are you going to let her get away with throwing things at me?" Brenda complained. She wadded the towel into a tight little ball, looking for a target. "Surely you could exact some sort of revenge for me. I'd do it myself but I've just been endangering my life, tramping through mosquito-infested waters and through alligator-ridden swamps to find the perfect Christmas tree for two ungrateful little chits. And the perfect tree turned out to be some straggly, misshapen bush!"

"There aren't alligators here," Trevor pointed out, "so technically your life wasn't really in danger. It's your duty as our aunt to do these things and *enjoy* them, isn't that right, Dad? So buck up, babe. We'll let you sing the first Christmas carol."

The tea towel hit Trevor's face dead center. "You *horrid* little boy!"

"Ouch, ouch," Trevor clutched at his chest, feigning a heart attack. "She spears with me with her unkind words." He drained the mug of hot chocolate. "More?" he asked hopefully, holding up the cup.

"No, you're going to bed soon," Jessica objected. "I swear, you're becoming a bottomless pit."

"He can have mine," Tara said, pushing the mug toward her brother. "I don't want any more."

Jessica intercepted it, catching it up before Trevor could snatch it out of her reach. "What if she still has the flu, Trev? Don't drink from the same mug," she chided. "Tara, do you feel sick? You've gone so pale."

"I think I still have the flu," Tara admitted, "or maybe I'm just still scared. I didn't like seeing you and Paul falling off the cliff."

"We didn't like it much either." Jessica exchanged a small smile with Paul.

"Hey, paper chains," Don said suddenly. "When I was a kid we used to make paper chains and hang them on the tree. I think I remember how to do it."

"I remember that," Robert agreed. "We should take all those musical notations we've thrown away and use them. We all love music. Does that work, Jessie? Brenda, we made a chain one year. We didn't have a tree so we made a chain of love."

Jessica grinned at Brenda as the woman visibly winced, horrified to be found out. "A love chain, Brenda? You're really a mushy girl after all, aren't you?"

"She's all sappy like you are, Jessie." Trevor was wearing an identical grin. "Brenda, you little romantic you. A *luv* chain."

"Why, Brenda." Dillon was outright smirking. "You've truly amazed me. I had no idea you were a marshmallow under all that sophistication."

"Don't start. Robert is making it all up as you know perfectly well." Brenda looked haughty, her nose in the air.

Brian wagged his finger at her. "Robert doesn't have the imagination to make something like that up, Brenda. You *did* make a love chain with him."

Tara protectively flung her arms around Brenda, glaring at everyone. "Leave her alone, all of you!" She pressed a kiss against Brenda's chin. "We can make as many chains as you want. Don't let them bother you."

Jessica met Brenda's gaze across the room. Tears glistened in the depths of Brenda's eyes. She sat very still, not moving a muscle. The two women simply stared at one another, caught in the moment. Brenda nuzzled the top of Tara's head briefly, her eyes still locked with Jessica's. "Thank you," she mouthed, blinking rapidly to rid herself of unwanted emotion.

"You're welcome," Jessica mouthed back with a watery smile.

Dillon felt his throat close, his heart swelling with pride at observing the exchange. Jessica brought her light to everyone. She could so easily have turned the twins against Brenda, against him. The children loved her beyond any other. Their loyalty to Jessica was strong. A single word from Jessica would have prevented the twins from even trying to work with all the different personalities around them. Jessica had been so generous in sharing them and she had instilled her giving nature in both of them. He knew, better than most, how Brenda often appeared cold and uncaring to others. He was proud of his children, that they saw beyond the barrier she presented to world to the real woman.

"There's always strings of popcorn," Paul pointed out. "Those are easy enough to make. We used to make those in your basement, Brian."

"We ate most of them," Dillon pointed out, laughing at the memory.

The next two hours were spent companionably, baking and coloring ornaments and stringing paper chains and popcorn. Dillon managed to lead them in Christmas carols that Paul and Brian turned into other much more ribald ballads. Brenda and Brian got into a popcorn fight until Trevor and Tara took their aunt's side and Brian was forced to cry uncle.

When Jessica could see that both Tara and Trevor were overtired and too flushed, she called a halt and took them both upstairs. She was surprised that both teenagers went without a murmur of protest.

Tara clutched her stomach. "I really don't feel very well, but I didn't want to ruin the fun," she admitted.

Little warning bells began going off in Jessica's head despite her determination not to worry. She rubbed at her temples, annoyed with herself for being so protective. Everyone got the flu, even she still felt sick.

"I wish we had played all those tricks on everyone," Trevor said suddenly to Tara. "Didn't that make you mad that they were blaming us for all those pranks while we were waiting for Jessica and Dad? It's so typical for adults to always blame kids for everything." He suddenly lunged for the bathroom.

"What do you mean they were blaming you for pranks?" Jessica tucked the blankets around Tara and smoothed back her hair. "Are you feeling any better, honey? I can get your father and we can take you to a doctor."

"I'm the one throwing my guts up," Trevor yelled from the bathroom.

"Sweetie, I'll be happy to take you to the doctor. It's just that I know you'd rather be boiled in oil than see the doc," Jessica said sympathetically.

They could hear Trevor noisily rinsing his mouth for the third time. "And it sucks that they thought we were going into their rooms. I wonder if someone's been going into Dad's room and he thinks it's us, too. Just because we're teenagers doesn't mean we don't have respect for other people's things," he said indignantly. He stumbled from the bathroom back to them, crossing the floor with an aggravated frown on his face. "I asked Brian point blank if he was in your room, Jessie, and if he'd burned incense and created one of his magic circles there, and he said no. And then he had the gall to tell me to stay out of his room."

"To stay the *hell* out of his room," Tara corrected. "He was really mad at us. I never went into his stupid room."

"Wait a minute." Jessica held up her hand. "What are you talking about? The others accused you of going into their rooms?"

Tara nodded. "Even Brenda and Robert thought we were playing pranks on them. I guess it's happened to everyone since we've been here and I don't think they believed us when we told them it was happening to us, too."

"What pranks?" Jessica wanted to know. "And where have I been?"

Trevor and Tara exchanged a slow grin. "With Dad," they said in unison.

Jessica blushed as she sat on the edge of Tara's bed. "I guess I deserved that. I'm sorry I've been in the studio working so much and that I've been going off with Dillon. I'll talk to Brian. He shouldn't have accused you. What do they think you've been doing?"

Trevor shrugged. "The usual teen-in-the-spooky-old-mansion stuff. Opening windows, leaving water running in the bathtub, moving things, writing weird leave-before-it's-too-late messages on mirrors. That sort of thing."

"Brian said no one else would be so childish." Tara was clearly offended. "Like I would want to find a stupid secret passageway and sneak into his dumb room!" Her gaze slid to her twin's face. "Well, Trevor and I did look for secret passageways, but just because it was fun. If we were going to try to convince everyone there was a ghost here, we'd have done a *much* better job," she declared. "At least Brenda and Robert said they believed us. Do you think Dad believes we're sneaking into people's rooms?" She sounded a little forlorn.

"Of course not, Tara. If your father thought you were doing such a thing, he would have spoken to you about it immediately. I'm sorry they accused you of such childish behavior. You're right, oftentimes an adult who isn't used to teenagers has a false idea of the things they do." Jessica stroked Tara's hair. "I noticed our resident ghost forgot to open the window tonight."

"Could there be a real ghost in the house?" Tara asked hopefully.

"The house isn't old enough," Trevor protested knowledgably. He'd read a lot on the subject. "Dad had it built after the fire. The contractor finished it while he was still in the burn center." When his sister and Jessica looked at him he shrugged with a sheepish grin. "Paul told me. I ask him questions about Dad. Sometimes he doesn't mind and other times he just sort of ignores me. You don't learn anything if you don't ask questions. A house has to be really old to have a ghost."

"Or there has to have been a murder in it," Tara agreed.

A chill went down Jessica's spine at Tara's words. She remembered the sound of the gunshots, the crackle of the flames, the heat and smoke. Standing up, she walked to the window, not wanting the twins to see the expression on her face. *Murder.* The word shimmered in her mind. Both children were watching her closely. Not wanting them to know what she was thinking, she changed the subject. "Did Brenda really take care of you and Tara this morning when you were sick? That amazes me."

Trevor laughed immediately. "She tried. She was as white as a sheet. The funny thing was, Robert wanted to go get you but she said no, they could handle it. I think she really wanted to, not only to give you and Dad time to work things out, but because she wanted to be the one to help us. The crazy part was, while she was being so nice, I was thinking Robert and Brenda might have tried to poison us."

Jessica looked at him sharply. "Why would you think something like that?"

"Well, we both drank a soda in their room and then we were sick. And I found a newspaper in their wastebasket with words cut out of it like for a ransom note. I had this wild idea they were going to hold us hostage or something until you paid them money. Or kill us and collect the insurance on us." He grinned, looking sheepish.

"I was sick *before* I drank the soda, that's why I drank it so fast." Tara scowled at her brother indignantly. "Brenda and Robert weren't trying to poison us!"

"I know that *now*." Trevor flung himself on his makeshift bed.

"You found *what* in Brenda's room?" Jessica tripped over Trevor's shoes and nearly fell on the bed. Don had confessed to attempting to blackmail Dillon. Why would Brenda and Robert have the remnants of a cut up newspaper in their room? What would be the point of Don's confessing and then trying to cast blame on someone else? Jessica could feel the strange shiver of apprehension snake down her spine. Unless someone else was involved. Someone far more sinister than Don. Jessica didn't like the implications of it at all.

"It was just an old newspaper," Trevor said, shrugging it off. "Some of the words had been cut out of it, but I didn't really have time to look at it closely."

Jessica sat down on the edge of the bed. Outside the rain had started again, pounding at the window and rattling branches against the house. "What is it you two used to call me?" she asked softly. The raindrops matched the rhythm in her heart.

"Magical girl," Tara's voice was drowsy. "You're our magical girl."

Jessica leaned over her to kiss her again. "Thank you, honey, I think I need to be magical girl again. I'm going down to the studio. If you need me, come get me." She needed to go somewhere and think and it always helped when she had a guitar in her hands. Her shoulder was aching, a reminder of the day's events, as she noiselessly crept down the hall to the wide staircase. The lights were off and the house had grown silent.

Dillon would be waiting for her to come to him. If she was too long he might go looking. She didn't want to be with him while she sorted things out. He distracted her, made her lose confidence in herself. *Magical girl.* Even her mother had used that name for her because she knew things. She knew things instinctively. Things like when what appeared to be an accident was really something much more sinister. Since coming here she had been relying on Dillon. Expecting Dillon to solve the mystery, to make it all better.

Lightning zigzagged across the sky and lit up the courtyard as she paused on the landing to look out through the glass doors. She could see the fir trees as they jerked in a macabre dance like wooden marionettes. Dillon didn't believe anyone was trying to hurt the children. Jessica believed it and if she was going to find the truth, she needed to rely on herself and her own judgment.

The sound room was empty, strangely eerie with the glass and instruments in the dark. She idly picked up one of Dillon's acoustic guitars, a *Martin* he particularly loved. She ran her fingers over the strings, heard the small jarring note not quite in tune. That was what the accidents were like, a note not quite in tune. She had to sort it all out just as she so efficiently tuned the guitar. She played there in the darkness, sitting on the edge of the instrument panel, her mind compiling the data for her. She closed her eyes and allowed the music, *Dillon's* music, to soothe her as she played.

She slipped a few random notes into the melody. Notes off-key, off-kilter, like the accidents that could have happened to anyone. Anyone. The word repeated like a refrain in her head. Random accidents. Secret passageways. Blackmail. Pieces of a puzzle like musical notations written on paper. Move them around, put them together differently, and she would have a masterpiece. Or a key.

Thunder crashed all too close, the clash of cymbals, the exclamation point after the melody. She opened her eyes just as another bolt of lightning lit up the world. A figure loomed up right in front of her, a dark shadow of terror. Jessica lunged to her feet, gripping the expensive guitar like a weapon.

Brenda stumbled backward with a frightened shriek. "Jess! It's me! Brenda!"

Her heart pounding too loudly, Jessica slowly lowered the guitar. "What in the world are you doing here?"

"Looking for you. Trevor told me where to find you. You're the only one who might believe me. I don't know who else to talk to." Brenda's hand shot out, prevented Jessica from turning on the light. "Don't, I can't look at you and say this." She took a deep calming breath. "I wanted to believe the kids were behind the pranks, but I don't think so. I think it's Vivian."

A chill went down Jessica's spine. Her eyes strained in the darkness to see Brenda's face, to read her expression.

"I'm not crazy, Jessie. I feel her at times." Brenda pressed a trembling hand to her mouth. "I think the kids or Dillon or maybe me, are in danger and she's trying to warn us. Vivian wasn't a bad person, and she believed in spirits. If she could come back to help set things right, she would. I've been afraid something was wrong for a while and the minute I came to the island, I was certain of it."

"You think Vivian is opening windows and drawing magic circles on the floor? Why, why would she do that, knowing how Dillon feels?" Jessica kept her voice very even. She didn't know if Brenda was attempting to frighten her, or if she really believed what she was saying.

"To protect you. To protect me. Dillon, the children. All of us. It was the only religion she knew." Brenda leaned closer to her, pleading with her. "Do you feel it, too? Tell me I haven't completely lost my mind. I don't want to end up like Viv."

Jessica carefully leaned the guitar against the wall. She didn't know if Vivian's presence was in the house helping her or if the next flash of lightning merely illuminated her brain. Like the notes blending into harmony, the pieces clicked into place.

"Since we came here, the accidents have all been random. I was trying to mold them, fit them into my idea that someone wanted to harm Trevor and Tara. But all the accidents could have hurt any of us. Anyone in the house. Do you see it, Brenda, the pattern?"

Brenda shook her head. "No, but you're chilling me to the bone."

"And the cape. The hooded figure. The dog didn't bark."

"You've lost me. Bark when?"

"When Trevor was buried under the landslide, Tara saw a hooded figure, but the dog didn't bark. So it wasn't a stranger hiding on the island, it was someone the dog knew." Jessica knew she was on the verge of discovery. It was all there for her to see. The pattern in the discordant notes. "Why were only the three of us sick? Why Tara and Trevor and me? None of you were sick." She pressed a hand to her mouth, her eyes wide. "It's the chocolate. My God, he poisoned the chocolate. He did everything. He shot Vivian, he must have, and he covered his tracks with the fire."

"What do you mean, he poisoned the chocolate? Dillon? You think Dillon tried to poison the twins?" Brenda sounded shocked.

"Not Dillon. Of course not Dillon. You can't believe he shot Vivian! It was never Dillon," Jessica was impatient. "You'll have to call the helicopter, have them pick up the kids and take them to the hospital and tell them to bring the police." She had to get to the twins, hold them in her arms, make certain they were alive and well.

The next flash of lightning revealed the dark, hooded figure standing so silently in the corner. Jessica saw him clearly, saw the ugly little gun in his hand. The light faded away, but she knew he was there. Real. Solid. A sinister demented being bent on murder. Brenda gave a frightened cry and Jessica thrust the woman behind her. She felt her way along the instrument panel for the switch to turn on the recorder.

There was a moment of silence while the rain came down and the wind howled and tugged at the house. While the gargoyles watched silently from the eaves.

Jessica forced a small smile, forced a calmness she didn't feel. "I knew it was you. It's going to break his heart all over again." There was deep regret in her voice. The knowledge of such a betrayal would hurt Dillon immensely. Some part of Jessica had known all along, but she hadn't wanted to see it. For Dillon's sake.

"You didn't know," Paul denied, his face so deep inside the hood they couldn't see him. He presented a frightening image, the grim reaper. All he needed was a long-handled scythe to complete the persona of death.

"Of course it had to be you. No one but you would know that someone was trying to blackmail Dillon."

"Your mother," he spat, "was so greedy. The money he gave her to care for the children wasn't enough. I wrote the checks out to her—she had enough."

"Not my mother," Jessica snarled back. "Don was blackmailing Dillon. She came here at Dillon's request to discuss it with him."

"I don't understand," Brenda said. "Paul, what are you doing? Why are you standing in that stupid cape with a gun pointed at us? And you'd better not be naked under that thing! Everyone's being so melodramatic! What are you talking about? Why would anyone want to blackmail Dillon?"

Jessica ignored her. She didn't dare take her eyes off of Paul. He was unstable and she had no idea what could set him off. But she knew he was perfectly capable of killing. He had done so numerous times. "You were the only one it could be, Paul. You had access to all the rooms through the passageways. You're the only one who has been here on a regular basis. Once I realized the accidents were random, directed toward everyone here, I knew they were designed to send everyone away. The landslide, the Christmas tree, the oil on the stairs. Even the chocolate. You thought if enough things happened, we'd all go away. That's what you wanted, wasn't it? You just wanted everyone to stay away from here." Her voice was soothing, the voice she had used for years on the children, a blend of sweetness and understanding.

"But you wouldn't go away," he said. "You brought them back here. *Her* children. Vivian was evil, an evil disgusting seductress who wouldn't leave us all alone."

Jessica's heart thudded. She heard it in his voice, the guilt, the seething hatred. It always came back to Vivian. She knew then. Her heart bled for Dillon. So much treachery, how did one survive it? She wanted to weep for them all. There wasn't going to be any miracle for the twins or Dillon this Christmas, only more heartache, more tragedy.

"You loved her." She said it simply, starkly, saying the words in the dark to the man who had calmly walked up the stairs, shot Vivian and her lover in cold blood and locked the other occupants in the room after ensuring the fire was raging.

"I *hated* her! I *despised* her!" Paul hissed the words. "She seduced me. I begged her to leave me alone, but she would crawl into my bed and I could never stop myself. She laughed at me, and she threatened to tell Dillon. He was the only friend, the only family I ever had. I wasn't going to let her destroy me. Or him. Phillip deserved to die, he used her to get at Dillon. He thought Dillon would pay him to leave Vivian alone."

"Where would he get an idea like that?" Brenda was far too quiet and that worried Jessica. She glanced at the other woman but couldn't see her clearly in the dark.

"What does it matter? None of it matters. He chose you. When I knocked you off the bluff and slipped myself, he saved you, not me. I couldn't believe it. He was never worth it. All these wasted years. His genius. I served his greatness, cared for him, *protected* him, *killed* for him, and he fell for another harlot." Paul shook his head so that the hooded cloak moved as if alive. "I gave him everything, and he chose you." He snarled the last words at her, like a rabid dog wanting to strike out.

Jessica forced a derisive laugh. She was inching her fingers along the wall seeking the guitar, her only weapon. "Is that how you lie to yourself at night in order to sleep, Paul? You betrayed him by sleeping with his wife. You probably brought Phillip Trent into Vivian's life. You let Dillon go through a trial, knew everyone believed he committed murder and yet you could have stopped it by telling the truth. You were responsible for the fire that burned him. You murdered my mother thinking she was blackmailing him. You left him open to blackmail and you arranged accidents that could have killed his children just to frighten them away from him. How in the world is that giving him everything? You made him a prisoner in this house and when it looked as if he might break free you started all over again to try to isolate him from the rest of the world."

"Shut up!" Pure venom dripped from Paul's voice. "Just shut up!"

"The biggest mistake you made was going after the children. Your plan backfired. You must have intercepted my letter telling him the children should be with him. You didn't want them here, did you? They were a threat to you. You wanted me to think Dillon was trying to hurt them, didn't you?" She looked at him steadily. "But, you see, I know Dillon. I knew he would *never* have killed Vivian or my mother or done harm to his children. So I brought the children here, knowing he would try to protect them."

"And delivered them right to me," Paul snarled.

"Put the gun down, Paul." Dillon's voice was weary and sad, a melody of smoke and blues. "It's over. We have to figure out how best to handle this." Dillon moved through the doorway.

While Dillon was so calm, Jessica wanted to scream. Were the children writhing in agony upstairs, while they talked to a madman with a gun? Her fingers found the neck of the guitar, circled, and gripped hard.

"There is only one way to handle it, Dillon," Paul said just as calmly. "I'm not about to be locked up for the rest of my life. I couldn't stand being interviewed behind bars while the band makes it to the top again."

Jessica knew. She always knew before things happened, even though she had doubted herself. There in the darkness with the rain coming down, she knew the precise moment Paul shifted the gun. She knew he was finished talking and that his finger was squeezing the trigger. Without hesitation, Jessica stepped solidly in front of Dillon and swung the guitar toward Paul with every ounce of strength she possessed.

She heard the bark of the gun, the simultaneous crack of the guitar as she hit Paul hard, and Dillon's husky cry of denial even as something knocked her legs out from under her. Jessica hit her head hard on the floor. She lay still, staring up at the figure in the hooded cloak. He was bent over, twisted. She blinked to clear her vision. Everything seemed hazy, a weird phosphorescent light was seeping into the room, a mist of colors and cold. The draft was icy, so that she could see the air as a foggy vapor. It seemed to slide between Paul and the other occupants of the room.

Paul screamed, a hoarse dark cry of rage and fear. For one moment the colors shifted and moved, formed the shimmering, translucent image of a woman in a flowing gown reaching out a long thin arm beckoning toward Paul. Dillon moved then, covering Jessica's body with his own, blocking her view of the strange apparition, so that she only heard the gun as it went off a second time.

"Vivian, don't leave me again!" Brenda's cry was anguished and she stumbled forward, her arms outstretched. Dillon caught her, dragging her down to the safety of the floor.

Jessica heard the body fall with a soft thud to the floor, and she found herself staring into Paul's wide-open eyes. She knew he was dead, with the life already drained from his body before he hit the floor. In the end, he had been determined to take Dillon with him, and she had been just as determined he would not.

Brenda's weeping was soft and brokenhearted. "Did you see her, Jessica? I told you I wasn't crazy. Did you see her?"

Dillon kicked the gun away from Paul's hand. "Call the doctor, Brenda, right now!" His voice was pure authority, snapping Brenda out of her sorrow. "Check on Tara and Trevor—make certain they're all right. And then call the police." His hands were running over Jessica's legs, searching for a wound, searching for the bullet hole that had knocked her to the floor.

There was no blood, no gaping wound, only a huge dark bruise already forming on her left thigh. The area was tender, painful, but neither Dillon nor Jessica knew who had struck her hard enough to knock her legs out from under her. Brenda had stood frozen, unable to move. They both stared at the strange mark, two circles, one inside the other, the center circle much darker. A circle of protection.

"I have to see to Paul," he said and she heard the heartbreak in his voice.

"He's beyond help, Dillon. Don't touch anything,"

Jessica cautioned gently. Now that it was over she began to shake almost uncontrollably. Her need to get to the children was paramount. Her need to comfort Dillon was just as great. More than anything else she was afraid for him. This time the truth had to be plain. "Wait for the police."

chapter
14

THE WHITE BIRD WINGED *its way across the wet sky. Far below, waves crashed against rock, foamed and sprayed, reaching toward the heavens, toward the small white dove as it flew with a glittering object in its beak.*

"Jessie, get out of bed," Tara insisted, jarring Jessica right out of her happy dream. "It's Christmas Eve, you can't just stay in bed!"

Jessica turned over with a small groan and pulled the blanket firmly over her head. "Go away, I'm never getting up again."

She wasn't going to face Christmas Eve. She didn't want to see the disappointment on the faces of the twins. She didn't want to face Dillon. She had seen him when the police took Paul's body away, when he told the truth about what had happened. Dillon looked like a man lost, with his heart and soul torn out. Reporters had been brutal, swarming to the hospital, nearly rioting at the police station. So many pictures, so many microphones thrust at him. It had to have been a nightmare for him. It had been for her. The police had the recording Jessica had made as well as Brenda's and Jessica's statements to back up Dillon's. The crime scene people had come and gone. Paul was dead by his own hand. They all said so. By mutual consent, they kept their knowledge of the apparition to themselves. There was no need to complicate the story to the police or the newspapers. And who would ever believe them?

"Jessie, really, get up." Tara dragged at the covers.

"I'll get her up," Dillon told his daughter gently. "You go play hostess, Tara. Tell everyone your Christmas story. They all need a feel-good story tonight. And Brian's made a special Christmas Eve feast. I believe he made pancakes."

Tara giggled as her father walked her to the door. "Not his famous pancakes! What a shocker." She leaned over to kiss his forehead as she went out.

Jessica heard the door close firmly and the lock turn. There was a mysterious rustle and then the room was flooded with music. Soft, beautiful strains of music. The swelling passion of the song she and Dillon had worked on so hard. She blinked back tears and sat up as he crossed the room to sit on the edge of her bed. The light was off and the room was dark, only the sliver of moon providing them with a streak of a silvery glow.

Jessica drew up her knees, rested her chin on them. "So what now, Dillon?" She asked it quietly, facing the worst, prepared for his rejection. He hadn't talked with her, hadn't come near her in days. He'd spent most of the time on the mainland.

Dillon reached out to her, his palm cupping her chin,

skin to skin. She realized then, that he wasn't wearing his gloves. "It's Christmas Eve, we wait for our miracle," he told her gently. "Don't tell me after believing all this time, you've suddenly had a crisis of faith." His thumb brushed along her chin, a slow sensual movement that made her shiver with awareness of him.

Jessica swept a trembling hand through her hair as it tumbled around her face. "I don't know what I think anymore, Dillon. I feel numb right now." It wasn't altogether true. When she looked at him, every part of her came alive. Heat coursed through her body, while her heart did a somersault and a multitude of butterfly wings brushed at the pit of her stomach. "I thought, with all that has happened, that . . ." she trailed off miserably. No matter what she said, it would be hurtful to him. How could she admit she thought he would retreat from her, from Trevor and Tara?

Dillon's smile was incredibly tender. "You didn't really think I would be so incredibly stupid as to send you and the children away again, did you? I wouldn't deserve you, Jess, if I'd been thinking of doing something that thick-skulled. I don't know that I deserve you now, but you offered and I'm holding on tight with both hands." He rubbed the bridge of his nose, suddenly looking vulnerable. "I thought about things, sitting up in my room, about treachery and betrayal and about letting life pass me by. I thought about courage and what it means. Courage was Don coming to me when he didn't have to and telling me how idiotic he had been. Courage was him willing to be kicked out of the band or even prosecuted. Courage is Brenda and Robert learning how to be an aunt and uncle to two children they are secretly terrified of. Courage is Brian standing in that kitchen and telling me his beliefs."

His hands framed her face. "Courage is a woman stepping between a man and death. You fought for me, Jess, even when I wouldn't do it myself. I'm not walking away from that. I'll never play the guitar again like I did, but I still have my voice and I still can write and produce songs. I have two children you gave back to me and God willing, I hope we have more. Tell me I still have you."

She melted into him, a long slow kiss that stole her breath and took her heart, that told him everything he wanted to know.

"Everyone's waiting for you," he whispered against her mouth.

Jessica hugged him hard, leapt out of bed, rushed for the bathroom. "Ten minutes," she called over her shoulder, "I have to shower." She peeled off her pajama top and flung it toward a chair.

Dillon's breath hitched in his throat as he saw her drawstring pants slide over the tempting curve of her bottom just as she disappeared into the other room. He stood up, a slow smile softening the edge of his mouth as he tossed his own shirt aside. He padded on bare feet to the bathroom door to watch her as she stepped under the cascade of hot water. She turned her head toward him just as he slowly pushed his jeans away from his hardened body. At once her gaze was on his heavy erection. Knowing she was looking hardened him more so that the ache grew and his need was instant and urgent.

"You missed me," she greeted, her smile pure invitation. The moment he stepped into the large compartment, she wrapped her hand around his thickness, warm and tight. "I missed you."

His hands moved over every inch of her he could touch, marveling that she could want him the way she did. Dillon caught the nape of her neck and turned up her head to fasten his mouth to hers. He wasn't gentle. He didn't feel gentle. He wanted to devour her. He fed there, his hands cupping her breasts, his thumbs circling her nipples.

She was driving him crazy with her bold caresses, stroking him even as her mouth was mating with his. Hot silken kisses; the earth spinning madly. The water running over their bodies and the steam rising around them. She was soft and pliant, as her body moved against his. One leg slid up to the curve of his hip, she pressed close, as wild as he was.

Dillon bent his head to the terrible bruise on her shoulder where Paul's elbow had cracked her hard enough to send her flying toward the edge of a cliff. His tongue eased the throbbing ache, and traveled lower to trace the outline of her breast. He felt her tremble in reaction. His mouth closed over her hard nipple, his teeth teasing gently before he suckled strongly. She gasped in reaction, arcing more fully into him. His hand shaped her every curve, slid lower to push into her body. She was wet and pulsing with her own need and he wanted all the time in the world to love her. To just lie beside her and bring her so much pleasure so she would know what she meant to him.

Jessica leaned forward to catch a little drop of water that ran from his shoulder to the muscles of his chest. She wasn't fast enough. Her tongue followed the little bead of moisture as it traveled across the ridges over his heart. She couldn't quite catch up and her arms slipped around his waist as she ducked her head to lap at the droplet, racing it over his flat belly. Her hand was still wrapped proprietarily around his heavy erection. She felt him swell more, thick, and hard, as she breathed warm air over him, as her tongue lapped at the droplets on his most sensitive tip.

Dillon went rigid, his body shuddering with pleasure as she took him into the heat of her mouth. The water cascaded down, sensitizing his skin. The roar started in his brain, the fire burned in his gut, a sweet ecstasy that shook him. Strains of their music penetrated into the shower, and fired his blood even more with the driving, impassioned beat. Her hips moved against his hand, her muscles were tight and clenching around his fingers.

"Jess." He said her name. Called to her. A pleading. A promise. "I need you now, this minute." Because there was nowhere else he would rather be than in her, with her, a part of her.

Her green gaze slid over him as she straightened. Took in every inch of him, the perfection of his face, the scars on his body, his heavy, thick evidence of his need for her. And she smiled in welcome. In happiness. Deliberately she turned and placed her hands carefully on the small half bench in the corner, presenting her rounded bottom and the smooth line of her back.

His hands went to her hips as he pulsed against her. She was more than ready for him, slick and hot and as eager as he was. Even as he pushed into her tight sheath, she pushed back, so that he filled her with a single surge. Molten lava raced through her, through him. He groaned, began to move hard and fast, thrusting deeply, wildly, a frenzy of white-hot pleasure for both of them. She was meeting every stroke, demanding more, her body gripping his, clenching and building a fiery friction that shook him all the way to his soul. And then she was rippling around him, milking him of his seed, so that his own orgasm ripped through him with such intensity her name was torn from his throat.

She always managed to surprise him. His Jessica, so unafraid of life, of passion, of showing her true feelings. She cried out with her release, her body spiraling out of control and she gave herself up to the pleasure, embraced it the way she did everything. It seemed to last forever. It seemed over far too fast. They collapsed together, holding each other, kissing each other, their hands greedy for the feel of each other's body.

Dillon caught her hair in his hand. "I can't get enough of kissing you." His mouth devoured her ravenously. "More, I need more."

"I thought you said everyone was waiting for us. It's been a lot longer than ten minutes," Jessica pointed out. "They'll send the twins."

"Promise me when you marry me, which will be very, very soon, I can spend a couple of weeks in bed with you. Just touching you. I love the way you feel." He reached past her to turn off the water.

Jessica stilled, stared up at him with the water running off her lashes. "You never mentioned marriage."

Dillon blinked down at her, managed to look boyishly

vulnerable. "I'm old-fashioned, I thought you knew I meant for life." He looked around, saw his jeans carelessly discarded on the floor. "I have a ring." He said it like a bribe.

"Dillon!" Flustered, Jessica wrapped her hair in a towel, staring at him wide-eyed. "You have a ring?"

She looked so beautiful with the confusion on her face, with the water beading on her petal soft skin and her large eyes bright with happiness, Dillon wanted to start all over again. He found the ring in his pocket and caught her hand. "I want us to be forever, Jess, forever."

The diamond sparkled at her as she smiled down at it. Then he was catching her up, throwing her on the bed in a tangle of sheets and arms and legs, his tongue lapping at every bead of water on her skin.

It was considerably longer than either of them expected before they were dressed and ready to join the others. Jessica's face was slightly red from the shadow on Dillon's jaw and the insides of her thighs held matching abrasions. She went with him willingly, confidently. Together they could manage to bring off Christmas.

She stopped in the doorway of the large room where the tree had been set up. Hundreds of tiny lights were woven in and out of the branches, highlighting the ornaments they had all made.

"So this is what you've been doing all this time," Jessica whispered, joy coursing through her as she looked at the lights on the Christmas tree, at the mound of brightly wrapped presents beneath the branches. "You've been playing Santa Claus."

He grinned at her, with his boyish, mischievous grin.

"I'm into the miracle business in a big way these days. I couldn't let Tara and Trevor be disappointed. They wanted their father back, didn't they?"

Jessica wrapped her arms around his neck and claimed his oh-so-beautiful mouth. Happiness blossomed inside of her. She had thought Paul's betrayal would have been the last straw, that it would have broken Dillon's spirit totally. Instead he had emerged to the other side, whole once more.

His kiss was gentle, relaxed, tasting of passion and hunger. Behind them Trevor groaned. "Are you two going to be doing that all night, because there are other rooms where you can be alone, in case you hadn't noticed."

"Don't tell them that." Brian slapped Trevor on the back. "We'll never have Christmas if you give them any ideas."

Dillon took his time, kissing Jessica. It mattered, kissing did, and he made a thorough job of it while the twins tapped their feet and the band members nudged one another. He lifted his head slowly, and smiled down into her upturned face. "I love you, Jessica, more than I can ever express, I love you."

She touched his mouth with a trembling fingertip. "Surprise! I love you right back." She would count that as her Christmas miracle. Dillon. Her other half.

"Dad!" Tara squeaked impatiently. "We all know what's going on here, so don't keep us in suspense. Are you or aren't you?"

Dillon and Jessica turned to look at the expectant faces gathered around them. "What are you talking about?" He put his arm around Jessica's shoulders, drawing her into the shelter of his body.

Trevor threw his hands up in the air. "So much for being suave. Jeeze, Dad, get a clue here. A little action on your part, you know?"

Don shook his head. "You disappoint me, Wentworth."

"Boyo." Brian slumped against the wall, a hand to his head. "You've destroyed my faith in true love."

Brenda stepped forward, caught Jessica's wrist and yanked her left hand up to their faces. "Oh, for heaven's sake, you are the most unobservant group on the face of the earth!" The ring glittered beneath the light.

"Holy cow, Dad." Trevor grinned from ear to ear. "You're amazing. I apologize. Profusely."

Jessica was kissed and hugged until Dillon rescued her, pulling her to him and waving the others off with a good-natured scowl. He turned off the overhead lights so that only the twinkling Christmas lights shone. A multitude of colors sparkled and glowed. "It's midnight. We should sing Christmas in," he announced, leaning down to steal another kiss.

Brenda settled close to Robert, resting her head on his chest. Brian sat across from the couple, on the floor, stretching out his long legs toward the tree. Don followed suit, dropping to the floor, his back against the couch, sprawling out, leaning back to look at the lights.

Dillon laced his fingers through Jessica's as he sat in the large armchair and pulled her beside him. Tara and Trevor immediately found a place on the floor close to their father and Jessica. Robert reached behind the chair where he was sitting and casually pulled out an acoustic guitar. Dillon's oldest, not expensive, but one he had carried with him for years. Robert handed it across the floor to Trevor who held it out to his father.

"Play for us tonight, Dad," Trevor said.

Jessica could feel Dillon stiffen beside her. He shook his head, took the guitar out of his son's hand and tried to give it to Jessica. "You play. I don't play anymore."

"Yes, you do," Jessica said, ignoring the instrument, "you just don't play for large crowds. We're family. All of us here together tonight. We're you're family, Dillon, and it's okay to be imperfect. Just play, don't be great, just play for us."

Dillon looked into her eyes. Green eyes. Guileless. Sincere. He glanced at the others watching him while he made his decision. The lights flickered and shimmied, winking at him as if in encouragement. He didn't have to do it all himself, he didn't have to be perfect. Sometimes people did get second chances. With a small sigh, he capitulated, bringing the guitar to him, cradling it in his arms like a lost lover. His longtime companion. His childhood friend when he was lonely. A small smile curved his mouth as he felt the familiar texture, the grain of the wood, the wide neck.

His fingers found the strings; his ear listened to the sound. He made the adjustments automatically, without thinking. He lived and breathed music: the notes that took on a life in his head. He still had that, a gift beyond comparison. He had his voice. It spilled out of him, his signature, a blend of edgy smoke and husky blues. He sang of hope and joy, love found, and families together. While he sang, his fingers found the familiar chords, moved over the strings with a remembered love. He didn't have the dexterity to play the fast riffs and the intricate melodies he often heard in his mind and composed, but he could do this, play for his family, and take pleasure in the gift of love.

They sang with him, all those he loved. Jessica's voice blended with his, in a perfect melding. Brenda was slightly out of tune, but he loved her all the more for it. Tara's voice held promise and Trevor's held enthusiasm. The pleasure of sitting in his home, surrounded by his family on Christmas Eve, was incomparable. His miracle.

A slight noise at the window distracted Jessica from the music and she frowned, looking beyond the glass pane to the darkened, wild storm. There was a small fluttering of white that settled on the outside windowsill. A storm-tossed bird, perhaps lost in the dark of night and the violence of the squall.

"There's a bird at the window," Jessica said softly, afraid if she spoke too loudly the white dove would vanish before anyone else saw it. She made her way with caution across the room while the others stayed motionless. "Birds aren't out at this time of night. Did it fly into the window?"

The bird looked bedraggled—a wet, unhappy, shivering dove. Jessica carefully opened the window, crooning to the creature, not wanting to frighten it away. To her astonishment, it waited calmly on the windowsill while she struggled to push one side of the window out against the fierce wind. Almost at once, the bird hopped onto her arm. She could feel it shaking, and immediately cupped its body in the warmth of her palms. It was carrying something in its beak. She could just make out the glint of gold between her hands. There was something else: a band on its leg. Jessica felt it drop into her palm as the bird rose, flapped its wings, and launched itself into the air. It flew around the room. As the bird passed over the twins, it opened its beak and dropped something between the twins. The bird made another fast circuit of the room while the lights played over its white feathers in a prism of colors that was mesmerizing and beautiful. The dove flew out the window, back into the night, winging its way toward some other shelter.

"What is it, Tara?" Trevor leaned in close as his sister lifted a gold chain for all of them to see. "It's a locket." It was small, heart-shaped, and intricately etched on the outside.

"I think it's real gold," Trevor said, lifting it up to peer at it more closely.

"Is it for me? Did someone get this for me? Where did this come from?" Tara looked around the room at the band members who had fallen silent as she held up the necklace. "Who gave it to me?"

Dillon leaned forward to get a closer look. Brenda's hand went to her throat in a curiously vulnerable gesture. Her gaze met Dillon's across the small space and she quickly shook her head. "I didn't, Dillon, I swear I didn't."

"It opens, doesn't it?" Trevor wrapped his arm around his sister's shoulder and peered at the delicate locket. "What's inside?"

Tara pressed the tiny catch and the locket popped open. There were two smiling faces, a two-year-old girl and an identical two-year-old boy. Both children were smiling. Their black, wavy hair framing their faces.

"Dad?" Tara looked at her father. "It's us, isn't it?"

Dillon nodded solemnly. "Your mother never took that necklace off. I didn't even know the pictures were inside of it."

Tara turned to Jessica, an awkward, uncertain expression on her young face. She didn't know what to think or feel about such a gift. Everyone was stunned, and had shocked looks on their faces. She didn't know whether to hug the locket to her, or to throw it away and cry a river of tears.

Jessica immediately hugged her. "What a beautiful gift. It is a day of miracles. Every child should know their mother wanted and loved them. I remember how precious that locket was to your mother. She wore it always, even when she had much more expensive jewelry. I think the necklace is proof of what she felt for you, even when she was too ill to show you."

Brenda caught Jessica's hand and squeezed it tightly. "Vivian always wore it, Tara—I teased her about her preferring it to diamonds. She said she had her reasons." Tears glittered in her eyes. "I know why now. I would never have taken it off either."

Tara kissed her aunt. "I'm glad you're here, Aunt Brenda," she confided. "I love you." She handed her the necklace. "Will you put it on me?"

Brenda nodded, her heart overflowing. "Absolutely I will."

"It was for both of us, Trev," Tara said. "She loved both of us after all. We'll share it." She leaned over to kiss her brother on the cheek.

Jessica settled in Dillon's lap, waited until the others were crowded around the twins, and she slowly opened her hand to show him what lay in her palm. The small ring was a mother's ring with two identical birthstones in it. They looked from the ring to one another without speaking.

Jessica closed her fingers around the precious gift the dove had left behind. It was better than diamonds. The most important gift ever given. Dillon's scarred fingers settled over hers, guarding the treasure, holding it close to their hearts. Trevor and Tara were theirs. They had their Christmas miracle and it was exactly what they needed.

Not sure what to read next?

Visit Pocket Books online at
www.SimonSays.com

Reading suggestions for
you and your reading group
New release news
Author appearances
Online chats with your favorite writers
Special offers
And much, much more!

1042

THE PASSION DOESN'T NEED TO END...

LOOK FOR THESE BREATHTAKING PERIOD ROMANCES FROM POCKET BOOKS

JULIA LONDON	**HIGHLANDER UNBOUND** On a mission to save his legacy he lost his heart.
LIZ CARLYLE	**A DEAL WITH THE DEVIL** She is a liar and possibly a murderess, but he's drawn to her with a passion he's never known.
CONNIE BROCKWAY	**MY SEDUCTION** In the company of a Highlander, no woman is ever entirely out of danger.
ANA LEIGH	**THE FRASERS: CLAY** They tamed the Wild West—but couldn't tame their love.
KRESLEY COLE	**THE PRICE OF PLEASURE** He came to her rescue—but does she want to be saved?
SABRINA JEFFRIES	**IN THE PRINCE'S BED** His legacy is the crown, but his destiny is her love.

www.simonsayslove.com • Wherever books are sold.

10412

LOVE IS IN THE AIR
WITH THESE UNFORGETTABLE
ROMANCES FROM
POCKET BOOKS

ROXANNE ST. CLAIRE   FRENCH TWIST

In the land of romance, love is
everywhere…but so is danger.

DORIEN KELLY   HOT NIGHTS IN BALLYMUIR

A passionate Irishman might be the
answer to an American woman's
dreams.

LORRAINE HEATH   SMOOTH TALKIN' STRANGER

Was it one night of uncontrollable
chemistry or the beginnings of the
love of a lifetime?

JANET CHAPMAN   THE SEDUCTIVE IMPOSTOR

He makes her want to risk
everything—but can she trust him?

CAROL GRACE   AN ACCIDENTAL GREEK WEDDING

Sparks are flying—only it's not
between the bride and groom!

JULIE KENNER   THE SPY WHO LOVES ME

He's Double-Oh-No. But she's
about to change that…

SUSAN SIZEMORE   I THIRST FOR YOU

A beautiful mortal becomes embraced
by darkness and passion when a
vampire desires her for all time.